Disney · PIXAR

FINDING DORY

GRAPHIC NOVEL

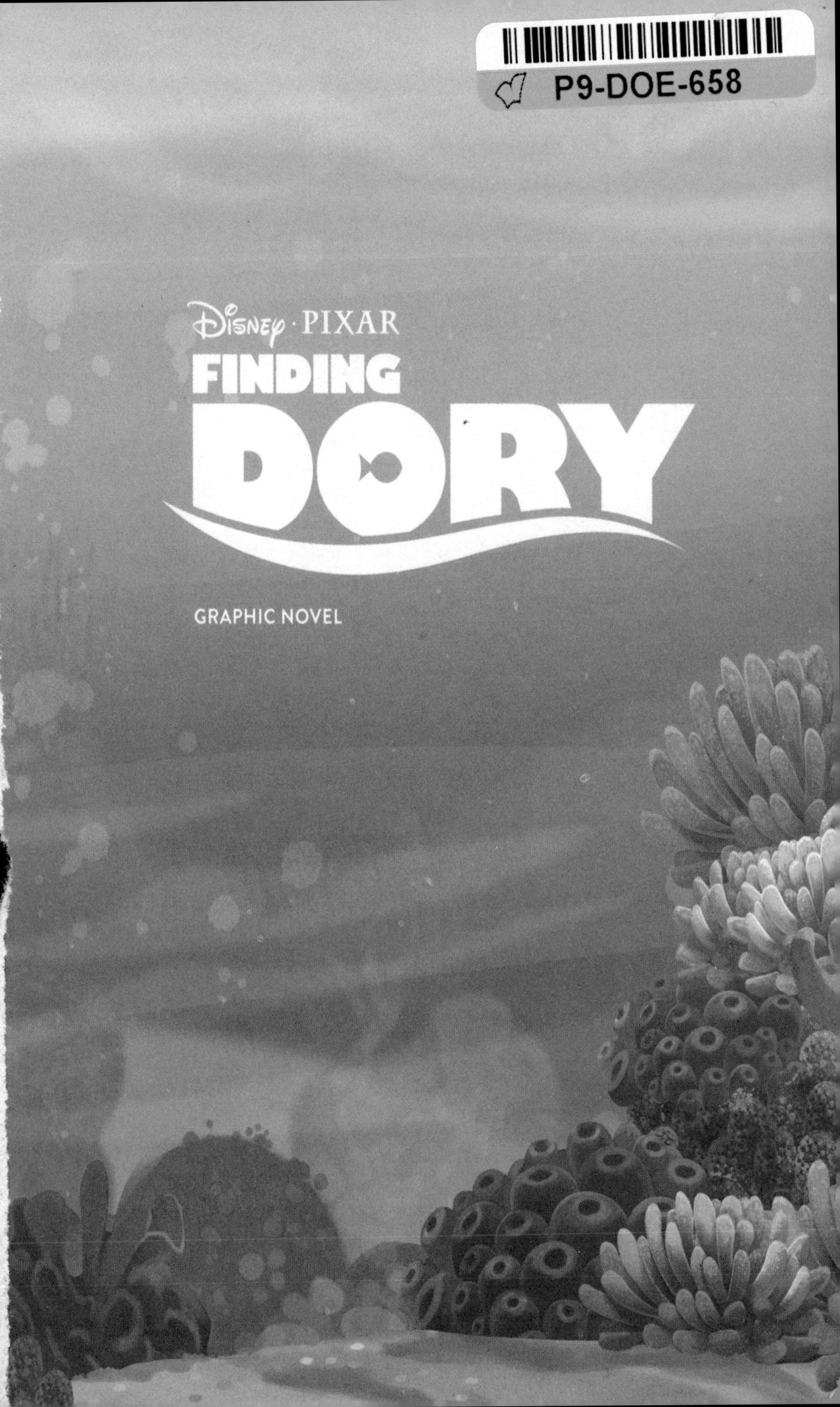

Also from Joe Books

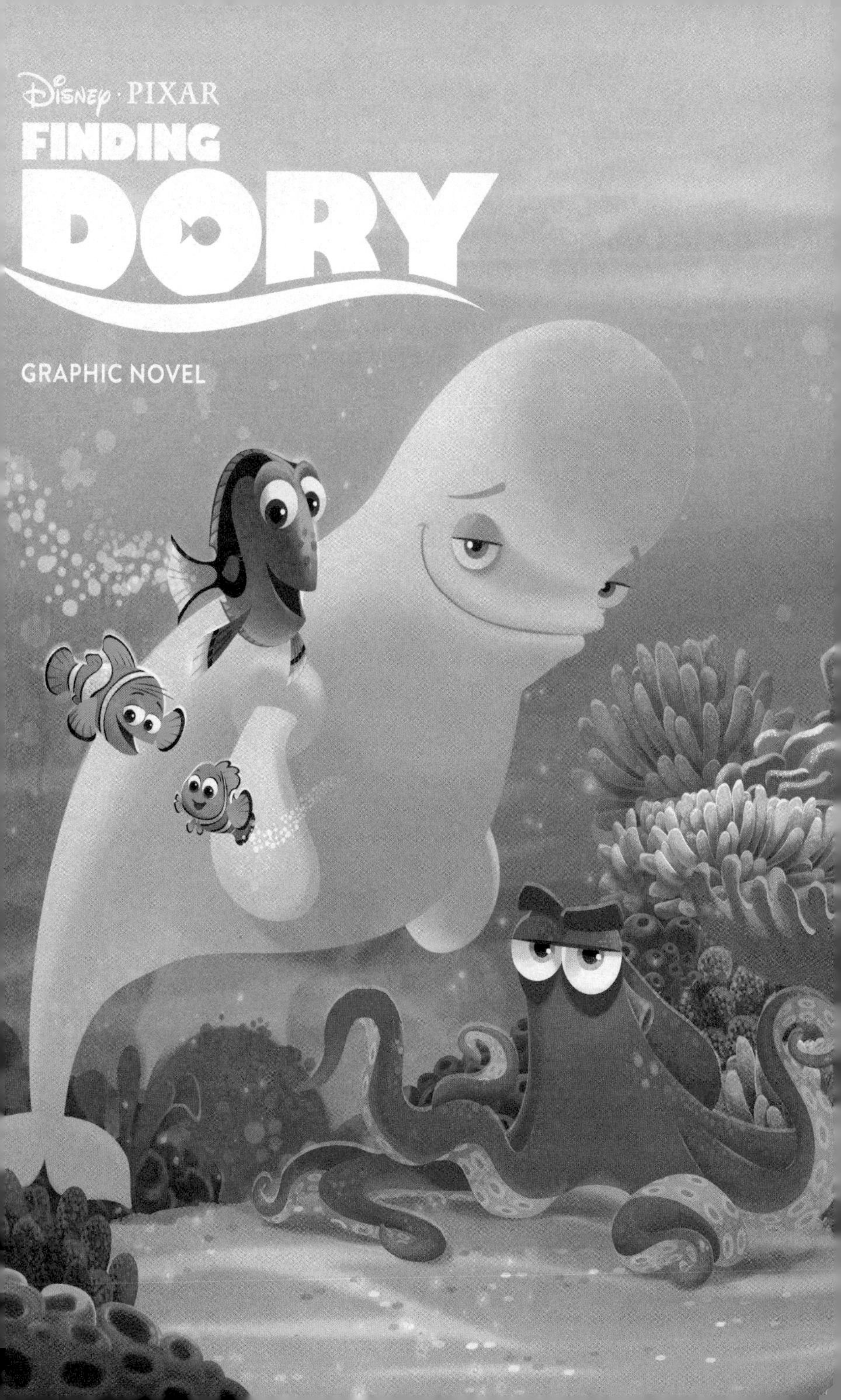
Disney · PIXAR
FINDING
DORY
GRAPHIC NOVEL

Published simultaneously in the United States and Canada by Joe Books Ltd,
489 College Street, Suite 203, Toronto, Ontario, M6G 1A5

www.joebooks.com

First Joe Books Edition: July 2016

print ISBN: 9781772753332
eISBN: 9781772753530

Library and Archives Canada Cataloguing in Publication
information is available upon request

Printed and bound in Canada
3 5 7 9 10 8 6 4 2 1

Contents

Living On the Reef   x

New Friends from
  the Marine Life Institute   3

The Story of the Movie in Comics   4

Back On the Reef   55

Friends and Family   59

Family Flashback   62

"Lunchtime"   64

"Little Lost Fish"   68

Visit the Marine Life Institute   74

Sea Stars   76

"Multiple Choice"   78

"Take Notice"   80

MLI Memories   82

"Incoming"   83
"Speaking Her Language"   90
Fin-tastic Friends   98
"Neighborhood Watch"   100
"Diver Drill"   108
How to Speak Whale   110
Sights to Sea   112
"Field of Screams"   114
"Home Sting Home"   117
"A Stand-Up Dad"   120
"Cruisin' with Crush"   124
"Not My Mother"   126
One Big Family   130
"Into the Deep"   132
Dear Dory   148
"Crab's Coral"   150

"A New Home" 152
The New Crew 154
"In the Dark" 156
"Hank Tells It Like It Is" 158
Hank's Driving School 160
"Piranhacuda" 166
"The Show Must Go On" 184
"Clam Chat" 187
"Clam Chat Interruptus" 189
"Intruder" 191
"Follow that Fish" 208
"Hero Day" 214
"Hide-and-Seek" 218
"Sleeping with the Fishes" 222
"Otterly Adorable" 224
"In Plain Sight" 226

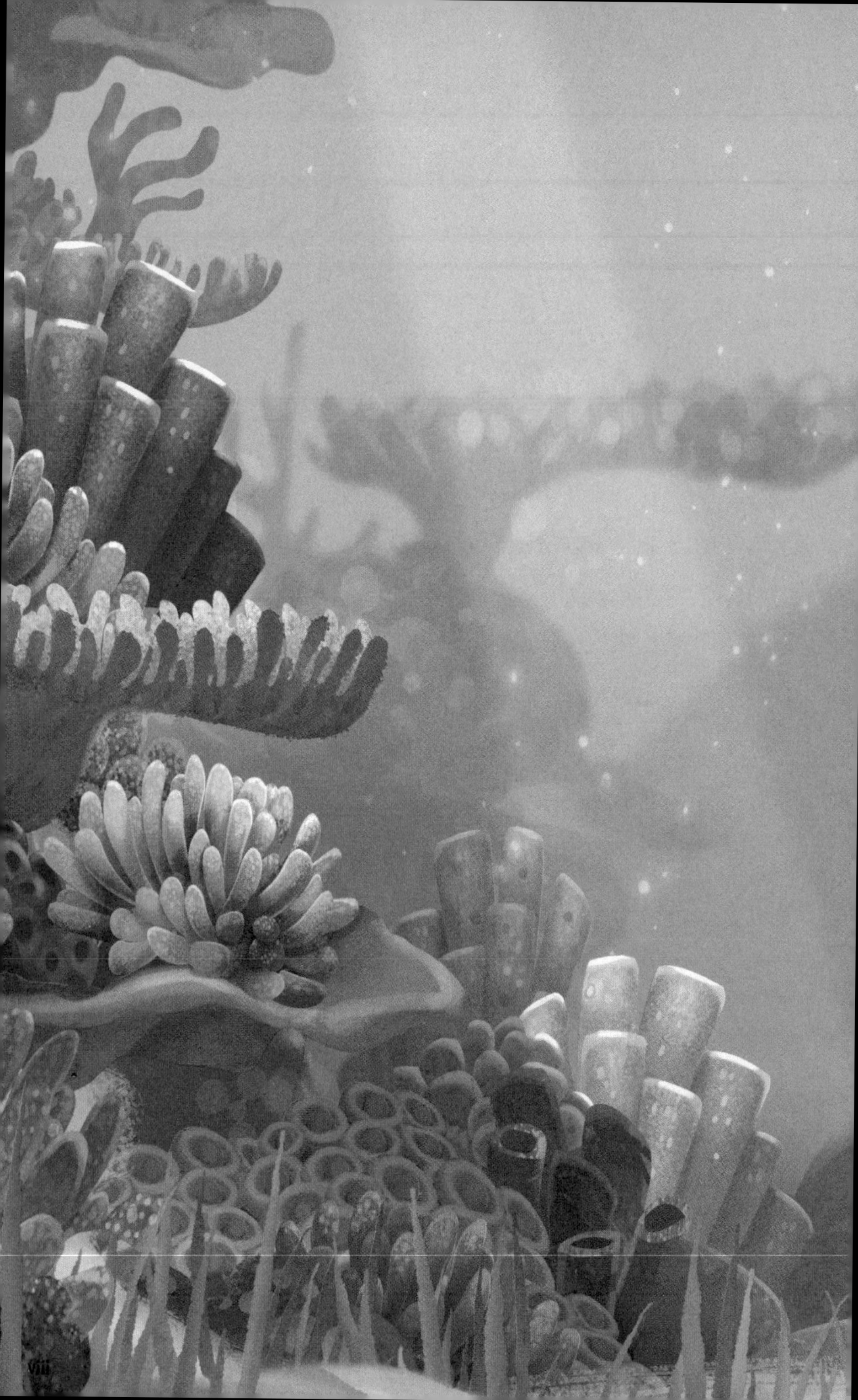

Disney · PIXAR

FINDING
DORY

GRAPHIC NOVEL

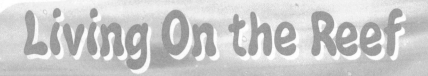

Living On the Reef

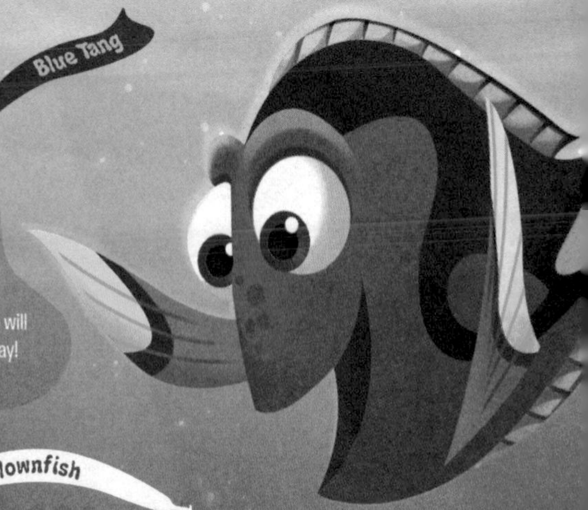

Dory

Blue Tang

As she tells any fish she meets, Dory suffers from short-term memory loss. Because of that, she cannot remember many things, the most important of which is... where are her parents? But Dory doesn't let this get in her way: she's probably the most positive and fearless fish in the ocean and sooner or later she will find them. She just needs to follow her own way!

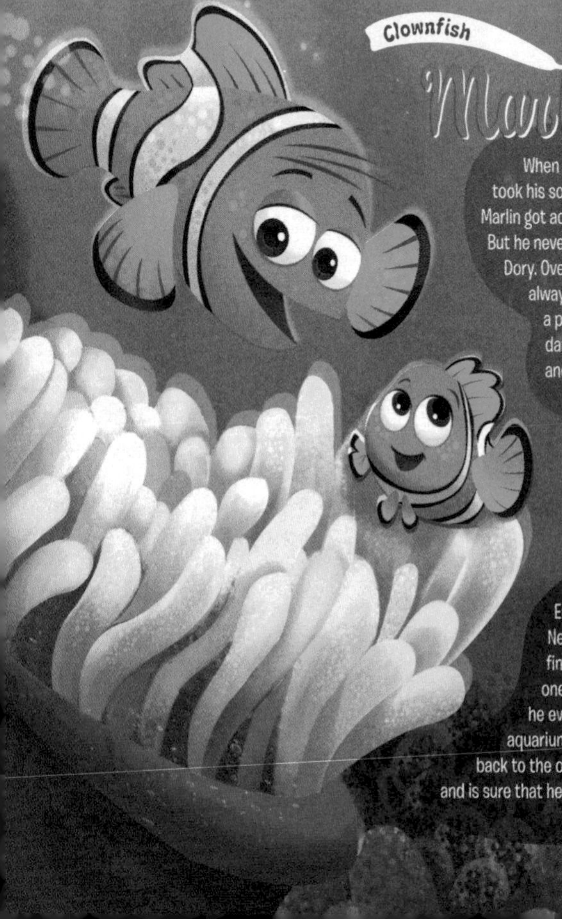

Marlin

Clownfish

When scuba divers took his son Nemo, a year ago, Marlin got across the ocean to save him. But he never would have made it without Dory. Overprotective and pessimistic, Marlin always expects the worst and just wishes to live a peaceful life on the reef, avoiding any possible danger. But he is also brave and kind-hearted, and would do anything to help his friend Dory.

Nemo

Clownfish

Enthusiastic, determined and adventurous, Nemo is never afraid of exploring. He has a lucky fin, but just like Dory he never lets it stop him: one year ago, with the help of some tank fish, he even managed to escape the dentist's aquarium he was placed in and he made it back to the ocean! Nemo loves his dad very much and is sure that he will always do the right thing.

Crush & Squirt

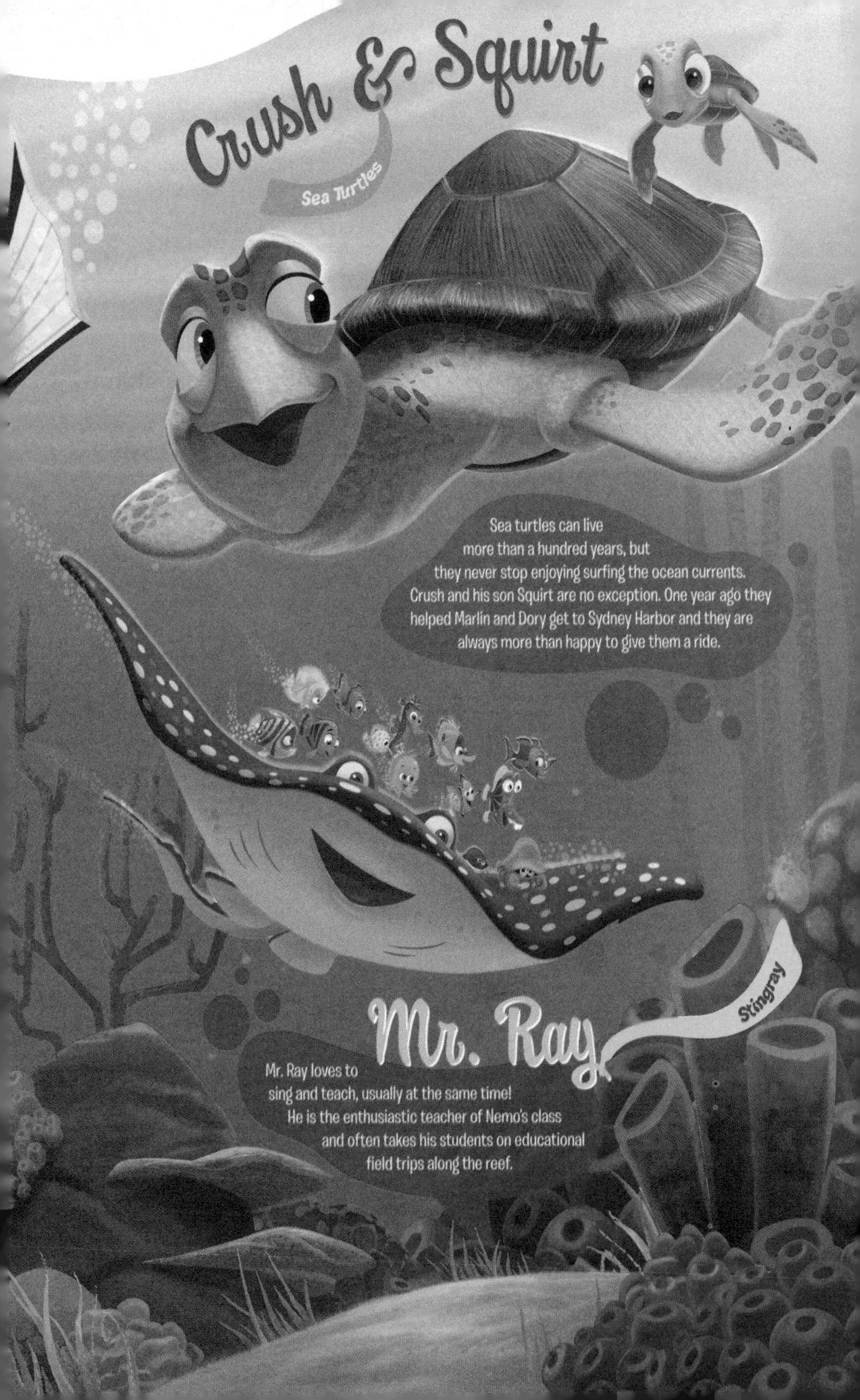
Sea Turtles
Stingray

Sea turtles can live more than a hundred years, but they never stop enjoying surfing the ocean currents. Crush and his son Squirt are no exception. One year ago they helped Marlin and Dory get to Sydney Harbor and they are always more than happy to give them a ride.

Mr. Ray

Mr. Ray loves to sing and teach, usually at the same time! He is the enthusiastic teacher of Nemo's class and often takes his students on educational field trips along the reef.

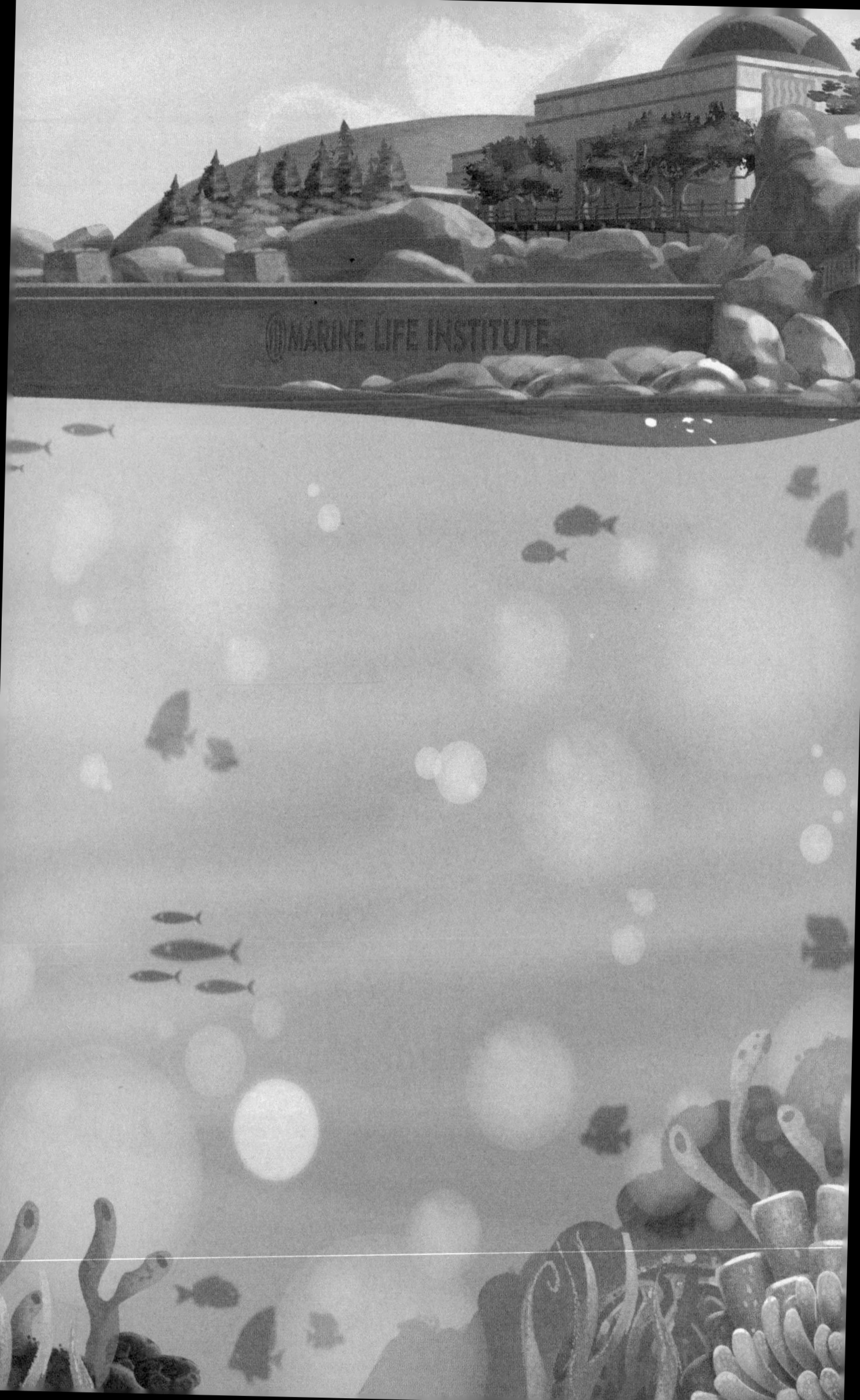
MARINE LIFE INSTITUTE

New Friends from
THE MARINE LIFE INSITUTE

Bailey
Beluga Whale

Brought into the Marine Life Institute because of a head injury, Bailey had a full recovery... but he refuses to believe it! Convinced his echolocation abilities are still damaged, he spends his days swimming in the tank near Destiny's, frequently arguing with her.

Whale Shark ### Destiny

Destiny was rescued by the Marine Life Institute due to her extreme nearsightedness: she can only see obstacles when they are close and has many troubles navigating her environment, her pool included. She speaks whale and used to communicate with a young fish through the MLI pipes, but she does not know where her friend is now.

Hank
Octopus

Hank has seven tentacles and three hearts, but only one desire: to never be sent back to the ocean again. Thanks to his camouflaging capabilities, he managed to escape his tank and is now trying to be transferred to another institute where he plans to live a long, solitary and boring life...

3

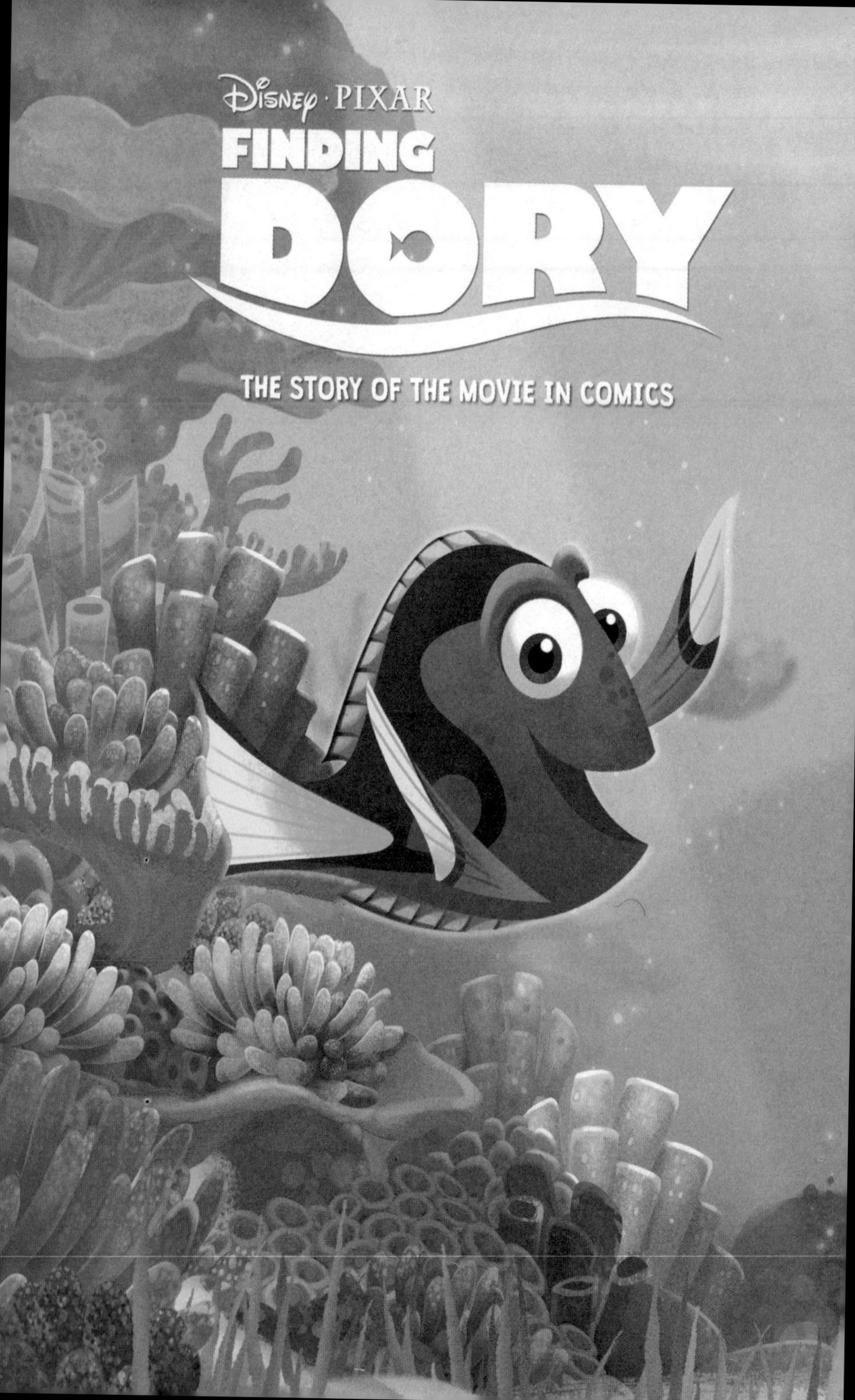
Disney · PIXAR
FINDING
DORY
THE STORY OF THE MOVIE IN COMICS

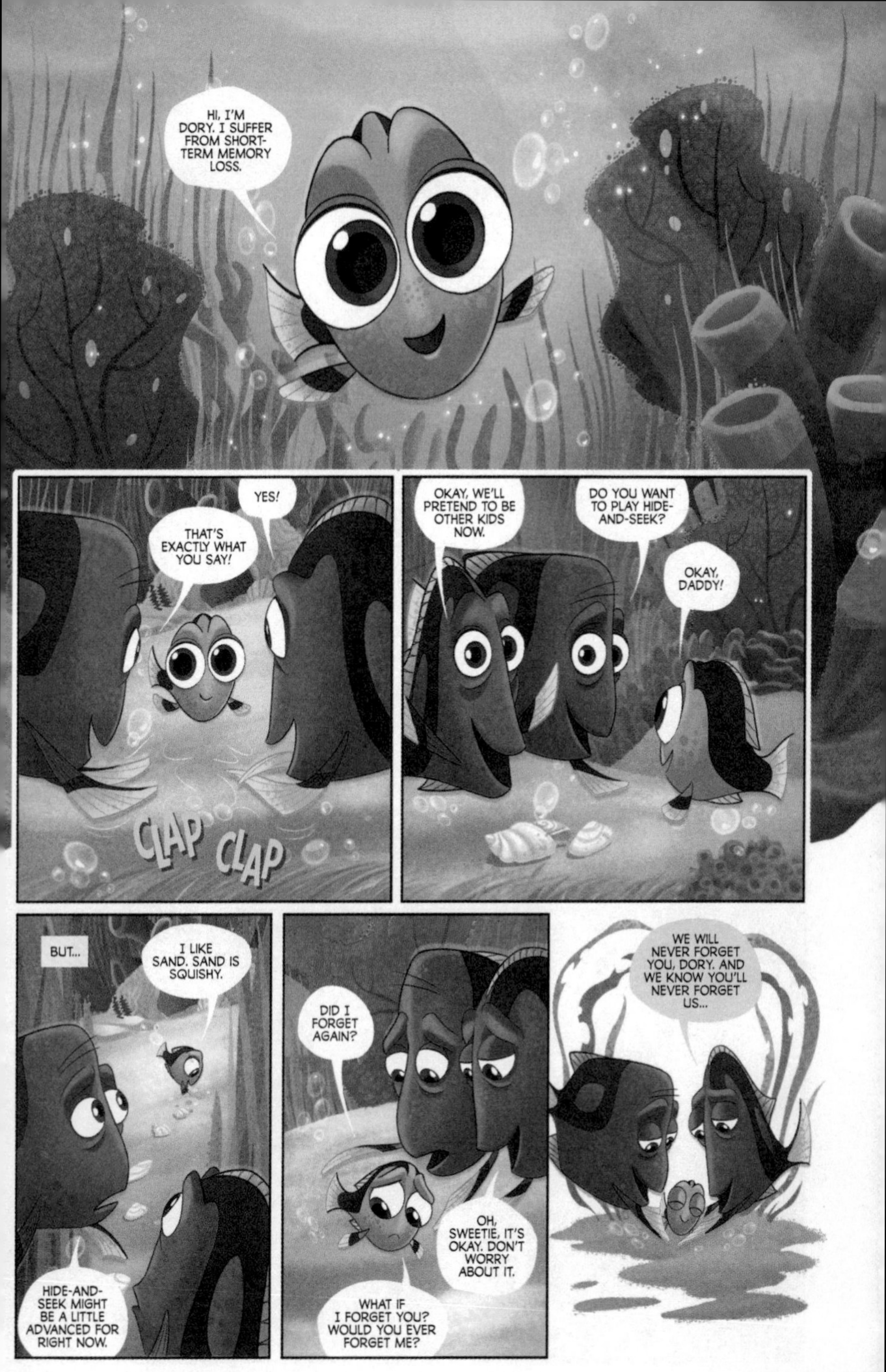
HI, I'M DORY. I SUFFER FROM SHORT-TERM MEMORY LOSS.
THAT'S EXACTLY WHAT YOU SAY!
YES!
CLAP CLAP
OKAY, WE'LL PRETEND TO BE OTHER KIDS NOW.
DO YOU WANT TO PLAY HIDE-AND-SEEK?
OKAY, DADDY!
BUT...
I LIKE SAND. SAND IS SQUISHY.
HIDE-AND-SEEK MIGHT BE A LITTLE ADVANCED FOR RIGHT NOW.
DID I FORGET AGAIN?
OH, SWEETIE, IT'S OKAY. DON'T WORRY ABOUT IT.
WHAT IF I FORGET YOU? WOULD YOU EVER FORGET ME?
WE WILL NEVER FORGET YOU, DORY. AND WE KNOW YOU'LL NEVER FORGET US...

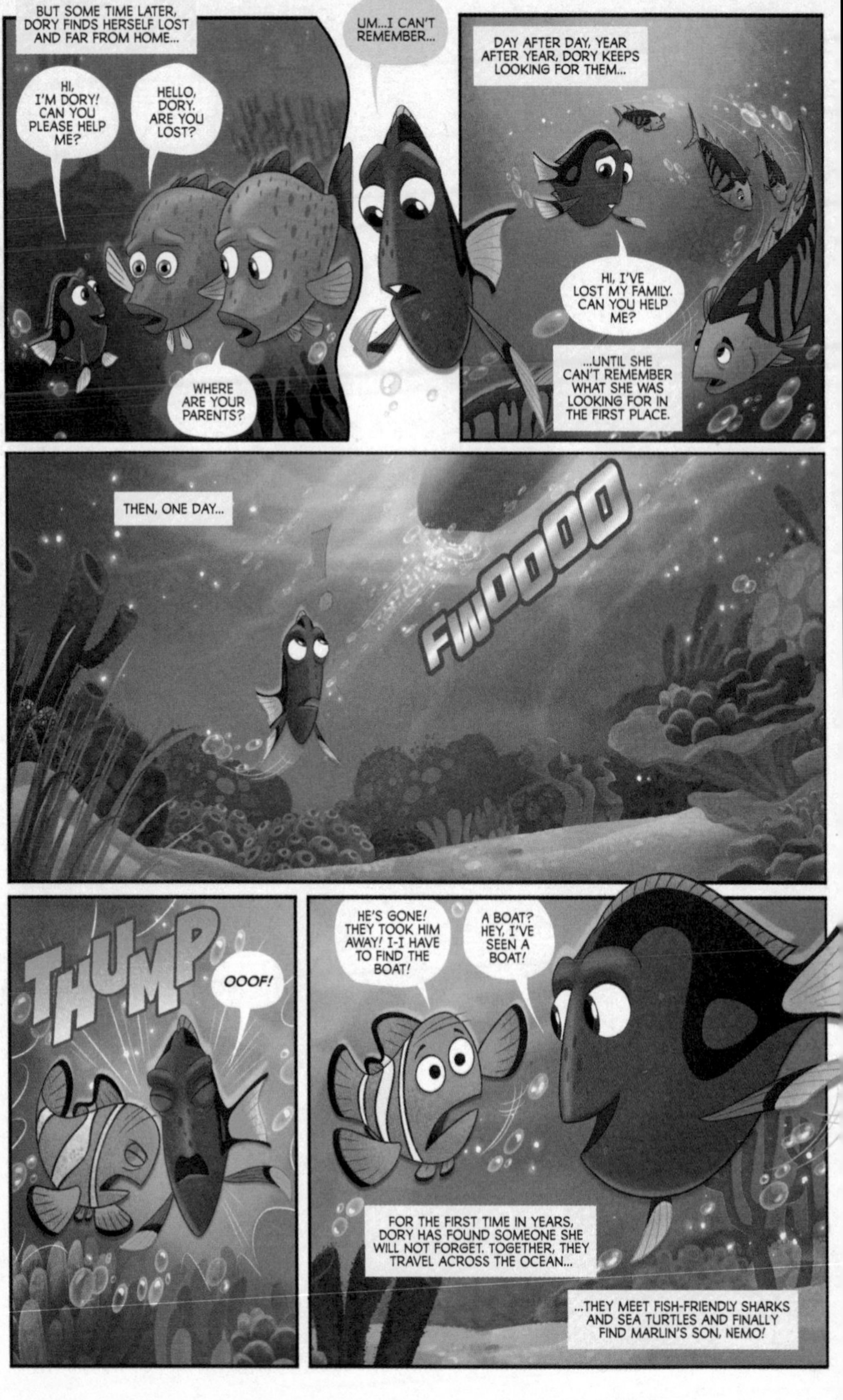

BUT SOME TIME LATER, DORY FINDS HERSELF LOST AND FAR FROM HOME...
HI, I'M DORY! CAN YOU PLEASE HELP ME?
HELLO, DORY. ARE YOU LOST?
WHERE ARE YOUR PARENTS?
UM...I CAN'T REMEMBER...
DAY AFTER DAY, YEAR AFTER YEAR, DORY KEEPS LOOKING FOR THEM...
HI, I'VE LOST MY FAMILY. CAN YOU HELP ME?
...UNTIL SHE CAN'T REMEMBER WHAT SHE WAS LOOKING FOR IN THE FIRST PLACE.
THEN, ONE DAY...
FWOOOOO
THUMP
OOOF!
HE'S GONE! THEY TOOK HIM AWAY! I-I HAVE TO FIND THE BOAT!
A BOAT? HEY, I'VE SEEN A BOAT!
FOR THE FIRST TIME IN YEARS, DORY HAS FOUND SOMEONE SHE WILL NOT FORGET. TOGETHER, THEY TRAVEL ACROSS THE OCEAN...
...THEY MEET FISH-FRIENDLY SHARKS AND SEA TURTLES AND FINALLY FIND MARLIN'S SON, NEMO!

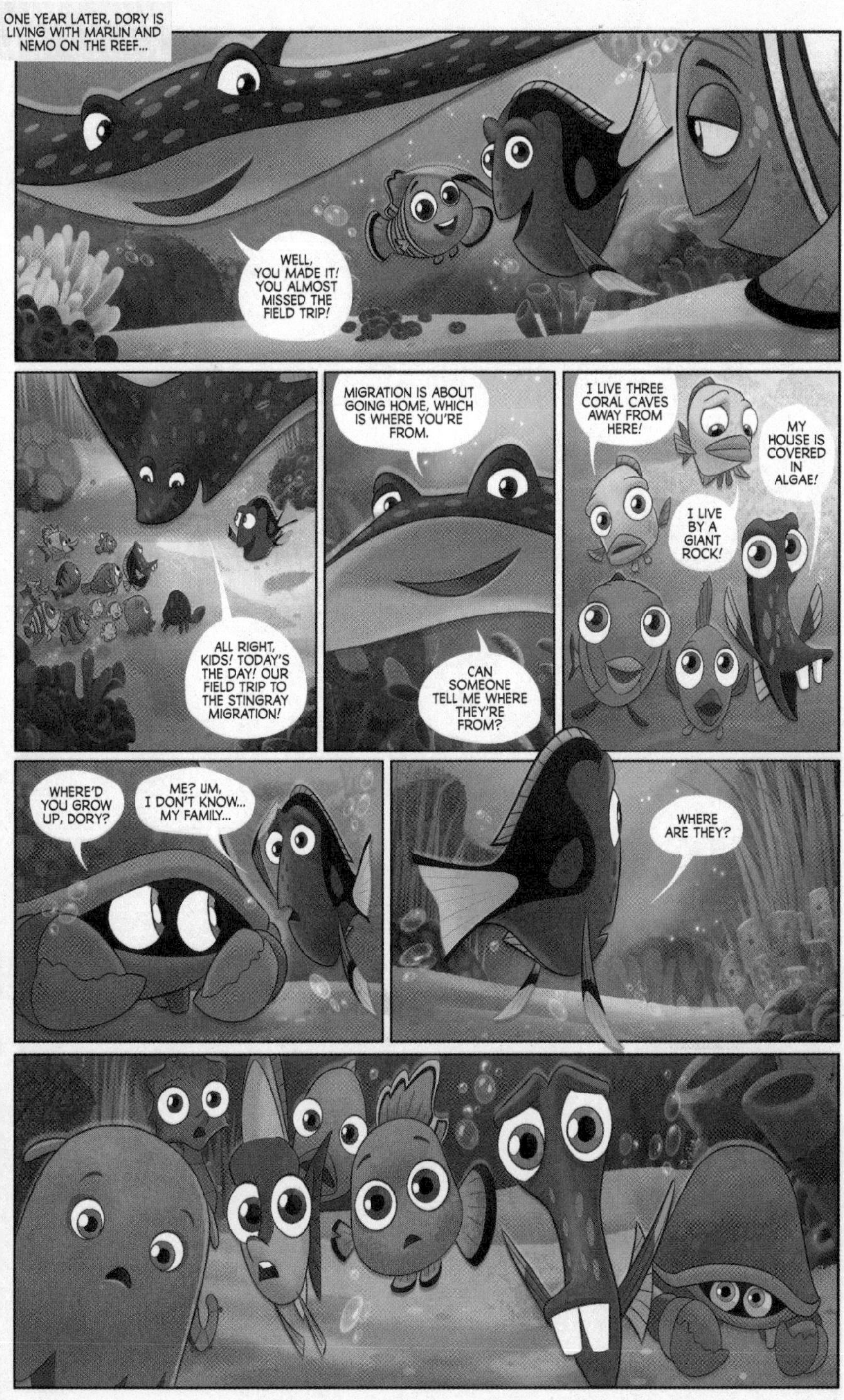
ONE YEAR LATER, DORY IS LIVING WITH MARLIN AND NEMO ON THE REEF...
WELL, YOU MADE IT! YOU ALMOST MISSED THE FIELD TRIP!
ALL RIGHT, KIDS! TODAY'S THE DAY! OUR FIELD TRIP TO THE STINGRAY MIGRATION!
MIGRATION IS ABOUT GOING HOME, WHICH IS WHERE YOU'RE FROM.
CAN SOMEONE TELL ME WHERE THEY'RE FROM?
I LIVE THREE CORAL CAVES AWAY FROM HERE!
MY HOUSE IS COVERED IN ALGAE!
I LIVE BY A GIANT ROCK!
WHERE'D YOU GROW UP, DORY?
ME? UM, I DON'T KNOW... MY FAMILY...
WHERE ARE THEY?

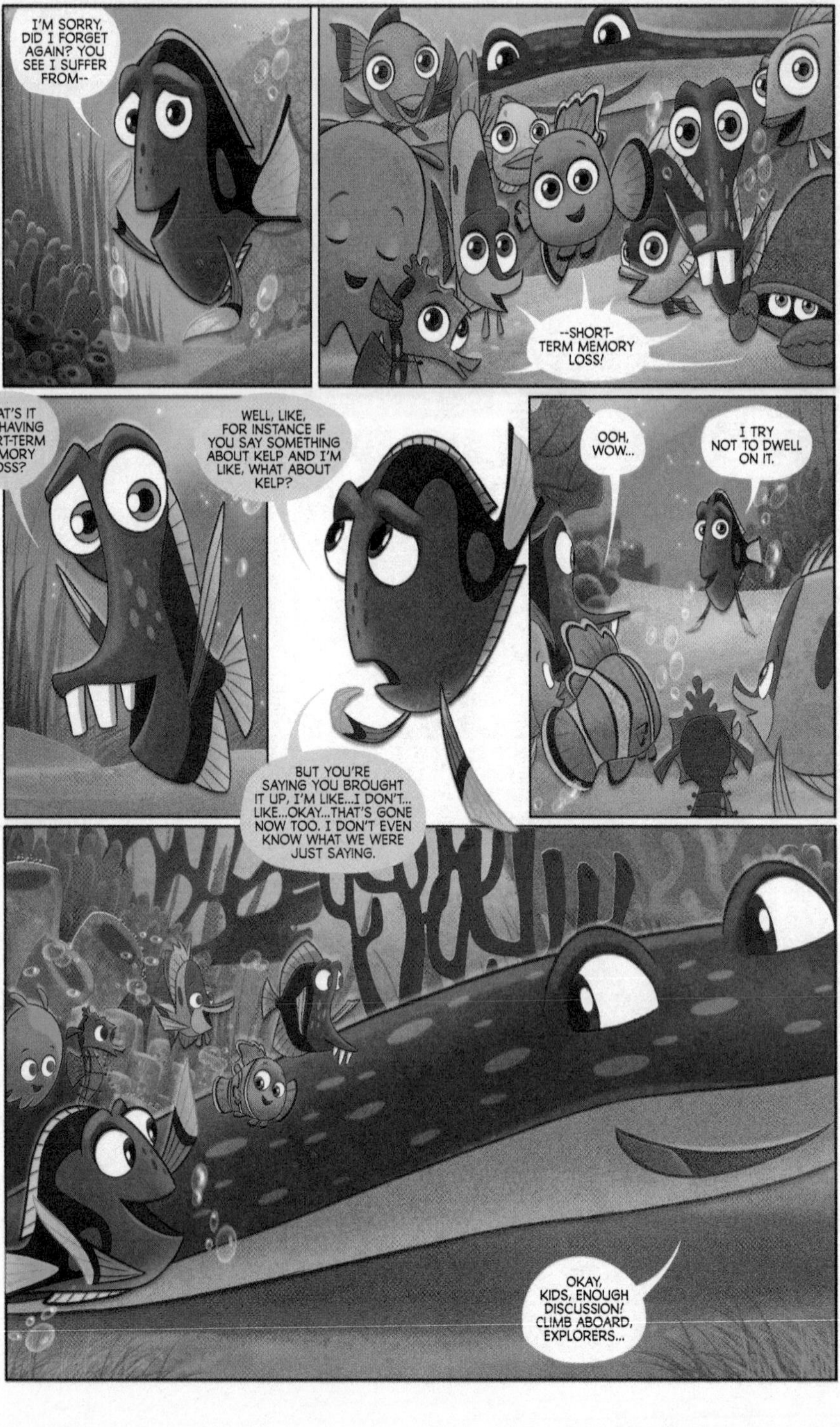
I'M SORRY, DID I FORGET AGAIN? YOU SEE I SUFFER FROM--
--SHORT-TERM MEMORY LOSS!
WHAT'S IT LIKE HAVING SHORT-TERM MEMORY LOSS?
WELL, LIKE, FOR INSTANCE IF YOU SAY SOMETHING ABOUT KELP AND I'M LIKE, WHAT ABOUT KELP?
BUT YOU'RE SAYING YOU BROUGHT IT UP, I'M LIKE...I DON'T... LIKE...OKAY...THAT'S GONE NOW TOO. I DON'T EVEN KNOW WHAT WE WERE JUST SAYING.
OOH, WOW...
I TRY NOT TO DWELL ON IT.
OKAY, KIDS, ENOUGH DISCUSSION! CLIMB ABOARD, EXPLORERS...

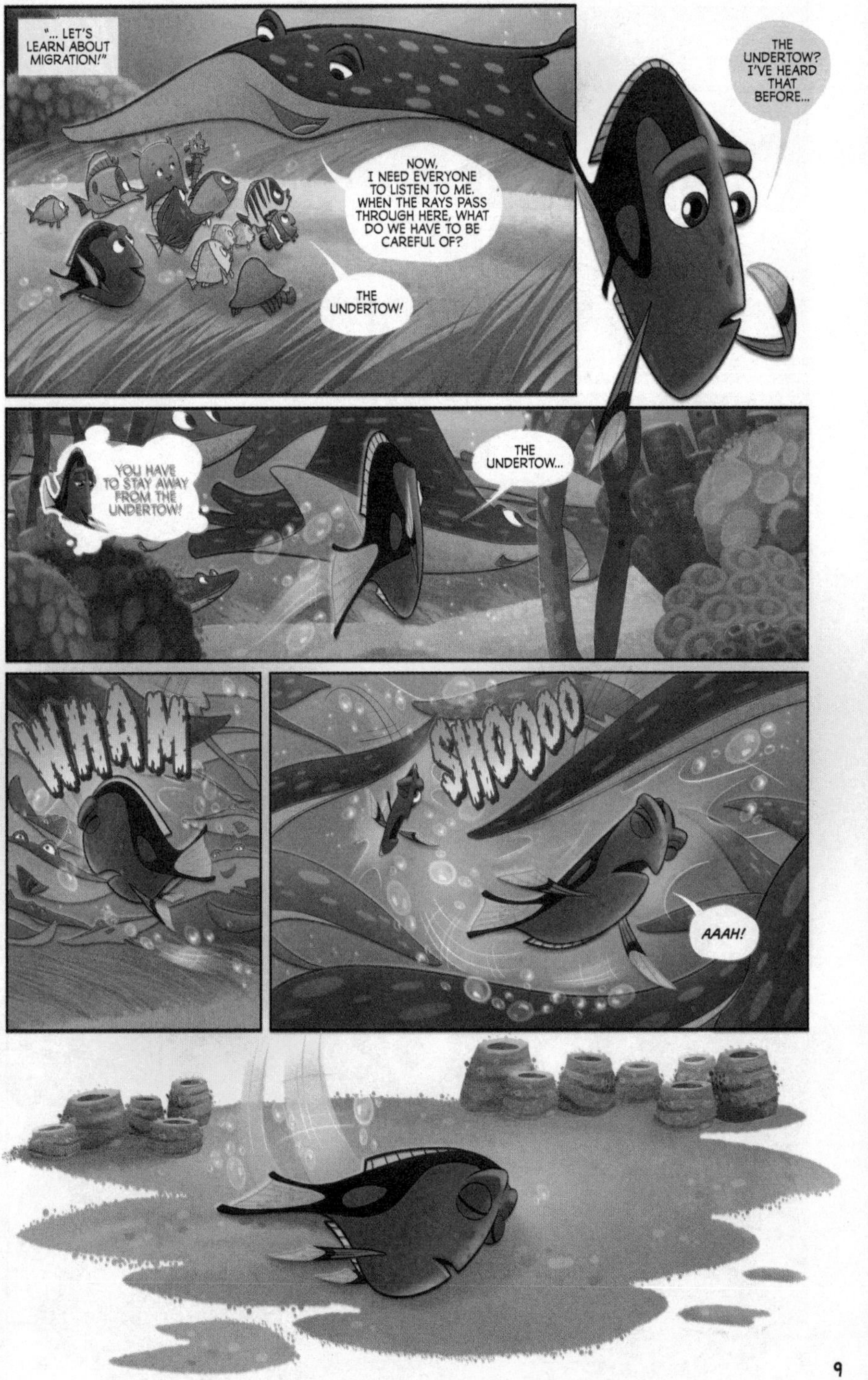
"... LET'S LEARN ABOUT MIGRATION!"
NOW, I NEED EVERYONE TO LISTEN TO ME. WHEN THE RAYS PASS THROUGH HERE, WHAT DO WE HAVE TO BE CAREFUL OF?
THE UNDERTOW!
THE UNDERTOW? I'VE HEARD THAT BEFORE...
YOU HAVE TO STAY AWAY FROM THE UNDERTOW!
THE UNDERTOW...
WHAM
SHOOOO
AAAH!

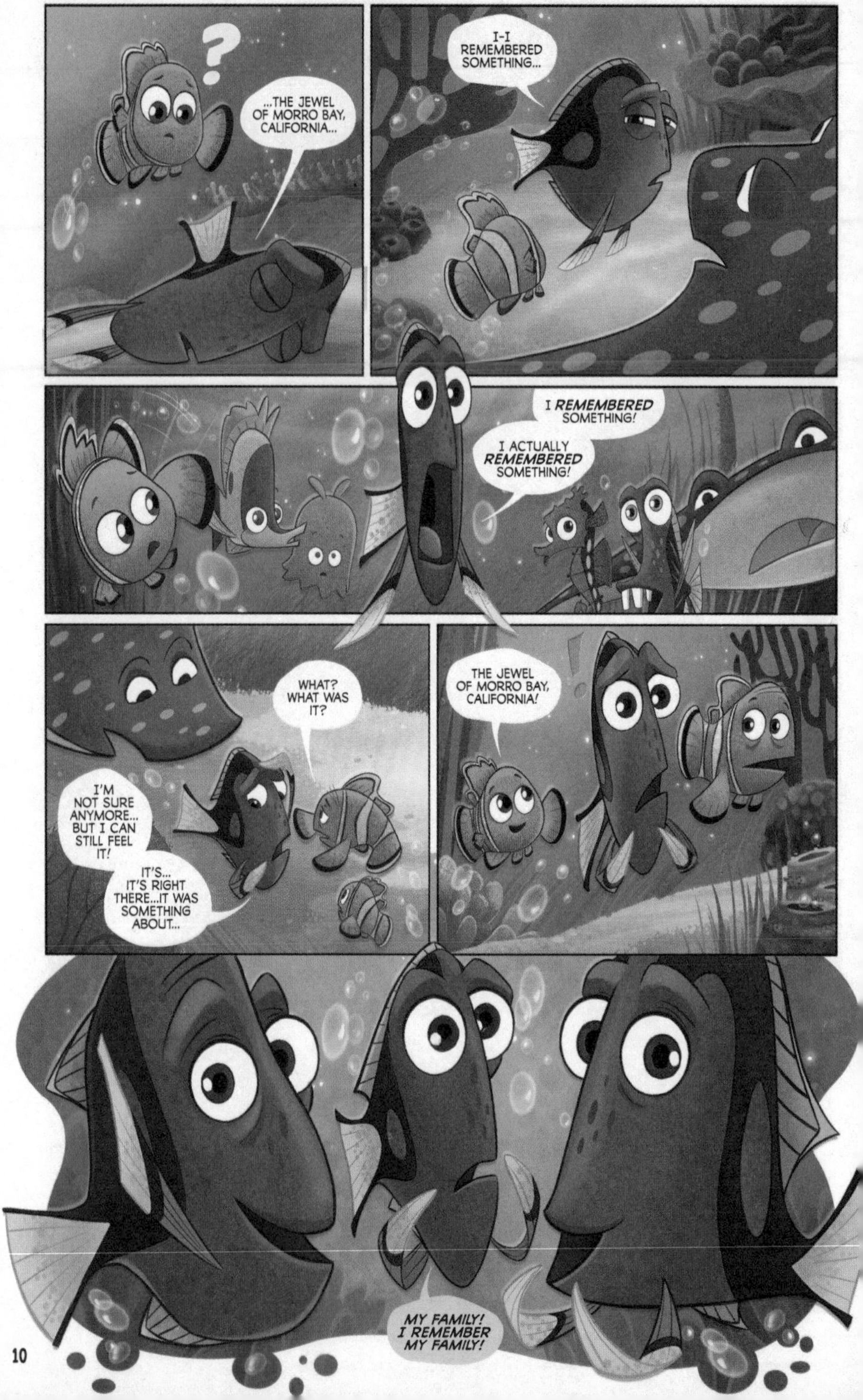
?
...THE JEWEL OF MORRO BAY, CALIFORNIA...
I-I REMEMBERED SOMETHING...
I *REMEMBERED* SOMETHING!
I ACTUALLY *REMEMBERED* SOMETHING!
WHAT? WHAT WAS IT?
I'M NOT SURE ANYMORE... BUT I CAN STILL FEEL IT!
IT'S... IT'S RIGHT THERE...IT WAS SOMETHING ABOUT...
THE JEWEL OF MORRO BAY, CALIFORNIA!
MY FAMILY! I REMEMBER MY FAMILY!

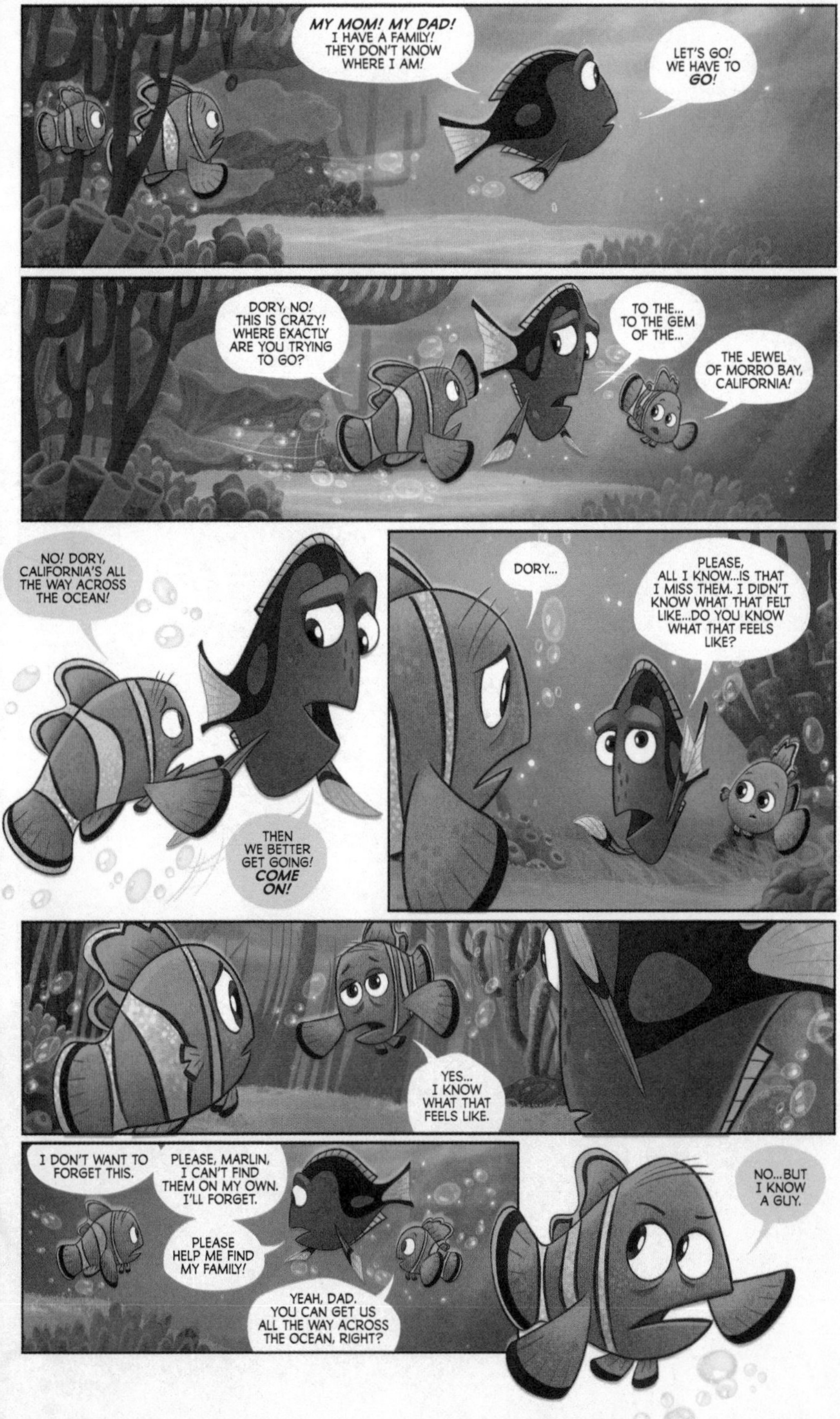
MY MOM! MY DAD! I HAVE A FAMILY! THEY DON'T KNOW WHERE I AM!
LET'S GO! WE HAVE TO GO!
DORY, NO! THIS IS CRAZY! WHERE EXACTLY ARE YOU TRYING TO GO?
TO THE... TO THE GEM OF THE...
THE JEWEL OF MORRO BAY, CALIFORNIA!
NO! DORY, CALIFORNIA'S ALL THE WAY ACROSS THE OCEAN!
THEN WE BETTER GET GOING! COME ON!
DORY...
PLEASE, ALL I KNOW...IS THAT I MISS THEM. I DIDN'T KNOW WHAT THAT FELT LIKE...DO YOU KNOW WHAT THAT FEELS LIKE?
YES... I KNOW WHAT THAT FEELS LIKE.
I DON'T WANT TO FORGET THIS.
PLEASE, MARLIN, I CAN'T FIND THEM ON MY OWN. I'LL FORGET.
PLEASE HELP ME FIND MY FAMILY!
YEAH, DAD. YOU CAN GET US ALL THE WAY ACROSS THE OCEAN, RIGHT?
NO...BUT I KNOW A GUY.

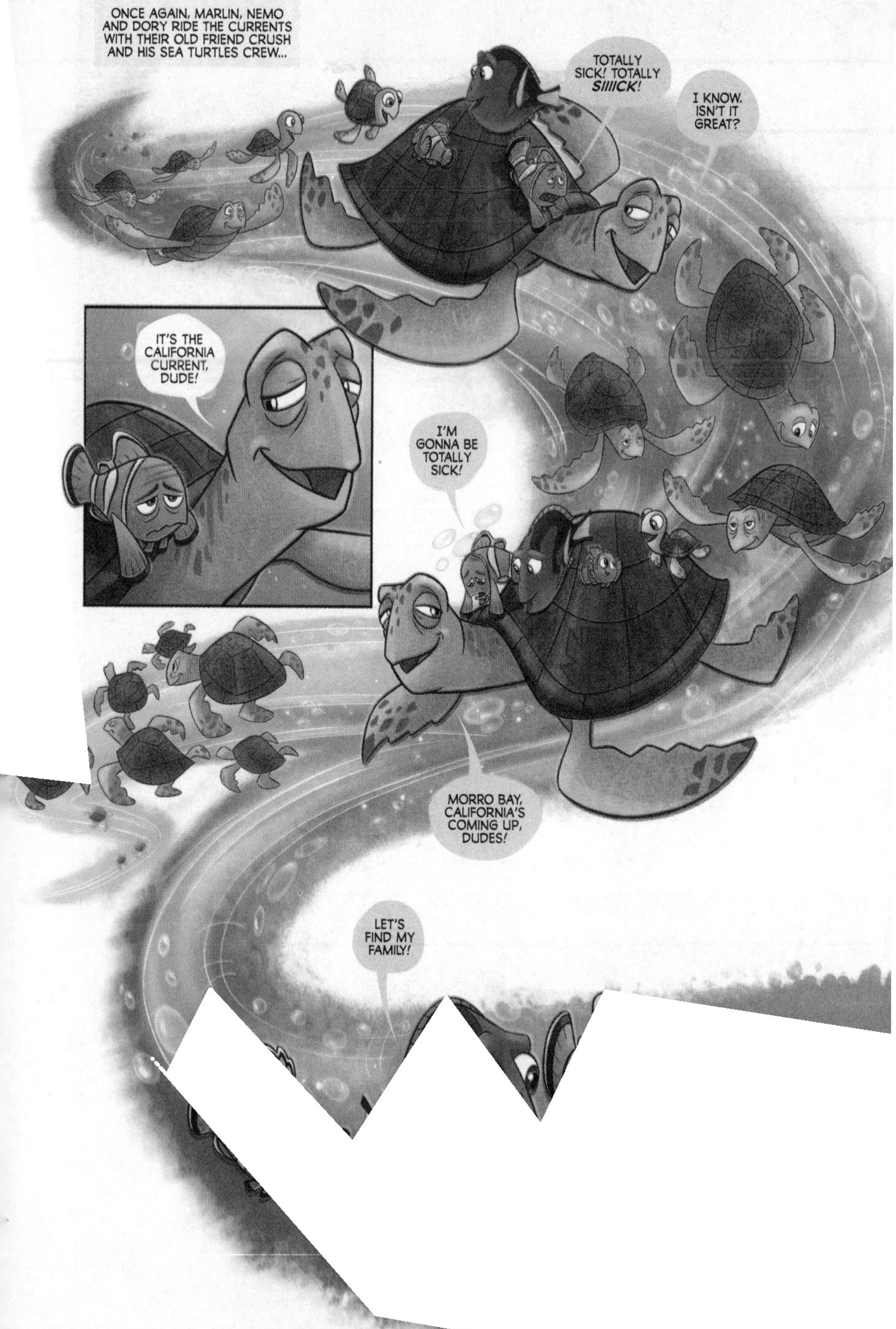
ONCE AGAIN, MARLIN, NEMO AND DORY RIDE THE CURRENTS WITH THEIR OLD FRIEND CRUSH AND HIS SEA TURTLES CREW...
TOTALLY SICK! TOTALLY SIIIICK!
I KNOW. ISN'T IT GREAT?
IT'S THE CALIFORNIA CURRENT, DUDE!
I'M GONNA BE TOTALLY SICK!
MORRO BAY, CALIFORNIA'S COMING UP, DUDES!
LET'S FIND MY FAMILY!

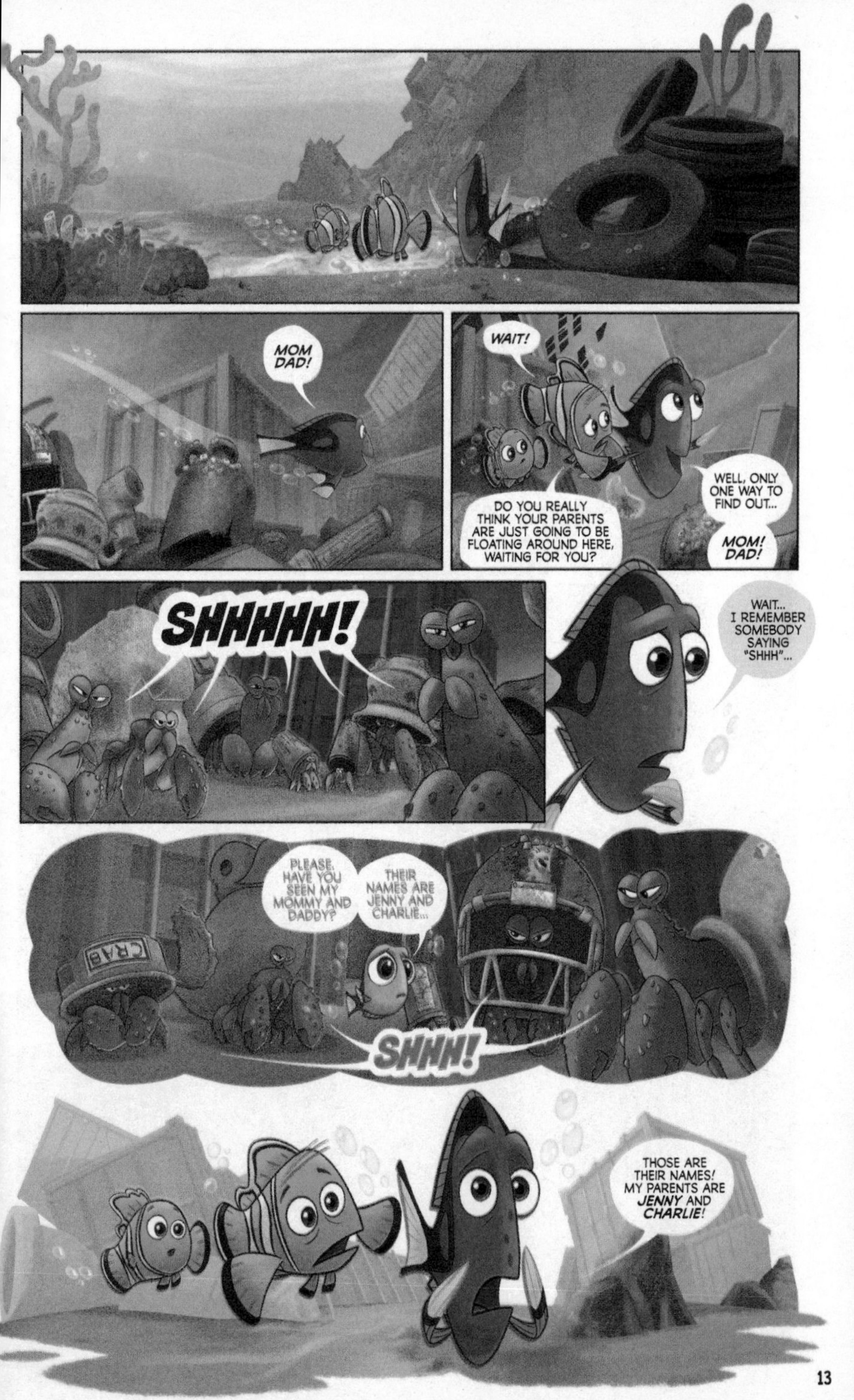
MOM
DAD!
WAIT!
DO YOU REALLY THINK YOUR PARENTS ARE JUST GOING TO BE FLOATING AROUND HERE, WAITING FOR YOU?
WELL, ONLY ONE WAY TO FIND OUT...
MOM! DAD!
SHHHHH!
WAIT... I REMEMBER SOMEBODY SAYING "SHHH"...
PLEASE, HAVE YOU SEEN MY MOMMY AND DADDY?
THEIR NAMES ARE JENNY AND CHARLIE...
CRAB
SHHH!
THOSE ARE THEIR NAMES! MY PARENTS ARE JENNY AND CHARLIE!

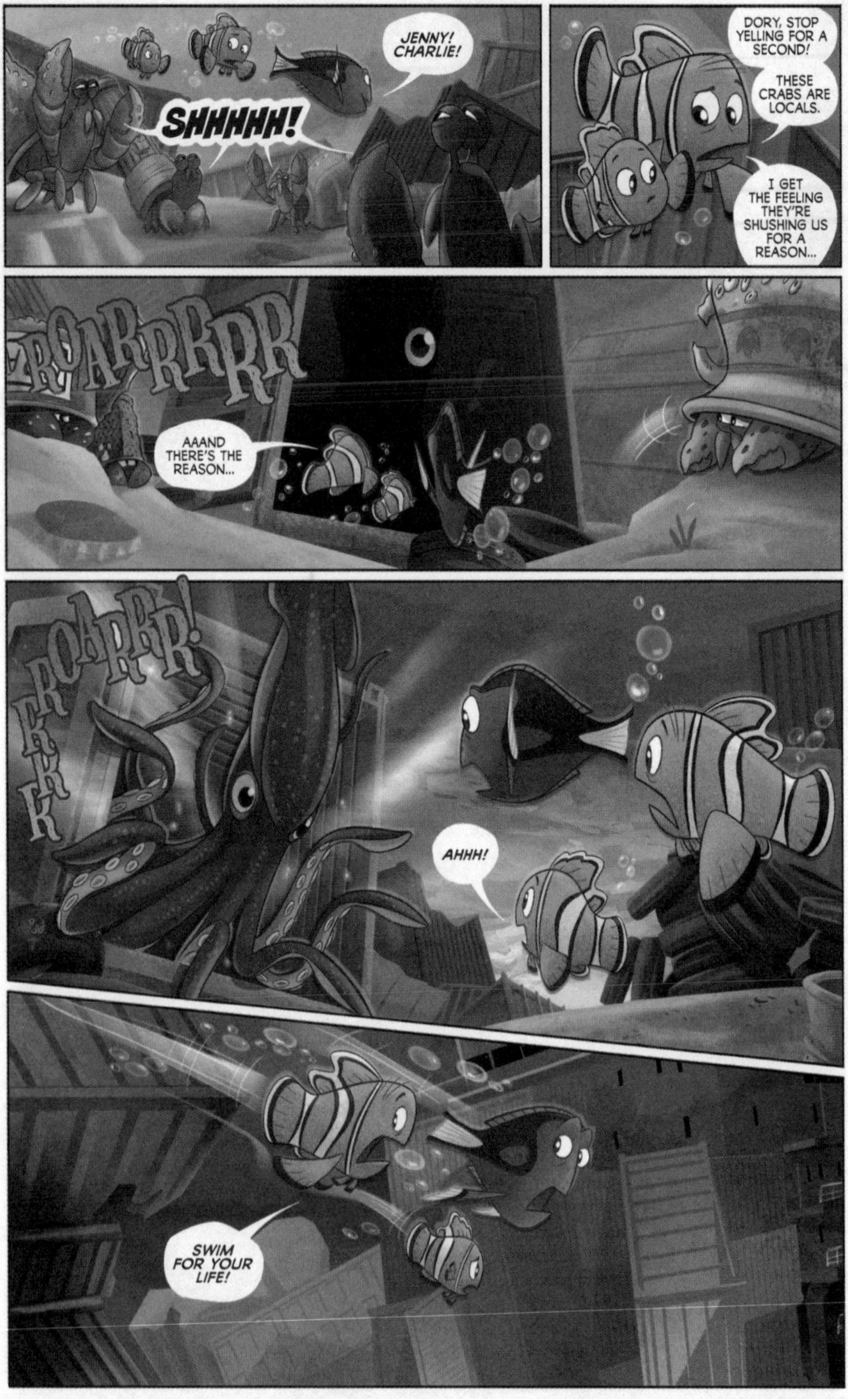
JENNY! CHARLIE!
SHHHHH!
DORY, STOP YELLING FOR A SECOND!
THESE CRABS ARE LOCALS.
I GET THE FEELING THEY'RE SHUSHING US FOR A REASON...
ROARRRRRR
AAAND THERE'S THE REASON...
ROARRR!
RRRR
AHHH!
SWIM FOR YOUR LIFE!

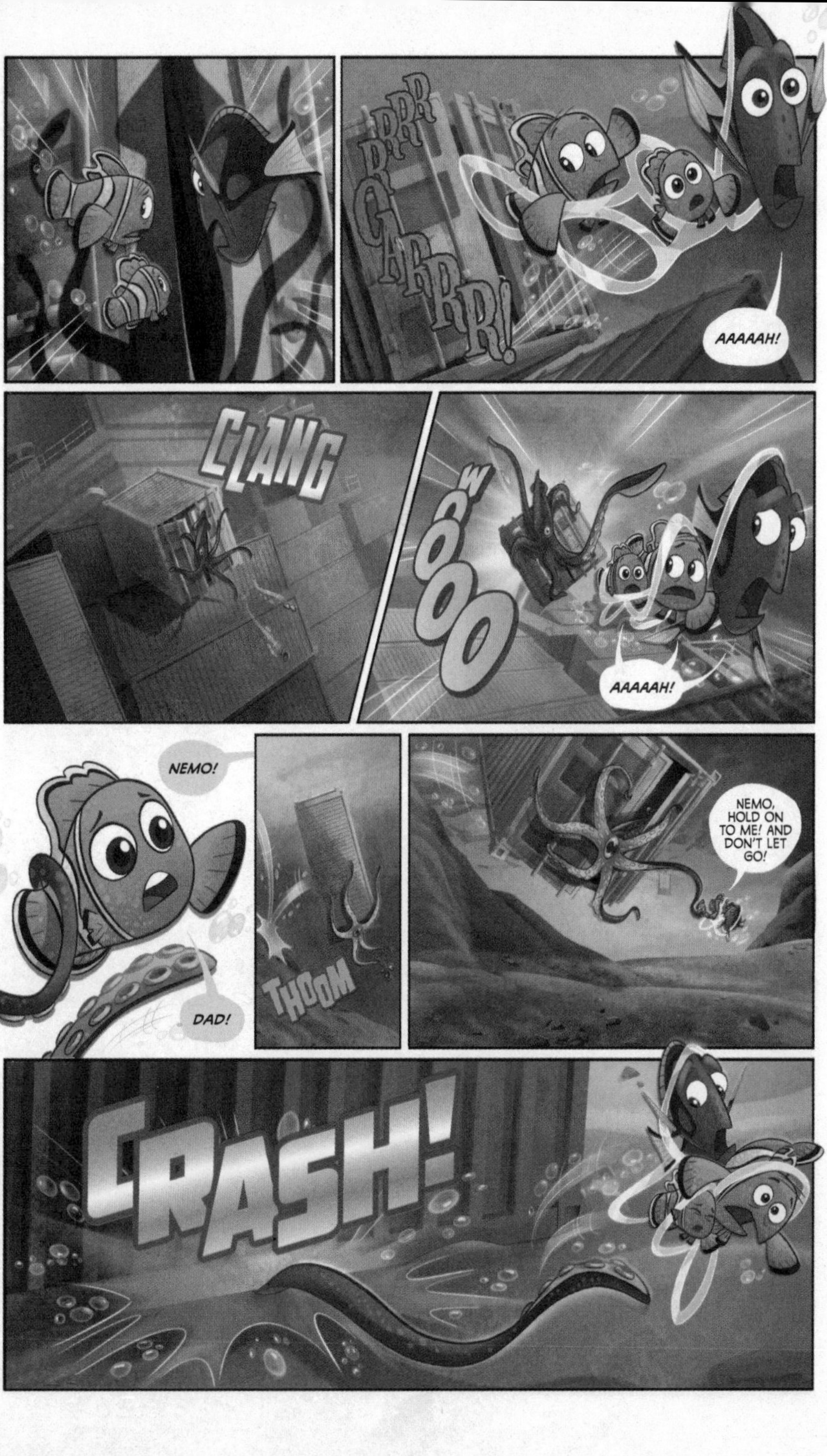
RRRRGARRRR!
AAAAAH!
CLANG
WOOOO
AAAAAH!
NEMO!
DAD!
THOOM
NEMO, HOLD ON TO ME! AND DON'T LET GO!
CRASH!

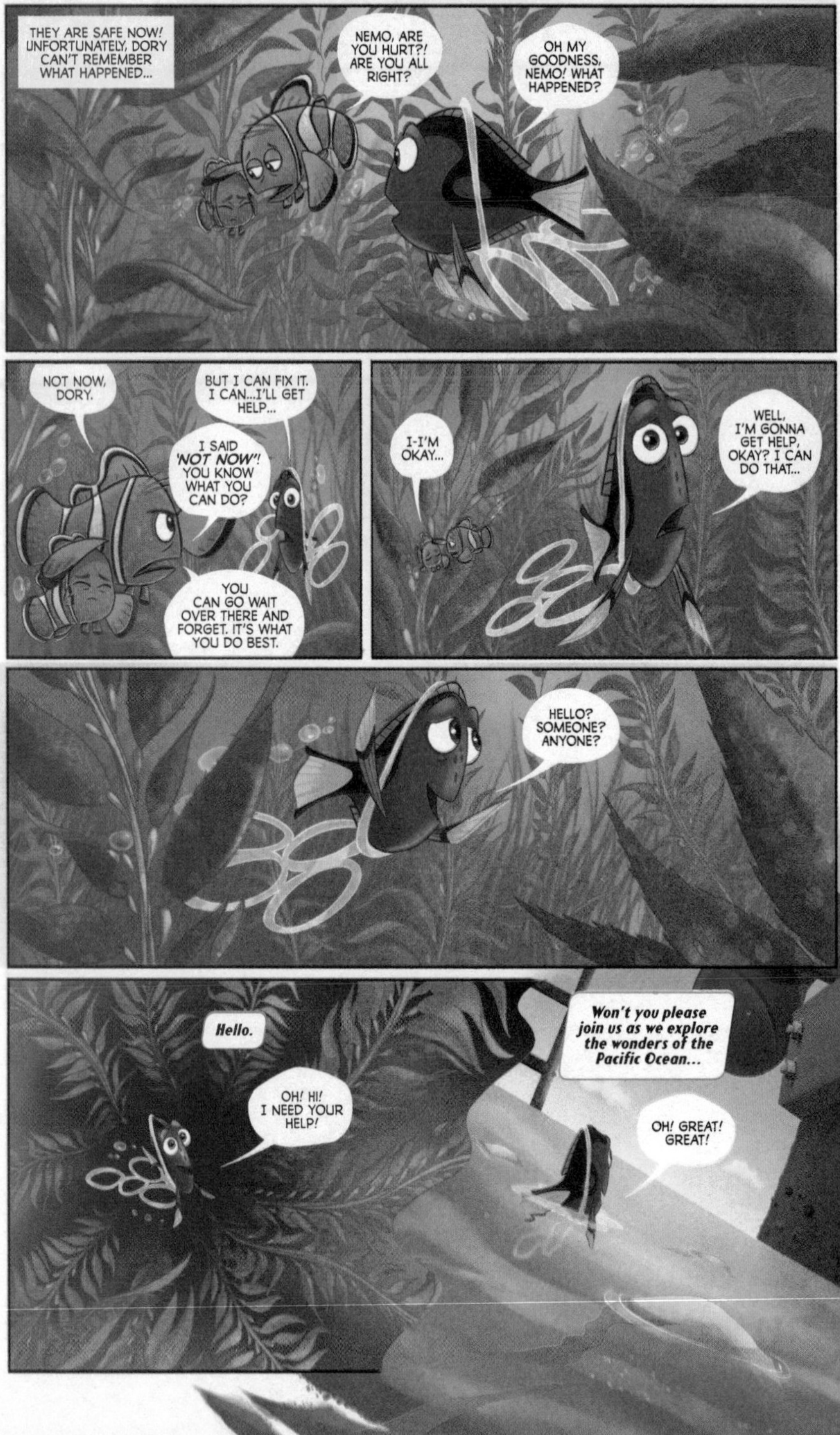
THEY ARE SAFE NOW! UNFORTUNATELY, DORY CAN'T REMEMBER WHAT HAPPENED...
NEMO, ARE YOU HURT?! ARE YOU ALL RIGHT?
OH MY GOODNESS, NEMO! WHAT HAPPENED?
NOT NOW, DORY.
BUT I CAN FIX IT. I CAN...I'LL GET HELP...
I SAID 'NOT NOW'! YOU KNOW WHAT YOU CAN DO?
YOU CAN GO WAIT OVER THERE AND FORGET. IT'S WHAT YOU DO BEST.
I-I'M OKAY...
WELL, I'M GONNA GET HELP, OKAY? I CAN DO THAT...
HELLO? SOMEONE? ANYONE?
Hello.
OH! HI! I NEED YOUR HELP!
Won't you please join us as we explore the wonders of the Pacific Ocean...
OH! GREAT! GREAT!

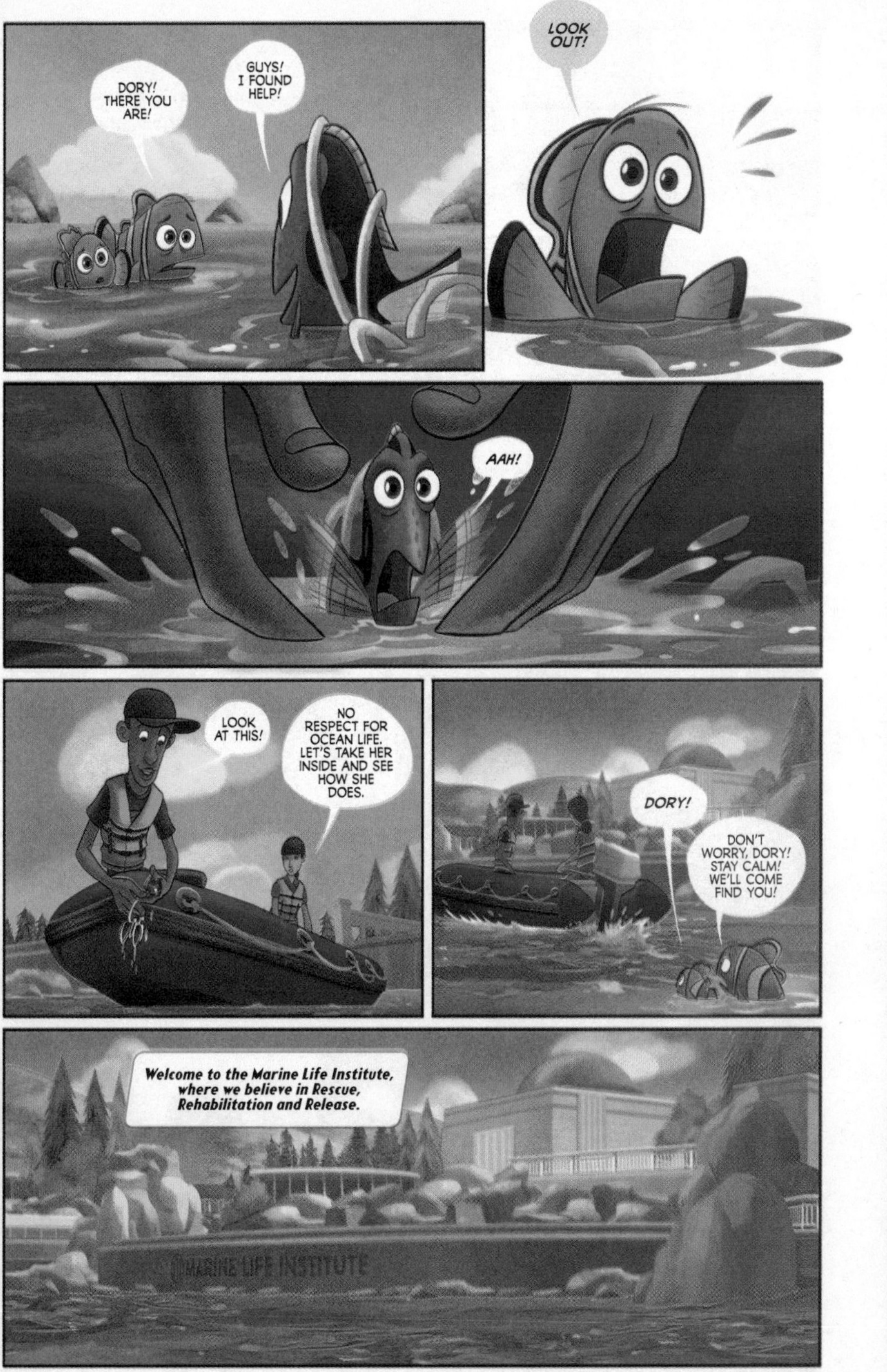
DORY! THERE YOU ARE!
GUYS! I FOUND HELP!
LOOK OUT!
AAH!
LOOK AT THIS!
NO RESPECT FOR OCEAN LIFE. LET'S TAKE HER INSIDE AND SEE HOW SHE DOES.
DORY!
DON'T WORRY, DORY! STAY CALM! WE'LL COME FIND YOU!
Welcome to the Marine Life Institute, where we believe in Rescue, Rehabilitation and Release.
MARINE LIFE INSTITUTE

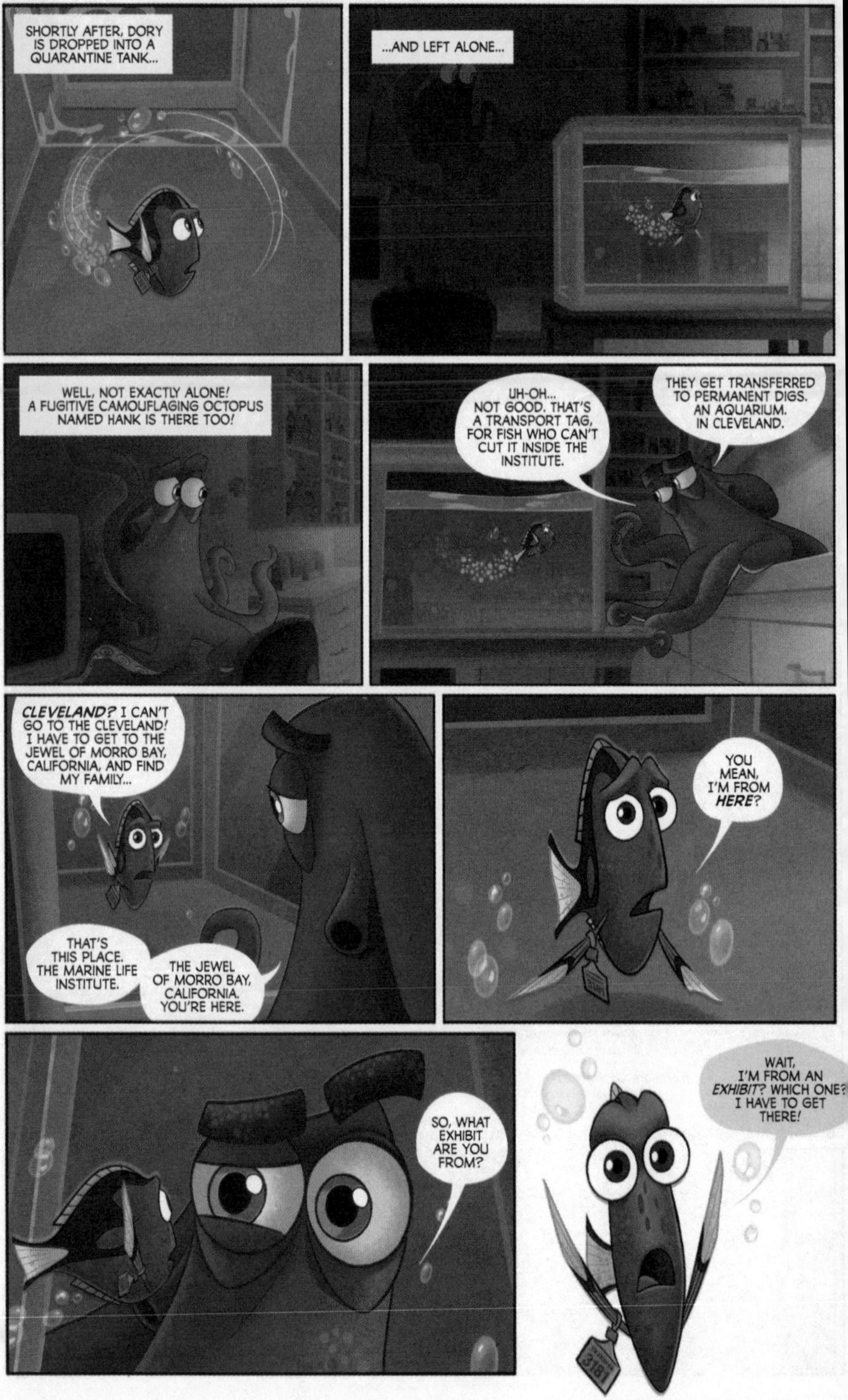
SHORTLY AFTER, DORY IS DROPPED INTO A QUARANTINE TANK...
...AND LEFT ALONE...
WELL, NOT EXACTLY ALONE! A FUGITIVE CAMOUFLAGING OCTOPUS NAMED HANK IS THERE TOO!
UH-OH... NOT GOOD. THAT'S A TRANSPORT TAG, FOR FISH WHO CAN'T CUT IT INSIDE THE INSTITUTE.
THEY GET TRANSFERRED TO PERMANENT DIGS. AN AQUARIUM. IN CLEVELAND.
CLEVELAND? I CAN'T GO TO THE CLEVELAND! I HAVE TO GET TO THE JEWEL OF MORRO BAY, CALIFORNIA, AND FIND MY FAMILY...
THAT'S THIS PLACE. THE MARINE LIFE INSTITUTE.
THE JEWEL OF MORRO BAY, CALIFORNIA. YOU'RE HERE.
YOU MEAN, I'M FROM HERE?
SO, WHAT EXHIBIT ARE YOU FROM?
WAIT, I'M FROM AN EXHIBIT? WHICH ONE? I HAVE TO GET THERE!
3181

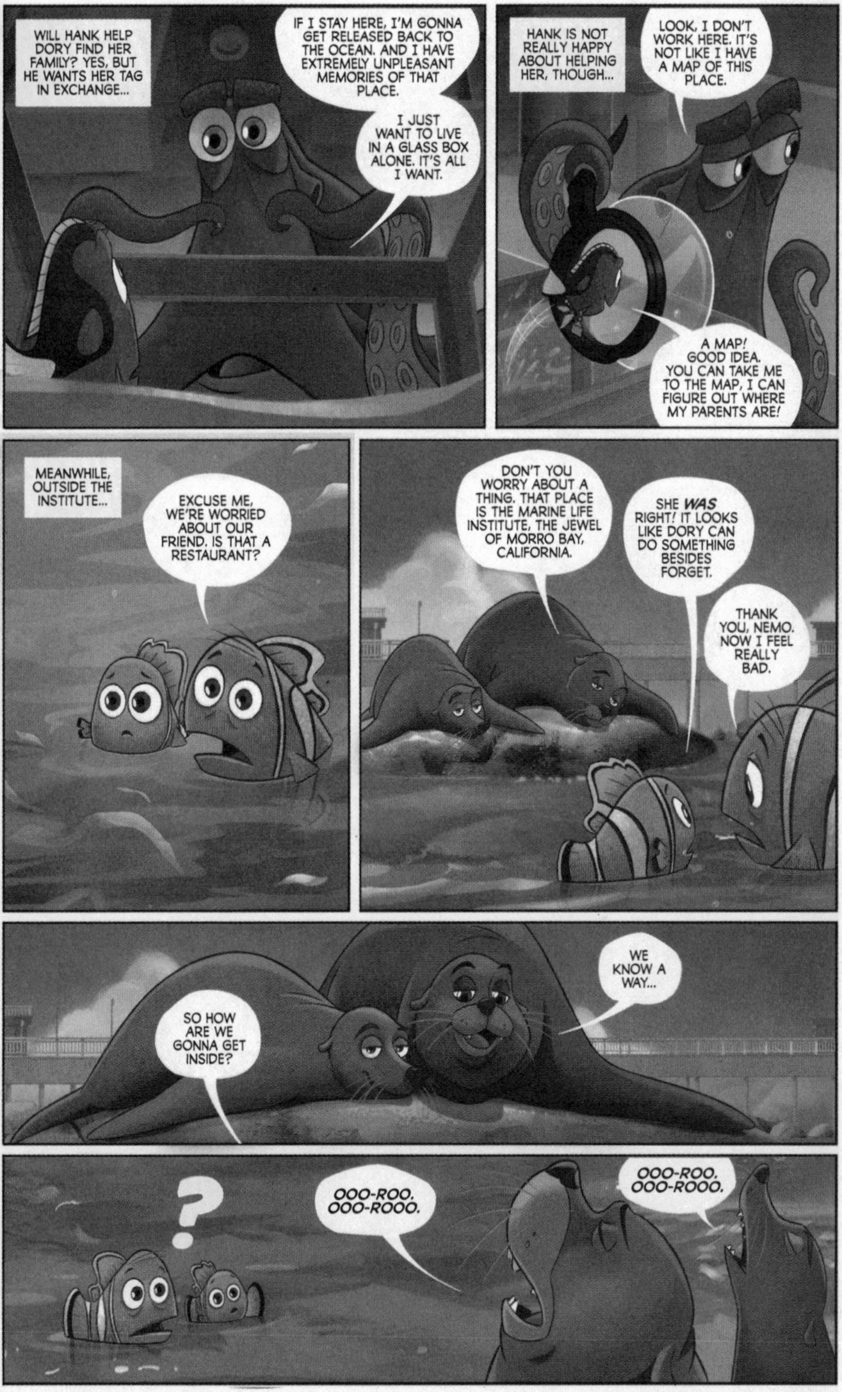
WILL HANK HELP DORY FIND HER FAMILY? YES, BUT HE WANTS HER TAG IN EXCHANGE...
IF I STAY HERE, I'M GONNA GET RELEASED BACK TO THE OCEAN. AND I HAVE EXTREMELY UNPLEASANT MEMORIES OF THAT PLACE.
I JUST WANT TO LIVE IN A GLASS BOX ALONE. IT'S ALL I WANT.
HANK IS NOT REALLY HAPPY ABOUT HELPING HER, THOUGH...
LOOK, I DON'T WORK HERE. IT'S NOT LIKE I HAVE A MAP OF THIS PLACE.
A MAP! GOOD IDEA. YOU CAN TAKE ME TO THE MAP, I CAN FIGURE OUT WHERE MY PARENTS ARE!
MEANWHILE, OUTSIDE THE INSTITUTE...
EXCUSE ME, WE'RE WORRIED ABOUT OUR FRIEND. IS THAT A RESTAURANT?
DON'T YOU WORRY ABOUT A THING. THAT PLACE IS THE MARINE LIFE INSTITUTE, THE JEWEL OF MORRO BAY, CALIFORNIA.
SHE *WAS* RIGHT! IT LOOKS LIKE DORY CAN DO SOMETHING BESIDES FORGET.
THANK YOU, NEMO. NOW I FEEL REALLY BAD.
SO HOW ARE WE GONNA GET INSIDE?
WE KNOW A WAY...
?
OOO-ROO. OOO-ROOO.
OOO-ROO. OOO-ROOO.

INSIDE THE *MLI*, HANK TAKES A NERVOUS DORY TO THE BACK OFFICES...

HANK, I'M SO GLAD I FOUND YOU. IT FEELS LIKE... *DESTINY!*

SHH! FOR WHAT MUST BE THE MILLIONTH TIME, IT'S *NOT* DESTINY!

THERE IT IS! THE MAP THEY WERE LOOKING FOR...

K-K-KEED... ZEE...ONE. KID ZONE!

NO KIDS! KIDS GRAB THINGS AND I'M NOT LOSING ANOTHER TENTACLE FOR YOU!

YOU LOST A TENTACLE?

WELL, THEN YOU'RE NOT AN OCTOPUS... YOU'RE A *SEPTOPUS!*

HEY, LOOK. SHELLS.

HEY, LOOK, SHELLS. I LIKE SHELLS.

THAT'S RIGHT, DEAR. DO YOU THINK YOU COULD FIND ME ANOTHER SHELL? PURPLE ONES ARE MY FAVORITE.

OKAY, MUMMY!

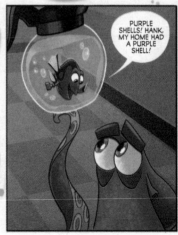

PURPLE SHELLS! HANK, MY HOME HAD A PURPLE SHELL!

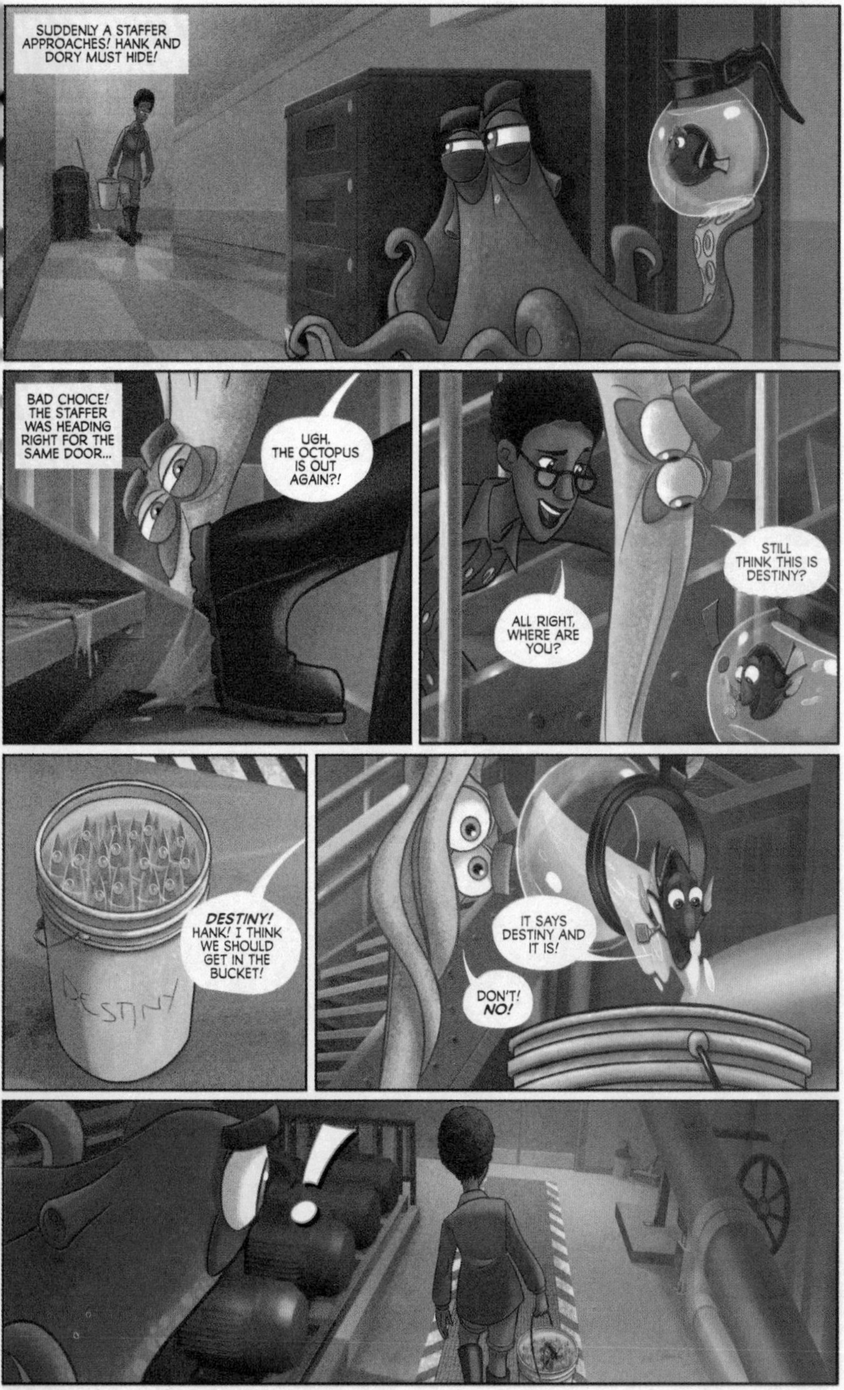
SUDDENLY A STAFFER APPROACHES! HANK AND DORY MUST HIDE!
BAD CHOICE! THE STAFFER WAS HEADING RIGHT FOR THE SAME DOOR...
UGH. THE OCTOPUS IS OUT AGAIN?!
STILL THINK THIS IS DESTINY?
ALL RIGHT, WHERE ARE YOU?
DESTINY! HANK! I THINK WE SHOULD GET IN THE BUCKET!
DESTINY
IT SAYS DESTINY AND IT IS!
DON'T! ***NO!***

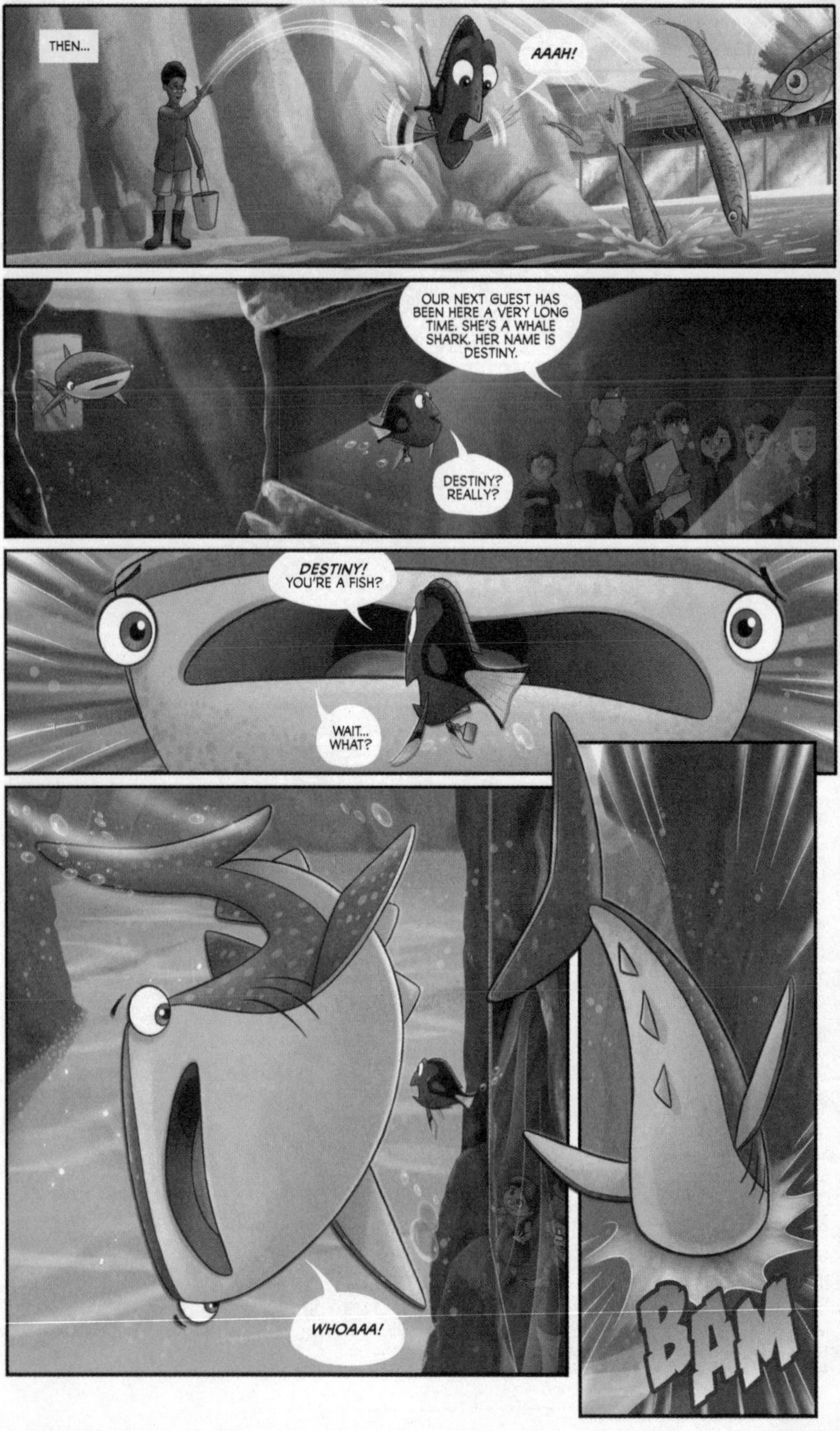
THEN...
AAAH!
OUR NEXT GUEST HAS BEEN HERE A VERY LONG TIME. SHE'S A WHALE SHARK. HER NAME IS DESTINY.
DESTINY? REALLY?
DESTINY! YOU'RE A FISH?
WAIT... WHAT?
WHOAAA!
BAM

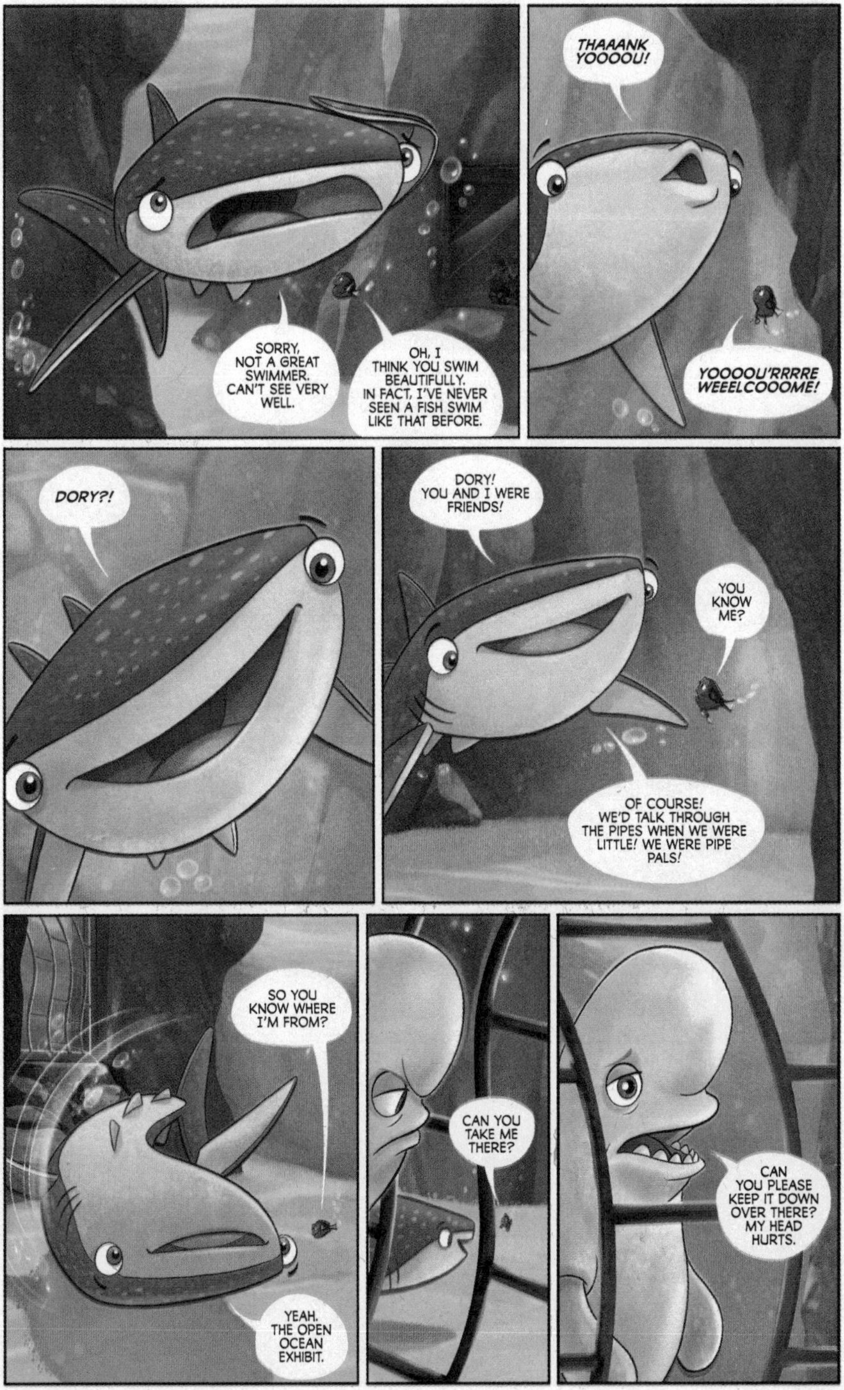
SORRY, NOT A GREAT SWIMMER. CAN'T SEE VERY WELL.
OH, I THINK YOU SWIM BEAUTIFULLY. IN FACT, I'VE NEVER SEEN A FISH SWIM LIKE THAT BEFORE.
THAAANK YOOOOU!
YOOOOU'RRRRE WEEELCOOOME!
DORY?!
DORY! YOU AND I WERE FRIENDS!
YOU KNOW ME?
OF COURSE! WE'D TALK THROUGH THE PIPES WHEN WE WERE LITTLE! WE WERE PIPE PALS!
SO YOU KNOW WHERE I'M FROM?
YEAH. THE OPEN OCEAN EXHIBIT.
CAN YOU TAKE ME THERE?
CAN YOU PLEASE KEEP IT DOWN OVER THERE? MY HEAD HURTS.

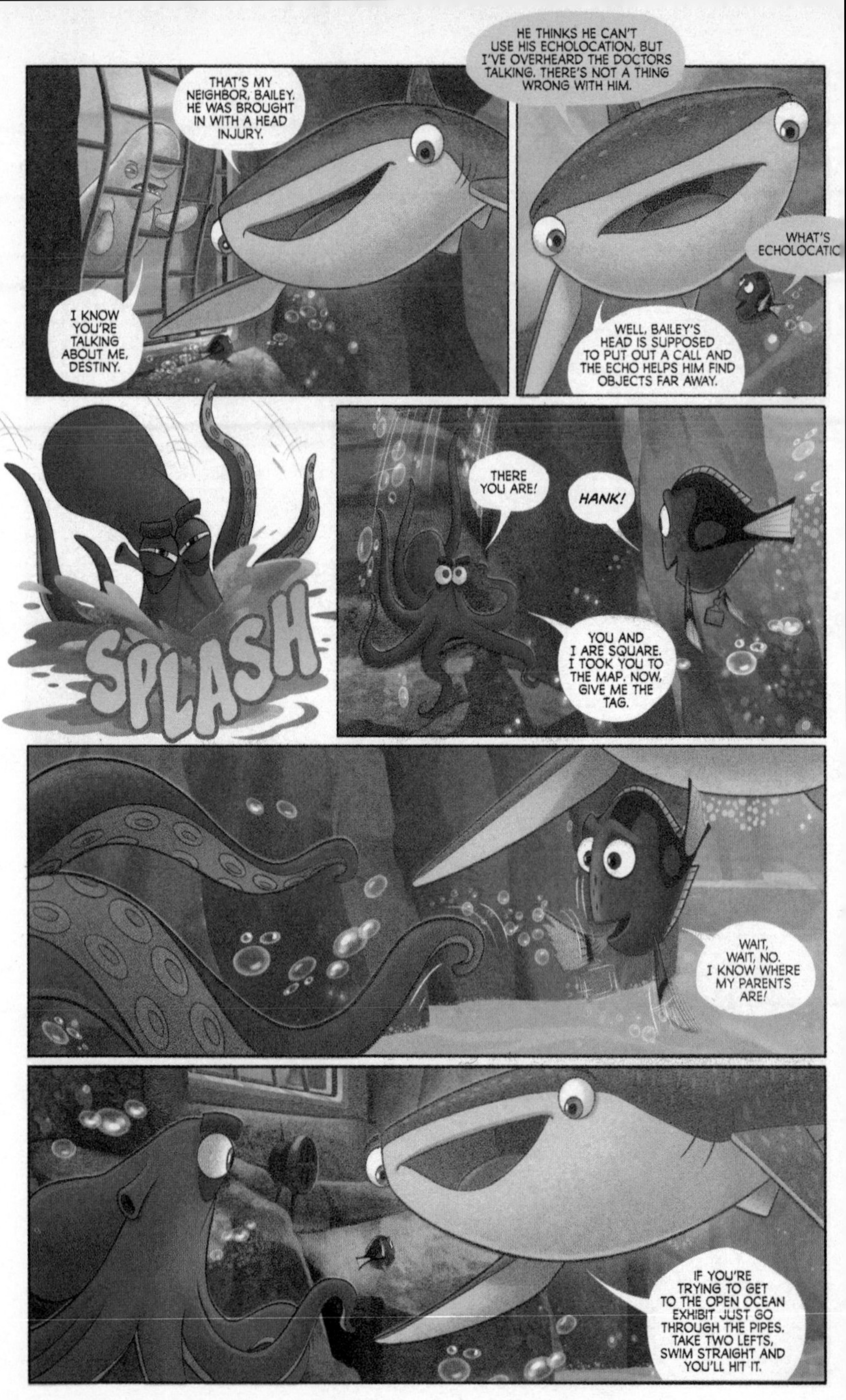
THAT'S MY NEIGHBOR, BAILEY. HE WAS BROUGHT IN WITH A HEAD INJURY.
I KNOW YOU'RE TALKING ABOUT ME, DESTINY.
HE THINKS HE CAN'T USE HIS ECHOLOCATION, BUT I'VE OVERHEARD THE DOCTORS TALKING. THERE'S NOT A THING WRONG WITH HIM.
WHAT'S ECHOLOCATIC
WELL, BAILEY'S HEAD IS SUPPOSED TO PUT OUT A CALL AND THE ECHO HELPS HIM FIND OBJECTS FAR AWAY.
SPLASH
THERE YOU ARE!
HANK!
YOU AND I ARE SQUARE. I TOOK YOU TO THE MAP. NOW, GIVE ME THE TAG.
WAIT, WAIT, NO. I KNOW WHERE MY PARENTS ARE!
IF YOU'RE TRYING TO GET TO THE OPEN OCEAN EXHIBIT JUST GO THROUGH THE PIPES. TAKE TWO LEFTS, SWIM STRAIGHT AND YOU'LL HIT IT.

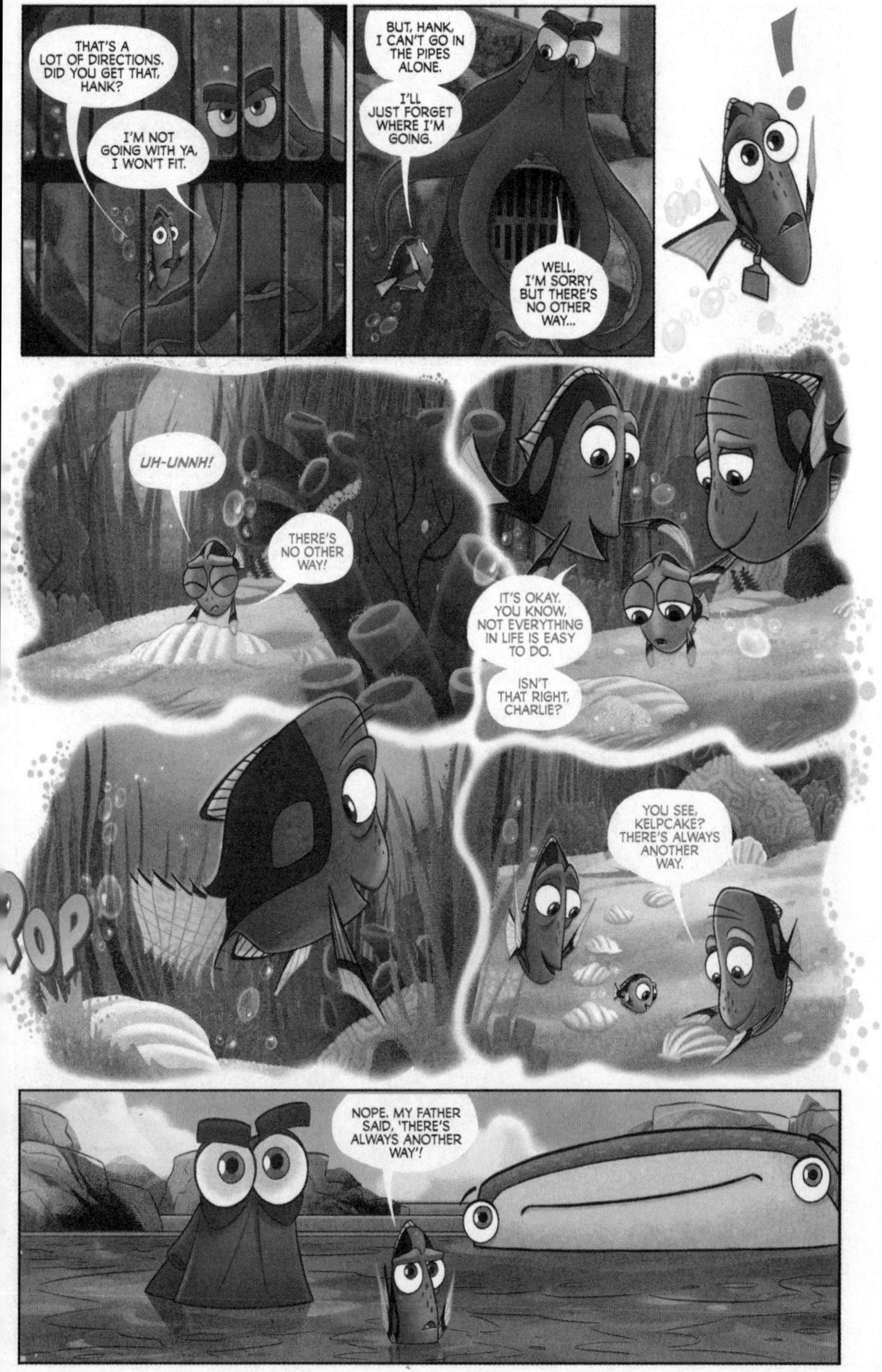
THAT'S A LOT OF DIRECTIONS. DID YOU GET THAT, HANK?
I'M NOT GOING WITH YA, I WON'T FIT.
BUT, HANK, I CAN'T GO IN THE PIPES ALONE.
I'LL JUST FORGET WHERE I'M GOING.
WELL, I'M SORRY BUT THERE'S NO OTHER WAY...
!
UH-UNNH!
THERE'S NO OTHER WAY!
IT'S OKAY. YOU KNOW, NOT EVERYTHING IN LIFE IS EASY TO DO.
ISN'T THAT RIGHT, CHARLIE?
POP
YOU SEE, KELPCAKE? THERE'S ALWAYS ANOTHER WAY.
NOPE. MY FATHER SAID, 'THERE'S ALWAYS ANOTHER WAY'!

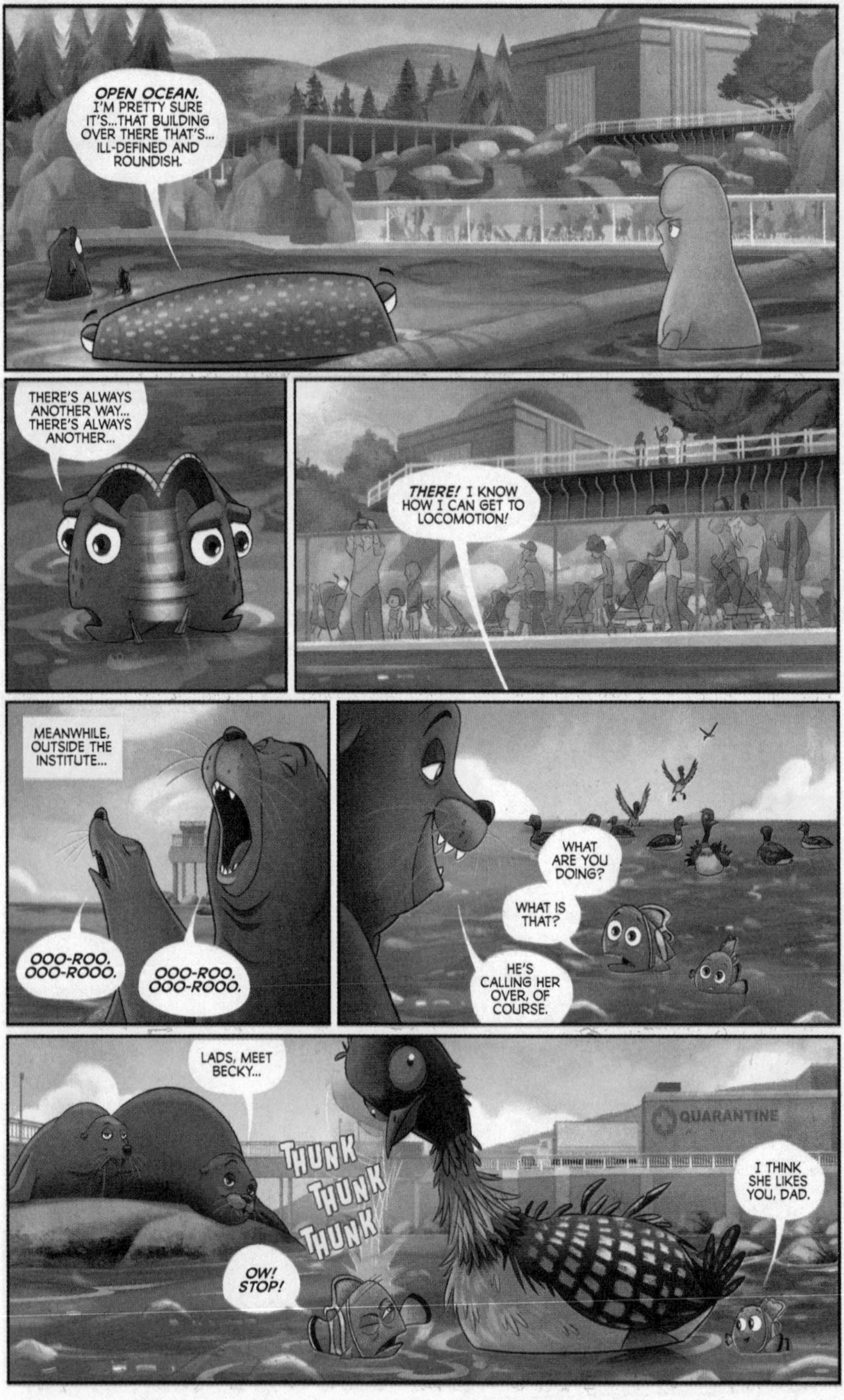
OPEN OCEAN. I'M PRETTY SURE IT'S...THAT BUILDING OVER THERE THAT'S... ILL-DEFINED AND ROUNDISH.
THERE'S ALWAYS ANOTHER WAY... THERE'S ALWAYS ANOTHER...
THERE! I KNOW HOW I CAN GET TO LOCOMOTION!
MEANWHILE, OUTSIDE THE INSTITUTE...
OOO-ROO. OOO-ROOO.
OOO-ROO. OOO-ROOO.
WHAT ARE YOU DOING?
WHAT IS THAT?
HE'S CALLING HER OVER, OF COURSE.
LADS, MEET BECKY...
QUARANTINE
THUNK
THUNK
THUNK
OW! STOP!
I THINK SHE LIKES YOU, DAD.

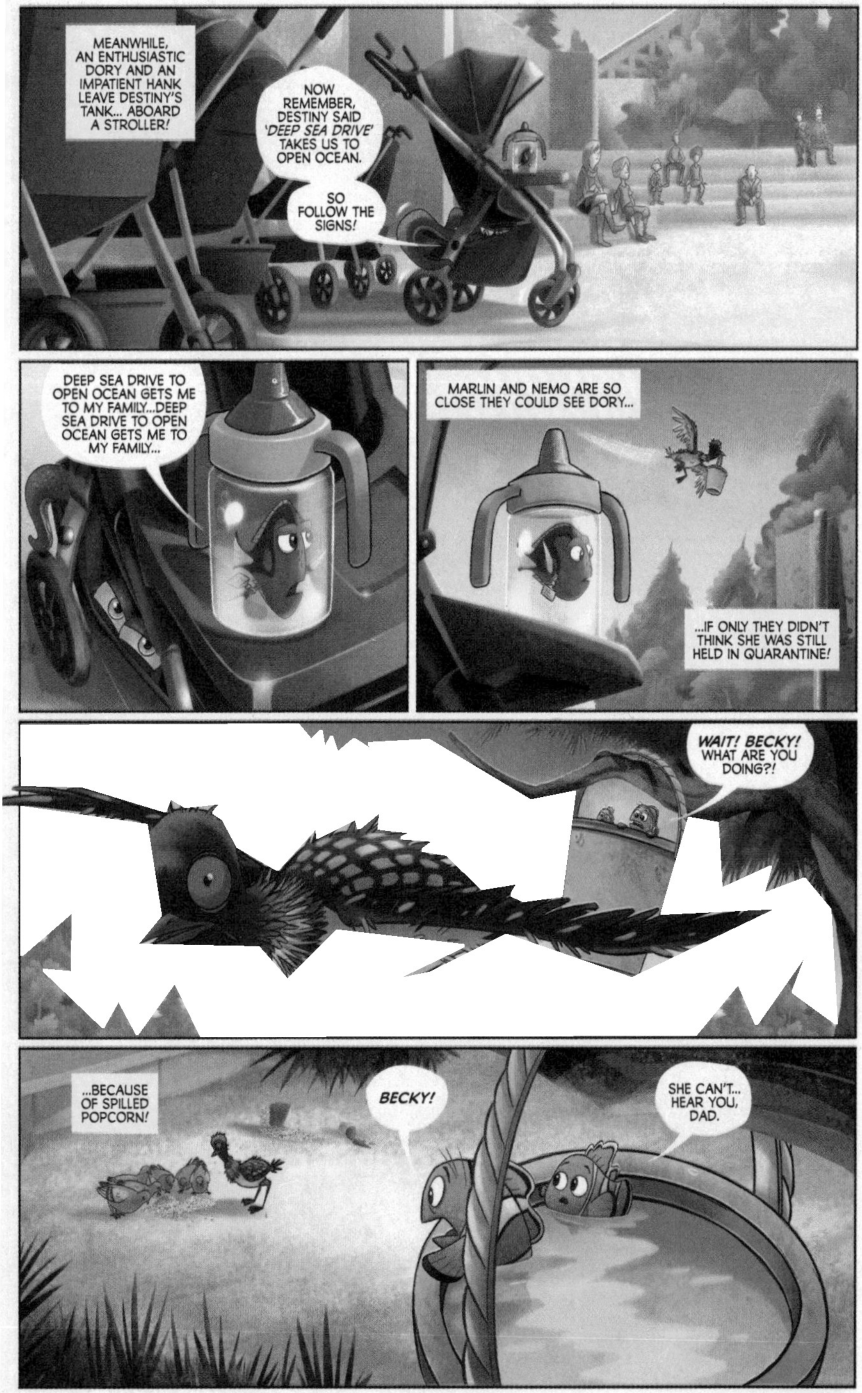
MEANWHILE, AN ENTHUSIASTIC DORY AND AN IMPATIENT HANK LEAVE DESTINY'S TANK... ABOARD A STROLLER!
NOW REMEMBER, DESTINY SAID *'DEEP SEA DRIVE'* TAKES US TO OPEN OCEAN.
SO FOLLOW THE SIGNS!
DEEP SEA DRIVE TO OPEN OCEAN GETS ME TO MY FAMILY...DEEP SEA DRIVE TO OPEN OCEAN GETS ME TO MY FAMILY...
MARLIN AND NEMO ARE SO CLOSE THEY COULD SEE DORY...
...IF ONLY THEY DIDN'T THINK SHE WAS STILL HELD IN QUARANTINE!
WAIT! BECKY! WHAT ARE YOU DOING?!
...BECAUSE OF SPILLED POPCORN!
BECKY!
SHE CAN'T... HEAR YOU, DAD.

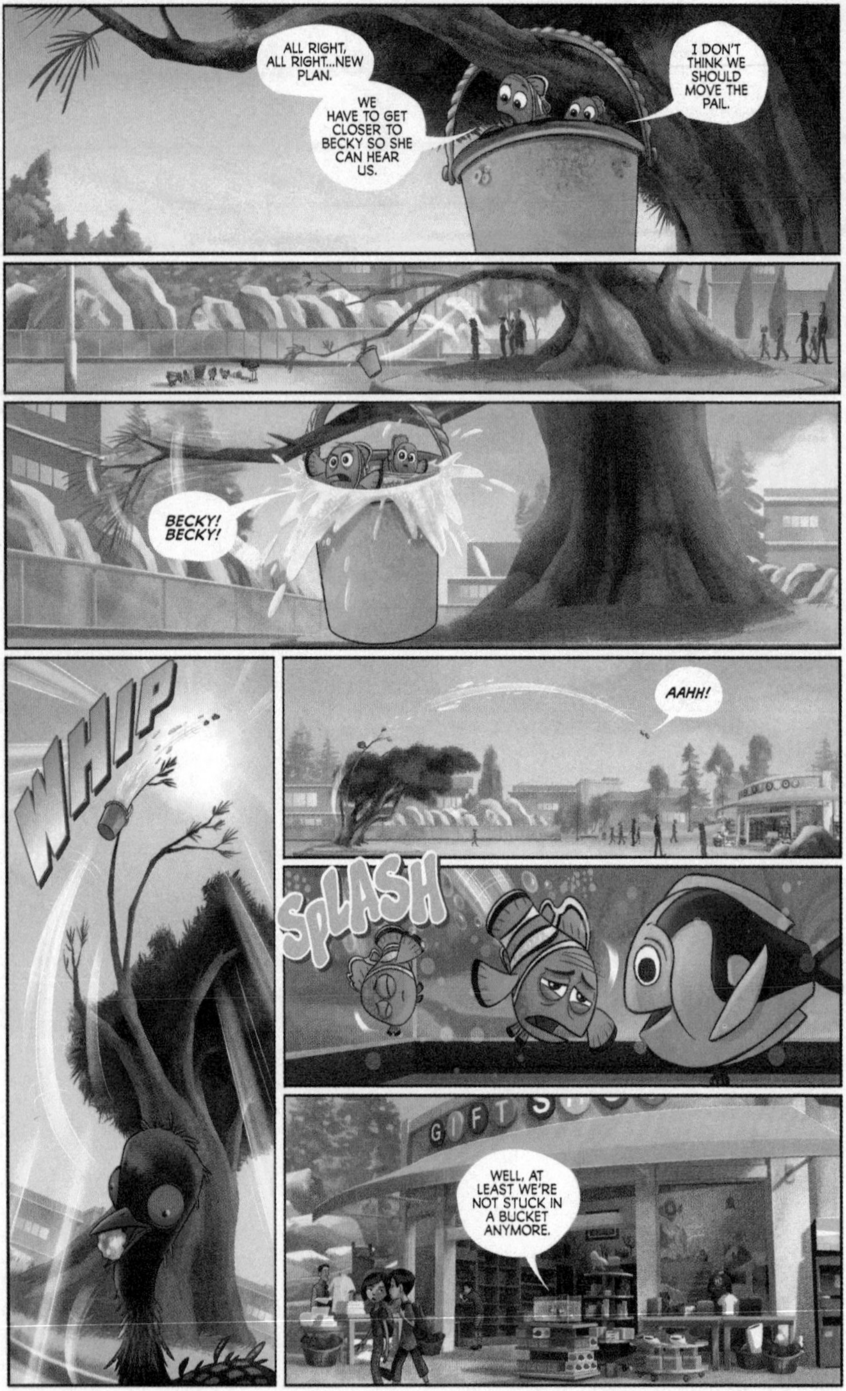
ALL RIGHT, ALL RIGHT...NEW PLAN.
WE HAVE TO GET CLOSER TO BECKY SO SHE CAN HEAR US.
I DON'T THINK WE SHOULD MOVE THE PAIL.
BECKY! BECKY!
WHIP
AAHH!
SPLASH
GIFT
WELL, AT LEAST WE'RE NOT STUCK IN A BUCKET ANYMORE.

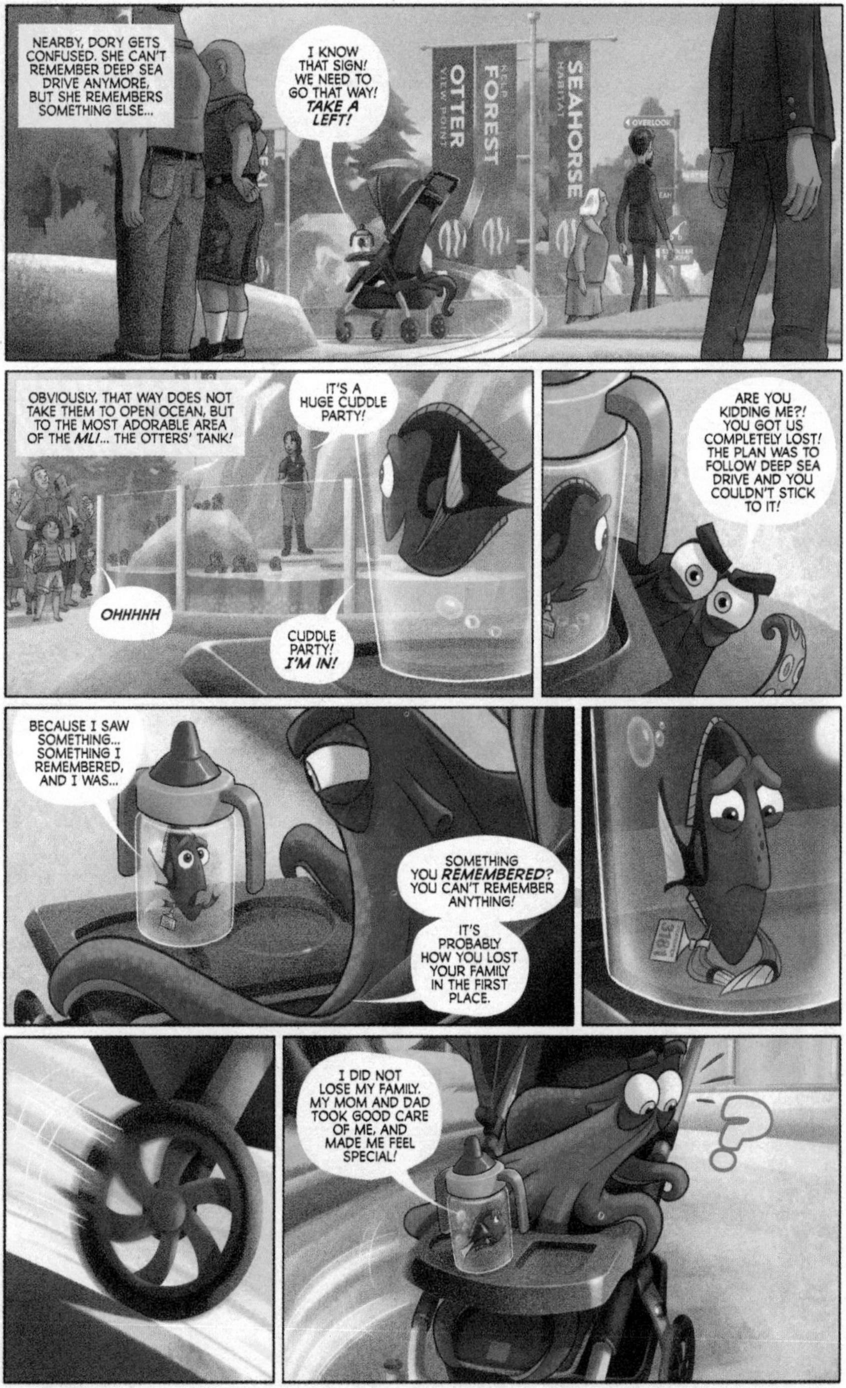
NEARBY, DORY GETS CONFUSED. SHE CAN'T REMEMBER DEEP SEA DRIVE ANYMORE, BUT SHE REMEMBERS SOMETHING ELSE...
I KNOW THAT SIGN! WE NEED TO GO THAT WAY! *TAKE A LEFT!*
OTTER
VIEW POINT
FOREST
SEAHORSE
HABITAT
OVERLOOK
OBVIOUSLY, THAT WAY DOES NOT TAKE THEM TO OPEN OCEAN, BUT TO THE MOST ADORABLE AREA OF THE *MLI*... THE OTTERS' TANK!
IT'S A HUGE CUDDLE PARTY!
OHHHHH
CUDDLE PARTY! *I'M IN!*
ARE YOU KIDDING ME?! YOU GOT US COMPLETELY LOST! THE PLAN WAS TO FOLLOW DEEP SEA DRIVE AND YOU COULDN'T STICK TO IT!
BECAUSE I SAW SOMETHING... SOMETHING I REMEMBERED, AND I WAS...
SOMETHING YOU *REMEMBERED*? YOU CAN'T REMEMBER ANYTHING!
IT'S PROBABLY HOW YOU LOST YOUR FAMILY IN THE FIRST PLACE.
I DID NOT LOSE MY FAMILY. MY MOM AND DAD TOOK GOOD CARE OF ME, AND MADE ME FEEL SPECIAL!
?

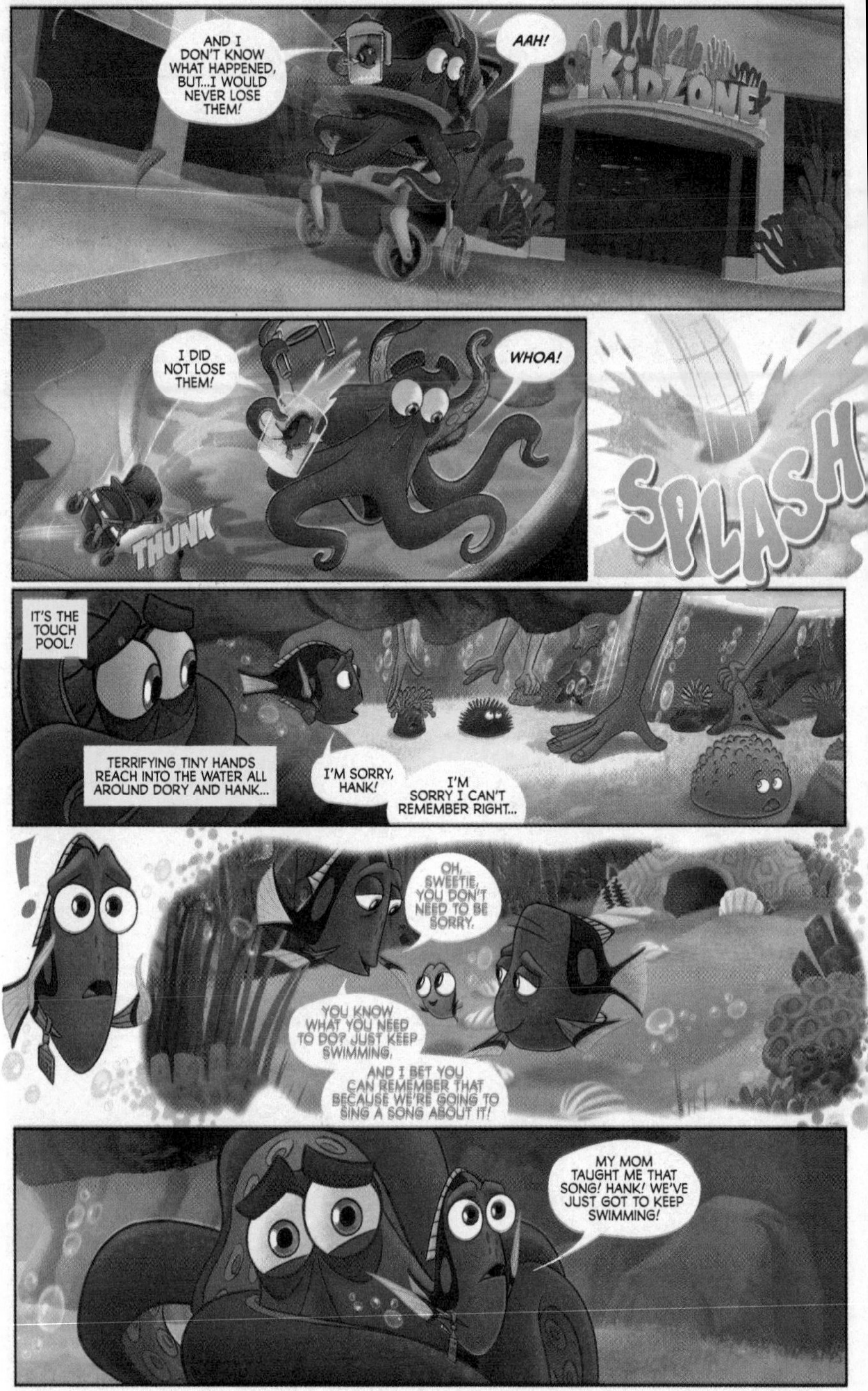
AND I DON'T KNOW WHAT HAPPENED, BUT...I WOULD NEVER LOSE THEM!
AAH!
KIDZONE
I DID NOT LOSE THEM!
WHOA!
THUNK
SPLASH
IT'S THE TOUCH POOL!
TERRIFYING TINY HANDS REACH INTO THE WATER ALL AROUND DORY AND HANK...
I'M SORRY, HANK!
I'M SORRY I CAN'T REMEMBER RIGHT...
!
OH, SWEETIE, YOU DON'T NEED TO BE SORRY.
YOU KNOW WHAT YOU NEED TO DO? JUST KEEP SWIMMING.
AND I BET YOU CAN REMEMBER THAT BECAUSE WE'RE GOING TO SING A SONG ABOUT IT!
MY MOM TAUGHT ME THAT SONG! HANK! WE'VE JUST GOT TO KEEP SWIMMING!

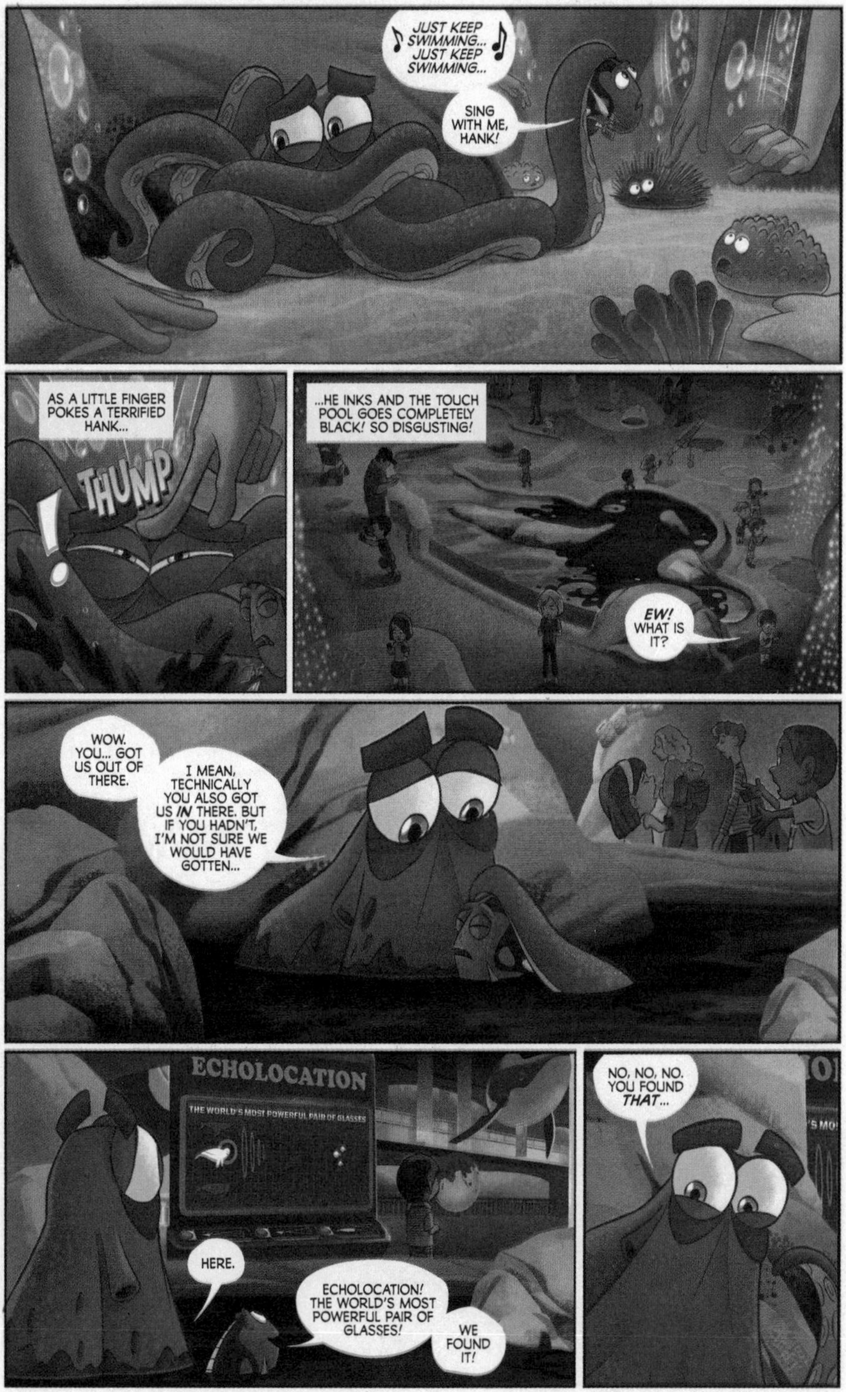
JUST KEEP SWIMMING... JUST KEEP SWIMMING...
SING WITH ME, HANK!
AS A LITTLE FINGER POKES A TERRIFIED HANK...
THUMP
!
...HE INKS AND THE TOUCH POOL GOES COMPLETELY BLACK! SO DISGUSTING!
EW! WHAT IS IT?
WOW. YOU... GOT US OUT OF THERE.
I MEAN, TECHNICALLY YOU ALSO GOT US IN THERE. BUT IF YOU HADN'T, I'M NOT SURE WE WOULD HAVE GOTTEN...
ECHOLOCATION
THE WORLD'S MOST POWERFUL PAIR OF GLASSES
HERE.
ECHOLOCATION! THE WORLD'S MOST POWERFUL PAIR OF GLASSES!
WE FOUND IT!
NO, NO, NO. YOU FOUND THAT...

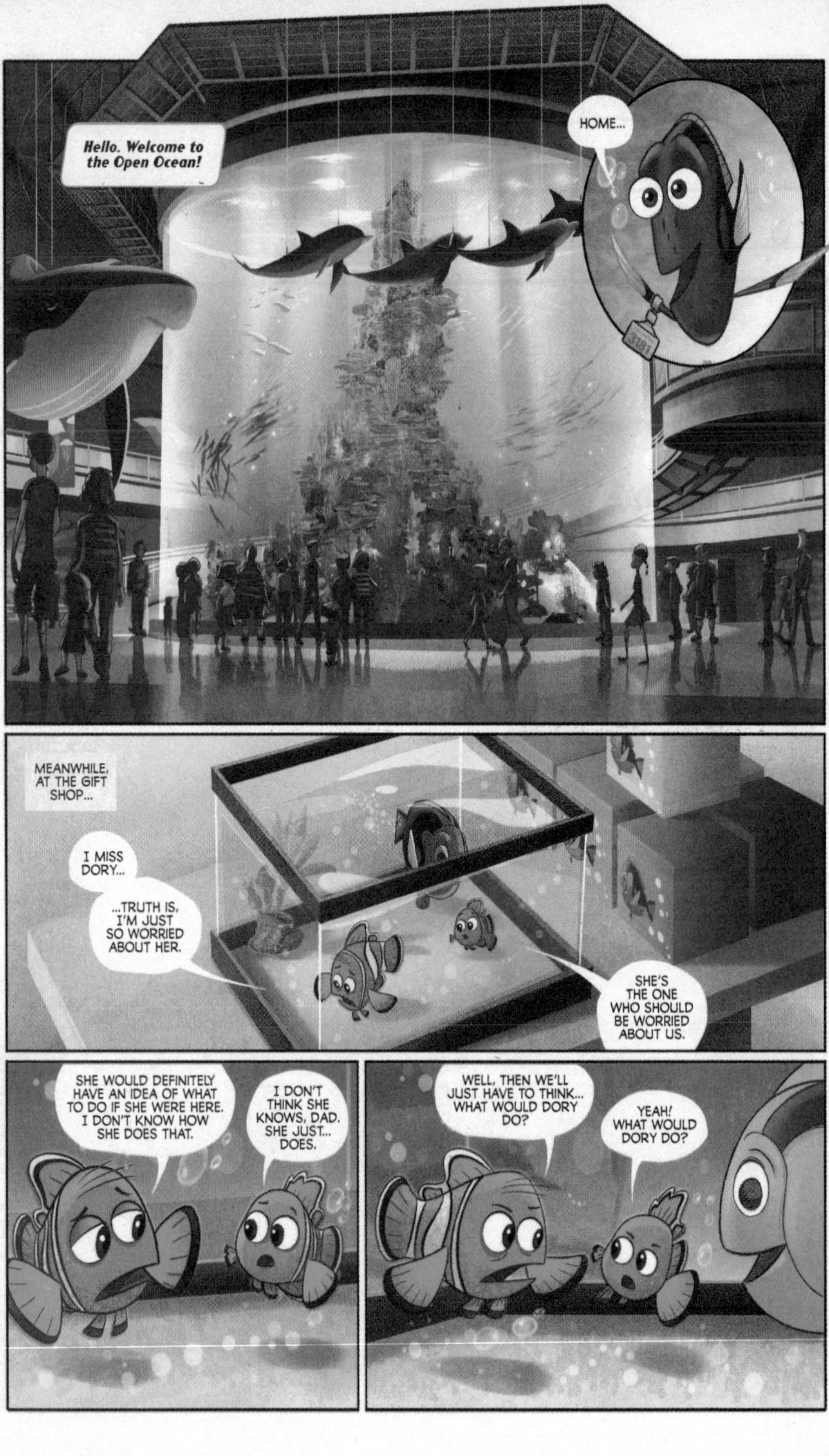
Hello. Welcome to the Open Ocean!
HOME...
3101
MEANWHILE, AT THE GIFT SHOP...
I MISS DORY...
...TRUTH IS, I'M JUST SO WORRIED ABOUT HER.
SHE'S THE ONE WHO SHOULD BE WORRIED ABOUT US.
SHE WOULD DEFINITELY HAVE AN IDEA OF WHAT TO DO IF SHE WERE HERE. I DON'T KNOW HOW SHE DOES THAT.
I DON'T THINK SHE KNOWS, DAD. SHE JUST... DOES.
WELL, THEN WE'LL JUST HAVE TO THINK... WHAT WOULD DORY DO?
YEAH! WHAT WOULD DORY DO?

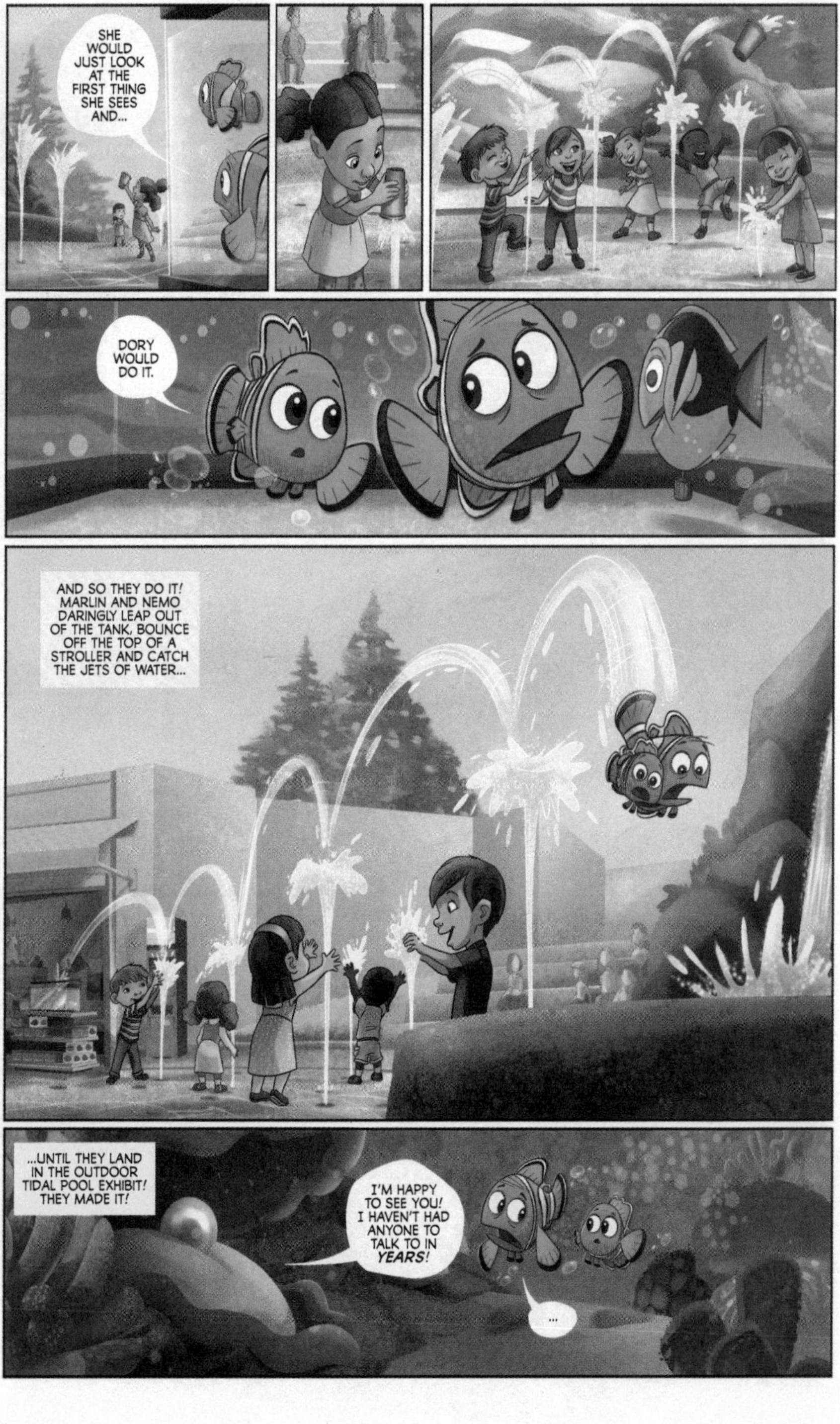
SHE WOULD JUST LOOK AT THE FIRST THING SHE SEES AND...
DORY WOULD DO IT.
AND SO THEY DO IT! MARLIN AND NEMO DARINGLY LEAP OUT OF THE TANK, BOUNCE OFF THE TOP OF A STROLLER AND CATCH THE JETS OF WATER...
...UNTIL THEY LAND IN THE OUTDOOR TIDAL POOL EXHIBIT! THEY MADE IT!
I'M HAPPY TO SEE YOU! I HAVEN'T HAD ANYONE TO TALK TO IN YEARS!
...

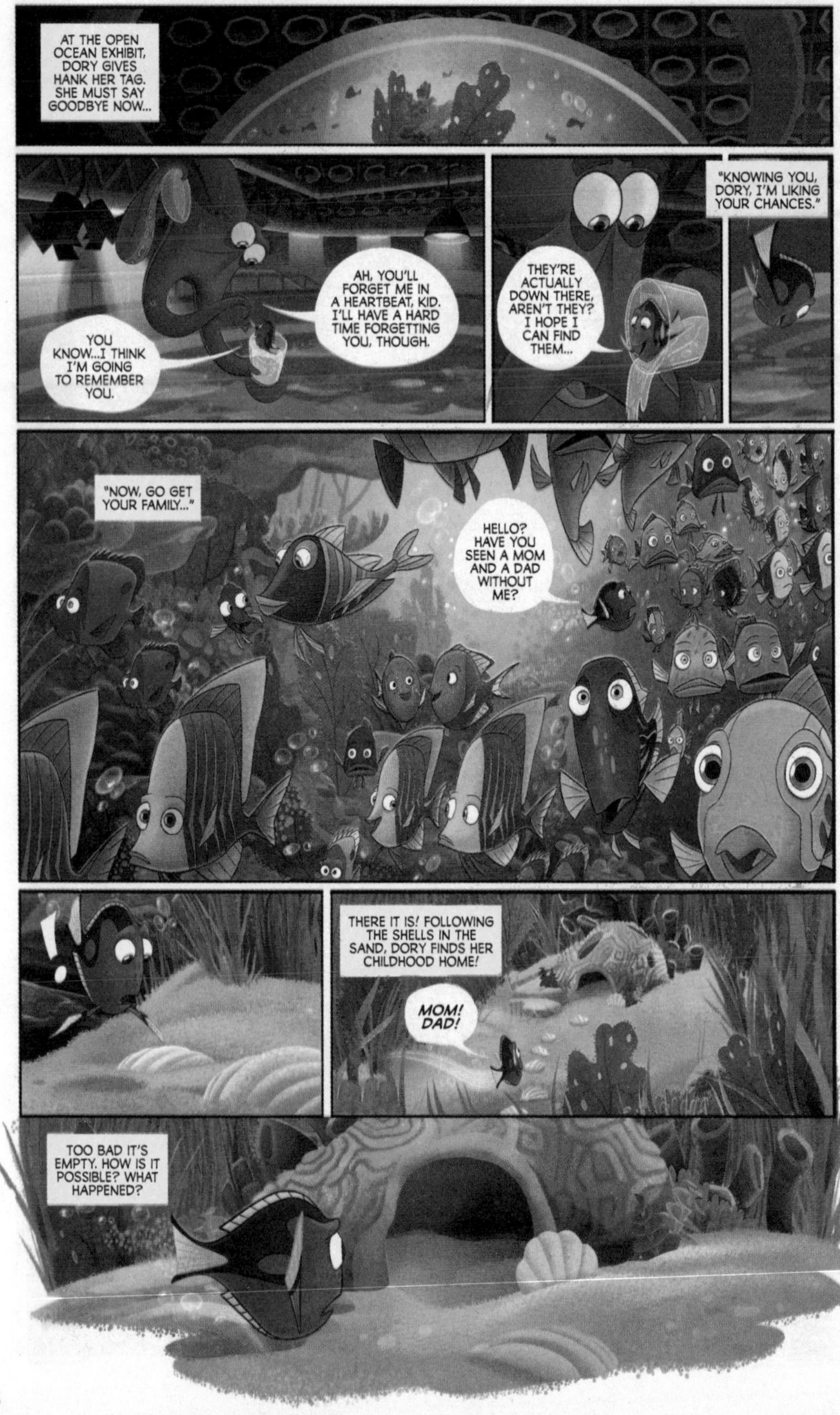
AT THE OPEN OCEAN EXHIBIT, DORY GIVES HANK HER TAG. SHE MUST SAY GOODBYE NOW...
YOU KNOW...I THINK I'M GOING TO REMEMBER YOU.
AH, YOU'LL FORGET ME IN A HEARTBEAT, KID. I'LL HAVE A HARD TIME FORGETTING YOU, THOUGH.
THEY'RE ACTUALLY DOWN THERE, AREN'T THEY? I HOPE I CAN FIND THEM...
"KNOWING YOU, DORY, I'M LIKING YOUR CHANCES."
"NOW, GO GET YOUR FAMILY..."
HELLO? HAVE YOU SEEN A MOM AND A DAD WITHOUT ME?
THERE IT IS! FOLLOWING THE SHELLS IN THE SAND, DORY FINDS HER CHILDHOOD HOME!
MOM! DAD!
TOO BAD IT'S EMPTY. HOW IS IT POSSIBLE? WHAT HAPPENED?

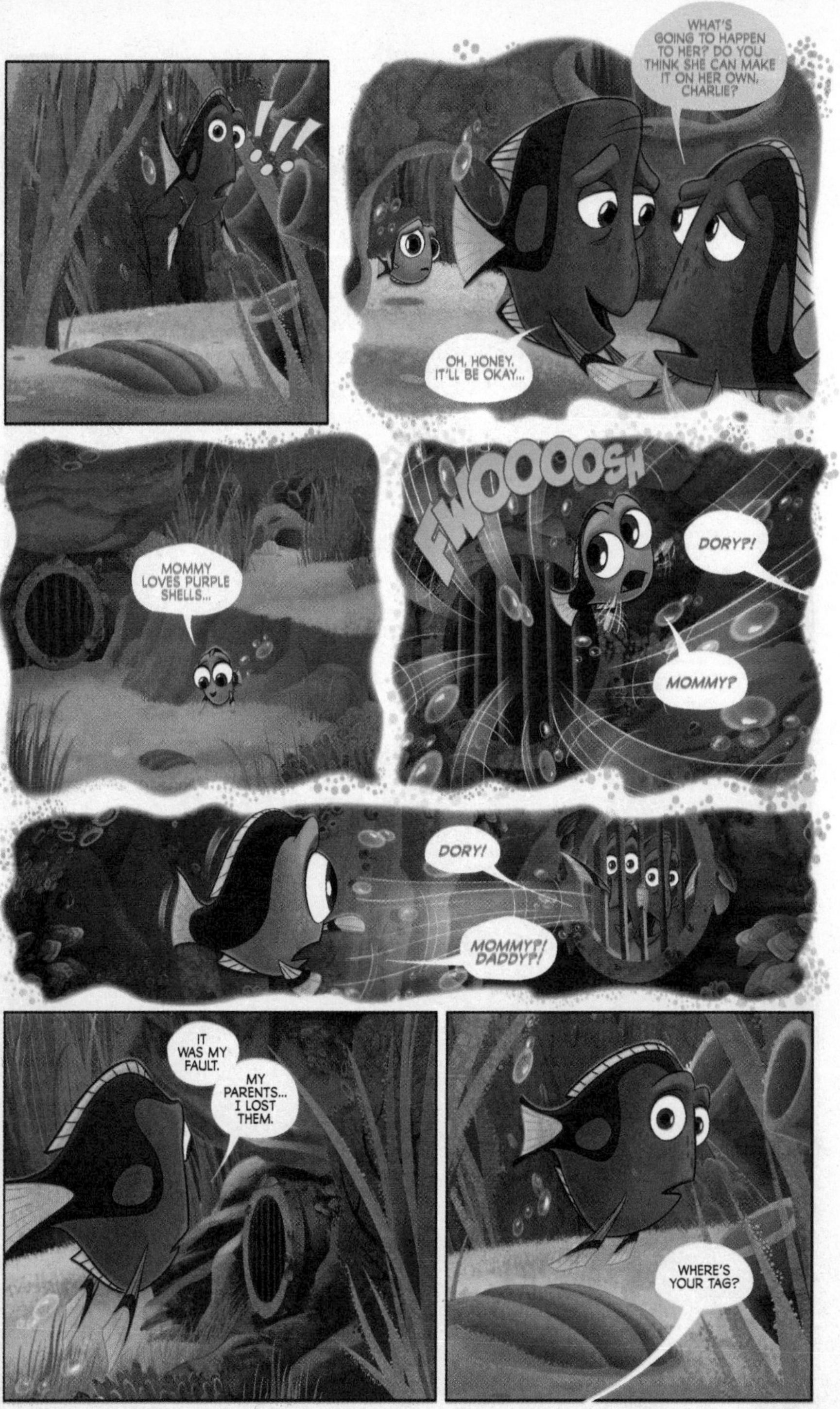
WHAT'S GOING TO HAPPEN TO HER? DO YOU THINK SHE CAN MAKE IT ON HER OWN, CHARLIE?
OH, HONEY. IT'LL BE OKAY...
MOMMY LOVES PURPLE SHELLS...
FWOOOOOSH
DORY?!
MOMMY?
DORY!
MOMMY?! DADDY?!
IT WAS MY FAULT.
MY PARENTS... I LOST THEM.
WHERE'S YOUR TAG?

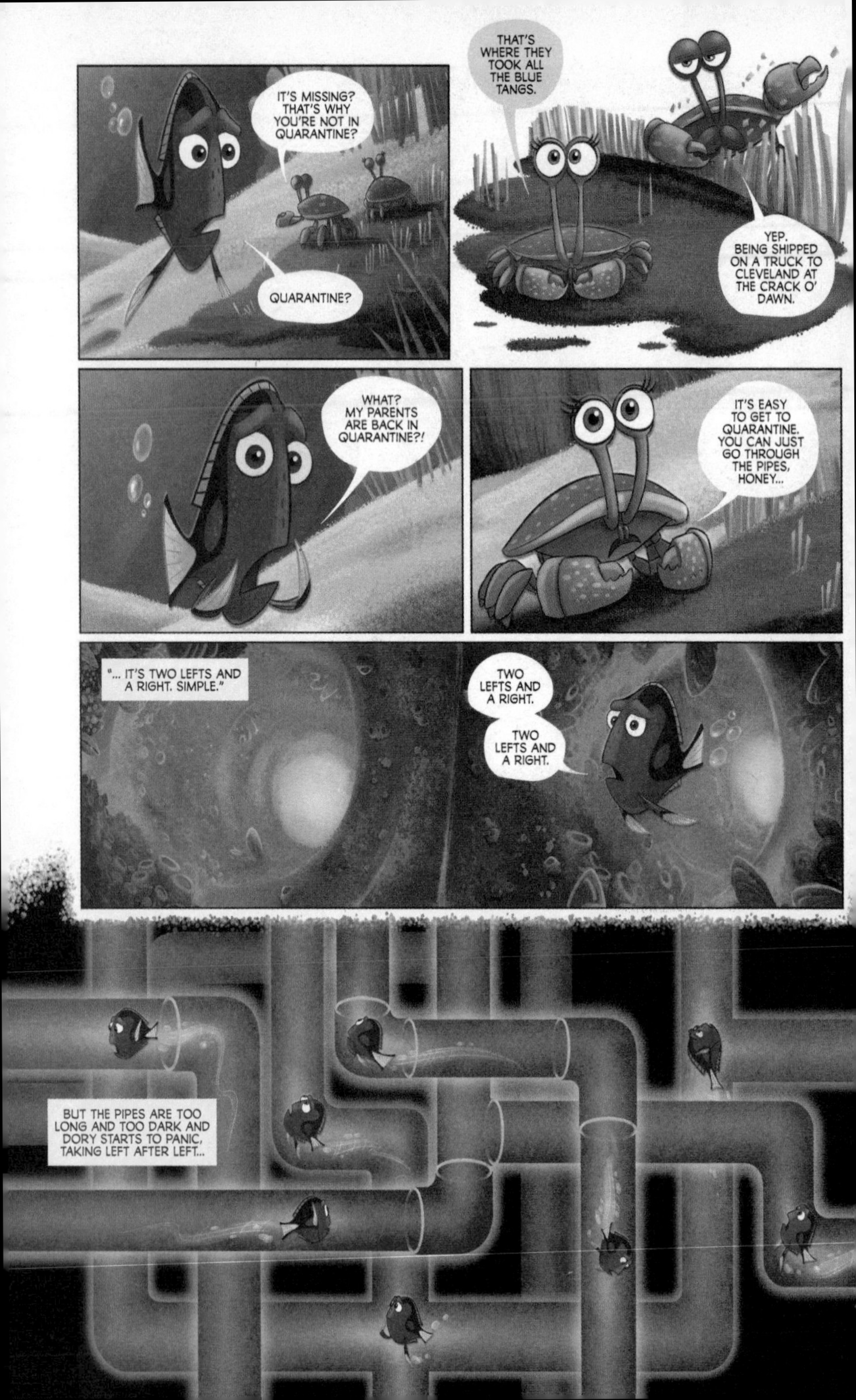
IT'S MISSING? THAT'S WHY YOU'RE NOT IN QUARANTINE?
QUARANTINE?
THAT'S WHERE THEY TOOK ALL THE BLUE TANGS.
YEP. BEING SHIPPED ON A TRUCK TO CLEVELAND AT THE CRACK O' DAWN.
WHAT? MY PARENTS ARE BACK IN QUARANTINE?!
IT'S EASY TO GET TO QUARANTINE. YOU CAN JUST GO THROUGH THE PIPES, HONEY...
"... IT'S TWO LEFTS AND A RIGHT. SIMPLE."
TWO LEFTS AND A RIGHT.
TWO LEFTS AND A RIGHT.
BUT THE PIPES ARE TOO LONG AND TOO DARK AND DORY STARTS TO PANIC, TAKING LEFT AFTER LEFT...

UNTIL...

OH NO... IT'S HAPPENING. I'M LOST. IT'S TOO HARD. I CAN'T REMEMBER!

I'M GONNA BE STUCK FOREVER IN THE PIPES!

THE PIPES! THE PIPE PALS!

DESTINEEE!

DORY?

I'M LOOOST IN THE PIIIPES AAAND MY PAAAAREEENTS AAARE IN QUAAARAAANTIIINE!

HAAANG OOON, DOOORY!

BAILEY! YOU'VE GOTTA USE YOUR ECHOLOCATION!

IT WORKS! BAILEY'S ECHOLOCATION IS NOT REALLY BROKEN... EXACTLY AS DESTINY HAS SAID!

I'M GETTING SOMETHING! I CAN SEE THE QUARANTINE! I CAN SEE EVERYTHING! AND I CAN SEE YOU!

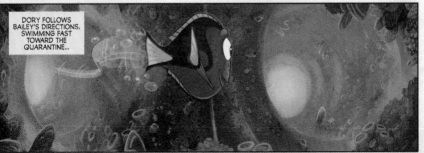

DORY FOLLOWS BAILEY'S DIRECTIONS, SWIMMING FAST TOWARD THE QUARANTINE...

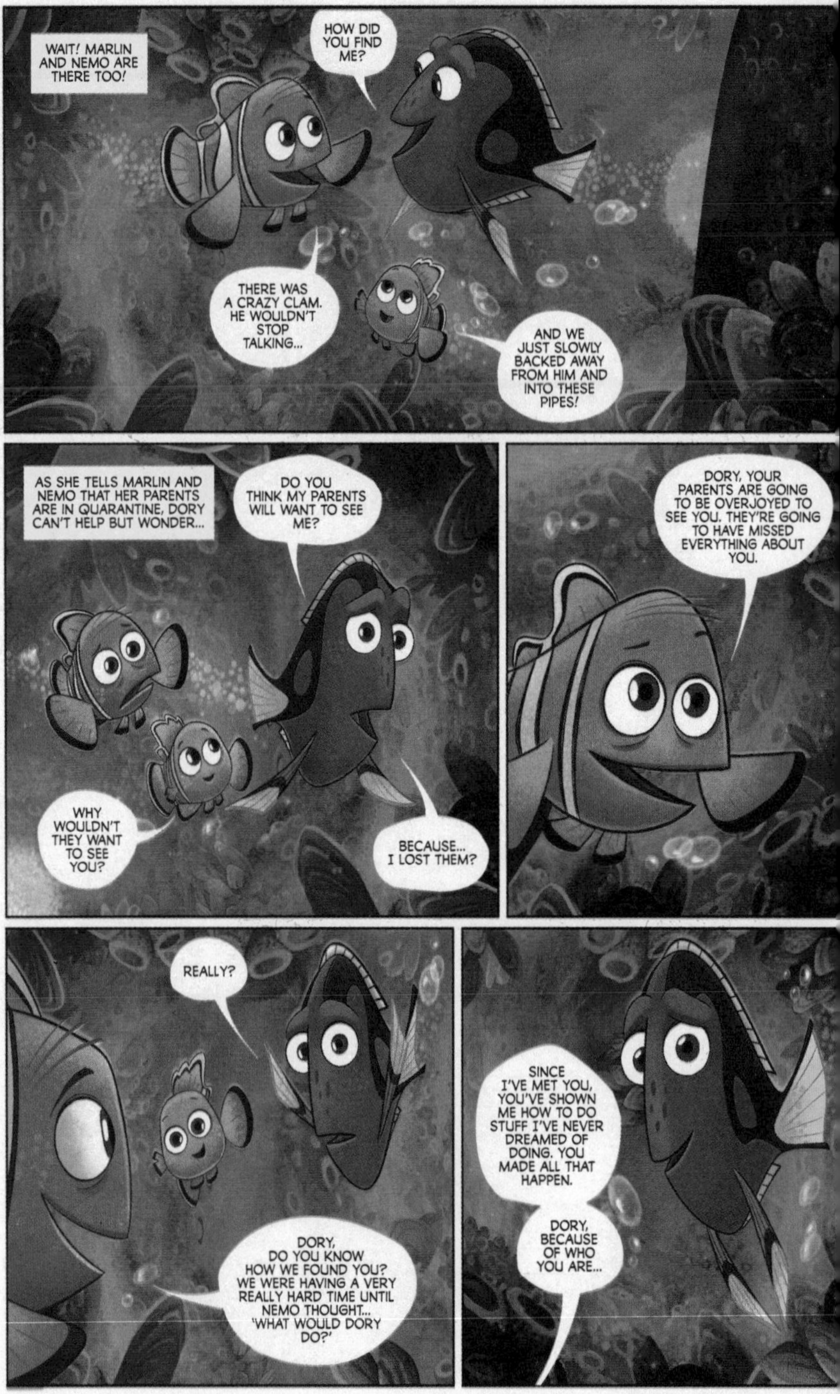
WAIT! MARLIN AND NEMO ARE THERE TOO!
HOW DID YOU FIND ME?
THERE WAS A CRAZY CLAM. HE WOULDN'T STOP TALKING...
AND WE JUST SLOWLY BACKED AWAY FROM HIM AND INTO THESE PIPES!
AS SHE TELLS MARLIN AND NEMO THAT HER PARENTS ARE IN QUARANTINE, DORY CAN'T HELP BUT WONDER...
DO YOU THINK MY PARENTS WILL WANT TO SEE ME?
WHY WOULDN'T THEY WANT TO SEE YOU?
BECAUSE... I LOST THEM?
DORY, YOUR PARENTS ARE GOING TO BE OVERJOYED TO SEE YOU. THEY'RE GOING TO HAVE MISSED EVERYTHING ABOUT YOU.
REALLY?
DORY, DO YOU KNOW HOW WE FOUND YOU? WE WERE HAVING A VERY REALLY HARD TIME UNTIL NEMO THOUGHT... 'WHAT WOULD DORY DO?'
SINCE I'VE MET YOU, YOU'VE SHOWN ME HOW TO DO STUFF I'VE NEVER DREAMED OF DOING. YOU MADE ALL THAT HAPPEN.
DORY, BECAUSE OF WHO YOU ARE...

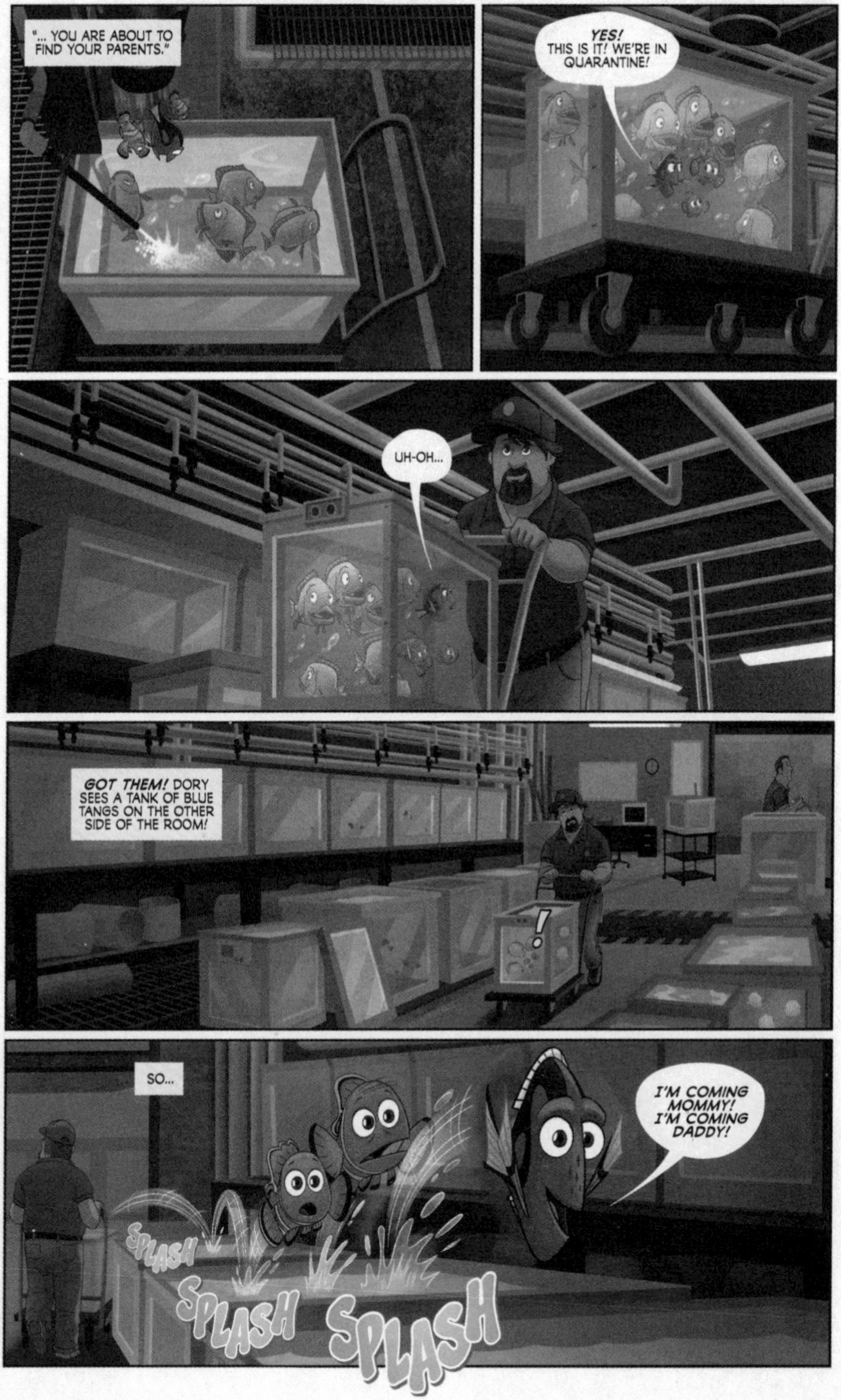
"... YOU ARE ABOUT TO FIND YOUR PARENTS."
YES! THIS IS IT! WE'RE IN QUARANTINE!
UH-OH...
GOT THEM! DORY SEES A TANK OF BLUE TANGS ON THE OTHER SIDE OF THE ROOM!
!
SO...
I'M COMING MOMMY! I'M COMING DADDY!
SPLASH
SPLASH
SPLASH

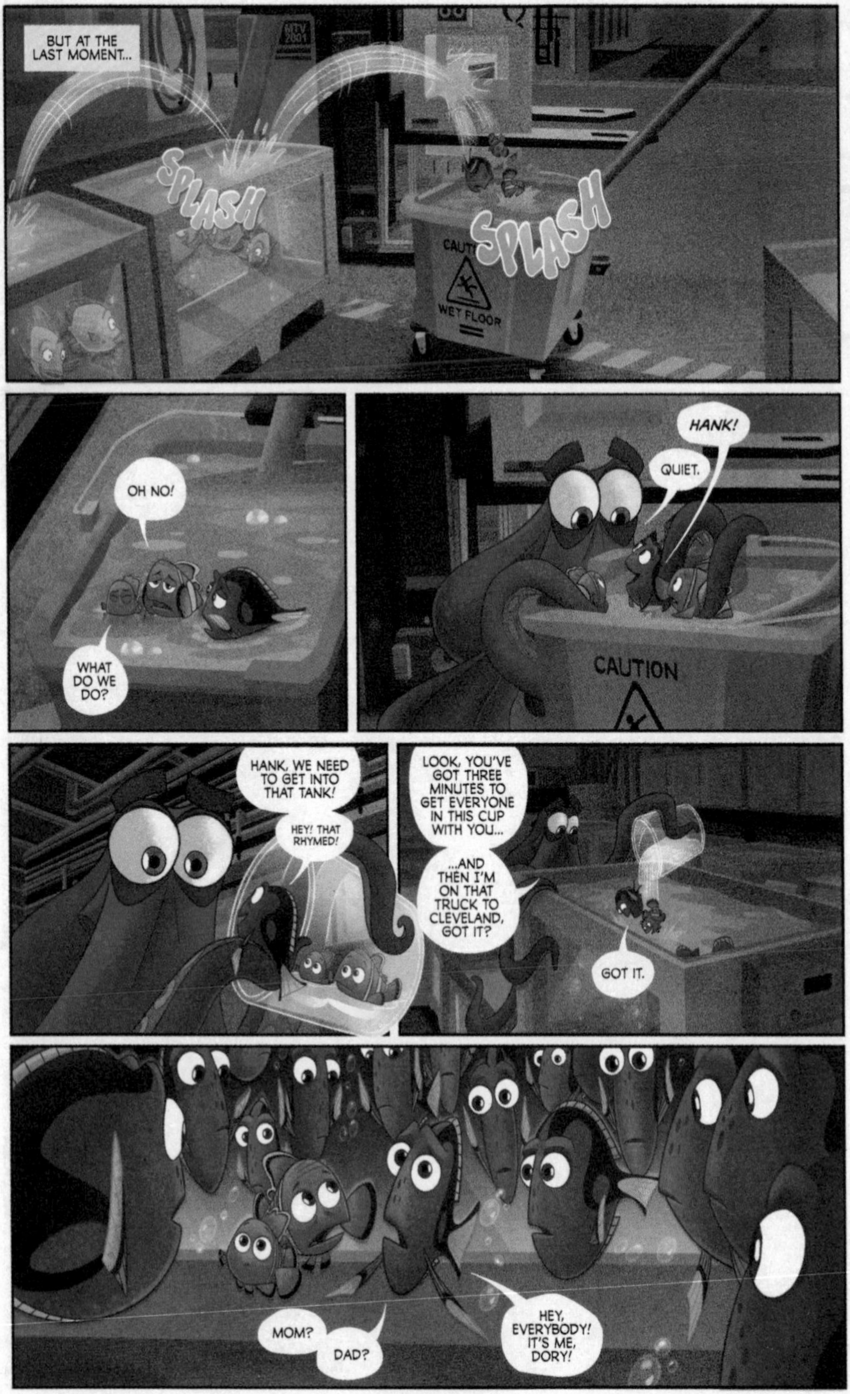

BUT AT THE LAST MOMENT...
SPLASH
SPLASH
CAUTION
WET FLOOR
OH NO!
WHAT DO WE DO?
HANK!
QUIET.
CAUTION
HANK, WE NEED TO GET INTO THAT TANK!
HEY! THAT RHYMED!
LOOK, YOU'VE GOT THREE MINUTES TO GET EVERYONE IN THIS CUP WITH YOU...
...AND THEN I'M ON THAT TRUCK TO CLEVELAND, GOT IT?
GOT IT.
MOM?
DAD?
HEY, EVERYBODY! IT'S ME, DORY!

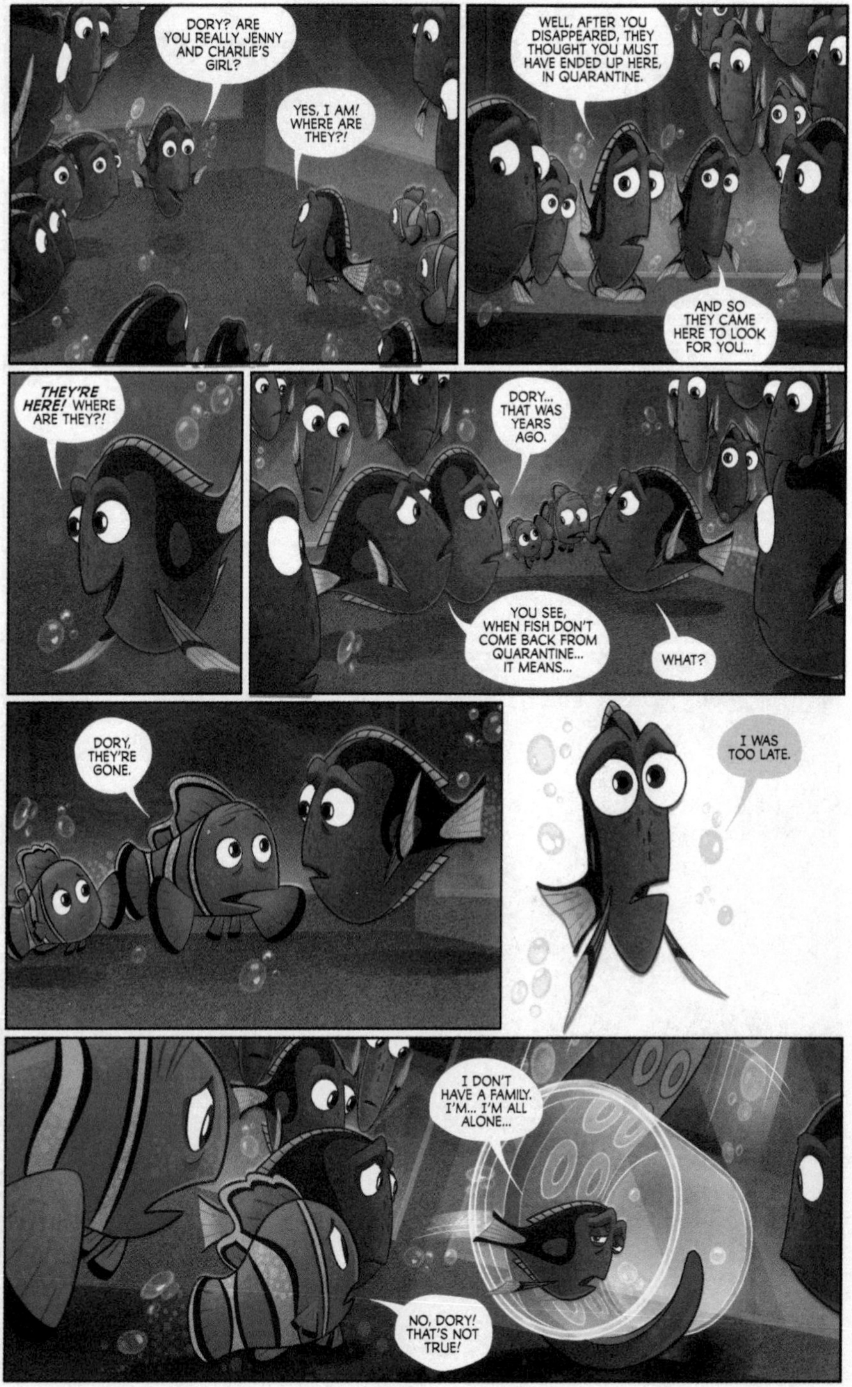
DORY? ARE YOU REALLY JENNY AND CHARLIE'S GIRL?
YES, I AM! WHERE ARE THEY?!
WELL, AFTER YOU DISAPPEARED, THEY THOUGHT YOU MUST HAVE ENDED UP HERE, IN QUARANTINE.
AND SO THEY CAME HERE TO LOOK FOR YOU...
THEY'RE HERE! WHERE ARE THEY?!
DORY... THAT WAS YEARS AGO.
YOU SEE, WHEN FISH DON'T COME BACK FROM QUARANTINE... IT MEANS...
WHAT?
DORY, THEY'RE GONE.
I WAS TOO LATE.
I DON'T HAVE A FAMILY. I'M... I'M ALL ALONE...
NO, DORY! THAT'S NOT TRUE!

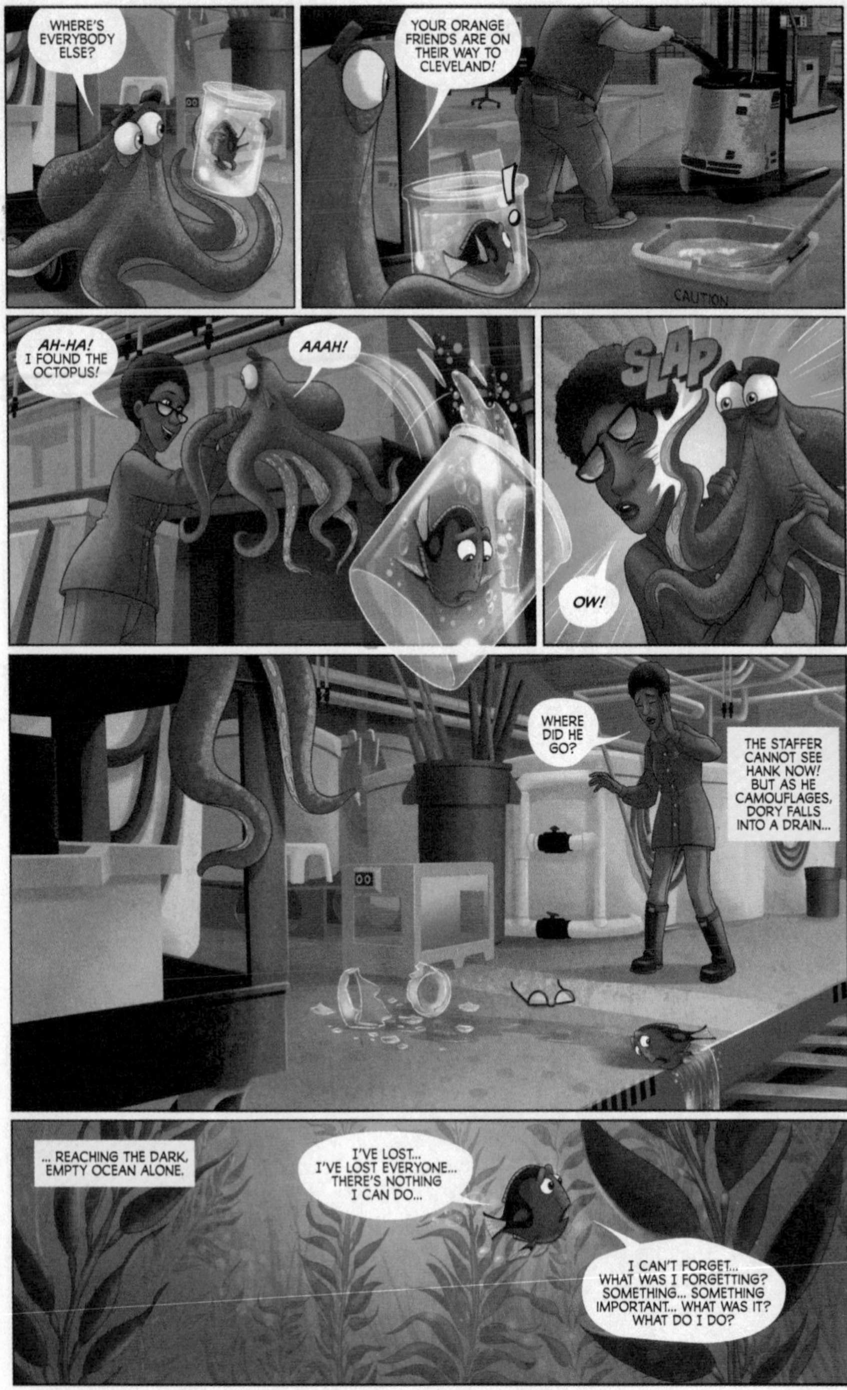
WHERE'S EVERYBODY ELSE?
YOUR ORANGE FRIENDS ARE ON THEIR WAY TO CLEVELAND!
!
CAUTION
AH-HA! I FOUND THE OCTOPUS!
AAAH!
SLAP
OW!
WHERE DID HE GO?
THE STAFFER CANNOT SEE HANK NOW! BUT AS HE CAMOUFLAGES, DORY FALLS INTO A DRAIN...
... REACHING THE DARK, EMPTY OCEAN ALONE.
I'VE LOST... I'VE LOST EVERYONE... THERE'S NOTHING I CAN DO...
I CAN'T FORGET... WHAT WAS I FORGETTING? SOMETHING... SOMETHING IMPORTANT... WHAT WAS IT? WHAT DO I DO?

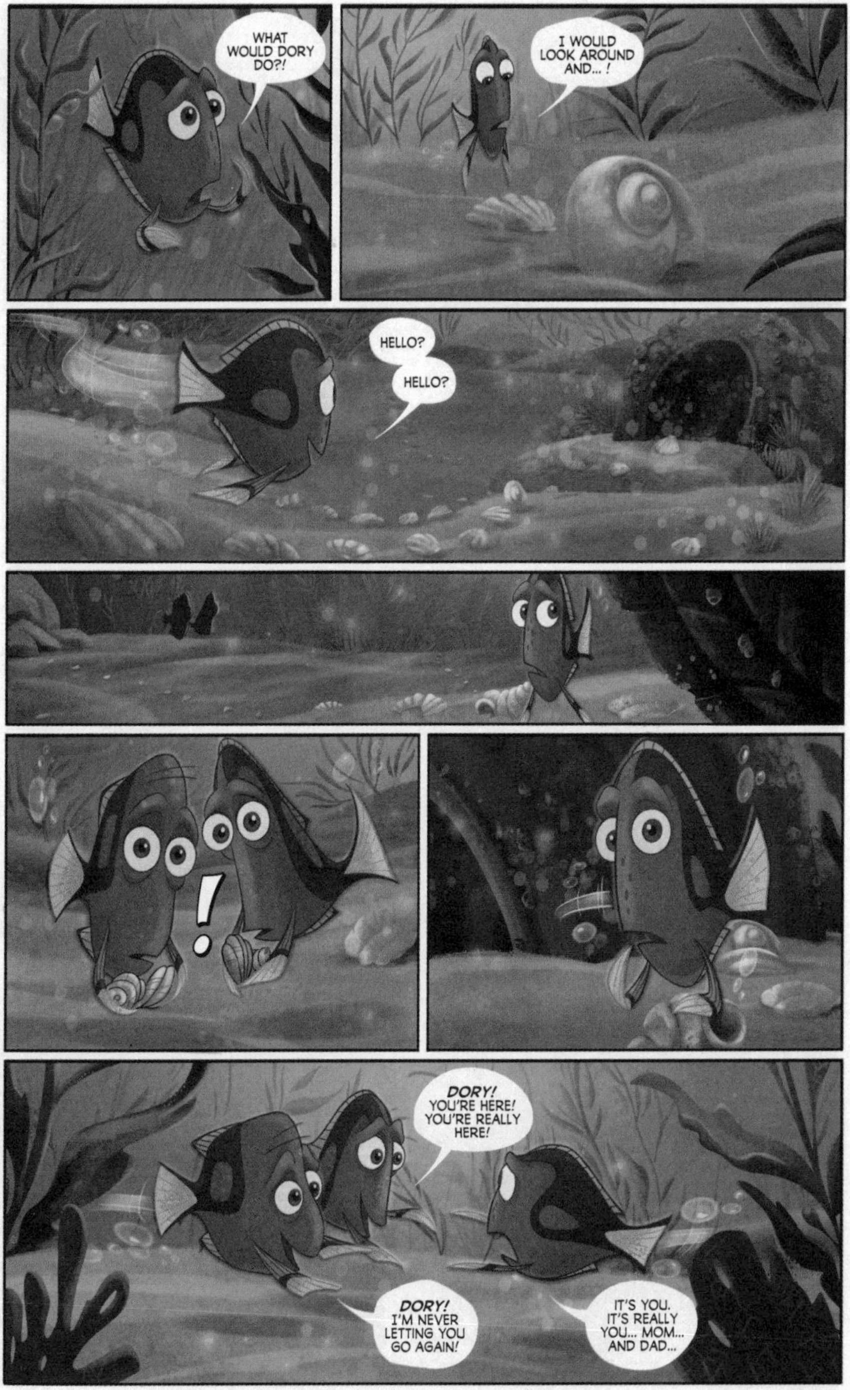
WHAT WOULD DORY DO?!
I WOULD LOOK AROUND AND... !
HELLO?
HELLO?
!
DORY! YOU'RE HERE! YOU'RE REALLY HERE!
DORY! I'M NEVER LETTING YOU GO AGAIN!
IT'S YOU. IT'S REALLY YOU... MOM... AND DAD...

I'M SO SORRY. I KNOW I'VE GOT A PROBLEM AND ALL THIS TIME I WANTED TO FIX IT AND I CAN'T...

DON'T YOU DARE BE SORRY. LOOK WHAT YOU DID! YOU FOUND US!

WE WENT TO QUARANTINE TO LOOK FOR YOU, BUT YOU WEREN'T THERE.

AND WE KNEW YOU MUST HAVE GOTTEN OUT THROUGH THE PIPES...

SO WE DID TOO. AND WE'VE STAYED IN THIS SPOT FOR YOU EVER SINCE.

BECAUSE WE THOUGHT YOU MIGHT COME BACK.

SO EVERY DAY, WE GO OUT AND LAY OUT...

SHELLS!

AND YOU FOUND US, BECAUSE YOU *REMEMBERED*.

IN YOUR OWN AMAZING, DORY WAY.

I DID. ALL BY MYSELF.

OH! I HAVEN'T BEEN ALL BY MYSELF...

"... MARLIN AND NEMO!"

SLAM

MARINE LIFE

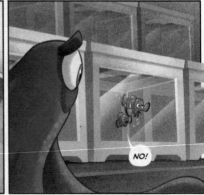

NO!

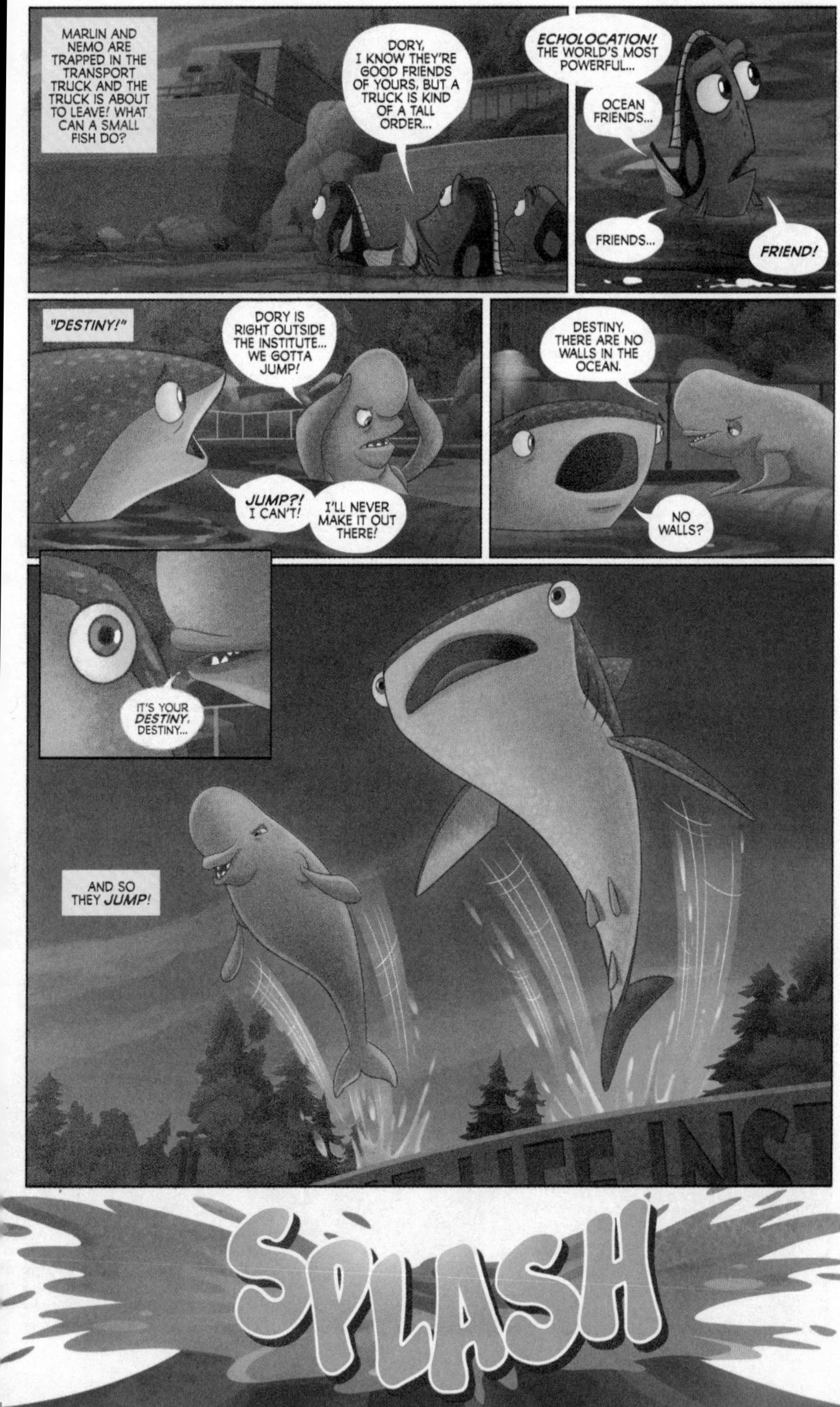
MARLIN AND NEMO ARE TRAPPED IN THE TRANSPORT TRUCK AND THE TRUCK IS ABOUT TO LEAVE! WHAT CAN A SMALL FISH DO?
DORY, I KNOW THEY'RE GOOD FRIENDS OF YOURS, BUT A TRUCK IS KIND OF A TALL ORDER...
ECHOLOCATION! THE WORLD'S MOST POWERFUL...
OCEAN FRIENDS...
FRIENDS...
FRIEND!
"DESTINY!"
DORY IS RIGHT OUTSIDE THE INSTITUTE... WE GOTTA JUMP!
JUMP?! I CAN'T!
I'LL NEVER MAKE IT OUT THERE!
DESTINY, THERE ARE NO WALLS IN THE OCEAN.
NO WALLS?
IT'S YOUR DESTINY, DESTINY...
AND SO THEY JUMP!
SPLASH

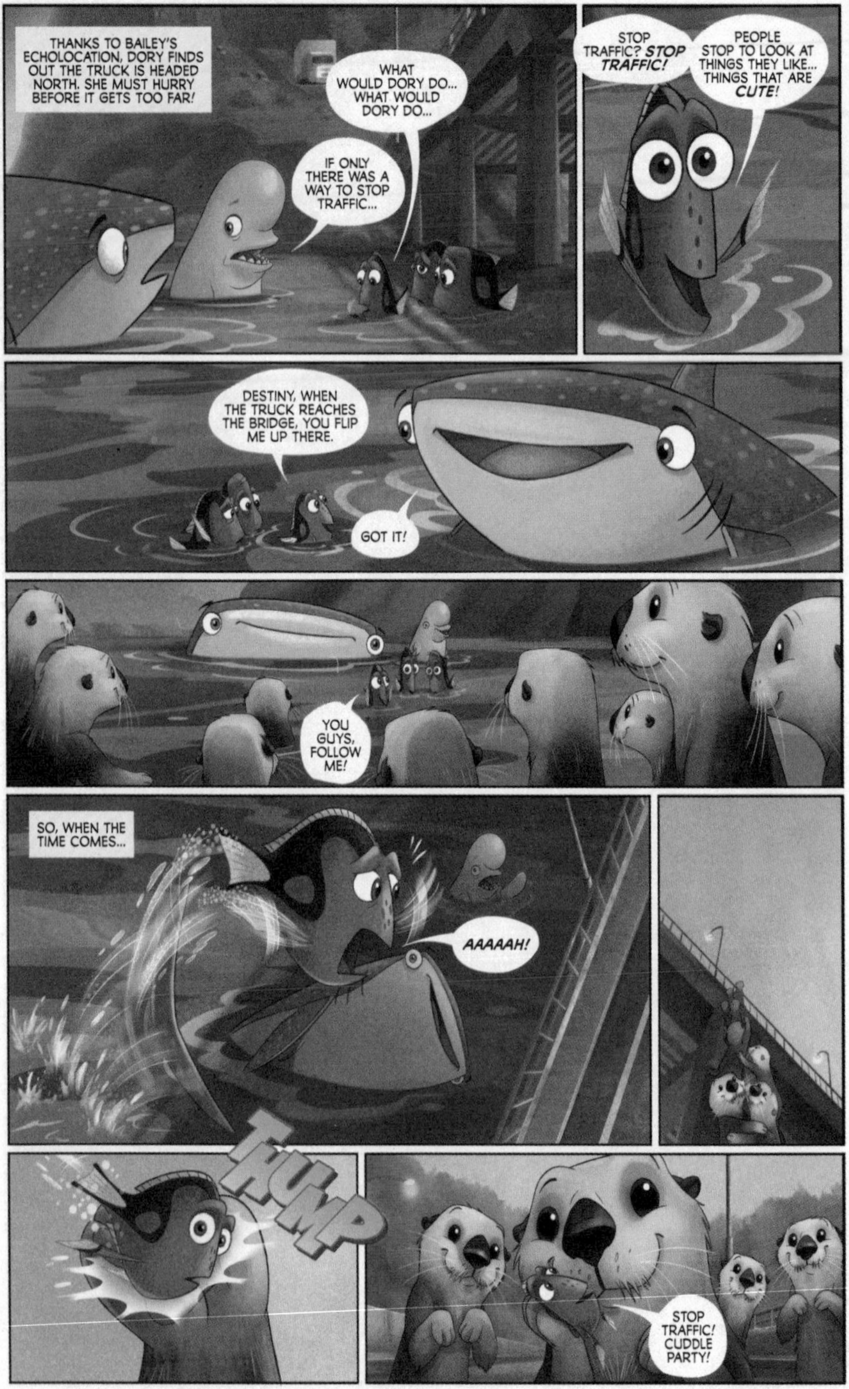

THANKS TO BAILEY'S ECHOLOCATION, DORY FINDS OUT THE TRUCK IS HEADED NORTH. SHE MUST HURRY BEFORE IT GETS TOO FAR!
WHAT WOULD DORY DO... WHAT WOULD DORY DO...
IF ONLY THERE WAS A WAY TO STOP TRAFFIC...
STOP TRAFFIC? STOP TRAFFIC!
PEOPLE STOP TO LOOK AT THINGS THEY LIKE... THINGS THAT ARE CUTE!
DESTINY, WHEN THE TRUCK REACHES THE BRIDGE, YOU FLIP ME UP THERE.
GOT IT!
YOU GUYS, FOLLOW ME!
SO, WHEN THE TIME COMES...
AAAAAH!
THUMP
STOP TRAFFIC! CUDDLE PARTY!

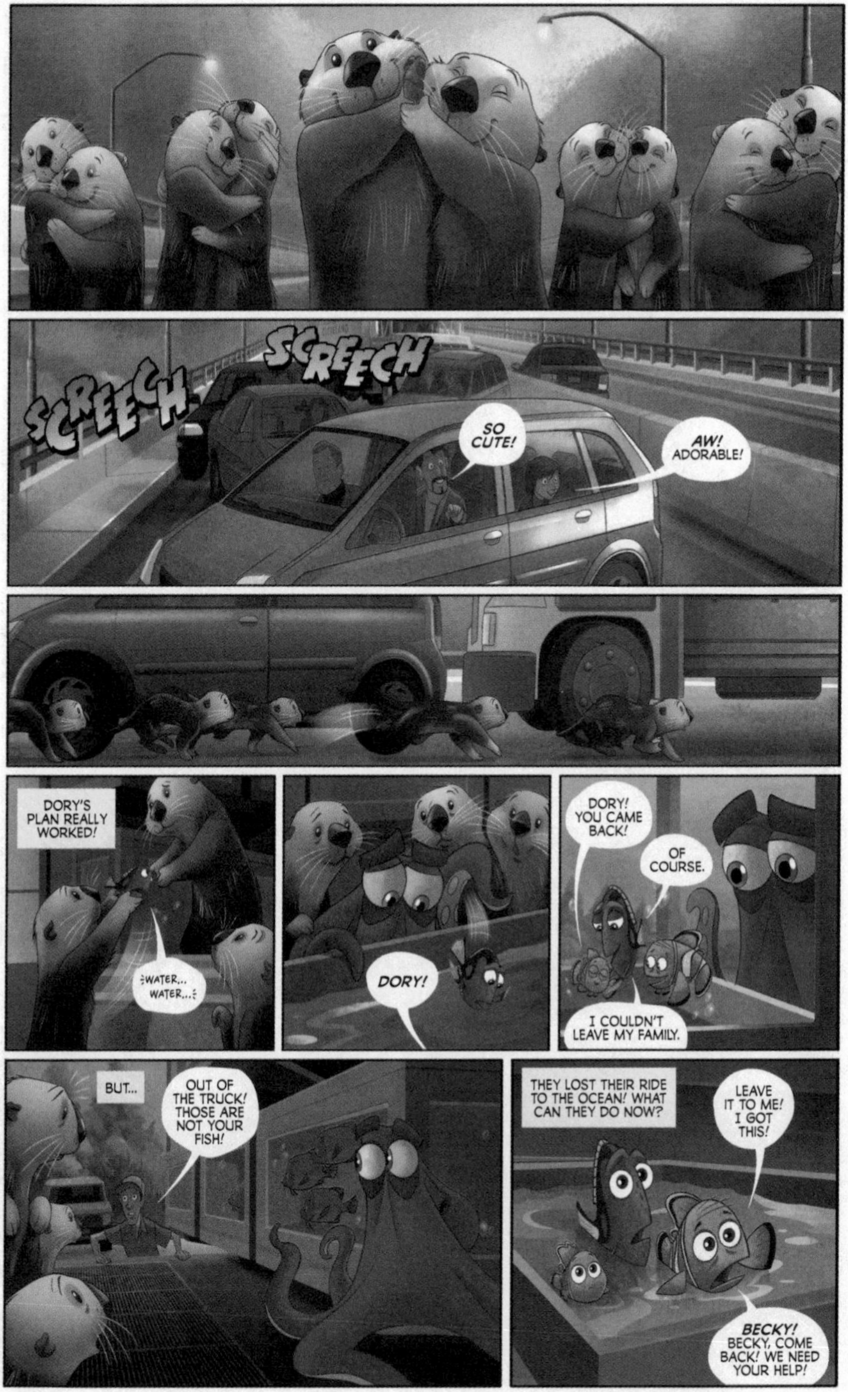
SCREECH
SCREECH
SO CUTE!
AW! ADORABLE!
DORY'S PLAN REALLY WORKED!
WATER... WATER...
DORY!
DORY! YOU CAME BACK!
OF COURSE.
I COULDN'T LEAVE MY FAMILY.
BUT...
OUT OF THE TRUCK! THOSE ARE NOT YOUR FISH!
THEY LOST THEIR RIDE TO THE OCEAN! WHAT CAN THEY DO NOW?
LEAVE IT TO ME! I GOT THIS!
BECKY! BECKY, COME BACK! WE NEED YOUR HELP!

BECKY ARRIVES! BUT AS SOON AS MARLIN AND NEMO HOP INTO THE PAIL...

...SHE TAKES OFF BEFORE DORY CAN GET IN!

BECKY, WAIT! WE NEED TO GO BACK!

BECKY! FETCH DORY!

BUT DORY IS STILL NOT READY TO LEAVE HANK...

YOU'RE NOT GOING TO THE CLEVELAND. YOU'RE COMING TO THE OCEAN WITH ME.

WHAT IS IT WITH YOU AND RUINING MY PLANS?

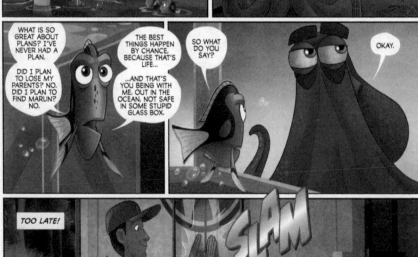

WHAT IS SO GREAT ABOUT PLANS? I'VE NEVER HAD A PLAN.

DID I PLAN TO LOSE MY PARENTS? NO. DID I PLAN TO FIND MARLIN? NO.

THE BEST THINGS HAPPEN BY CHANCE, BECAUSE THAT'S LIFE...

...AND THAT'S YOU BEING WITH ME, OUT IN THE OCEAN, NOT SAFE IN SOME STUPID GLASS BOX.

SO WHAT DO YOU SAY?

OKAY.

TOO LATE!

SLAM

MARINE LIFE INSTITUTE OF CLEVELAND

NOT GOOD.

48

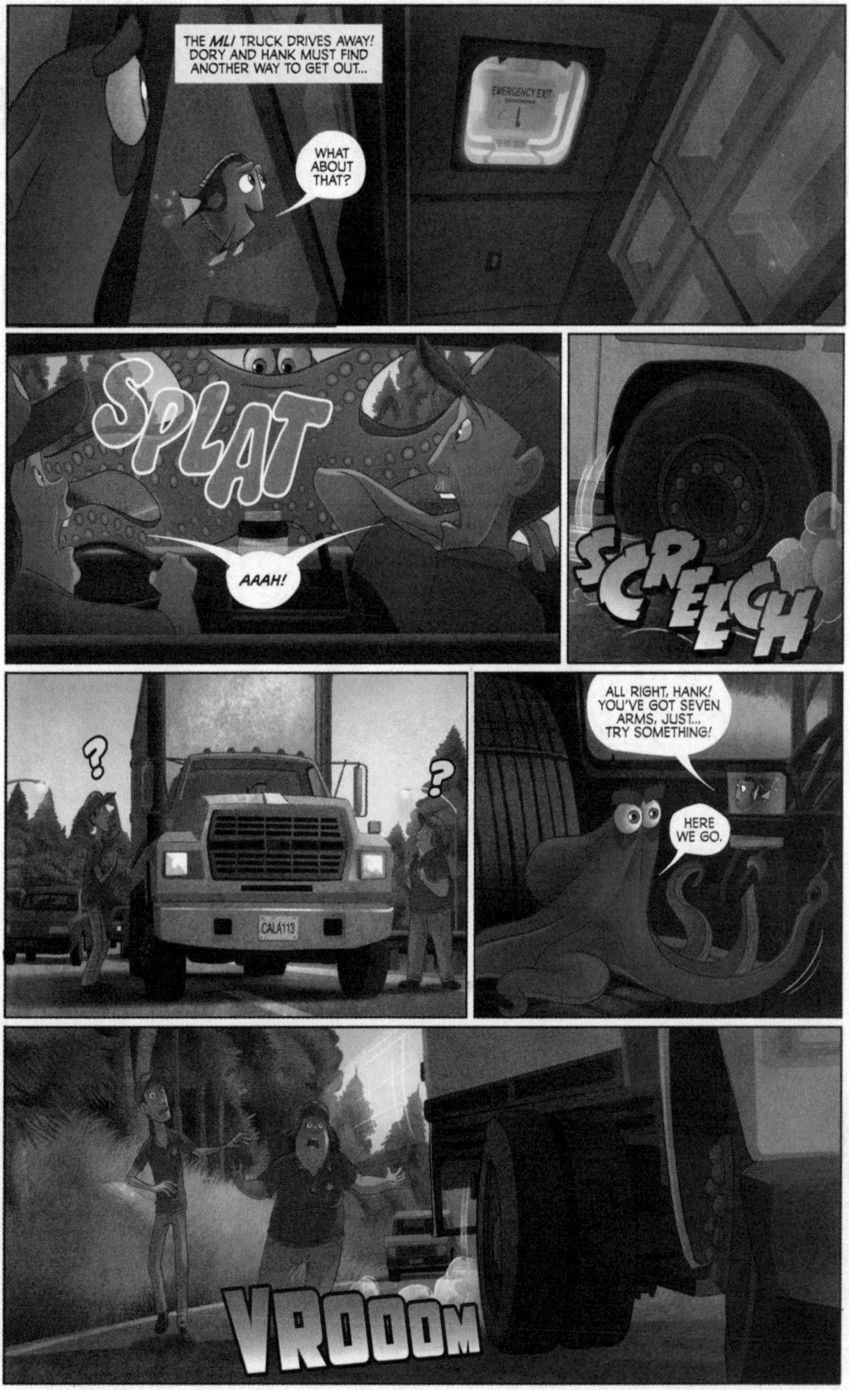
THE *MLI* TRUCK DRIVES AWAY! DORY AND HANK MUST FIND ANOTHER WAY TO GET OUT...
WHAT ABOUT THAT?
EMERGENCY EXIT
SPLAT
AAAH!
SCREEECH
CALA113
ALL RIGHT, HANK! YOU'VE GOT SEVEN ARMS, JUST... TRY SOMETHING!
HERE WE GO.
VROOOM

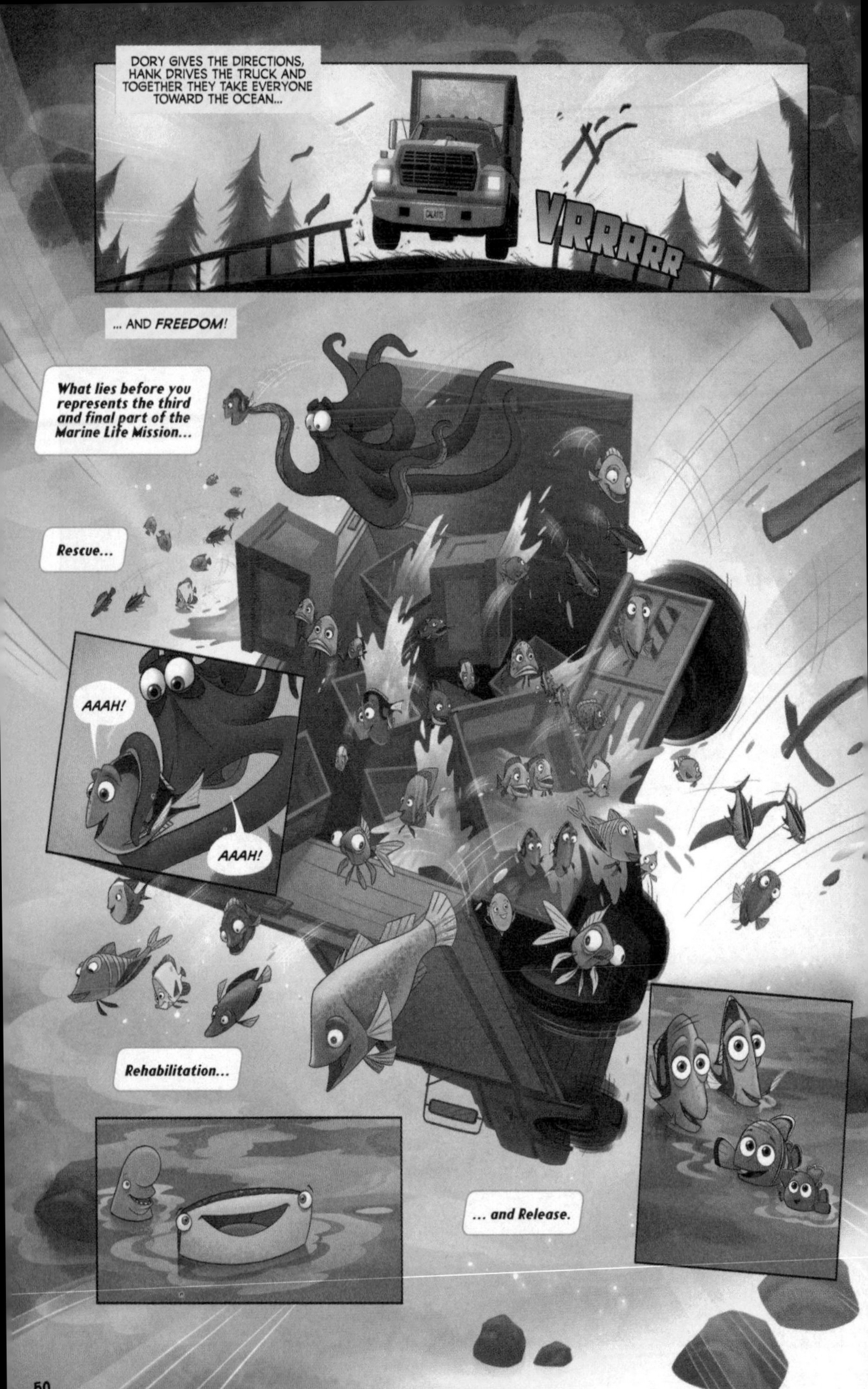
DORY GIVES THE DIRECTIONS, HANK DRIVES THE TRUCK AND TOGETHER THEY TAKE EVERYONE TOWARD THE OCEAN...
VRRRRR
... AND FREEDOM!
What lies before you represents the third and final part of the Marine Life Mission...
Rescue...
AAAH!
AAAH!
Rehabilitation...
... and Release.

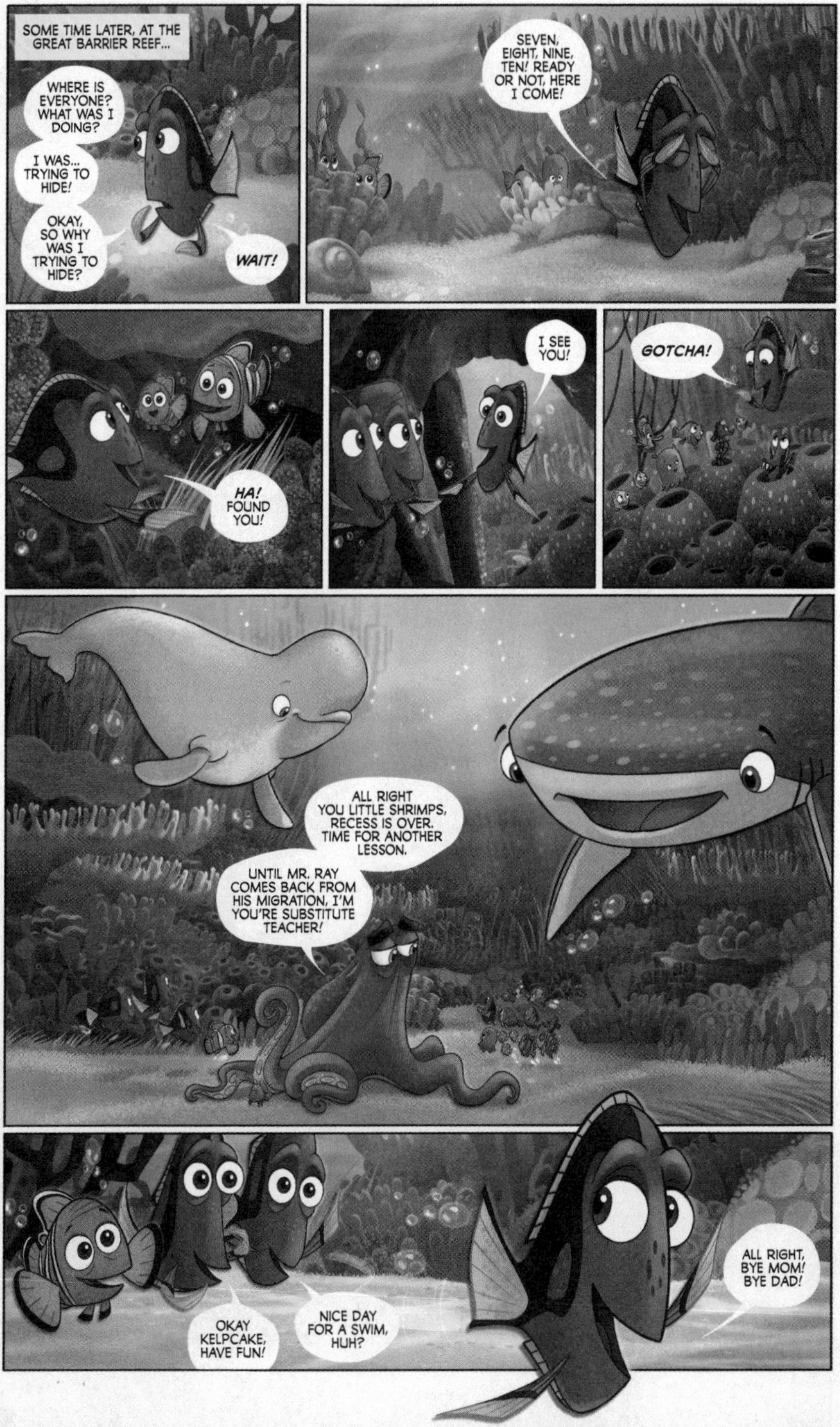
SOME TIME LATER, AT THE GREAT BARRIER REEF...
WHERE IS EVERYONE? WHAT WAS I DOING?
I WAS... TRYING TO HIDE!
OKAY, SO WHY WAS I TRYING TO HIDE?
WAIT!
SEVEN, EIGHT, NINE, TEN! READY OR NOT, HERE I COME!
HA! FOUND YOU!
I SEE YOU!
GOTCHA!
ALL RIGHT YOU LITTLE SHRIMPS, RECESS IS OVER. TIME FOR ANOTHER LESSON.
UNTIL MR. RAY COMES BACK FROM HIS MIGRATION, I'M YOU'RE SUBSTITUTE TEACHER!
OKAY KELPCAKE, HAVE FUN!
NICE DAY FOR A SWIM, HUH?
ALL RIGHT, BYE MOM! BYE DAD!

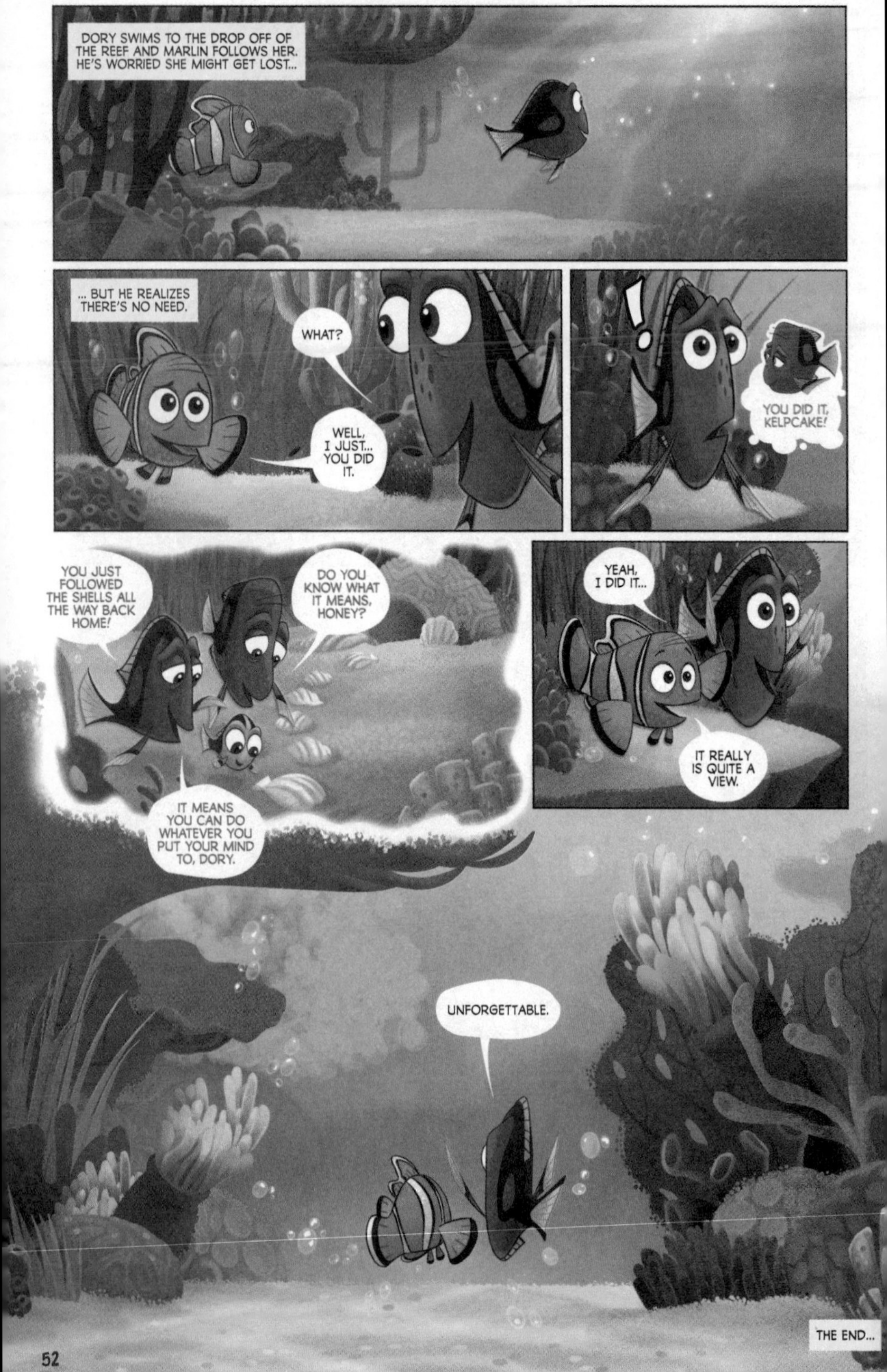
DORY SWIMS TO THE DROP OFF OF THE REEF AND MARLIN FOLLOWS HER. HE'S WORRIED SHE MIGHT GET LOST...
... BUT HE REALIZES THERE'S NO NEED.
WHAT?
WELL, I JUST... YOU DID IT.
!
YOU DID IT, KELPCAKE!
YOU JUST FOLLOWED THE SHELLS ALL THE WAY BACK HOME!
DO YOU KNOW WHAT IT MEANS, HONEY?
IT MEANS YOU CAN DO WHATEVER YOU PUT YOUR MIND TO, DORY.
YEAH, I DID IT...
IT REALLY IS QUITE A VIEW.
UNFORGETTABLE.
THE END...

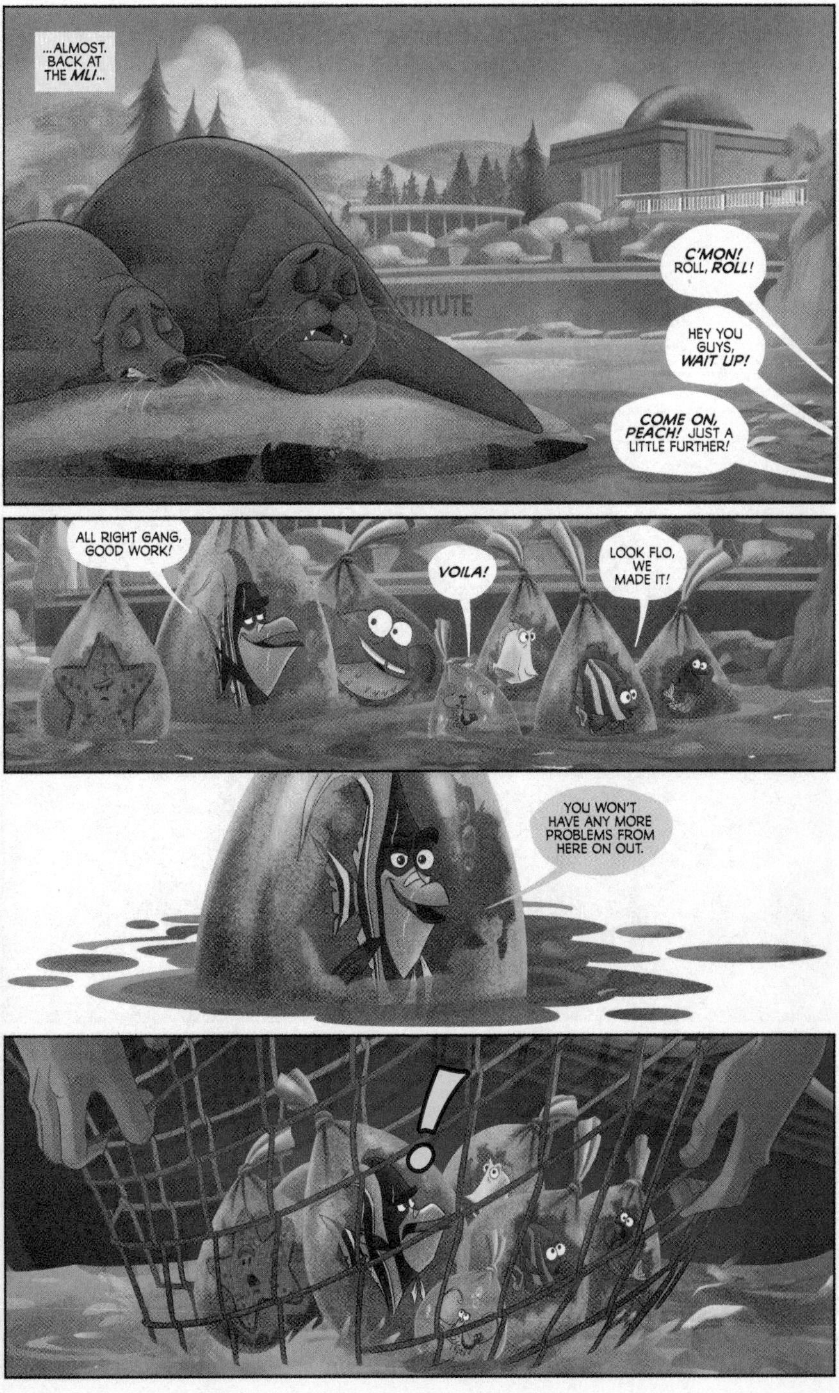
...ALMOST. BACK AT THE *MLI*...
INSTITUTE
C'MON! ROLL, ***ROLL***!
HEY YOU GUYS, ***WAIT UP!***
COME ON, PEACH! JUST A LITTLE FURTHER!
ALL RIGHT GANG, GOOD WORK!
VOILA!
LOOK FLO, WE MADE IT!
YOU WON'T HAVE ANY MORE PROBLEMS FROM HERE ON OUT.
!

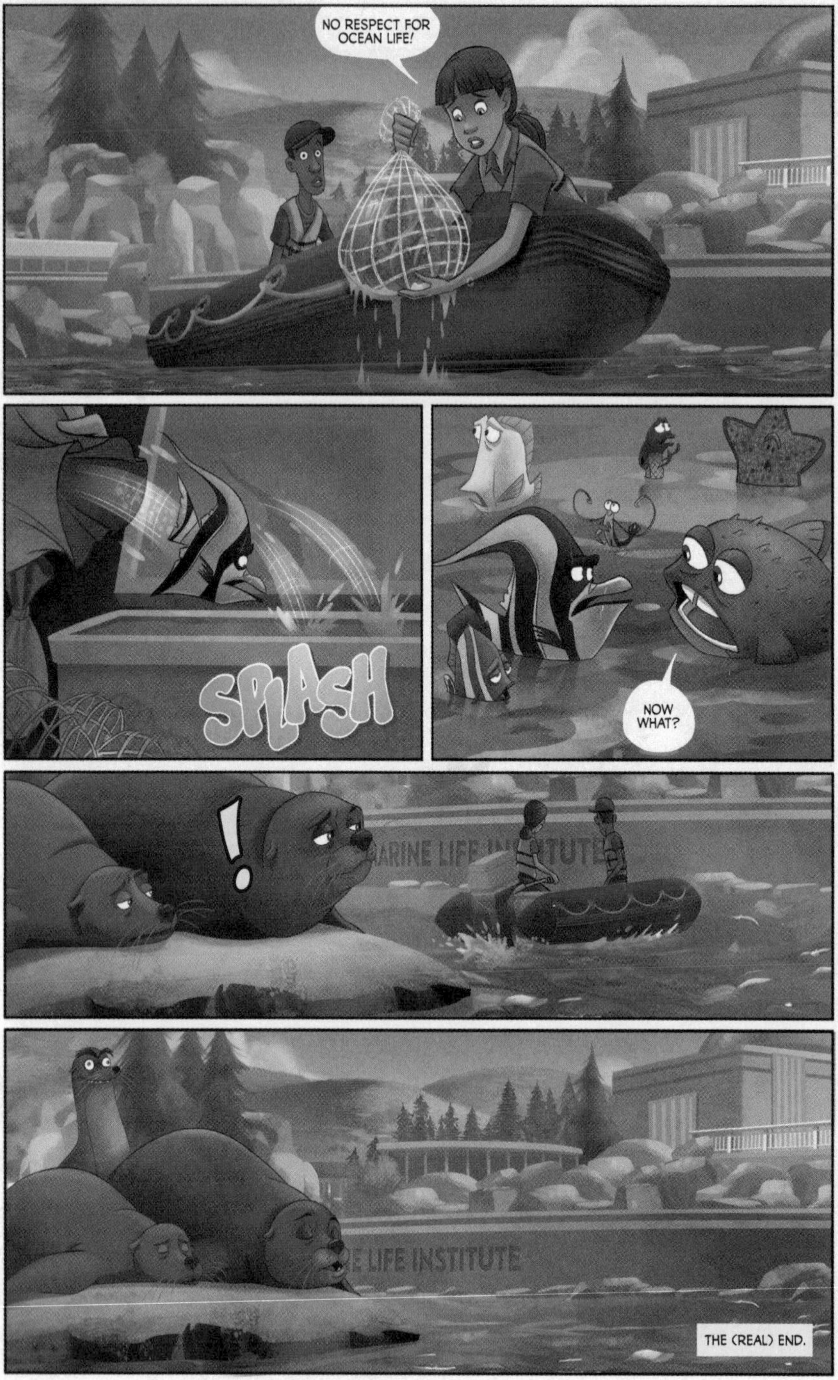
NO RESPECT FOR OCEAN LIFE!
SPLASH
NOW WHAT?
!
MARINE LIFE INSTITUTE
E LIFE INSTITUTE
THE (REAL) END.

Back On the Reef

Jenny & Charlie

Blue Tang

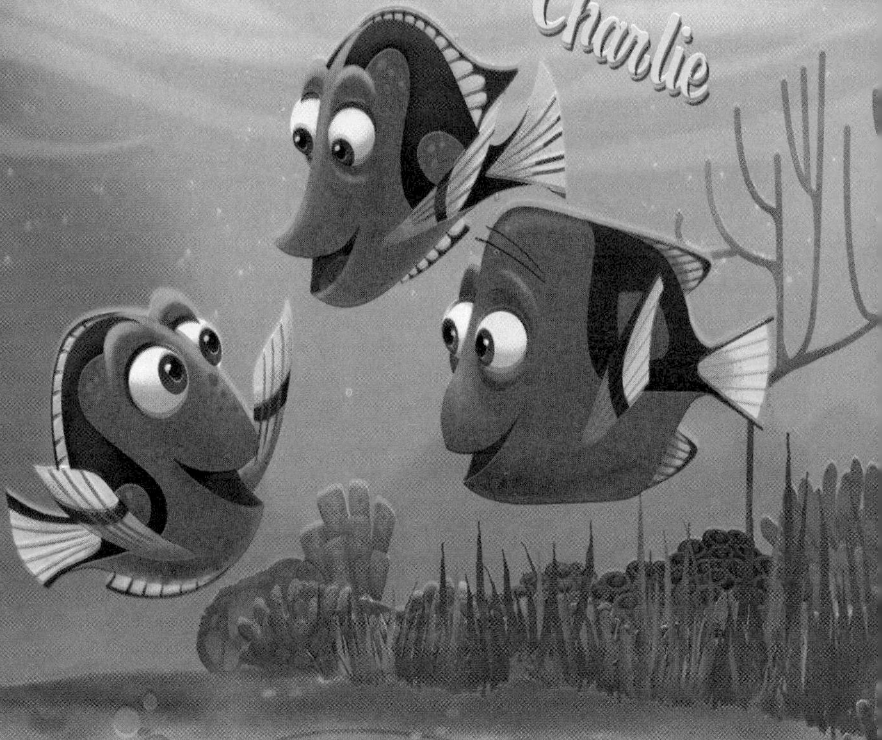

Dory's mom and dad have always known how special their beloved daughter is. Not because she suffers from short-term memory loss, but because despite of that she can do whatever she puts her mind to. Since the day Dory got lost, Jenny and Charlie knew she would have found them, no matter what. And she did!

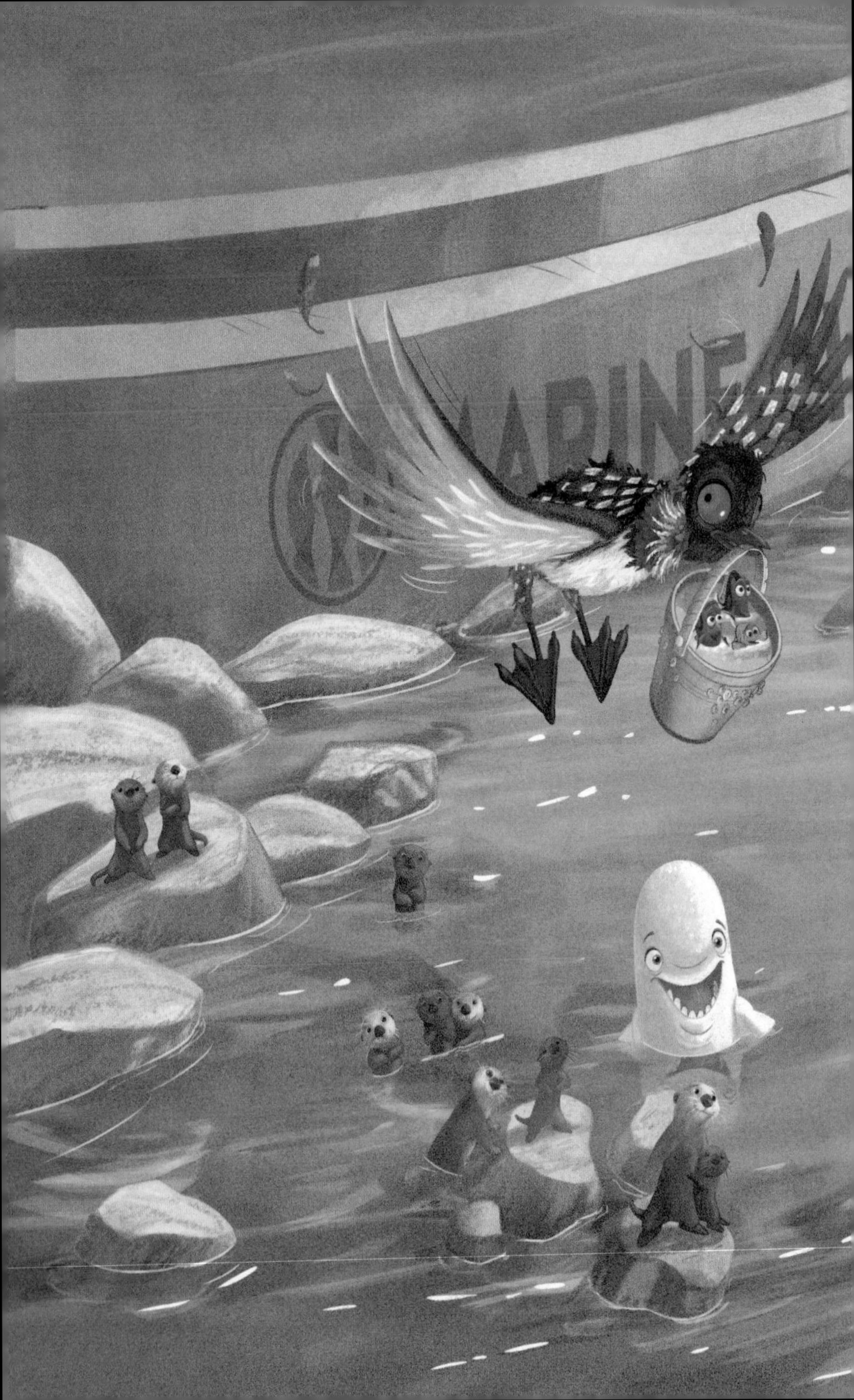

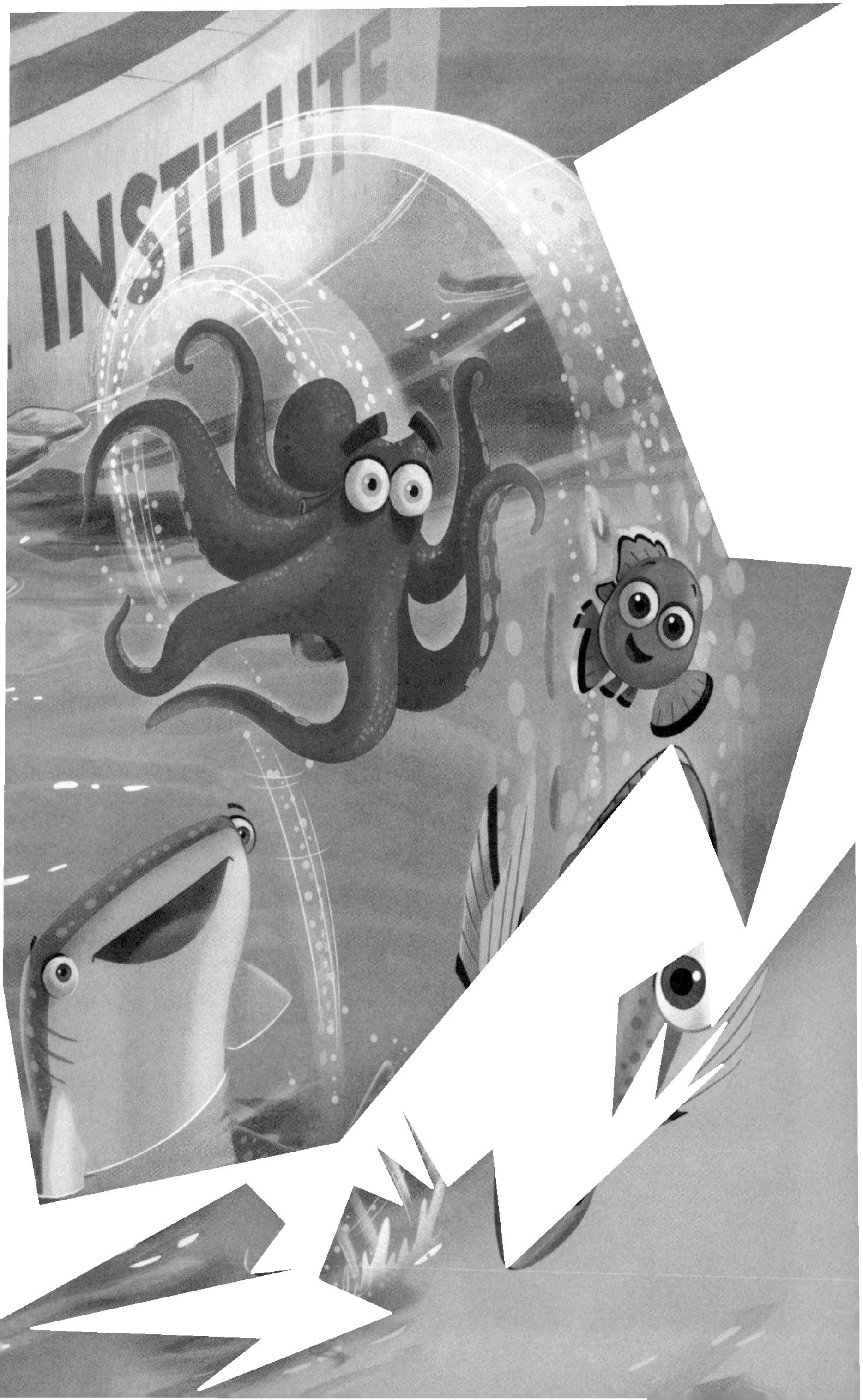
INSTITUTE

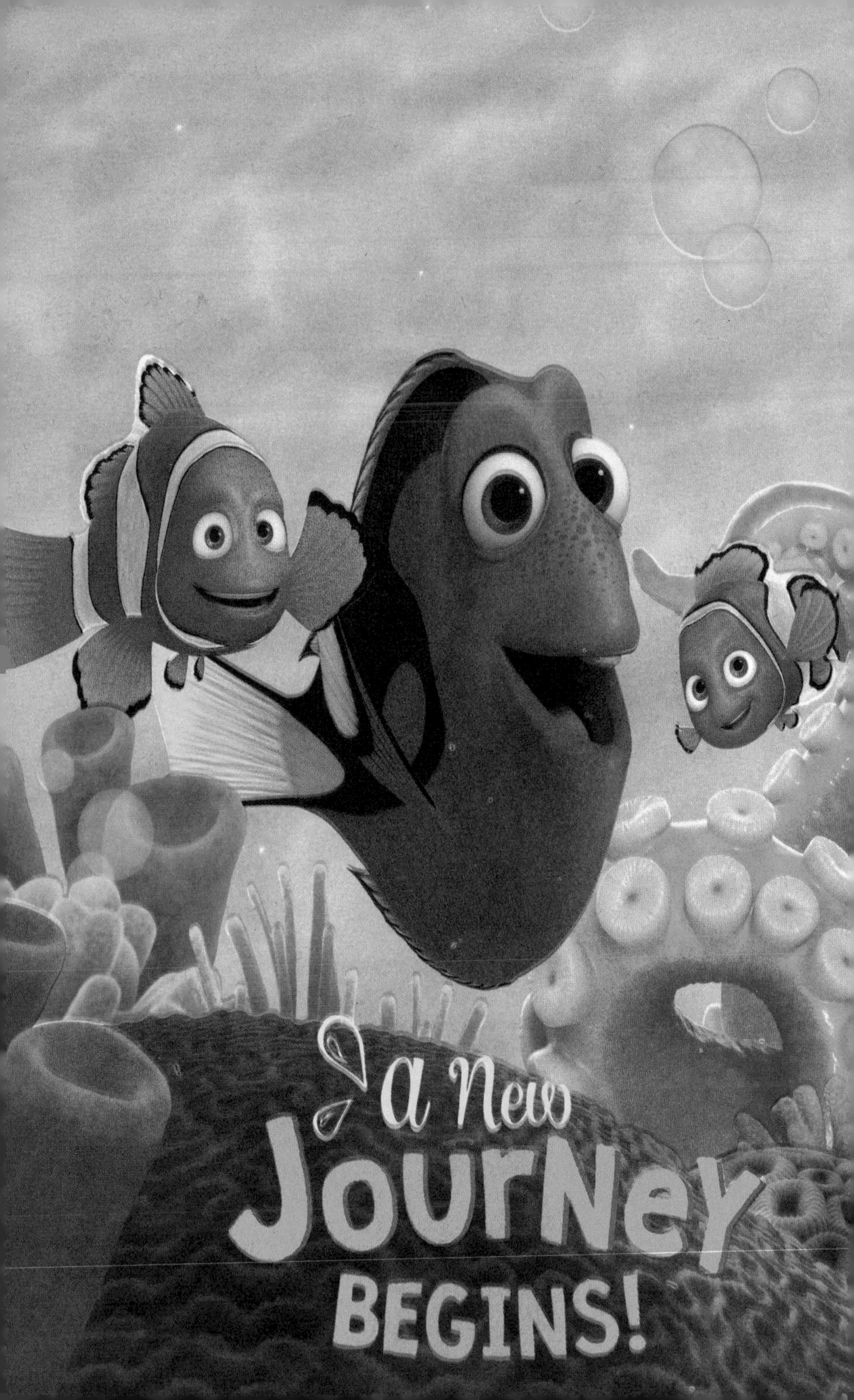
a New
JourNey
BEGINS!

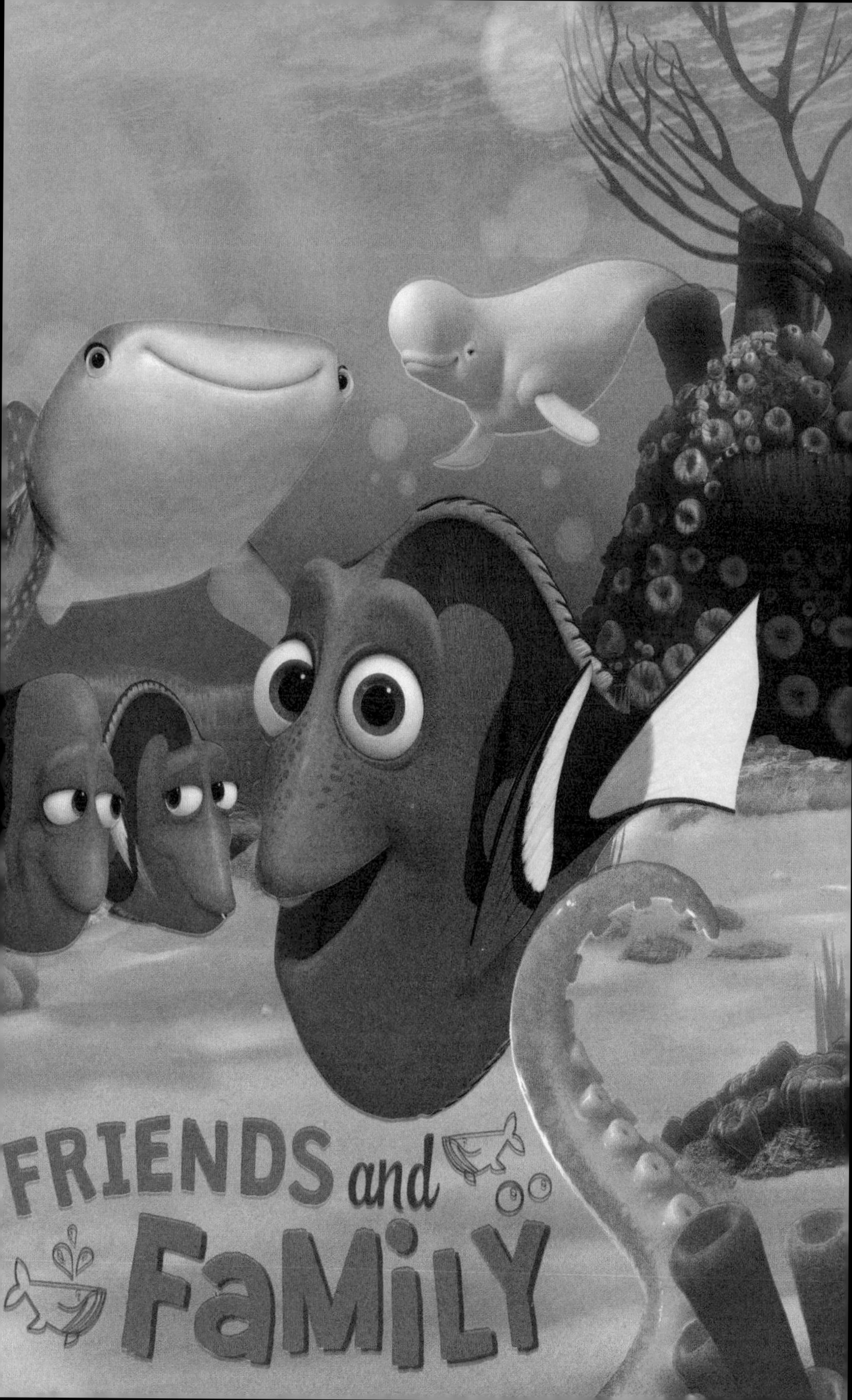
FRIENDS and
FaMiLY

FRIENDS and FAMILY

Along with her pals Nemo and Marlin, Dory swims across the ocean to find her family, meeting lots of fun characters along the way. Once she's reunited with her parents, Dory realizes she's one lucky fish, because she has more than one family: Her parents, Nemo and Marlin, and a whole school of fin-tastic friends!

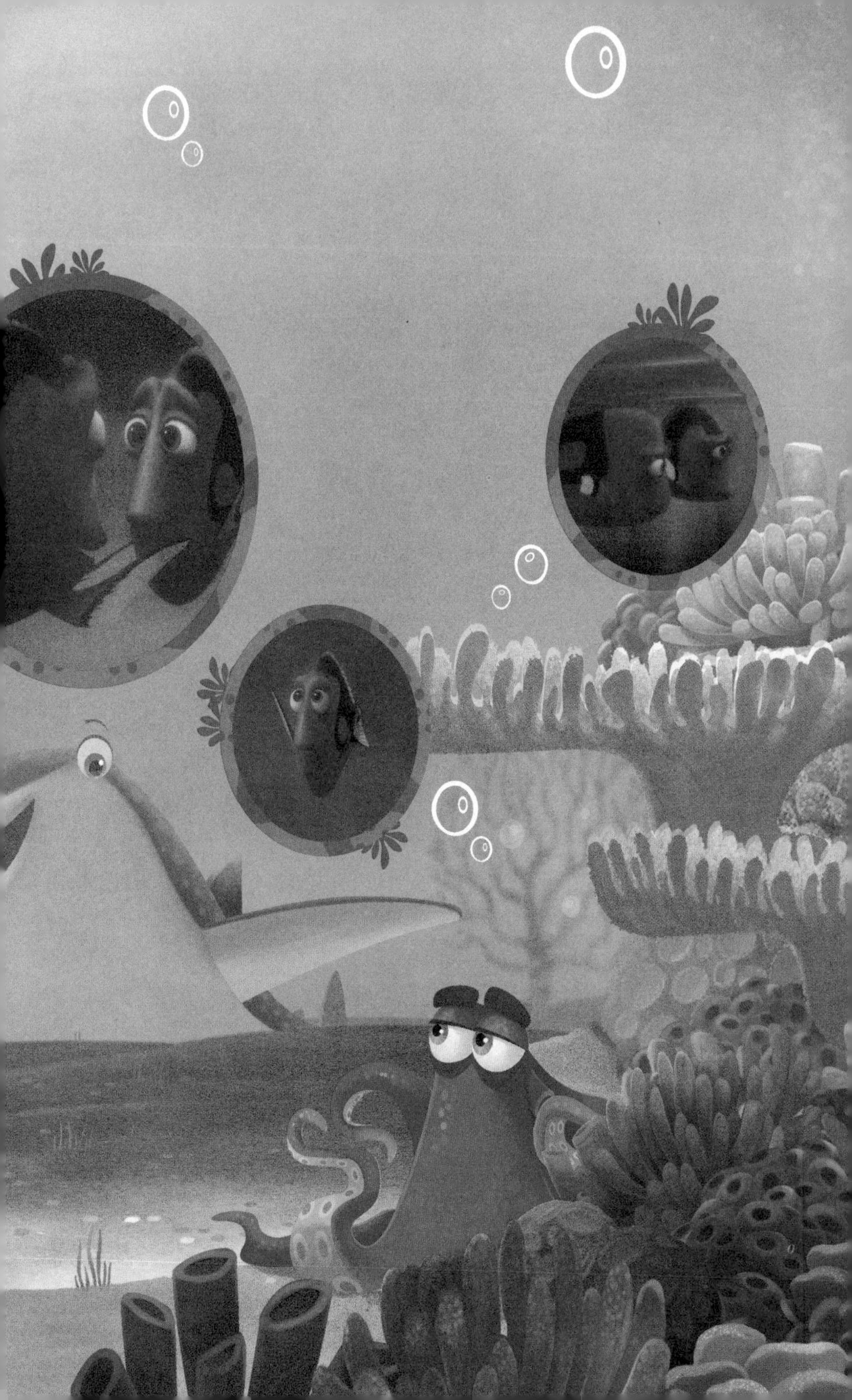

Family FLASHBACK

Led by memories of her childhood, Dory rediscovers the family she almost forgot!

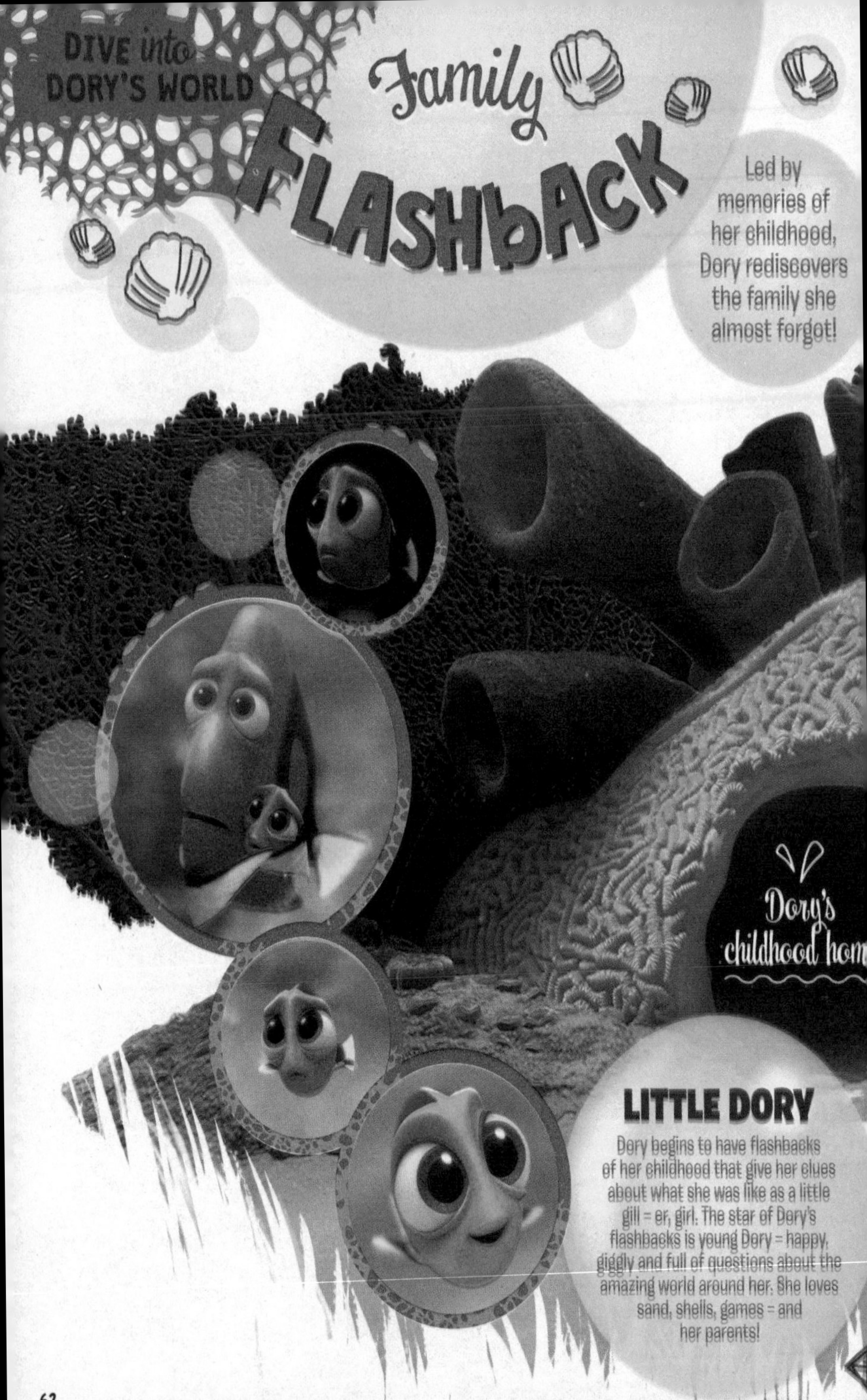
Dory's childhood hom

LITTLE DORY

Dory begins to have flashbacks of her childhood that give her clues about what she was like as a little gill – er, girl. The star of Dory's flashbacks is young Dory – happy, giggly and full of questions about the amazing world around her. She loves sand, shells, games – and her parents!

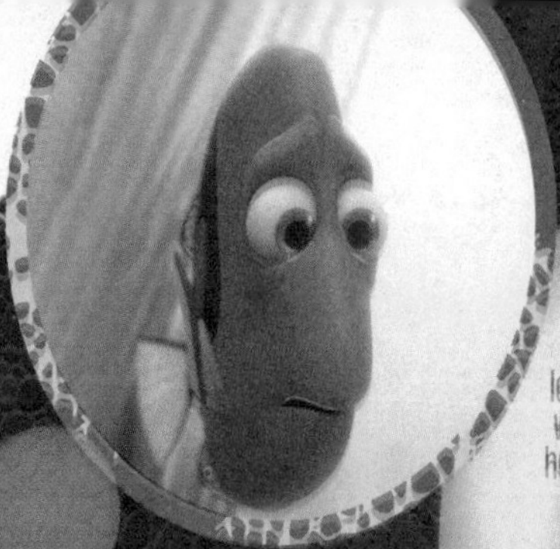

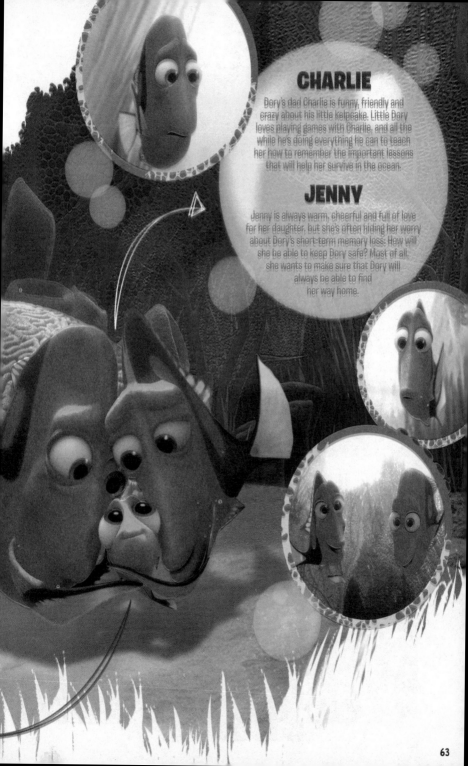

CHARLIE

Dory's dad Charlie is funny, friendly and crazy about his little kelpcake. Little Dory loves playing games with Charlie, and all the while he's doing everything he can to teach her how to remember the important lessons that will help her survive in the ocean.

JENNY

Jenny is always warm, cheerful and full of love for her daughter, but she's often hiding her worry about Dory's short-term memory loss: How will she be able to keep Dory safe? Most of all, she wants to make sure that Dory will always be able to find her way home.

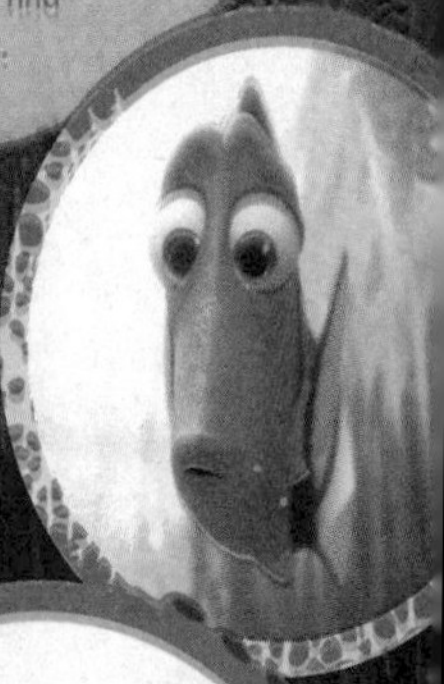

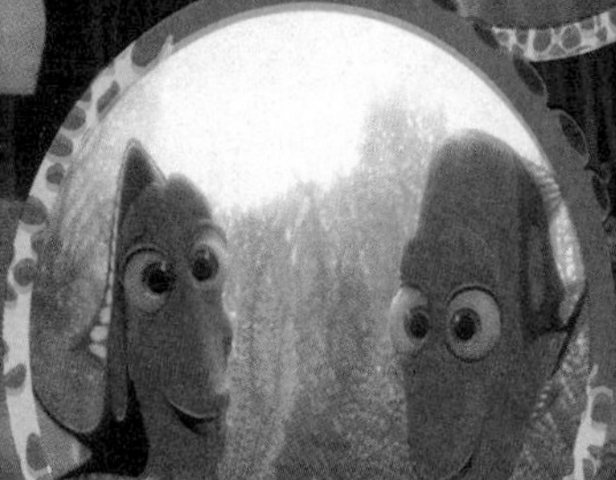

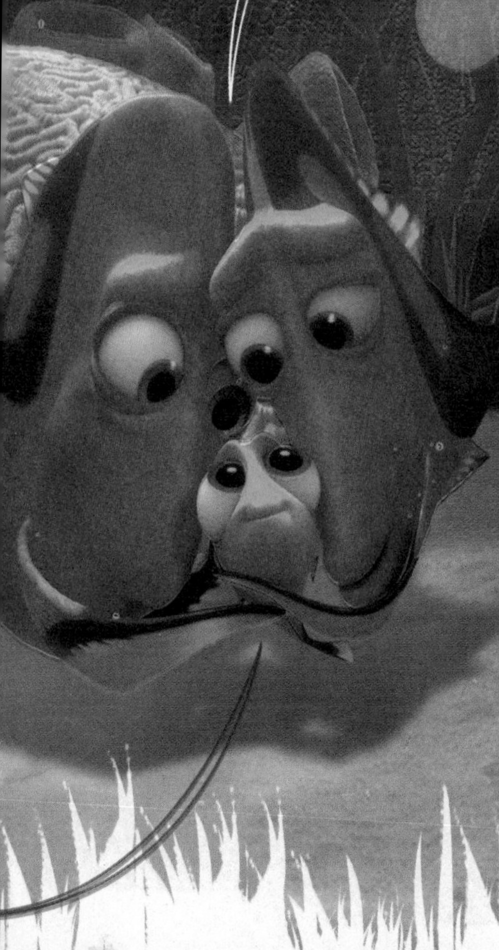

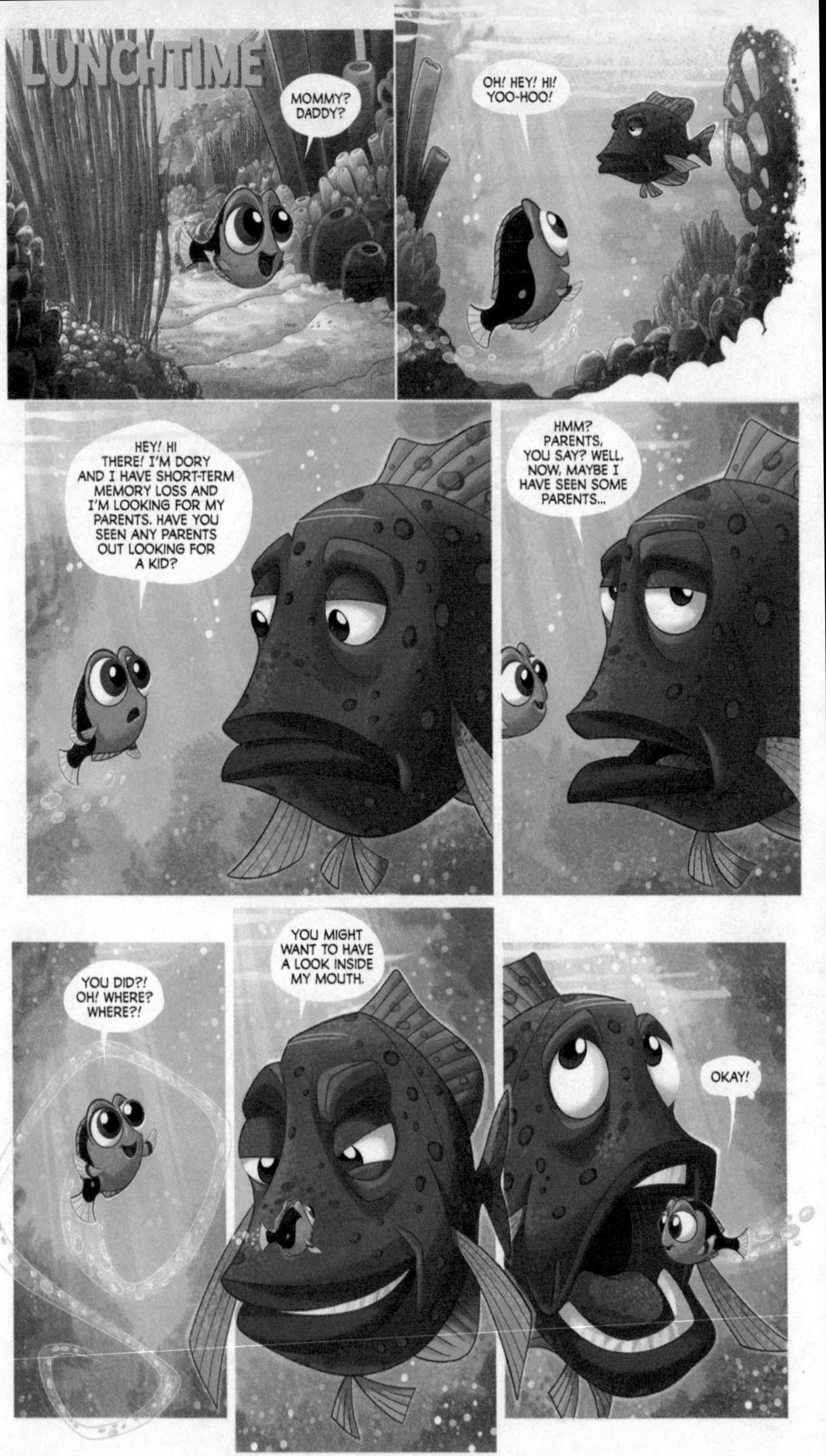
LUNCHTIME
MOMMY? DADDY?
OH! HEY! HI! YOO-HOO!
HEY! HI THERE! I'M DORY AND I HAVE SHORT-TERM MEMORY LOSS AND I'M LOOKING FOR MY PARENTS. HAVE YOU SEEN ANY PARENTS OUT LOOKING FOR A KID?
HMM? PARENTS, YOU SAY? WELL, NOW, MAYBE I HAVE SEEN SOME PARENTS...
YOU DID?! OH! WHERE? WHERE?!
YOU MIGHT WANT TO HAVE A LOOK INSIDE MY MOUTH.
OKAY!

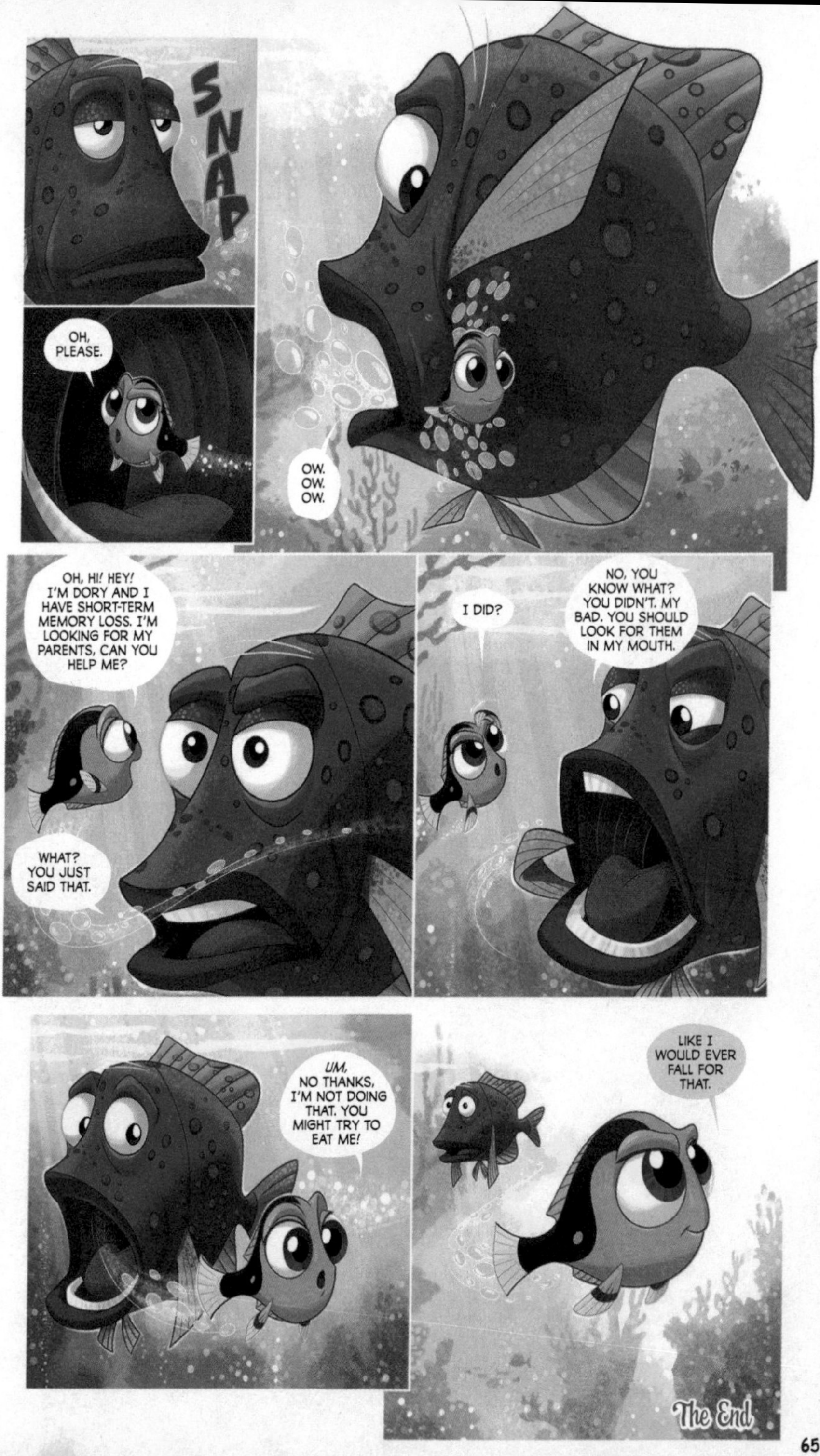
SNAP
OH, PLEASE.
OW. OW. OW.
OH, HI! HEY! I'M DORY AND I HAVE SHORT-TERM MEMORY LOSS. I'M LOOKING FOR MY PARENTS, CAN YOU HELP ME?
WHAT? YOU JUST SAID THAT.
I DID?
NO, YOU KNOW WHAT? YOU DIDN'T. MY BAD. YOU SHOULD LOOK FOR THEM IN MY MOUTH.
UM, NO THANKS, I'M NOT DOING THAT. YOU MIGHT TRY TO EAT ME!
LIKE I WOULD EVER FALL FOR THAT.
The End

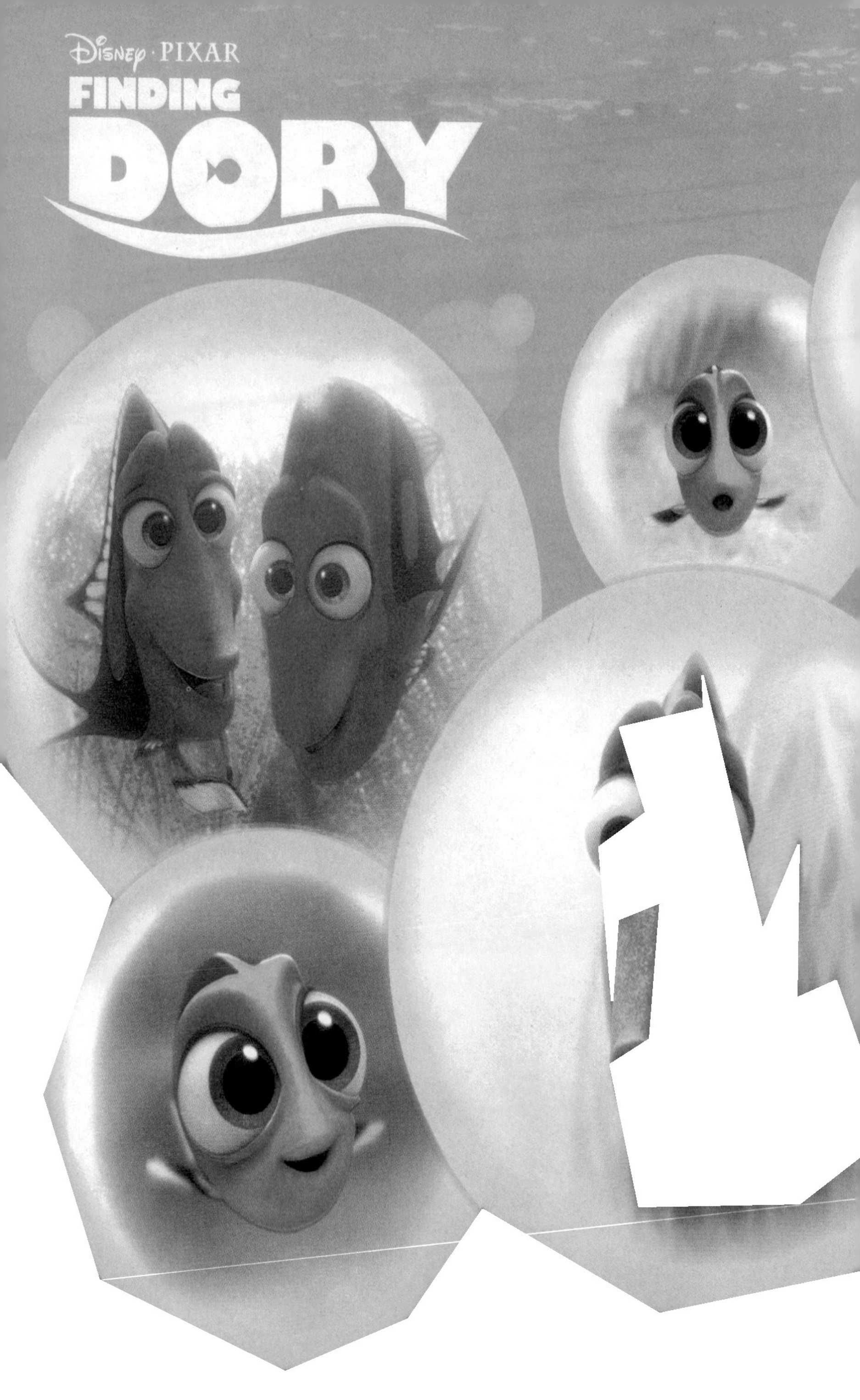
Disney · PIXAR
FINDING
DORY

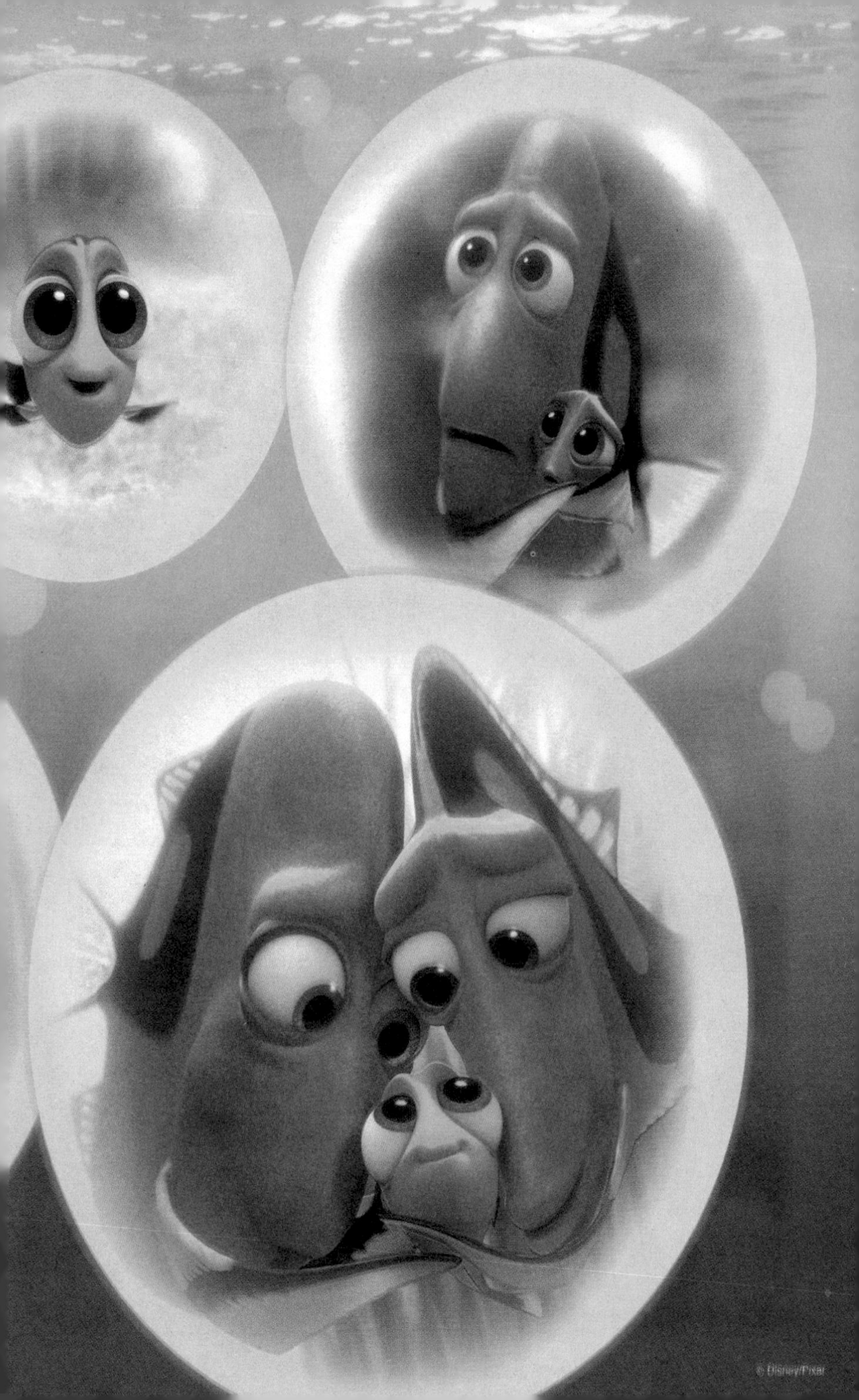

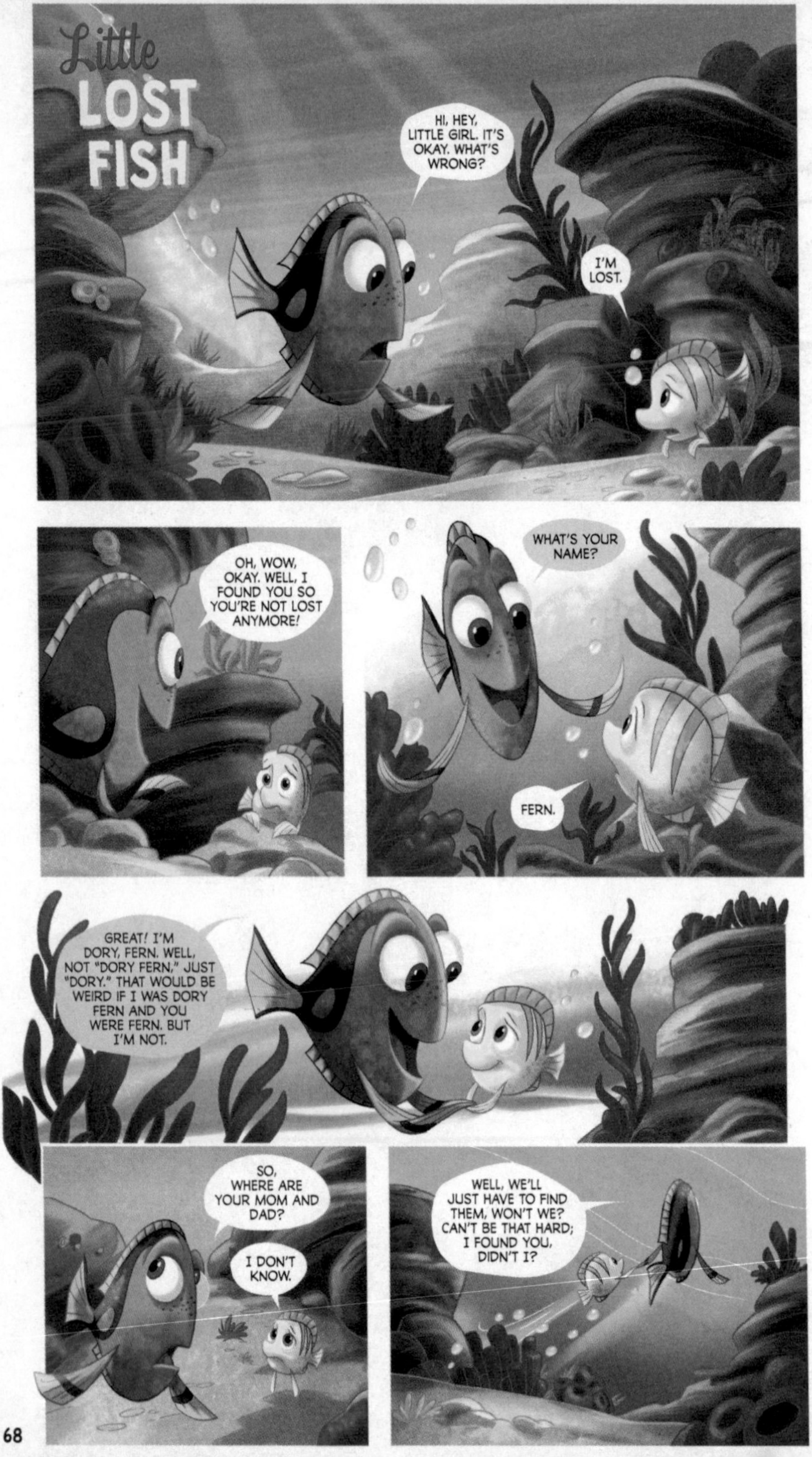
Little LOST FISH
HI, HEY, LITTLE GIRL. IT'S OKAY. WHAT'S WRONG?
I'M LOST.
OH, WOW, OKAY. WELL, I FOUND YOU SO YOU'RE NOT LOST ANYMORE!
WHAT'S YOUR NAME?
FERN.
GREAT! I'M DORY, FERN. WELL, NOT "DORY FERN," JUST "DORY." THAT WOULD BE WEIRD IF I WAS DORY FERN AND YOU WERE FERN. BUT I'M NOT.
SO, WHERE ARE YOUR MOM AND DAD?
I DON'T KNOW.
WELL, WE'LL JUST HAVE TO FIND THEM, WON'T WE? CAN'T BE THAT HARD; I FOUND YOU, DIDN'T I?

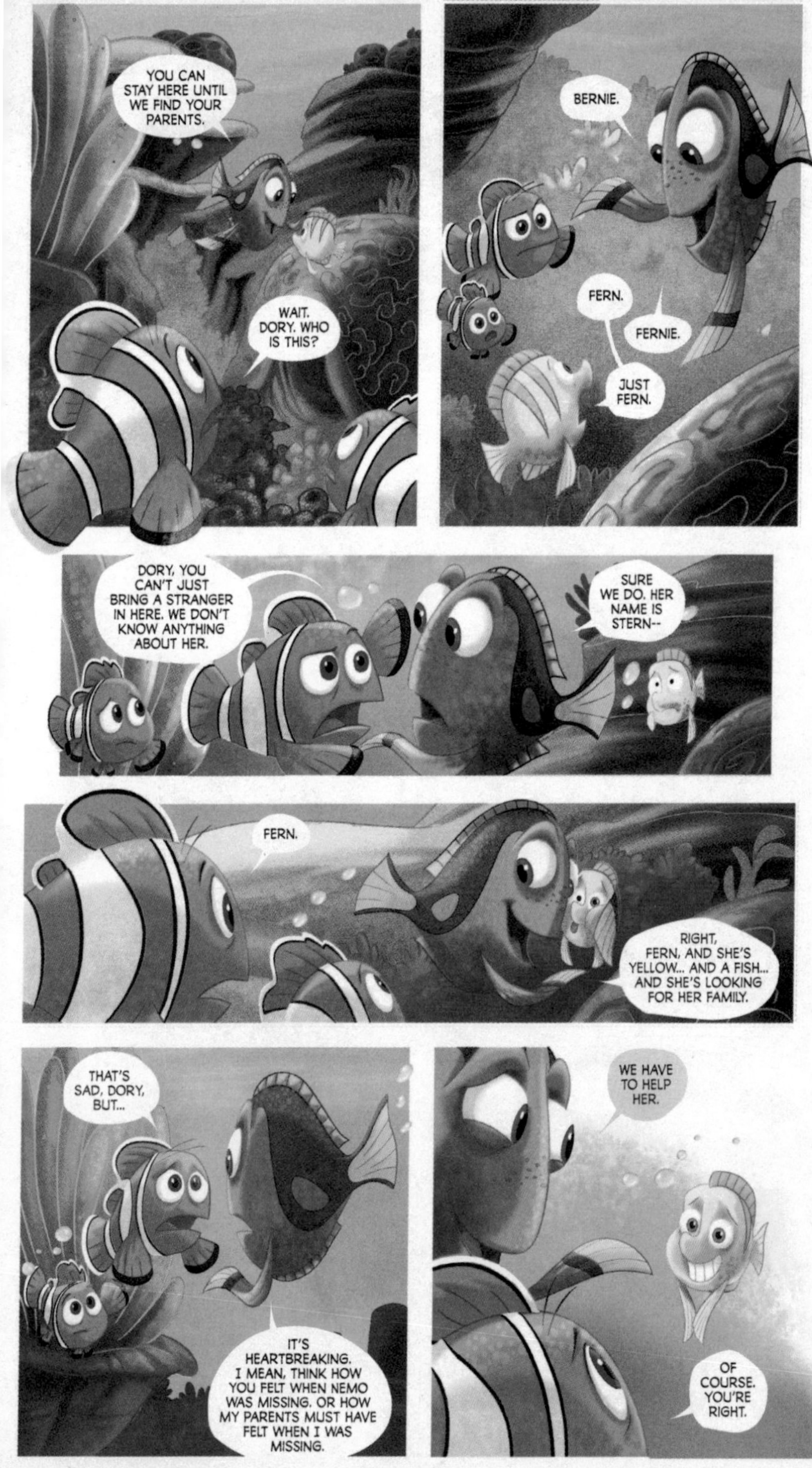
YOU CAN STAY HERE UNTIL WE FIND YOUR PARENTS.
WAIT. DORY. WHO IS THIS?
BERNIE.
FERN.
FERNIE.
JUST FERN.
DORY, YOU CAN'T JUST BRING A STRANGER IN HERE. WE DON'T KNOW ANYTHING ABOUT HER.
SURE WE DO. HER NAME IS STERN--
FERN.
RIGHT, FERN, AND SHE'S YELLOW... AND A FISH... AND SHE'S LOOKING FOR HER FAMILY.
THAT'S SAD, DORY, BUT...
IT'S HEARTBREAKING. I MEAN, THINK HOW YOU FELT WHEN NEMO WAS MISSING. OR HOW MY PARENTS MUST HAVE FELT WHEN I WAS MISSING.
WE HAVE TO HELP HER.
OF COURSE. YOU'RE RIGHT.

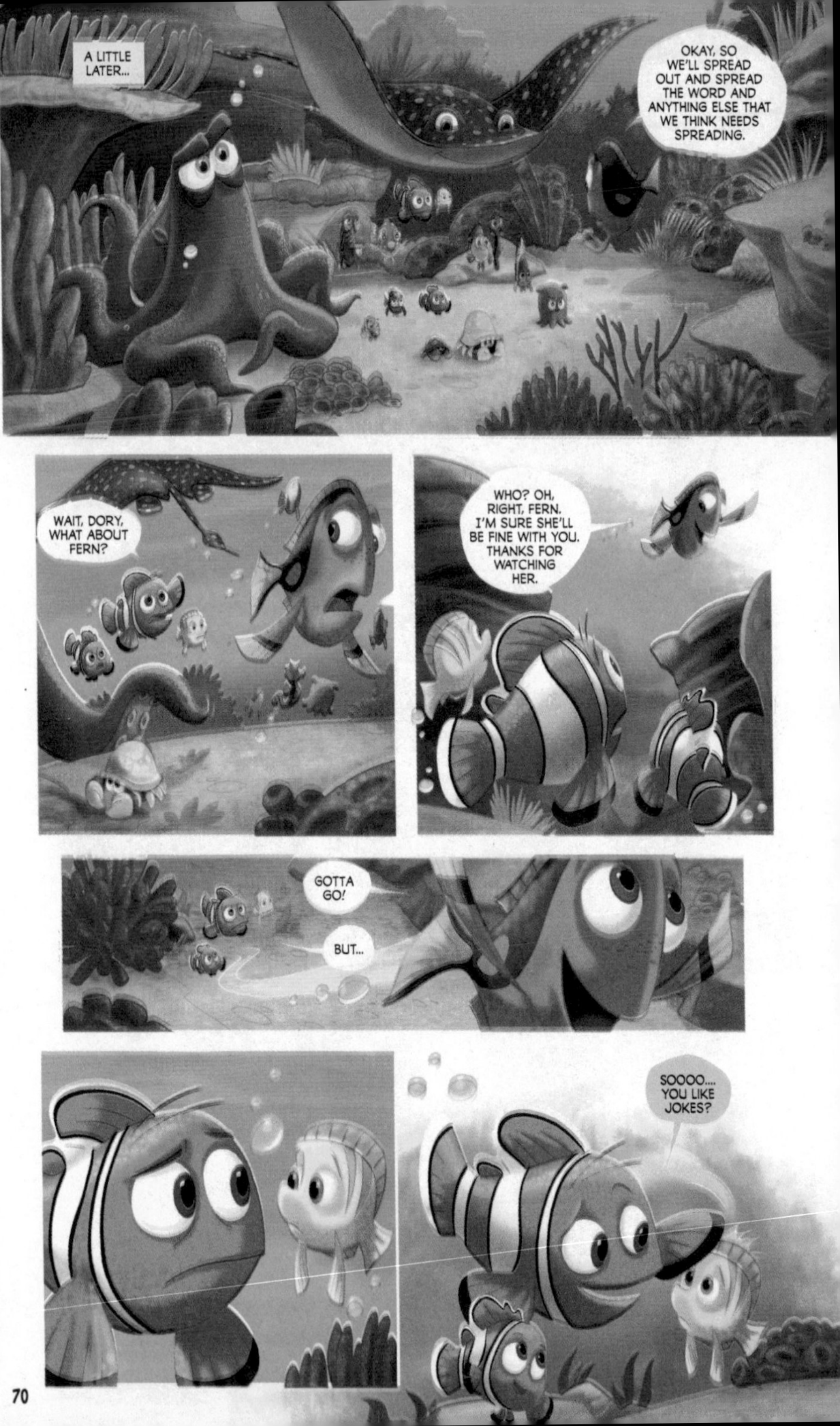
A LITTLE LATER...
OKAY, SO WE'LL SPREAD OUT AND SPREAD THE WORD AND ANYTHING ELSE THAT WE THINK NEEDS SPREADING.
WAIT, DORY, WHAT ABOUT FERN?
WHO? OH, RIGHT, FERN. I'M SURE SHE'LL BE FINE WITH YOU. THANKS FOR WATCHING HER.
GOTTA GO!
BUT...
SOOOO.... YOU LIKE JOKES?

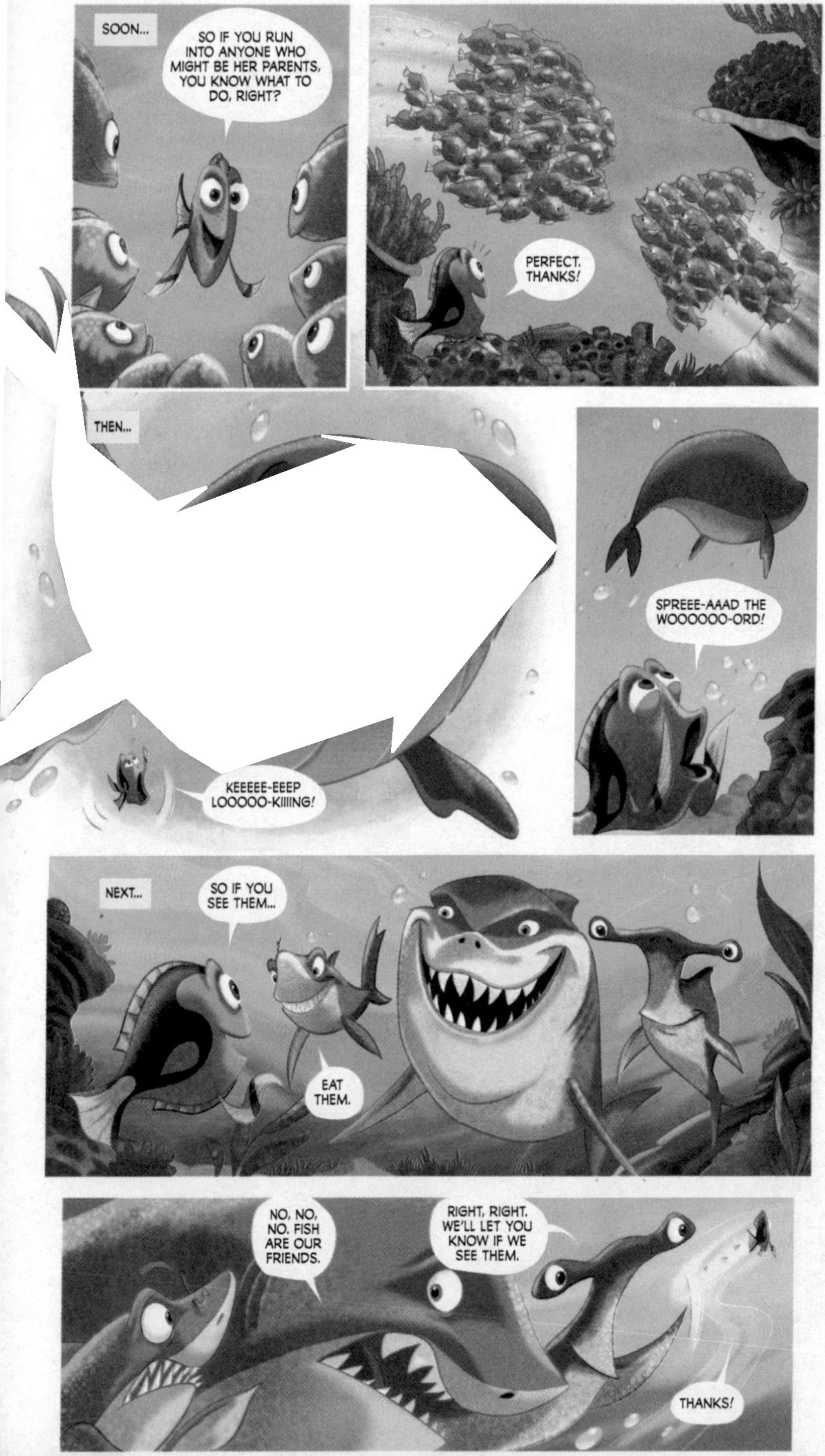
SOON...
SO IF YOU RUN INTO ANYONE WHO MIGHT BE HER PARENTS, YOU KNOW WHAT TO DO, RIGHT?
PERFECT. THANKS!
THEN...
KEEEEE-EEEP LOOOOO-KIIIING!
SPREEE-AAAD THE WOOOOOO-ORD!
NEXT...
SO IF YOU SEE THEM...
EAT THEM.
NO, NO, NO. FISH ARE OUR FRIENDS.
RIGHT, RIGHT. WE'LL LET YOU KNOW IF WE SEE THEM.
THANKS!

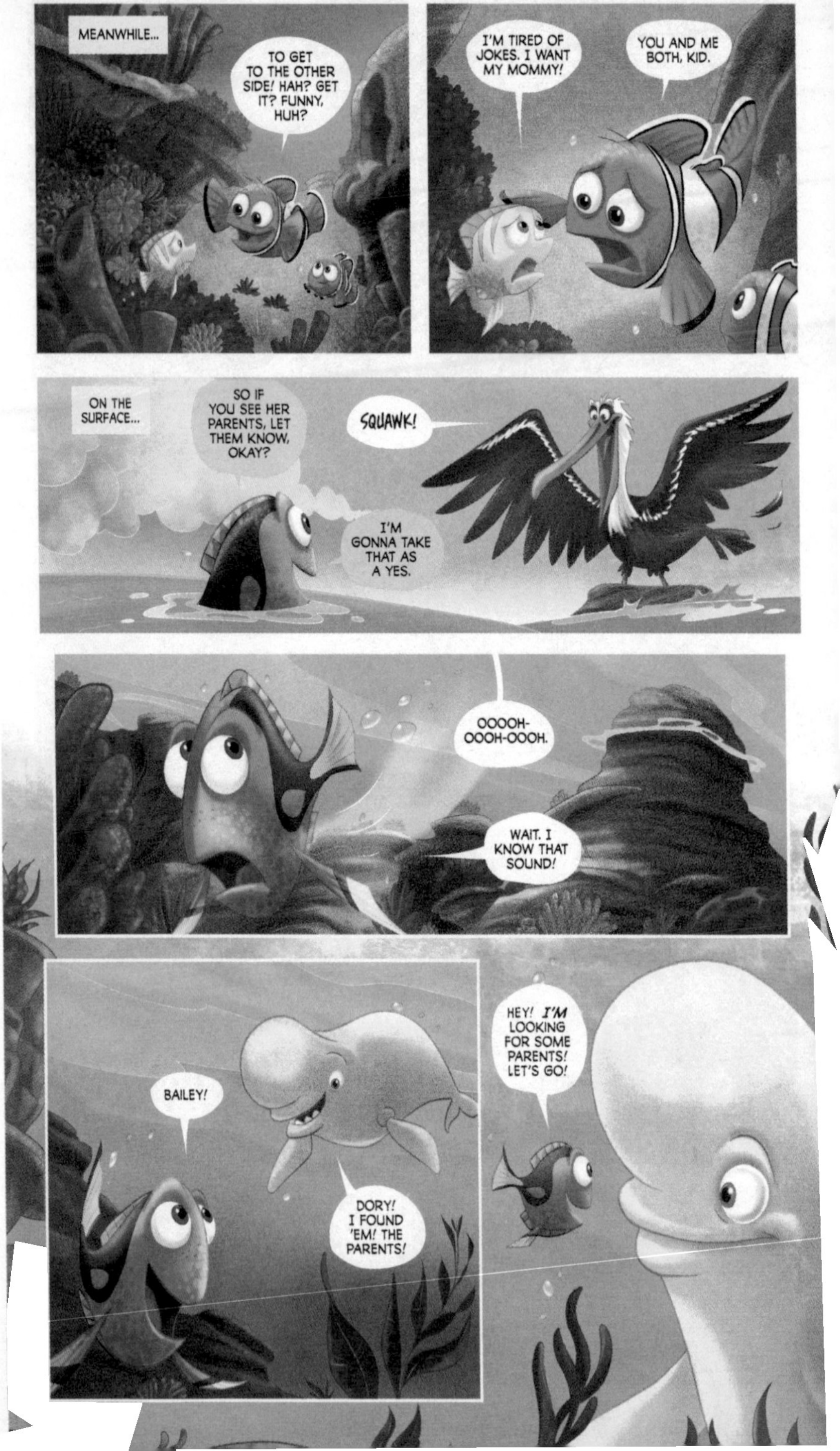
MEANWHILE...
TO GET TO THE OTHER SIDE! HAH? GET IT? FUNNY, HUH?
I'M TIRED OF JOKES. I WANT MY MOMMY!
YOU AND ME BOTH, KID.
ON THE SURFACE...
SO IF YOU SEE HER PARENTS, LET THEM KNOW, OKAY?
SQUAWK!
I'M GONNA TAKE THAT AS A YES.
OOOOH-OOOH-OOOH.
WAIT. I KNOW THAT SOUND!
BAILEY!
DORY! I FOUND 'EM! THE PARENTS!
HEY! I'M LOOKING FOR SOME PARENTS! LET'S GO!

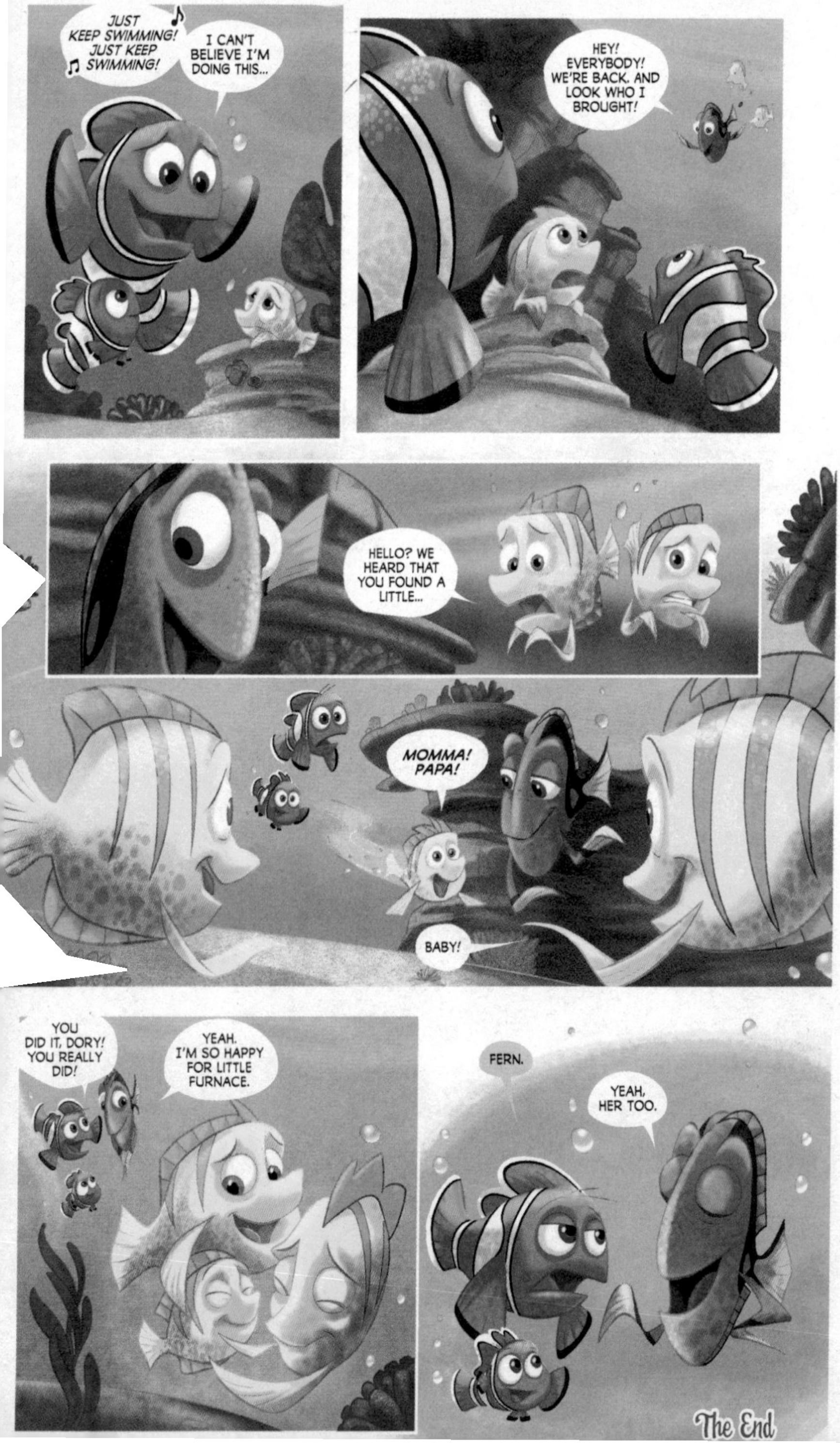
JUST KEEP SWIMMING! JUST KEEP SWIMMING!
I CAN'T BELIEVE I'M DOING THIS...
HEY! EVERYBODY! WE'RE BACK. AND LOOK WHO I BROUGHT!
HELLO? WE HEARD THAT YOU FOUND A LITTLE...
MOMMA! PAPA!
BABY!
YOU DID IT, DORY! YOU REALLY DID!
YEAH. I'M SO HAPPY FOR LITTLE FURNACE.
FERN.
YEAH, HER TOO.
The End

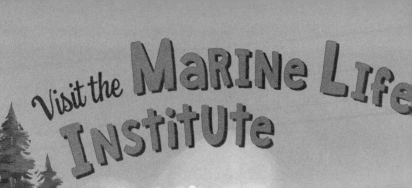

Visit the Marine Life Institute

Dory, Nemo, and Marlin's adventures take them to the Marine Life Institute, a place dedicated to the rescue, rehabilitation, and release of sea creatures of all shapes and sizes!

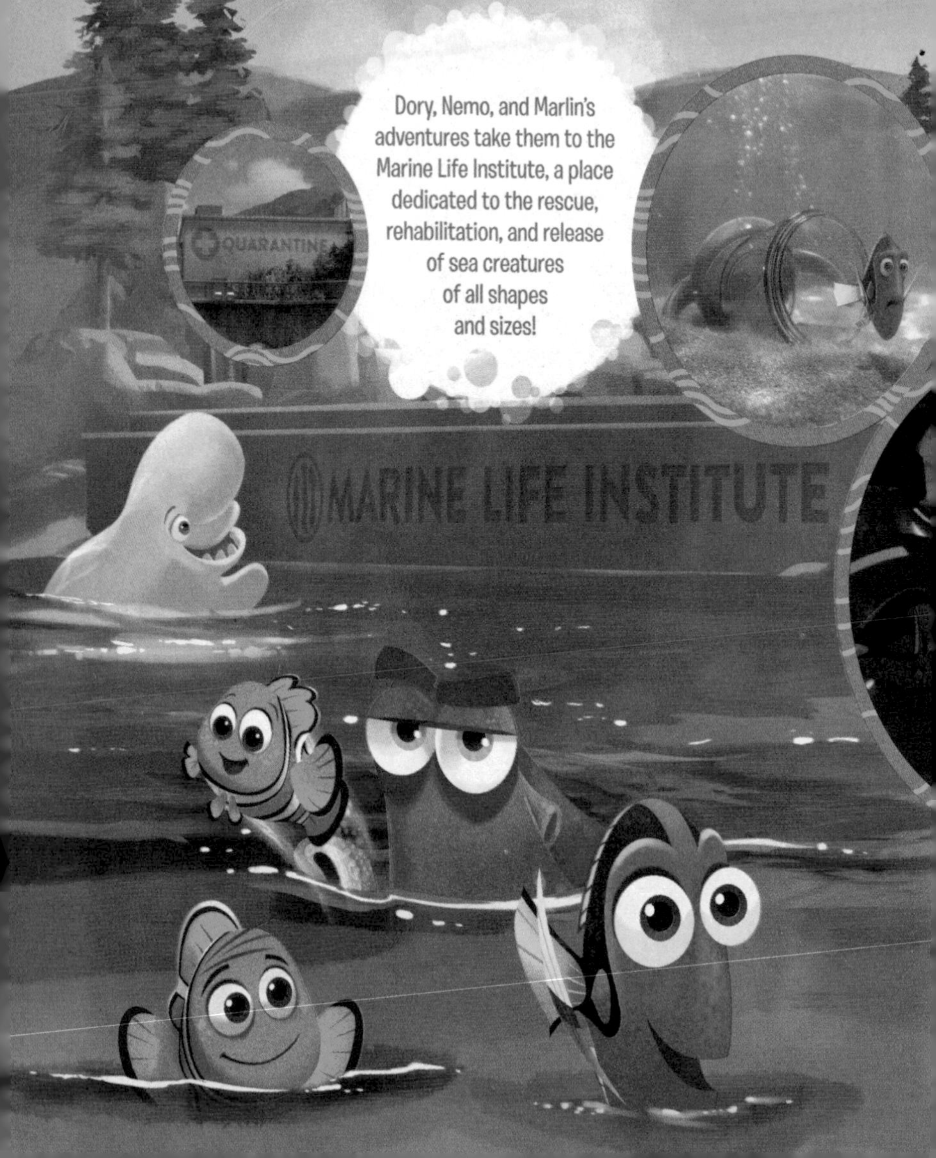
QUARANTINE
MARINE LIFE INSTITUTE

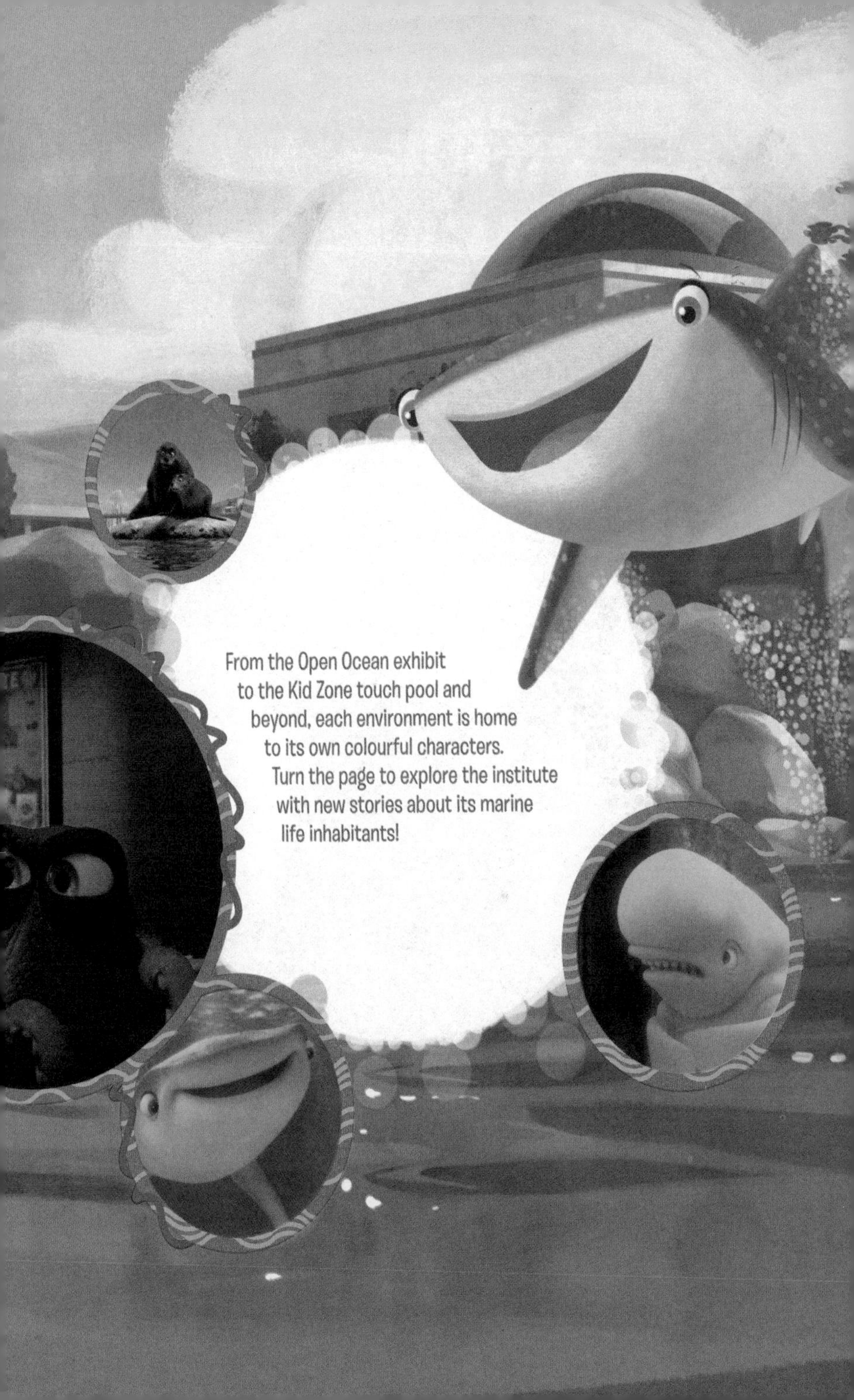

From the Open Ocean exhibit to the Kid Zone touch pool and beyond, each environment is home to its own colourful characters. Turn the page to explore the institute with new stories about its marine life inhabitants!

DIVE into DORY'S WORLD

Sea STARS

From the open ocean to the tanks at MLI, Dory and her friends always make a splash.

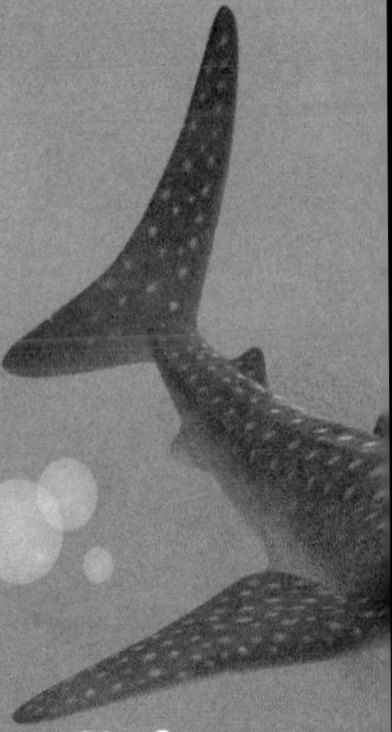

Dory

SCIENTIFIC NAME:
Paracanthurus hepatus (aka blue tang, surgeonfish, blue barber)
HOME: Coral reef
For Dory, living next door to Marlin and Nemo is a blast – thanks to her short-term memory loss, every day is a new adventure! But one day she remembers that she has a family of her own, so she sets out with her clownfish chums to find them. Her search leads her to the Marine Life Institute in Morro Bay, California, where she meets a tankful of new friends!

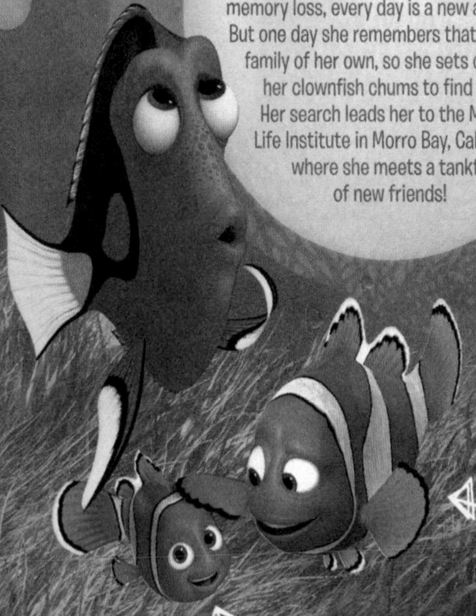

Hank

SCIENTIFIC NAME:
Octopus vulgaris (aka common octopus)
HOME: Marine Life Institute (MLI)
Hank is actually a septopus – he lost an arm at some point, but that hasn't prevented him from becoming MLI's greatest escape artist.

He uses his 7 limbs and crafty camouflage to help Dory make her way around the Institute.

Nemo

SCIENTIFIC NAME:
Amphiprion percula (aka clown anemonefish, clownfish)
HOME: Coral reef
Dory's super-loyal friend Nemo is her biggest supporter – always ready to lend a helping fin. He's even ready to swim across the ocean with her!

Marlin

SCIENTIFIC NAME:
Amphiprion percula (aka clown anemonefish, clownfish)
HOME: Coral reef
Nemo's dad Marlin worries a lot about his son – and Dory too – so he's not excited about another journey across the ocean. But he knows what it's like to miss your family, so he just has to help Dory find hers.

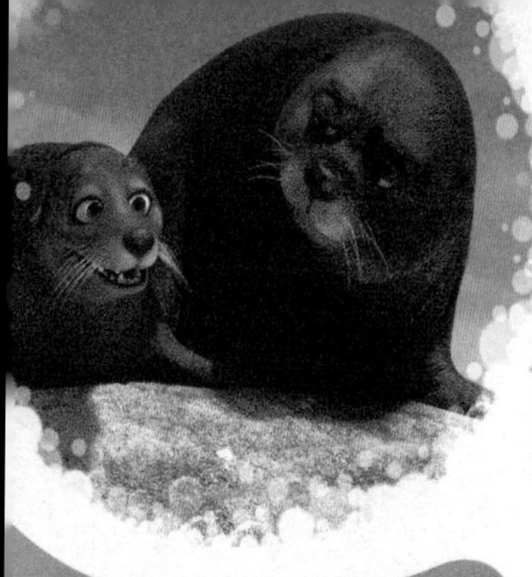

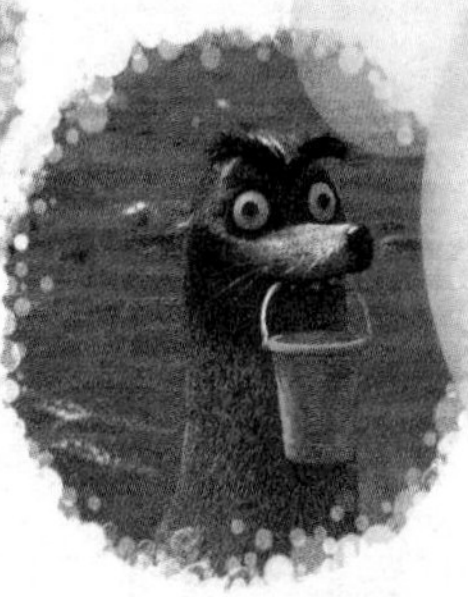

Rudder, Fluke and Gerald

SCIENTIFIC NAME:
Otariinae (aka sea lion)
HOME: Morro Bay, outside MLI
Lazy sea lions Fluke and Rudder are preoccupied with keeping Gerald off their favorite rock, but they do find time to chip in and help Dory, Nemo and Marlin on their adventure.

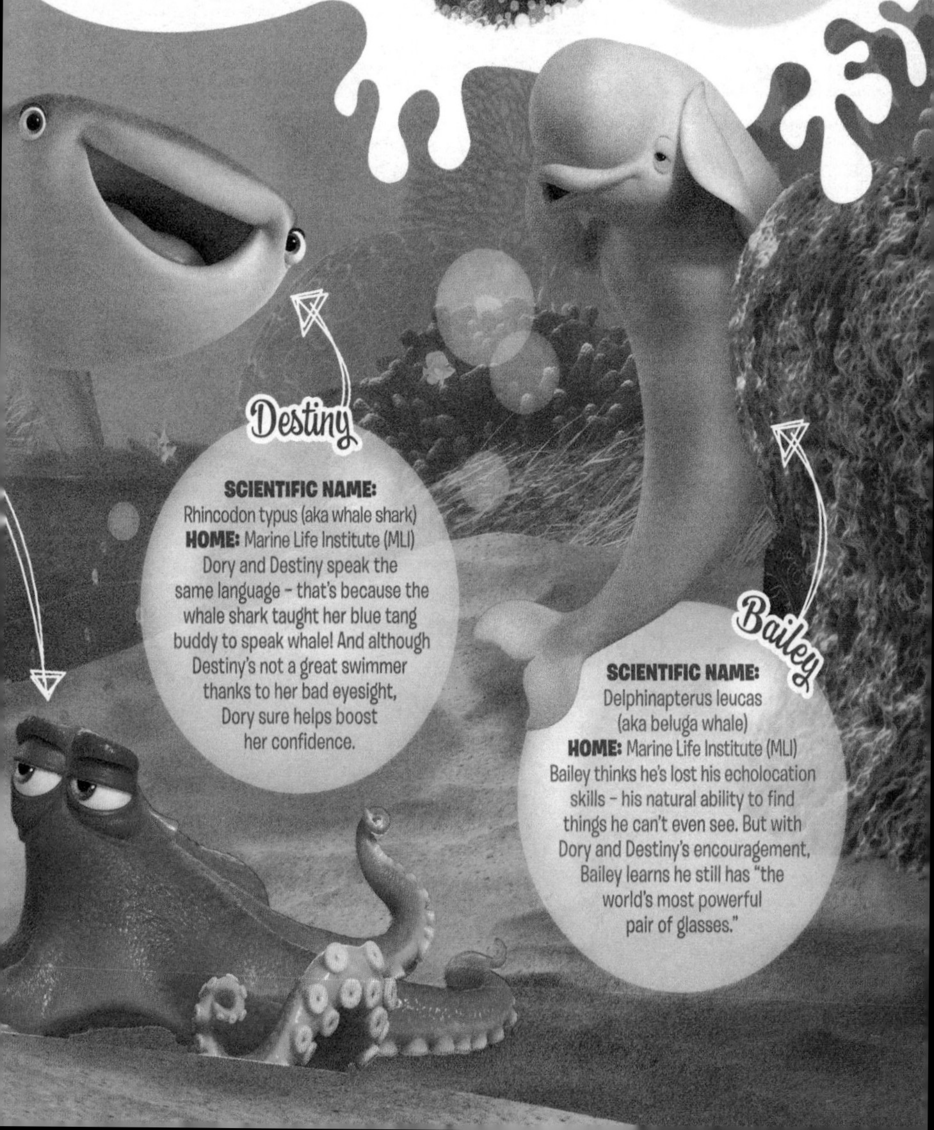

Destiny

SCIENTIFIC NAME:
Rhincodon typus (aka whale shark)
HOME: Marine Life Institute (MLI)
Dory and Destiny speak the same language – that's because the whale shark taught her blue tang buddy to speak whale! And although Destiny's not a great swimmer thanks to her bad eyesight, Dory sure helps boost her confidence.

Bailey

SCIENTIFIC NAME:
Delphinapterus leucas (aka beluga whale)
HOME: Marine Life Institute (MLI)
Bailey thinks he's lost his echolocation skills – his natural ability to find things he can't even see. But with Dory and Destiny's encouragement, Bailey learns he still has "the world's most powerful pair of glasses."

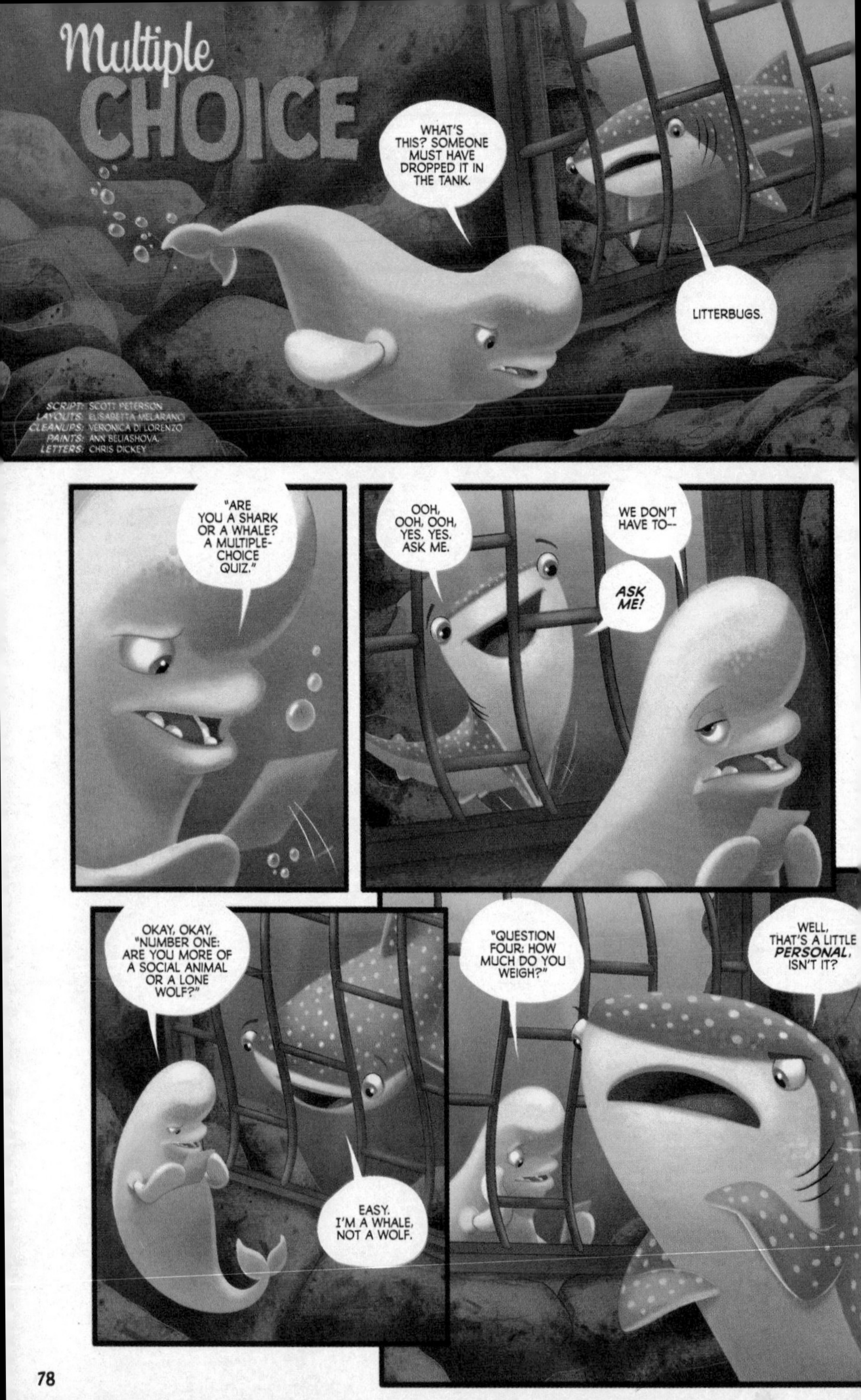
Multiple CHOICE
WHAT'S THIS? SOMEONE MUST HAVE DROPPED IT IN THE TANK.
LITTERBUGS.
SCRIPT: SCOTT PETERSON
LAYOUTS: ELISABETTA MELARANCI
CLEANUPS: VERONICA DI LORENZO
PAINTS: ANN BELIASHOVA.
LETTERS: CHRIS DICKEY
"ARE YOU A SHARK OR A WHALE? A MULTIPLE-CHOICE QUIZ."
OOH, OOH, OOH, YES. YES. ASK ME.
WE DON'T HAVE TO--
ASK ME!
OKAY, OKAY, "NUMBER ONE: ARE YOU MORE OF A SOCIAL ANIMAL OR A LONE WOLF?"
EASY. I'M A WHALE, NOT A WOLF.
"QUESTION FOUR: HOW MUCH DO YOU WEIGH?"
WELL, THAT'S A LITTLE PERSONAL, ISN'T IT?

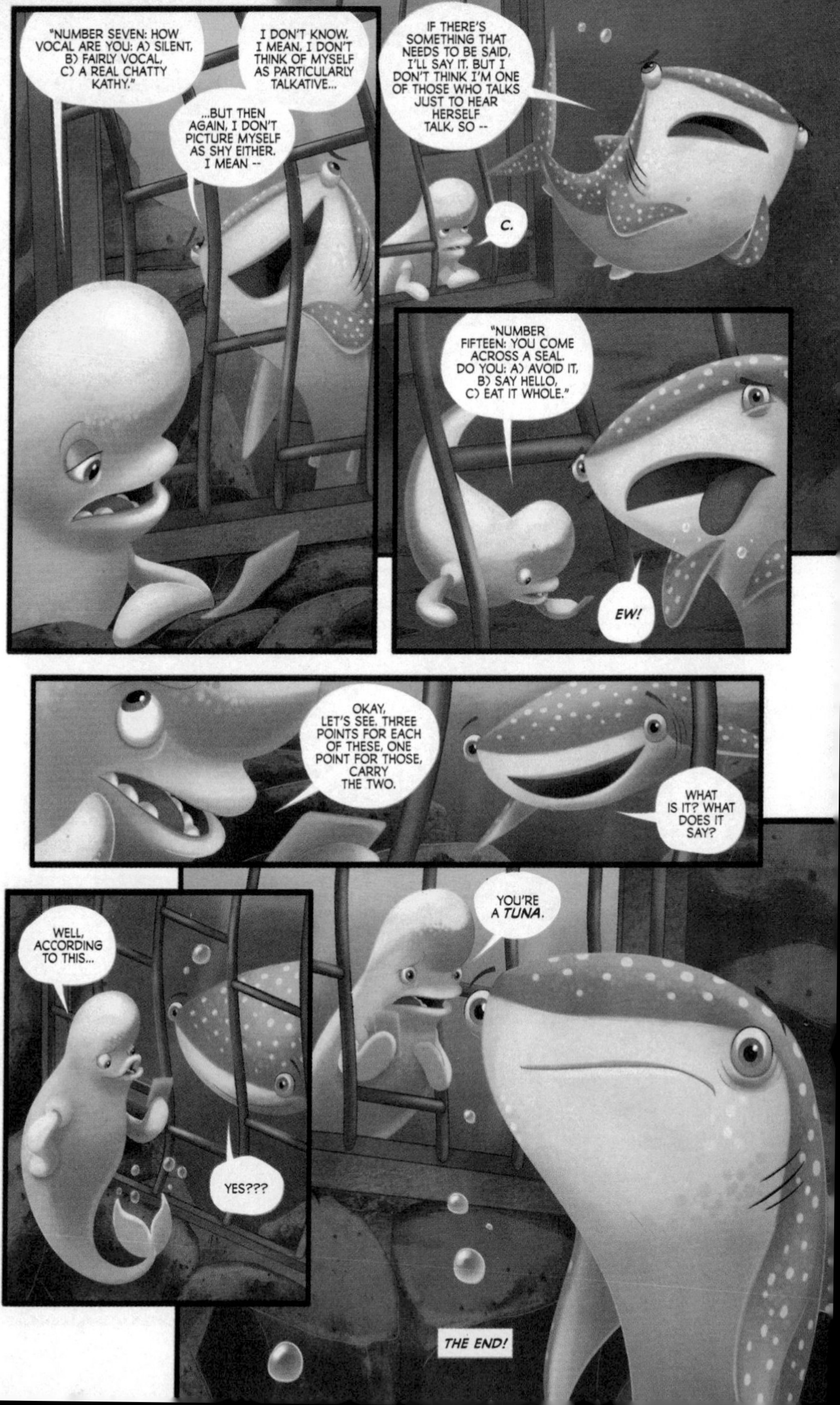
"NUMBER SEVEN: HOW VOCAL ARE YOU: A) SILENT, B) FAIRLY VOCAL, C) A REAL CHATTY KATHY."
I DON'T KNOW. I MEAN, I DON'T THINK OF MYSELF AS PARTICULARLY TALKATIVE...
...BUT THEN AGAIN, I DON'T PICTURE MYSELF AS SHY EITHER. I MEAN --
IF THERE'S SOMETHING THAT NEEDS TO BE SAID, I'LL SAY IT. BUT I DON'T THINK I'M ONE OF THOSE WHO TALKS JUST TO HEAR HERSELF TALK, SO --
C.
"NUMBER FIFTEEN: YOU COME ACROSS A SEAL. DO YOU: A) AVOID IT, B) SAY HELLO, C) EAT IT WHOLE."
EW!
OKAY, LET'S SEE. THREE POINTS FOR EACH OF THESE, ONE POINT FOR THOSE, CARRY THE TWO.
WHAT IS IT? WHAT DOES IT SAY?
WELL, ACCORDING TO THIS...
YES???
YOU'RE A TUNA.
THE END!

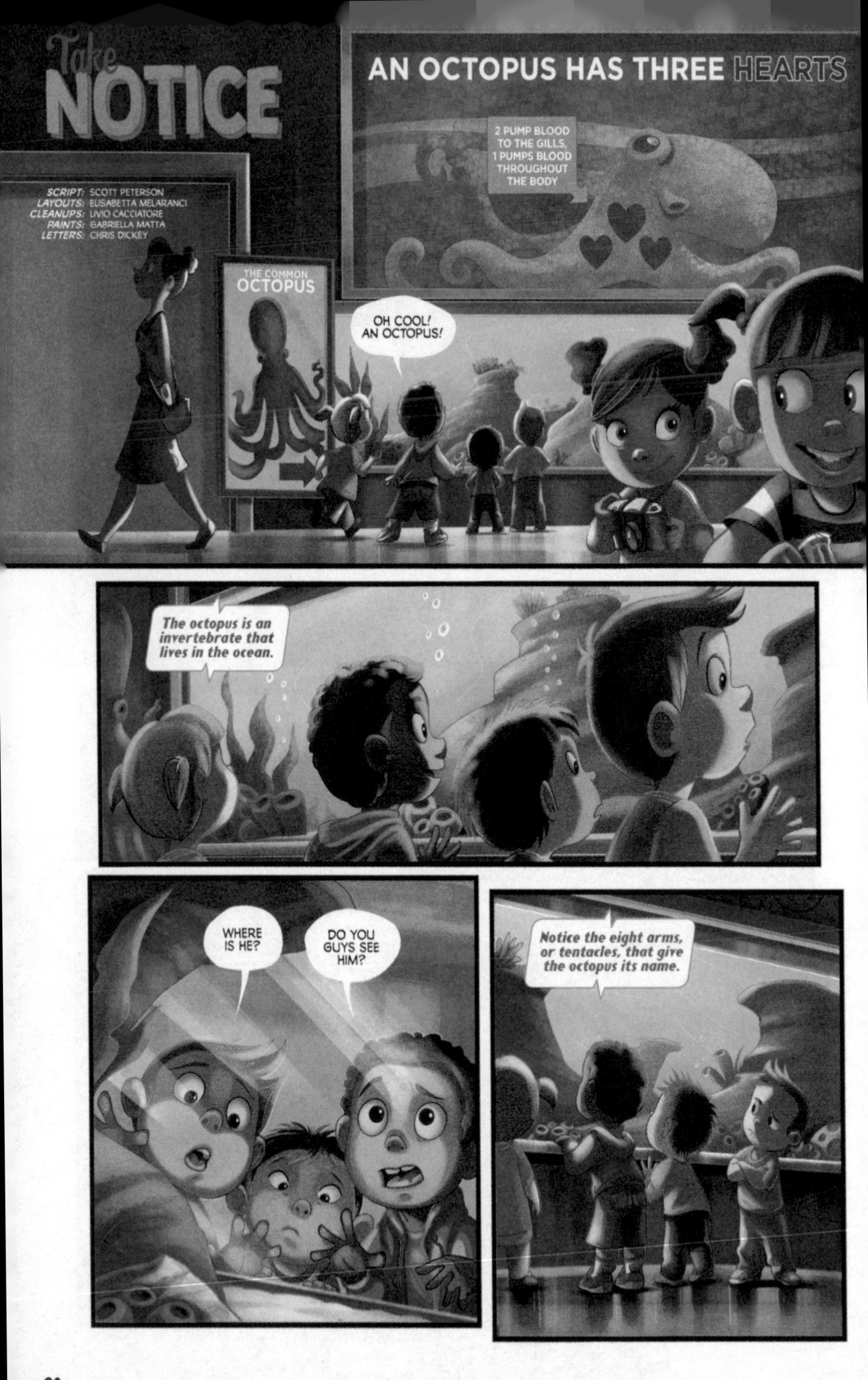
Take NOTICE
AN OCTOPUS HAS THREE HEARTS
SCRIPT: SCOTT PETERSON
LAYOUTS: ELISABETTA MELARANCI
CLEANUPS: LIVIO CACCIATORE
PAINTS: GABRIELLA MATTA
LETTERS: CHRIS DICKEY
2 PUMP BLOOD TO THE GILLS, 1 PUMPS BLOOD THROUGHOUT THE BODY
THE COMMON OCTOPUS
OH COOL! AN OCTOPUS!
The octopus is an invertebrate that lives in the ocean.
WHERE IS HE?
DO YOU GUYS SEE HIM?
Notice the eight arms, or tentacles, that give the octopus its name.

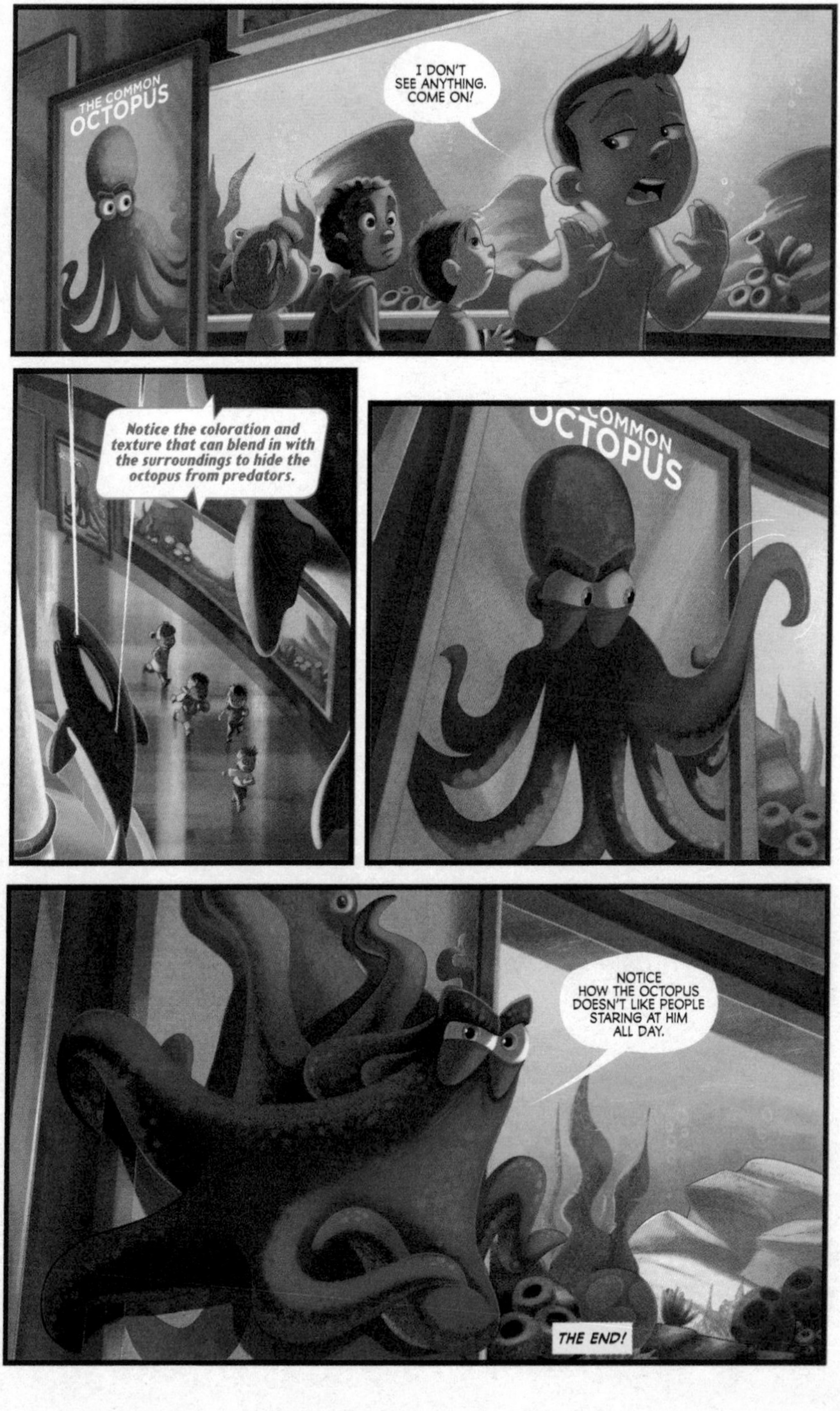
THE COMMON OCTOPUS
I DON'T SEE ANYTHING. COME ON!
Notice the coloration and texture that can blend in with the surroundings to hide the octopus from predators.
COMMON OCTOPUS
NOTICE HOW THE OCTOPUS DOESN'T LIKE PEOPLE STARING AT HIM ALL DAY.
THE END!

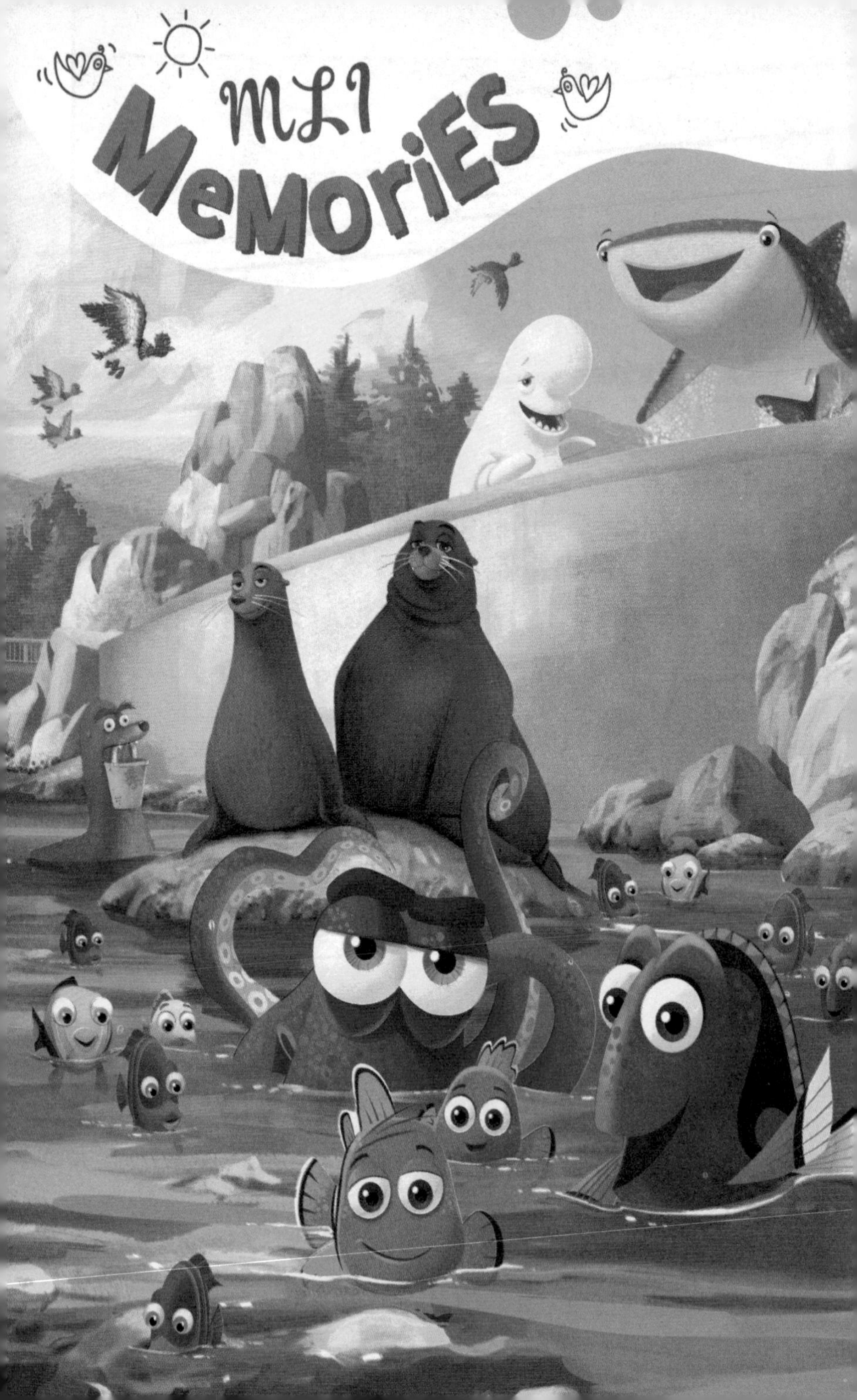
MLI
Memories

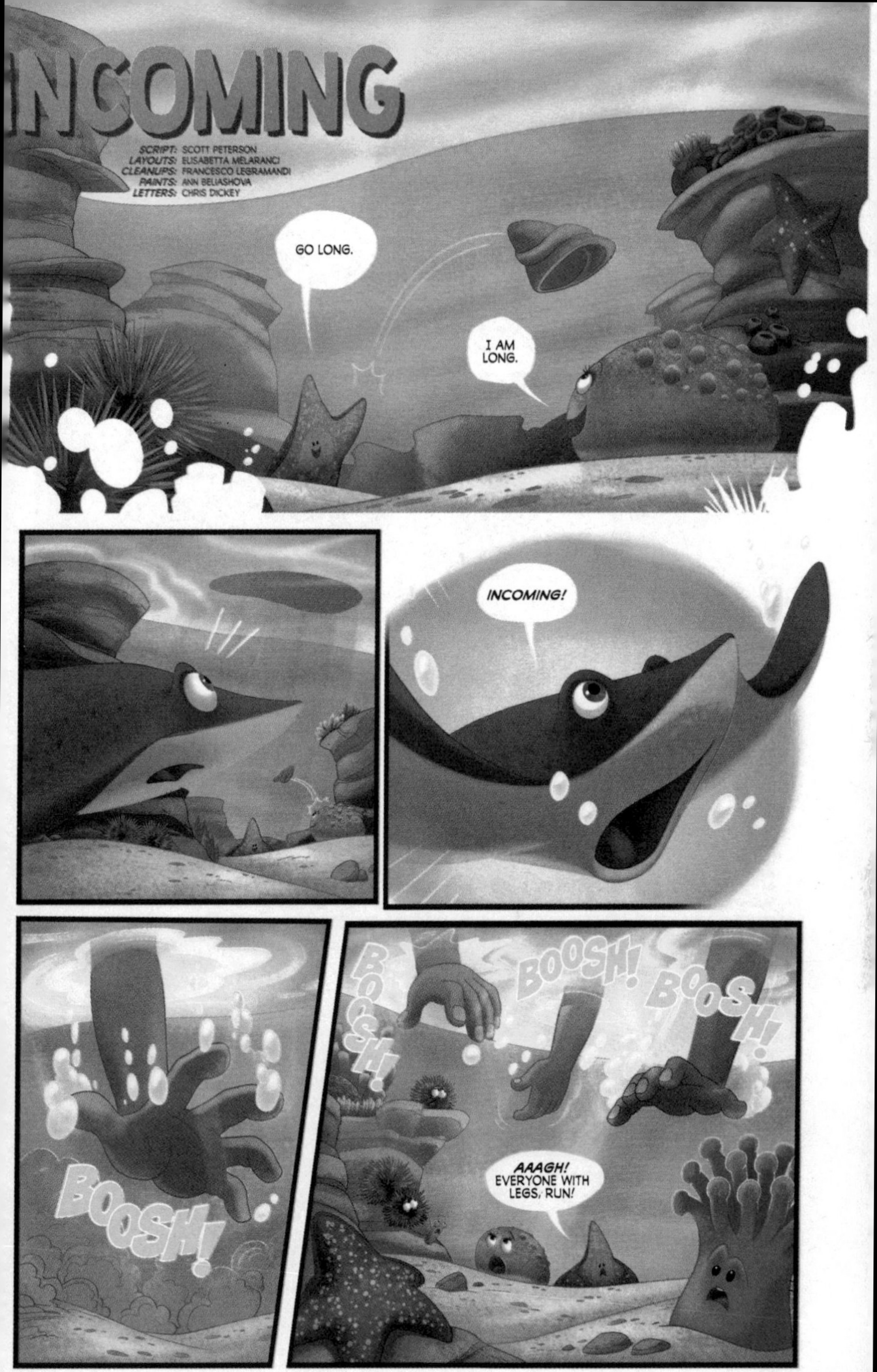
NCOMING
SCRIPT: SCOTT PETERSON
LAYOUTS: ELISABETTA MELARANCI
CLEANUPS: FRANCESCO LEGRAMANDI
PAINTS: ANN BELIASHOVA
LETTERS: CHRIS DICKEY
GO LONG.
I AM LONG.
INCOMING!
BOOSH!
BOOSH!
BOOSH!
BOOSH!
AAAGH! EVERYONE WITH LEGS, RUN!

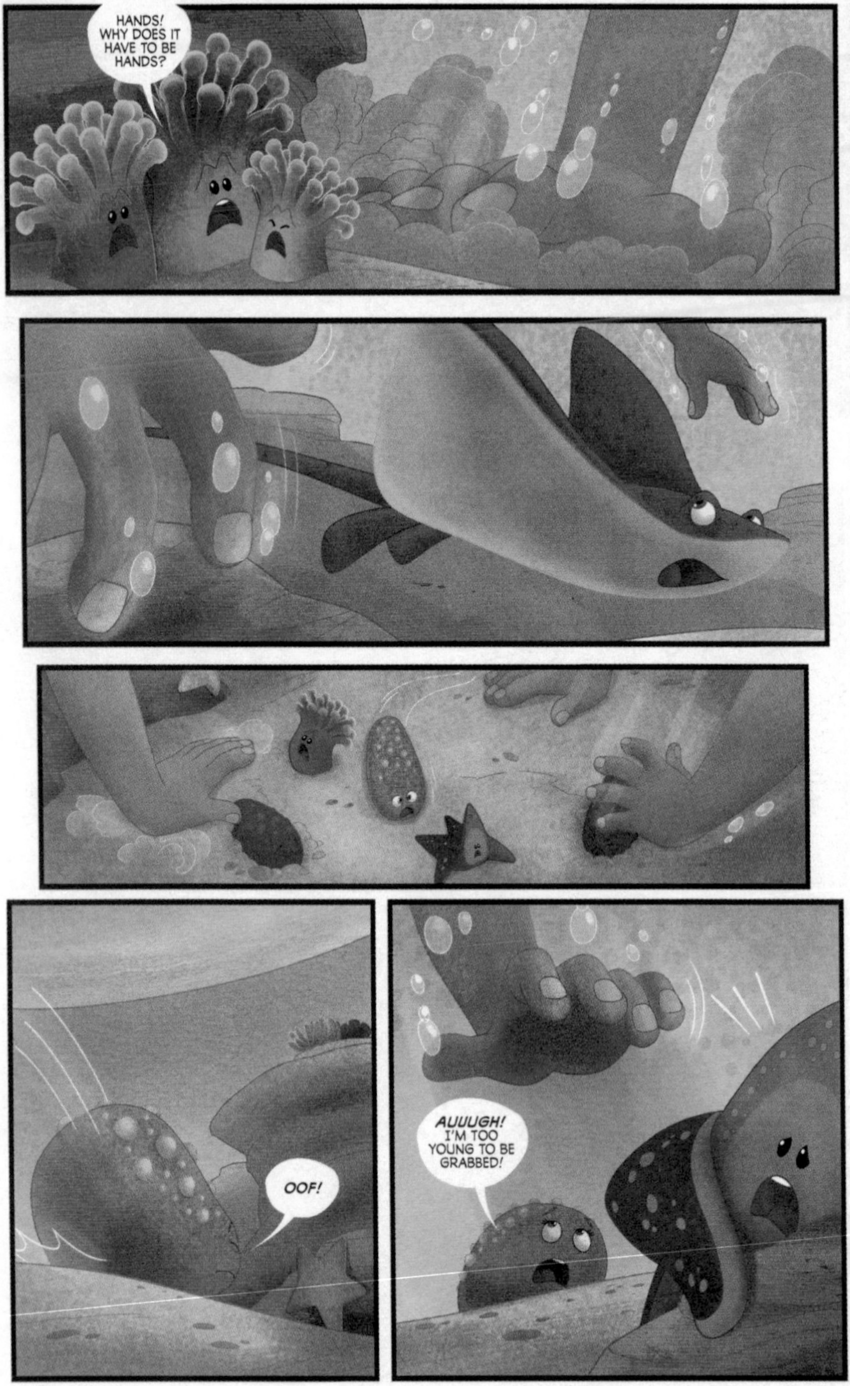
HANDS! WHY DOES IT HAVE TO BE HANDS?
OOF!
AUUUGH! I'M TOO YOUNG TO BE GRABBED!

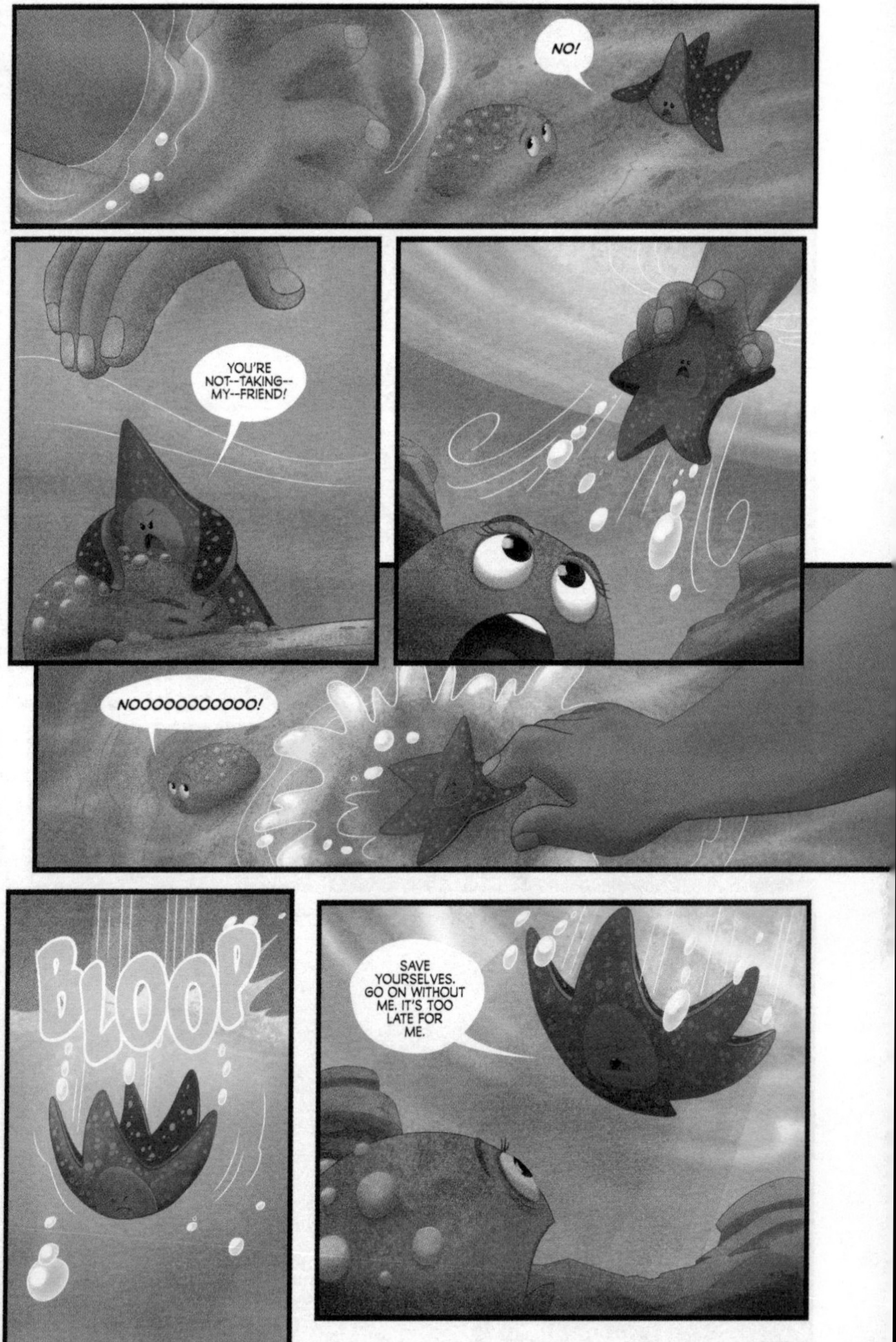
NO!
YOU'RE NOT--TAKING--MY--FRIEND!
NOOOOOOOOOOO!
BLOOP
SAVE YOURSELVES. GO ON WITHOUT ME. IT'S TOO LATE FOR ME.

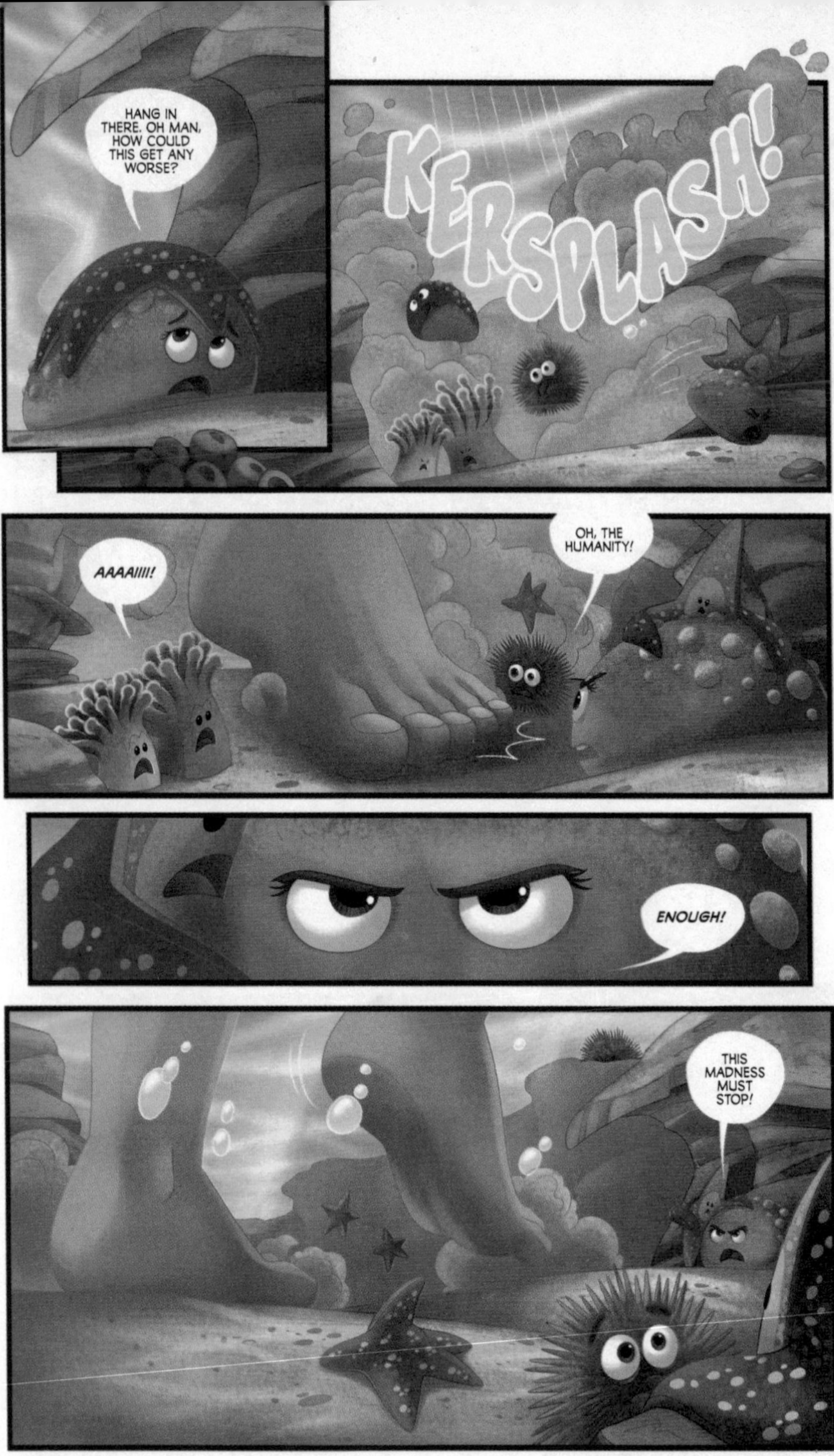
HANG IN THERE. OH MAN, HOW COULD THIS GET ANY WORSE?
KERSPLASH!
AAAAIIII!
OH, THE HUMANITY!
ENOUGH!
THIS MADNESS MUST STOP!

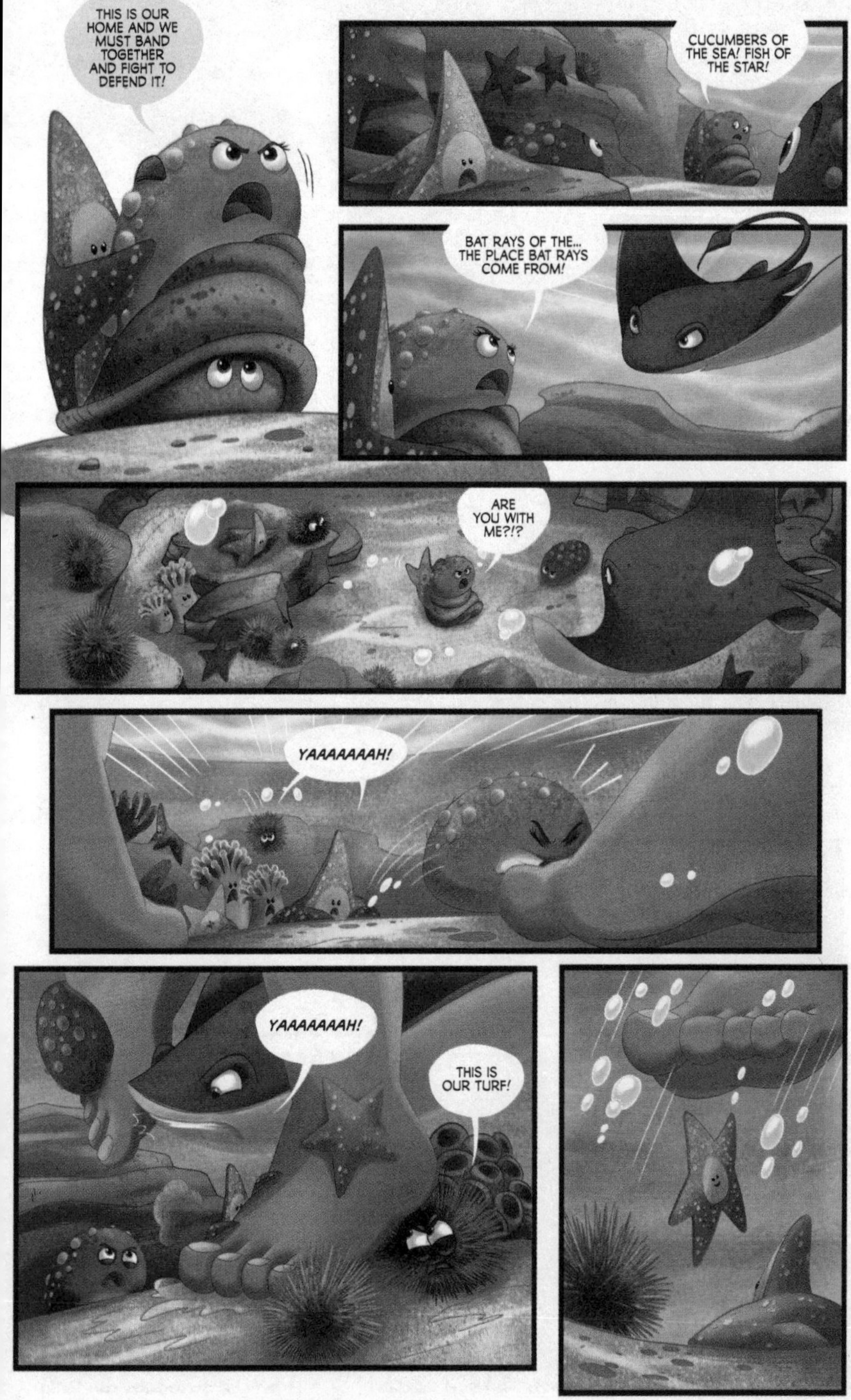
THIS IS OUR HOME AND WE MUST BAND TOGETHER AND FIGHT TO DEFEND IT!
CUCUMBERS OF THE SEA! FISH OF THE STAR!
BAT RAYS OF THE... THE PLACE BAT RAYS COME FROM!
ARE YOU WITH ME?!?
YAAAAAAAH!
YAAAAAAAH!
THIS IS OUR TURF!

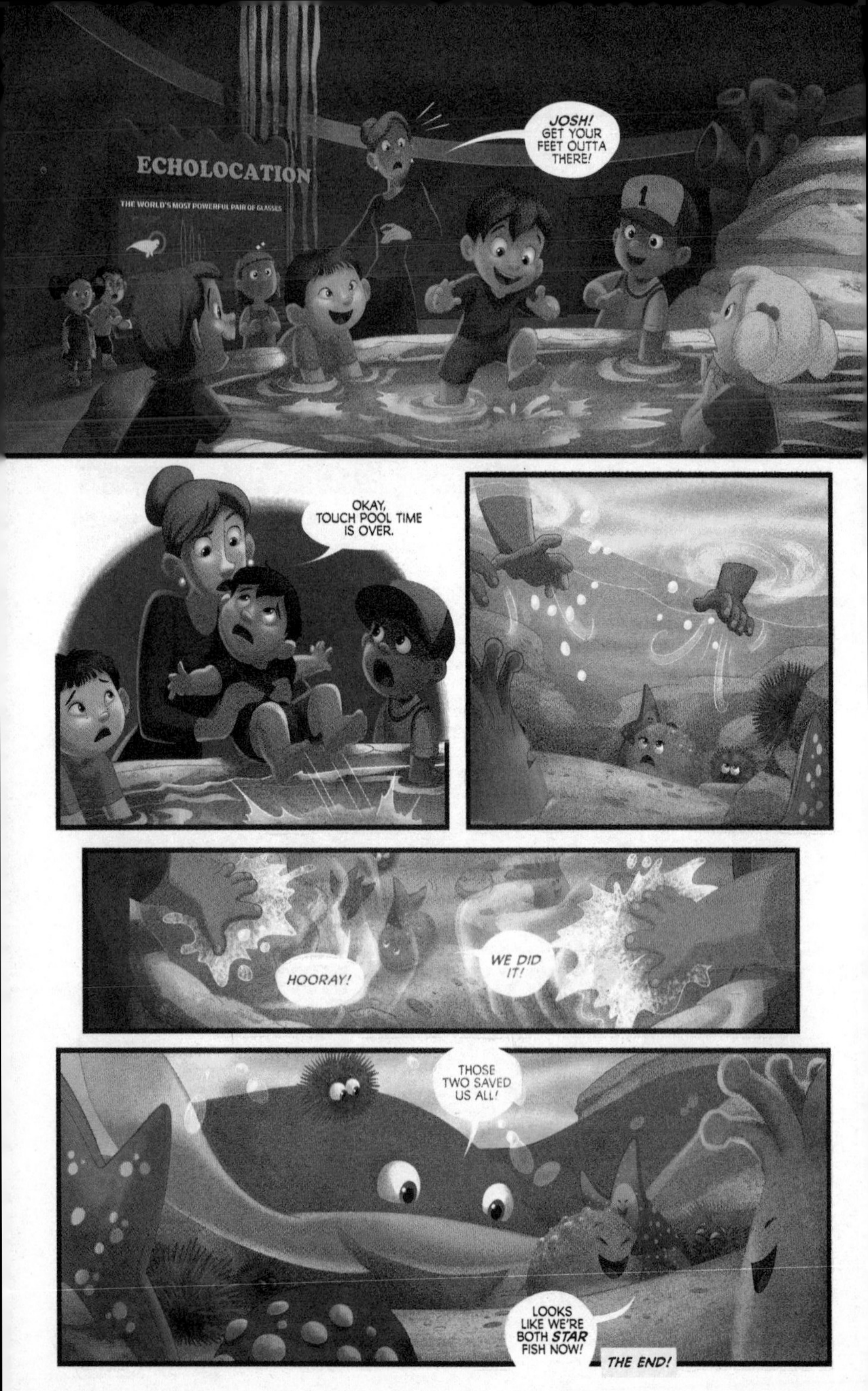
ECHOLOCATION
THE WORLD'S MOST POWERFUL PAIR OF GLASSES
JOSH! GET YOUR FEET OUTTA THERE!
OKAY, TOUCH POOL TIME IS OVER.
HOORAY!
WE DID IT!
THOSE TWO SAVED US ALL!
LOOKS LIKE WE'RE BOTH STAR FISH NOW!
THE END!

FROM "SPEAKING HER LANGUAGE"

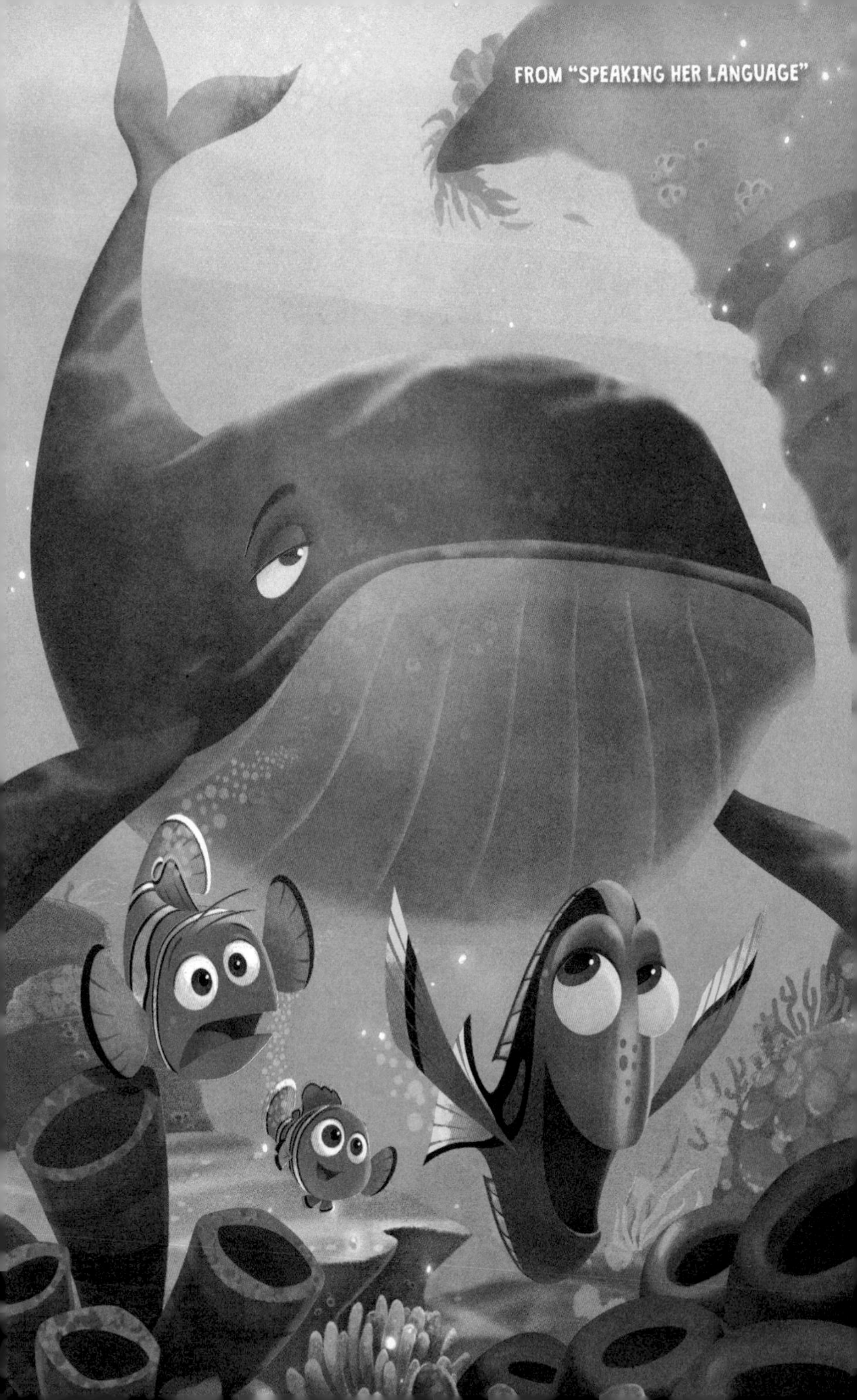

EAKING Her LANGUAGE

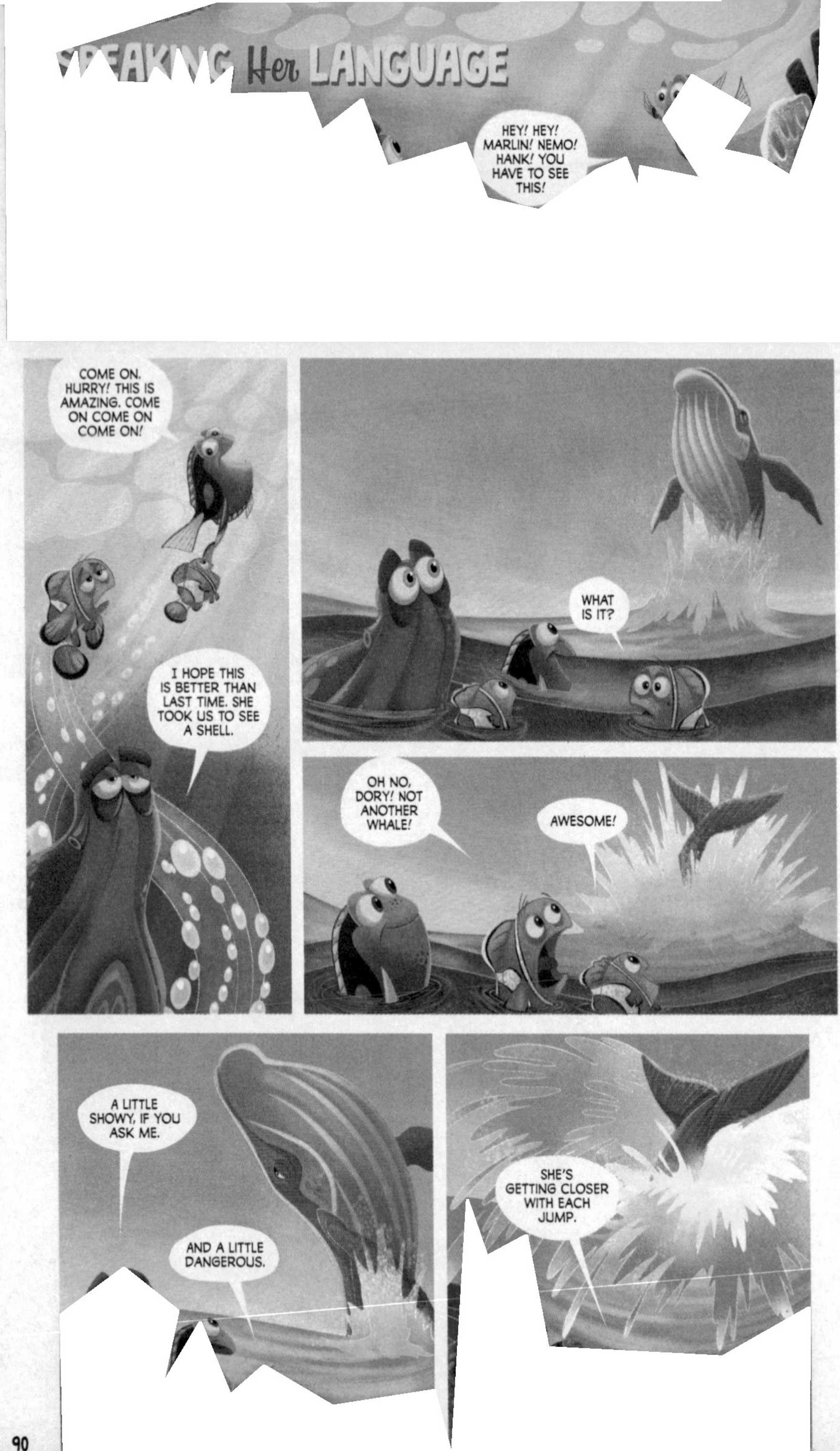

HEY! HEY! MARLIN! NEMO! HANK! YOU HAVE TO SEE THIS!
COME ON. HURRY! THIS IS AMAZING. COME ON COME ON COME ON!
I HOPE THIS IS BETTER THAN LAST TIME. SHE TOOK US TO SEE A SHELL.
WHAT IS IT?
OH NO, DORY! NOT ANOTHER WHALE!
AWESOME!
A LITTLE SHOWY, IF YOU ASK ME.
AND A LITTLE DANGEROUS.
SHE'S GETTING CLOSER WITH EACH JUMP.

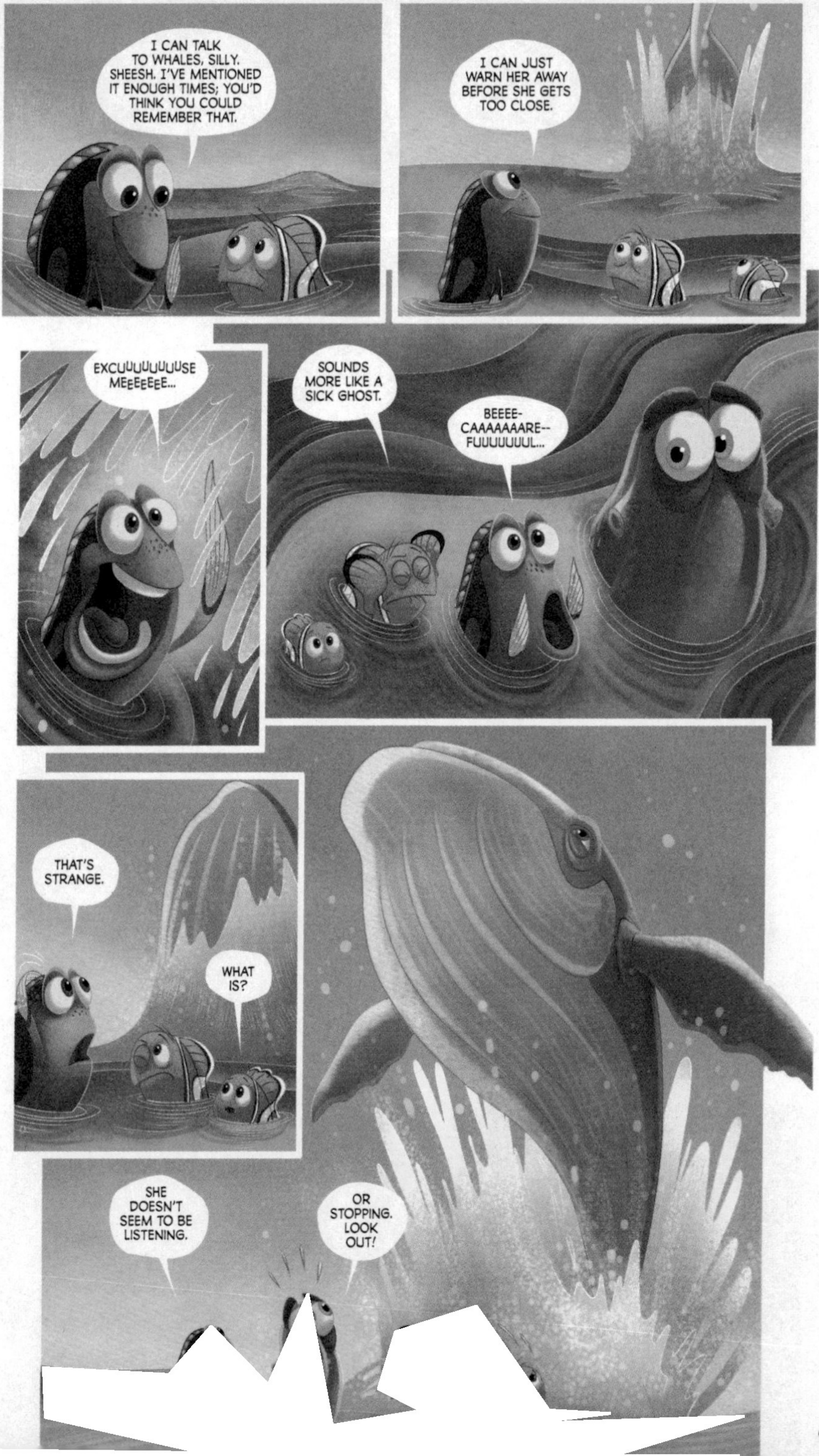

I CAN TALK TO WHALES, SILLY. SHEESH. I'VE MENTIONED IT ENOUGH TIMES; YOU'D THINK YOU COULD REMEMBER THAT.
I CAN JUST WARN HER AWAY BEFORE SHE GETS TOO CLOSE.
EXCUUUUUUUUSE MEEEEEEE...
SOUNDS MORE LIKE A SICK GHOST.
BEEEE-CAAAAAAARE--FUUUUUUUL...
THAT'S STRANGE.
WHAT IS?
SHE DOESN'T SEEM TO BE LISTENING.
OR STOPPING. LOOK OUT!

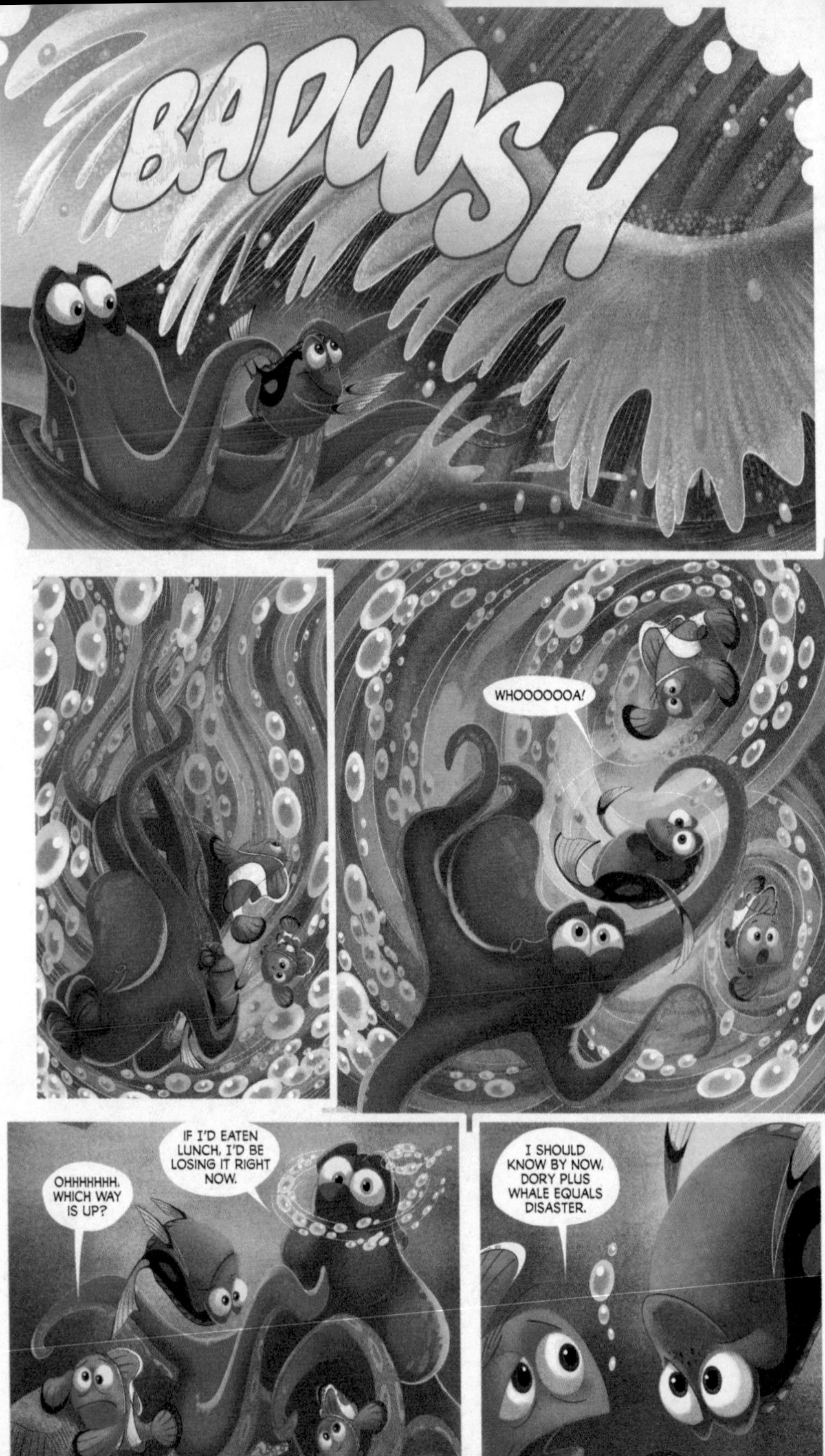
BADOOSH
WHOOOOOOA!
OHHHHHHH. WHICH WAY IS UP?
IF I'D EATEN LUNCH, I'D BE LOSING IT RIGHT NOW.
I SHOULD KNOW BY NOW, DORY PLUS WHALE EQUALS DISASTER.

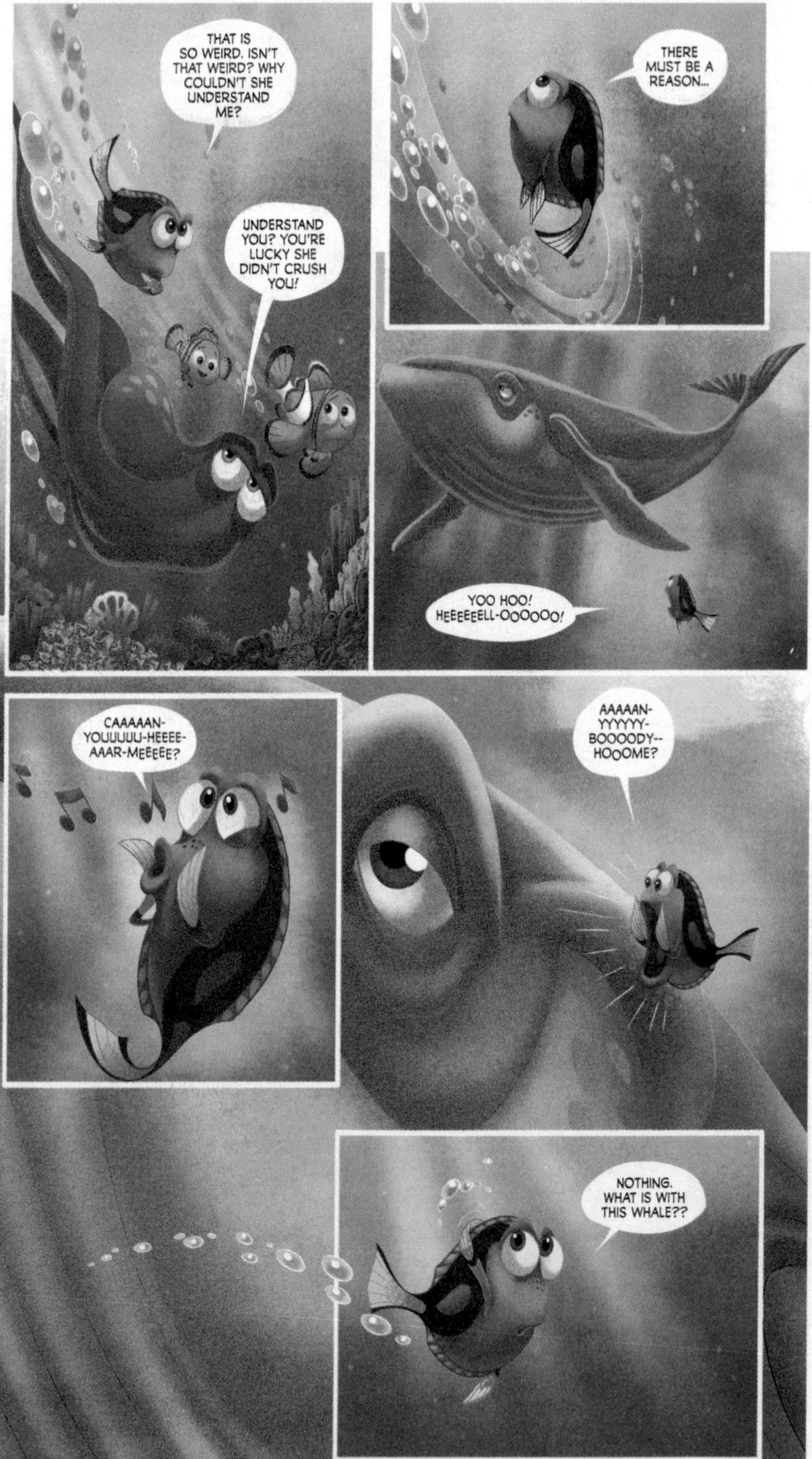
THAT IS SO WEIRD. ISN'T THAT WEIRD? WHY COULDN'T SHE UNDERSTAND ME?
UNDERSTAND YOU? YOU'RE LUCKY SHE DIDN'T CRUSH YOU!
THERE MUST BE A REASON...
YOO HOO! HEEEEEELL-OOOOOO!
CAAAAAN-YOUUUUU-HEEEE-AAAR-MEEEEE?
AAAAAN-YYYYYY-BOOOODY--HOOOME?
NOTHING. WHAT IS WITH THIS WHALE??

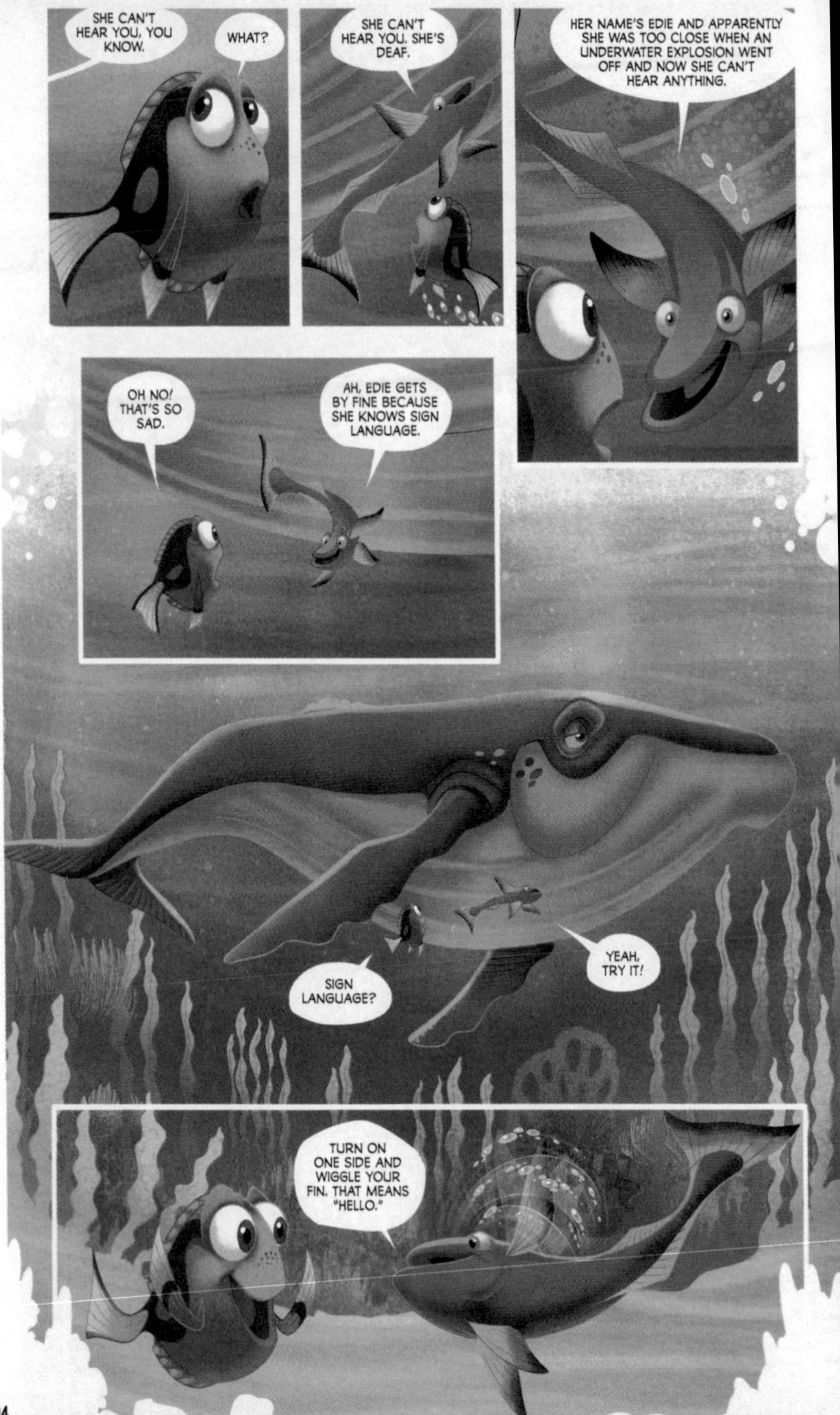
SHE CAN'T HEAR YOU, YOU KNOW.
WHAT?
SHE CAN'T HEAR YOU. SHE'S DEAF.
HER NAME'S EDIE AND APPARENTLY SHE WAS TOO CLOSE WHEN AN UNDERWATER EXPLOSION WENT OFF AND NOW SHE CAN'T HEAR ANYTHING.
OH NO! THAT'S SO SAD.
AH, EDIE GETS BY FINE BECAUSE SHE KNOWS SIGN LANGUAGE.
SIGN LANGUAGE?
YEAH, TRY IT!
TURN ON ONE SIDE AND WIGGLE YOUR FIN. THAT MEANS "HELLO."

OKAY...

HELLO.

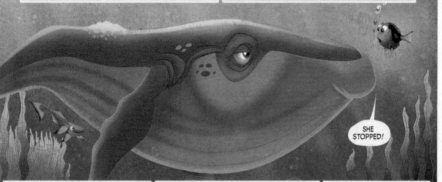

SHE STOPPED!

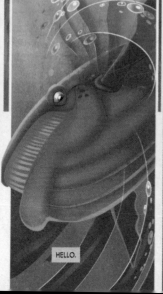

HELLO.

SHE HEARD ME! I MEAN, SHE SAW ME! WE TALKED!

SHOW ME MORE! SHOW ME MORE!

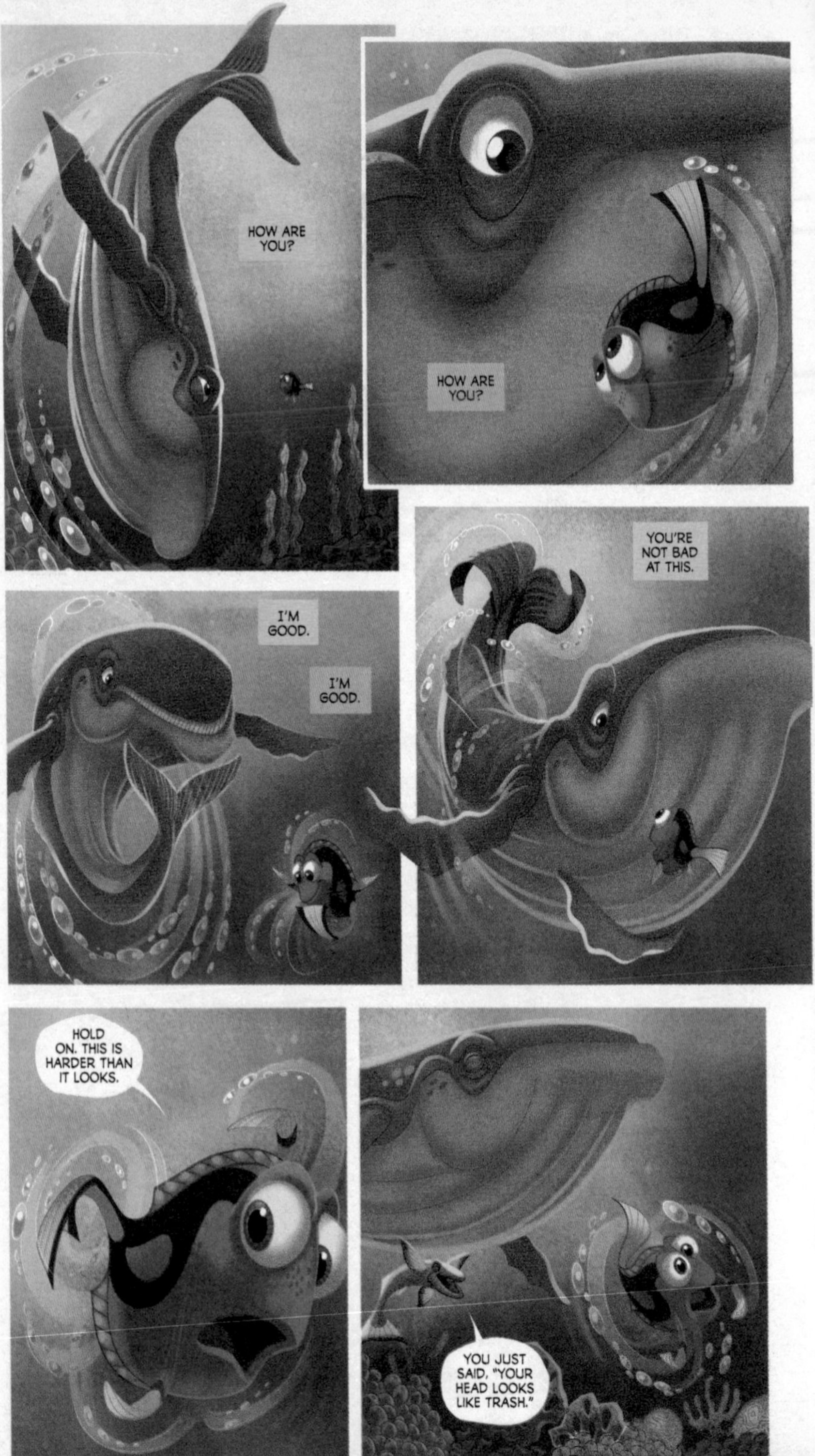
HOW ARE YOU?
HOW ARE YOU?
I'M GOOD.
I'M GOOD.
YOU'RE NOT BAD AT THIS.
HOLD ON. THIS IS HARDER THAN IT LOOKS.
YOU JUST SAID, "YOUR HEAD LOOKS LIKE TRASH."

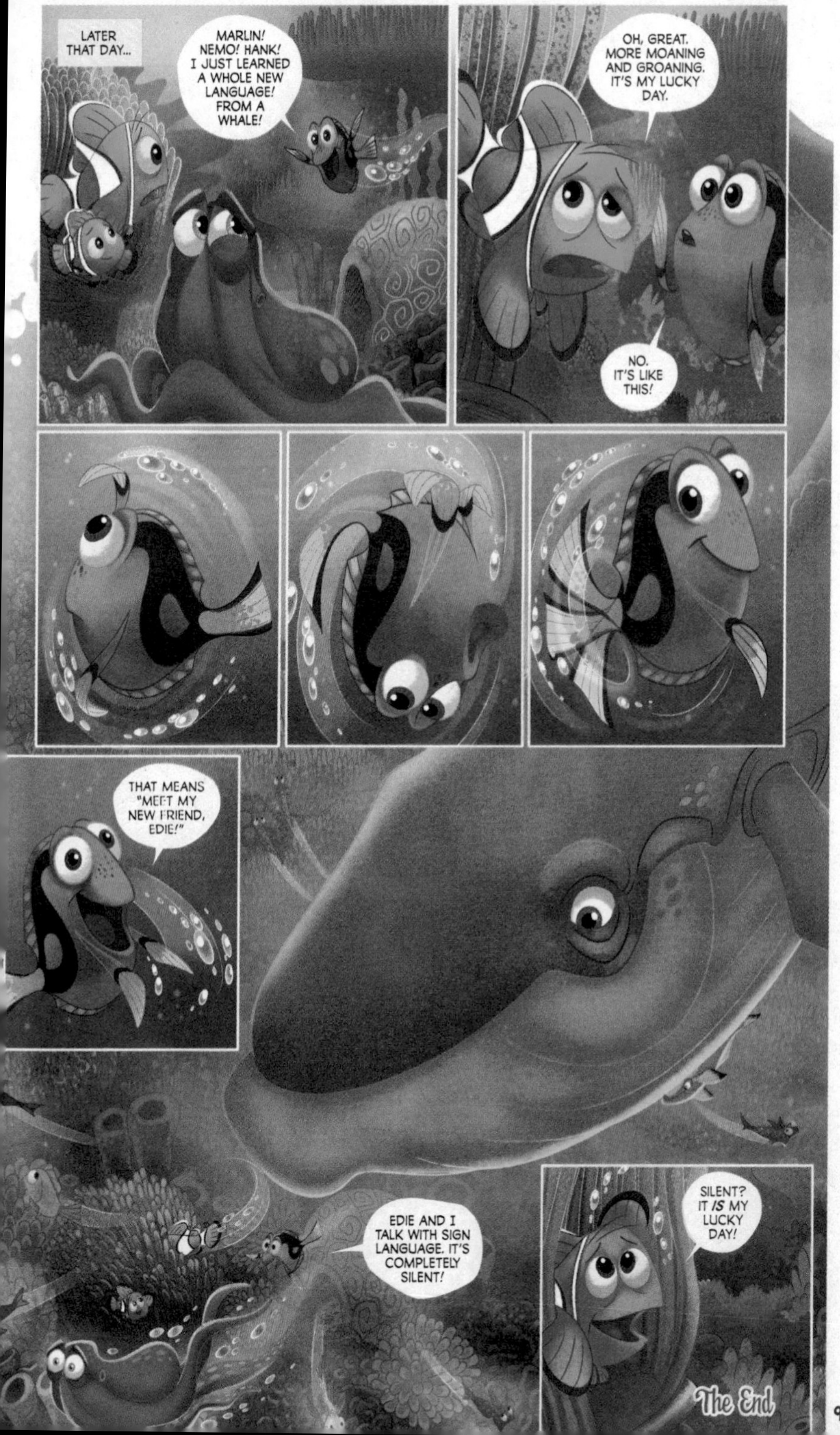
LATER THAT DAY...
MARLIN! NEMO! HANK! I JUST LEARNED A WHOLE NEW LANGUAGE! FROM A WHALE!
OH, GREAT. MORE MOANING AND GROANING. IT'S MY LUCKY DAY.
NO. IT'S LIKE THIS!
THAT MEANS "MEET MY NEW FRIEND, EDIE!"
EDIE AND I TALK WITH SIGN LANGUAGE. IT'S COMPLETELY SILENT!
SILENT? IT IS MY LUCKY DAY!
The End

FIN-TASTIC Friends

Life is always colorful on the coral reef where Dory, Nemo and Marlin live!

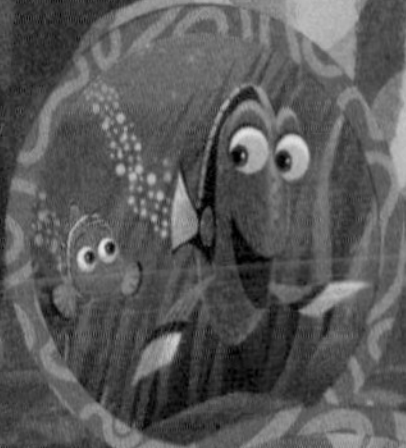

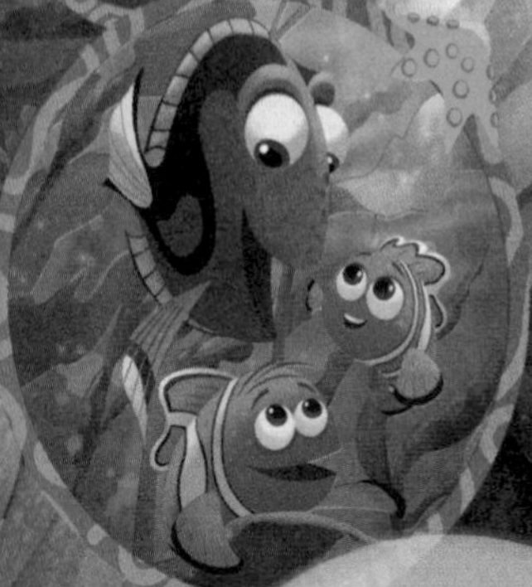

Marlin & Nemo's house

DORY

Everyone loves Dory, the little blue tang with a big heart. She's always sunny and eager to help anyone she meets. When she helped Marlin find his son Nemo, they all became best friends. Now she's part of their family. But Dory realizes that somewhere in the great wide ocean, she has her own family, and she wants to find them. Thanks to her short-term memory loss, Dory has her own way of doing everything – and sometimes it may seem a bit odd, but it always seems to work! As Dory says, "There's always another way!"

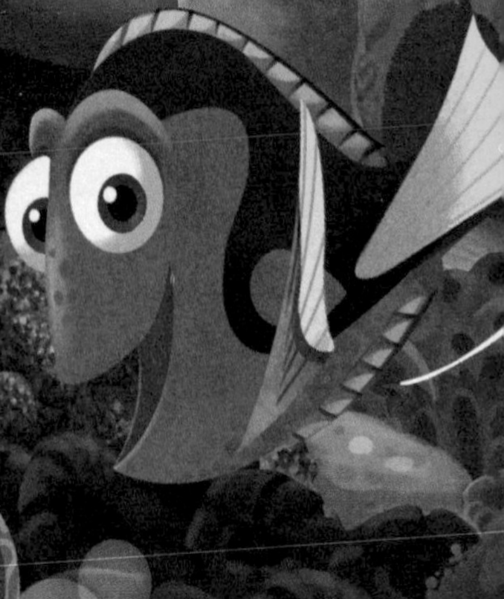

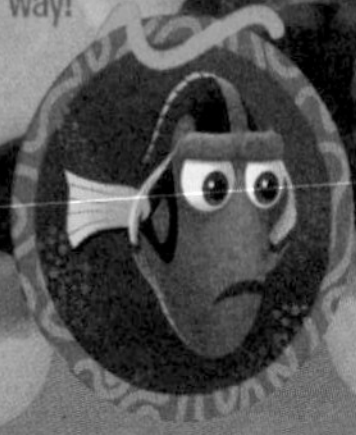

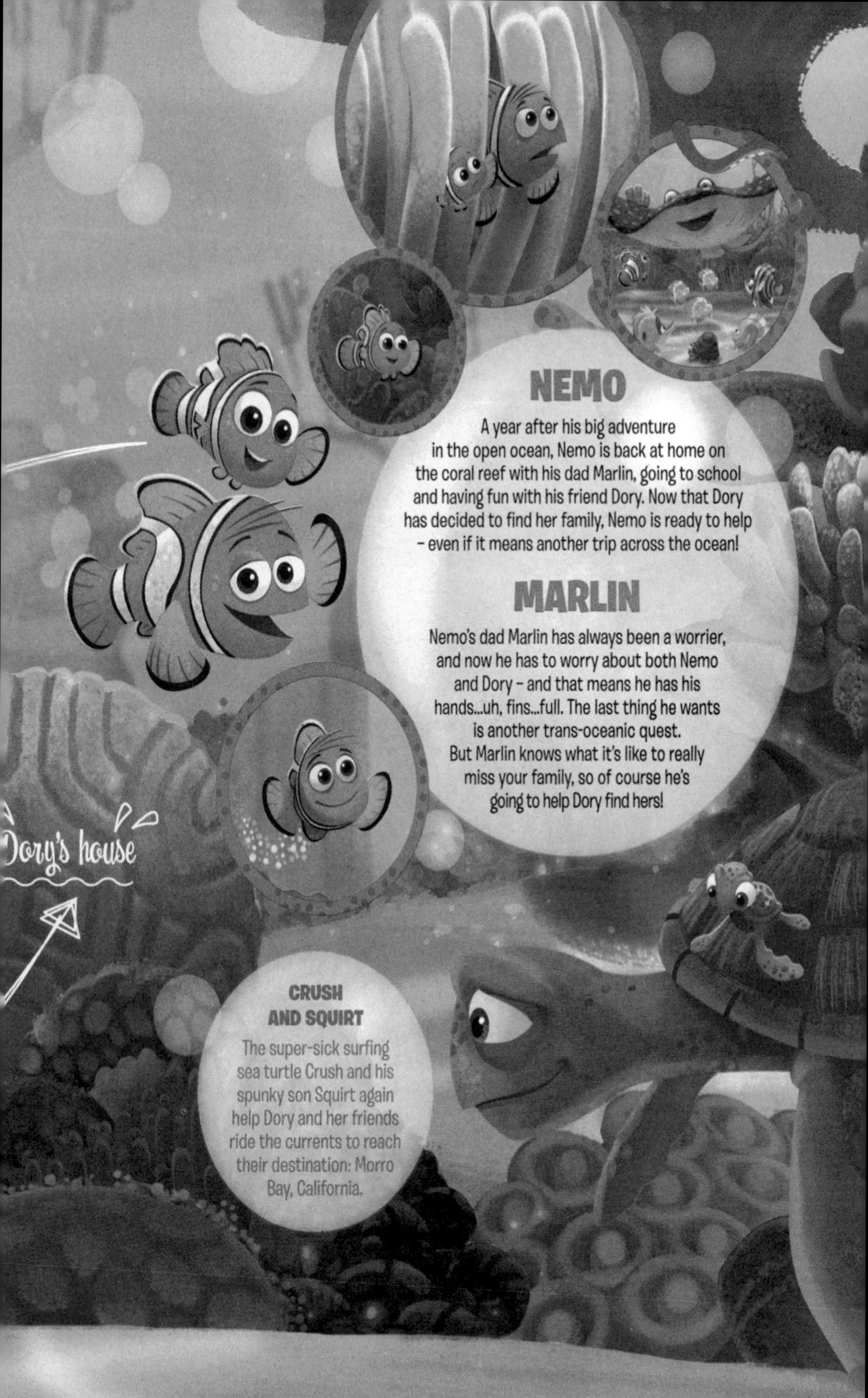
Dory's house

NEMO

A year after his big adventure in the open ocean, Nemo is back at home on the coral reef with his dad Marlin, going to school and having fun with his friend Dory. Now that Dory has decided to find her family, Nemo is ready to help – even if it means another trip across the ocean!

MARLIN

Nemo's dad Marlin has always been a worrier, and now he has to worry about both Nemo and Dory – and that means he has his hands...uh, fins...full. The last thing he wants is another trans-oceanic quest. But Marlin knows what it's like to really miss your family, so of course he's going to help Dory find hers!

CRUSH AND SQUIRT

The super-sick surfing sea turtle Crush and his spunky son Squirt again help Dory and her friends ride the currents to reach their destination: Morro Bay, California.

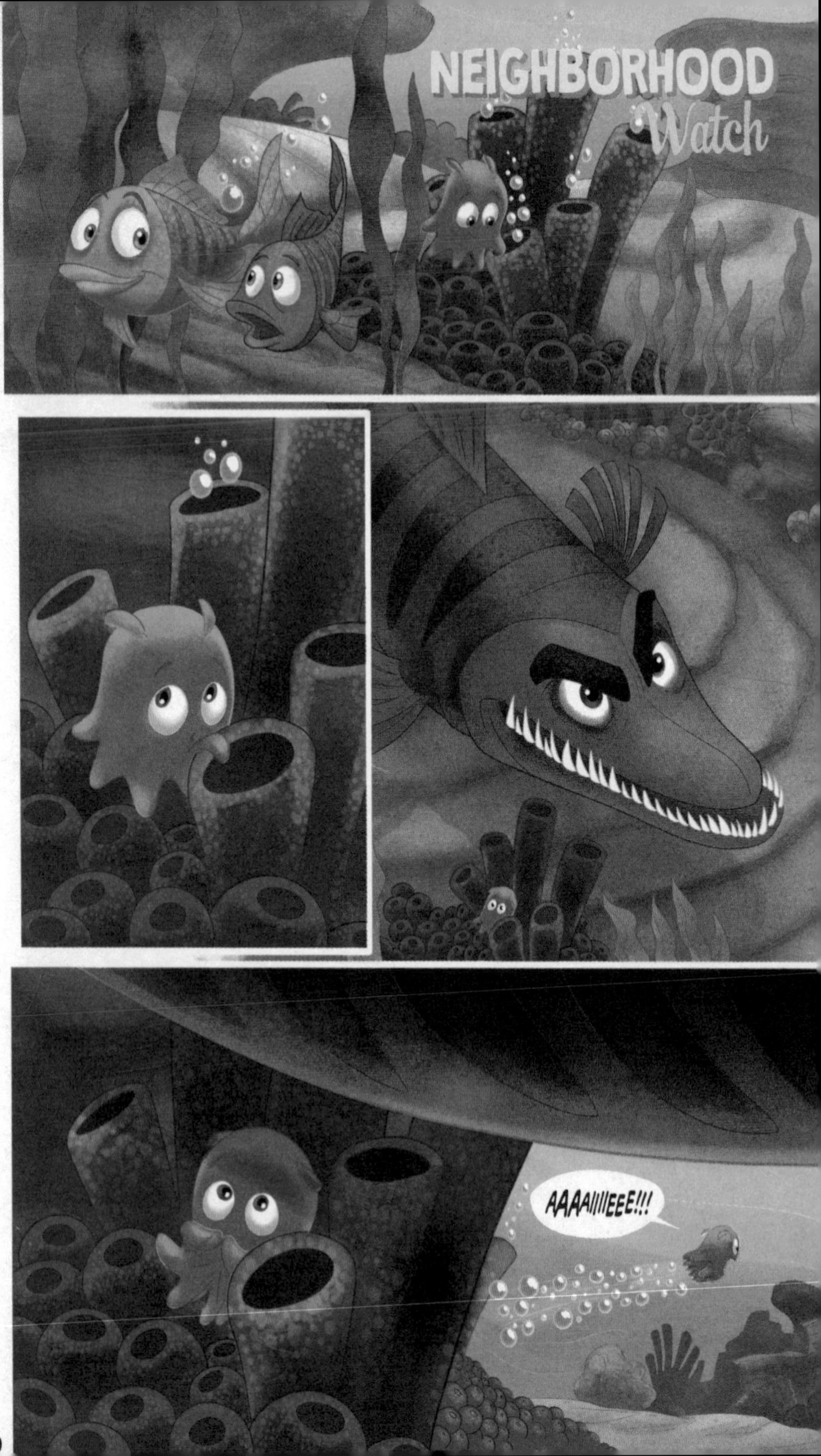
NEIGHBORHOOD Watch
AAAAIIIIEEE!!!

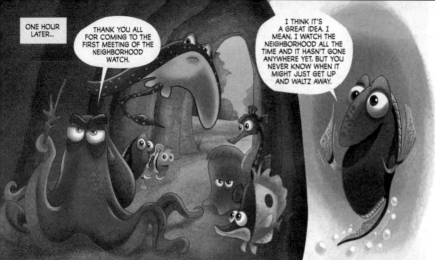

ONE HOUR LATER...

THANK YOU ALL FOR COMING TO THE FIRST MEETING OF THE NEIGHBORHOOD WATCH.

I THINK IT'S A GREAT IDEA. I MEAN, I WATCH THE NEIGHBORHOOD ALL THE TIME AND IT HASN'T GONE ANYWHERE YET, BUT YOU NEVER KNOW WHEN IT MIGHT JUST GET UP AND WALTZ AWAY.

NO, THE POINT OF NEIGHBORHOOD WATCH IS TO KEEP AN EYE ON OUR NEIGHBORHOOD AND EACH OTHER TO ENSURE OUR SAFETY.

PEARL HERE SAW A VERY DANGEROUS DEEP SEA LIZARDFISH IN OUR AREA SO WE NEED TO WORK TOGETHER TO KEEP WATCH.

AUGH! THERE HE IS!

IS THAT WHAT WE SHOULD SAY IF WE SEE HIM?

YES, DORY.

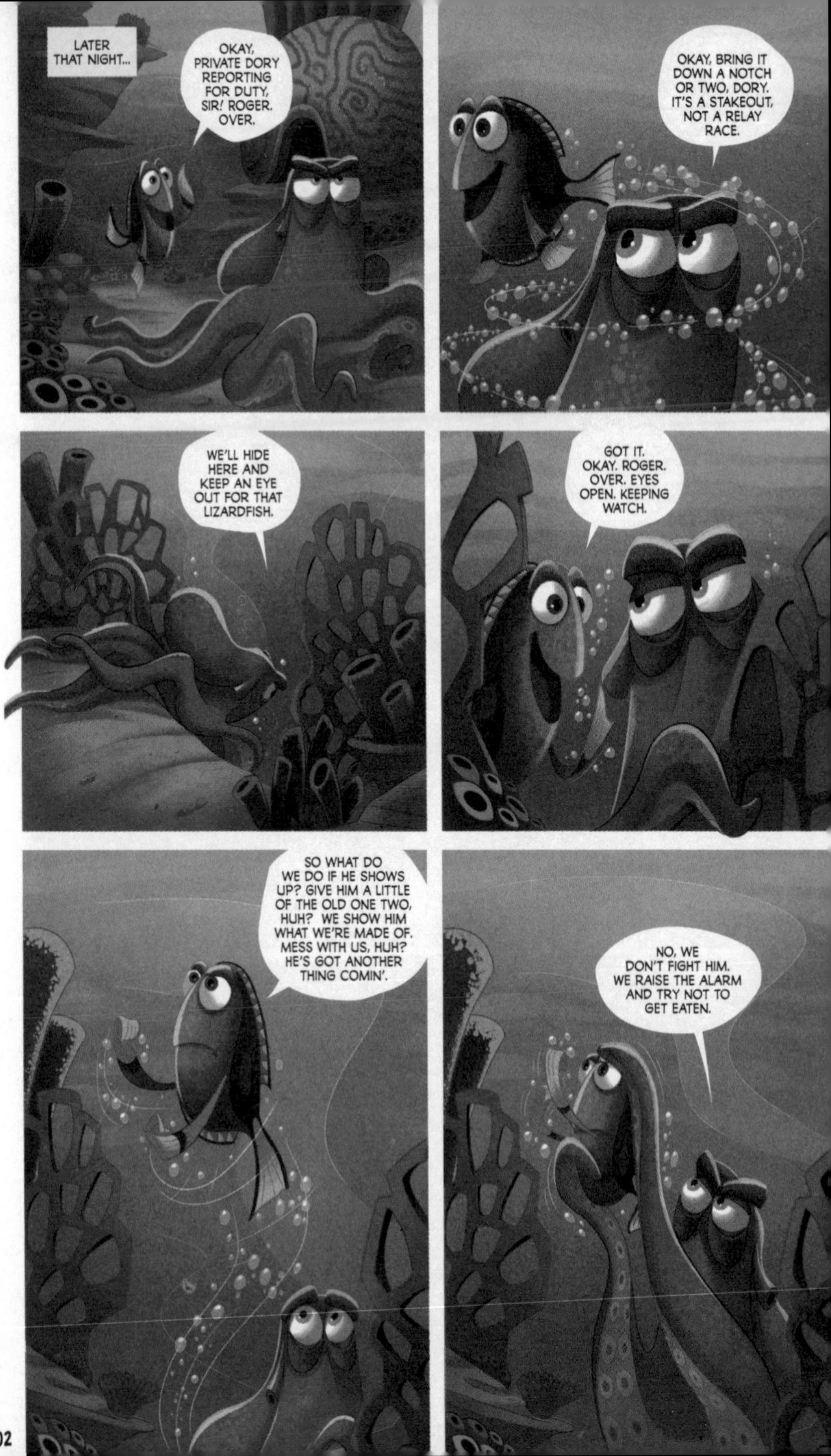
LATER THAT NIGHT...
OKAY, PRIVATE DORY REPORTING FOR DUTY, SIR! ROGER. OVER.
OKAY, BRING IT DOWN A NOTCH OR TWO, DORY. IT'S A STAKEOUT, NOT A RELAY RACE.
WE'LL HIDE HERE AND KEEP AN EYE OUT FOR THAT LIZARDFISH.
GOT IT. OKAY. ROGER. OVER. EYES OPEN. KEEPING WATCH.
SO WHAT DO WE DO IF HE SHOWS UP? GIVE HIM A LITTLE OF THE OLD ONE TWO, HUH? WE SHOW HIM WHAT WE'RE MADE OF. MESS WITH US, HUH? HE'S GOT ANOTHER THING COMIN'.
NO, WE DON'T FIGHT HIM. WE RAISE THE ALARM AND TRY NOT TO GET EATEN.

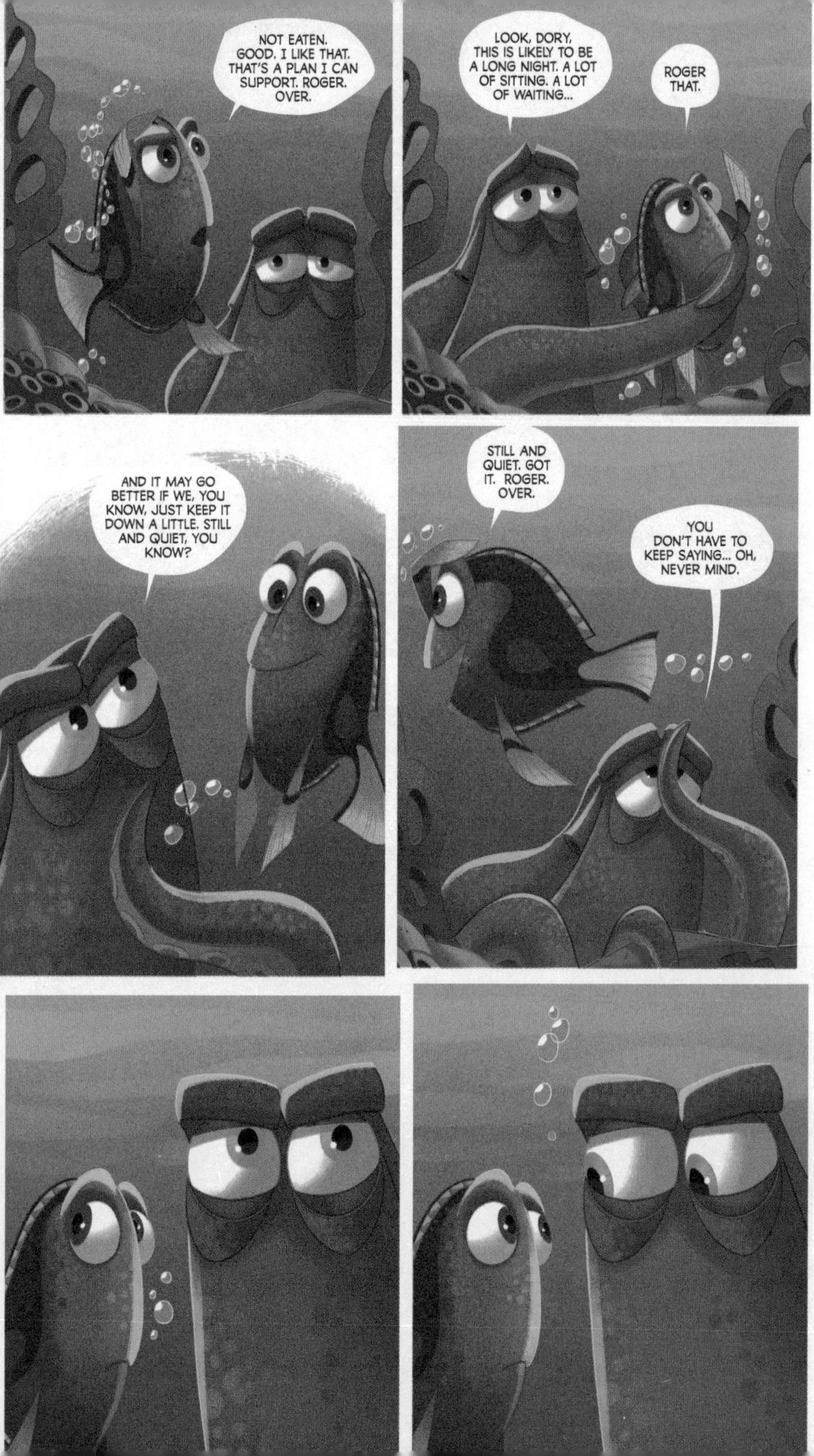
NOT EATEN. GOOD. I LIKE THAT. THAT'S A PLAN I CAN SUPPORT. ROGER. OVER.
LOOK, DORY, THIS IS LIKELY TO BE A LONG NIGHT. A LOT OF SITTING. A LOT OF WAITING...
ROGER THAT.
AND IT MAY GO BETTER IF WE, YOU KNOW, JUST KEEP IT DOWN A LITTLE. STILL AND QUIET, YOU KNOW?
STILL AND QUIET. GOT IT. ROGER. OVER.
YOU DON'T HAVE TO KEEP SAYING... OH, NEVER MIND.

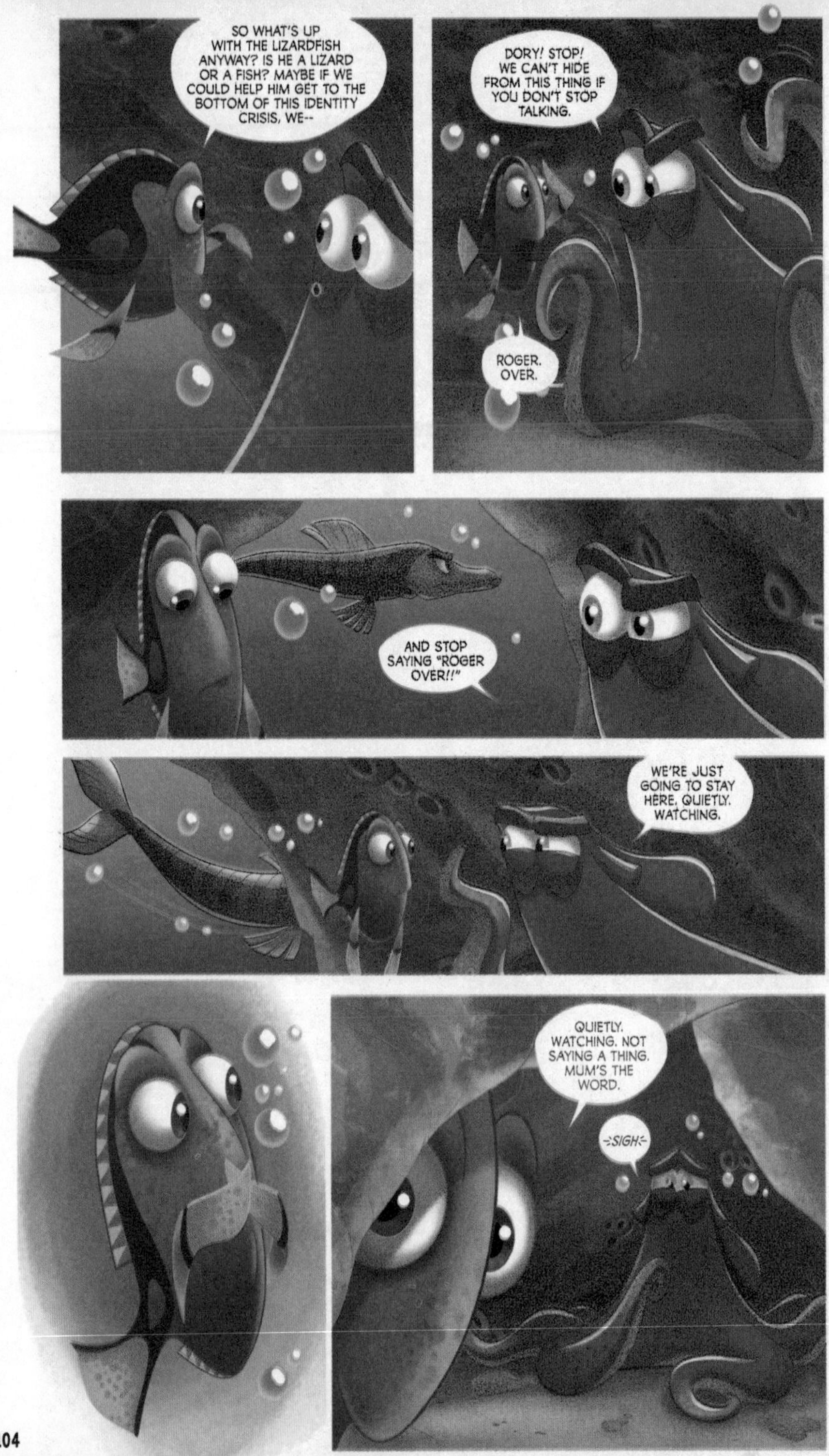
SO WHAT'S UP WITH THE LIZARDFISH ANYWAY? IS HE A LIZARD OR A FISH? MAYBE IF WE COULD HELP HIM GET TO THE BOTTOM OF THIS IDENTITY CRISIS, WE--
DORY! STOP! WE CAN'T HIDE FROM THIS THING IF YOU DON'T STOP TALKING.
ROGER. OVER.
AND STOP SAYING "ROGER OVER!!"
WE'RE JUST GOING TO STAY HERE, QUIETLY. WATCHING.
QUIETLY. WATCHING. NOT SAYING A THING. MUM'S THE WORD.
SIGH

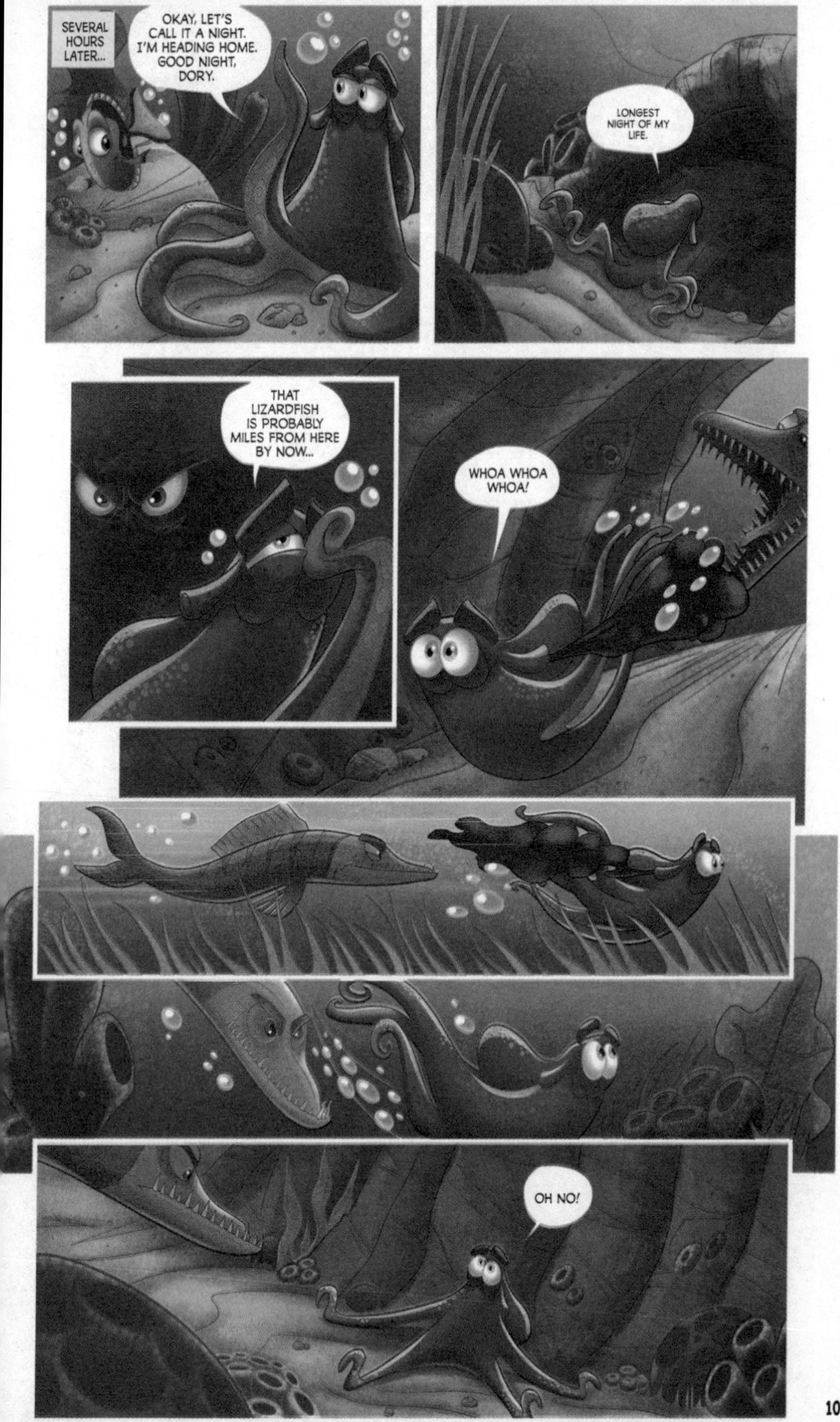
SEVERAL HOURS LATER...
OKAY, LET'S CALL IT A NIGHT. I'M HEADING HOME. GOOD NIGHT, DORY.
LONGEST NIGHT OF MY LIFE.
THAT LIZARDFISH IS PROBABLY MILES FROM HERE BY NOW...
WHOA WHOA WHOA!
OH NO!

UGH! HE EVEN HAS TEETH ON HIS TONGUE.
HEY!
THAT'S MY FRIEND!
AUGH! THERE HE IS!
OVER HERE!

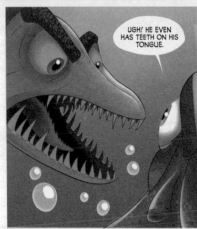

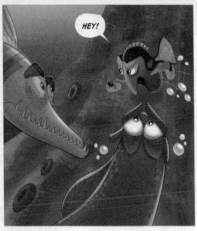

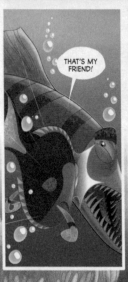

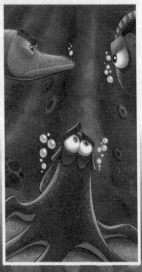

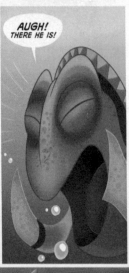

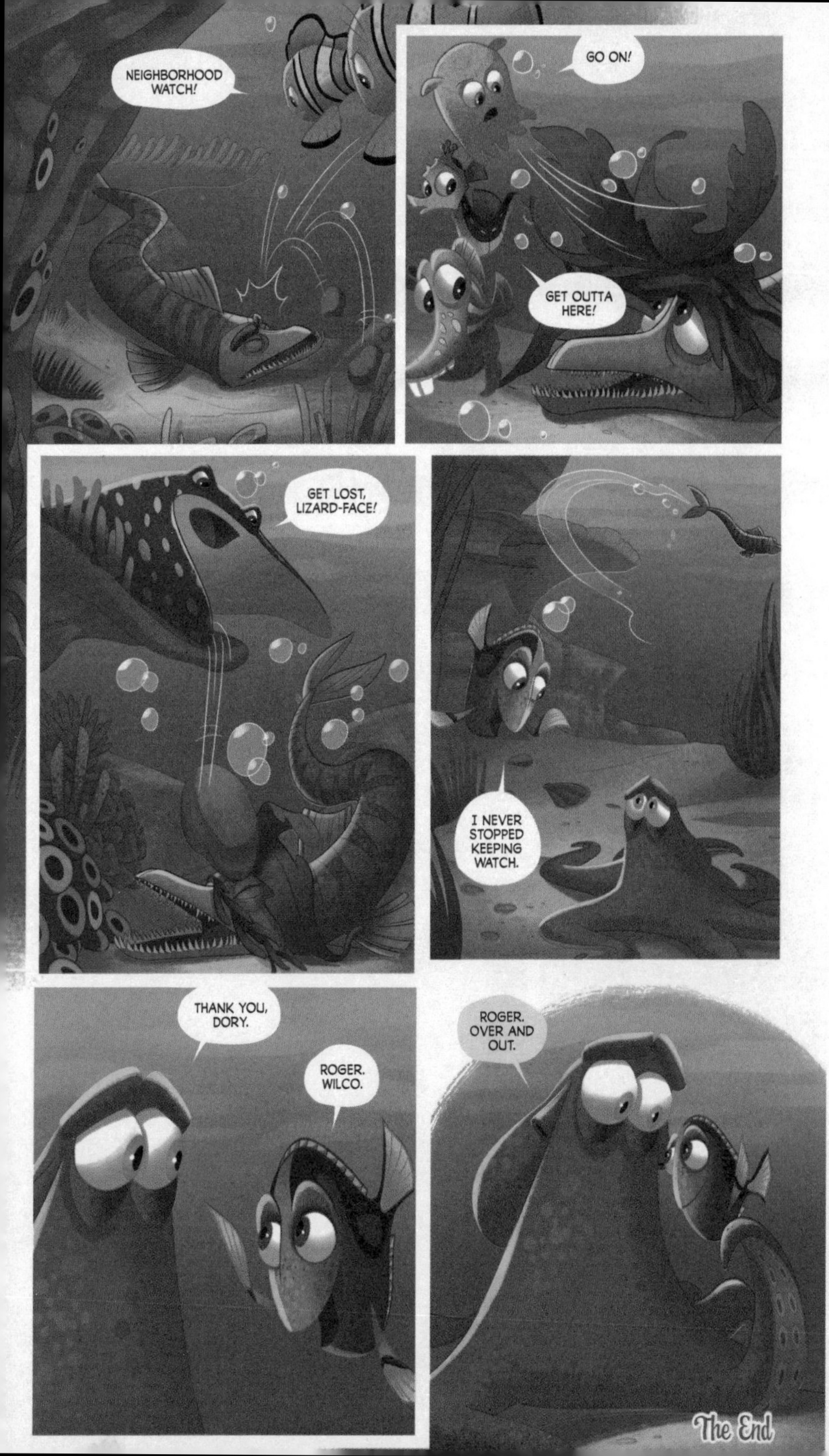
NEIGHBORHOOD WATCH!
GO ON!
GET OUTTA HERE!
GET LOST, LIZARD-FACE!
I NEVER STOPPED KEEPING WATCH.
THANK YOU, DORY.
ROGER. WILCO.
ROGER. OVER AND OUT.
The End

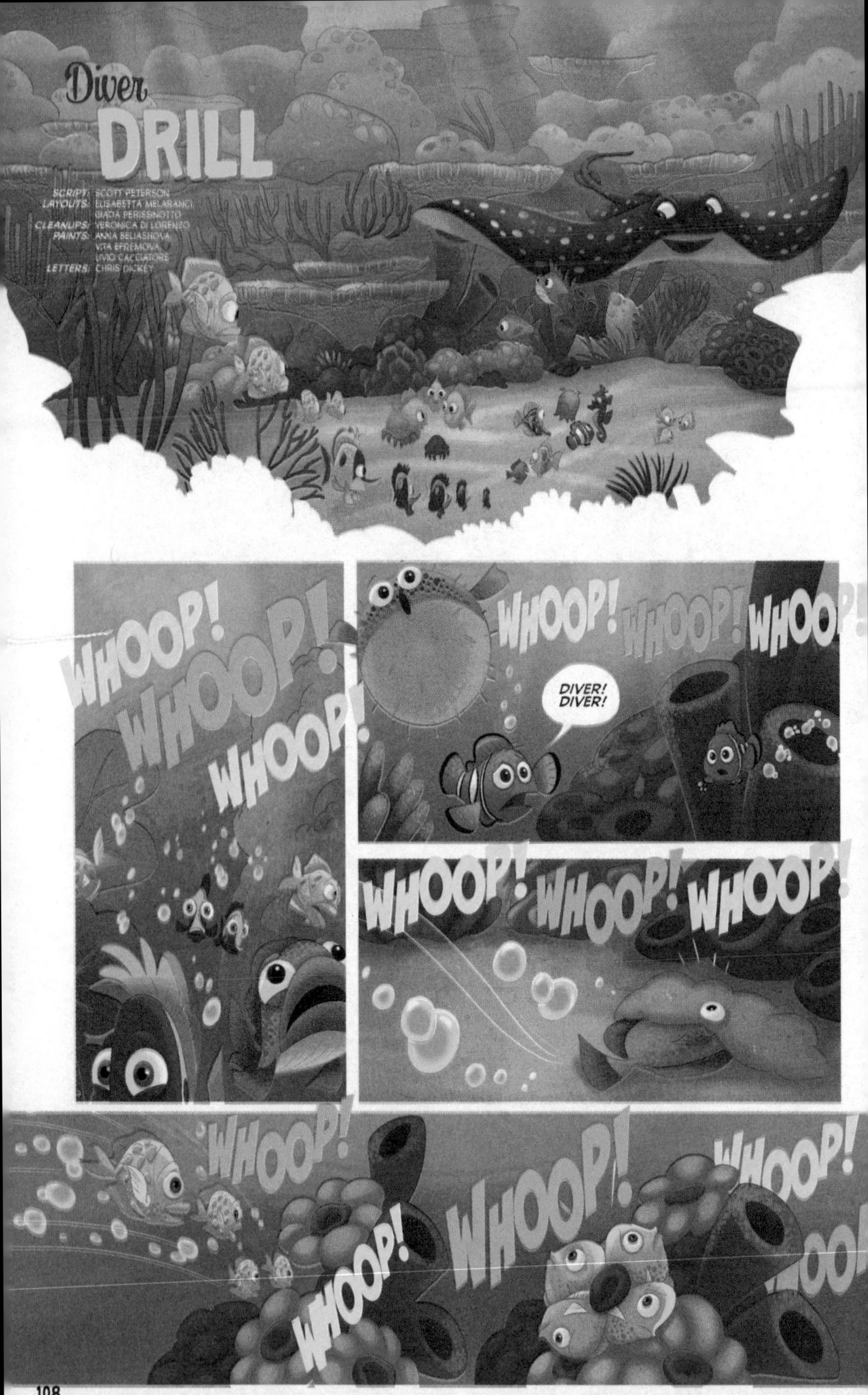
Diver DRILL
SCRIPT: SCOTT PETERSON
LAYOUTS: ELISABETTA MELARANCI
GIADA PERISSINOTTO
CLEANUPS: VERONICA DI LORENZO
PAINTS: ANNA BELIASHOVA
VITA EFREMOVA
LIVIO CACCIATORE
LETTERS: CHRIS DICKEY
WHOOP! WHOOP! WHOOP!
WHOOP! WHOOP! WHOOP!
DIVER! DIVER!
WHOOP! WHOOP! WHOOP!
WHOOP! WHOOP! WHOOP! WHOOP!

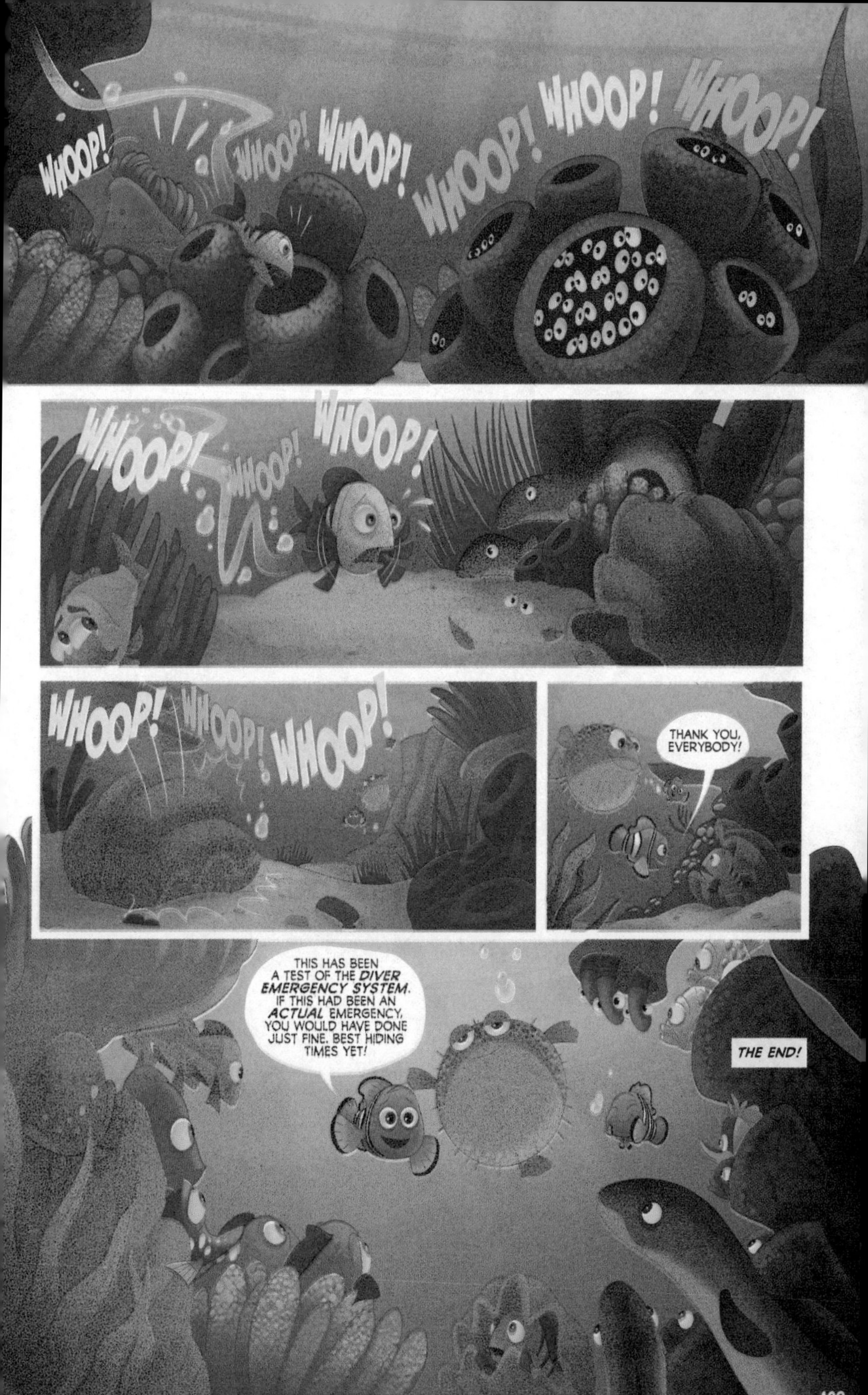
WHOOP! WHOOP! WHOOP! WHOOP! WHOOP! WHOOP!
WHOOP! WHOOP! WHOOP!
WHOOP! WHOOP! WHOOP!
THANK YOU, EVERYBODY!
THIS HAS BEEN A TEST OF THE DIVER EMERGENCY SYSTEM. IF THIS HAD BEEN AN ACTUAL EMERGENCY, YOU WOULD HAVE DONE JUST FINE. BEST HIDING TIMES YET!
THE END!

How to Speak Whale

Dory is fluent in a second language, and that's been super-useful during her adventures. In case you're ever stranded in the ocean and meet a friendly whale who might be able to help, here are a few phrases that will come in handy.

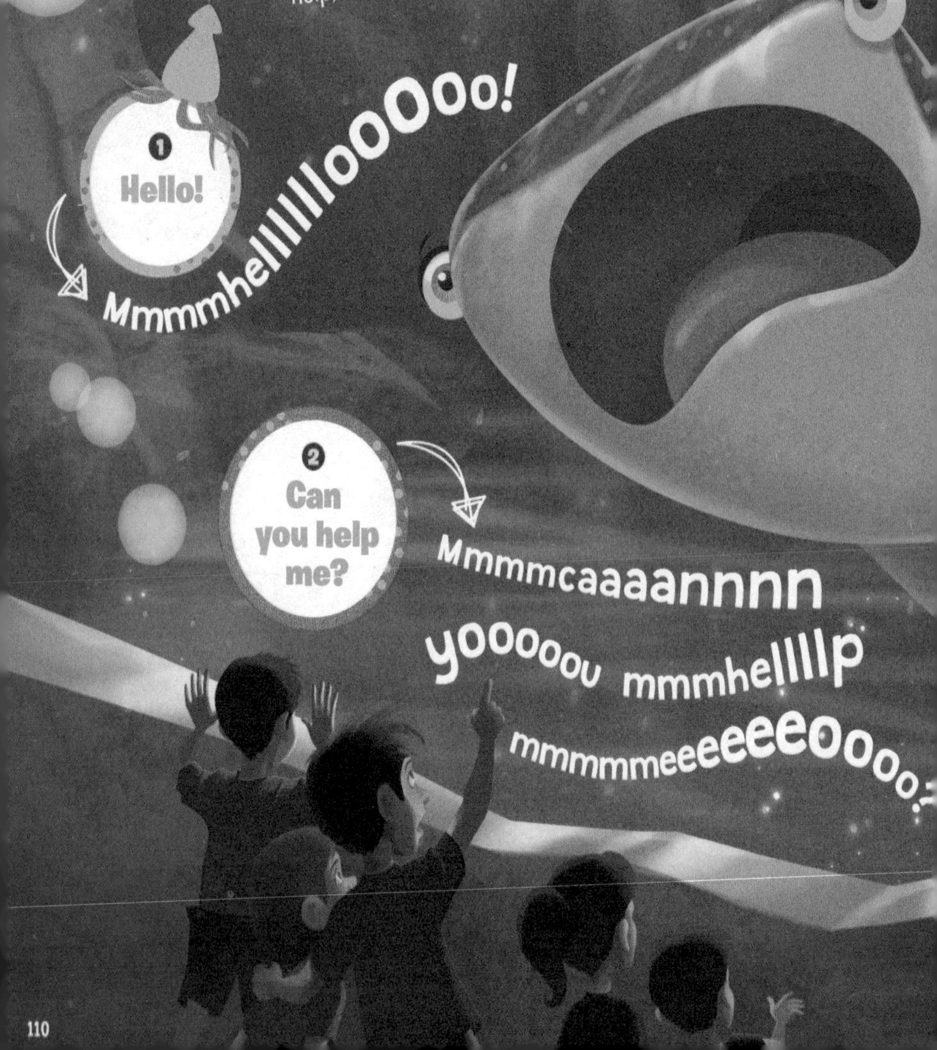

1 Hello!

Mmmmhellllllooooooo!

2 Can you help me?

Mmmmcaaaannnnn yoooooou mmmhellllp mmmmmeeeeeeeoooo?

FOR BASIC WHALE, START EACH PHRASE
WITH A LOW RUMBLE, THEN RAISE YOUR
VOICE HIGHER, THEN BRING IT BACK DOWN
AND END WITH AN "O" OR "OOOH" SOUND.

4 You're welcome.

Mmmmmyoooooou're welllllcommmmmmeooo

3 Thank you.

Mmmthaannnkkkk yoooooooou!

MmmmIIIIIeee aaammm noooottt kriiiiiiillllllloooooo!

5 I am not krill.

ALTHOUGH SOME WHALES SPEAK
WITH DIFFERENT DIALECTS,
BASIC WHALE USUALLY WORKS.
USE CAUTION, THOUGH – EVEN FLUENT
WHALE SPEAKERS ARE SOMETIMES
MISTAKEN FOR DINNER!

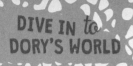

Sights to SEA

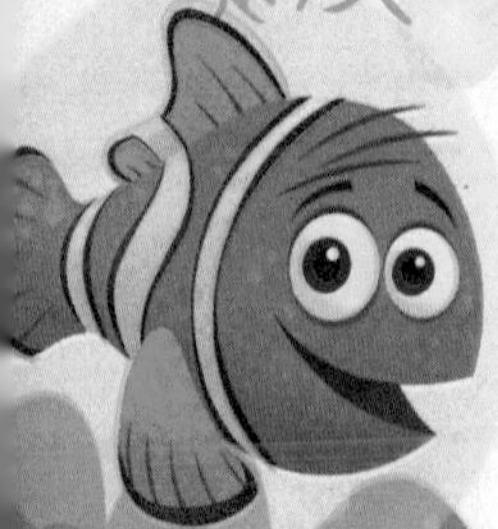

Take a swim through some of the exciting places where Dory, Nemo and Marlin find adventure in *Finding Dory*!

CORAL REEF

The coral reef is home to Dory, Nemo and Marlin – and a brilliant world of amazing creatures, including crabs, seahorses, urchins, sponges...and of course, coral!

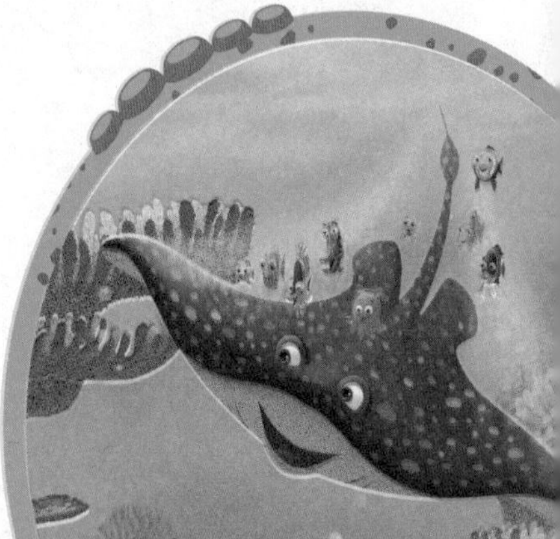

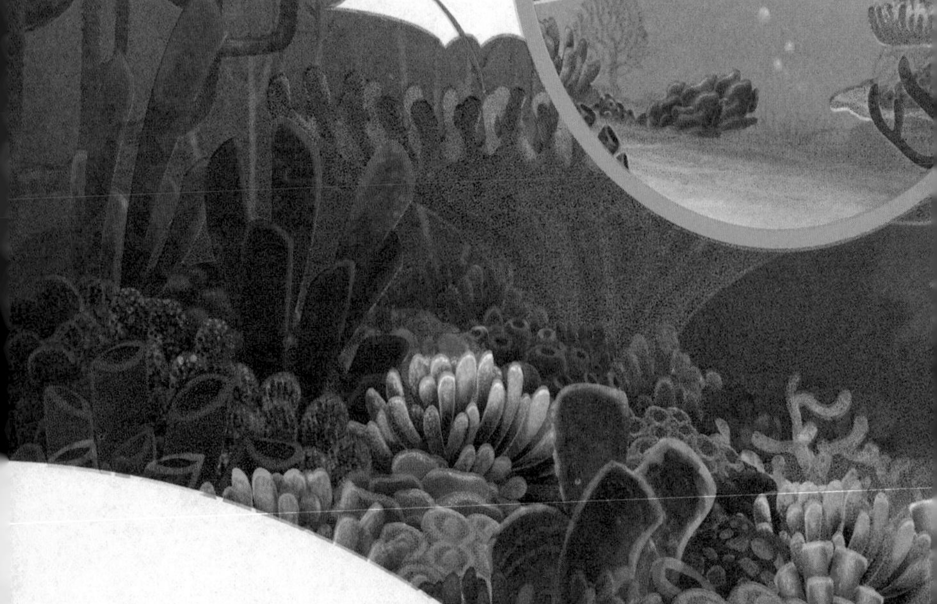

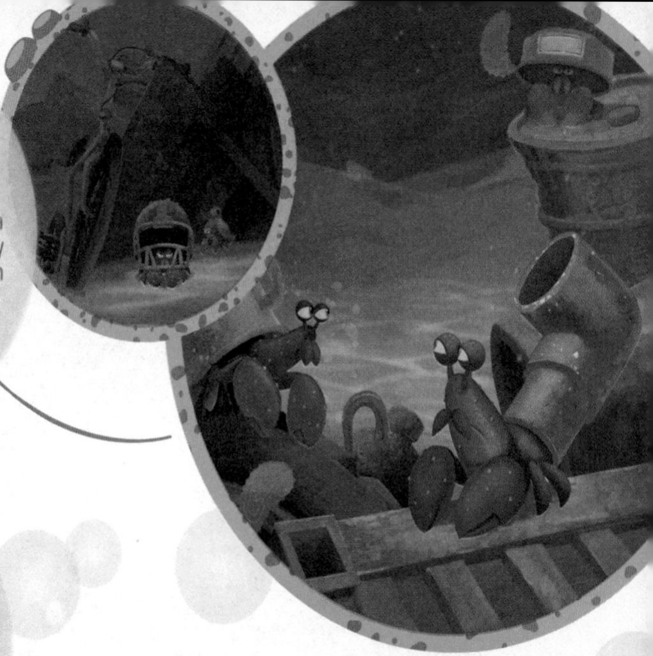

SHIPPING LANES

As Dory, Nemo and Marlin near California, they pass through an area of ocean where cargo ships regularly chug back and forth. With that much traffic, it's no wonder there are potentially dangerous obstacles like sunken container ships!

SANDY PATCH SCHOOL

Dory likes to go along on field trips with Nemo and his classmates at his school on the coral reef. But his teacher, Mr. Ray, is not always so excited to have Dory on board!

DORY'S AND NEMO'S HOMES

Dory lives in a coral cave right next door to Marlin and Nemo's anemone home. It's a cozy arrangement – except when Dory forgets that the anemone stings!

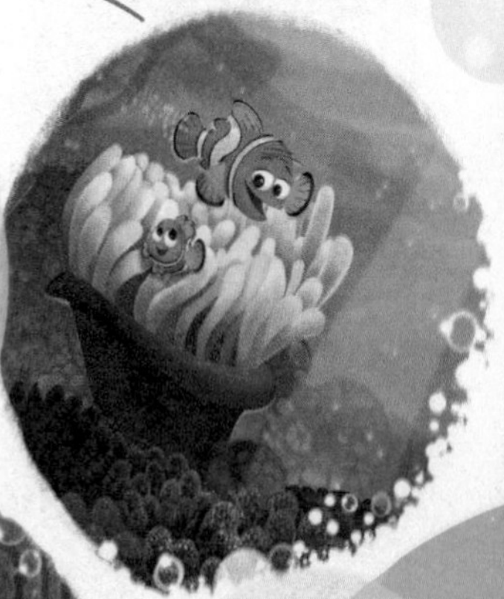

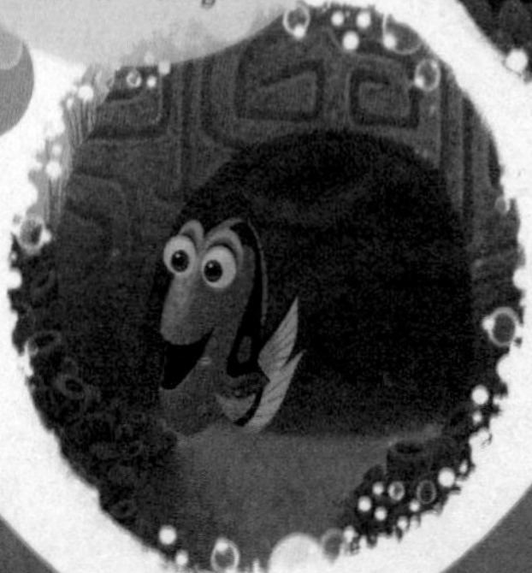

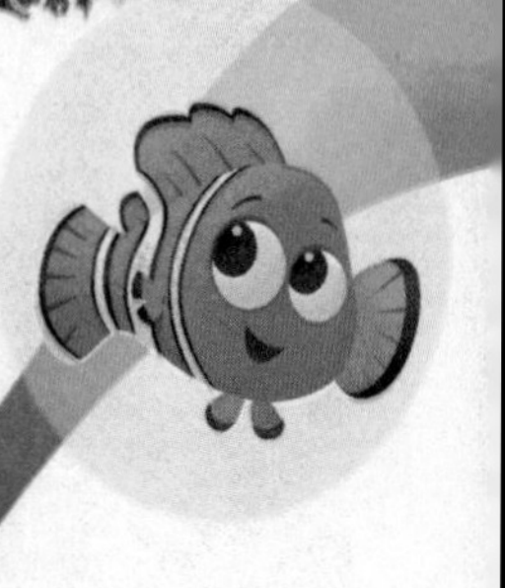

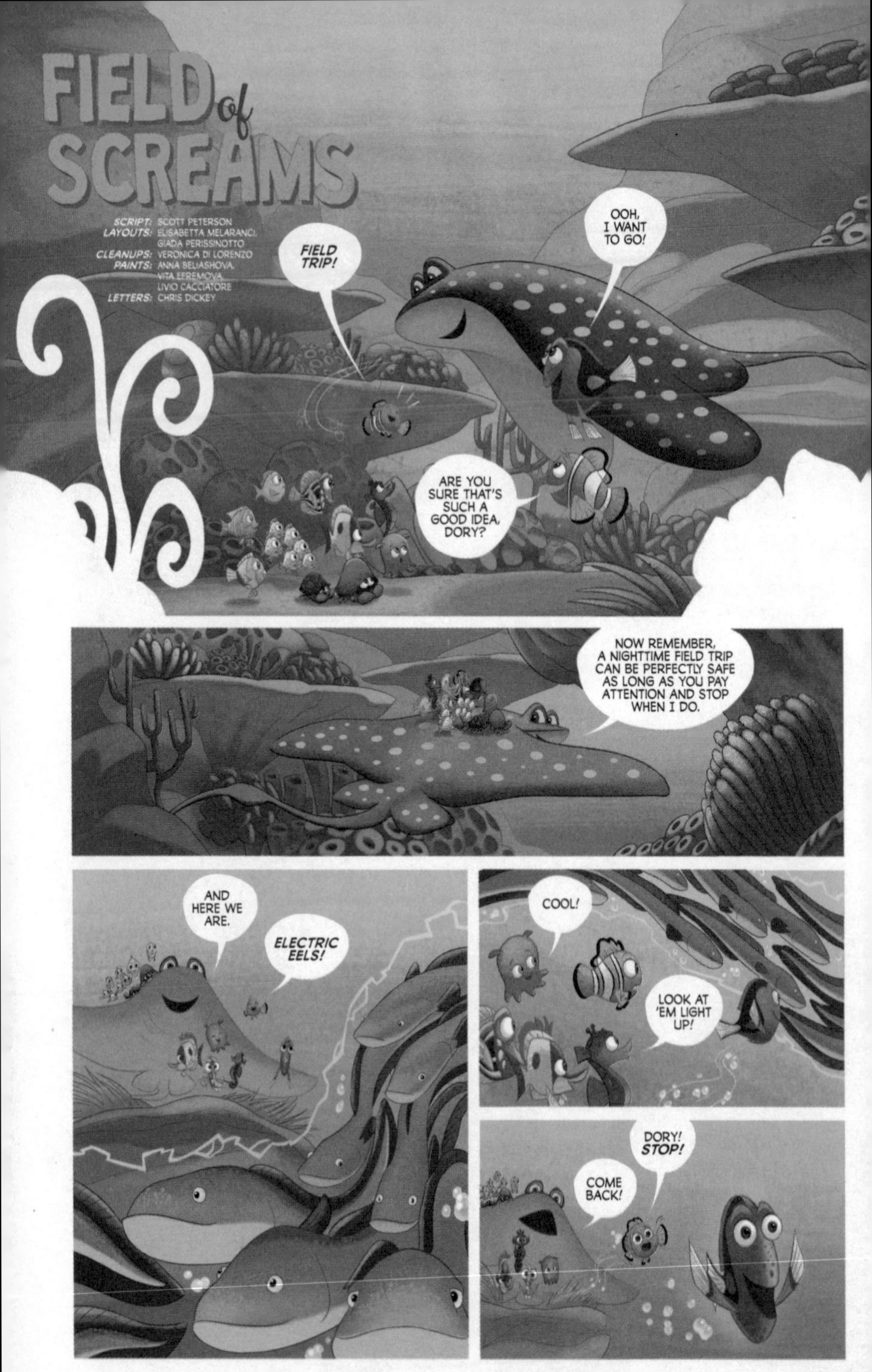
FIELD of SCREAMS
SCRIPT: SCOTT PETERSON
LAYOUTS: ELISABETTA MELARANCI, GIADA PERISSINOTTO
CLEANUPS: VERONICA DI LORENZO
PAINTS: ANNA BELIASHOVA, VITA EFREMOVA, LIVIO CACCIATORE
LETTERS: CHRIS DICKEY
FIELD TRIP!
OOH, I WANT TO GO!
ARE YOU SURE THAT'S SUCH A GOOD IDEA, DORY?
NOW REMEMBER, A NIGHTTIME FIELD TRIP CAN BE PERFECTLY SAFE AS LONG AS YOU PAY ATTENTION AND STOP WHEN I DO.
AND HERE WE ARE.
ELECTRIC EELS!
COOL!
LOOK AT 'EM LIGHT UP!
DORY! STOP!
COME BACK!

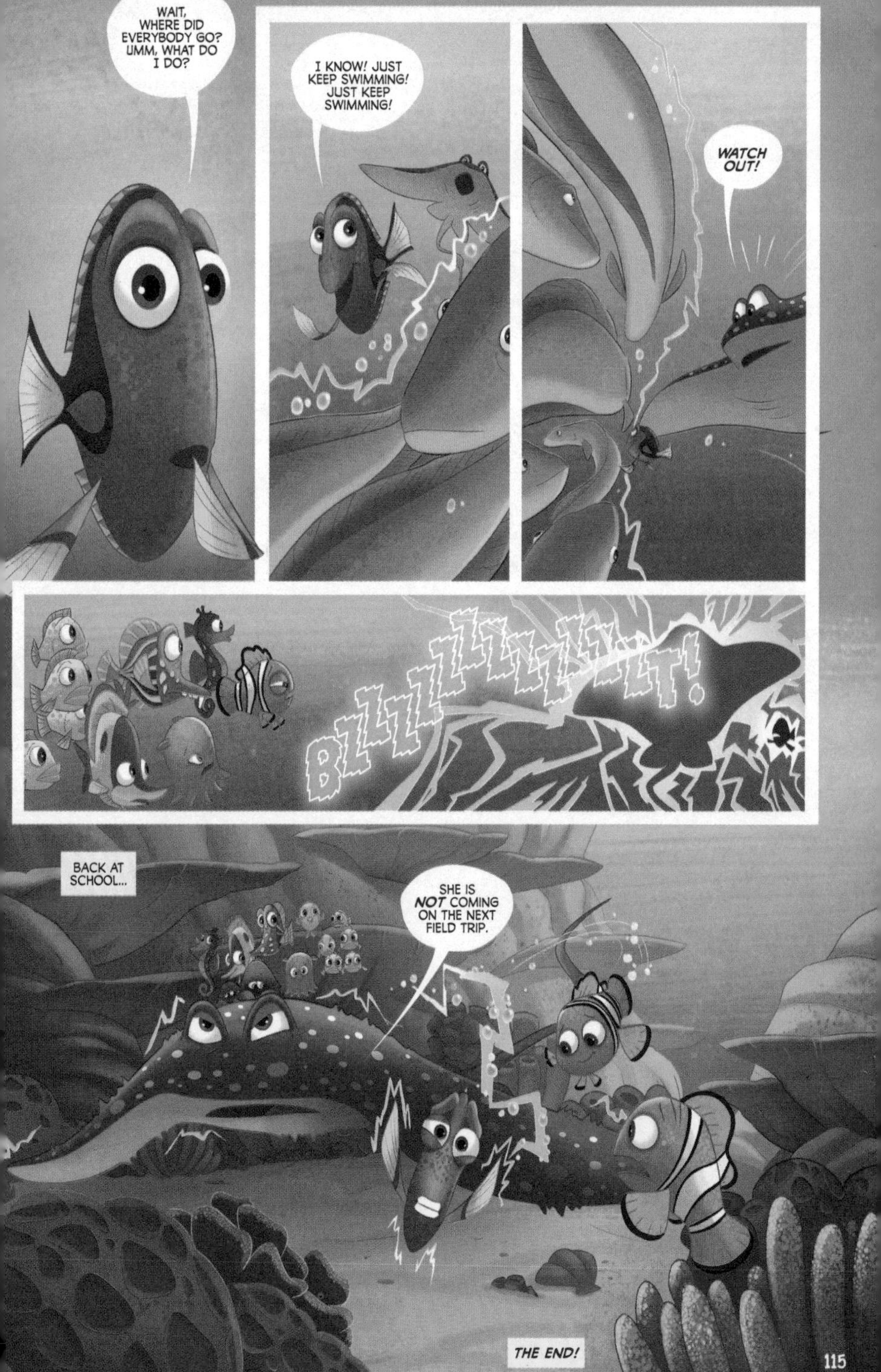
WAIT, WHERE DID EVERYBODY GO? UMM, WHAT DO I DO?
I KNOW! JUST KEEP SWIMMING! JUST KEEP SWIMMING!
WATCH OUT!
BZZZZZZZZZZZZT!
BACK AT SCHOOL...
SHE IS *NOT* COMING ON THE NEXT FIELD TRIP.
THE END!

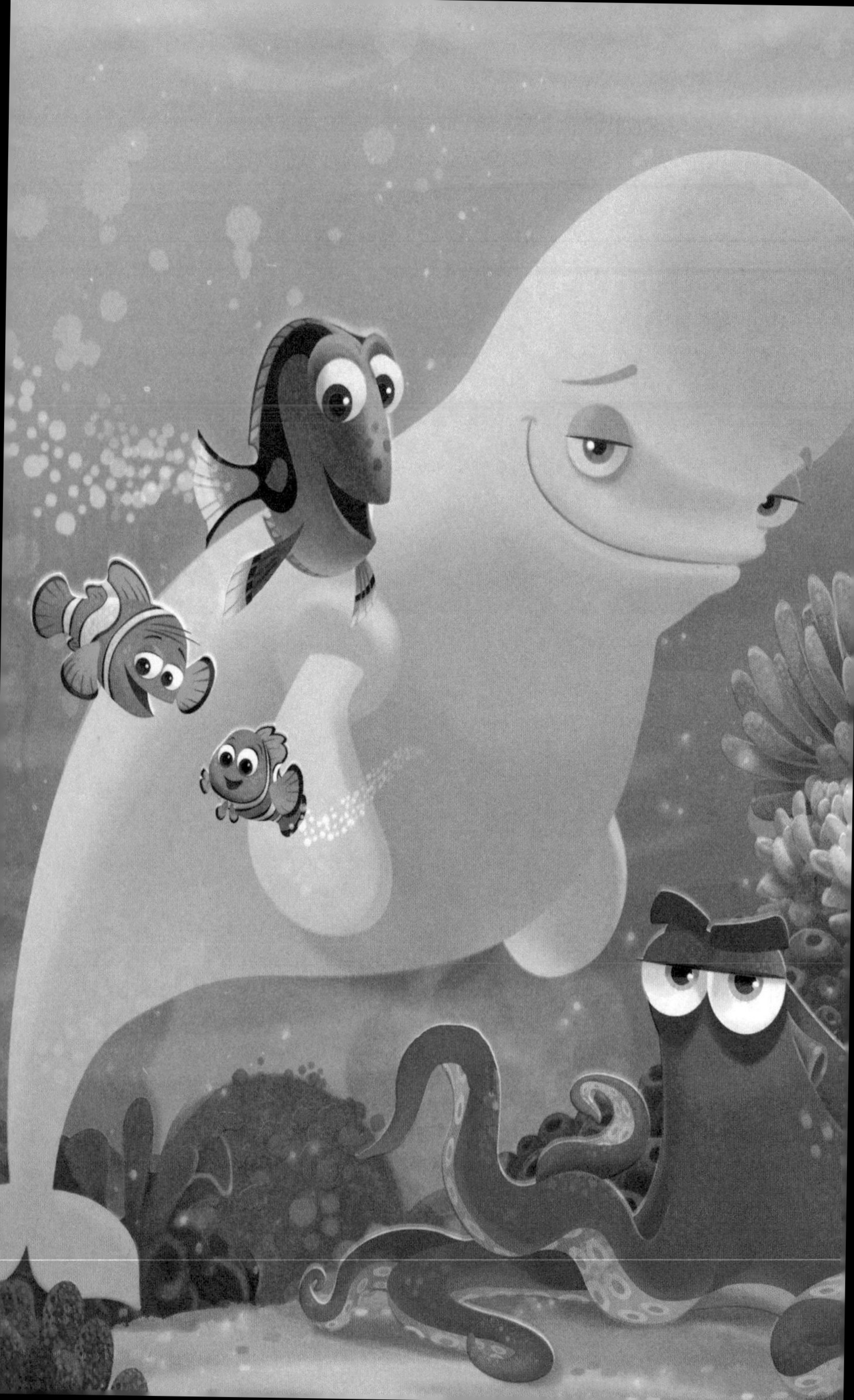

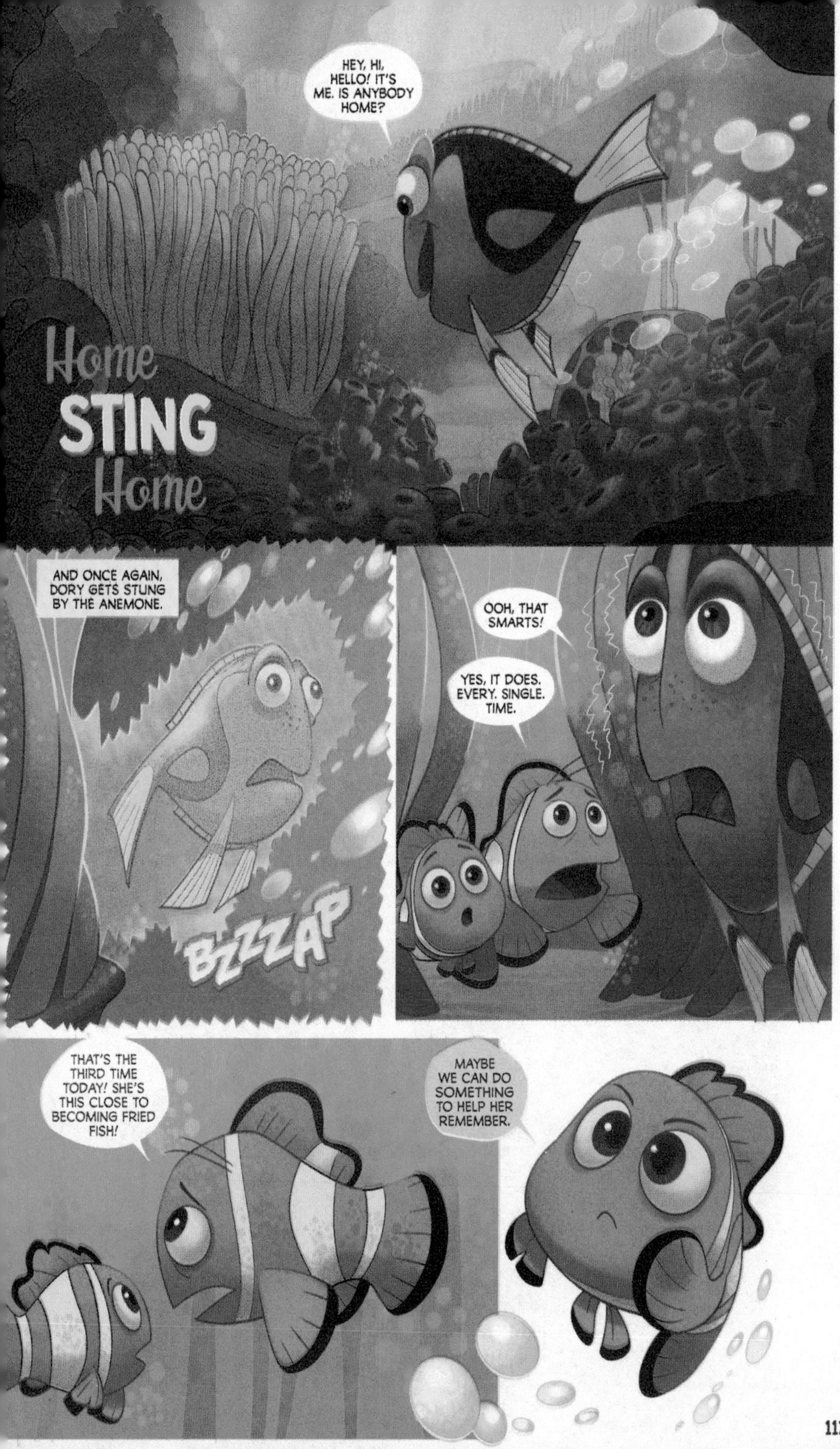
HEY, HI, HELLO! IT'S ME. IS ANYBODY HOME?
Home STING Home
AND ONCE AGAIN, DORY GETS STUNG BY THE ANEMONE.
BZZZAP
OOH, THAT SMARTS!
YES, IT DOES. EVERY. SINGLE. TIME.
THAT'S THE THIRD TIME TODAY! SHE'S THIS CLOSE TO BECOMING FRIED FISH!
MAYBE WE CAN DO SOMETHING TO HELP HER REMEMBER.

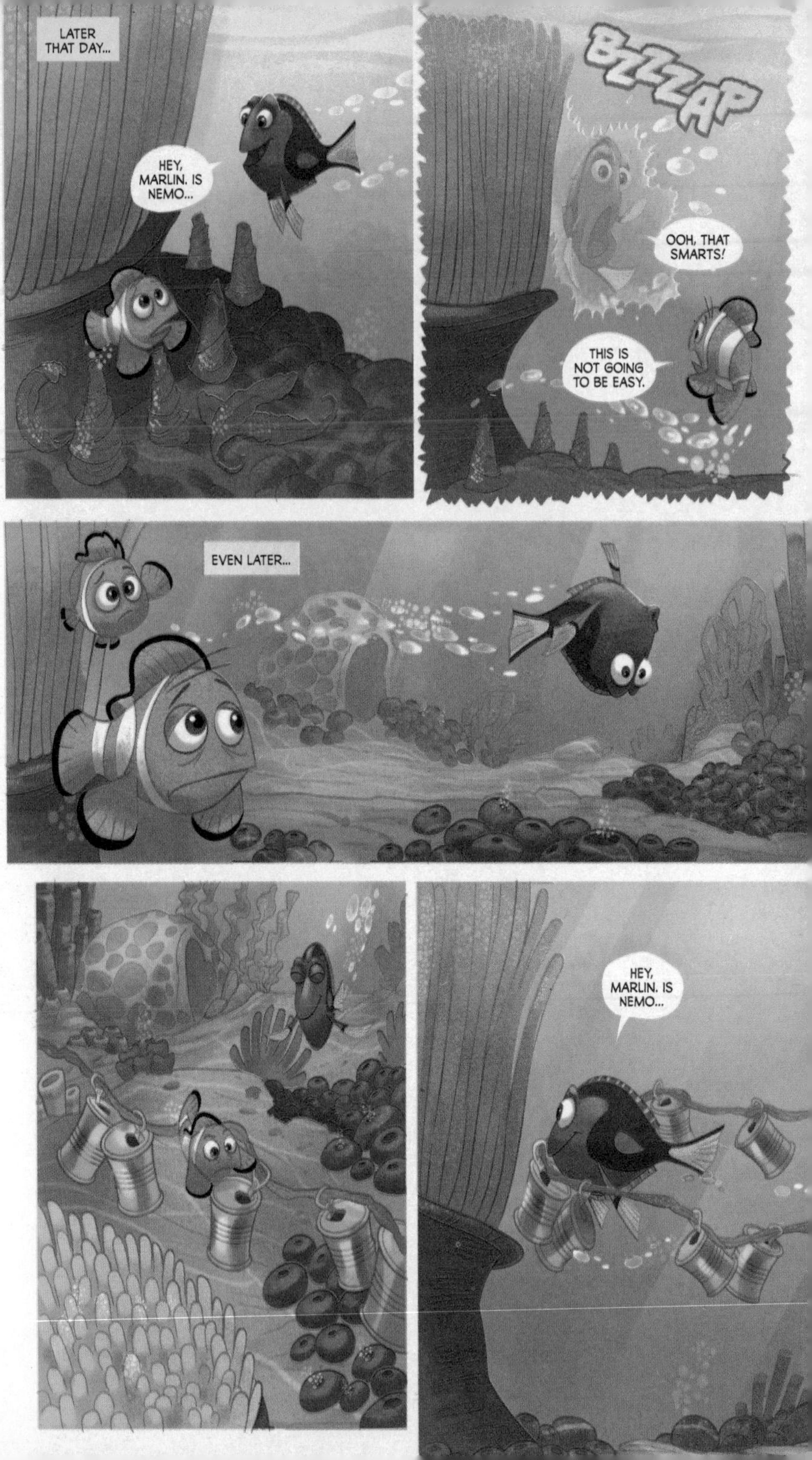
LATER THAT DAY...
HEY, MARLIN. IS NEMO...
BZZZAP
OOH, THAT SMARTS!
THIS IS NOT GOING TO BE EASY.
EVEN LATER...
HEY, MARLIN. IS NEMO...

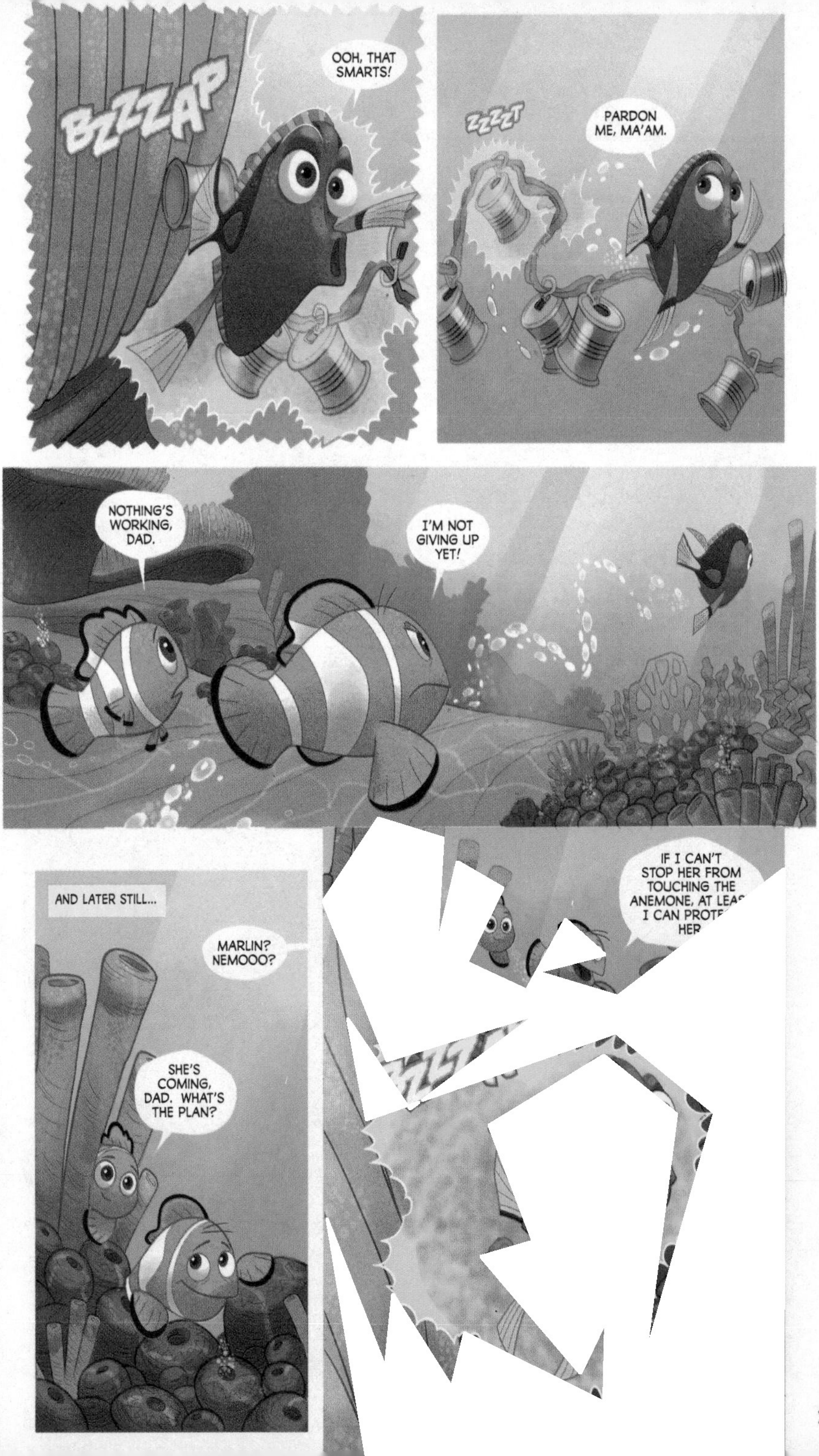
BZZZAP
OOH, THAT SMARTS!
ZZZZT
PARDON ME, MA'AM.
NOTHING'S WORKING, DAD.
I'M NOT GIVING UP YET!
AND LATER STILL...
MARLIN? NEMOOO?
SHE'S COMING, DAD. WHAT'S THE PLAN?
IF I CAN'T STOP HER FROM TOUCHING THE ANEMONE, AT LEAS
I CAN PROTE
HER

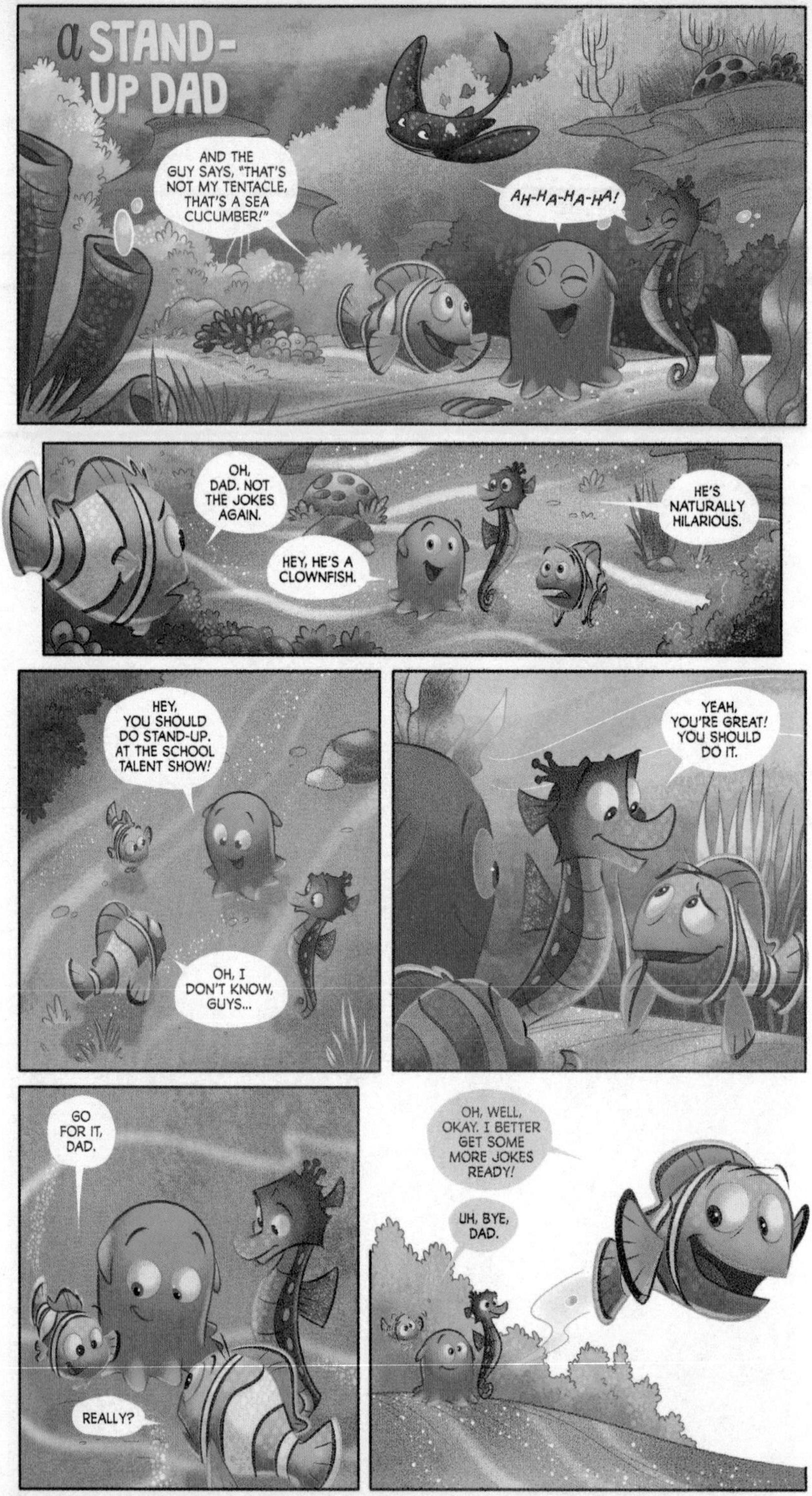
a STAND-UP DAD
AND THE GUY SAYS, "THAT'S NOT MY TENTACLE, THAT'S A SEA CUCUMBER!"
AH-HA-HA-HA!
OH, DAD. NOT THE JOKES AGAIN.
HEY, HE'S A CLOWNFISH.
HE'S NATURALLY HILARIOUS.
HEY, YOU SHOULD DO STAND-UP. AT THE SCHOOL TALENT SHOW!
OH, I DON'T KNOW, GUYS...
YEAH, YOU'RE GREAT! YOU SHOULD DO IT.
GO FOR IT, DAD.
REALLY?
OH, WELL, OKAY. I BETTER GET SOME MORE JOKES READY!
UH, BYE, DAD.

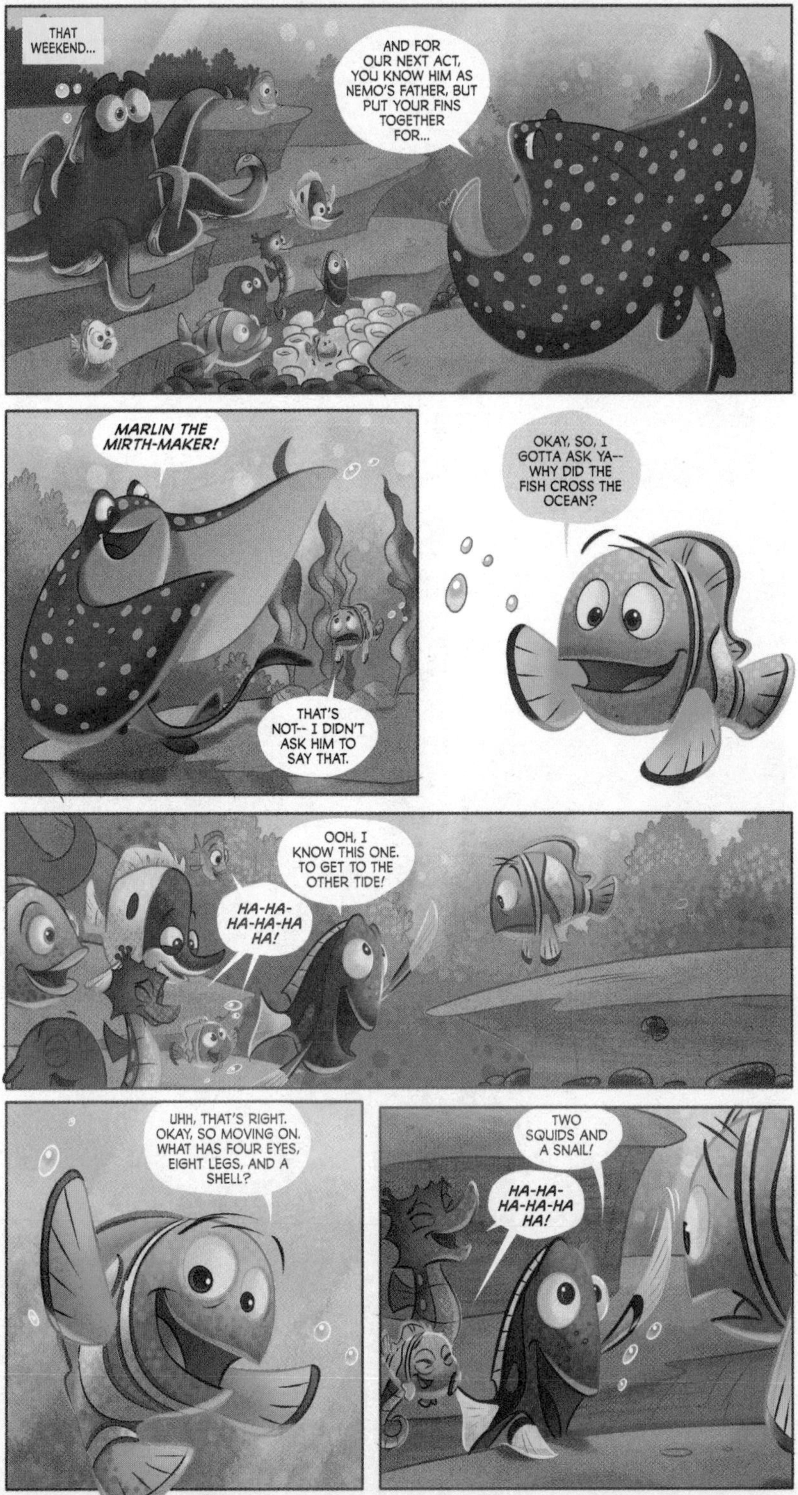
THAT WEEKEND...
AND FOR OUR NEXT ACT, YOU KNOW HIM AS NEMO'S FATHER, BUT PUT YOUR FINS TOGETHER FOR...
MARLIN THE MIRTH-MAKER!
THAT'S NOT-- I DIDN'T ASK HIM TO SAY THAT.
OKAY, SO, I GOTTA ASK YA-- WHY DID THE FISH CROSS THE OCEAN?
HA-HA-HA-HA-HA HA!
OOH, I KNOW THIS ONE. TO GET TO THE OTHER *TIDE!*
UHH, THAT'S RIGHT. OKAY, SO MOVING ON. WHAT HAS FOUR EYES, EIGHT LEGS, AND A SHELL?
TWO SQUIDS AND A SNAIL!
HA-HA-HA-HA-HA HA!

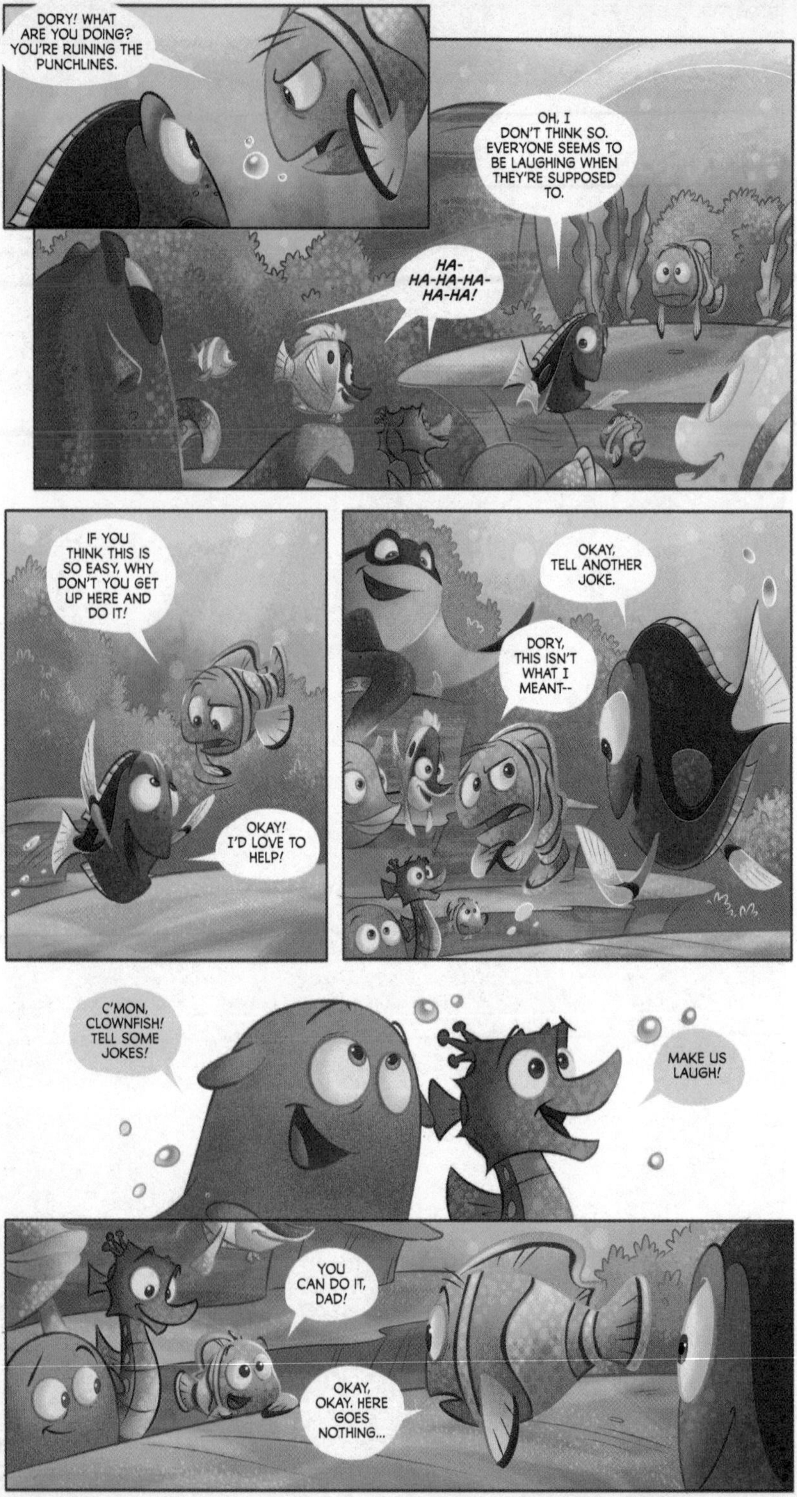
DORY! WHAT ARE YOU DOING? YOU'RE RUINING THE PUNCHLINES.
OH, I DON'T THINK SO. EVERYONE SEEMS TO BE LAUGHING WHEN THEY'RE SUPPOSED TO.
HA-HA-HA-HA-HA-HA!
IF YOU THINK THIS IS SO EASY, WHY DON'T YOU GET UP HERE AND DO IT!
OKAY! I'D LOVE TO HELP!
OKAY, TELL ANOTHER JOKE.
DORY, THIS ISN'T WHAT I MEANT--
C'MON, CLOWNFISH! TELL SOME JOKES!
MAKE US LAUGH!
YOU CAN DO IT, DAD!
OKAY, OKAY. HERE GOES NOTHING...

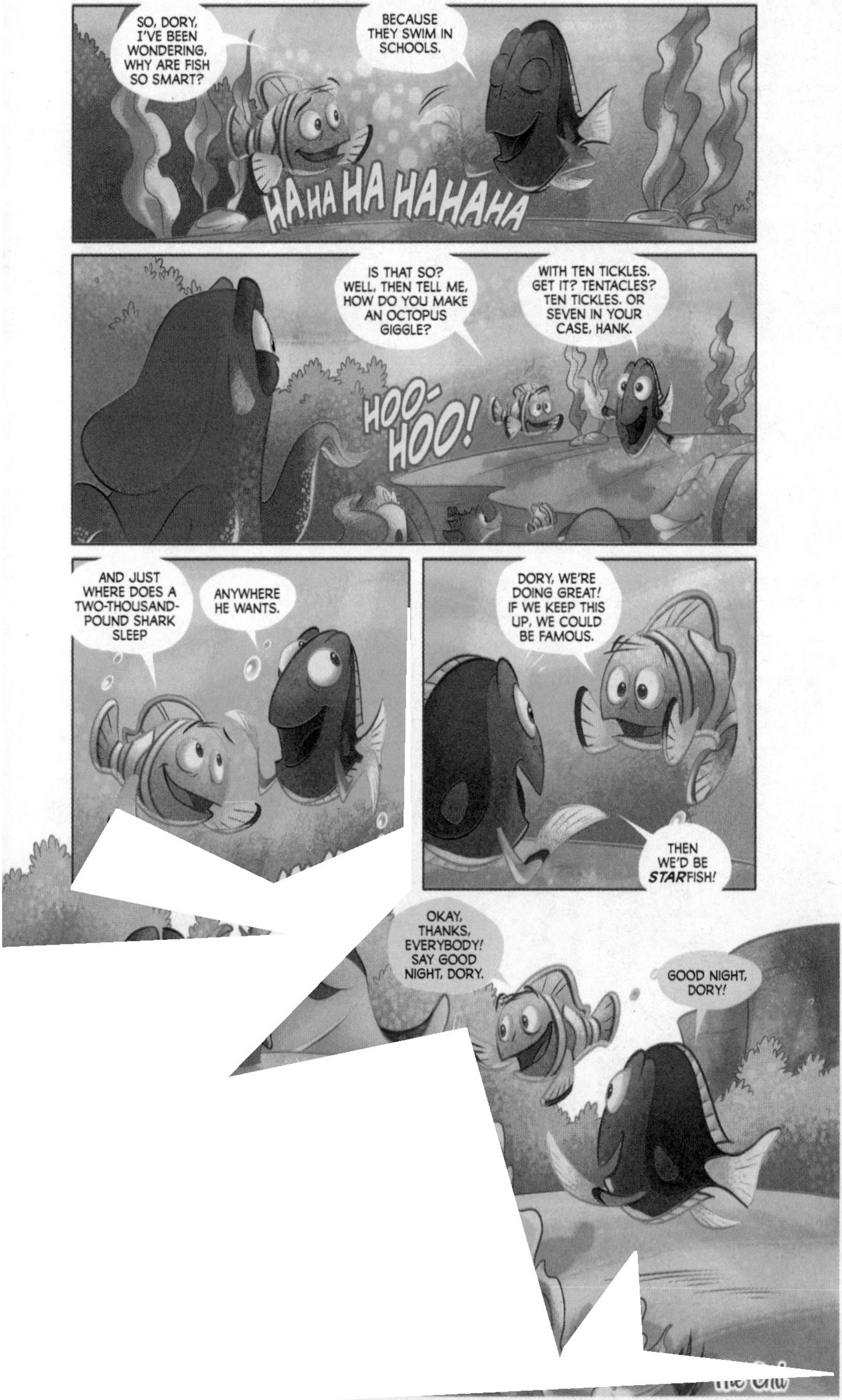
SO, DORY, I'VE BEEN WONDERING, WHY ARE FISH SO SMART?
BECAUSE THEY SWIM IN SCHOOLS.
HA HA HA HAHAHA
IS THAT SO? WELL, THEN TELL ME, HOW DO YOU MAKE AN OCTOPUS GIGGLE?
WITH TEN TICKLES. GET IT? TENTACLES? TEN TICKLES. OR SEVEN IN YOUR CASE, HANK.
HOO-HOO!
AND JUST WHERE DOES A TWO-THOUSAND-POUND SHARK SLEEP
ANYWHERE HE WANTS.
DORY, WE'RE DOING GREAT! IF WE KEEP THIS UP, WE COULD BE FAMOUS.
THEN WE'D BE STARFISH!
OKAY, THANKS, EVERYBODY! SAY GOOD NIGHT, DORY.
GOOD NIGHT, DORY!

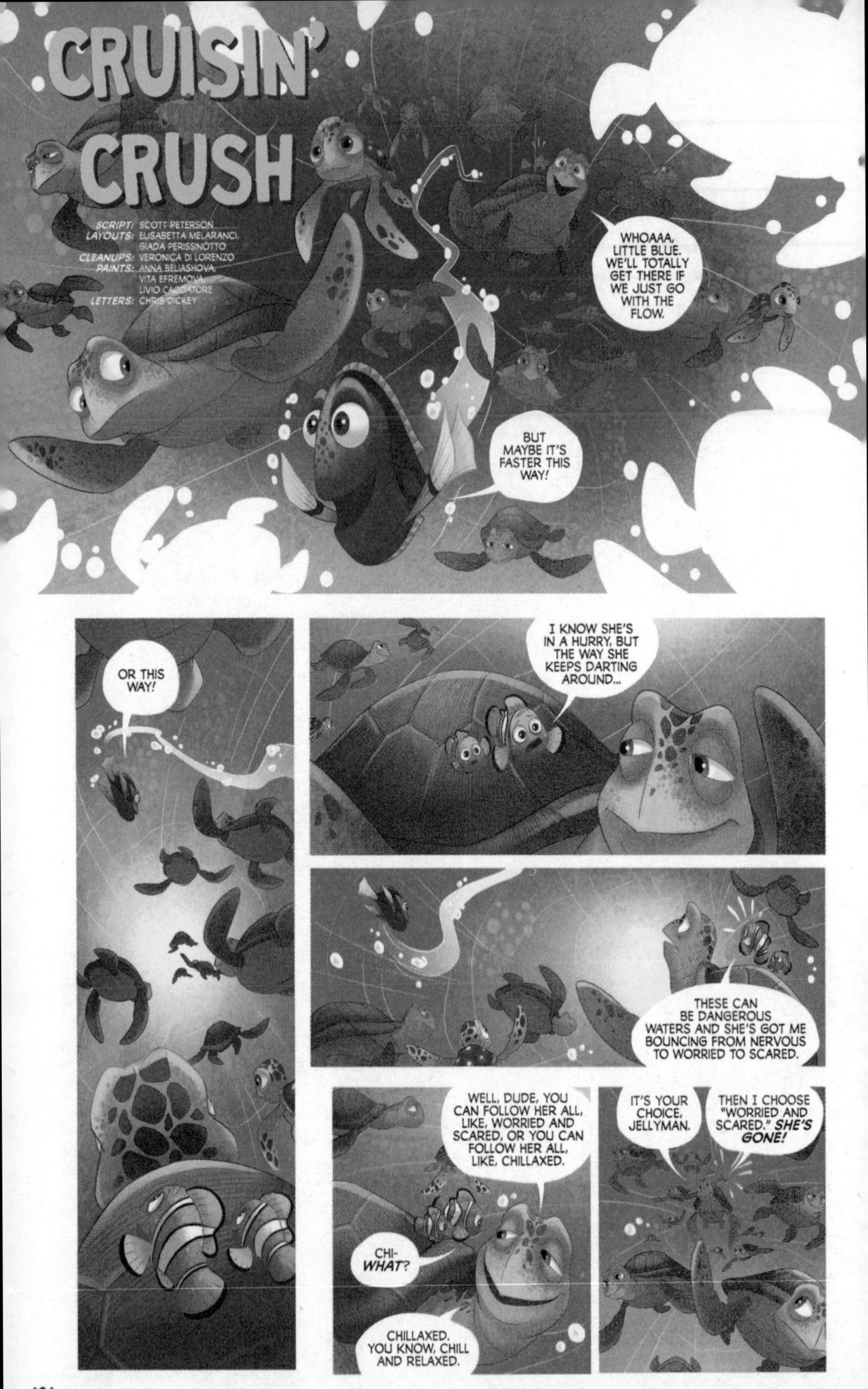
CRUISIN' CRUSH
SCRIPT: SCOTT PETERSON
LAYOUTS: ELISABETTA MELARANCI, GIADA PERISSINOTTO
CLEANUPS: VERONICA DI LORENZO
PAINTS: ANNA BELIASHOVA, VITA EFREMOVA, LIVIO CACCIATORE
LETTERS: CHRIS DICKEY
WHOAAA, LITTLE BLUE. WE'LL TOTALLY GET THERE IF WE JUST GO WITH THE FLOW.
BUT MAYBE IT'S FASTER THIS WAY!
OR THIS WAY!
I KNOW SHE'S IN A HURRY, BUT THE WAY SHE KEEPS DARTING AROUND...
THESE CAN BE DANGEROUS WATERS AND SHE'S GOT ME BOUNCING FROM NERVOUS TO WORRIED TO SCARED.
WELL, DUDE, YOU CAN FOLLOW HER ALL, LIKE, WORRIED AND SCARED, OR YOU CAN FOLLOW HER ALL, LIKE, CHILLAXED.
CHI-*WHAT*?
CHILLAXED. YOU KNOW, CHILL AND RELAXED.
IT'S YOUR CHOICE, JELLYMAN.
THEN I CHOOSE "WORRIED AND SCARED." ***SHE'S GONE!***

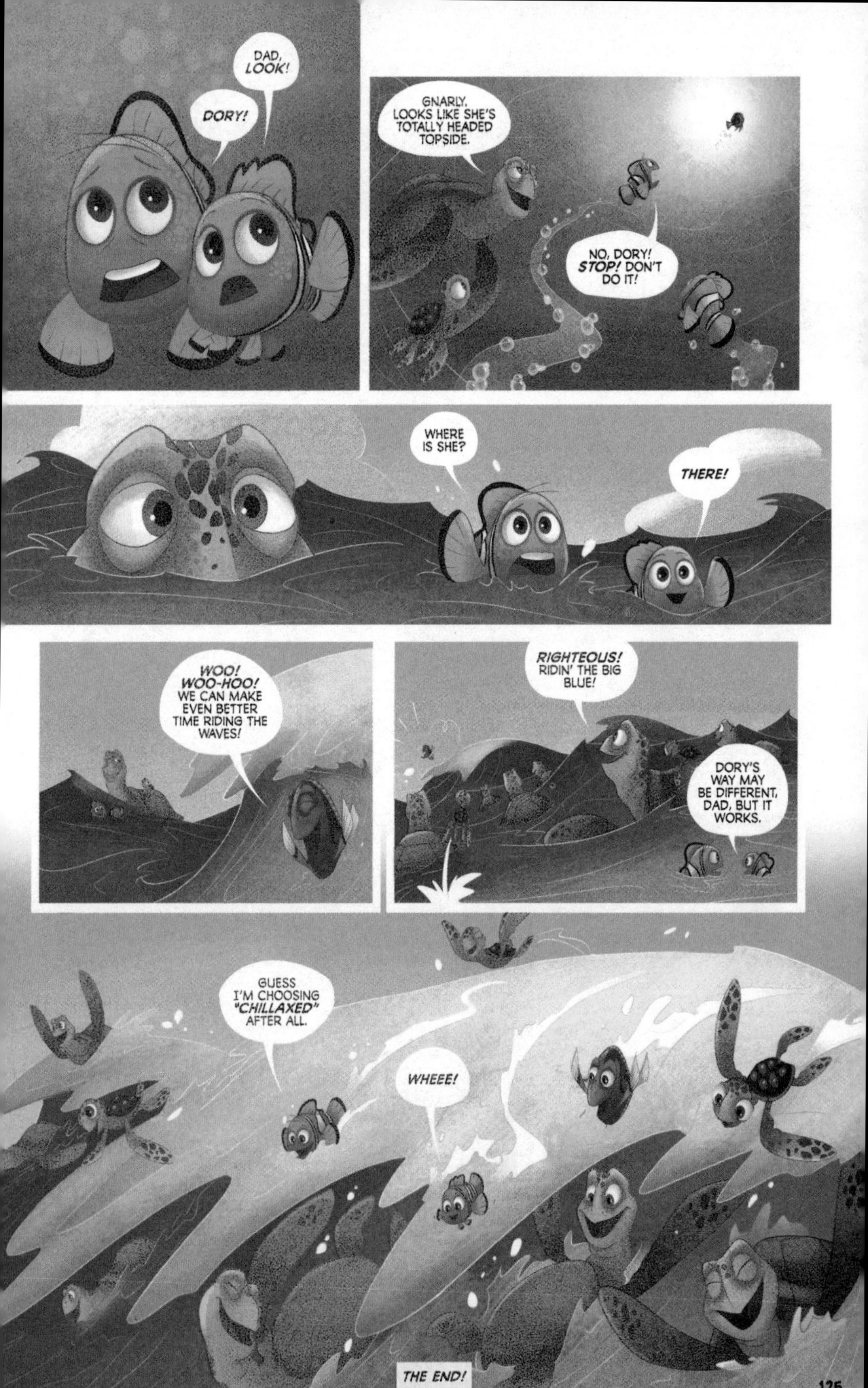
DAD, LOOK!
DORY!
GNARLY. LOOKS LIKE SHE'S TOTALLY HEADED TOPSIDE.
NO, DORY! STOP! DON'T DO IT!
WHERE IS SHE?
THERE!
WOO! WOO-HOO! WE CAN MAKE EVEN BETTER TIME RIDING THE WAVES!
RIGHTEOUS! RIDIN' THE BIG BLUE!
DORY'S WAY MAY BE DIFFERENT, DAD, BUT IT WORKS.
GUESS I'M CHOOSING "CHILLAXED" AFTER ALL.
WHEEE!
THE END!

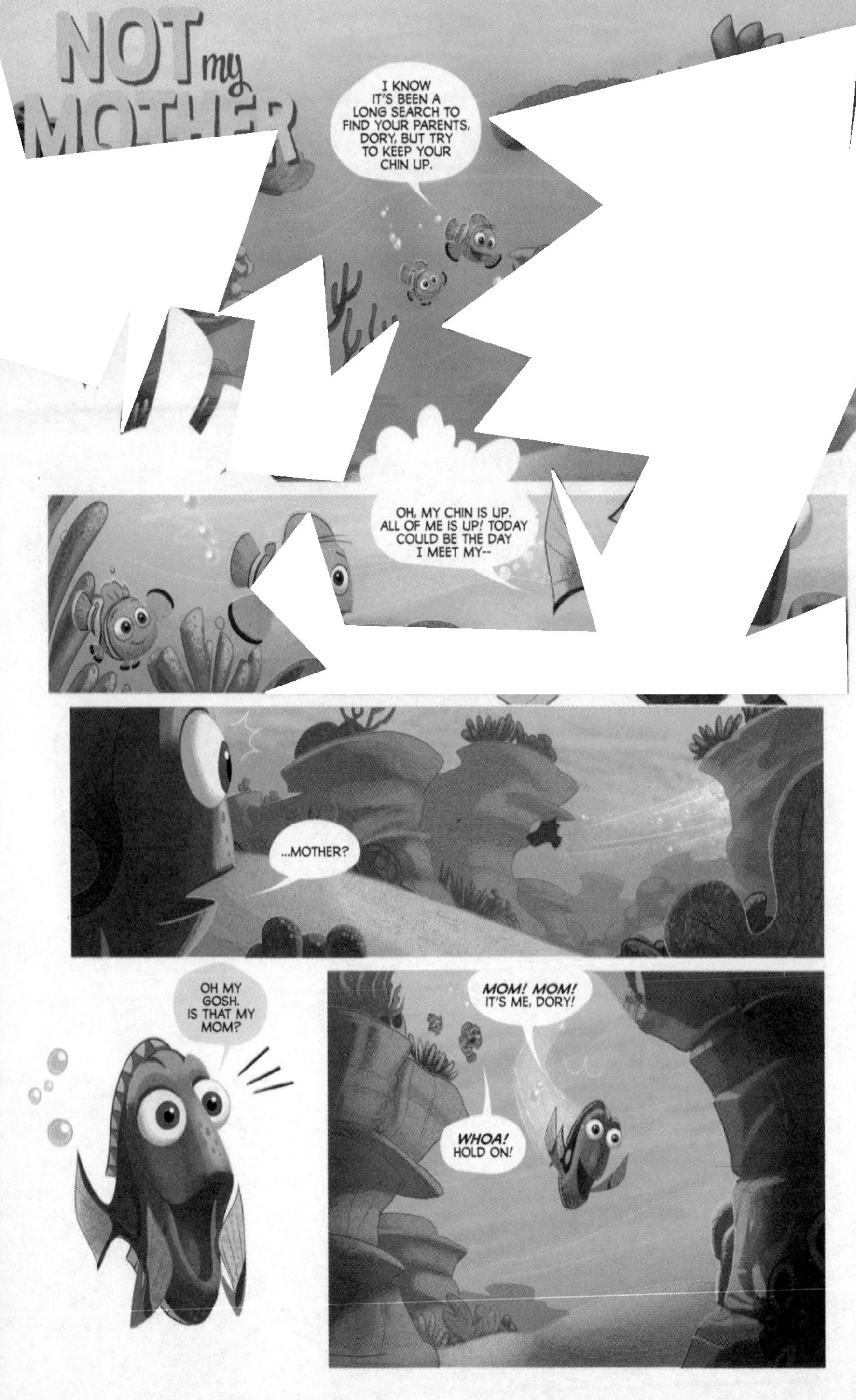
NOT my MOTHER
I KNOW IT'S BEEN A LONG SEARCH TO FIND YOUR PARENTS, DORY, BUT TRY TO KEEP YOUR CHIN UP.
OH, MY CHIN IS UP. ALL OF ME IS UP! TODAY COULD BE THE DAY I MEET MY--
...MOTHER?
OH MY GOSH. IS THAT MY MOM?
MOM! MOM! IT'S ME, DORY!
WHOA! HOLD ON!

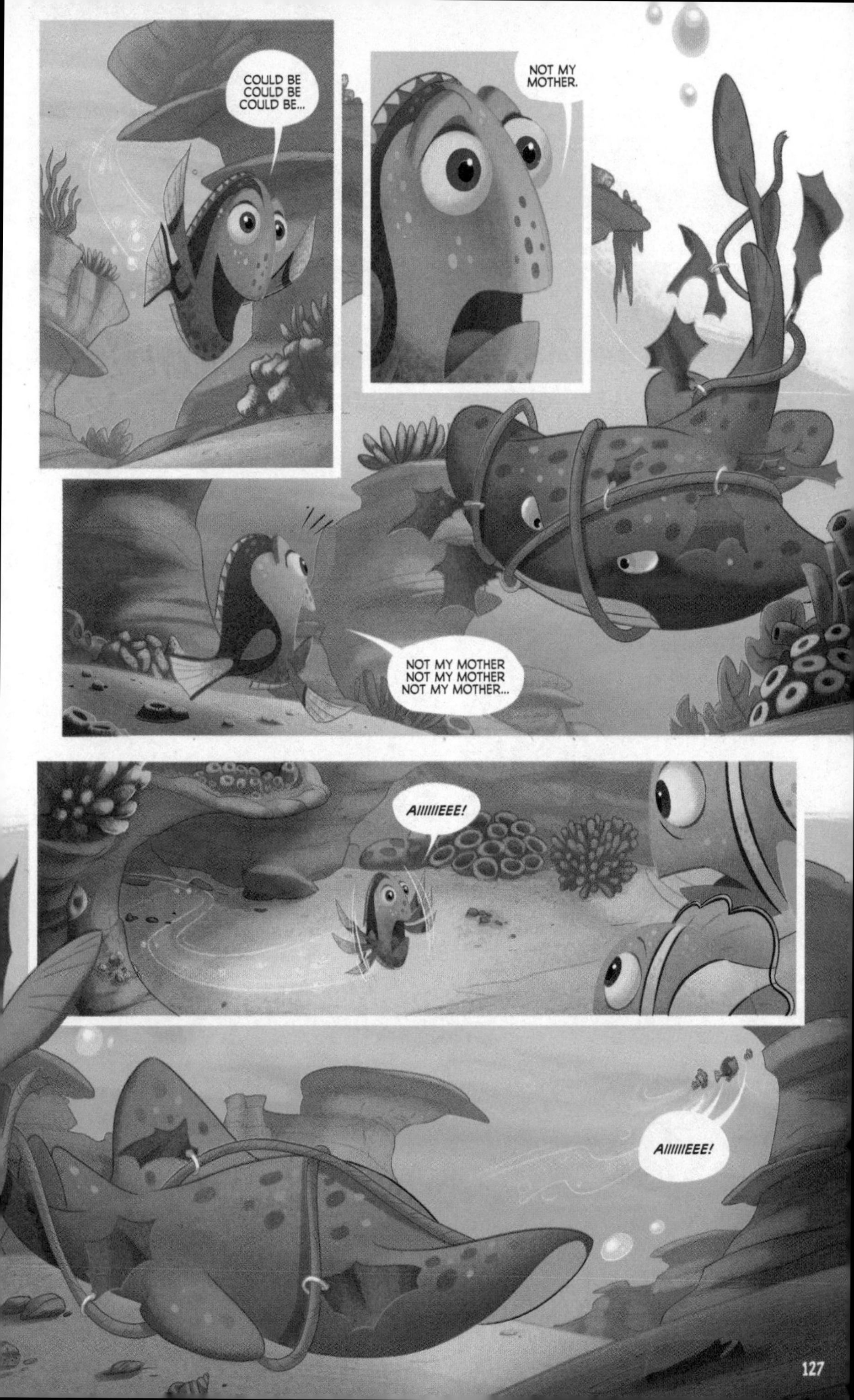
COULD BE
COULD BE
COULD BE...
NOT MY MOTHER.
NOT MY MOTHER NOT MY MOTHER NOT MY MOTHER...
AIIIIIEEE!
AIIIIIEEE!

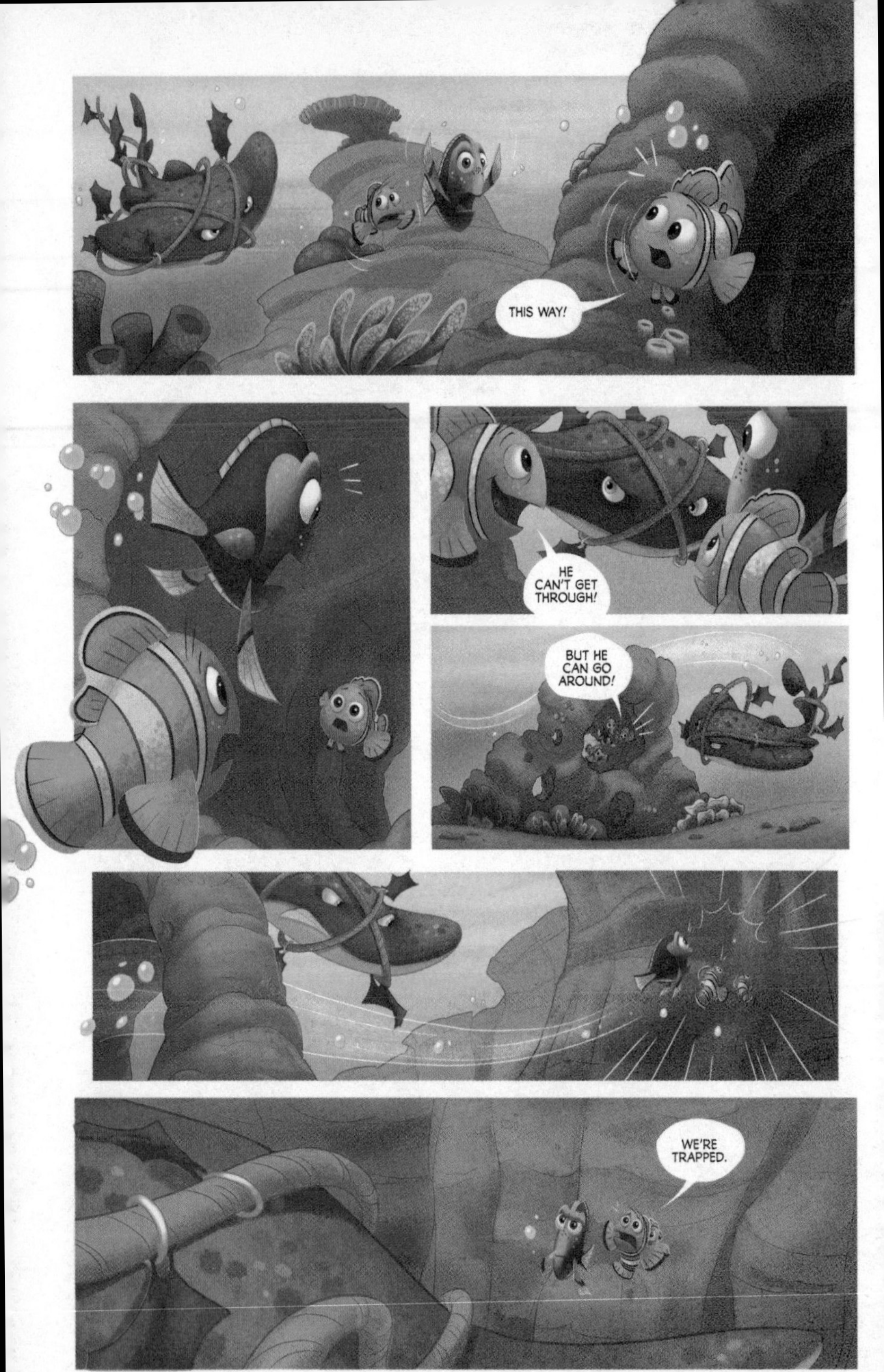
THIS WAY!
HE CAN'T GET THROUGH!
BUT HE CAN GO AROUND!
WE'RE TRAPPED.

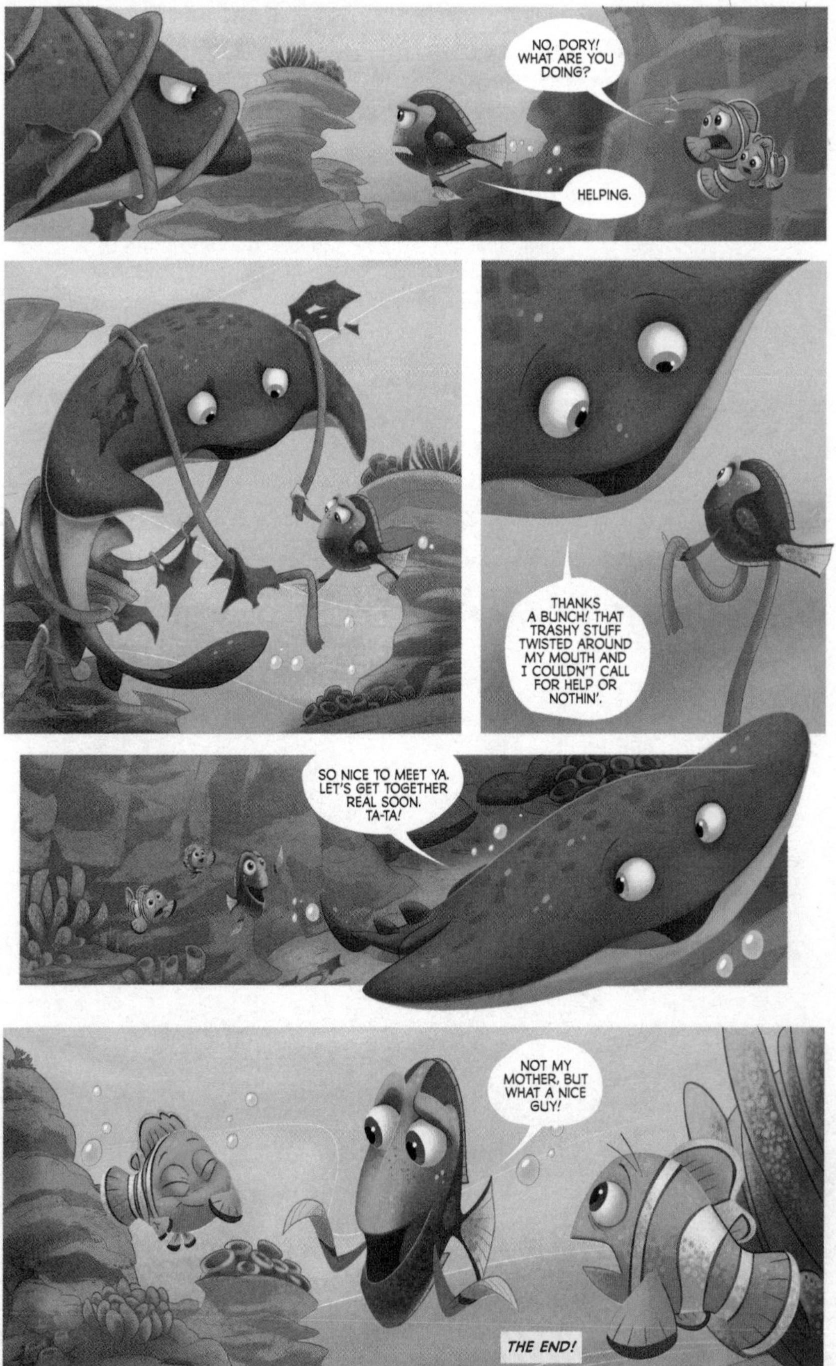
NO, DORY! WHAT ARE YOU DOING?
HELPING.
THANKS A BUNCH! THAT TRASHY STUFF TWISTED AROUND MY MOUTH AND I COULDN'T CALL FOR HELP OR NOTHIN'.
SO NICE TO MEET YA. LET'S GET TOGETHER REAL SOON. TA-TA!
NOT MY MOTHER, BUT WHAT A NICE GUY!
THE END!

One BiG FAMILY

Everyone loves Dory – she has friends and family all over the ocean!

BAILEY
Beluga whale Bailey's echolocation skills can really come in handy – if you can coax him into using them!

DESTINY
Dory's childhood "pipe pal," Destiny the whale shark, used to converse with Dory through the pipes at the MLI.

HANK
Cranky Hank is one sour cephalopod, but he has a real soft – make that squishy – spot for Dory.

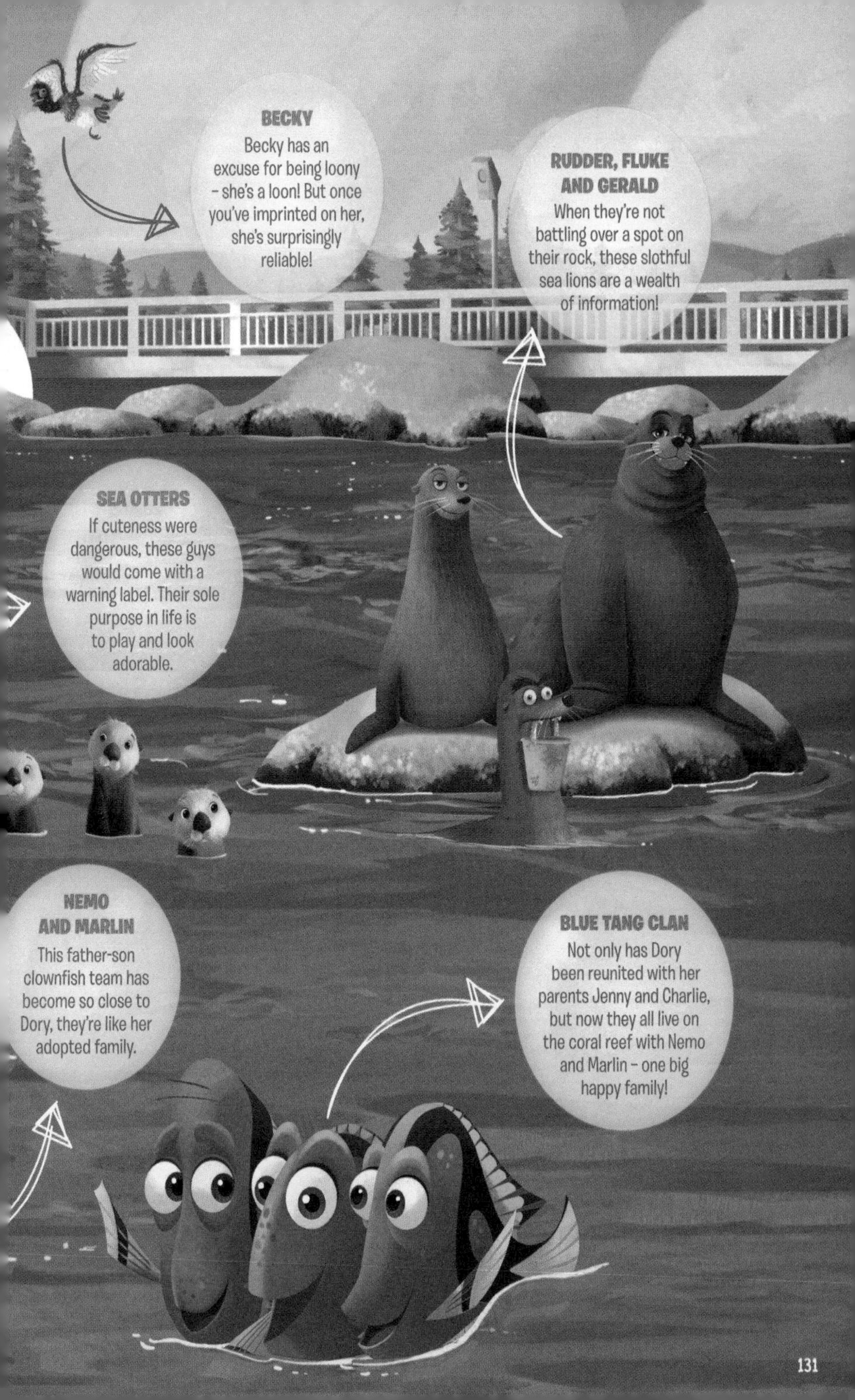

BECKY

Becky has an excuse for being loony – she's a loon! But once you've imprinted on her, she's surprisingly reliable!

RUDDER, FLUKE AND GERALD

When they're not battling over a spot on their rock, these slothful sea lions are a wealth of information!

SEA OTTERS

If cuteness were dangerous, these guys would come with a warning label. Their sole purpose in life is to play and look adorable.

NEMO AND MARLIN

This father-son clownfish team has become so close to Dory, they're like her adopted family.

BLUE TANG CLAN

Not only has Dory been reunited with her parents Jenny and Charlie, but now they all live on the coral reef with Nemo and Marlin – one big happy family!

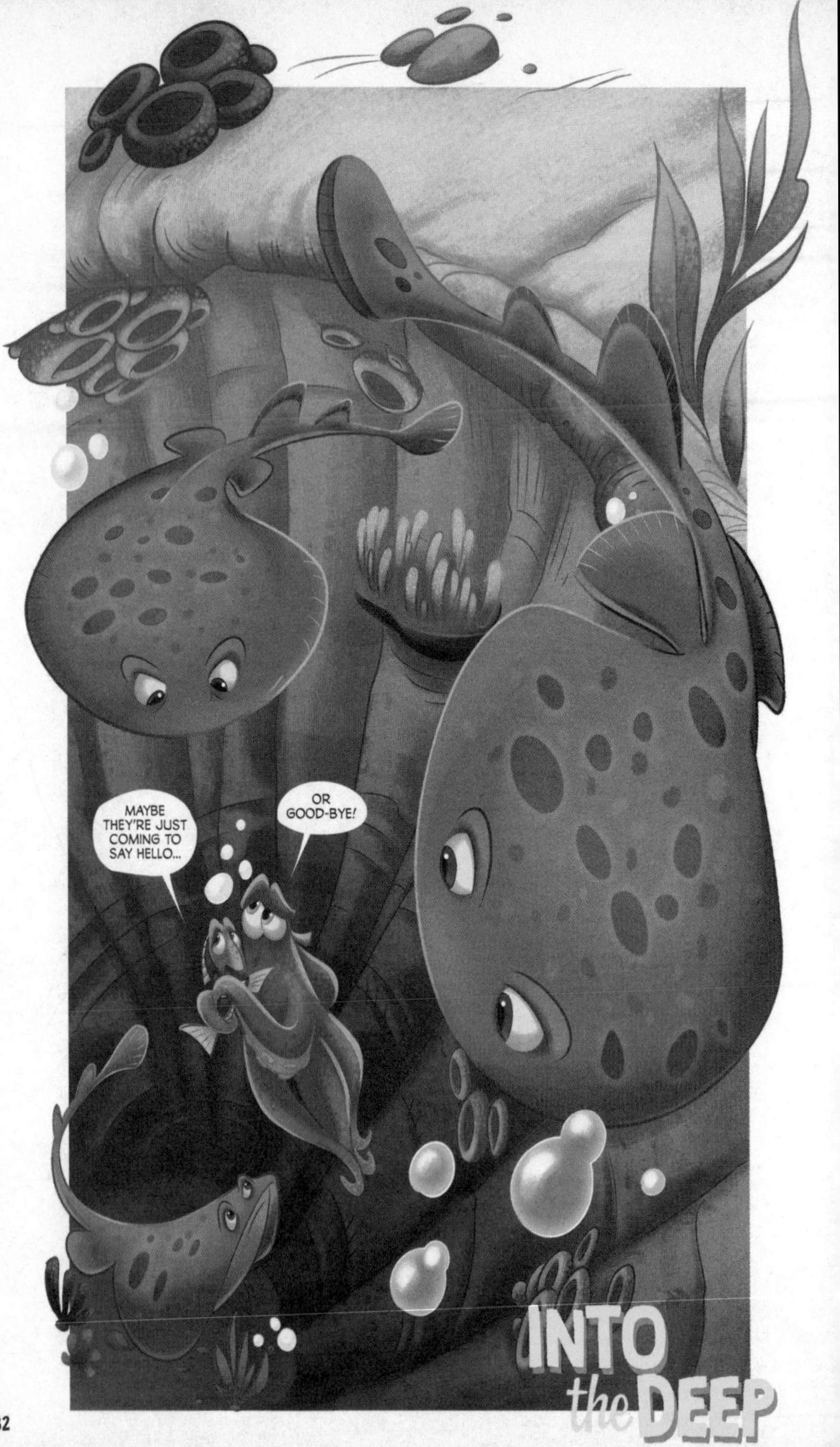
MAYBE THEY'RE JUST COMING TO SAY HELLO...
OR GOOD-BYE!
INTO the DEEP

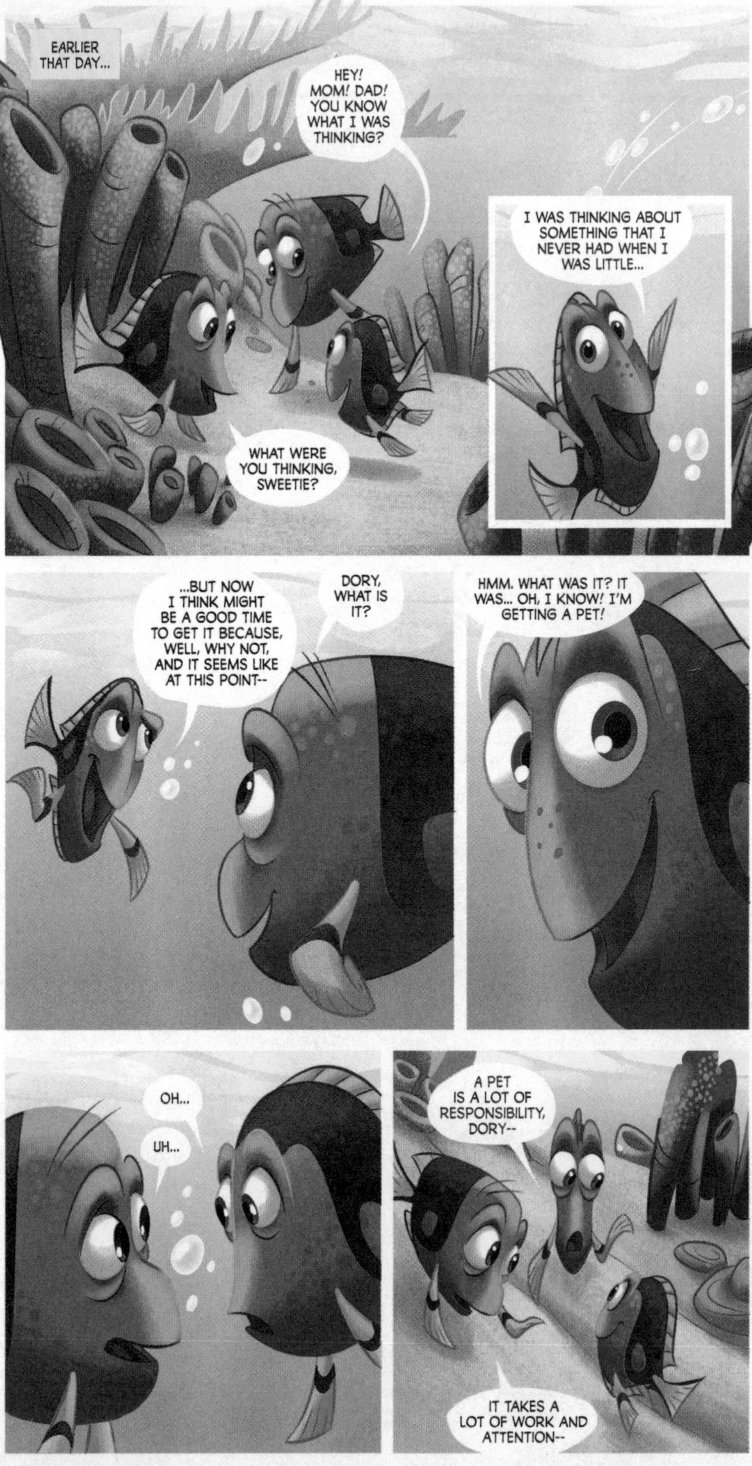
EARLIER THAT DAY...
HEY! MOM! DAD! YOU KNOW WHAT I WAS THINKING?
WHAT WERE YOU THINKING, SWEETIE?
I WAS THINKING ABOUT SOMETHING THAT I NEVER HAD WHEN I WAS LITTLE...
...BUT NOW I THINK MIGHT BE A GOOD TIME TO GET IT BECAUSE, WELL, WHY NOT, AND IT SEEMS LIKE AT THIS POINT--
DORY, WHAT IS IT?
HMM. WHAT WAS IT? IT WAS... OH, I KNOW! I'M GETTING A PET!
OH...
UH...
A PET IS A LOT OF RESPONSIBILITY, DORY--
IT TAKES A LOT OF WORK AND ATTENTION--

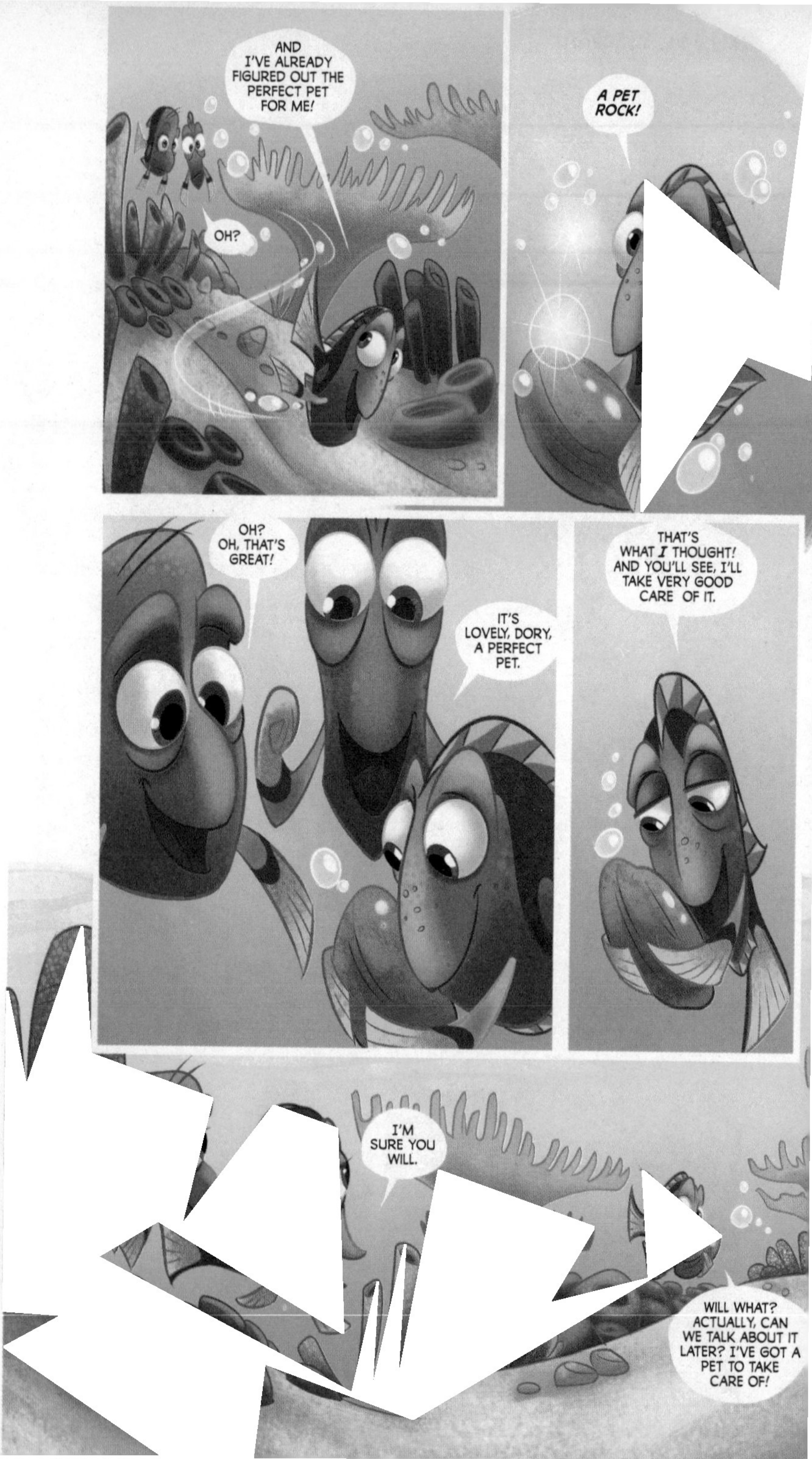
AND I'VE ALREADY FIGURED OUT THE PERFECT PET FOR ME!
OH?
A PET ROCK!
OH? OH, THAT'S GREAT!
IT'S LOVELY, DORY, A PERFECT PET.
THAT'S WHAT I THOUGHT! AND YOU'LL SEE, I'LL TAKE VERY GOOD CARE OF IT.
I'M SURE YOU WILL.
WILL WHAT? ACTUALLY, CAN WE TALK ABOUT IT LATER? I'VE GOT A PET TO TAKE CARE OF!

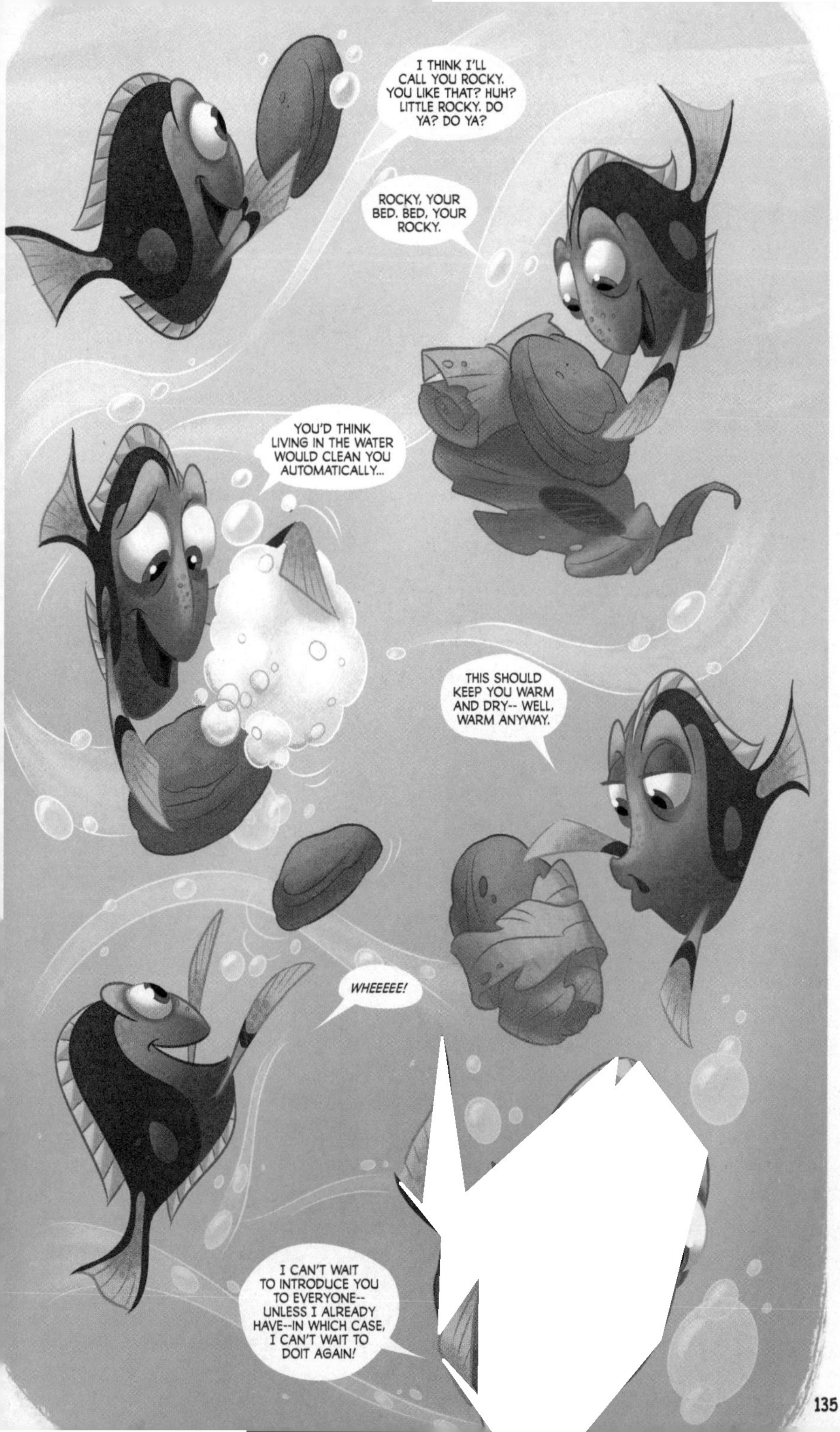
I THINK I'LL CALL YOU ROCKY. YOU LIKE THAT? HUH? LITTLE ROCKY. DO YA? DO YA?
ROCKY, YOUR BED. BED, YOUR ROCKY.
YOU'D THINK LIVING IN THE WATER WOULD CLEAN YOU AUTOMATICALLY...
THIS SHOULD KEEP YOU WARM AND DRY-- WELL, WARM ANYWAY.
WHEEEEE!
I CAN'T WAIT TO INTRODUCE YOU TO EVERYONE-- UNLESS I ALREADY HAVE--IN WHICH CASE, I CAN'T WAIT TO DOIT AGAIN!

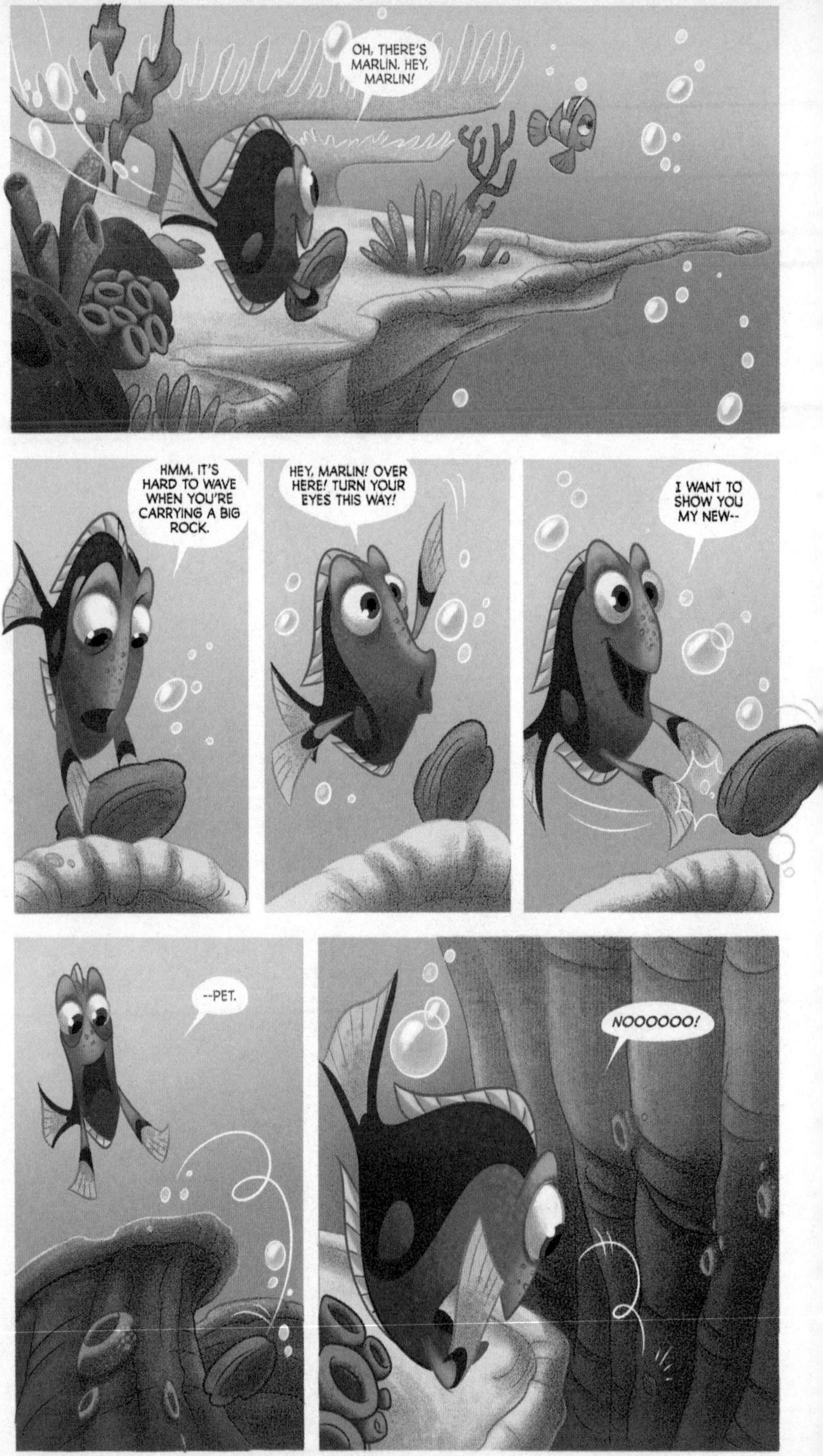
OH, THERE'S MARLIN. HEY, MARLIN!
HMM. IT'S HARD TO WAVE WHEN YOU'RE CARRYING A BIG ROCK.
HEY, MARLIN! OVER HERE! TURN YOUR EYES THIS WAY!
I WANT TO SHOW YOU MY NEW--
--PET.
NOOOOOO!

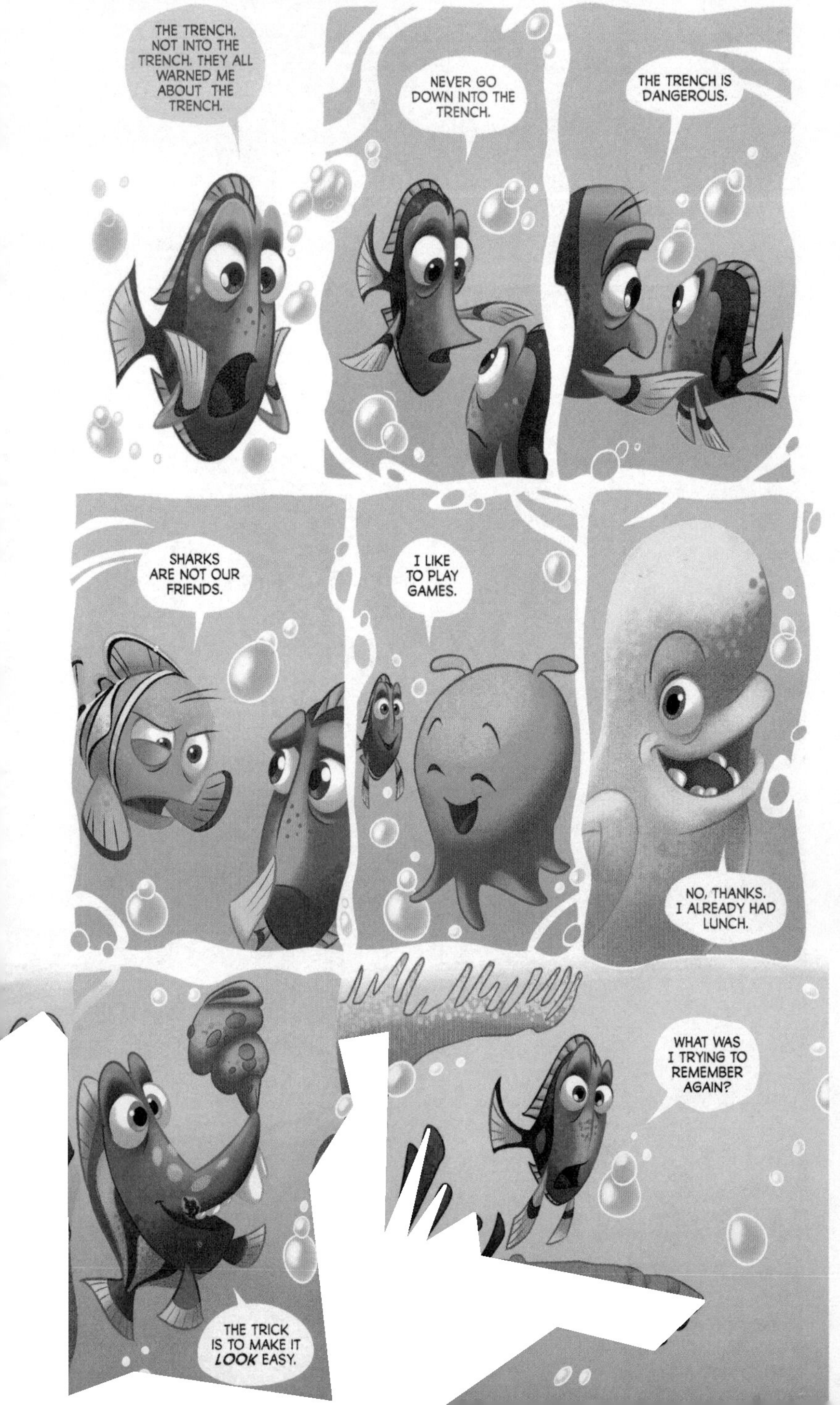
THE TRENCH. NOT INTO THE TRENCH. THEY ALL WARNED ME ABOUT THE TRENCH.
NEVER GO DOWN INTO THE TRENCH.
THE TRENCH IS DANGEROUS.
SHARKS ARE NOT OUR FRIENDS.
I LIKE TO PLAY GAMES.
NO, THANKS. I ALREADY HAD LUNCH.
THE TRICK IS TO MAKE IT *LOOK* EASY.
WHAT WAS I TRYING TO REMEMBER AGAIN?

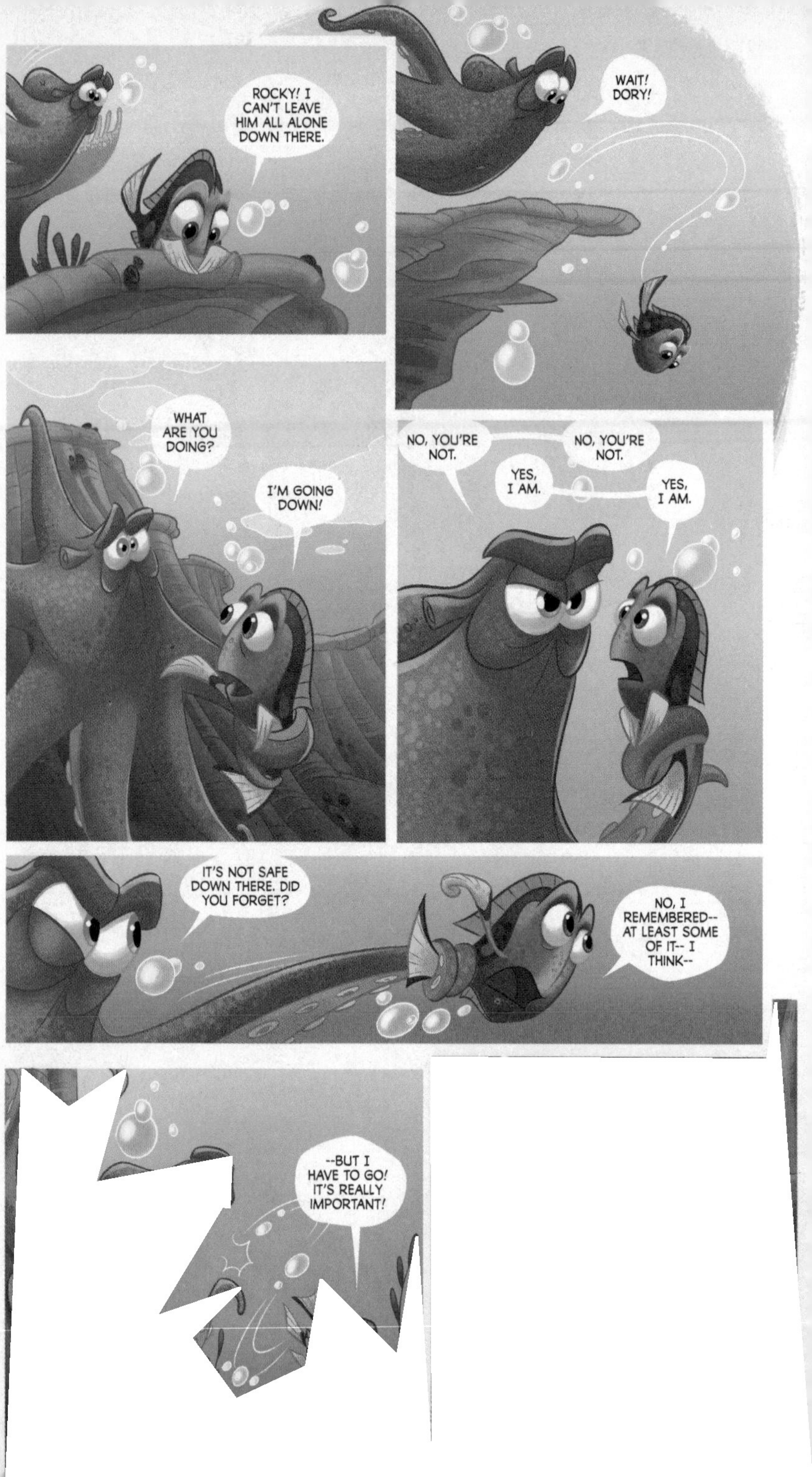
ROCKY! I CAN'T LEAVE HIM ALL ALONE DOWN THERE.
WAIT! DORY!
WHAT ARE YOU DOING?
I'M GOING DOWN!
NO, YOU'RE NOT.
YES, I AM.
NO, YOU'RE NOT.
YES, I AM.
IT'S NOT SAFE DOWN THERE. DID YOU FORGET?
NO, I REMEMBERED-- AT LEAST SOME OF IT-- I THINK--
--BUT I HAVE TO GO! IT'S REALLY IMPORTANT!

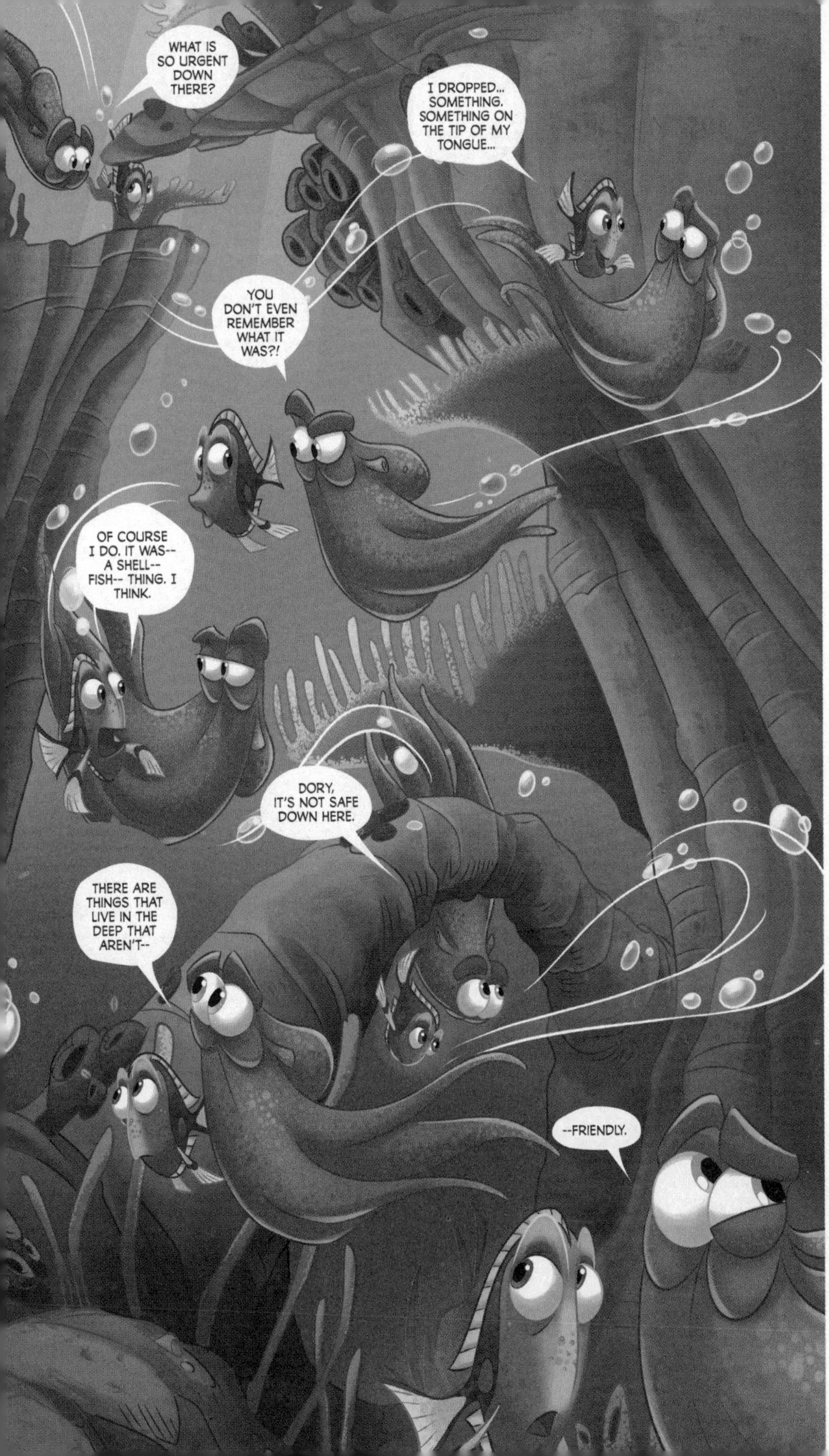
WHAT IS SO URGENT DOWN THERE?
I DROPPED... SOMETHING. SOMETHING ON THE TIP OF MY TONGUE...
YOU DON'T EVEN REMEMBER WHAT IT WAS?!
OF COURSE I DO. IT WAS-- A SHELL-- FISH-- THING. I THINK.
DORY, IT'S NOT SAFE DOWN HERE.
THERE ARE THINGS THAT LIVE IN THE DEEP THAT AREN'T--
--FRIENDLY.

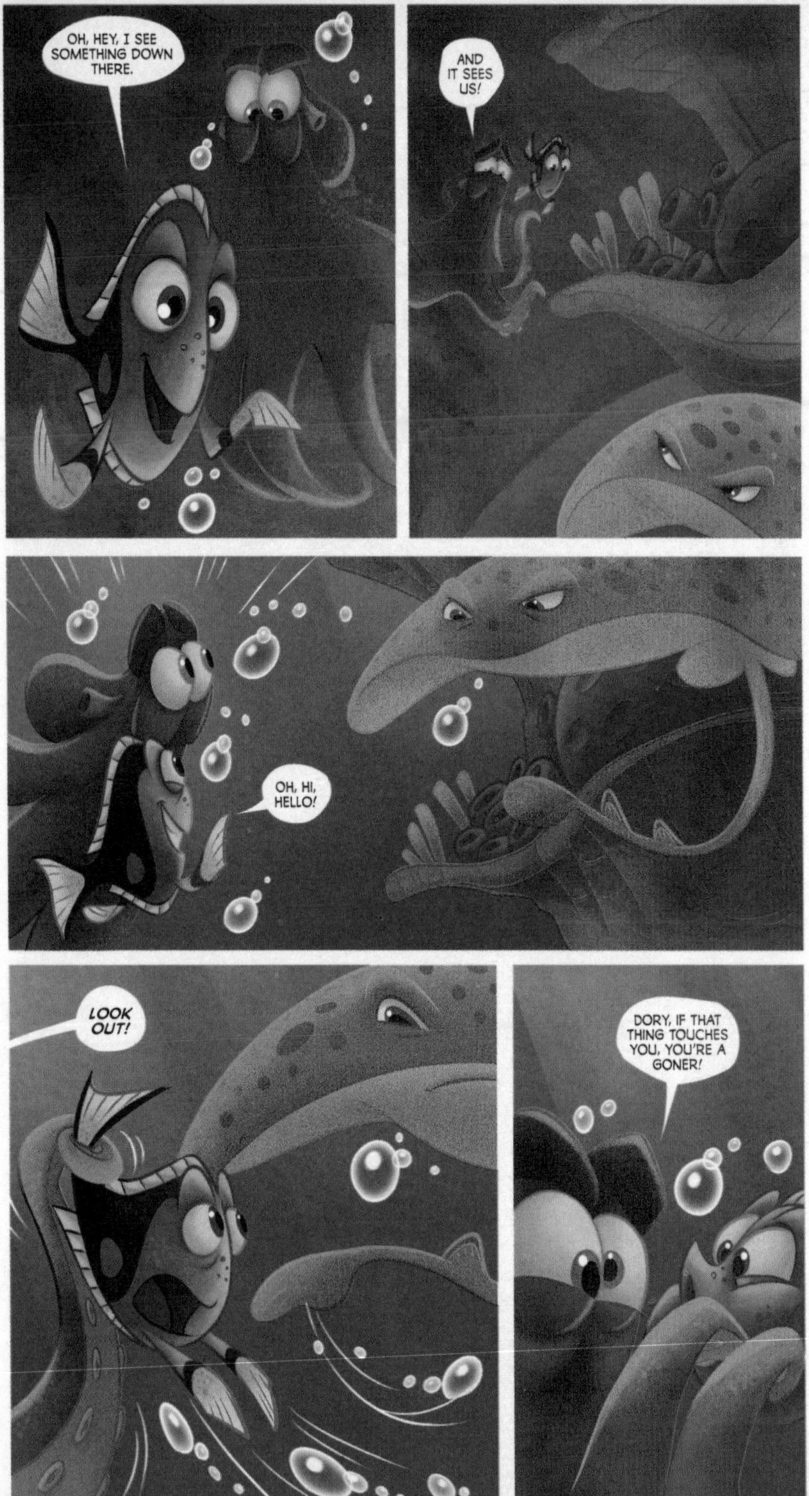
OH, HEY, I SEE SOMETHING DOWN THERE.
AND IT SEES US!
OH, HI, HELLO!
LOOK OUT!
DORY, IF THAT THING TOUCHES YOU, YOU'RE A GONER!

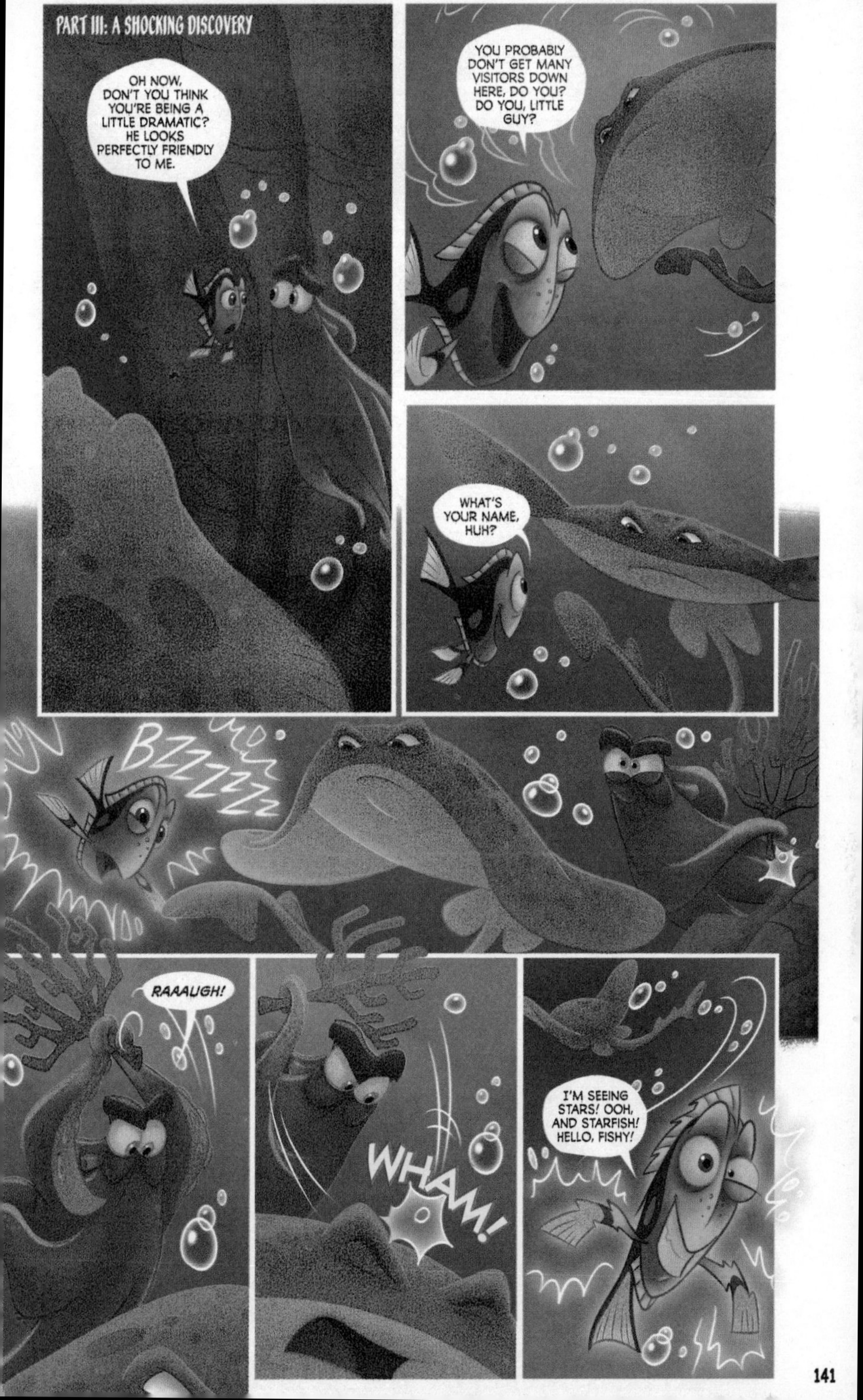
PART III: A SHOCKING DISCOVERY
OH NOW, DON'T YOU THINK YOU'RE BEING A LITTLE DRAMATIC? HE LOOKS PERFECTLY FRIENDLY TO ME.
YOU PROBABLY DON'T GET MANY VISITORS DOWN HERE, DO YOU? DO YOU, LITTLE GUY?
WHAT'S YOUR NAME, HUH?
BZZZZZZZ
RAAAUGH!
WHAM!
I'M SEEING STARS! OOH, AND STARFISH! HELLO, FISHY!

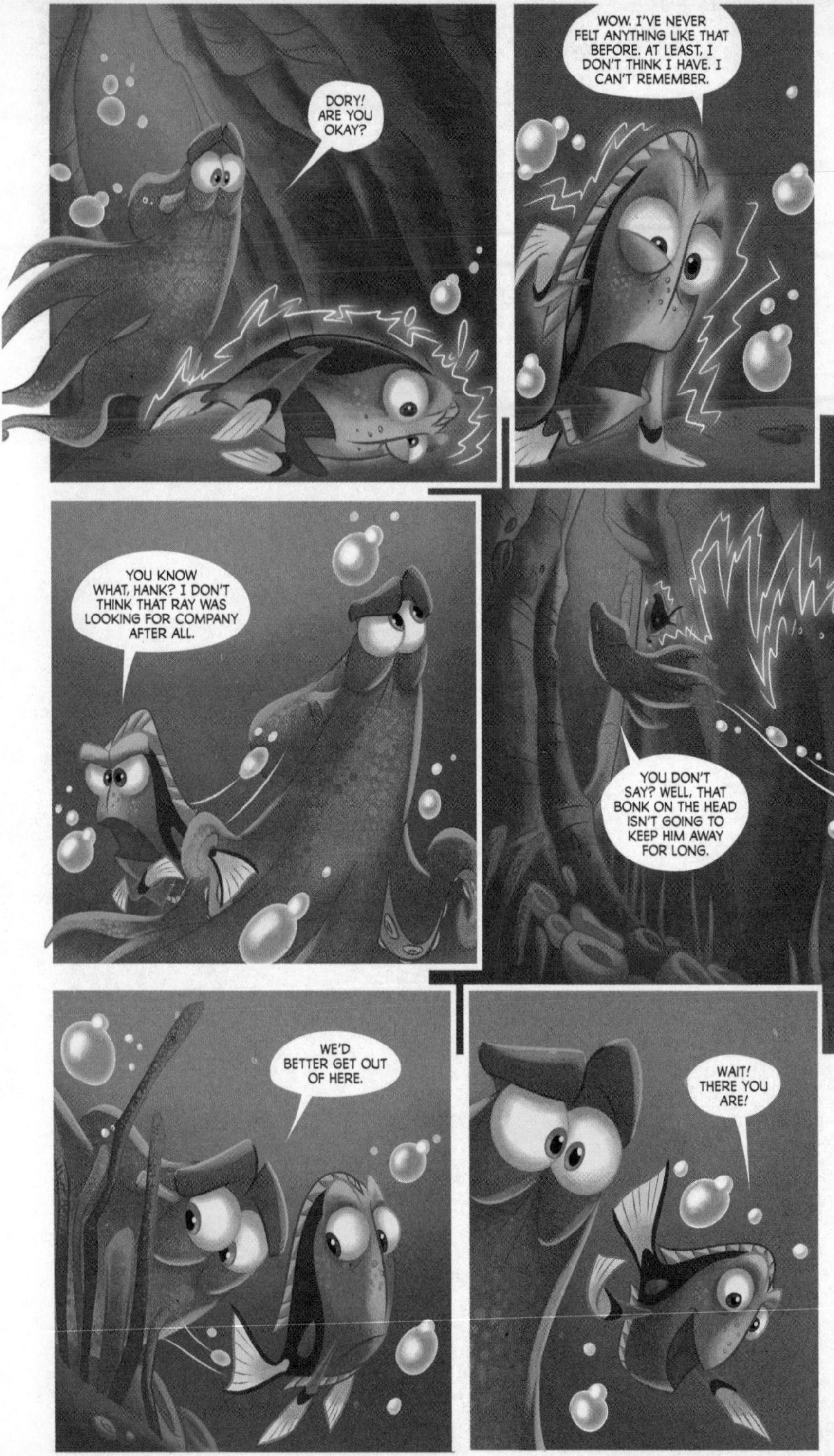
DORY! ARE YOU OKAY?
WOW. I'VE NEVER FELT ANYTHING LIKE THAT BEFORE. AT LEAST, I DON'T THINK I HAVE. I CAN'T REMEMBER.
YOU KNOW WHAT, HANK? I DON'T THINK THAT RAY WAS LOOKING FOR COMPANY AFTER ALL.
YOU DON'T SAY? WELL, THAT BONK ON THE HEAD ISN'T GOING TO KEEP HIM AWAY FOR LONG.
WE'D BETTER GET OUT OF HERE.
WAIT! THERE YOU ARE!

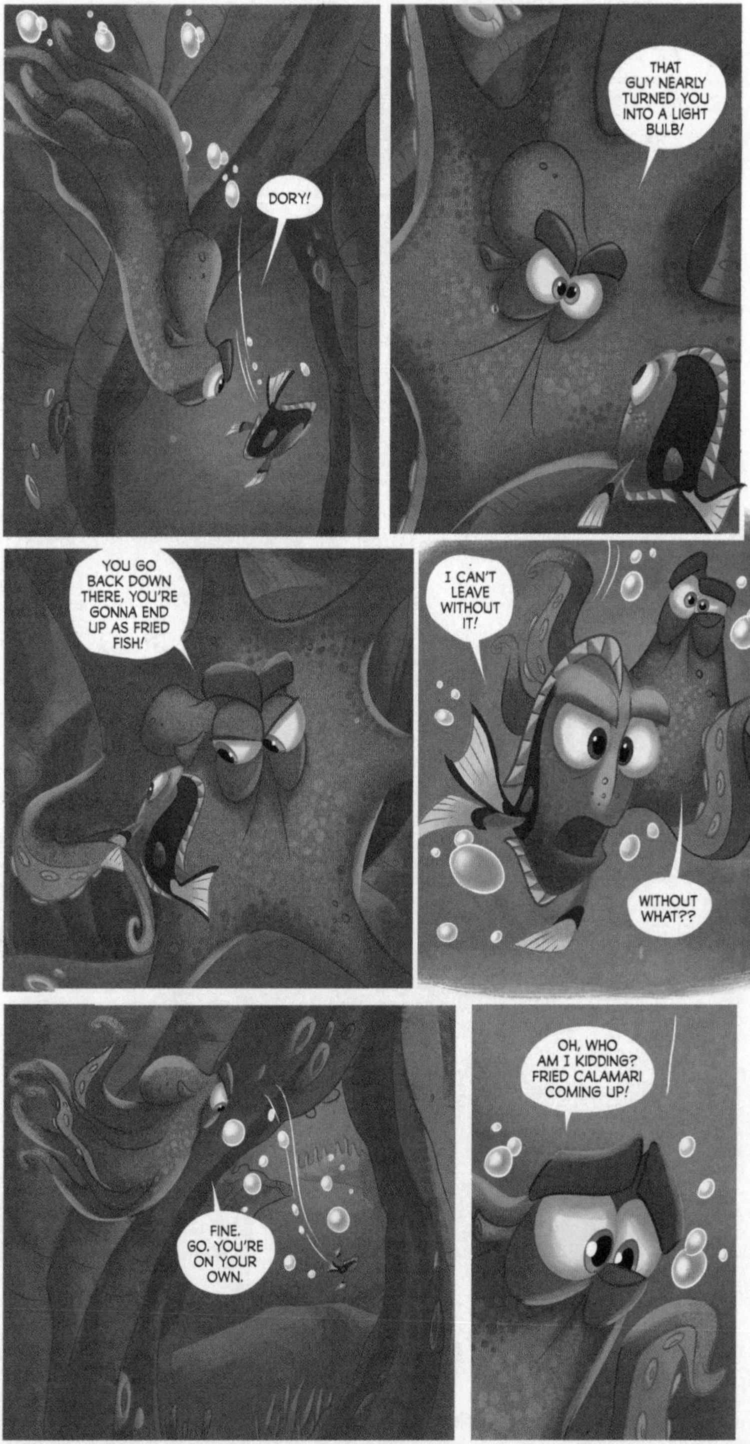
DORY!
THAT GUY NEARLY TURNED YOU INTO A LIGHT BULB!
YOU GO BACK DOWN THERE, YOU'RE GONNA END UP AS FRIED FISH!
I CAN'T LEAVE WITHOUT IT!
WITHOUT WHAT??
FINE. GO. YOU'RE ON YOUR OWN.
OH, WHO AM I KIDDING? FRIED CALAMARI COMING UP!

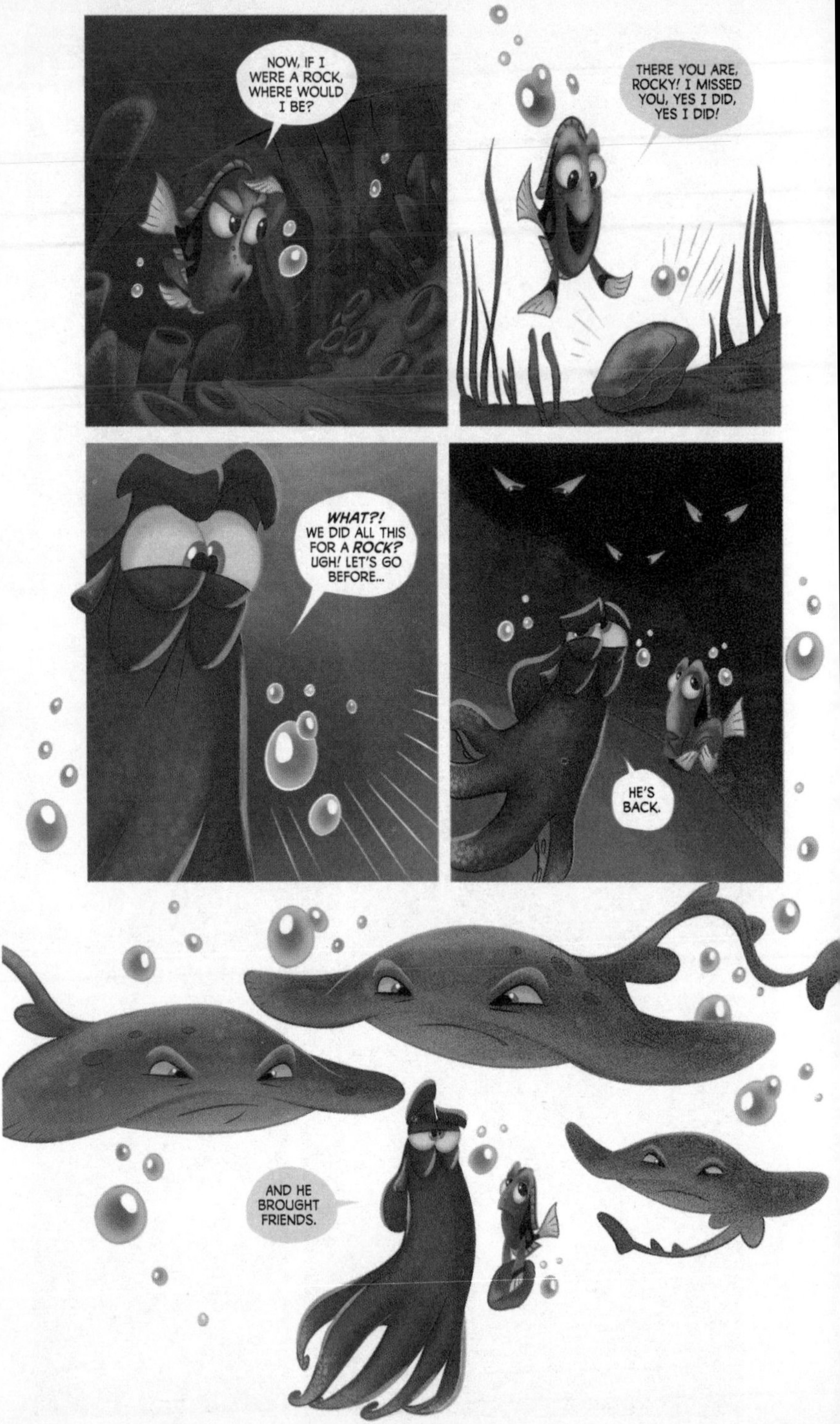
NOW, IF I WERE A ROCK, WHERE WOULD I BE?
THERE YOU ARE, ROCKY! I MISSED YOU, YES I DID, YES I DID!
WHAT?! WE DID ALL THIS FOR A ROCK? UGH! LET'S GO BEFORE...
HE'S BACK.
AND HE BROUGHT FRIENDS.

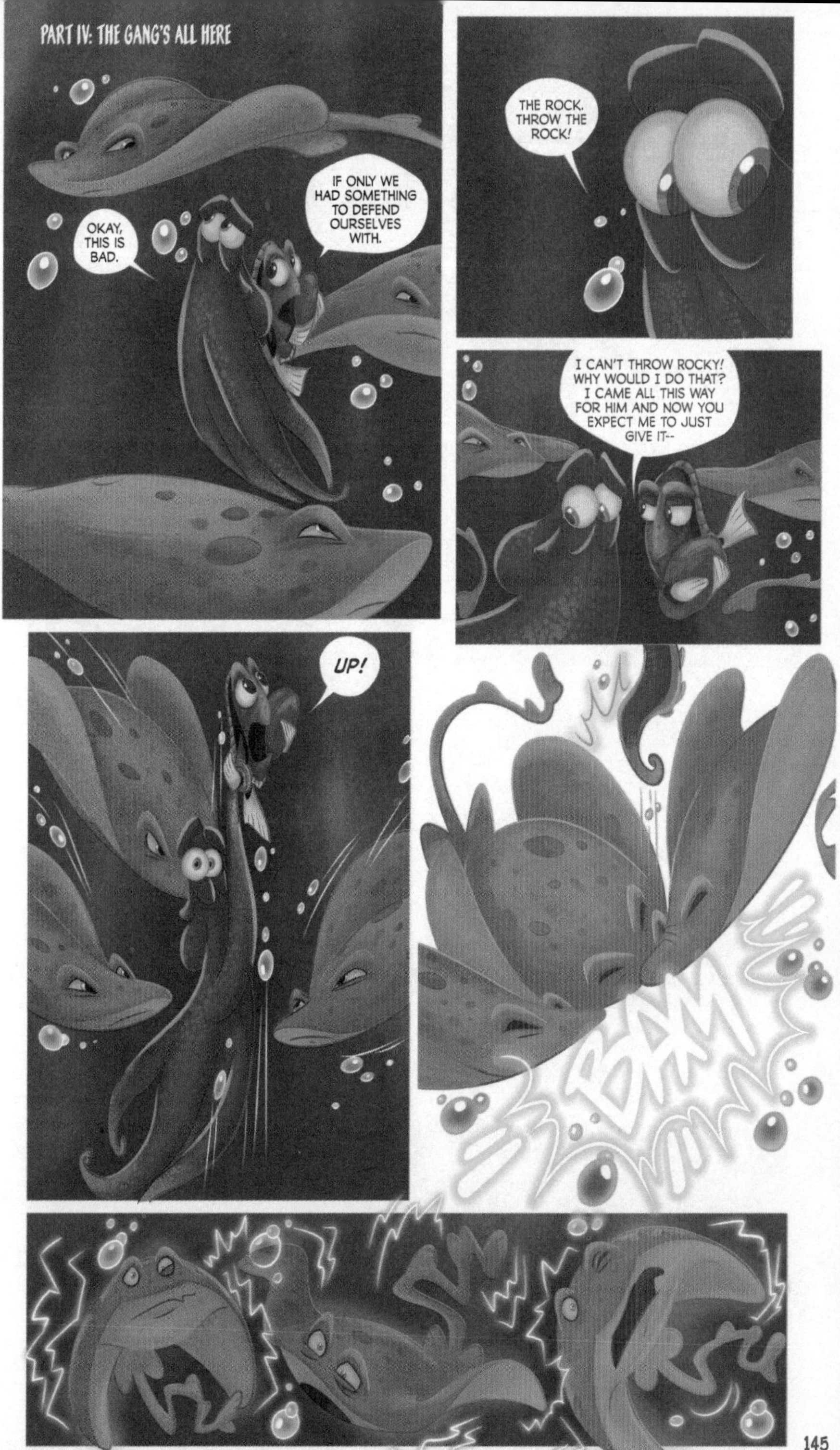
OKAY, THIS IS BAD.
IF ONLY WE HAD SOMETHING TO DEFEND OURSELVES WITH.
THE ROCK. THROW THE ROCK!
I CAN'T THROW ROCKY! WHY WOULD I DO THAT? I CAME ALL THIS WAY FOR HIM AND NOW YOU EXPECT ME TO JUST GIVE IT--
UP!
BAM

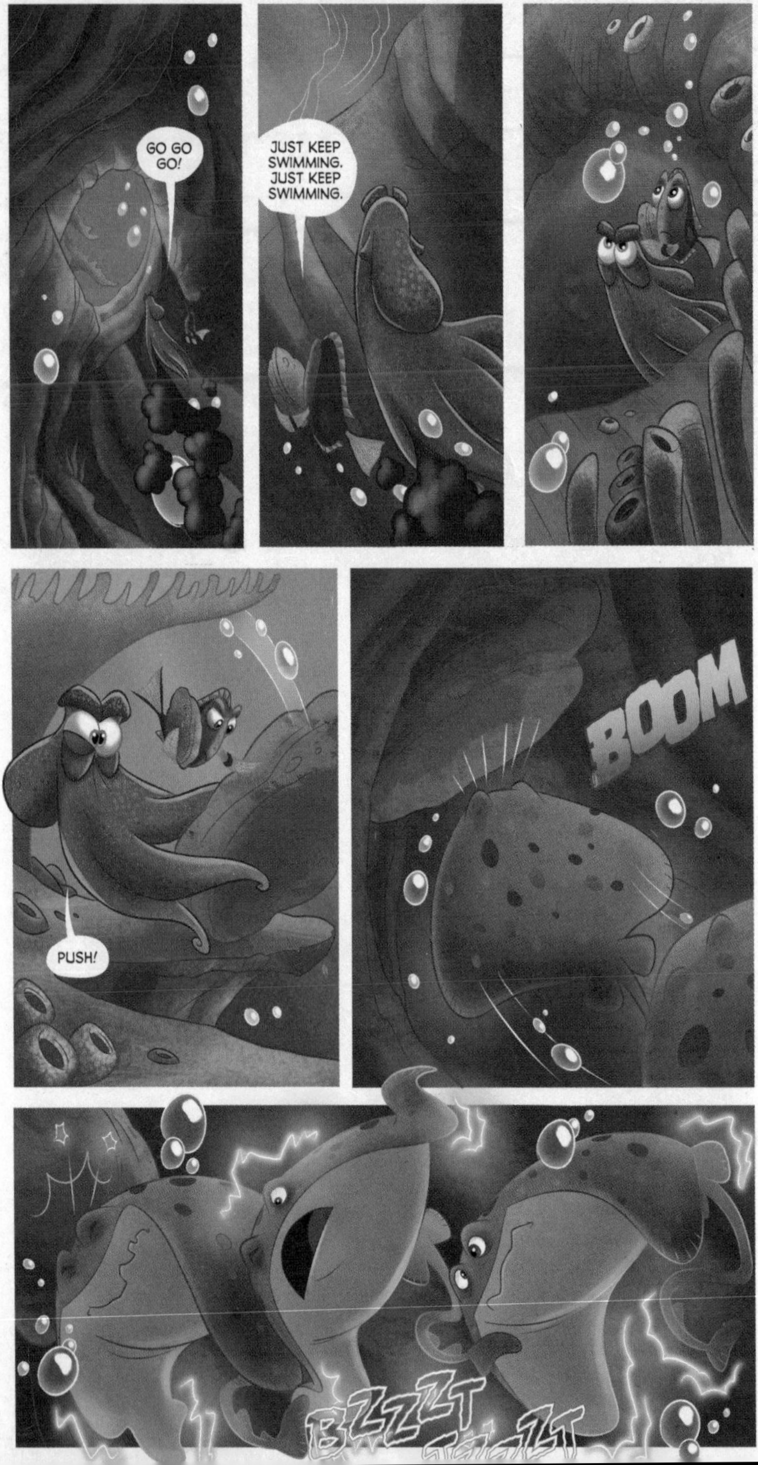
GO GO GO!
JUST KEEP SWIMMING. JUST KEEP SWIMMING.
PUSH!
BOOM
BZZZT

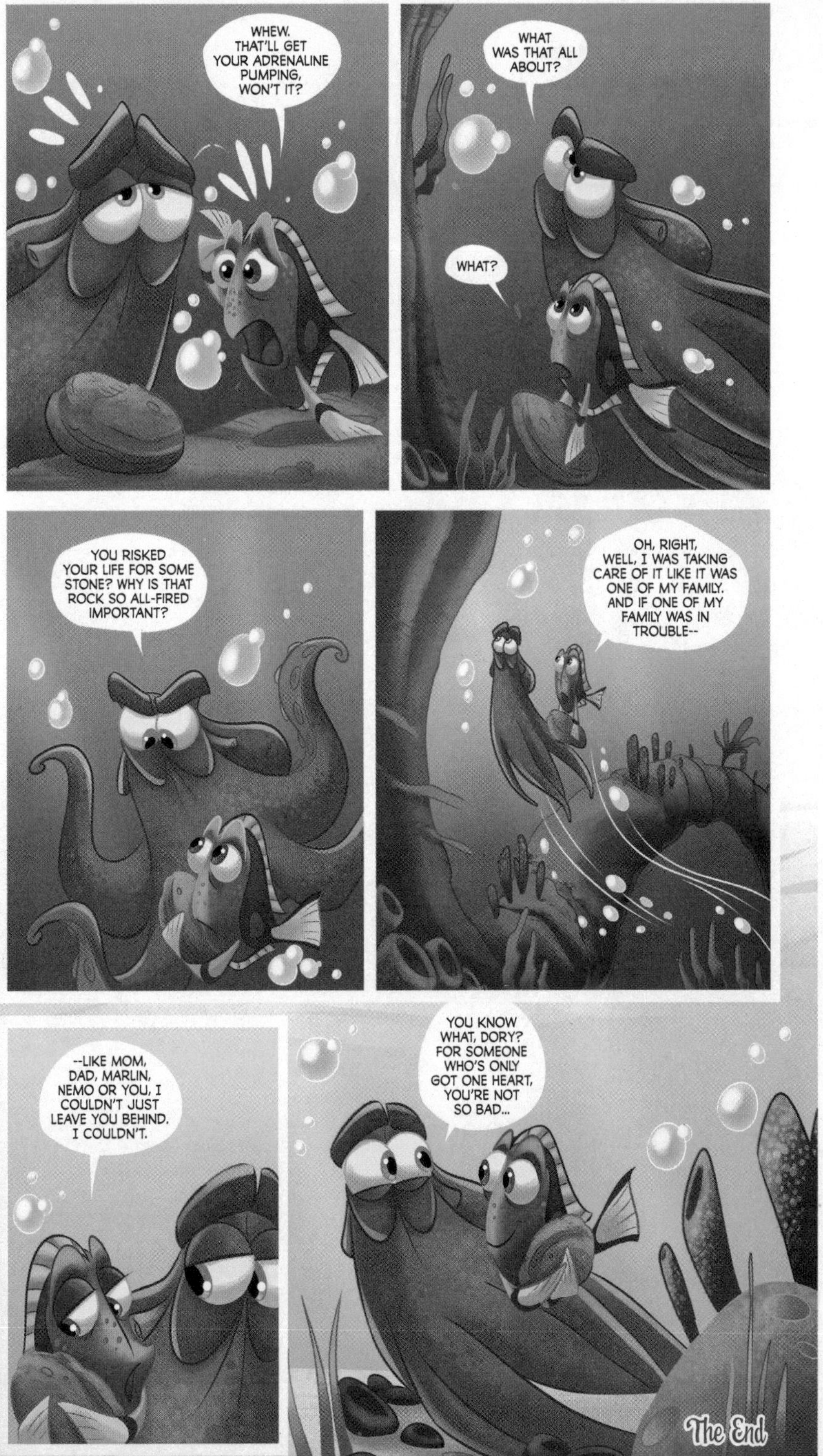
WHEW. THAT'LL GET YOUR ADRENALINE PUMPING, WON'T IT?
WHAT WAS THAT ALL ABOUT?
WHAT?
YOU RISKED YOUR LIFE FOR SOME STONE? WHY IS THAT ROCK SO ALL-FIRED IMPORTANT?
OH, RIGHT, WELL, I WAS TAKING CARE OF IT LIKE IT WAS ONE OF MY FAMILY. AND IF ONE OF MY FAMILY WAS IN TROUBLE--
--LIKE MOM, DAD, MARLIN, NEMO OR YOU, I COULDN'T JUST LEAVE YOU BEHIND. I COULDN'T.
YOU KNOW WHAT, DORY? FOR SOMEONE WHO'S ONLY GOT ONE HEART, YOU'RE NOT SO BAD...
The End

THINK TANK

Dear DORY

Dory learned a lot during her adventure, and now she's full of good advice!

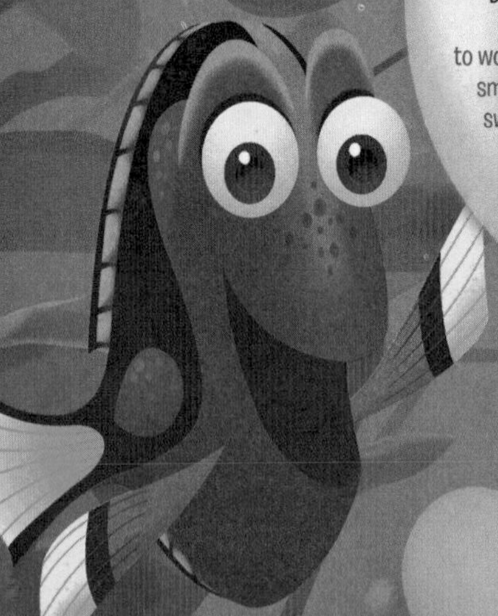

DEAR DORY:

I would like to play basketball, but everyone says I'm too small. What do you think?

Justa Minnow

Dear Justa: Being small doesn't mean you can't play, it just means you might have to work harder. My friend Nemo has one fin that's smaller than everyone else's but he's a great swimmer. And my short-term memory loss makes doing some things harder, but I don't quit, I keep trying. So don't give up – just keep swimming...or, err, dribbling!

DEAR DORY:

I just started at a new school, and I've tried and tried, but I can't seem to make any new friends. You have lots of friends – do you have any advice?

Friendly Finley

Dear Fin: Boy, I know how important friends are! I could never have made it across the ocean to find my parents without help from all my best buddies. When I meet someone, I introduce myself and just try to "go with the flow," and see where it leads. I don't go in with a big major plan or anything. Of course, I try to be as helpful as possible, and everyone seems to appreciate that. So if you see someone who might need help, just introduce yourself and offer to lend a hand...or fin! And if that doesn't work, keep trying...there's always another way!

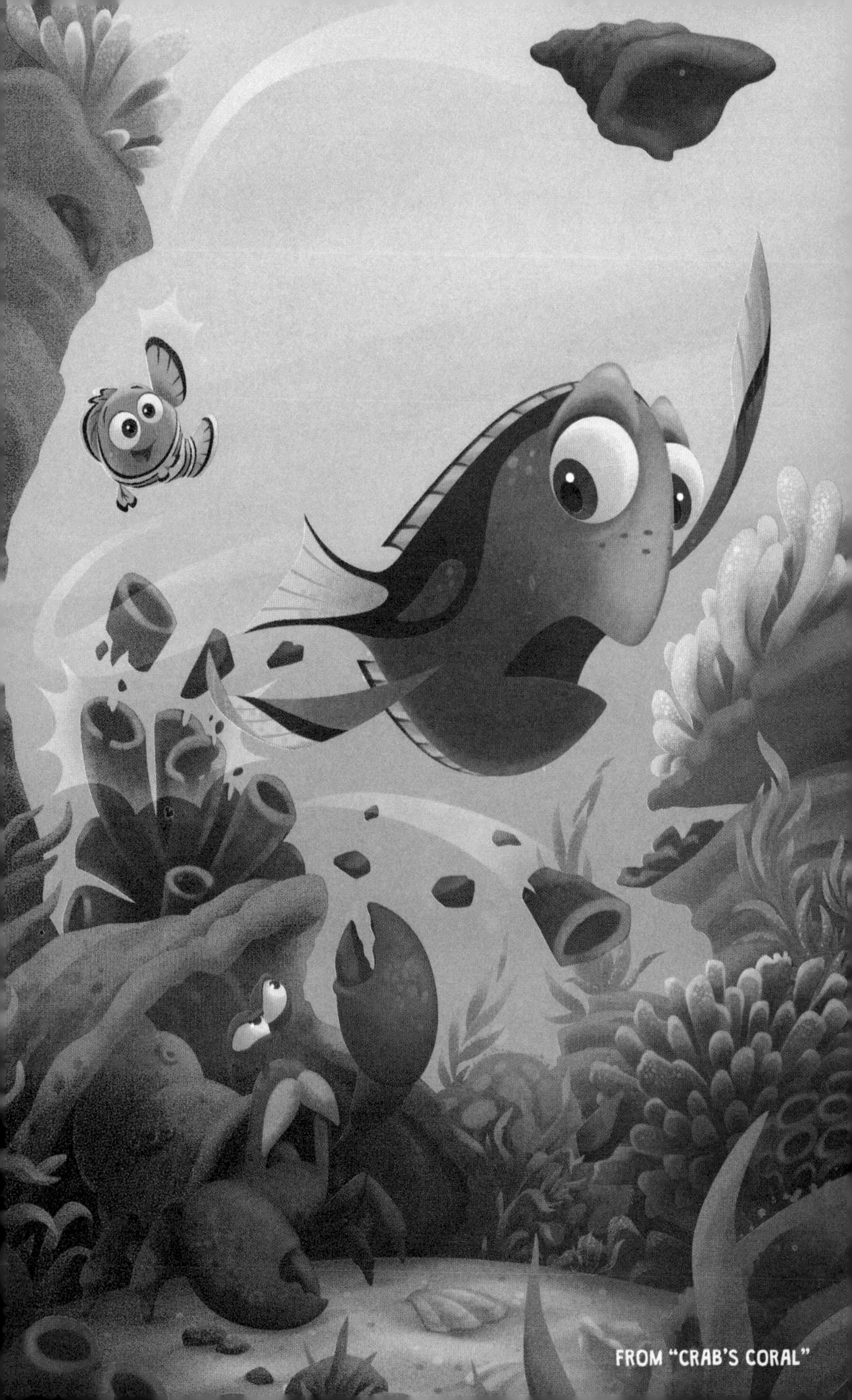

FROM "CRAB'S CORAL"

CRAB'S CORAL

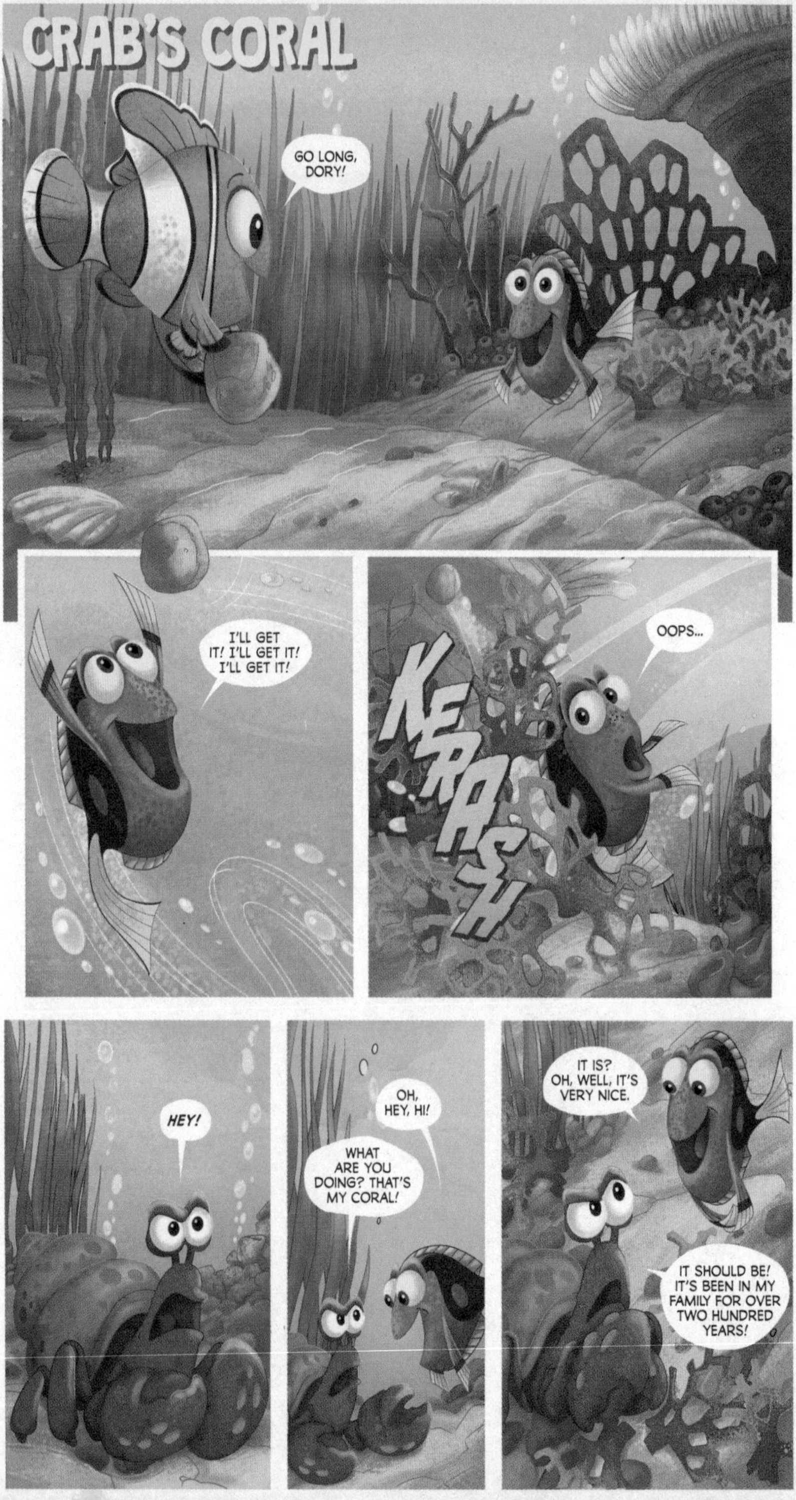
GO LONG, DORY!
I'LL GET IT! I'LL GET IT! I'LL GET IT!
KERASH
OOPS...
HEY!
OH, HEY, HI!
WHAT ARE YOU DOING? THAT'S MY CORAL!
IT IS? OH, WELL, IT'S VERY NICE.
IT SHOULD BE! IT'S BEEN IN MY FAMILY FOR OVER TWO HUNDRED YEARS!

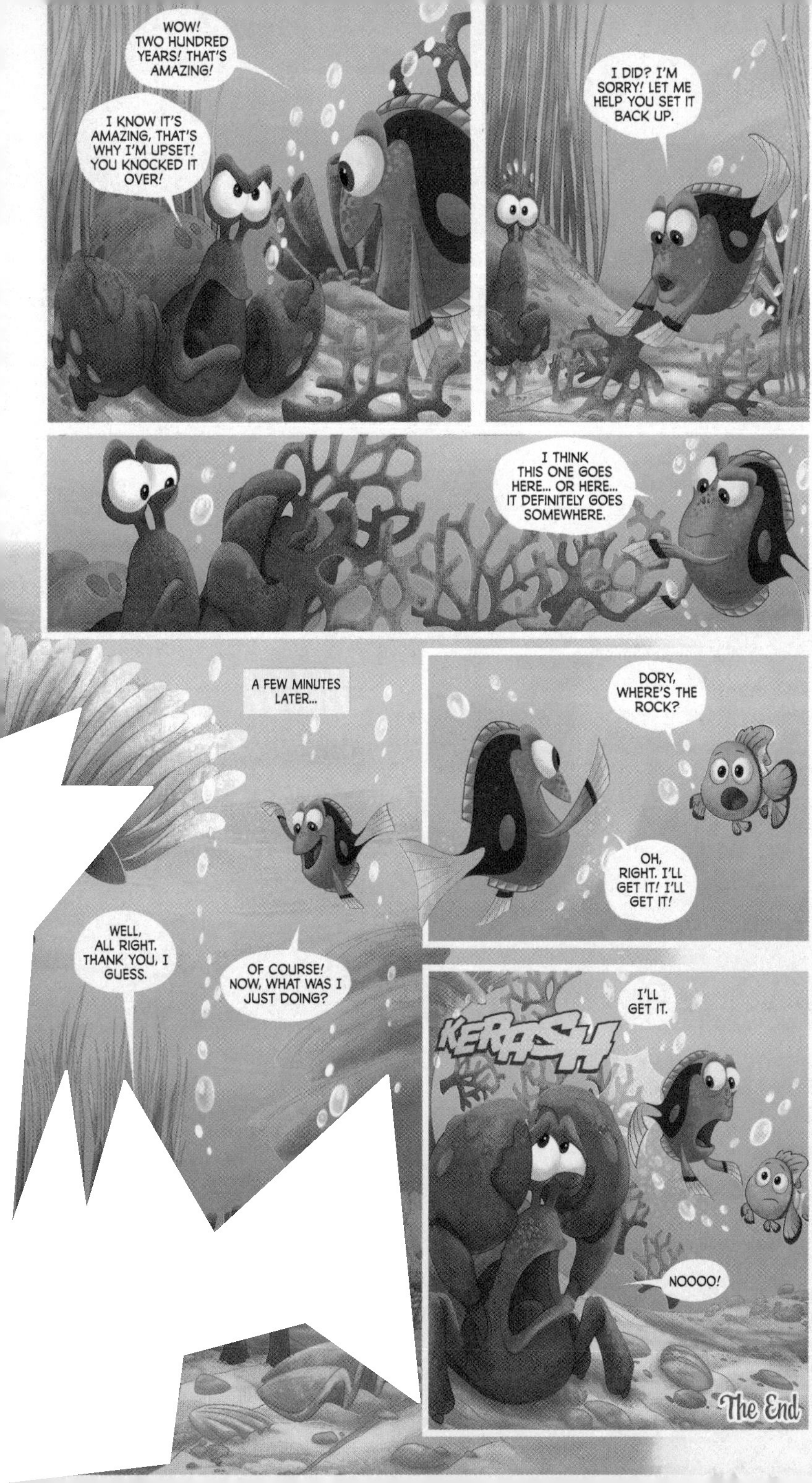
WOW! TWO HUNDRED YEARS! THAT'S AMAZING!
I KNOW IT'S AMAZING, THAT'S WHY I'M UPSET! YOU KNOCKED IT OVER!
I DID? I'M SORRY! LET ME HELP YOU SET IT BACK UP.
I THINK THIS ONE GOES HERE... OR HERE... IT DEFINITELY GOES SOMEWHERE.
A FEW MINUTES LATER...
WELL, ALL RIGHT. THANK YOU, I GUESS.
OF COURSE! NOW, WHAT WAS I JUST DOING?
DORY, WHERE'S THE ROCK?
OH, RIGHT. I'LL GET IT! I'LL GET IT!
I'LL GET IT.
KERASH
NOOOO!
The End

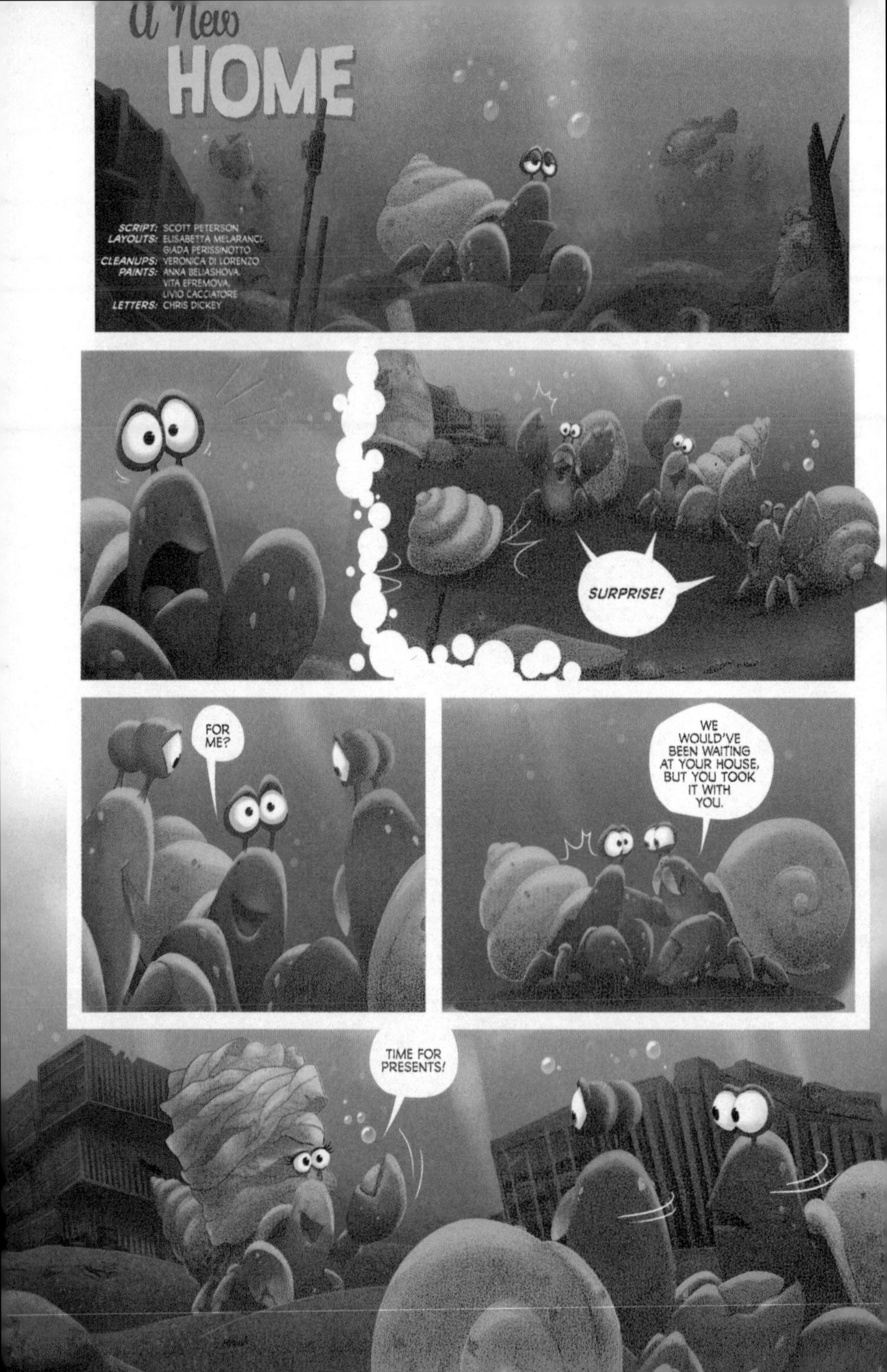
A New HOME
SCRIPT: SCOTT PETERSON
LAYOUTS: ELISABETTA MELARANCI, GIADA PERISSINOTTO
CLEANUPS: VERONICA DI LORENZO
PAINTS: ANNA BELIASHOVA, VITA EFREMOVA, LIVIO CACCIATORE
LETTERS: CHRIS DICKEY
SURPRISE!
FOR ME?
WE WOULD'VE BEEN WAITING AT YOUR HOUSE, BUT YOU TOOK IT WITH YOU.
TIME FOR PRESENTS!

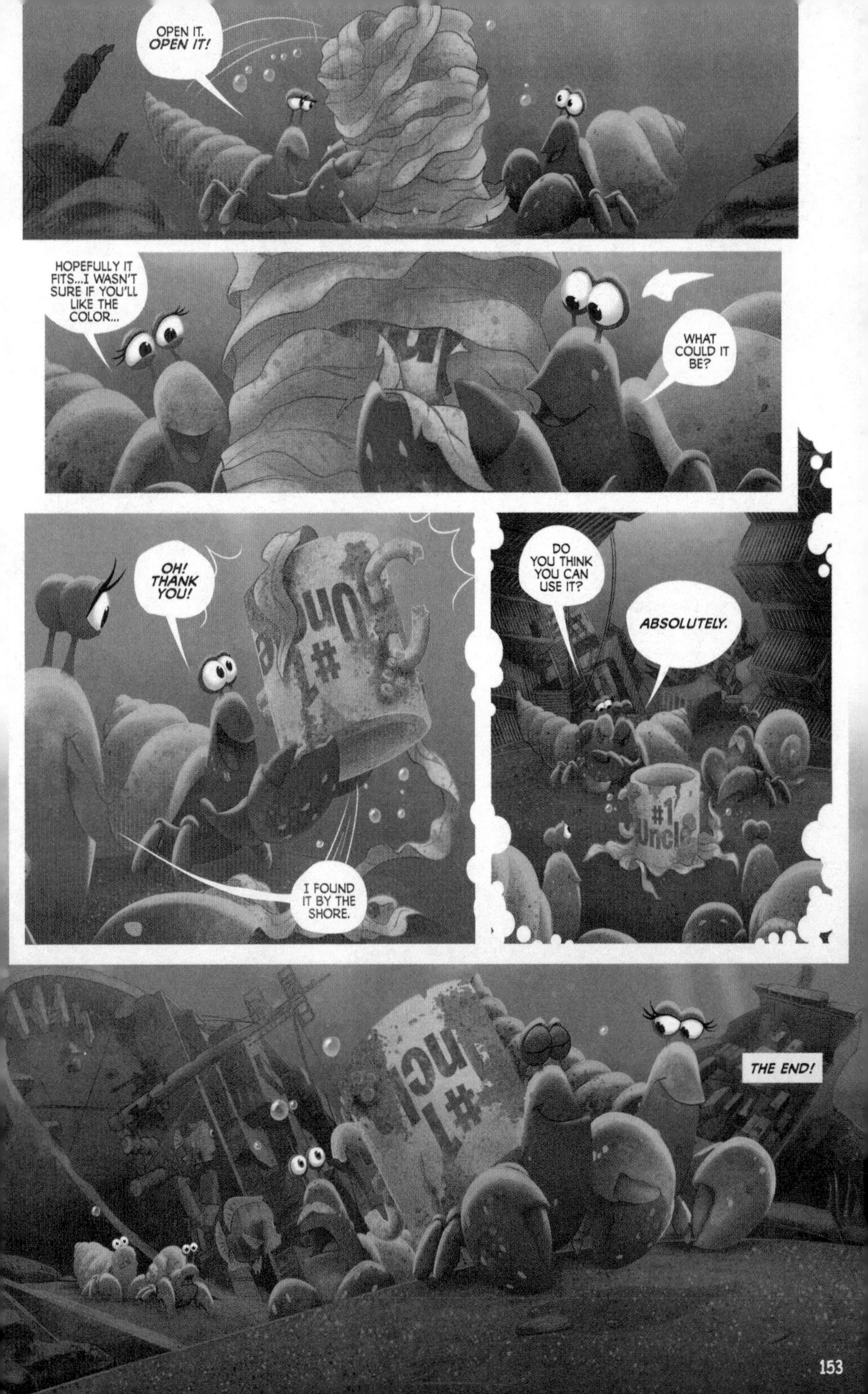
OPEN IT. OPEN IT!
HOPEFULLY IT FITS...I WASN'T SURE IF YOU'LL LIKE THE COLOR...
WHAT COULD IT BE?
OH! THANK YOU!
I FOUND IT BY THE SHORE.
DO YOU THINK YOU CAN USE IT?
ABSOLUTELY.
#1 Uncle
THE END!

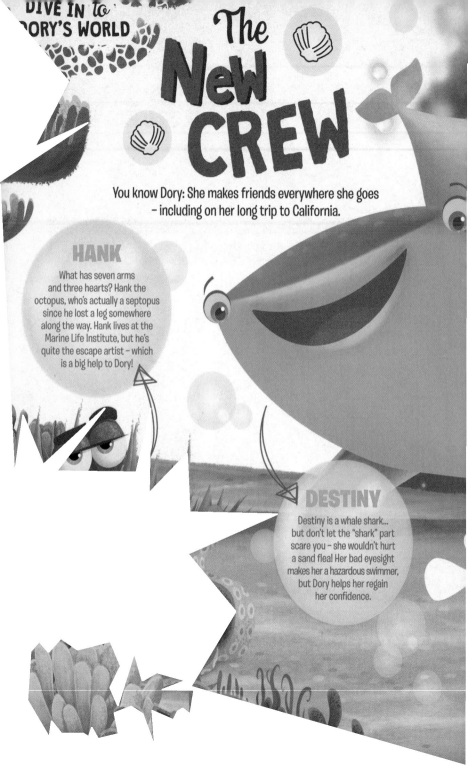

The New CREW

You know Dory: She makes friends everywhere she goes – including on her long trip to California.

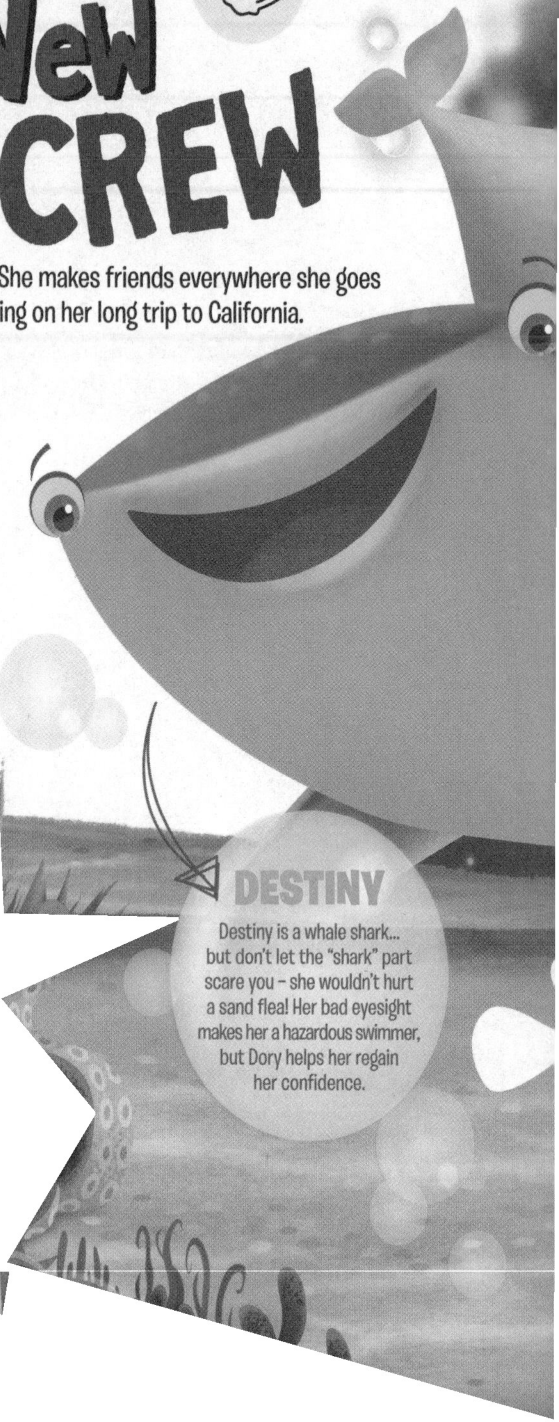

HANK

What has seven arms and three hearts? Hank the octopus, who's actually a septopus since he lost a leg somewhere along the way. Hank lives at the Marine Life Institute, but he's quite the escape artist – which is a big help to Dory!

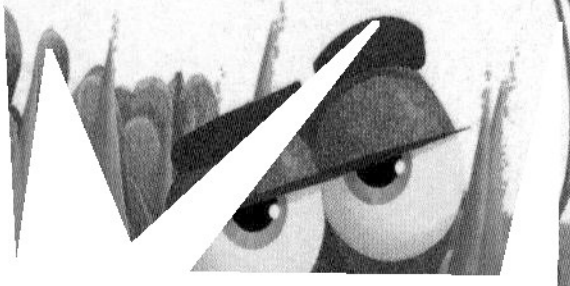

DESTINY

Destiny is a whale shark... but don't let the "shark" part scare you – she wouldn't hurt a sand flea! Her bad eyesight makes her a hazardous swimmer, but Dory helps her regain her confidence.

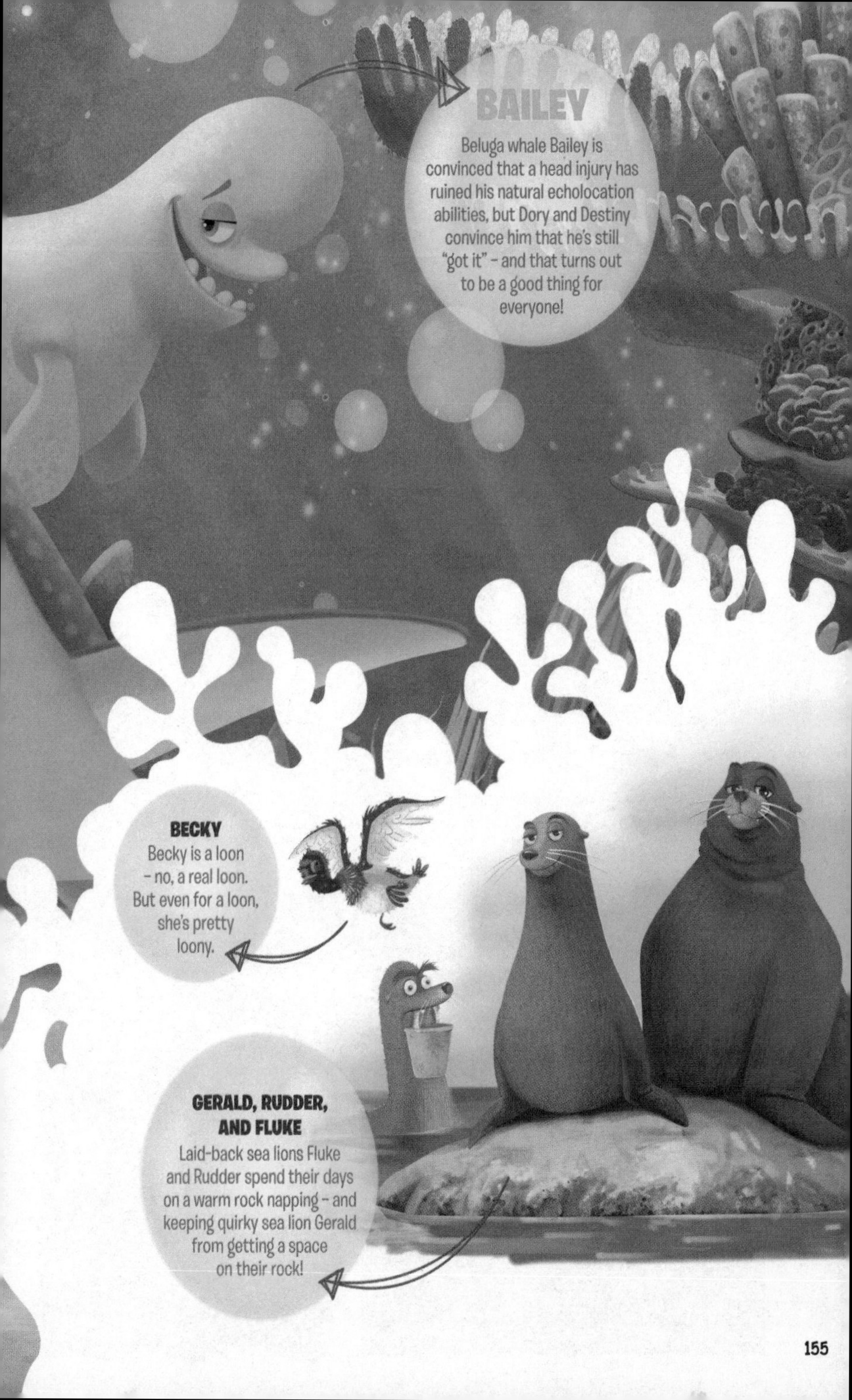

BAILEY

Beluga whale Bailey is convinced that a head injury has ruined his natural echolocation abilities, but Dory and Destiny convince him that he's still "got it" – and that turns out to be a good thing for everyone!

BECKY

Becky is a loon – no, a real loon. But even for a loon, she's pretty loony.

GERALD, RUDDER, AND FLUKE

Laid-back sea lions Fluke and Rudder spend their days on a warm rock napping – and keeping quirky sea lion Gerald from getting a space on their rock!

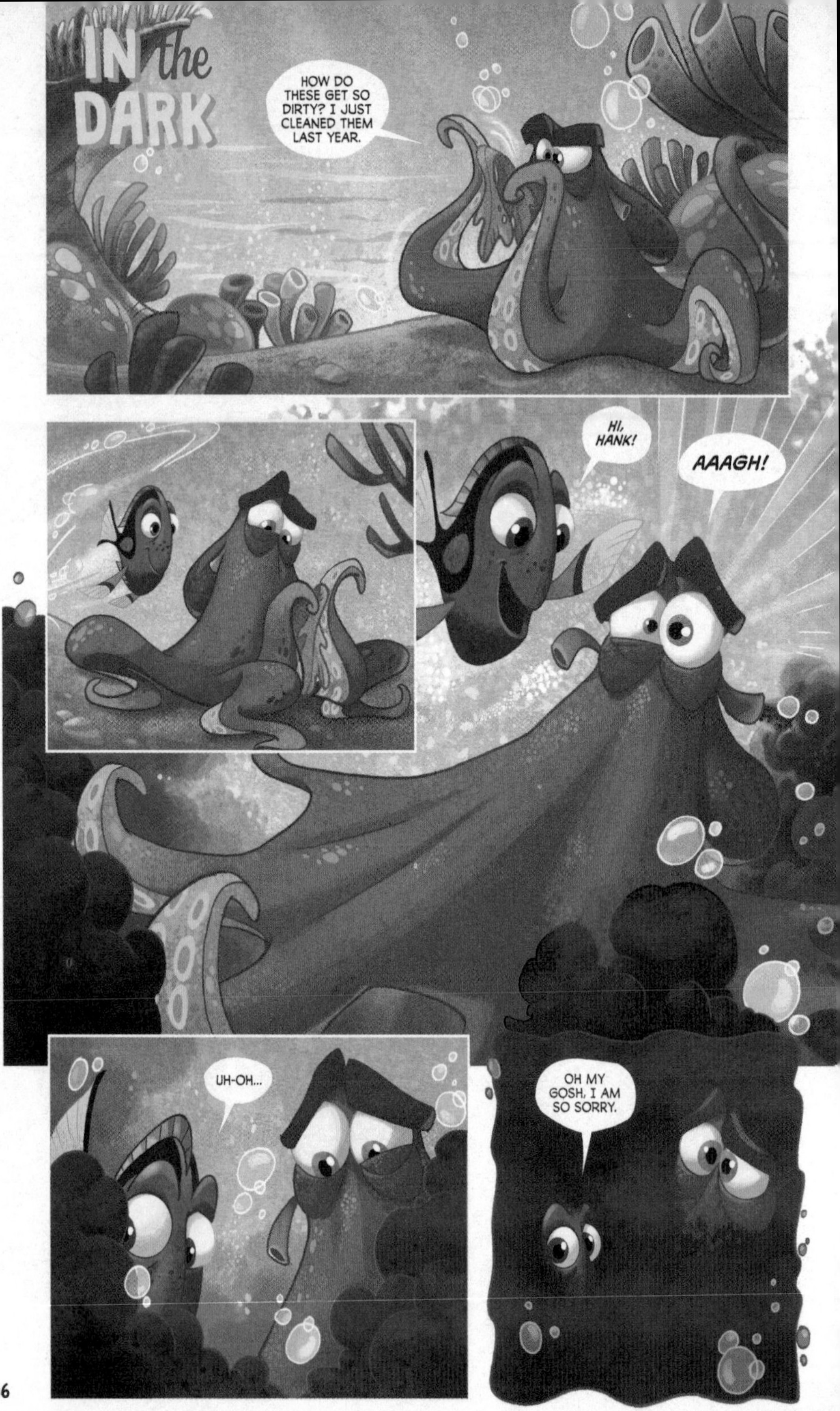
IN the DARK
HOW DO THESE GET SO DIRTY? I JUST CLEANED THEM LAST YEAR.
HI, HANK!
AAAGH!
UH-OH...
OH MY GOSH, I AM SO SORRY.

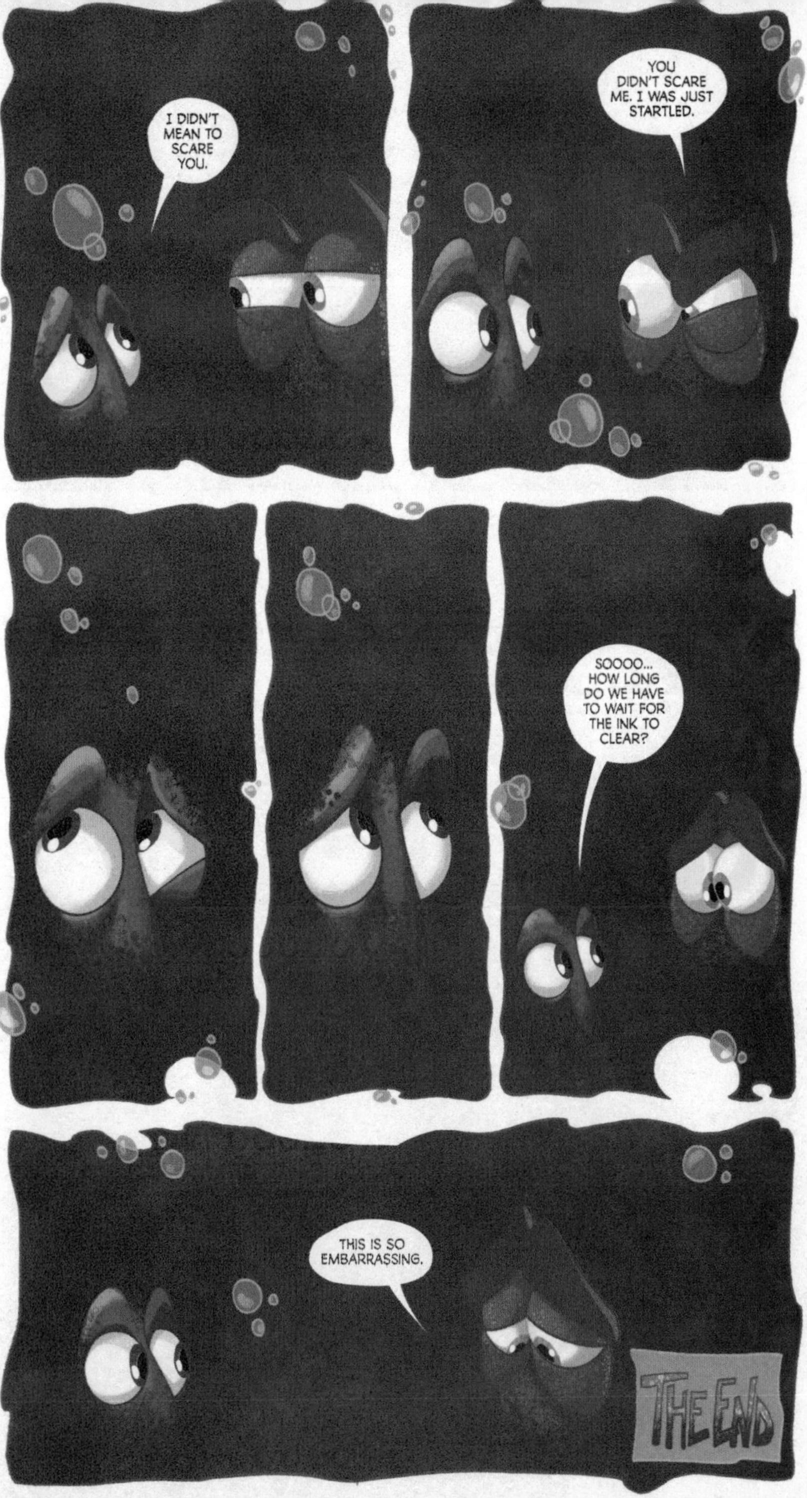
I DIDN'T MEAN TO SCARE YOU.
YOU DIDN'T SCARE ME. I WAS JUST STARTLED.
SOOOO... HOW LONG DO WE HAVE TO WAIT FOR THE INK TO CLEAR?
THIS IS SO EMBARRASSING.
THE END

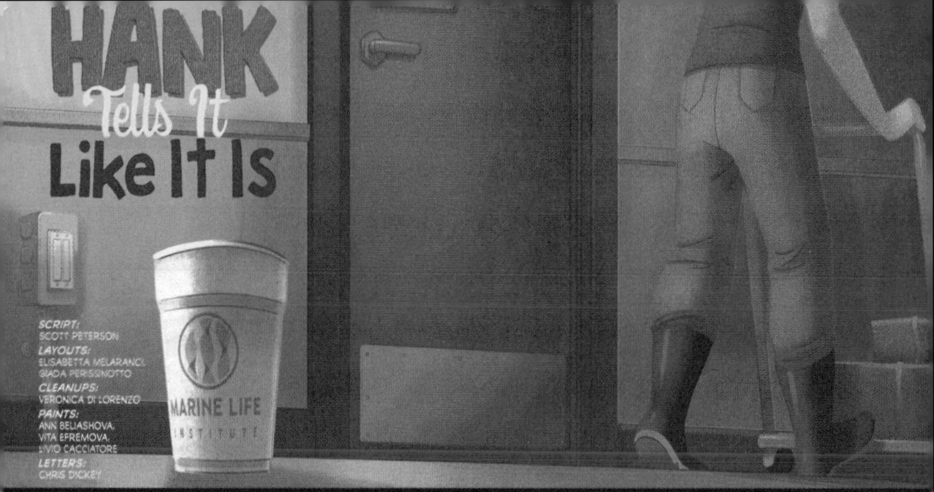
HANK
Tells It
Like It Is
SCRIPT:
SCOTT PETERSON
LAYOUTS:
ELISABETTA MELARANCI
GIADA PERISSINOTTO
CLEANUPS:
VERONICA DI LORENZO
PAINTS:
ANN BELIASHOVA,
VITA EFREMOVA,
LIVIO CACCIATORE
LETTERS:
CHRIS DICKEY
MARINE LIFE
INSTITUTE

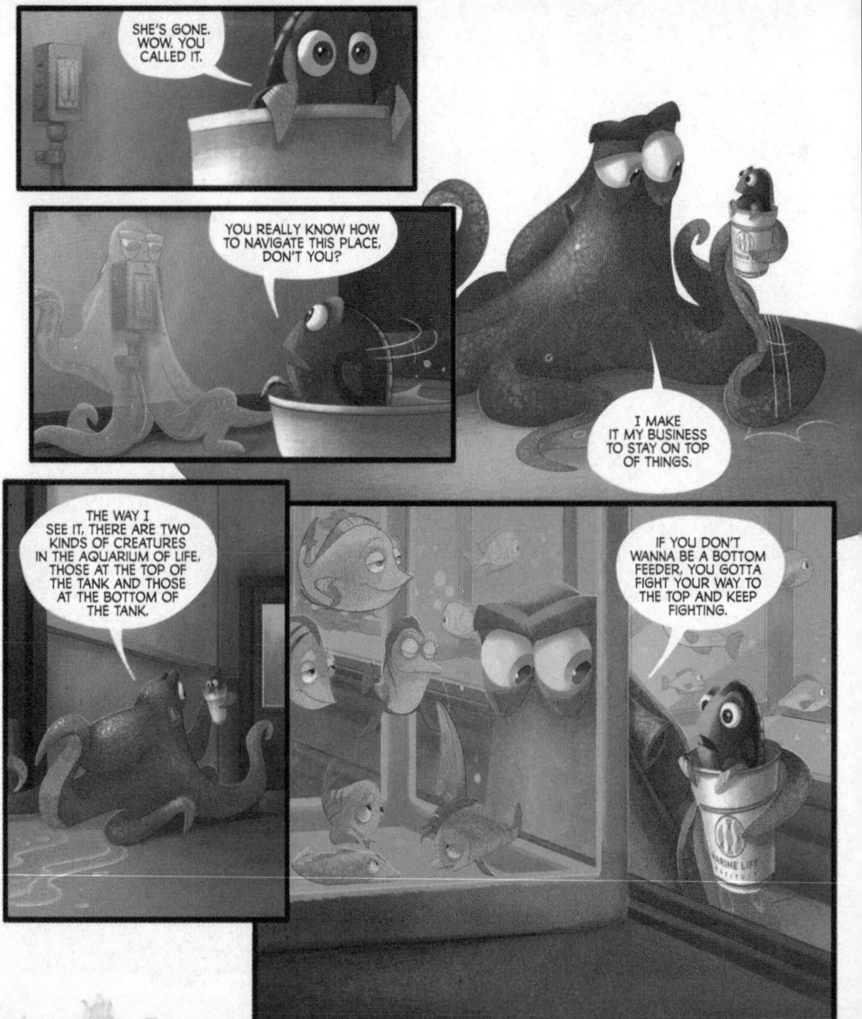
SHE'S GONE. WOW. YOU CALLED IT.
YOU REALLY KNOW HOW TO NAVIGATE THIS PLACE, DON'T YOU?
I MAKE IT MY BUSINESS TO STAY ON TOP OF THINGS.
THE WAY I SEE IT, THERE ARE TWO KINDS OF CREATURES IN THE AQUARIUM OF LIFE, THOSE AT THE TOP OF THE TANK AND THOSE AT THE BOTTOM OF THE TANK.
IF YOU DON'T WANNA BE A BOTTOM FEEDER, YOU GOTTA FIGHT YOUR WAY TO THE TOP AND KEEP FIGHTING.

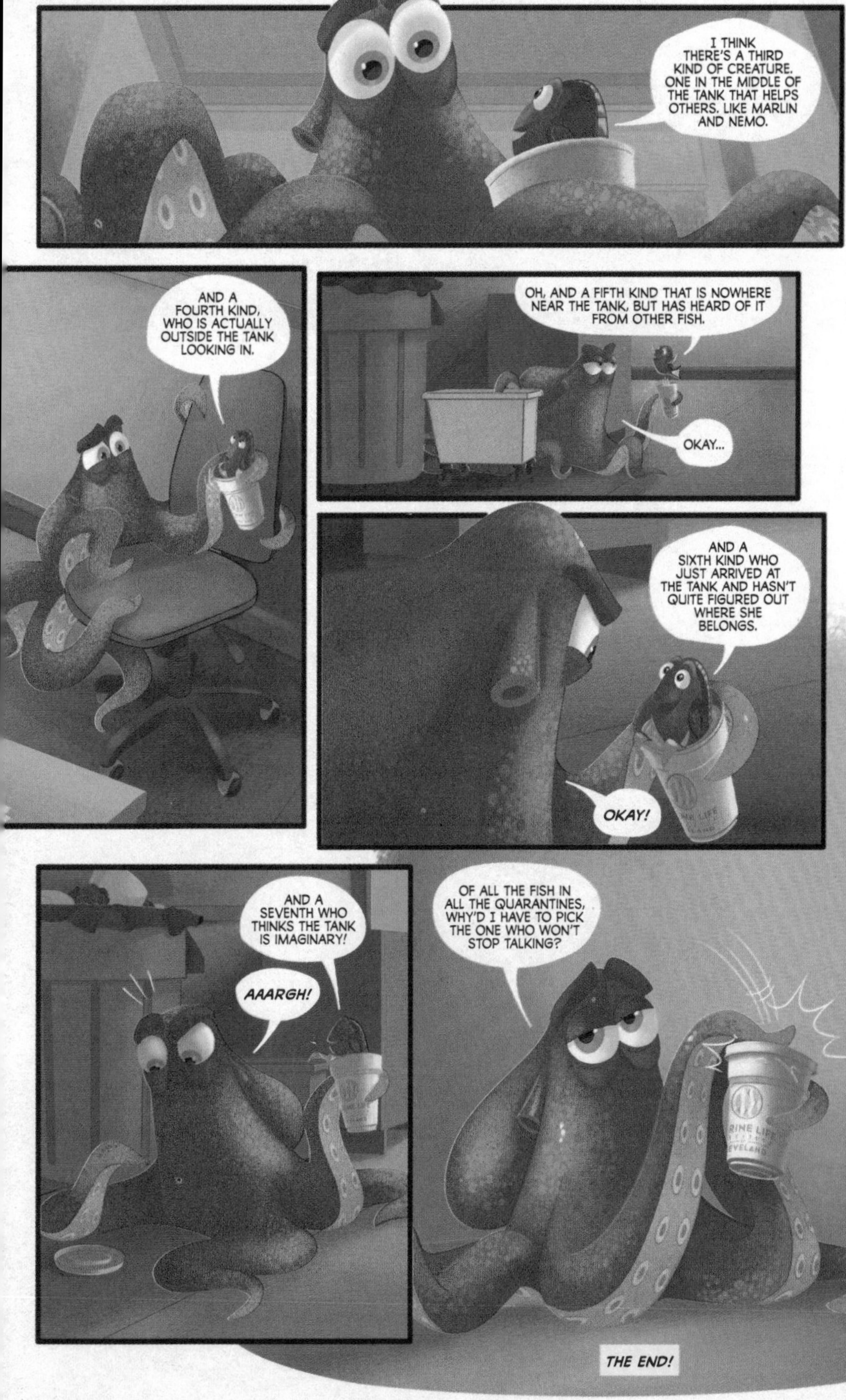
I THINK THERE'S A THIRD KIND OF CREATURE. ONE IN THE MIDDLE OF THE TANK THAT HELPS OTHERS. LIKE MARLIN AND NEMO.
AND A FOURTH KIND, WHO IS ACTUALLY OUTSIDE THE TANK LOOKING IN.
OH, AND A FIFTH KIND THAT IS NOWHERE NEAR THE TANK, BUT HAS HEARD OF IT FROM OTHER FISH.
OKAY...
AND A SIXTH KIND WHO JUST ARRIVED AT THE TANK AND HASN'T QUITE FIGURED OUT WHERE SHE BELONGS.
OKAY!
AND A SEVENTH WHO THINKS THE TANK IS IMAGINARY!
AAARGH!
OF ALL THE FISH IN ALL THE QUARANTINES, WHY'D I HAVE TO PICK THE ONE WHO WON'T STOP TALKING?
THE END!

Hank's Driving SCHOOL

WARNING: THESE DRIVING TIPS APPLY ONLY TO THOSE WITH SEVEN OR MORE ARMS.

Who needs a license when you have seven tentacles?

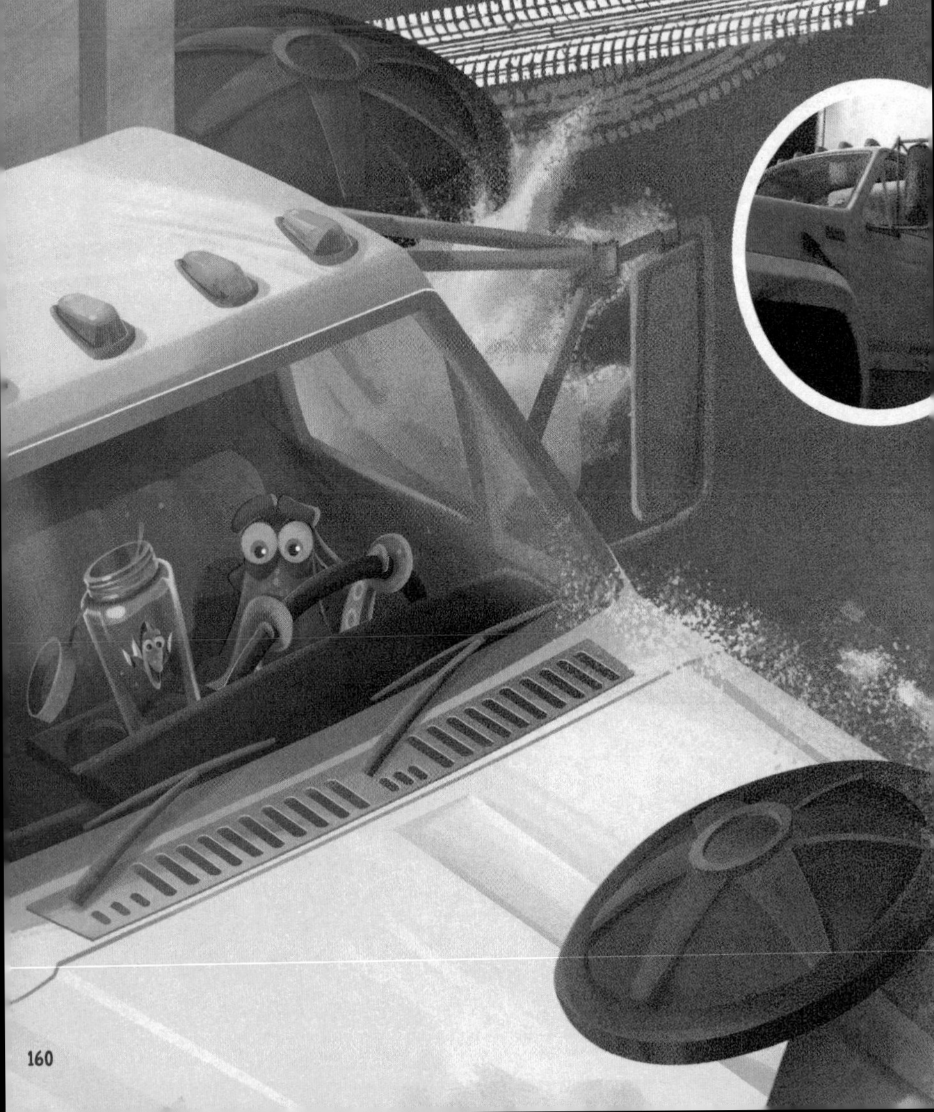

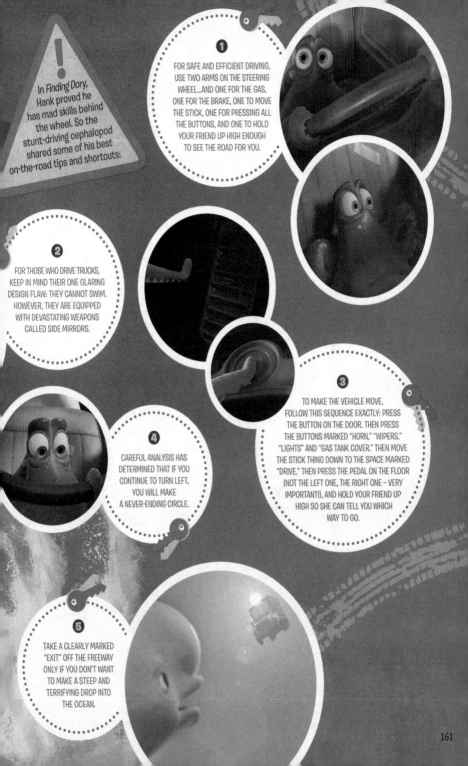

In *Finding Dory*, Hank proved he has mad skills behind the wheel. So the stunt-driving cephalopod shared some of his best on-the-road tips and shortcuts:

1

FOR SAFE AND EFFICIENT DRIVING, USE TWO ARMS ON THE STEERING WHEEL...AND ONE FOR THE GAS, ONE FOR THE BRAKE, ONE TO MOVE THE STICK, ONE FOR PRESSING ALL THE BUTTONS, AND ONE TO HOLD YOUR FRIEND UP HIGH ENOUGH TO SEE THE ROAD FOR YOU.

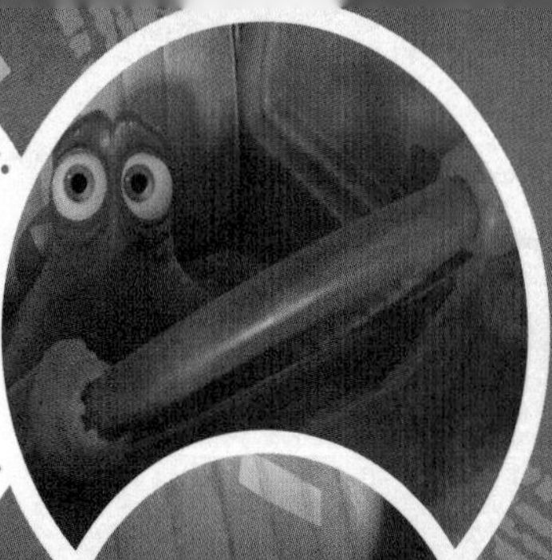

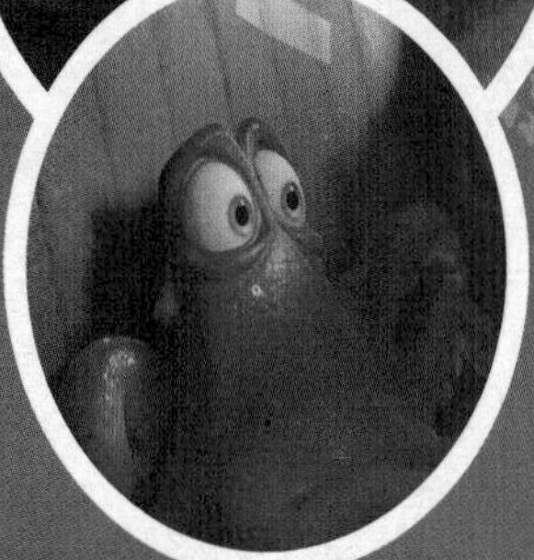

2

FOR THOSE WHO DRIVE TRUCKS, KEEP IN MIND THEIR ONE GLARING DESIGN FLAW: THEY CANNOT SWIM. HOWEVER, THEY ARE EQUIPPED WITH DEVASTATING WEAPONS CALLED SIDE MIRRORS.

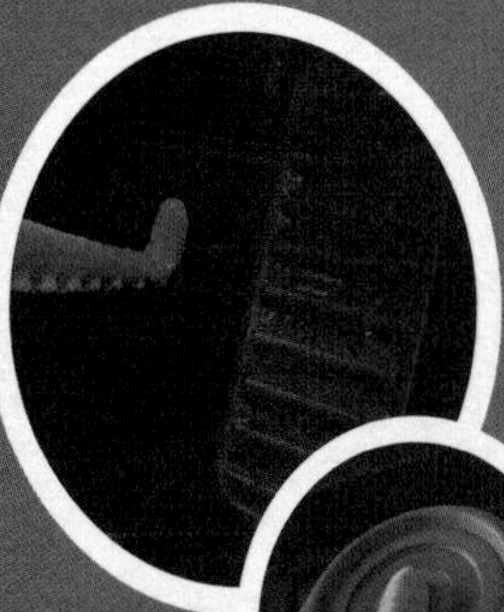

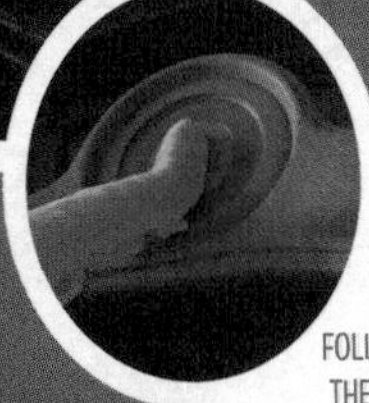

3

TO MAKE THE VEHICLE MOVE, FOLLOW THIS SEQUENCE EXACTLY: PRESS THE BUTTON ON THE DOOR. THEN PRESS THE BUTTONS MARKED "HORN," "WIPERS," "LIGHTS" AND "GAS TANK COVER." THEN MOVE THE STICK THING DOWN TO THE SPACE MARKED "DRIVE." THEN PRESS THE PEDAL ON THE FLOOR (NOT THE LEFT ONE, THE RIGHT ONE – VERY IMPORTANT!), AND HOLD YOUR FRIEND UP HIGH SO SHE CAN TELL YOU WHICH WAY TO GO.

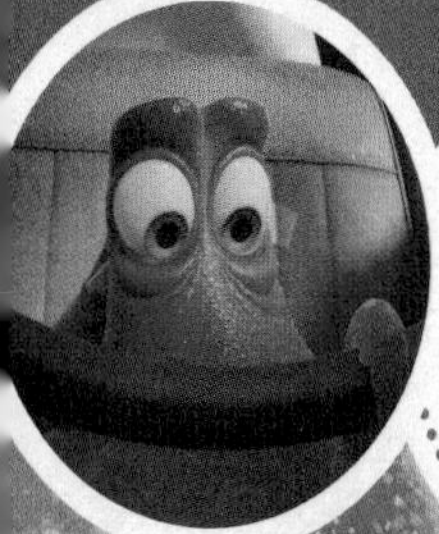

4

CAREFUL ANALYSIS HAS DETERMINED THAT IF YOU CONTINUE TO TURN LEFT, YOU WILL MAKE A NEVER-ENDING CIRCLE.

5

TAKE A CLEARLY MARKED "EXIT" OFF THE FREEWAY ONLY IF YOU DON'T WANT TO MAKE A STEEP AND TERRIFYING DROP INTO THE OCEAN.

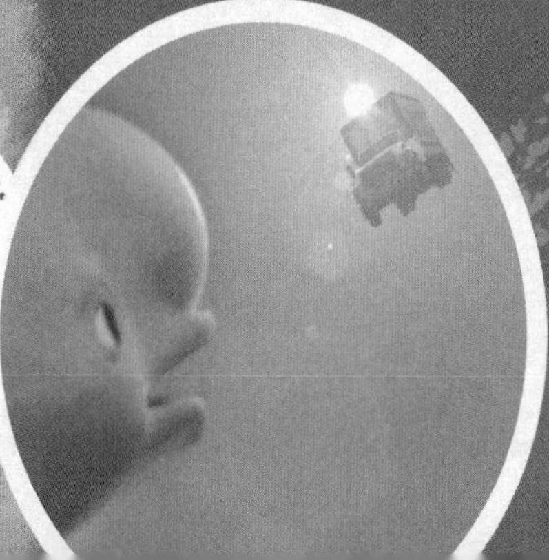

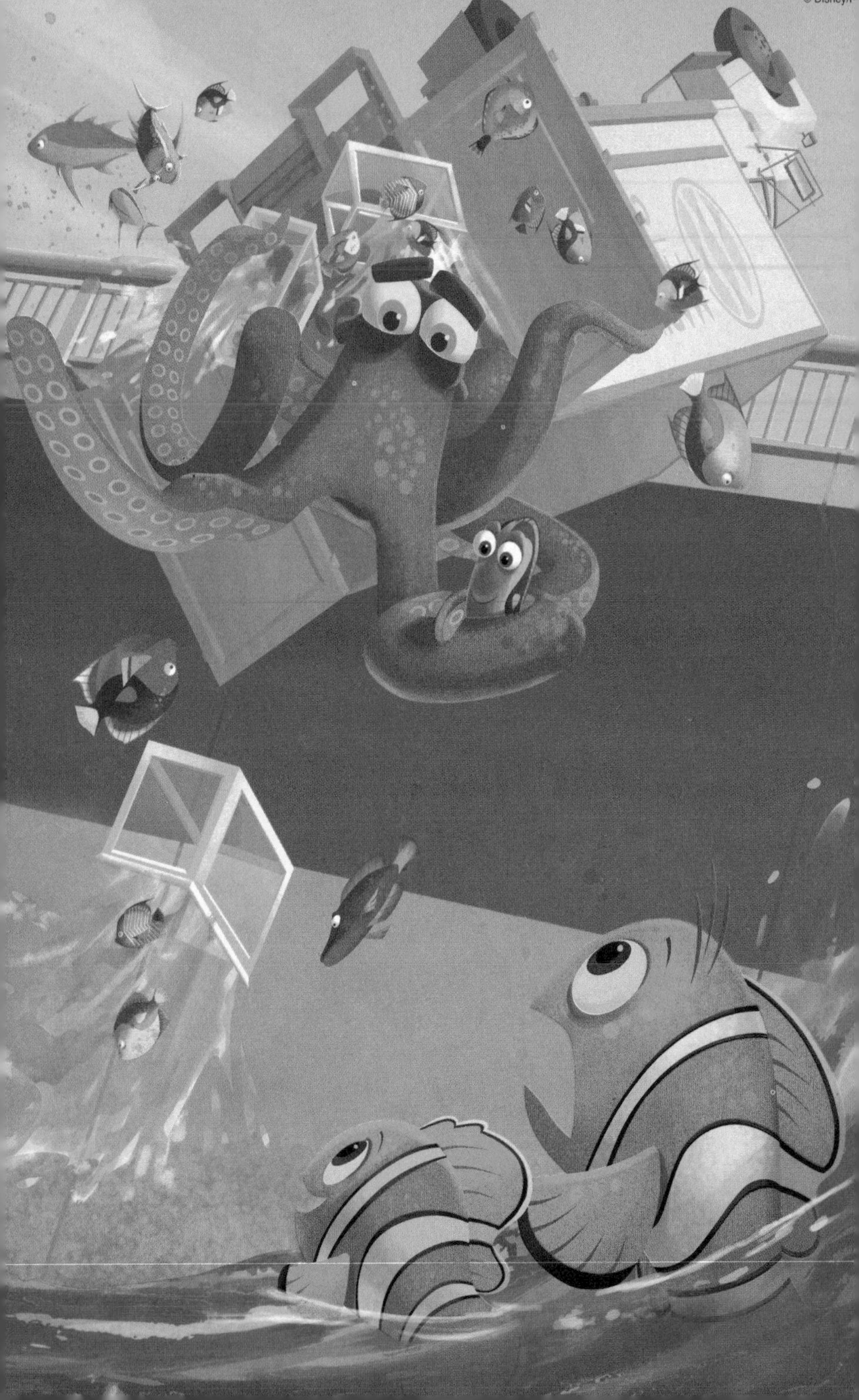

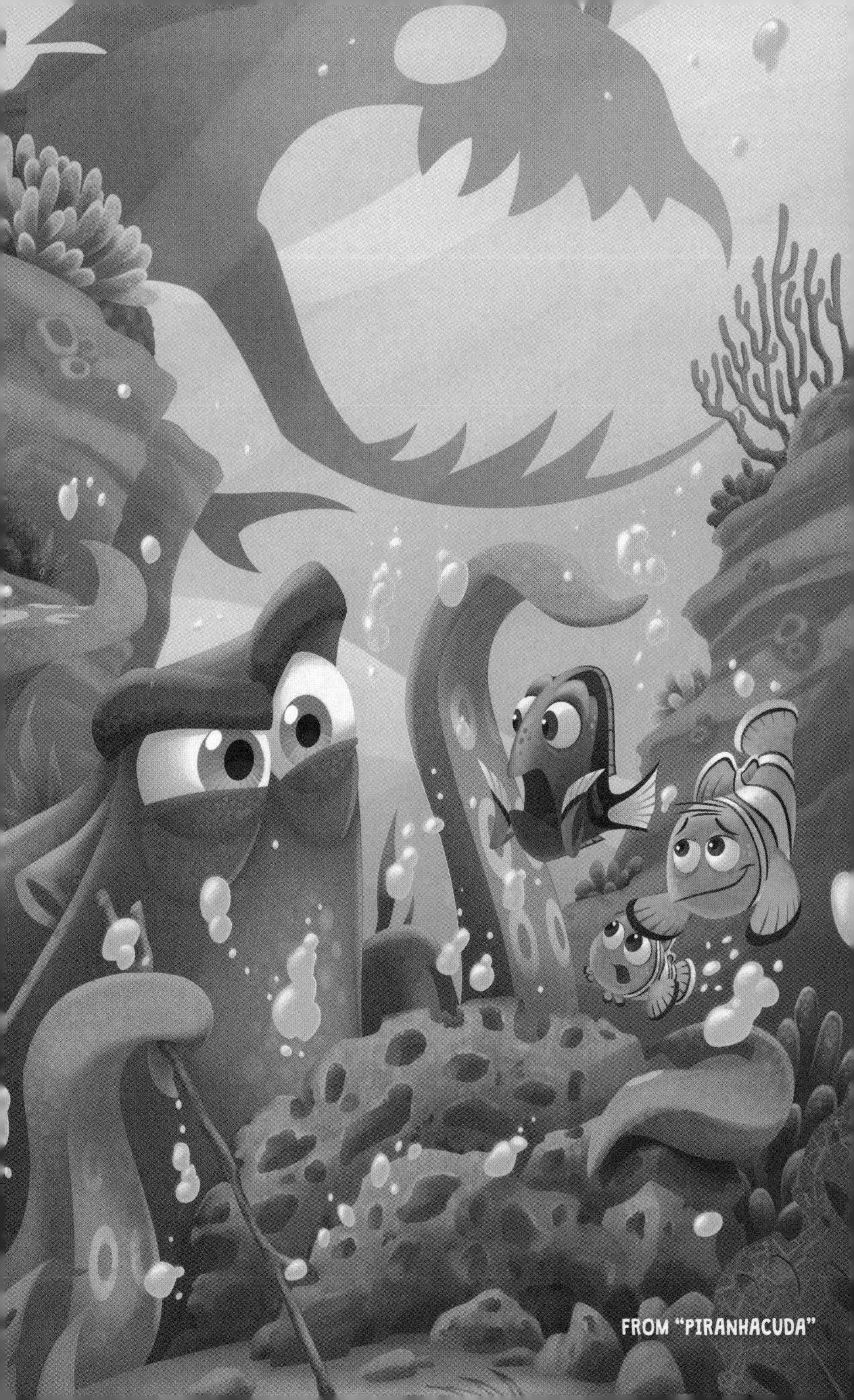

FROM “PIRANHACUDA”

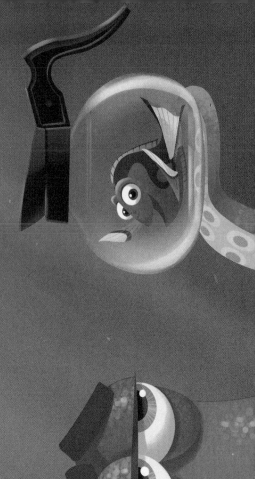

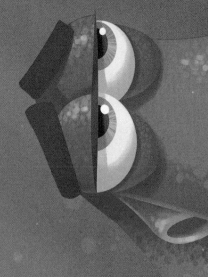

Disney · PIXAR
FINDING DORY

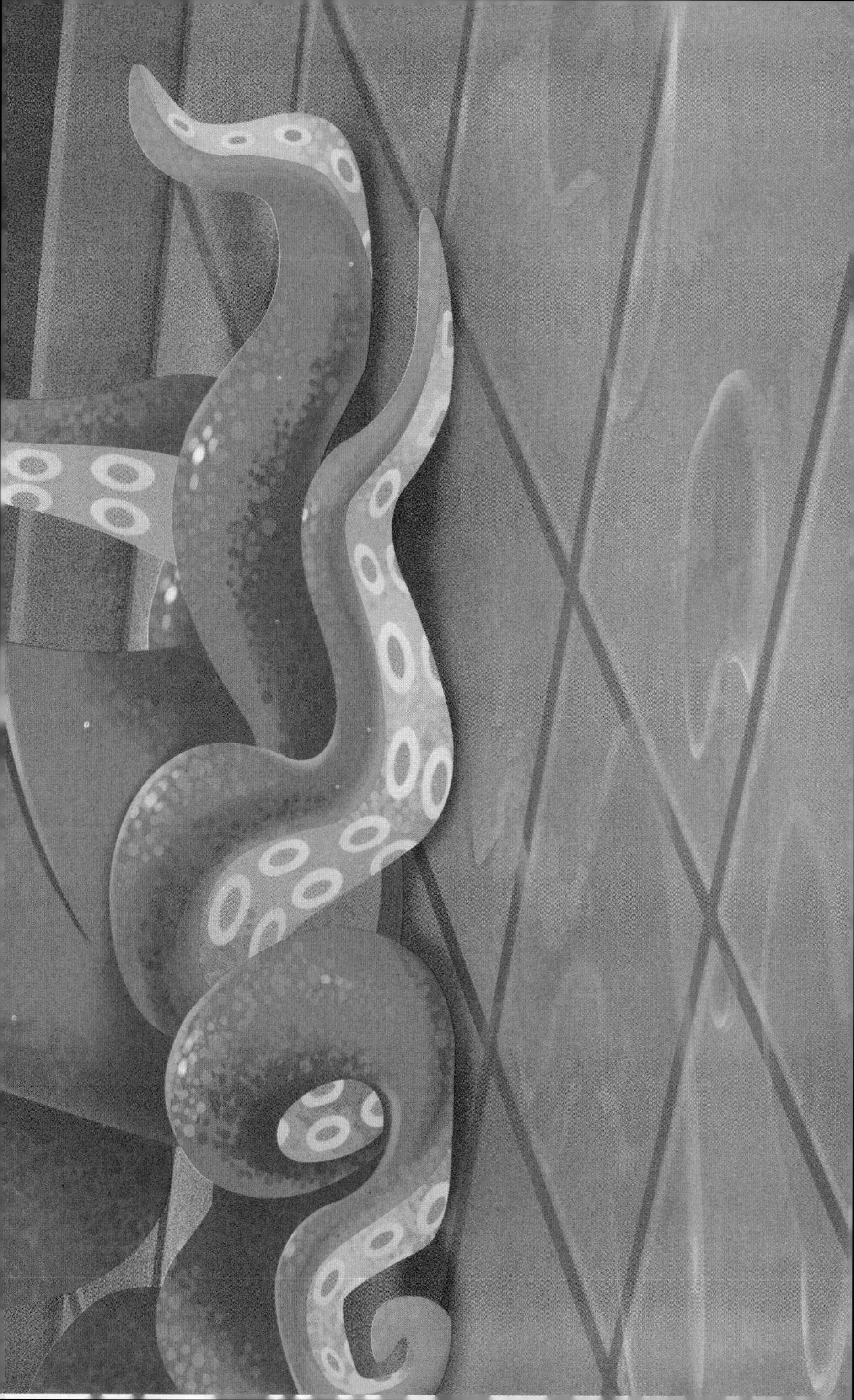

PIRANHACUDA

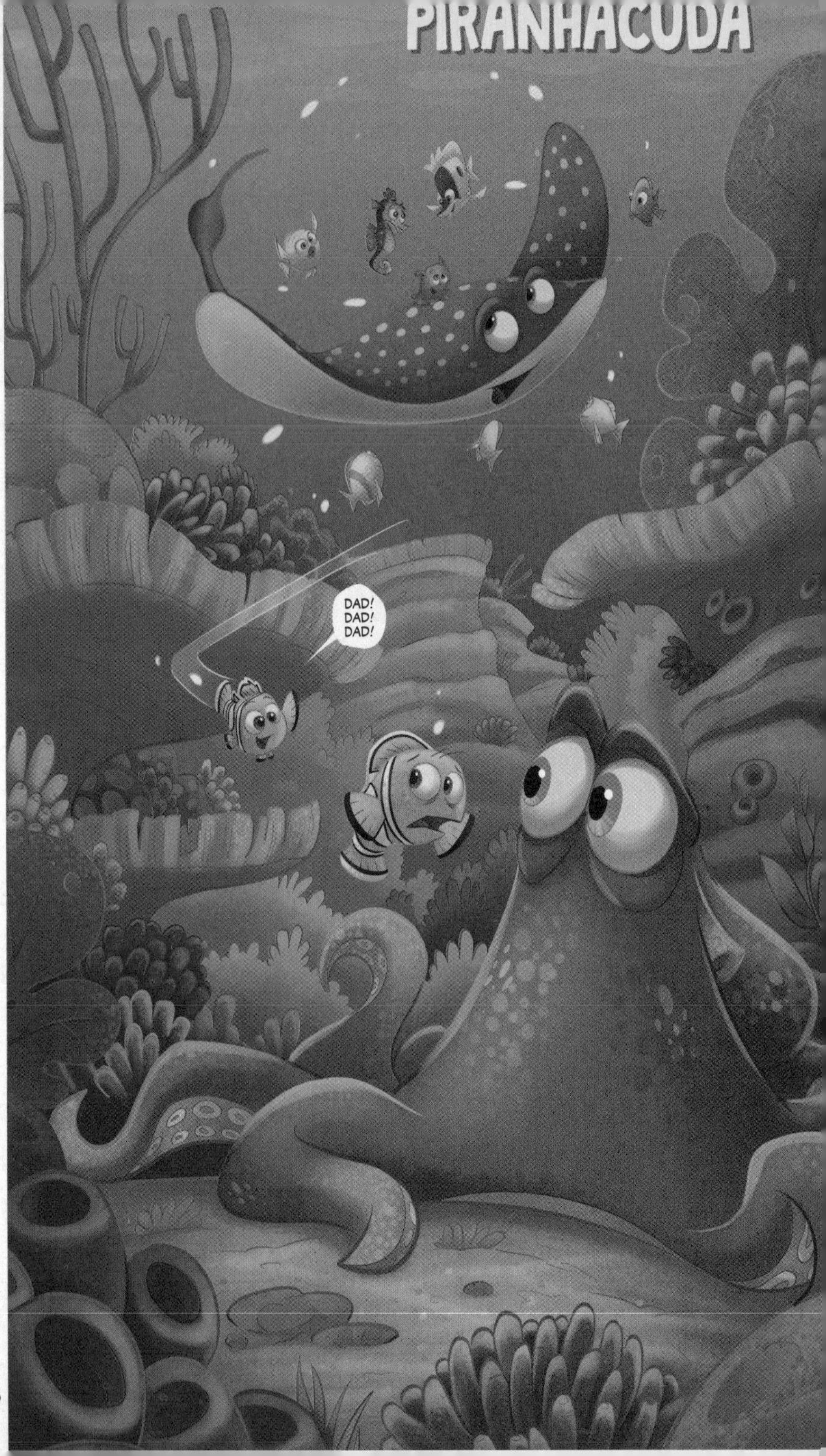
DAD! DAD! DAD!

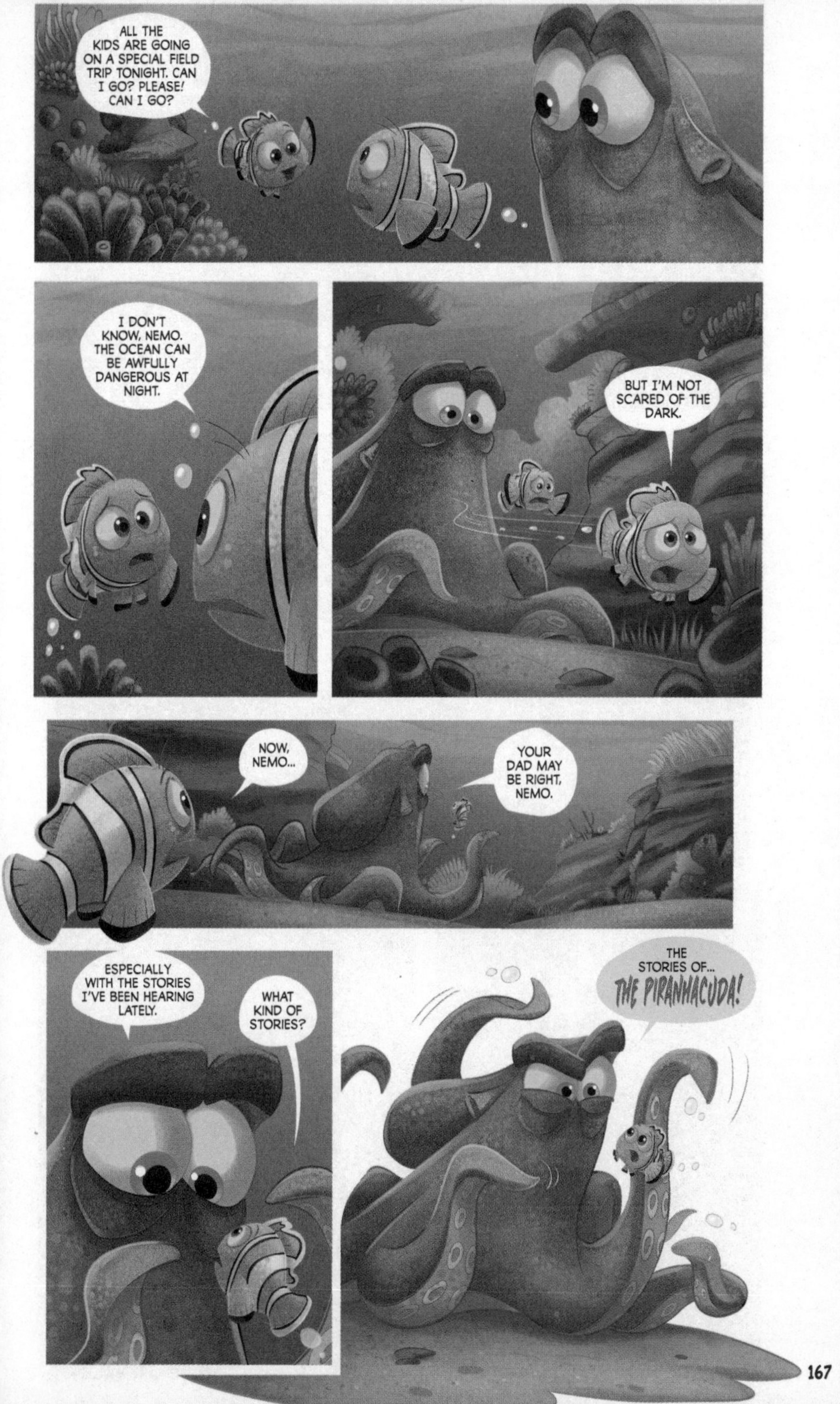
ALL THE KIDS ARE GOING ON A SPECIAL FIELD TRIP TONIGHT. CAN I GO? PLEASE! CAN I GO?
I DON'T KNOW, NEMO. THE OCEAN CAN BE AWFULLY DANGEROUS AT NIGHT.
BUT I'M NOT SCARED OF THE DARK.
NOW, NEMO...
YOUR DAD MAY BE RIGHT, NEMO.
ESPECIALLY WITH THE STORIES I'VE BEEN HEARING LATELY.
WHAT KIND OF STORIES?
THE STORIES OF... THE PIRANHACUDA!

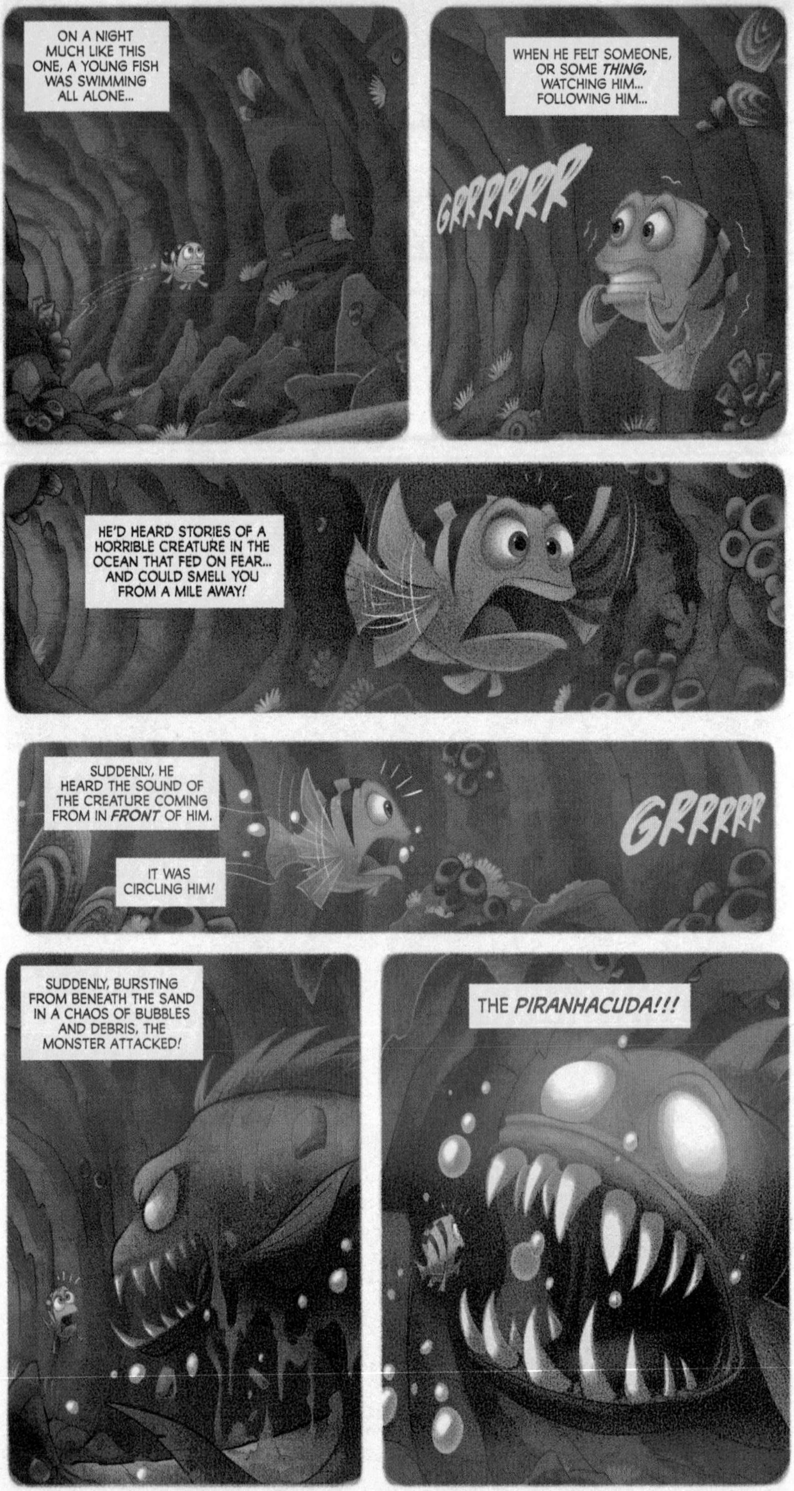
ON A NIGHT MUCH LIKE THIS ONE, A YOUNG FISH WAS SWIMMING ALL ALONE...
WHEN HE FELT SOMEONE, OR SOME *THING,* WATCHING HIM... FOLLOWING HIM...
GRRRRRR
HE'D HEARD STORIES OF A HORRIBLE CREATURE IN THE OCEAN THAT FED ON FEAR... AND COULD SMELL YOU FROM A MILE AWAY!
SUDDENLY, HE HEARD THE SOUND OF THE CREATURE COMING FROM IN *FRONT* OF HIM.
IT WAS CIRCLING HIM!
GRRRRR
SUDDENLY, BURSTING FROM BENEATH THE SAND IN A CHAOS OF BUBBLES AND DEBRIS, THE MONSTER ATTACKED!
THE *PIRANHACUDA!!!*

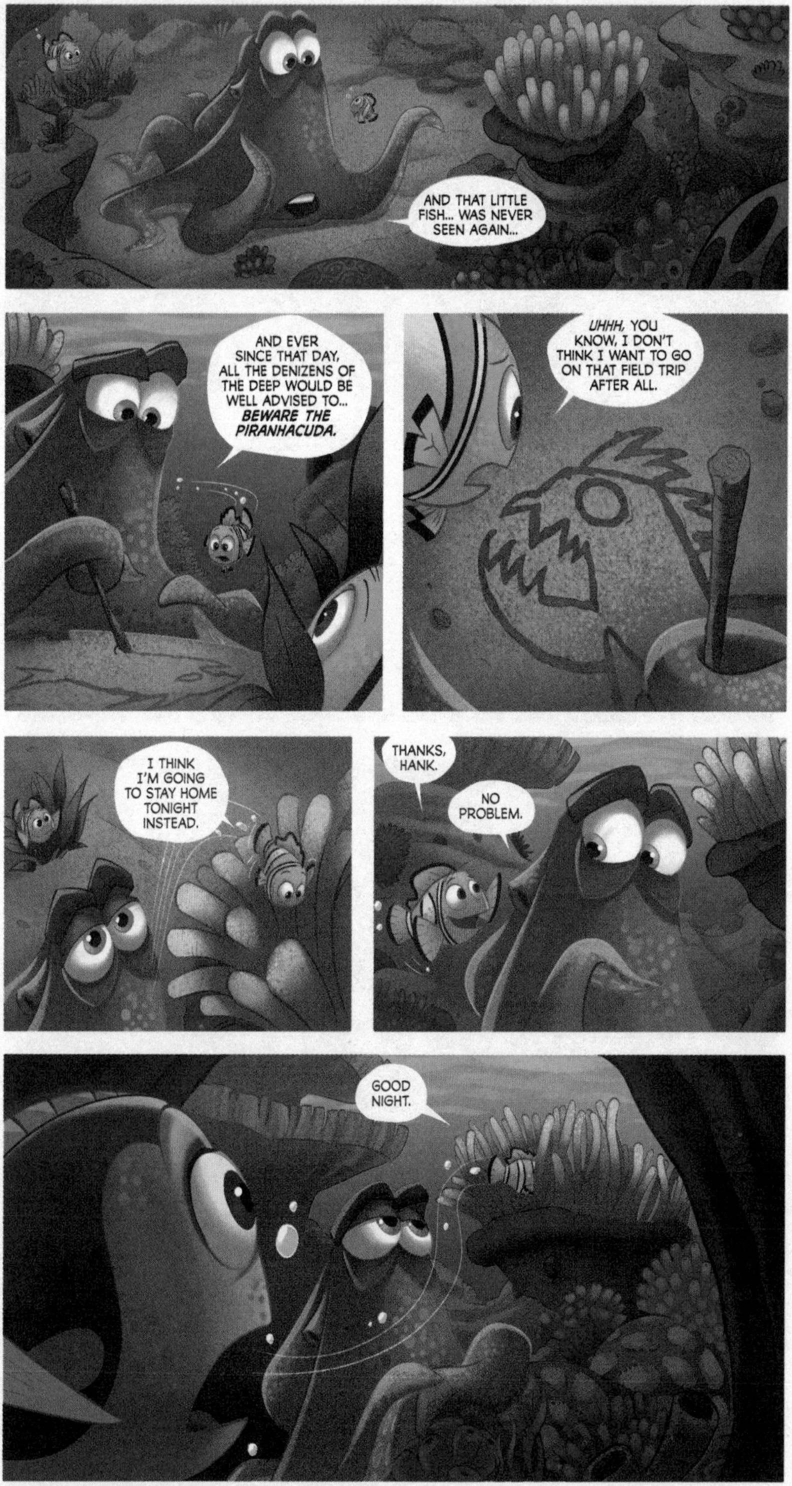
AND THAT LITTLE FISH... WAS NEVER SEEN AGAIN...
AND EVER SINCE THAT DAY, ALL THE DENIZENS OF THE DEEP WOULD BE WELL ADVISED TO... *BEWARE THE PIRANHACUDA.*
UHHH, YOU KNOW, I DON'T THINK I WANT TO GO ON THAT FIELD TRIP AFTER ALL.
I THINK I'M GOING TO STAY HOME TONIGHT INSTEAD.
THANKS, HANK.
NO PROBLEM.
GOOD NIGHT.

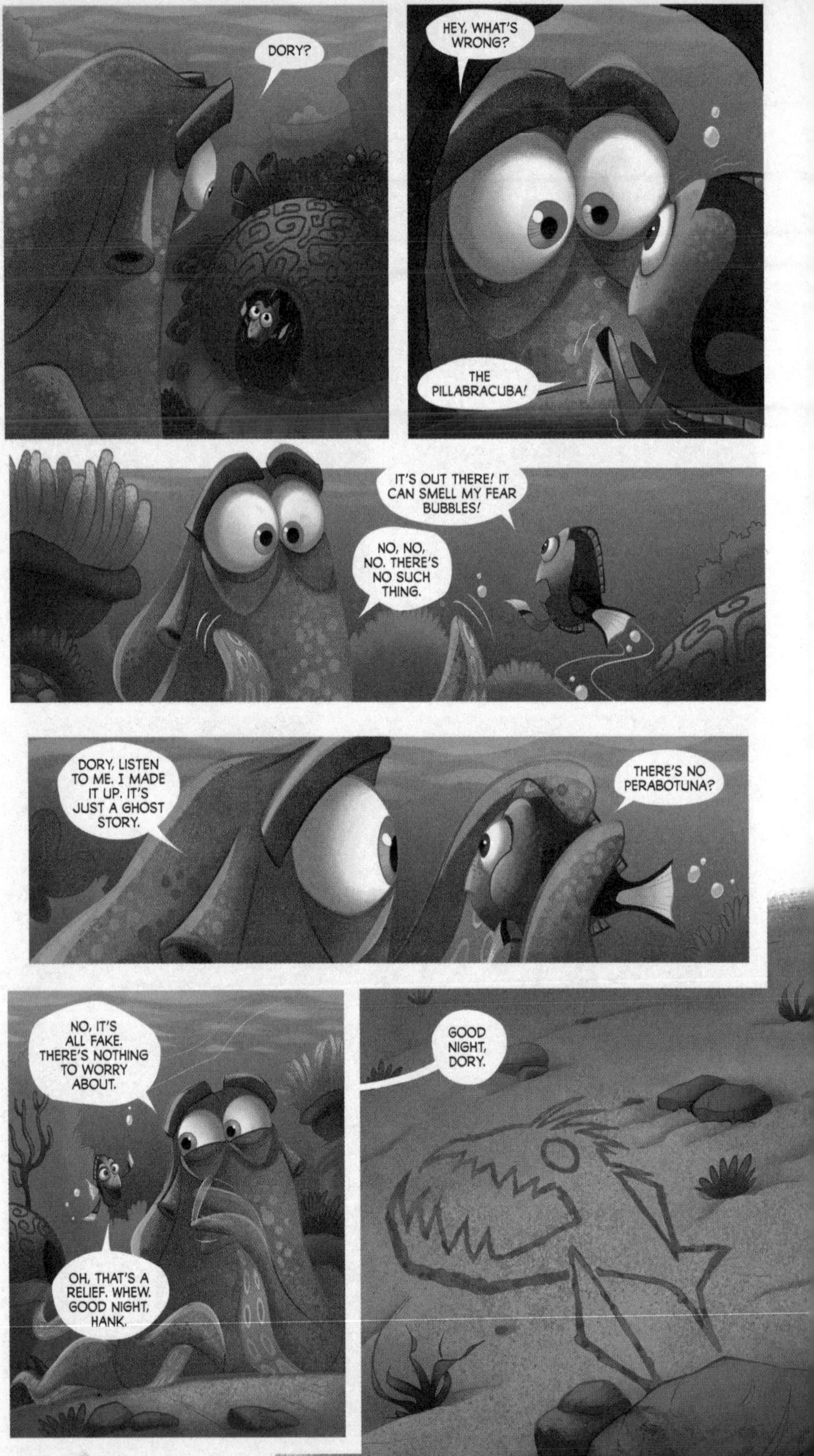
DORY?
HEY, WHAT'S WRONG?
THE PILLABRACUBA!
IT'S OUT THERE! IT CAN SMELL MY FEAR BUBBLES!
NO, NO, NO. THERE'S NO SUCH THING.
DORY, LISTEN TO ME. I MADE IT UP. IT'S JUST A GHOST STORY.
THERE'S NO PERABOTUNA?
NO, IT'S ALL FAKE. THERE'S NOTHING TO WORRY ABOUT.
OH, THAT'S A RELIEF. WHEW. GOOD NIGHT, HANK.
GOOD NIGHT, DORY.

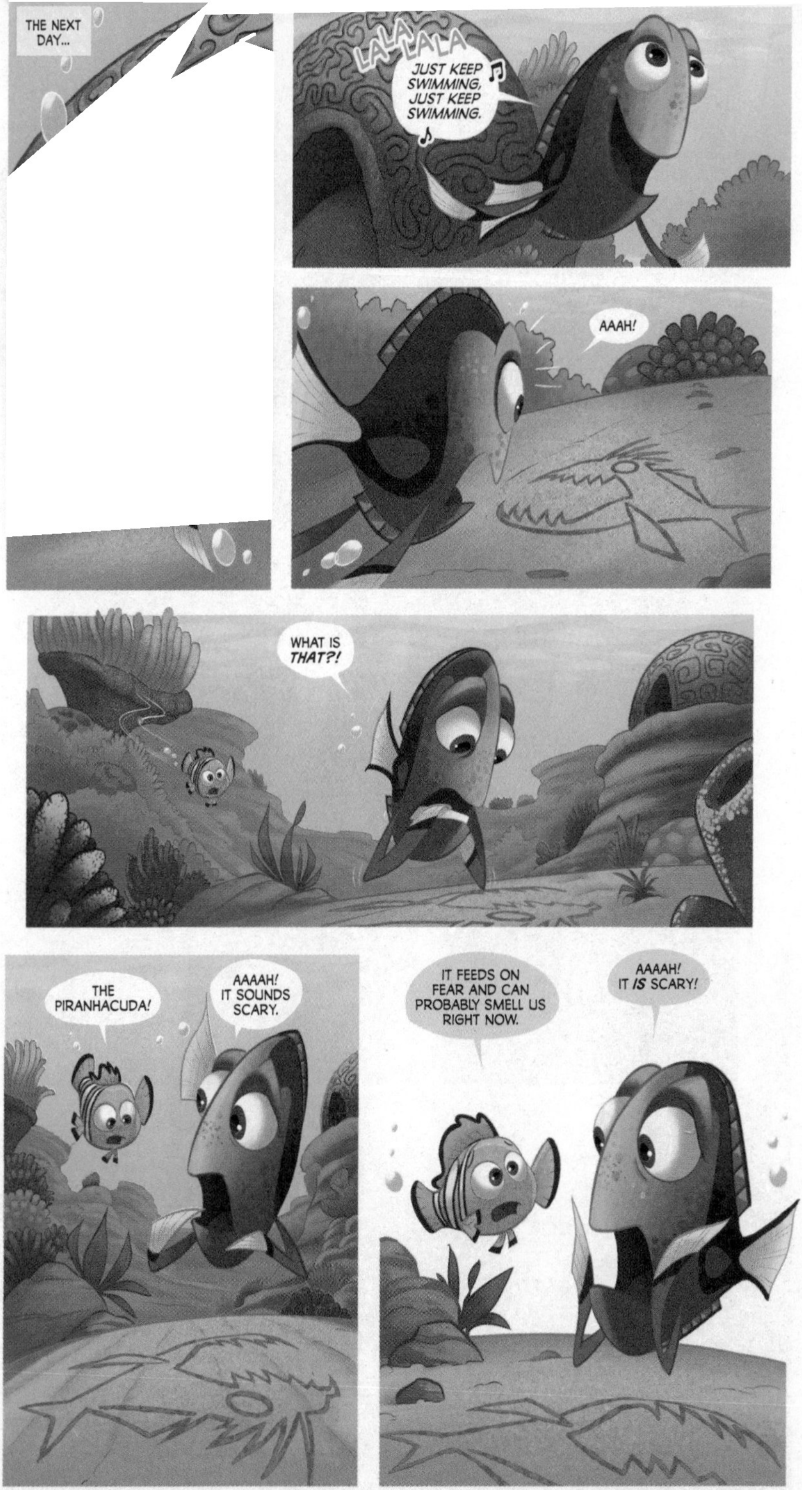
THE NEXT DAY...
LA LA LA LA
JUST KEEP SWIMMING, JUST KEEP SWIMMING.
AAAH!
WHAT IS THAT?!
THE PIRANHACUDA!
AAAAH! IT SOUNDS SCARY.
IT FEEDS ON FEAR AND CAN PROBABLY SMELL US RIGHT NOW.
AAAAH! IT IS SCARY!

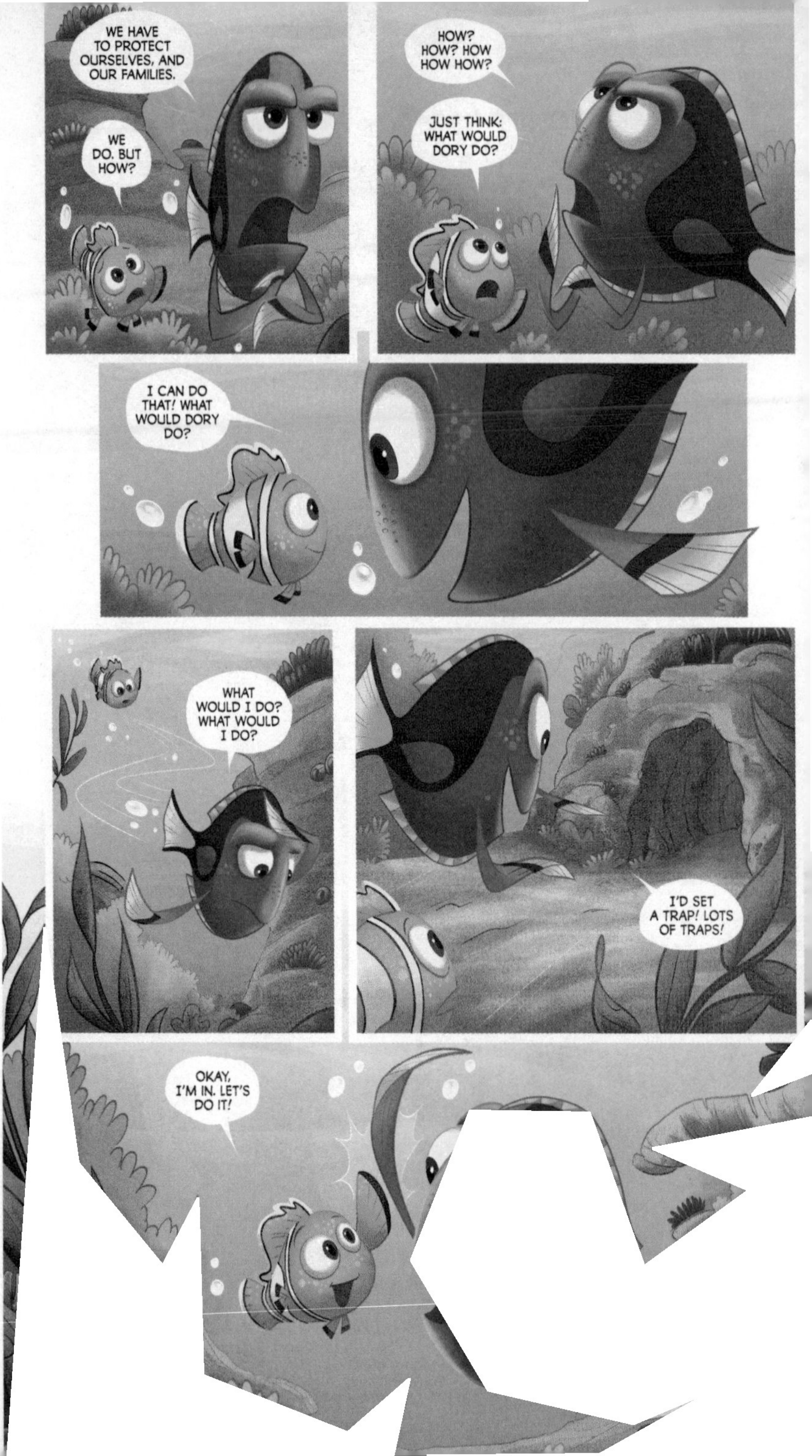
WE HAVE TO PROTECT OURSELVES, AND OUR FAMILIES.
WE DO. BUT HOW?
HOW? HOW? HOW HOW HOW?
JUST THINK: WHAT WOULD DORY DO?
I CAN DO THAT! WHAT WOULD DORY DO?
WHAT WOULD I DO? WHAT WOULD I DO?
I'D SET A TRAP! LOTS OF TRAPS!
OKAY, I'M IN. LET'S DO IT!

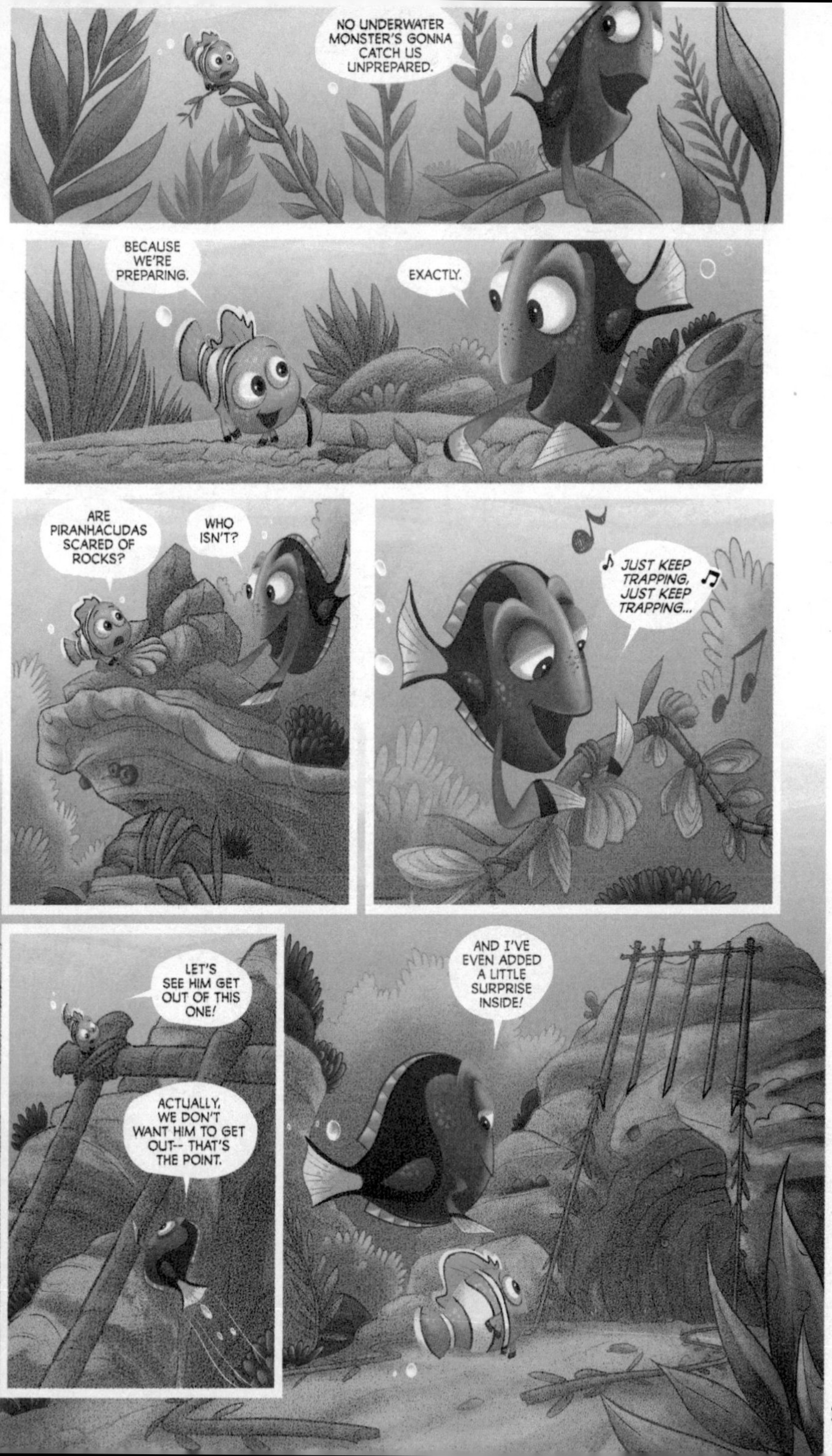
NO UNDERWATER MONSTER'S GONNA CATCH US UNPREPARED.
BECAUSE WE'RE PREPARING.
EXACTLY.
ARE PIRANHACUDAS SCARED OF ROCKS?
WHO ISN'T?
JUST KEEP TRAPPING, JUST KEEP TRAPPING...
LET'S SEE HIM GET OUT OF THIS ONE!
ACTUALLY, WE DON'T WANT HIM TO GET OUT-- THAT'S THE POINT.
AND I'VE EVEN ADDED A LITTLE SURPRISE INSIDE!

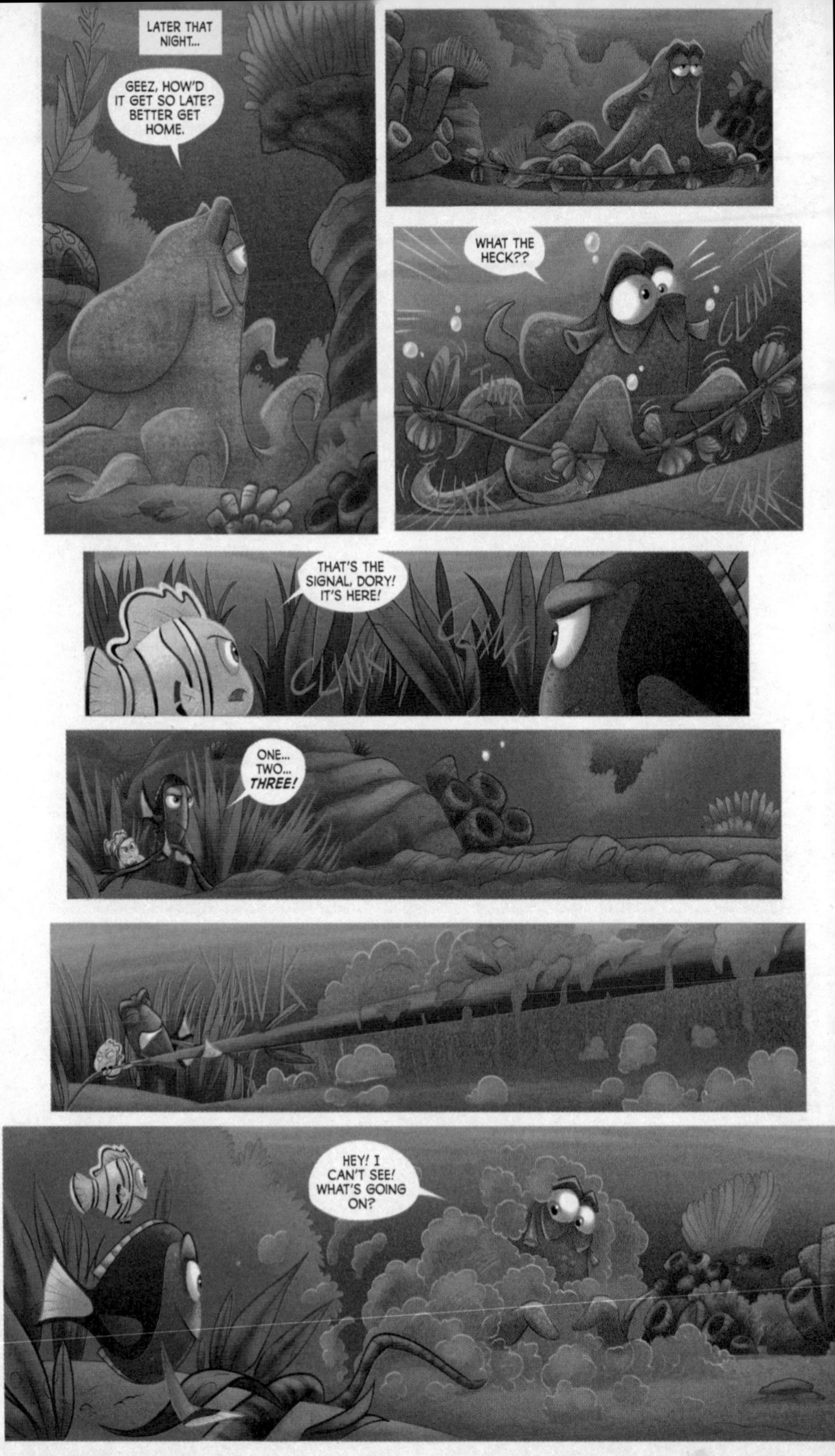
LATER THAT NIGHT...
GEEZ, HOW'D IT GET SO LATE? BETTER GET HOME.
WHAT THE HECK??
CLINK
TINK
CLINK
CLINK
THAT'S THE SIGNAL, DORY! IT'S HERE!
CLINK!
CLINK
ONE... TWO... THREE!
YANK
HEY! I CAN'T SEE! WHAT'S GOING ON?

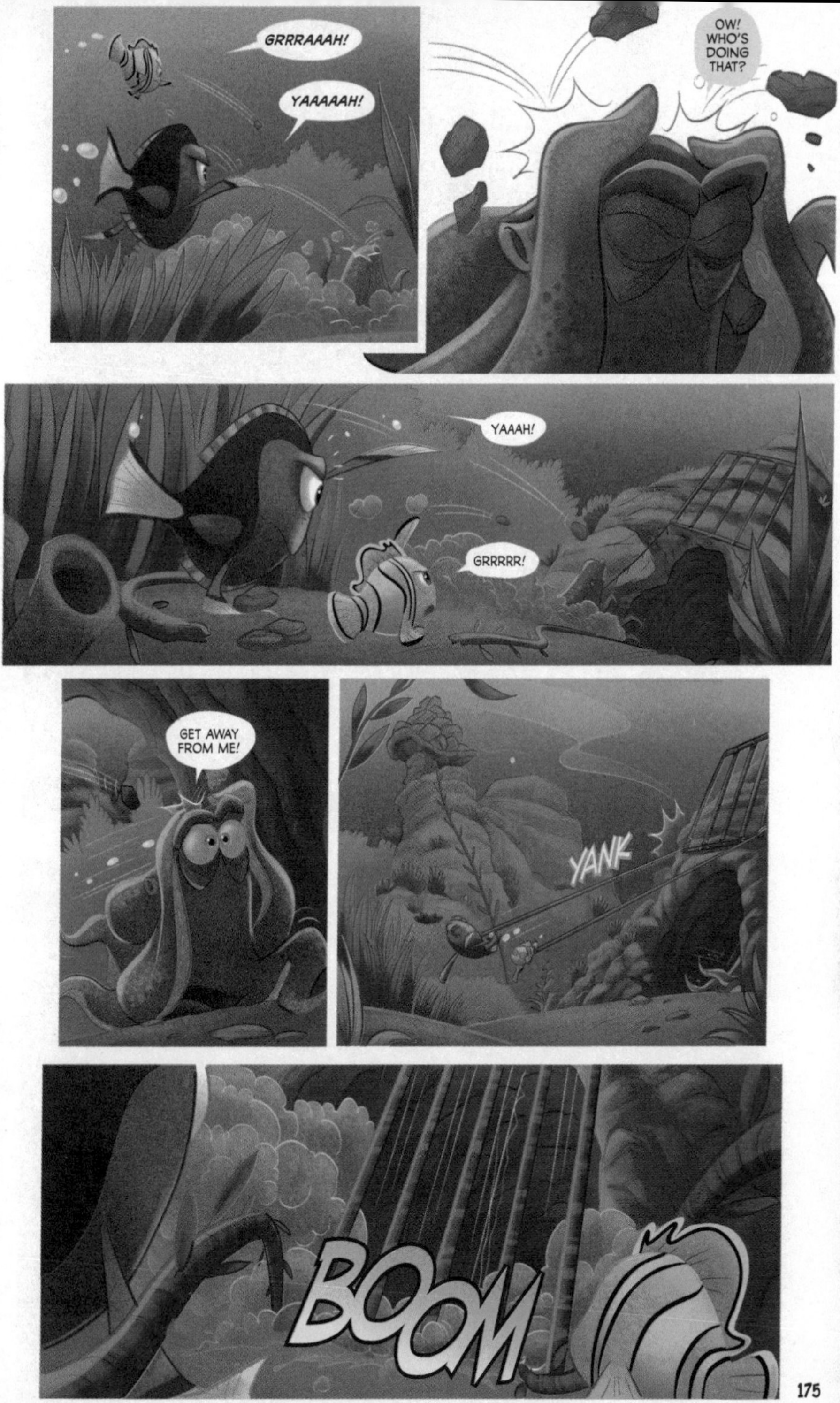

GRRRAAAH!
YAAAAAH!
OW! WHO'S DOING THAT?
YAAAH!
GRRRRR!
GET AWAY FROM ME!
YANK
BOOM

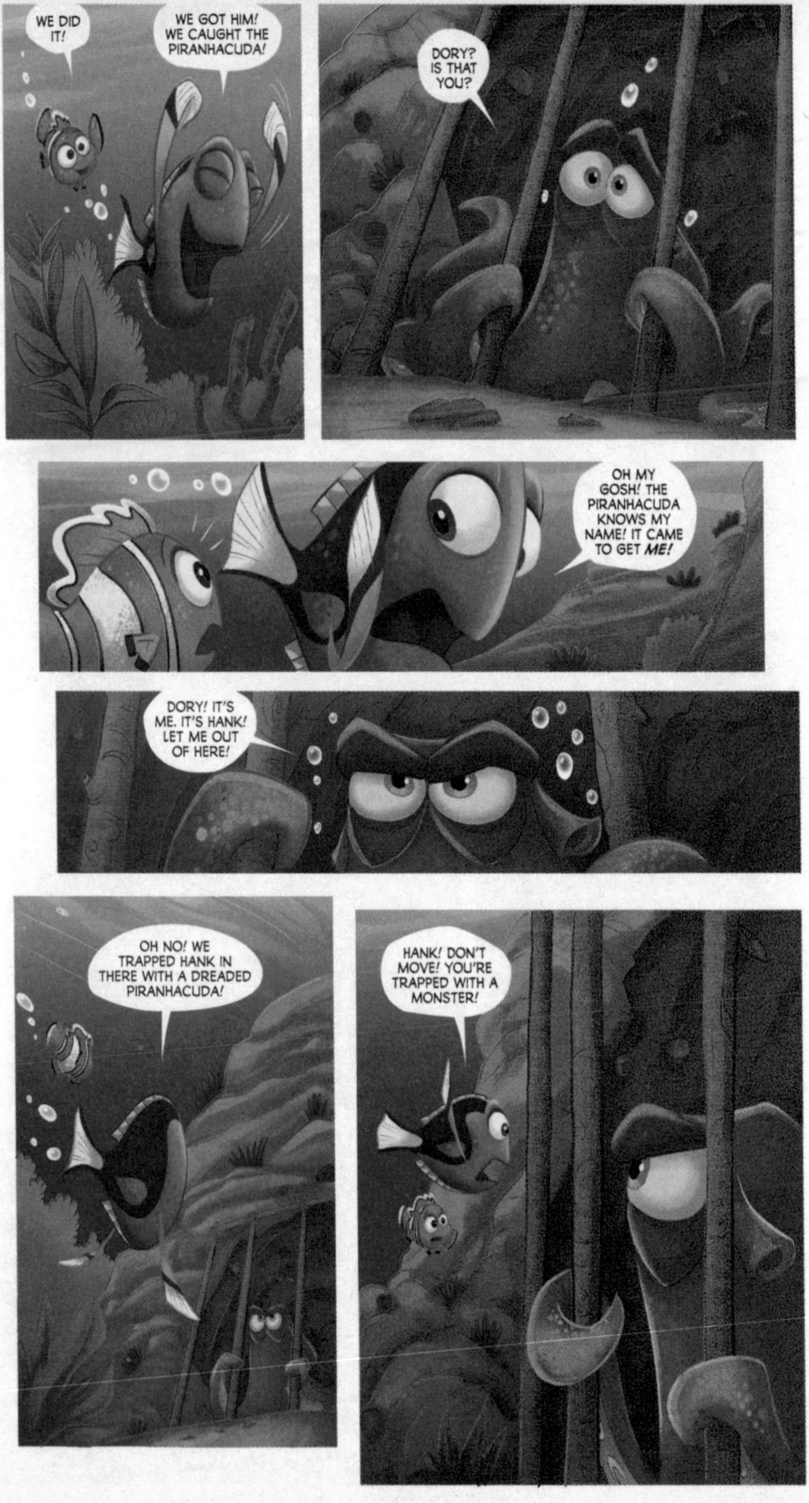

WE DID IT!
WE GOT HIM! WE CAUGHT THE PIRANHACUDA!
DORY? IS THAT YOU?
OH MY GOSH! THE PIRANHACUDA KNOWS MY NAME! IT CAME TO GET ME!
DORY! IT'S ME. IT'S HANK! LET ME OUT OF HERE!
OH NO! WE TRAPPED HANK IN THERE WITH A DREADED PIRANHACUDA!
HANK! DON'T MOVE! YOU'RE TRAPPED WITH A MONSTER!

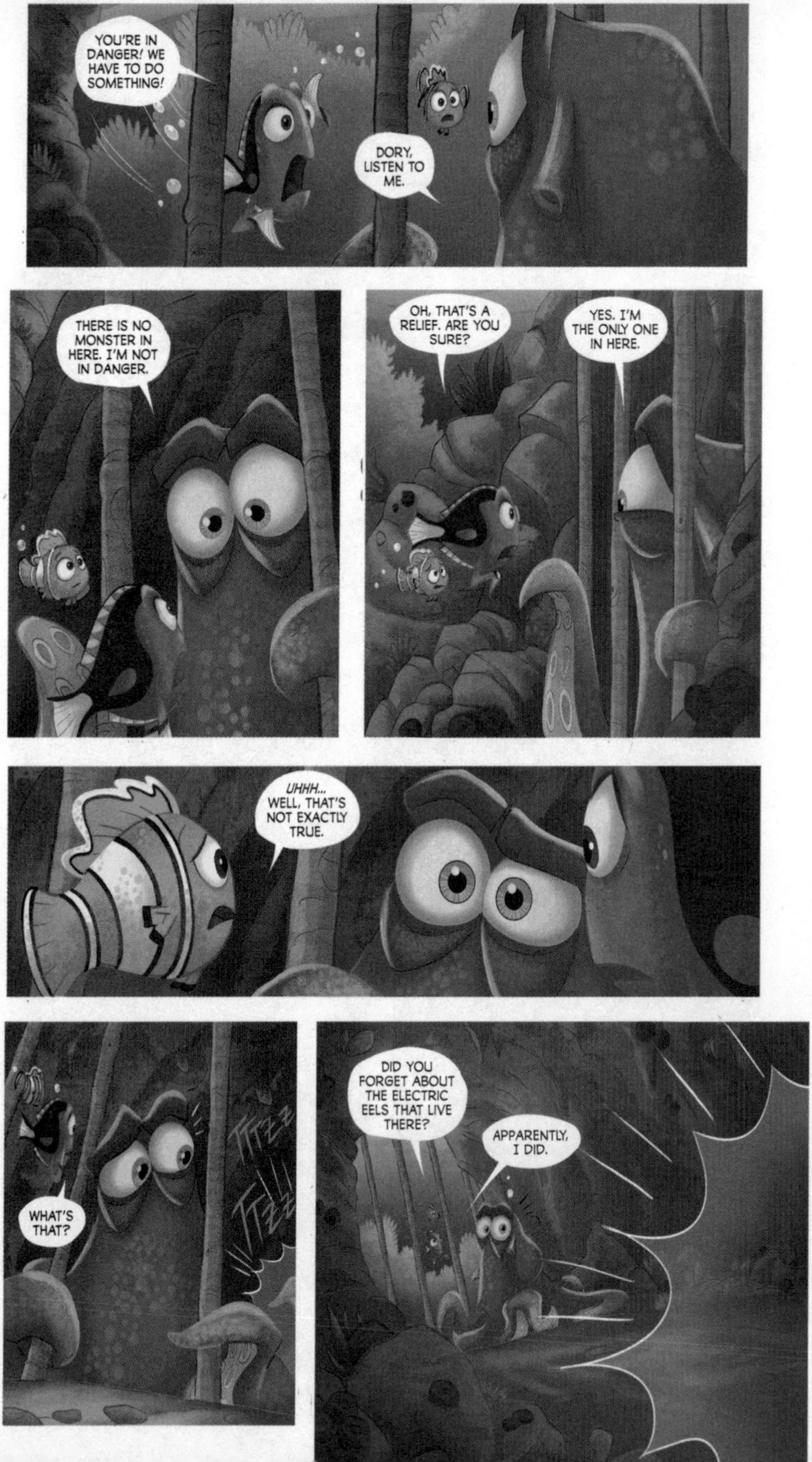
YOU'RE IN DANGER! WE HAVE TO DO SOMETHING!
DORY, LISTEN TO ME.
THERE IS NO MONSTER IN HERE. I'M NOT IN DANGER.
OH, THAT'S A RELIEF. ARE YOU SURE?
YES. I'M THE ONLY ONE IN HERE.
UHHH... WELL, THAT'S NOT EXACTLY TRUE.
WHAT'S THAT?
DID YOU FORGET ABOUT THE ELECTRIC EELS THAT LIVE THERE?
APPARENTLY, I DID.

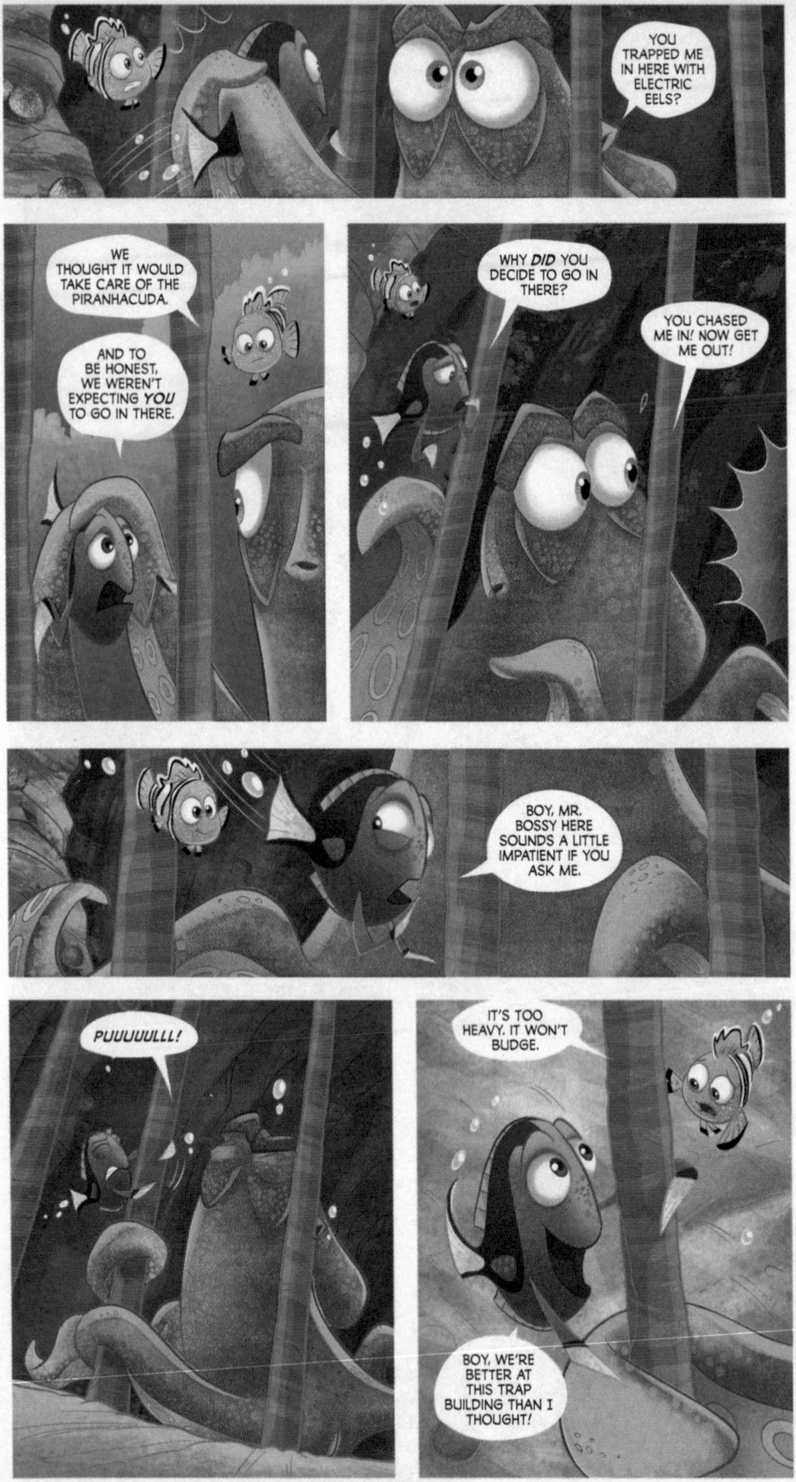
YOU TRAPPED ME IN HERE WITH ELECTRIC EELS?
WE THOUGHT IT WOULD TAKE CARE OF THE PIRANHACUDA.
AND TO BE HONEST, WE WEREN'T EXPECTING *YOU* TO GO IN THERE.
WHY *DID* YOU DECIDE TO GO IN THERE?
YOU CHASED ME IN! NOW GET ME OUT!
BOY, MR. BOSSY HERE SOUNDS A LITTLE IMPATIENT IF YOU ASK ME.
PUUUUULLL!
IT'S TOO HEAVY. IT WON'T BUDGE.
BOY, WE'RE BETTER AT THIS TRAP BUILDING THAN I THOUGHT!

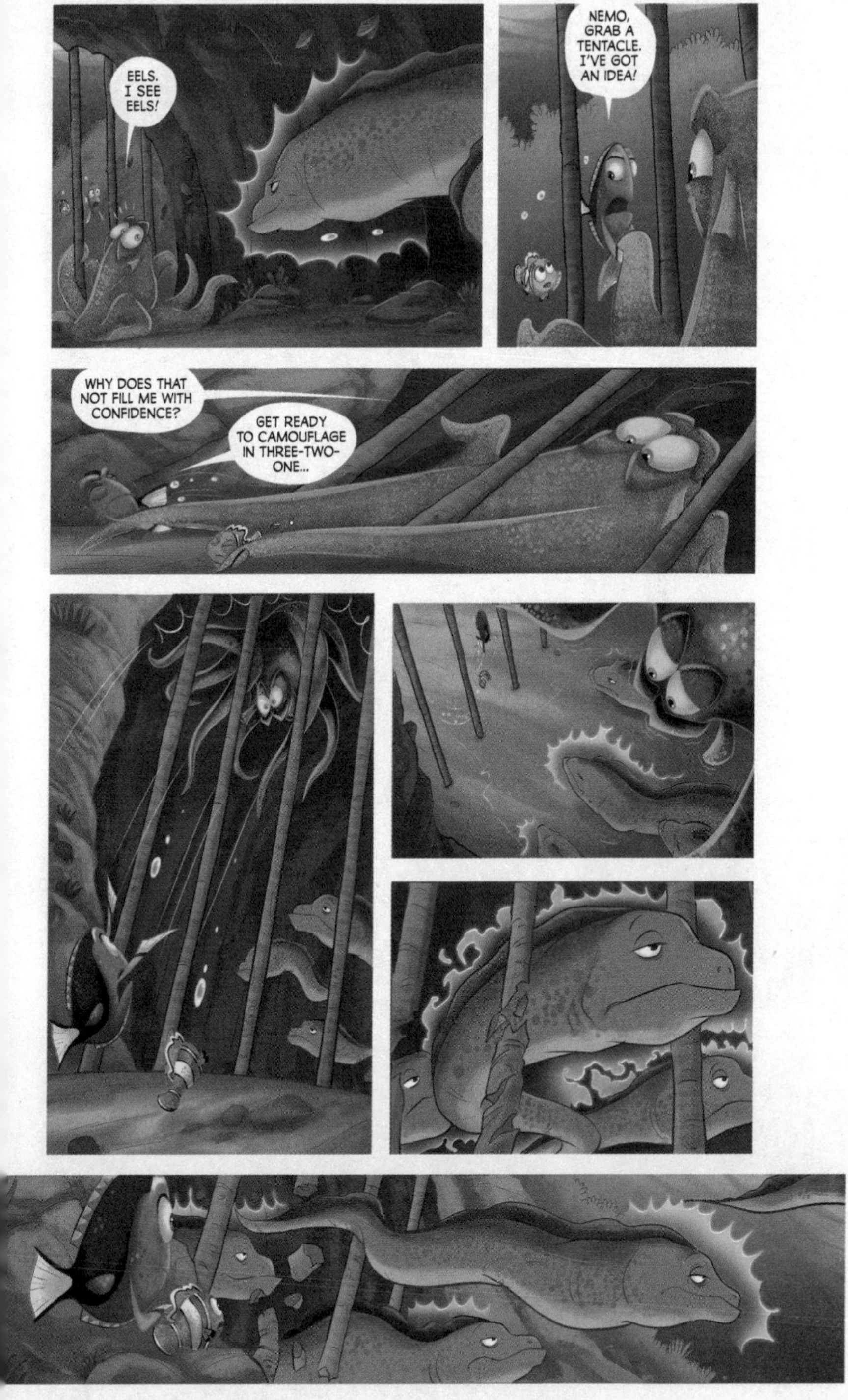
EELS.
I SEE
EELS!
NEMO,
GRAB A
TENTACLE.
I'VE GOT
AN IDEA!
WHY DOES THAT
NOT FILL ME WITH
CONFIDENCE?
GET READY
TO CAMOUFLAGE
IN THREE-TWO-
ONE...

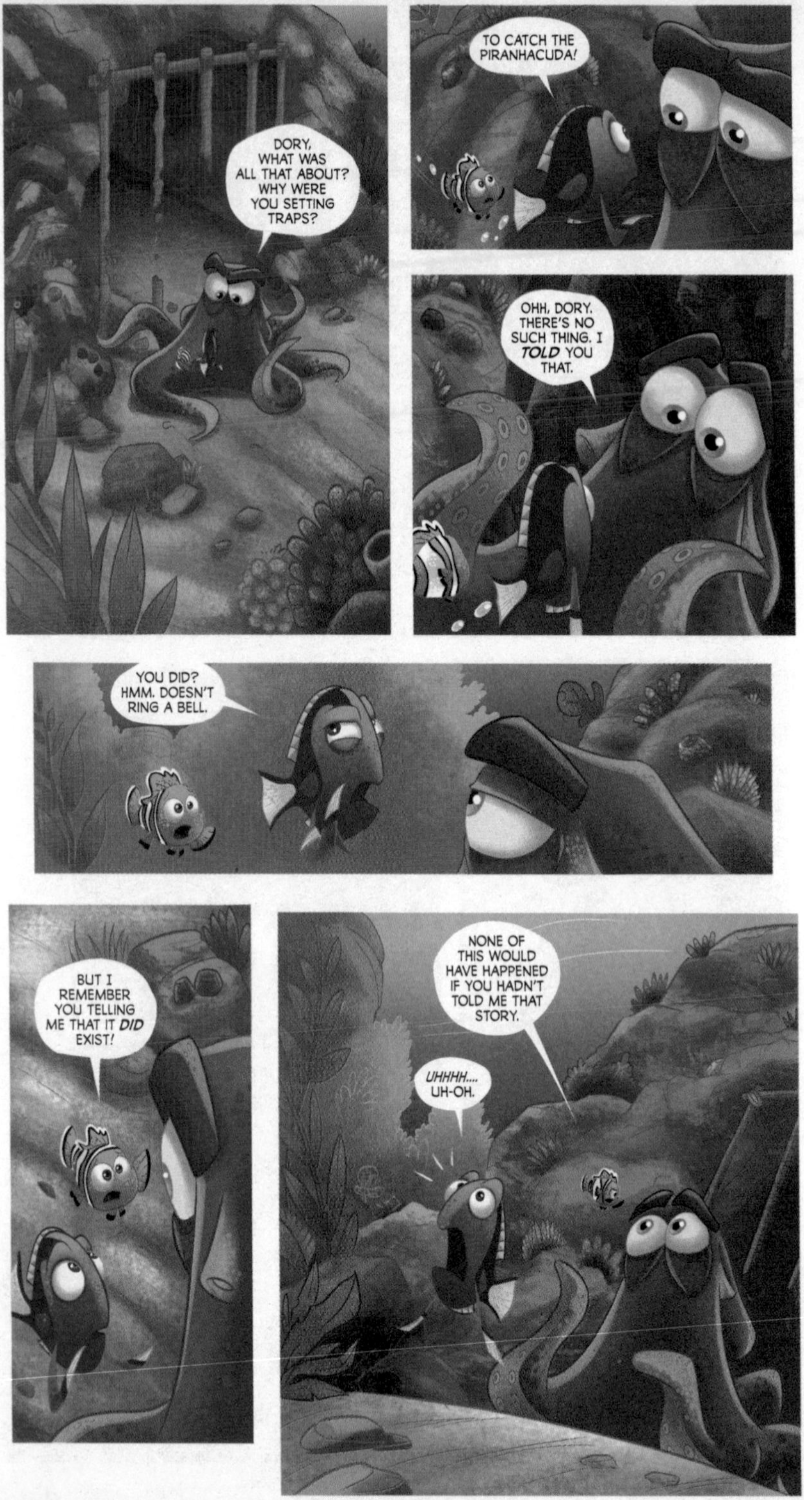
DORY, WHAT WAS ALL THAT ABOUT? WHY WERE YOU SETTING TRAPS?
TO CATCH THE PIRANHACUDA!
OHH, DORY. THERE'S NO SUCH THING. I *TOLD* YOU THAT.
YOU DID? HMM. DOESN'T RING A BELL.
BUT I REMEMBER YOU TELLING ME THAT IT *DID* EXIST!
NONE OF THIS WOULD HAVE HAPPENED IF YOU HADN'T TOLD ME THAT STORY.
UHHHH.... UH-OH.

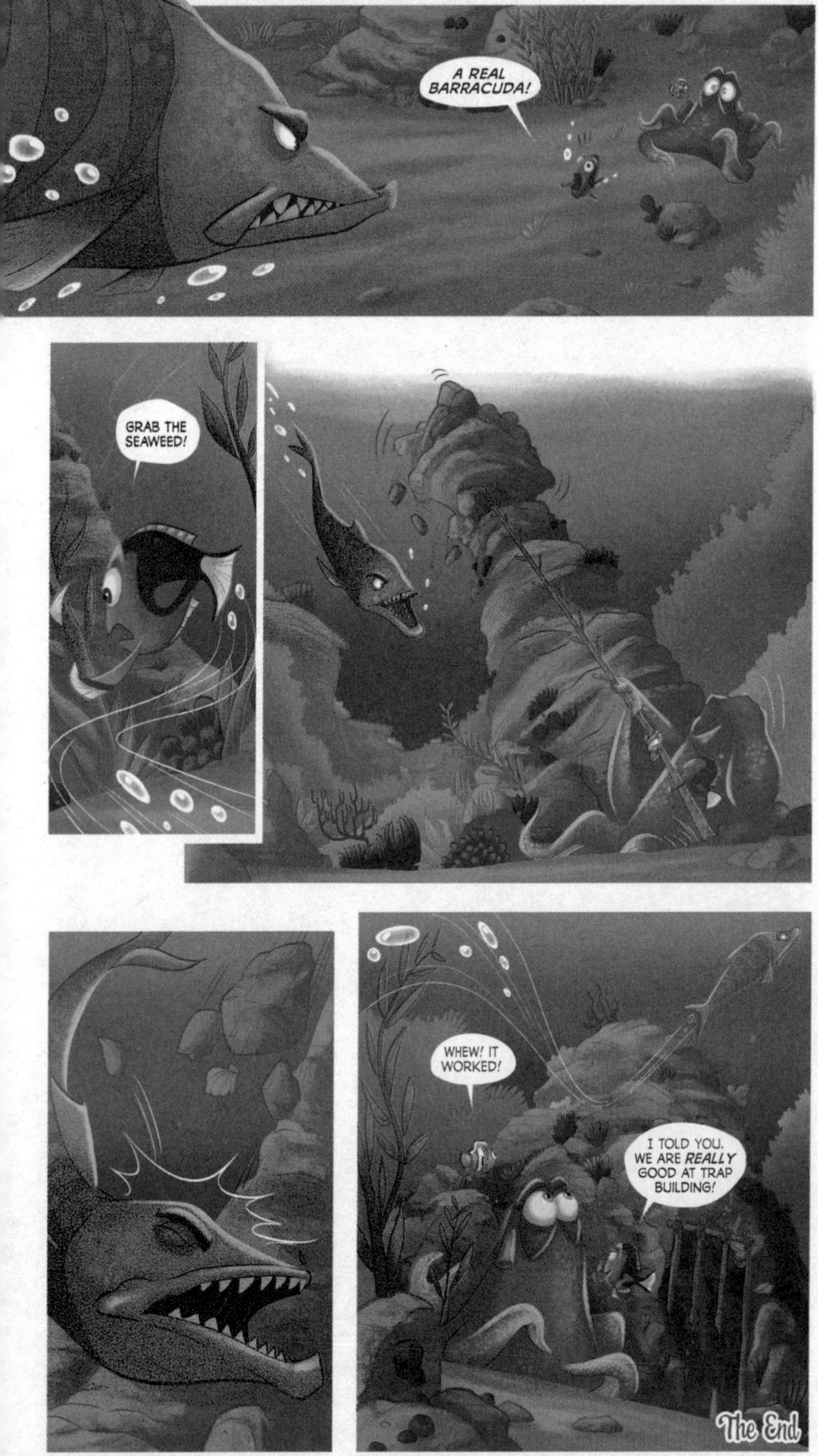
A REAL BARRACUDA!
GRAB THE SEAWEED!
WHEW! IT WORKED!
I TOLD YOU. WE ARE *REALLY* GOOD AT TRAP BUILDING!
The End

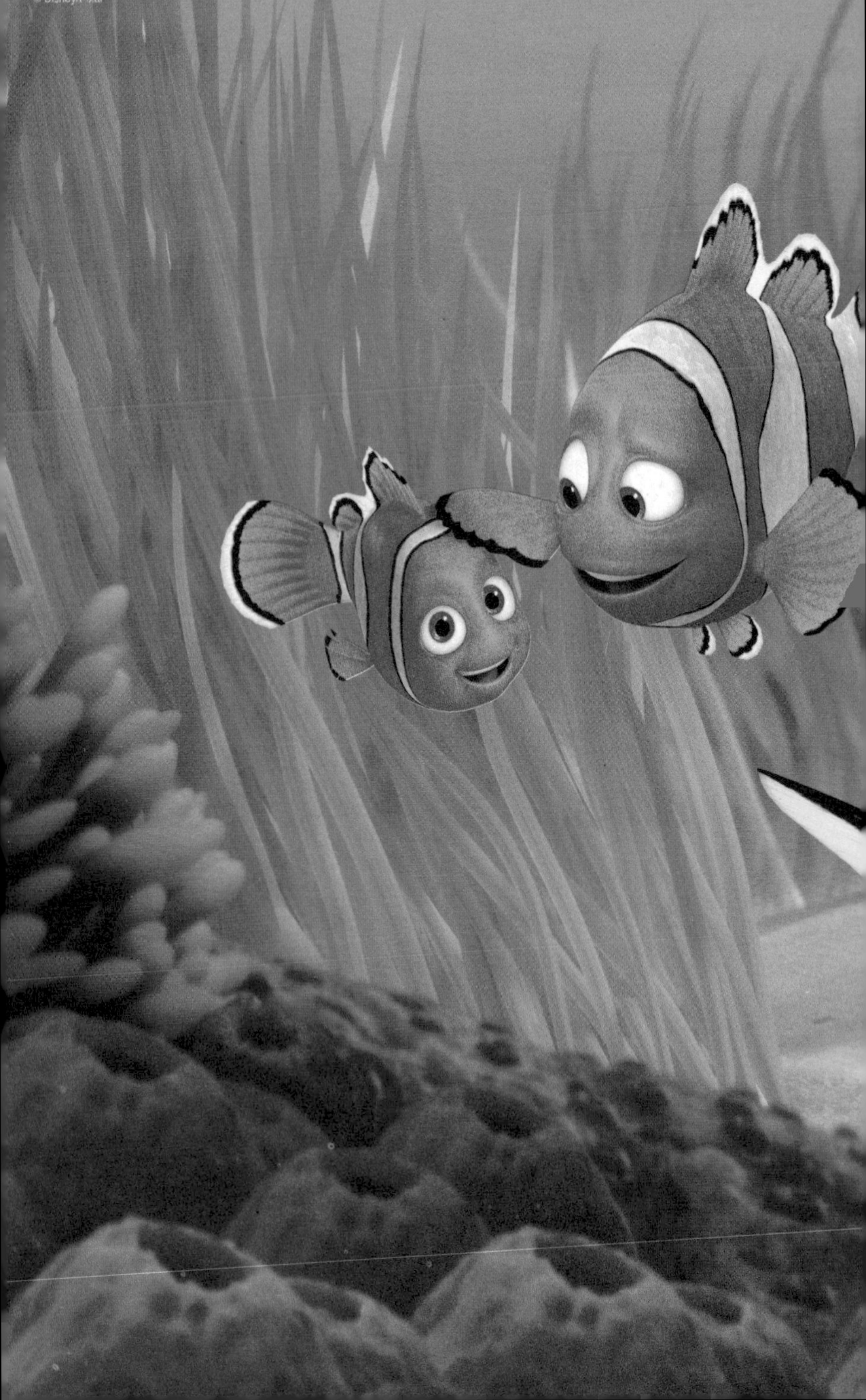

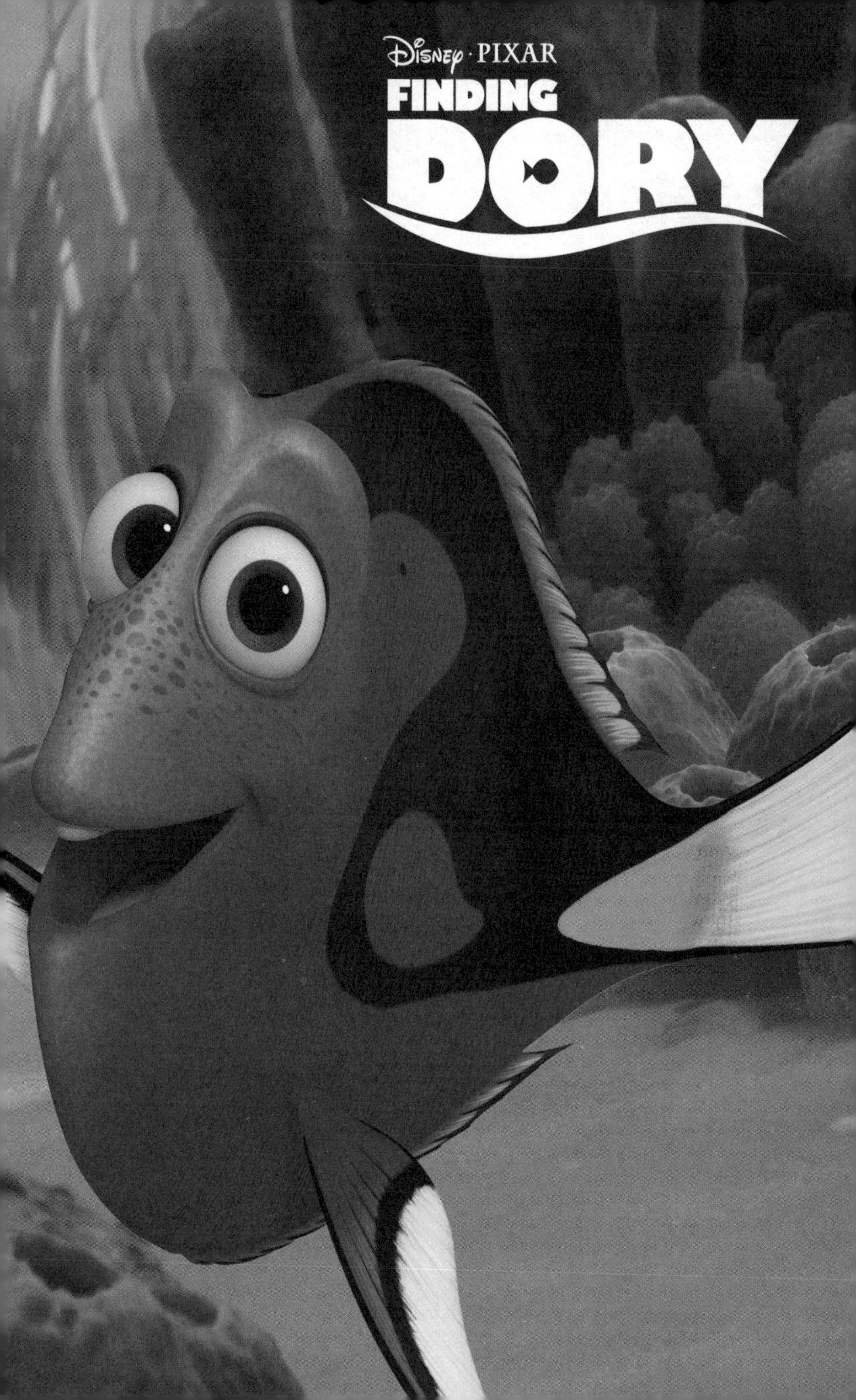
Disney · PIXAR
FINDING
DORY

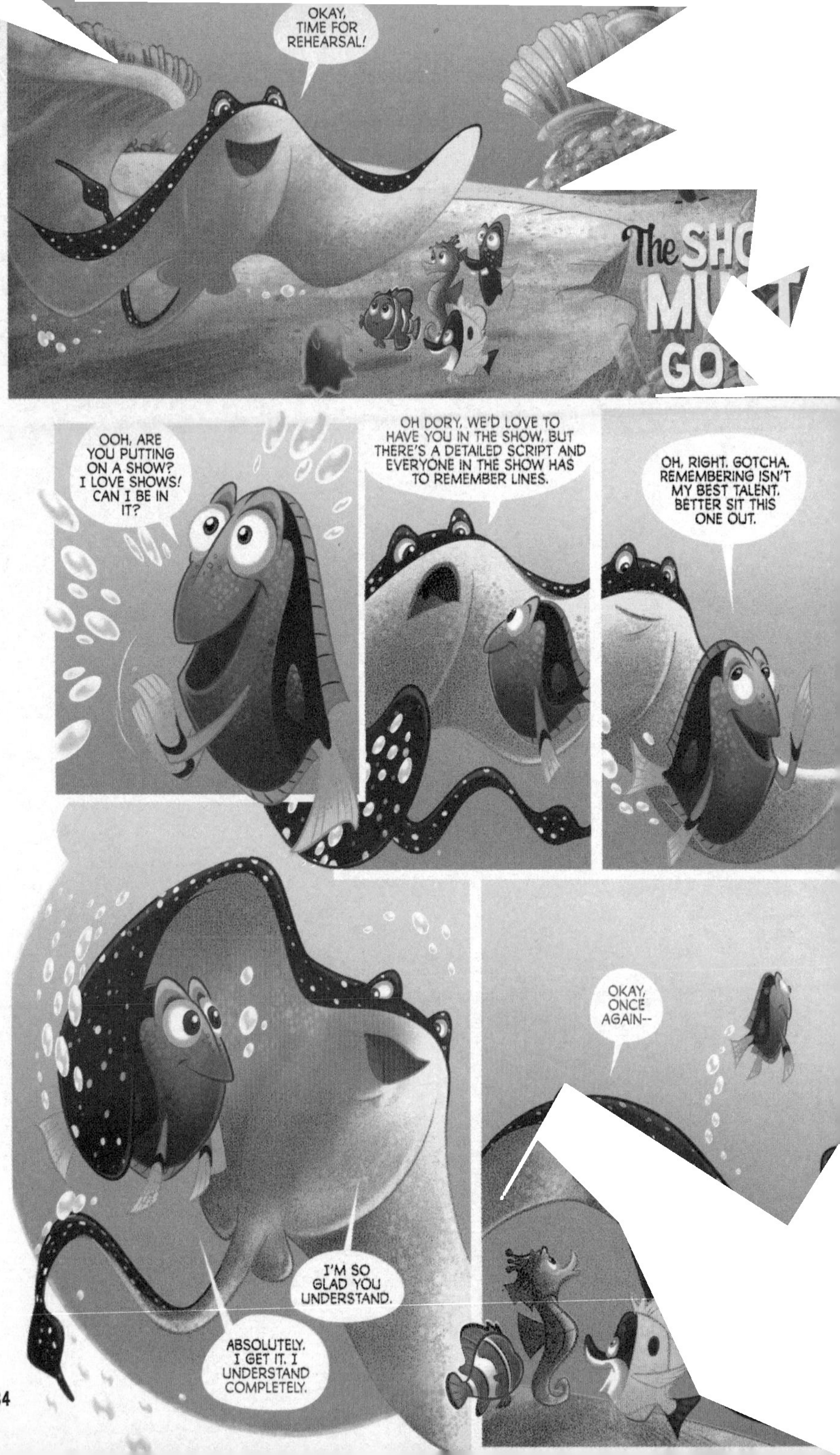
The SHO
MU
GO
OKAY, TIME FOR REHEARSAL!
OOH, ARE YOU PUTTING ON A SHOW? I LOVE SHOWS! CAN I BE IN IT?
OH DORY, WE'D LOVE TO HAVE YOU IN THE SHOW, BUT THERE'S A DETAILED SCRIPT AND EVERYONE IN THE SHOW HAS TO REMEMBER LINES.
OH, RIGHT. GOTCHA. REMEMBERING ISN'T MY BEST TALENT. BETTER SIT THIS ONE OUT.
I'M SO GLAD YOU UNDERSTAND.
ABSOLUTELY. I GET IT. I UNDERSTAND COMPLETELY.
OKAY, ONCE AGAIN--

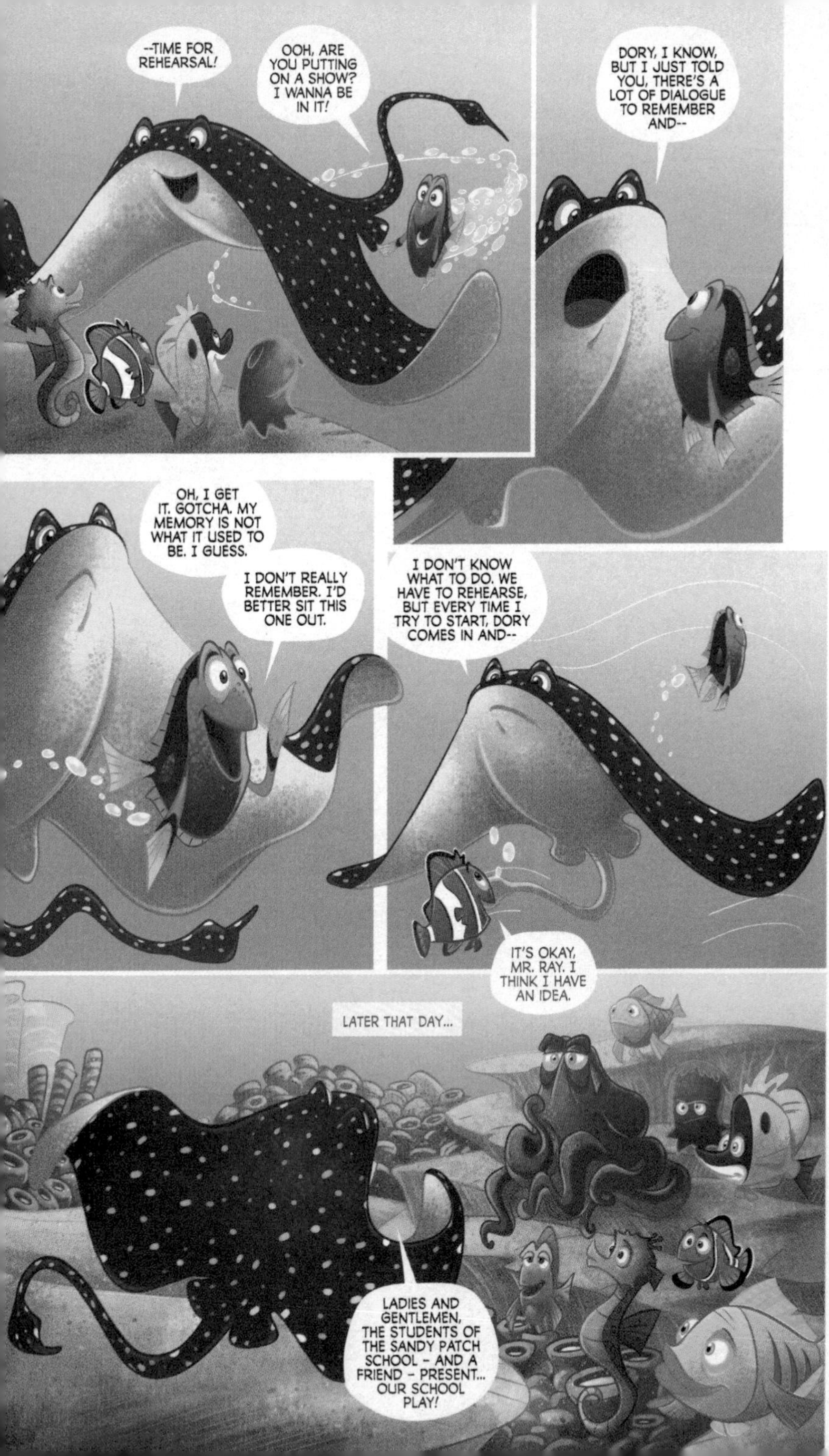
--TIME FOR REHEARSAL!
OOH, ARE YOU PUTTING ON A SHOW? I WANNA BE IN IT!
DORY, I KNOW, BUT I JUST TOLD YOU, THERE'S A LOT OF DIALOGUE TO REMEMBER AND--
OH, I GET IT. GOTCHA. MY MEMORY IS NOT WHAT IT USED TO BE. I GUESS.
I DON'T REALLY REMEMBER. I'D BETTER SIT THIS ONE OUT.
I DON'T KNOW WHAT TO DO. WE HAVE TO REHEARSE, BUT EVERY TIME I TRY TO START, DORY COMES IN AND--
IT'S OKAY, MR. RAY. I THINK I HAVE AN IDEA.
LATER THAT DAY...
LADIES AND GENTLEMEN, THE STUDENTS OF THE SANDY PATCH SCHOOL - AND A FRIEND - PRESENT... OUR SCHOOL PLAY!

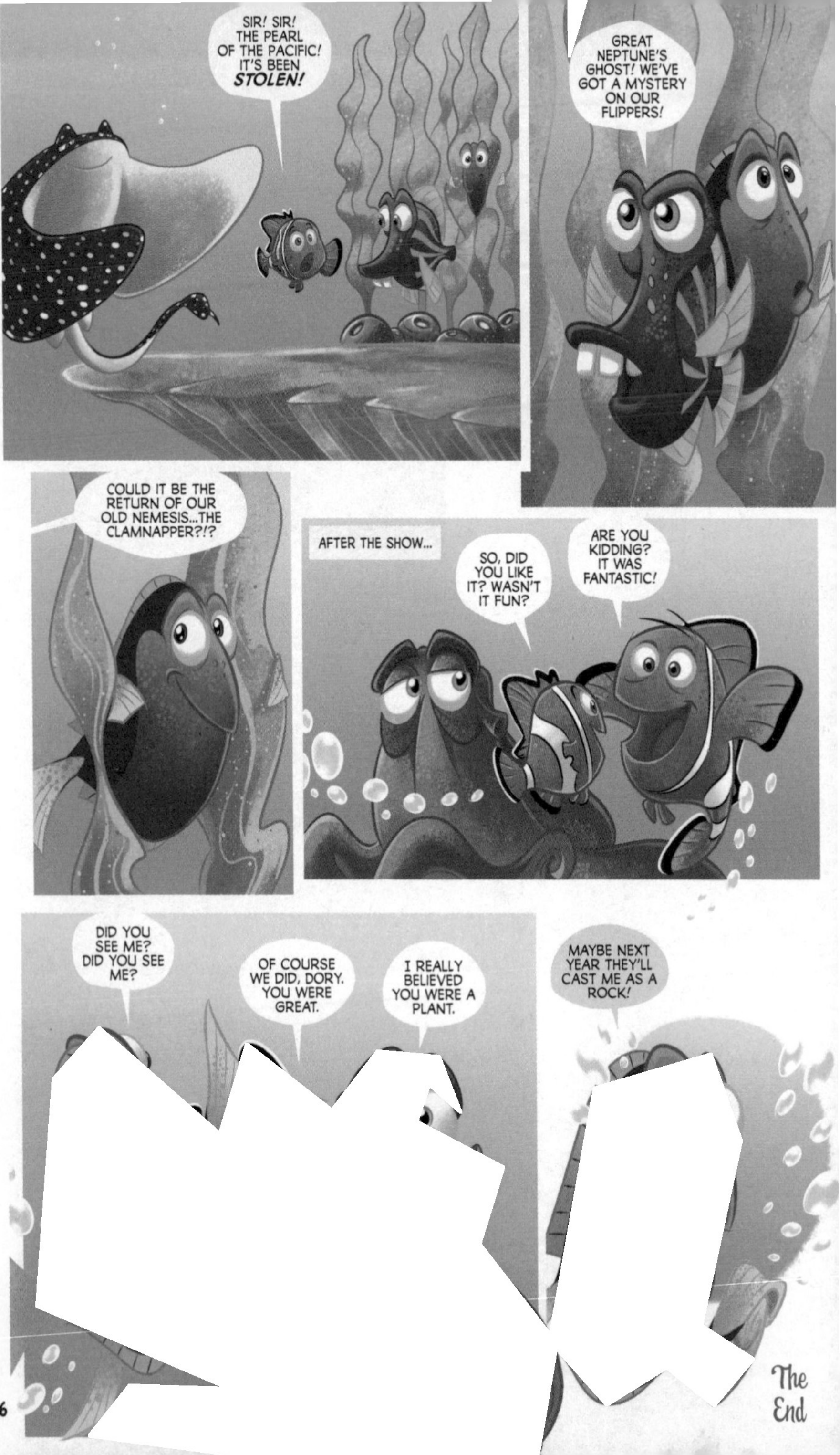
SIR! SIR! THE PEARL OF THE PACIFIC! IT'S BEEN **STOLEN!**
GREAT NEPTUNE'S GHOST! WE'VE GOT A MYSTERY ON OUR FLIPPERS!
COULD IT BE THE RETURN OF OUR OLD NEMESIS...THE CLAMNAPPER?!?
AFTER THE SHOW...
SO, DID YOU LIKE IT? WASN'T IT FUN?
ARE YOU KIDDING? IT WAS FANTASTIC!
DID YOU SEE ME? DID YOU SEE ME?
OF COURSE WE DID, DORY. YOU WERE GREAT.
I REALLY BELIEVED YOU WERE A PLANT.
MAYBE NEXT YEAR THEY'LL CAST ME AS A ROCK!
The End

CLAM Chat

A GOOD LISTENER. THAT'S A VALUABLE TRAIT IN A VISITOR, IN ANYONE REALLY. WOULDN'T YOU AGREE?

I JUST HATE THOSE GUYS WHO TALK AND TALK AND DON'T LET YOU GET A WORD IN EDGEWISE, RIGHT?

...

...

I MEAN, I'LL LISTEN. I'M ALL EARS. SERIOUSLY, IT'S NOT LIKE I HAVE EYES OR ANYTHING. WELL, I DON'T TECHNICALLY HAVE EARS EITHER, BUT I CAN HEAR. I DON'T KNOW WHY, IT'S A MIRACLE OF MODERN SCIENCE!

BUT THERE'S SUCH A THING AS "GIVE AND TAKE."

SHELLY AND I HAD THAT. GIVE AND TAKE.

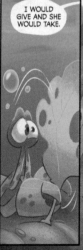

I WOULD GIVE AND SHE WOULD TAKE.

BUT YOU DON'T WANT TO GET ME STARTED ON THAT SUBJECT; I'LL TALK ALL NIGHT.

187

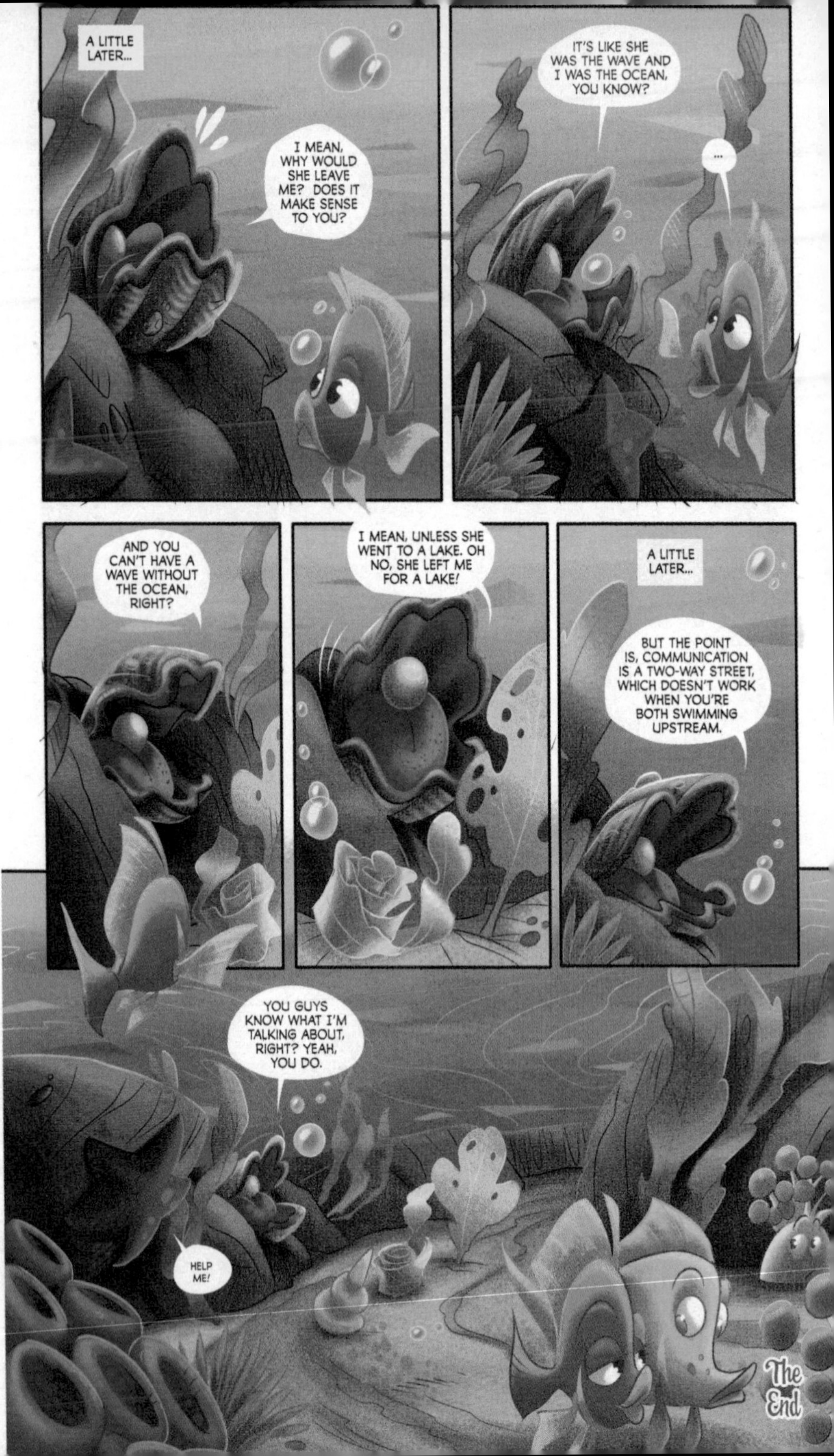
A LITTLE LATER...
I MEAN, WHY WOULD SHE LEAVE ME? DOES IT MAKE SENSE TO YOU?
IT'S LIKE SHE WAS THE WAVE AND I WAS THE OCEAN, YOU KNOW?
...
AND YOU CAN'T HAVE A WAVE WITHOUT THE OCEAN, RIGHT?
I MEAN, UNLESS SHE WENT TO A LAKE. OH NO, SHE LEFT ME FOR A LAKE!
A LITTLE LATER...
BUT THE POINT IS, COMMUNICATION IS A TWO-WAY STREET, WHICH DOESN'T WORK WHEN YOU'RE BOTH SWIMMING UPSTREAM.
YOU GUYS KNOW WHAT I'M TALKING ABOUT, RIGHT? YEAH, YOU DO.
HELP ME!
The End

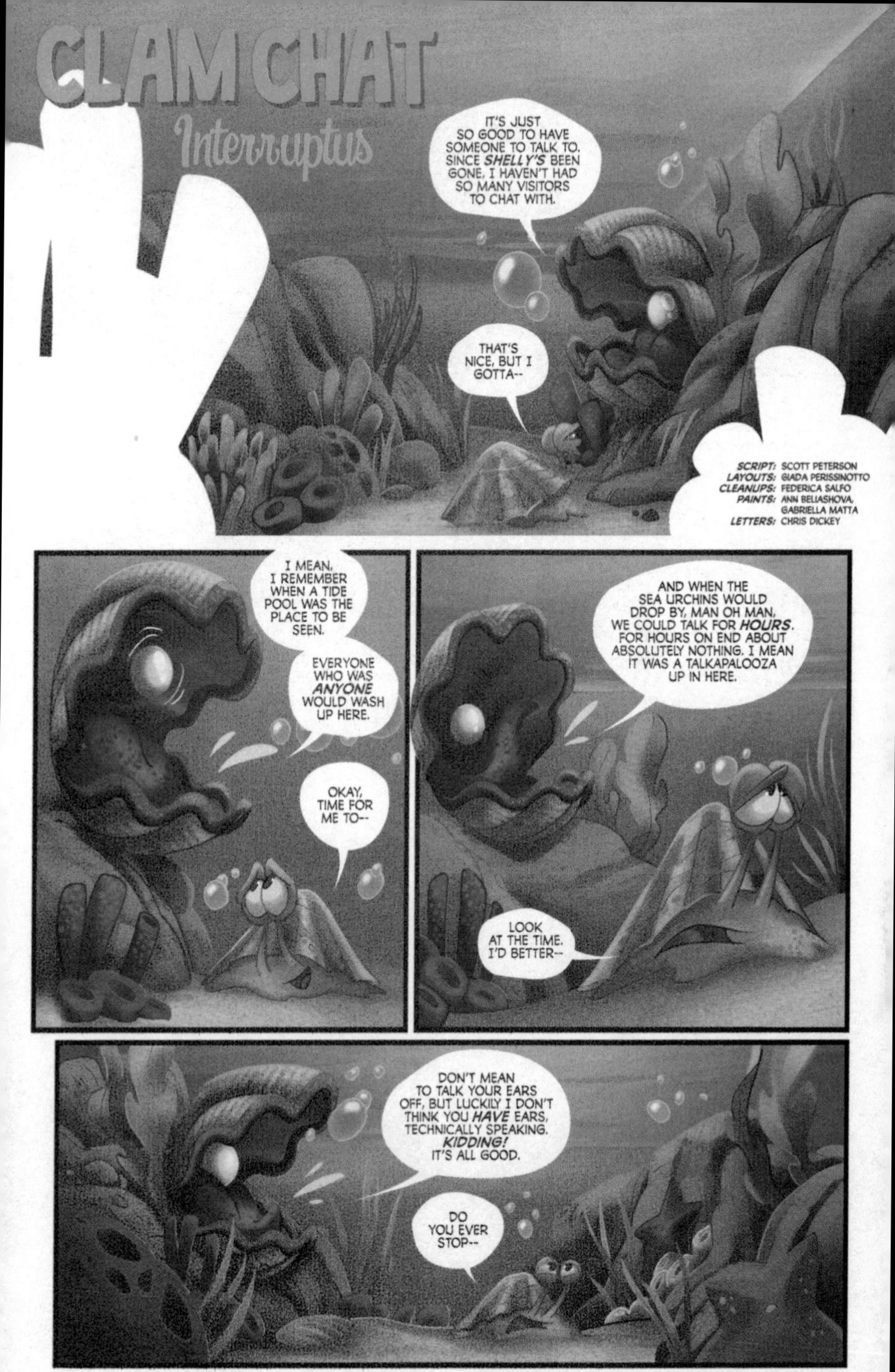
CLAM CHAT
Interruptus
IT'S JUST SO GOOD TO HAVE SOMEONE TO TALK TO. SINCE SHELLY'S BEEN GONE, I HAVEN'T HAD SO MANY VISITORS TO CHAT WITH.
THAT'S NICE, BUT I GOTTA--
SCRIPT: SCOTT PETERSON
LAYOUTS: GIADA PERISSINOTTO
CLEANUPS: FEDERICA SALFO
PAINTS: ANN BELIASHOVA, GABRIELLA MATTA
LETTERS: CHRIS DICKEY
I MEAN, I REMEMBER WHEN A TIDE POOL WAS THE PLACE TO BE SEEN.
EVERYONE WHO WAS ANYONE WOULD WASH UP HERE.
OKAY, TIME FOR ME TO--
AND WHEN THE SEA URCHINS WOULD DROP BY, MAN OH MAN, WE COULD TALK FOR HOURS. FOR HOURS ON END ABOUT ABSOLUTELY NOTHING. I MEAN IT WAS A TALKAPALOOZA UP IN HERE.
LOOK AT THE TIME. I'D BETTER--
DON'T MEAN TO TALK YOUR EARS OFF, BUT LUCKILY I DON'T THINK YOU HAVE EARS, TECHNICALLY SPEAKING. KIDDING! IT'S ALL GOOD.
DO YOU EVER STOP--

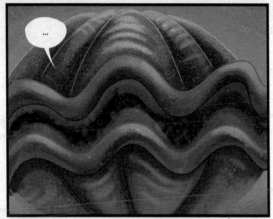

AND IT'S LIKE I ALWAYS SAY--

...

HELLO... SHUCK.

SHELLY?

PHEW. THAT SEEMED AWKWARD. OKAY, WELL, I'D BETTER GET GOING BEFORE --

OOF!

AAAAAAAAAARGH! SHELLY, WHY DID YOU LEAVE ME? *WHYYYY?* WHAT'S HE GOT THAT I HAVEN'T GOT? BESIDES A FANCY SHELL AND A SLIME TRAIL THAT STRETCHES FROM HERE TO THE NORTH PACIFIC!

IT'S ALWAYS THE QUIET ONES, I TELL YOU; YOU JUST CAN'T TRUST 'EM. *AAAAAAAUGH!*

THE END!

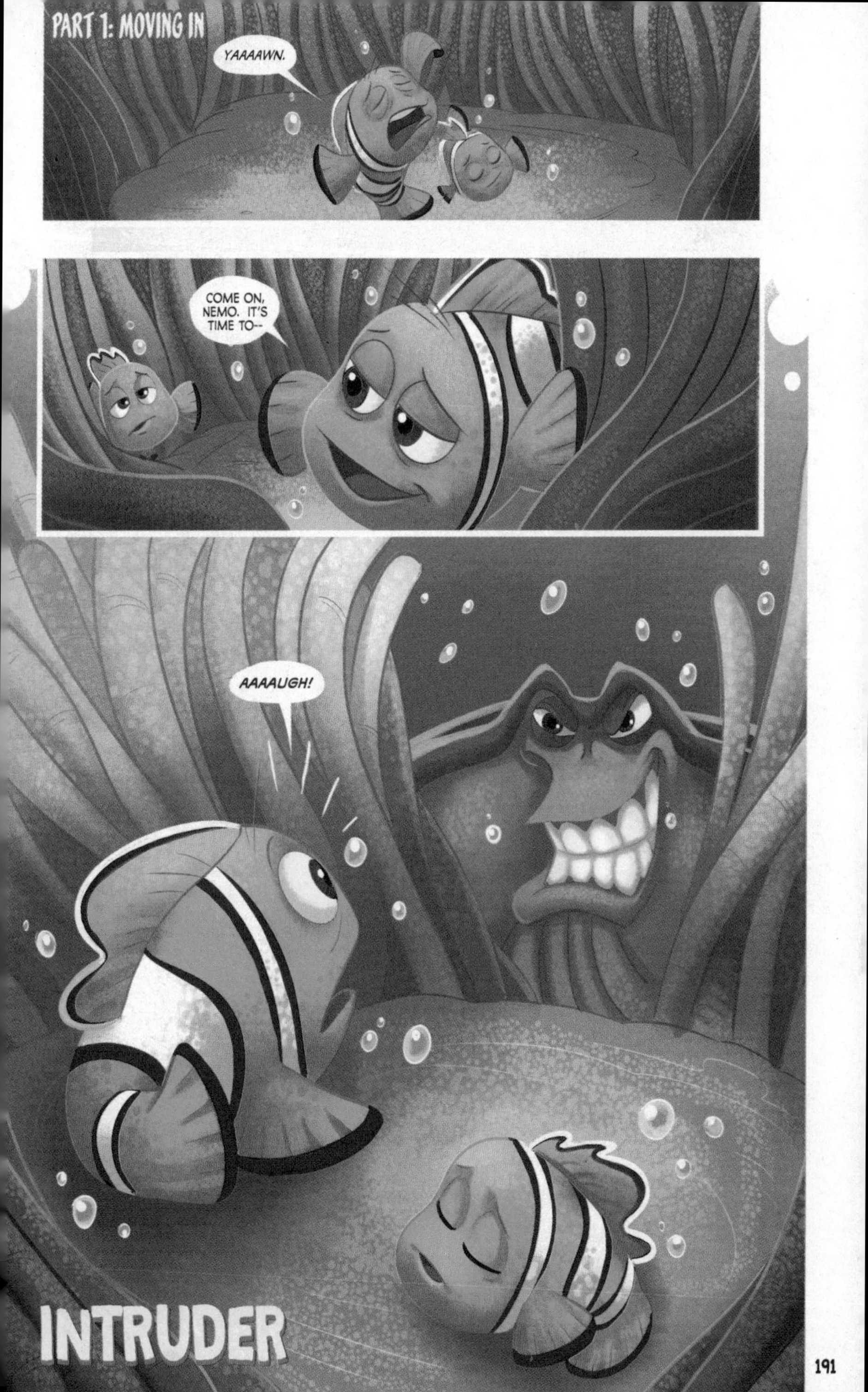
PART 1: MOVING IN
YAAAAWN.
COME ON, NEMO. IT'S TIME TO--
AAAAUGH!
INTRUDER

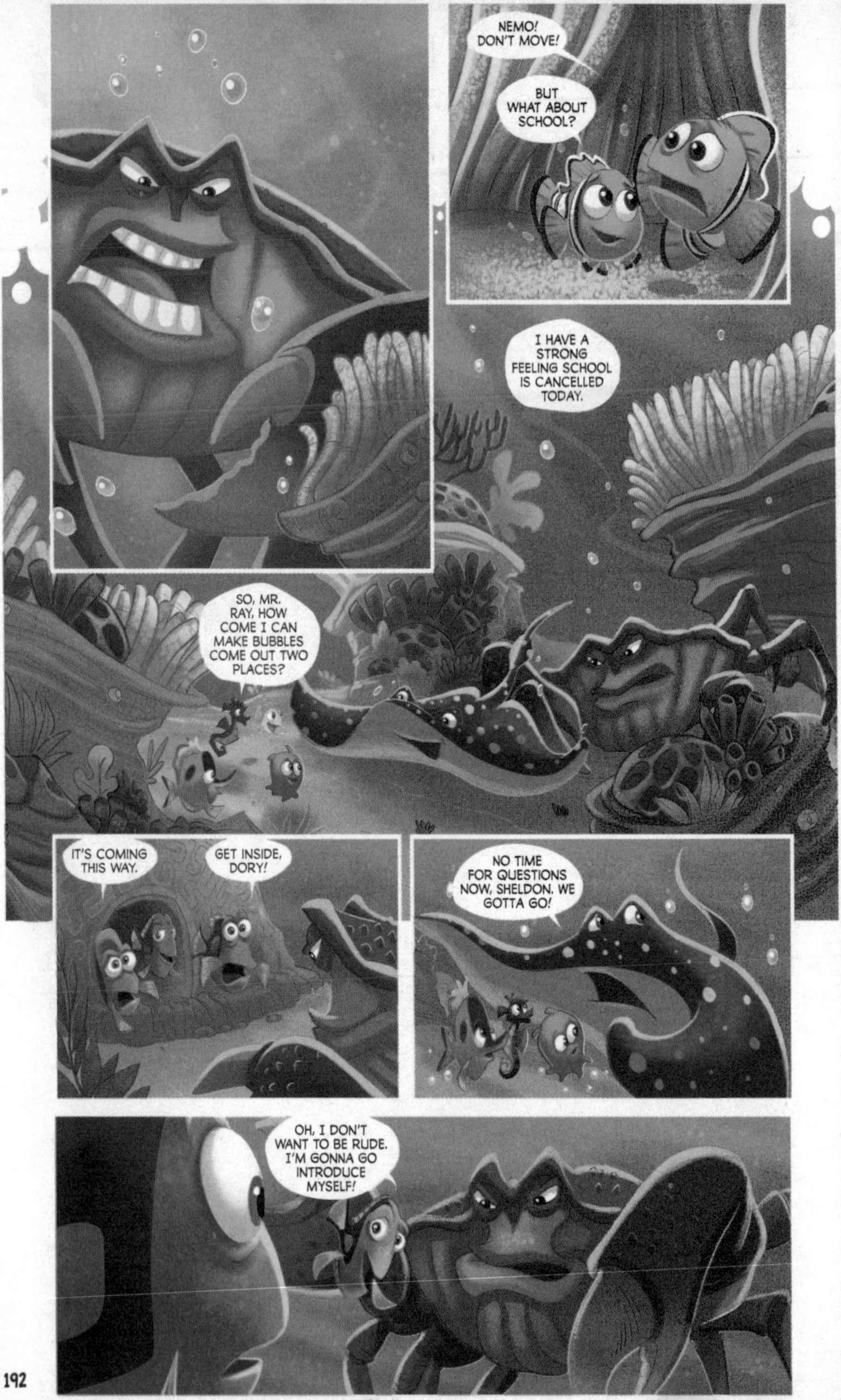
NEMO! DON'T MOVE!
BUT WHAT ABOUT SCHOOL?
I HAVE A STRONG FEELING SCHOOL IS CANCELLED TODAY.
SO, MR. RAY, HOW COME I CAN MAKE BUBBLES COME OUT TWO PLACES?
IT'S COMING THIS WAY.
GET INSIDE, DORY!
NO TIME FOR QUESTIONS NOW, SHELDON. WE GOTTA GO!
OH, I DON'T WANT TO BE RUDE. I'M GONNA GO INTRODUCE MYSELF!

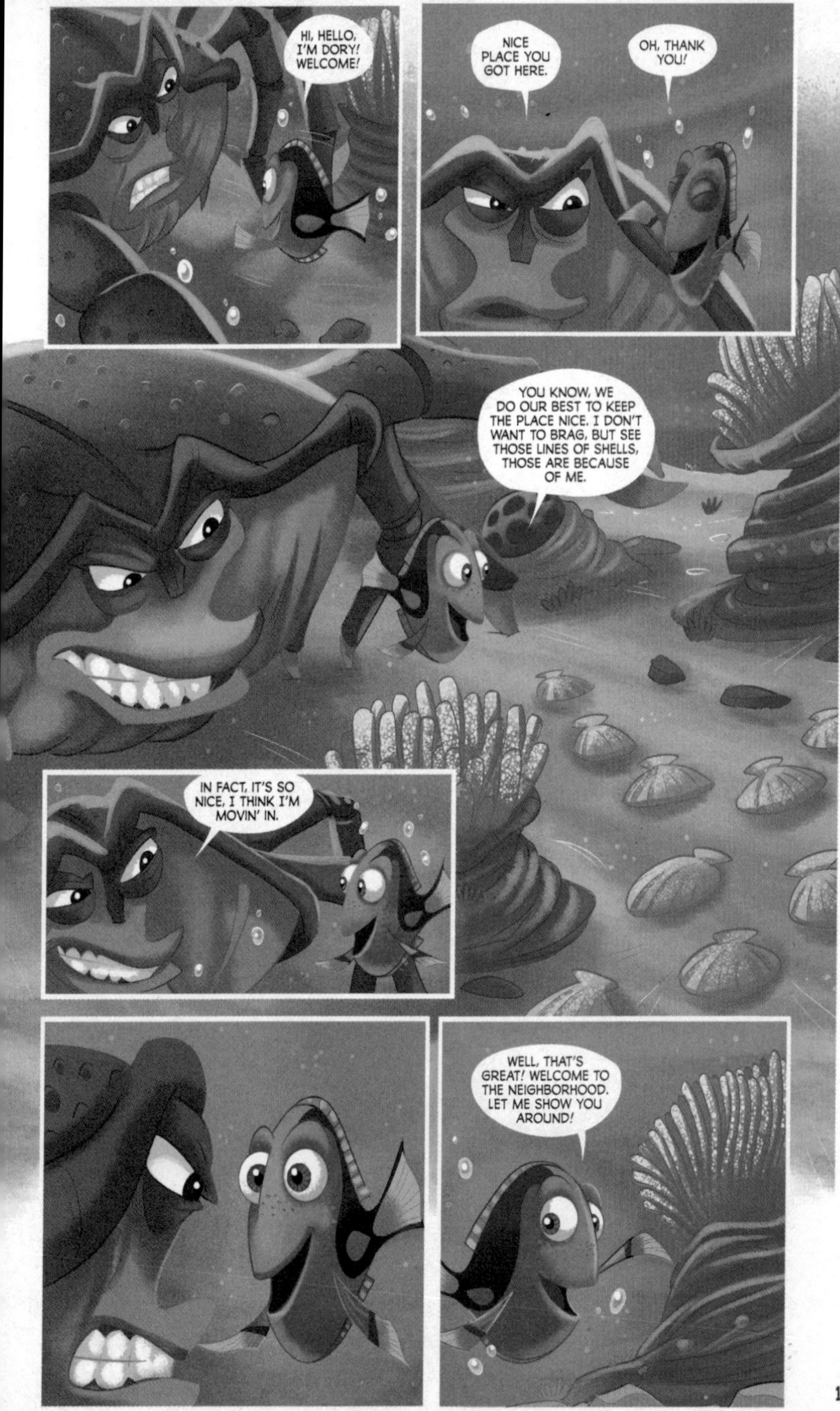
HI, HELLO, I'M DORY! WELCOME!
NICE PLACE YOU GOT HERE.
OH, THANK YOU!
YOU KNOW, WE DO OUR BEST TO KEEP THE PLACE NICE. I DON'T WANT TO BRAG, BUT SEE THOSE LINES OF SHELLS, THOSE ARE BECAUSE OF ME.
IN FACT, IT'S SO NICE, I THINK I'M MOVIN' IN.
WELL, THAT'S GREAT! WELCOME TO THE NEIGHBORHOOD. LET ME SHOW YOU AROUND!

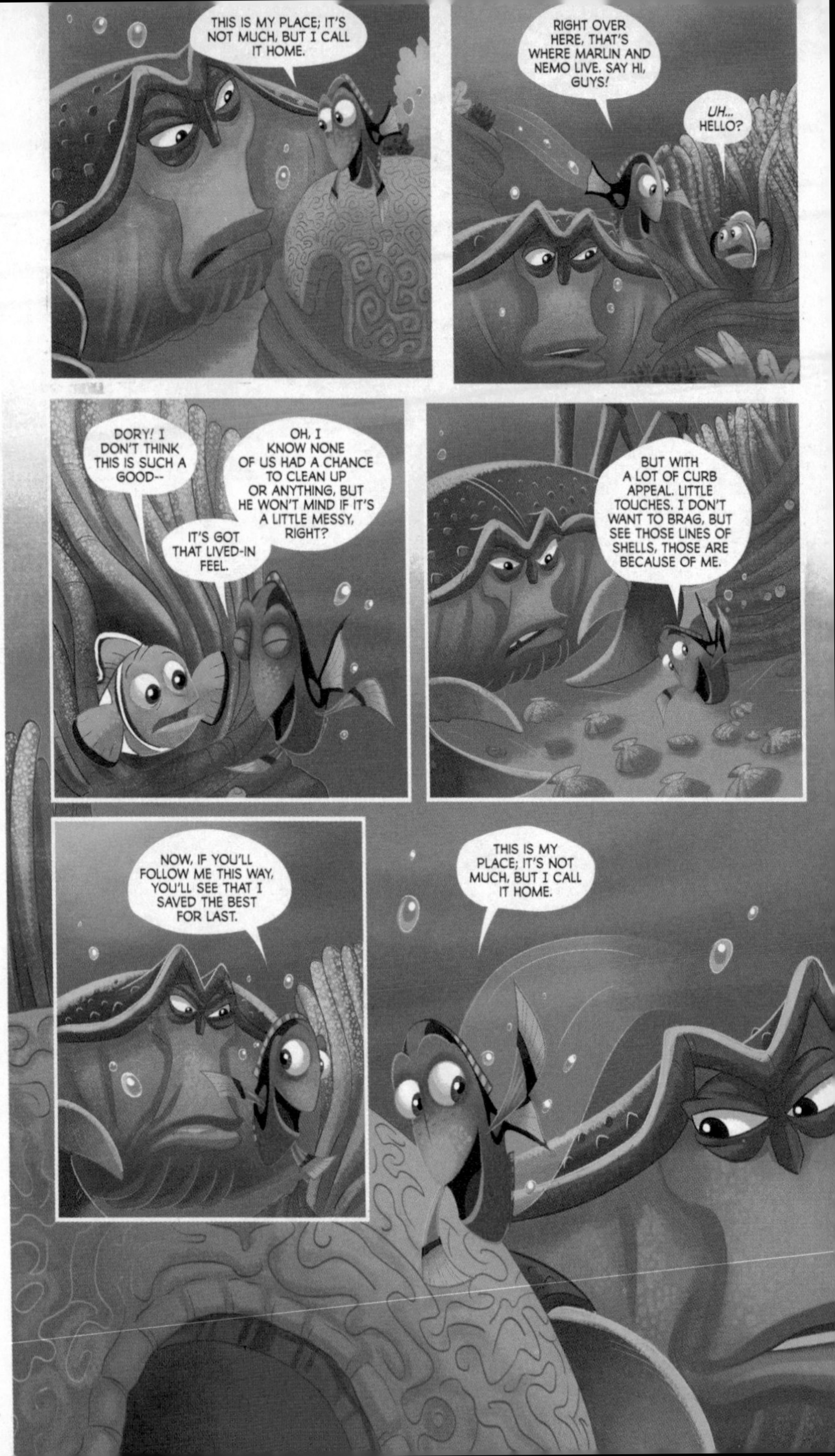
THIS IS MY PLACE; IT'S NOT MUCH, BUT I CALL IT HOME.
RIGHT OVER HERE, THAT'S WHERE MARLIN AND NEMO LIVE. SAY HI, GUYS!
UH... HELLO?
DORY! I DON'T THINK THIS IS SUCH A GOOD--
OH, I KNOW NONE OF US HAD A CHANCE TO CLEAN UP OR ANYTHING, BUT HE WON'T MIND IF IT'S A LITTLE MESSY, RIGHT?
IT'S GOT THAT LIVED-IN FEEL.
BUT WITH A LOT OF CURB APPEAL. LITTLE TOUCHES. I DON'T WANT TO BRAG, BUT SEE THOSE LINES OF SHELLS, THOSE ARE BECAUSE OF ME.
NOW, IF YOU'LL FOLLOW ME THIS WAY, YOU'LL SEE THAT I SAVED THE BEST FOR LAST.
THIS IS MY PLACE; IT'S NOT MUCH, BUT I CALL IT HOME.

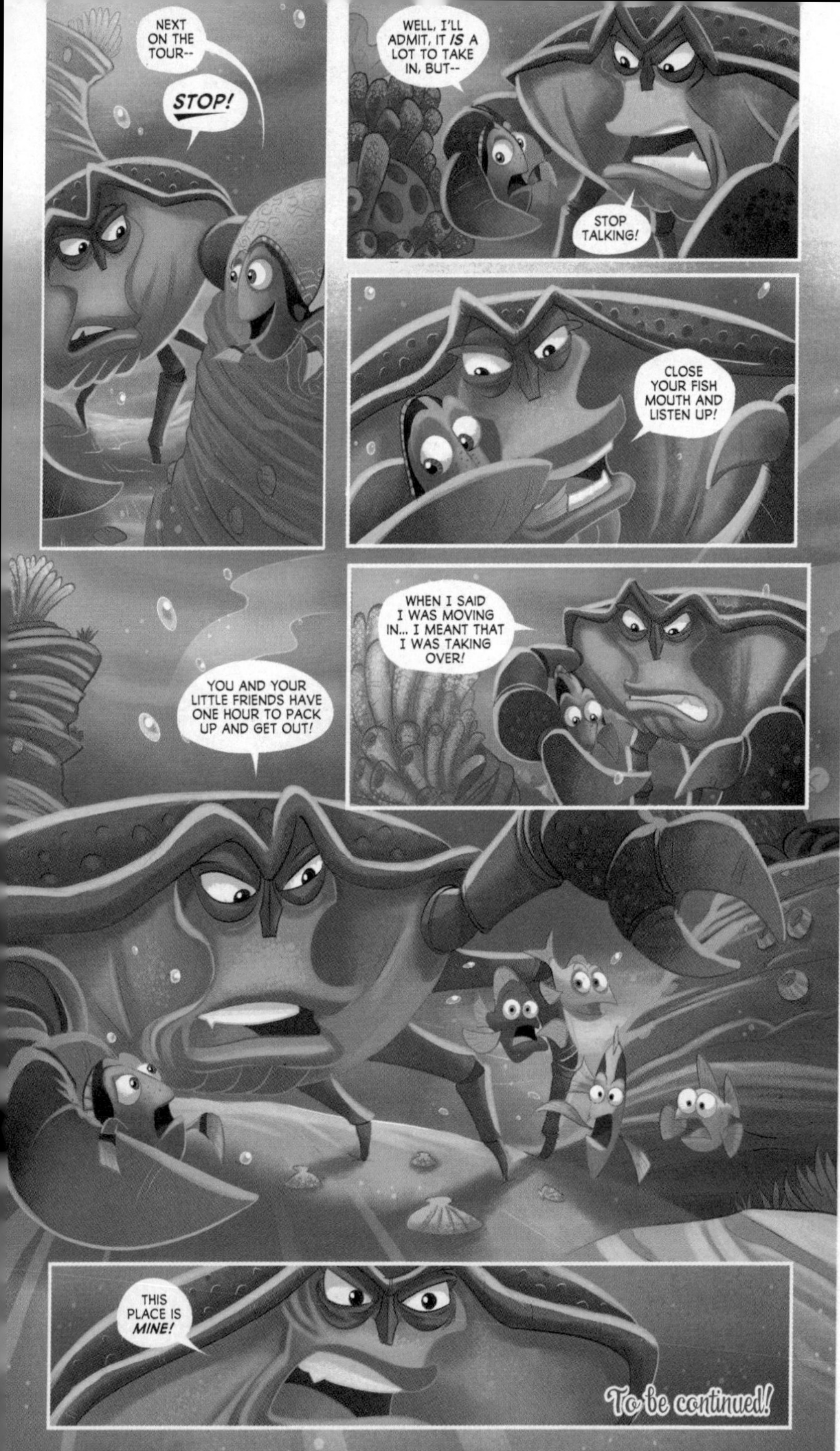
NEXT ON THE TOUR--
STOP!
WELL, I'LL ADMIT, IT *IS* A LOT TO TAKE IN, BUT--
STOP TALKING!
CLOSE YOUR FISH MOUTH AND LISTEN UP!
WHEN I SAID I WAS MOVING IN... I MEANT THAT I WAS TAKING OVER!
YOU AND YOUR LITTLE FRIENDS HAVE ONE HOUR TO PACK UP AND GET OUT!
THIS PLACE IS *MINE!*
To be continued!

PART 2: GET OUT

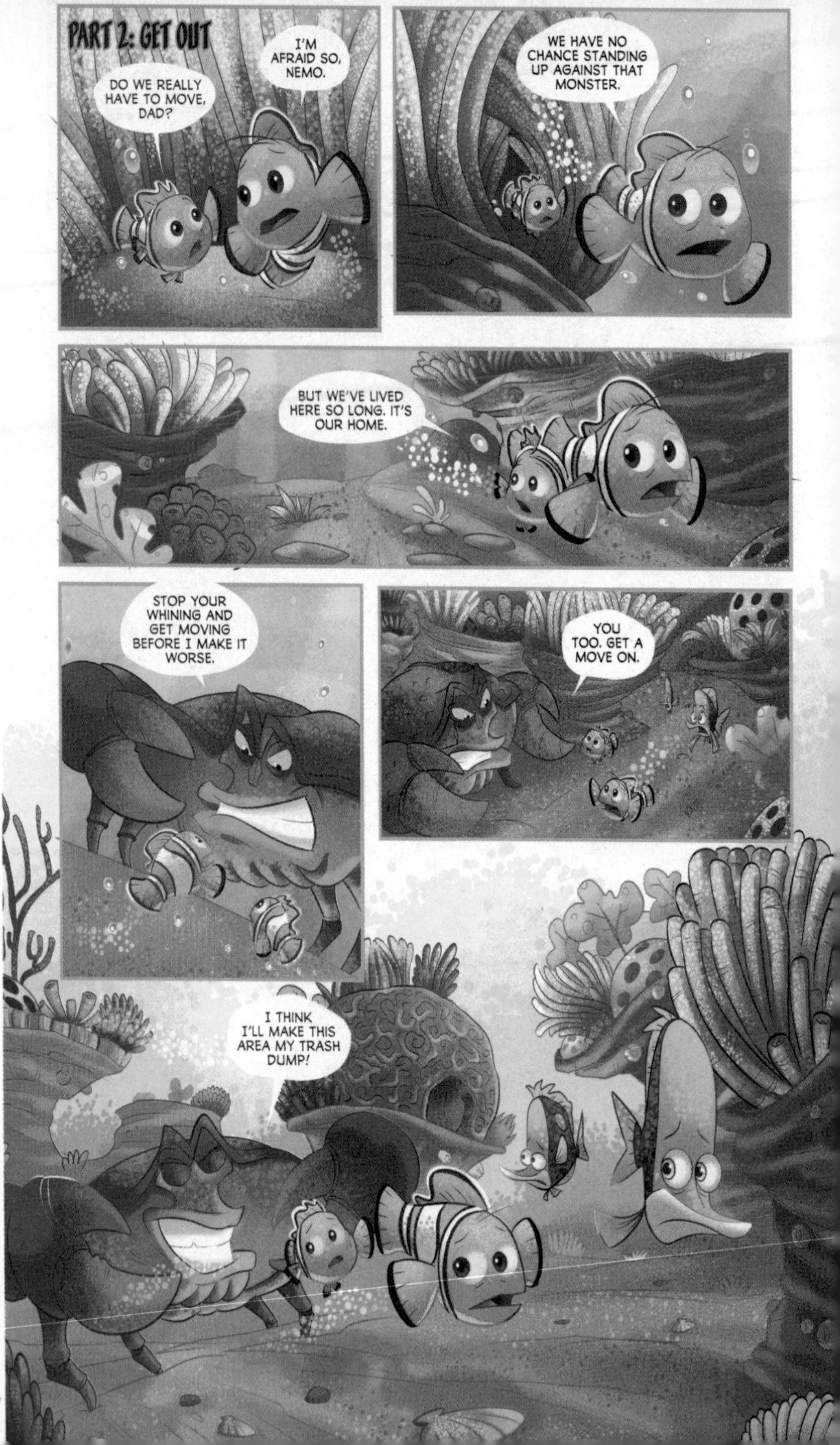

DO WE REALLY HAVE TO MOVE, DAD?
I'M AFRAID SO, NEMO.
WE HAVE NO CHANCE STANDING UP AGAINST THAT MONSTER.
BUT WE'VE LIVED HERE SO LONG. IT'S OUR HOME.
STOP YOUR WHINING AND GET MOVING BEFORE I MAKE IT WORSE.
YOU TOO. GET A MOVE ON.
I THINK I'LL MAKE THIS AREA MY TRASH DUMP!

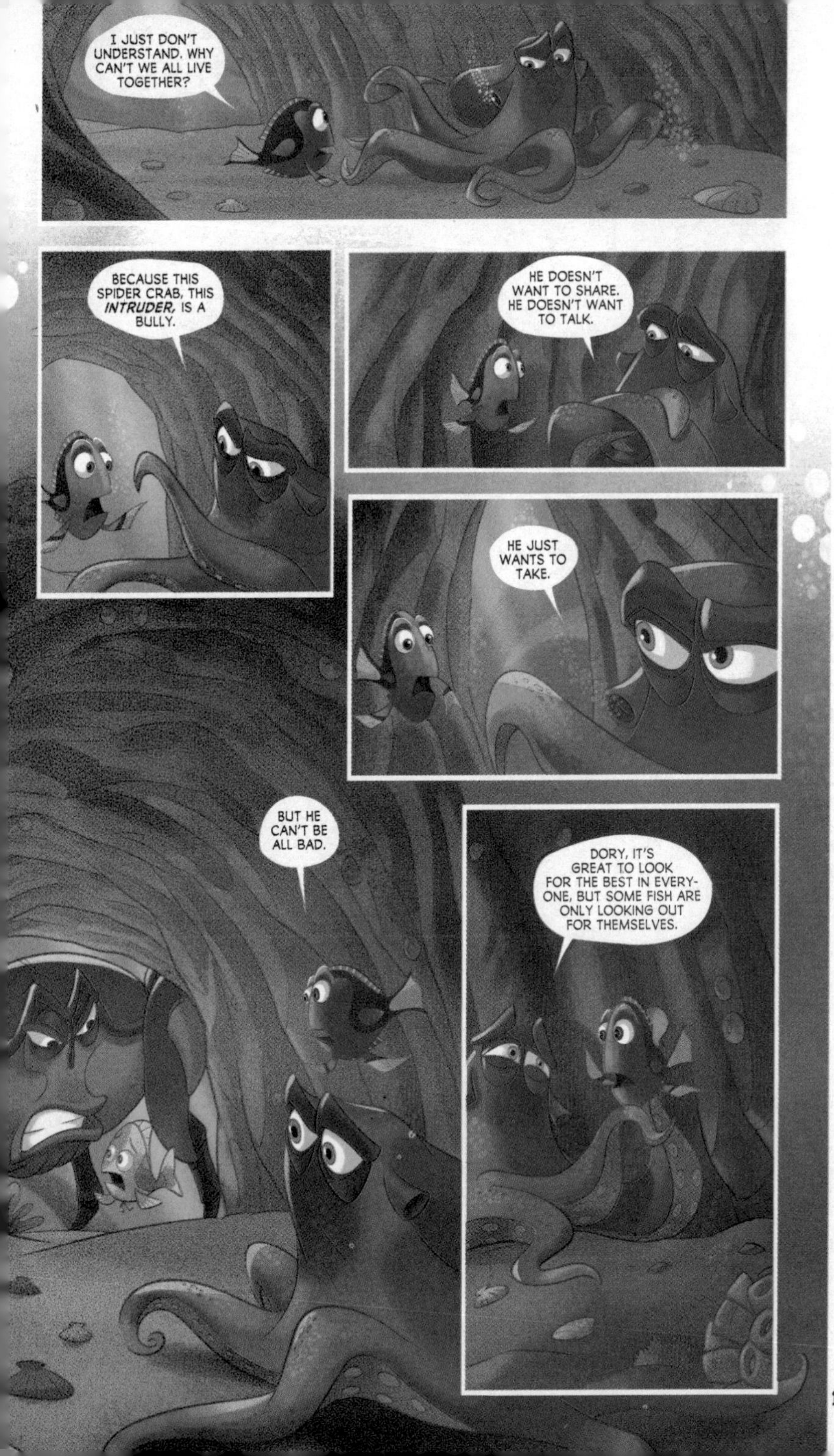
I JUST DON'T UNDERSTAND. WHY CAN'T WE ALL LIVE TOGETHER?
BECAUSE THIS SPIDER CRAB, THIS *INTRUDER,* IS A BULLY.
HE DOESN'T WANT TO SHARE. HE DOESN'T WANT TO TALK.
HE JUST WANTS TO TAKE.
BUT HE CAN'T BE ALL BAD.
DORY, IT'S GREAT TO LOOK FOR THE BEST IN EVERY-ONE, BUT SOME FISH ARE ONLY LOOKING OUT FOR THEMSELVES.

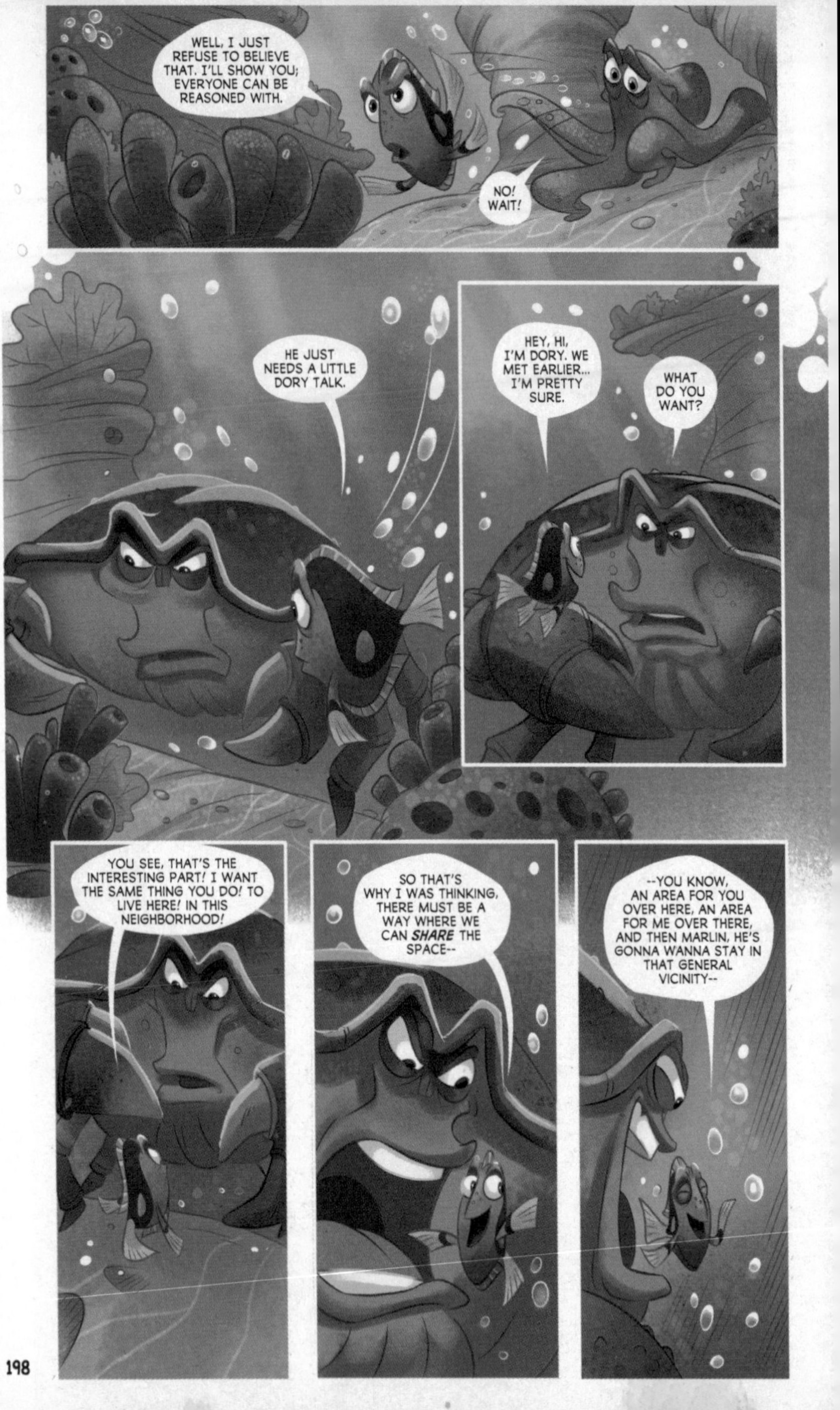
WELL, I JUST REFUSE TO BELIEVE THAT. I'LL SHOW YOU; EVERYONE CAN BE REASONED WITH.
NO! WAIT!
HE JUST NEEDS A LITTLE DORY TALK.
HEY, HI, I'M DORY. WE MET EARLIER... I'M PRETTY SURE.
WHAT DO YOU WANT?
YOU SEE, THAT'S THE INTERESTING PART! I WANT THE SAME THING YOU DO! TO LIVE HERE! IN THIS NEIGHBORHOOD!
SO THAT'S WHY I WAS THINKING, THERE MUST BE A WAY WHERE WE CAN *SHARE* THE SPACE--
--YOU KNOW, AN AREA FOR YOU OVER HERE, AN AREA FOR ME OVER THERE, AND THEN MARLIN, HE'S GONNA WANNA STAY IN THAT GENERAL VICINITY--

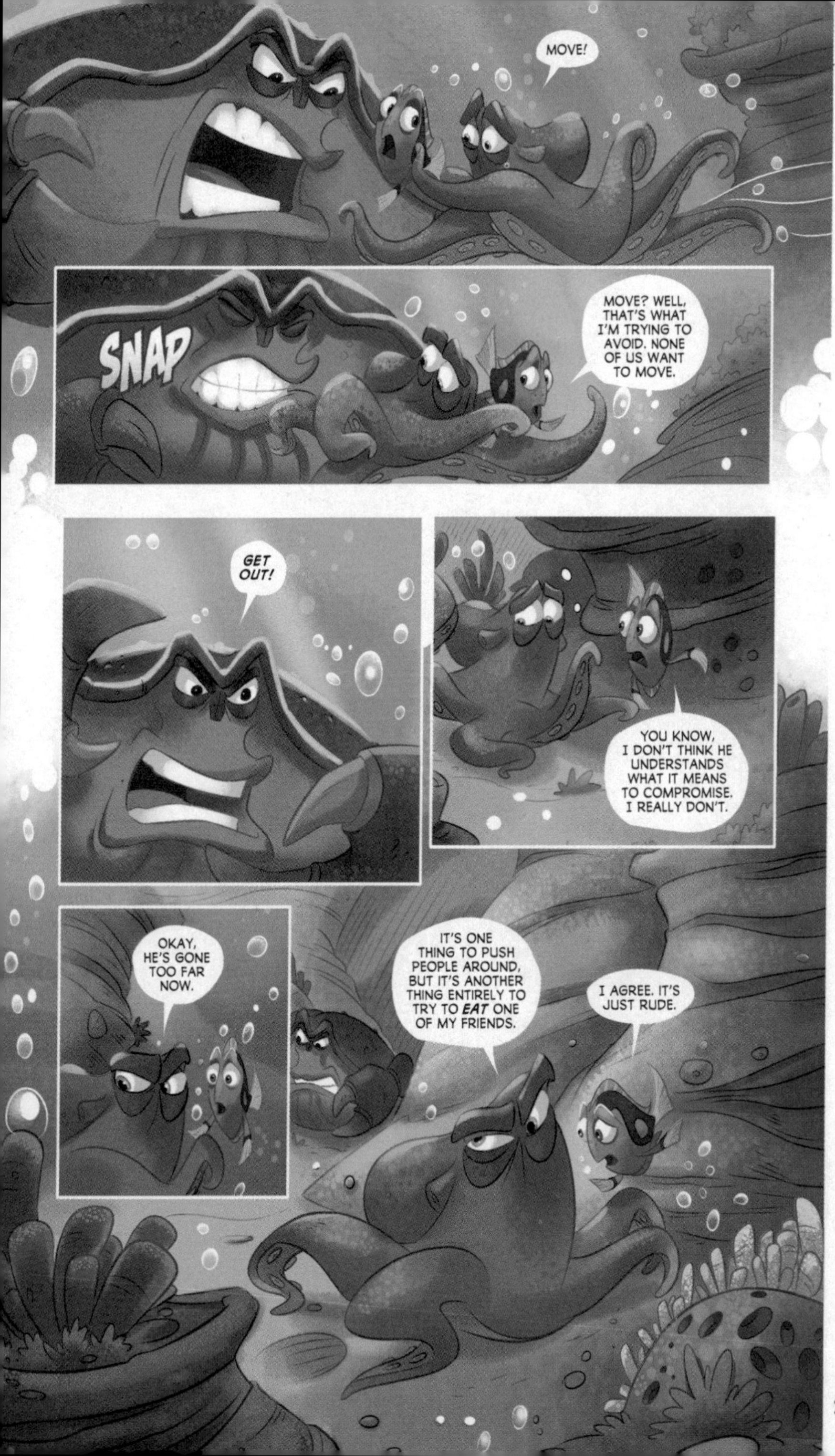
MOVE!
SNAP
MOVE? WELL, THAT'S WHAT I'M TRYING TO AVOID. NONE OF US WANT TO MOVE.
GET OUT!
YOU KNOW, I DON'T THINK HE UNDERSTANDS WHAT IT MEANS TO COMPROMISE. I REALLY DON'T.
OKAY, HE'S GONE TOO FAR NOW.
IT'S ONE THING TO PUSH PEOPLE AROUND, BUT IT'S ANOTHER THING ENTIRELY TO TRY TO *EAT* ONE OF MY FRIENDS.
I AGREE. IT'S JUST RUDE.

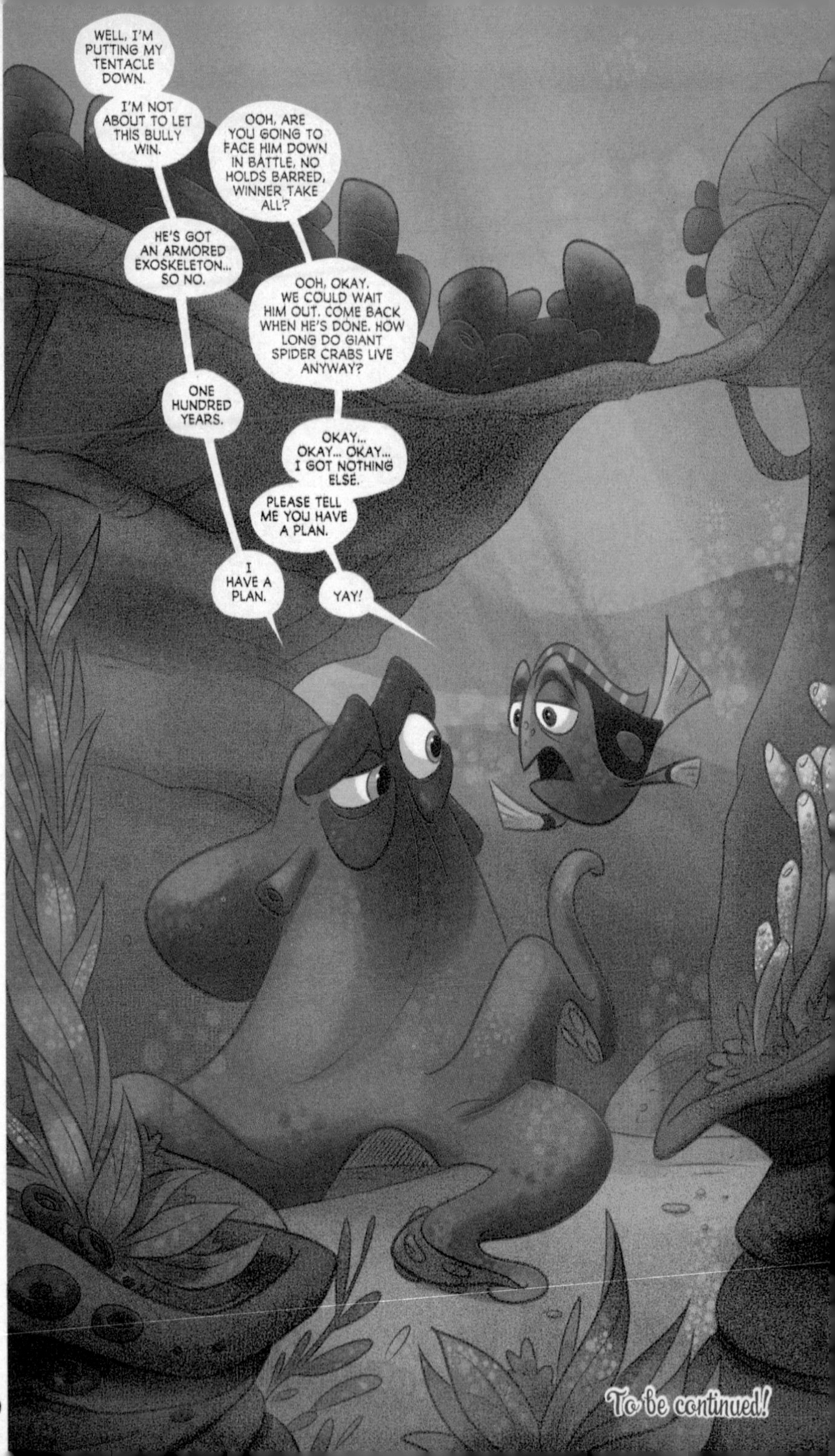
WELL, I'M PUTTING MY TENTACLE DOWN.
I'M NOT ABOUT TO LET THIS BULLY WIN.
OOH, ARE YOU GOING TO FACE HIM DOWN IN BATTLE, NO HOLDS BARRED, WINNER TAKE ALL?
HE'S GOT AN ARMORED EXOSKELETON... SO NO.
OOH, OKAY. WE COULD WAIT HIM OUT. COME BACK WHEN HE'S DONE. HOW LONG DO GIANT SPIDER CRABS LIVE ANYWAY?
ONE HUNDRED YEARS.
OKAY... OKAY... OKAY... I GOT NOTHING ELSE.
PLEASE TELL ME YOU HAVE A PLAN.
I HAVE A PLAN.
YAY!
To be continued!

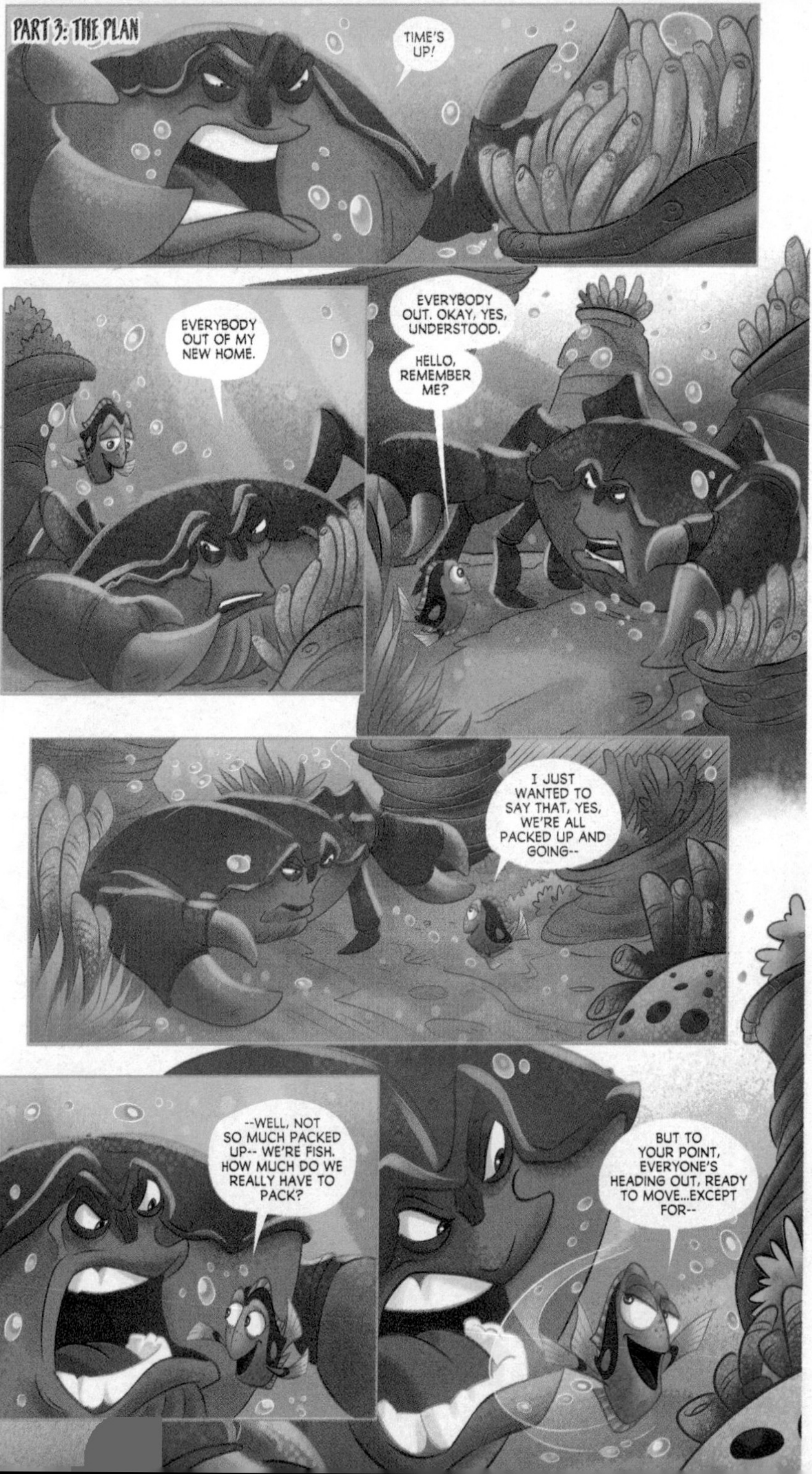
PART 3: THE PLAN
TIME'S UP!
EVERYBODY OUT OF MY NEW HOME.
EVERYBODY OUT. OKAY, YES, UNDERSTOOD.
HELLO, REMEMBER ME?
I JUST WANTED TO SAY THAT, YES, WE'RE ALL PACKED UP AND GOING--
--WELL, NOT SO MUCH PACKED UP-- WE'RE FISH. HOW MUCH DO WE REALLY HAVE TO PACK?
BUT TO YOUR POINT, EVERYONE'S HEADING OUT, READY TO MOVE...EXCEPT FOR--

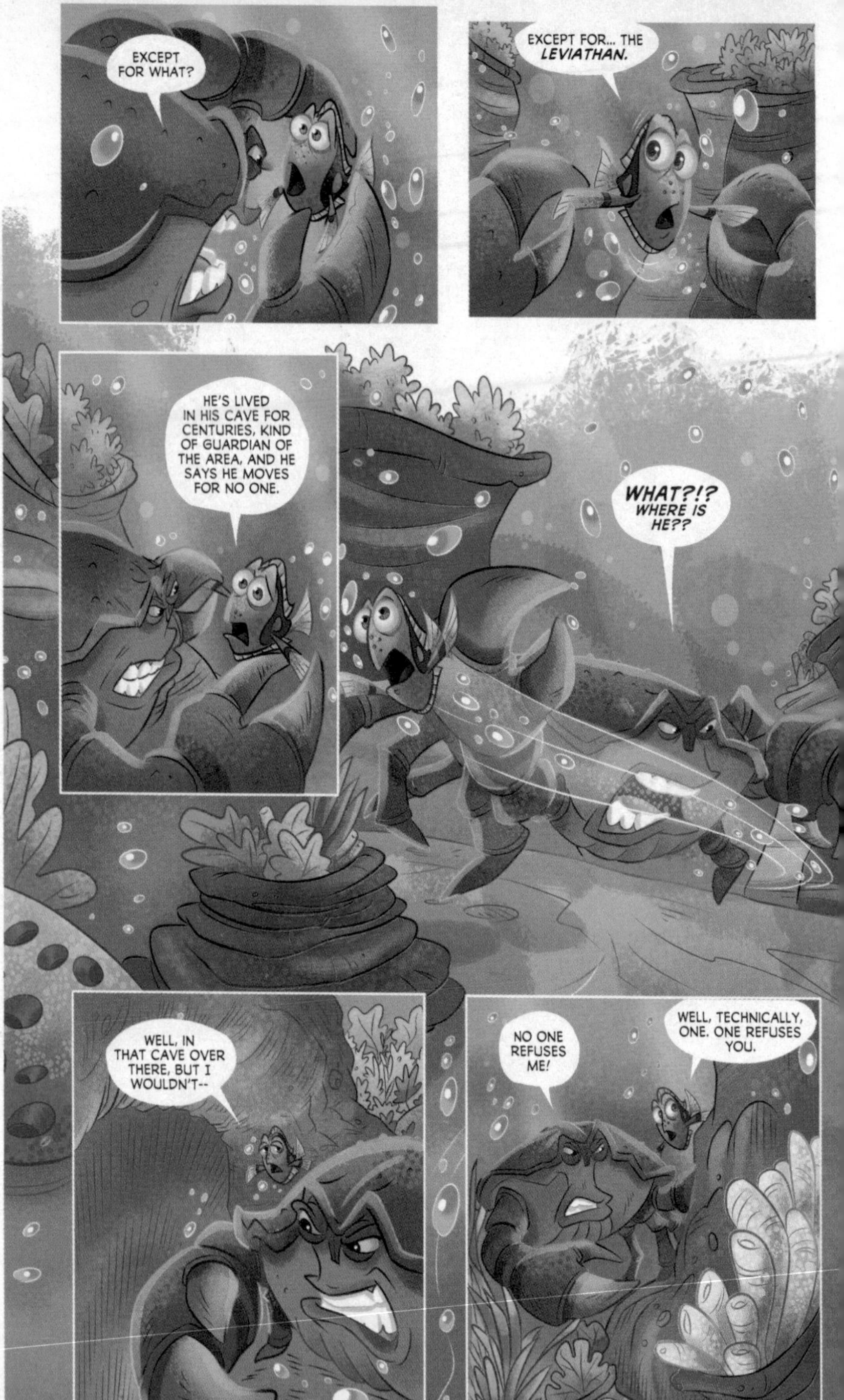
EXCEPT FOR WHAT?
EXCEPT FOR... THE LEVIATHAN.
HE'S LIVED IN HIS CAVE FOR CENTURIES, KIND OF GUARDIAN OF THE AREA, AND HE SAYS HE MOVES FOR NO ONE.
WHAT?!? WHERE IS HE??
WELL, IN THAT CAVE OVER THERE, BUT I WOULDN'T--
NO ONE REFUSES ME!
WELL, TECHNICALLY, ONE. ONE REFUSES YOU.

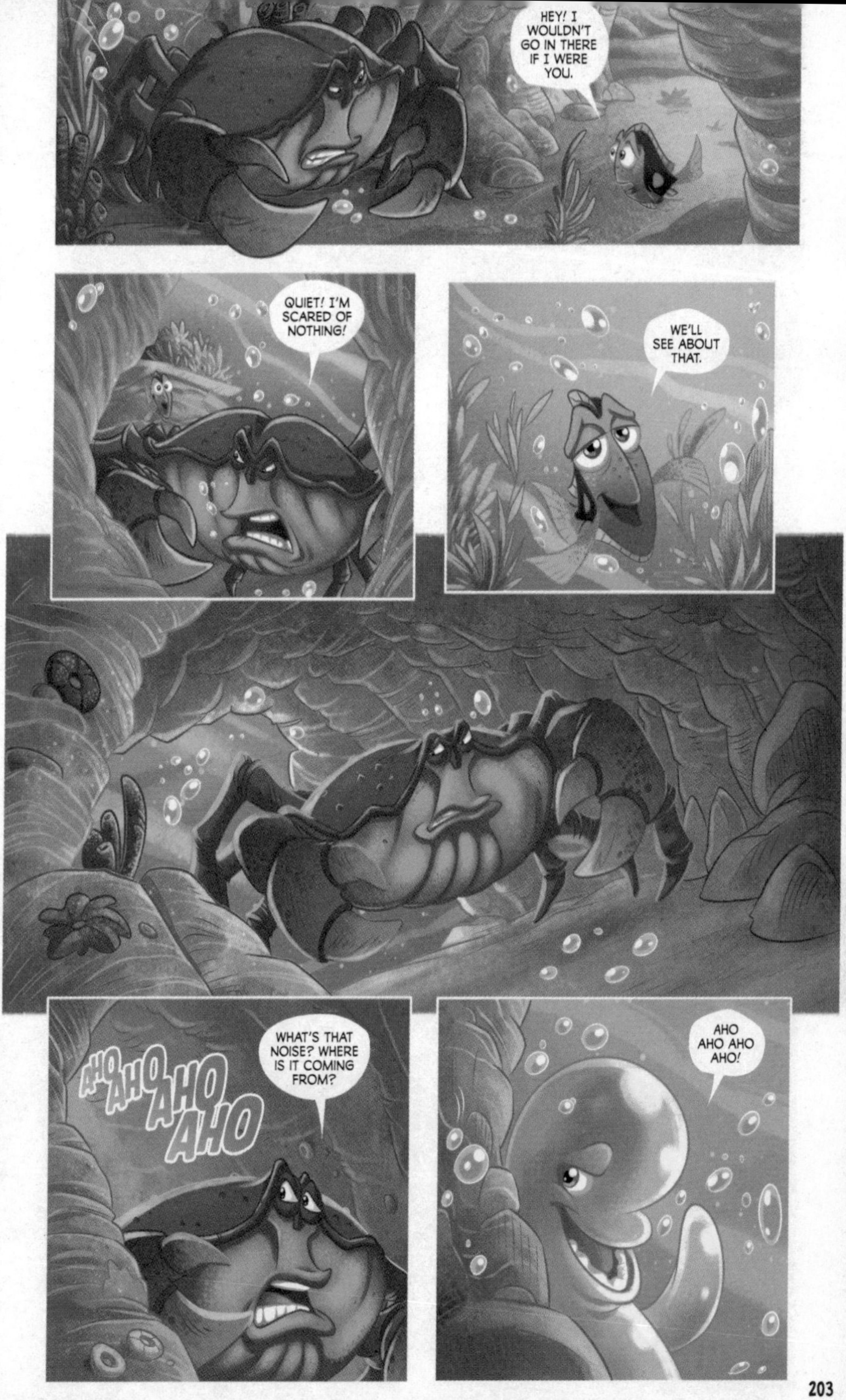
HEY! I WOULDN'T GO IN THERE IF I WERE YOU.
QUIET! I'M SCARED OF NOTHING!
WE'LL SEE ABOUT THAT.
AHO AHO AHO AHO
WHAT'S THAT NOISE? WHERE IS IT COMING FROM?
AHO AHO AHO AHO!

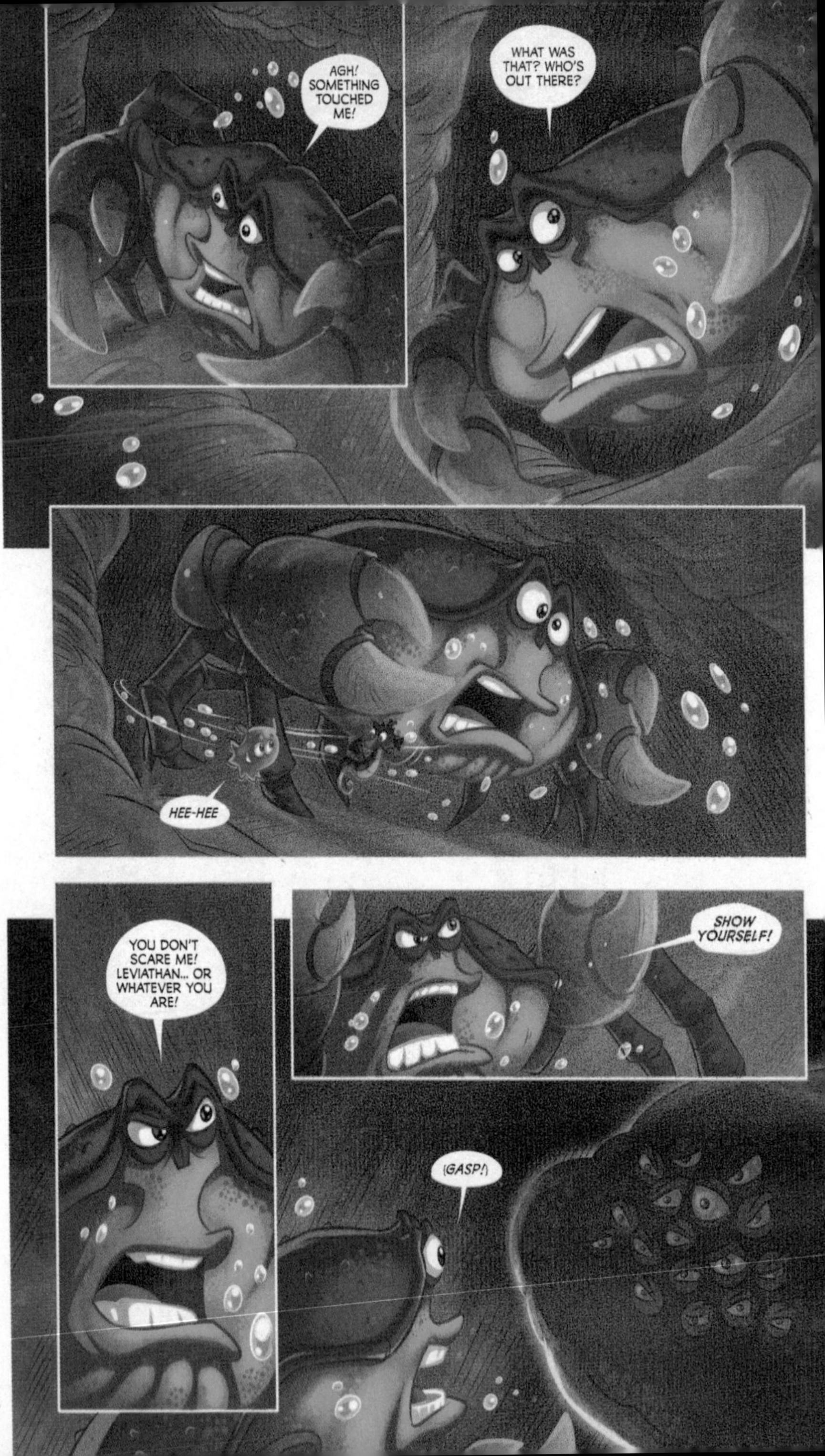
AGH! SOMETHING TOUCHED ME!
WHAT WAS THAT? WHO'S OUT THERE?
HEE-HEE
YOU DON'T SCARE ME! LEVIATHAN... OR WHATEVER YOU ARE!
SHOW YOURSELF!
(GASP!)

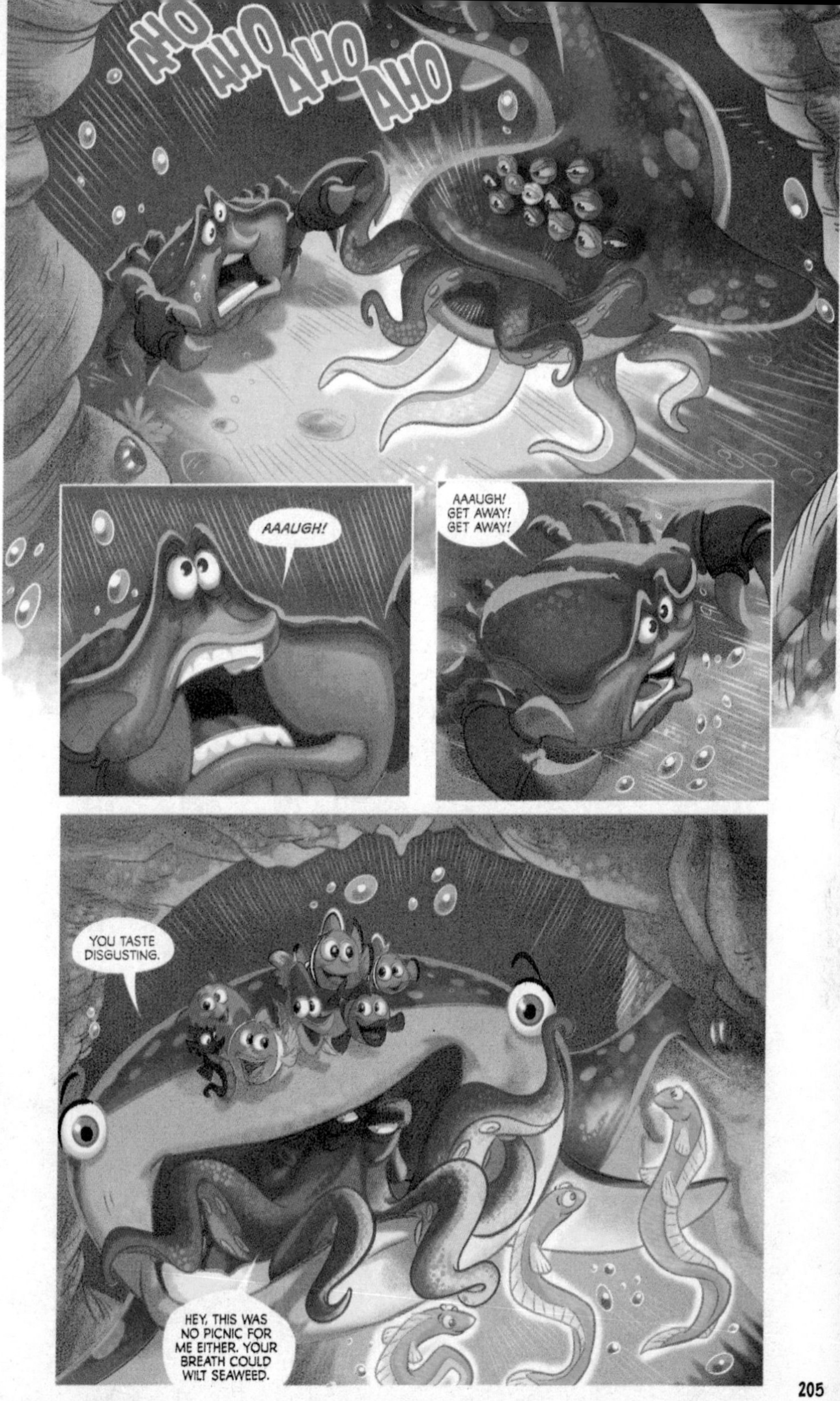
AAAUGH!
AAAUGH! GET AWAY! GET AWAY!
YOU TASTE DISGUSTING.
HEY, THIS WAS NO PICNIC FOR ME EITHER. YOUR BREATH COULD WILT SEAWEED.

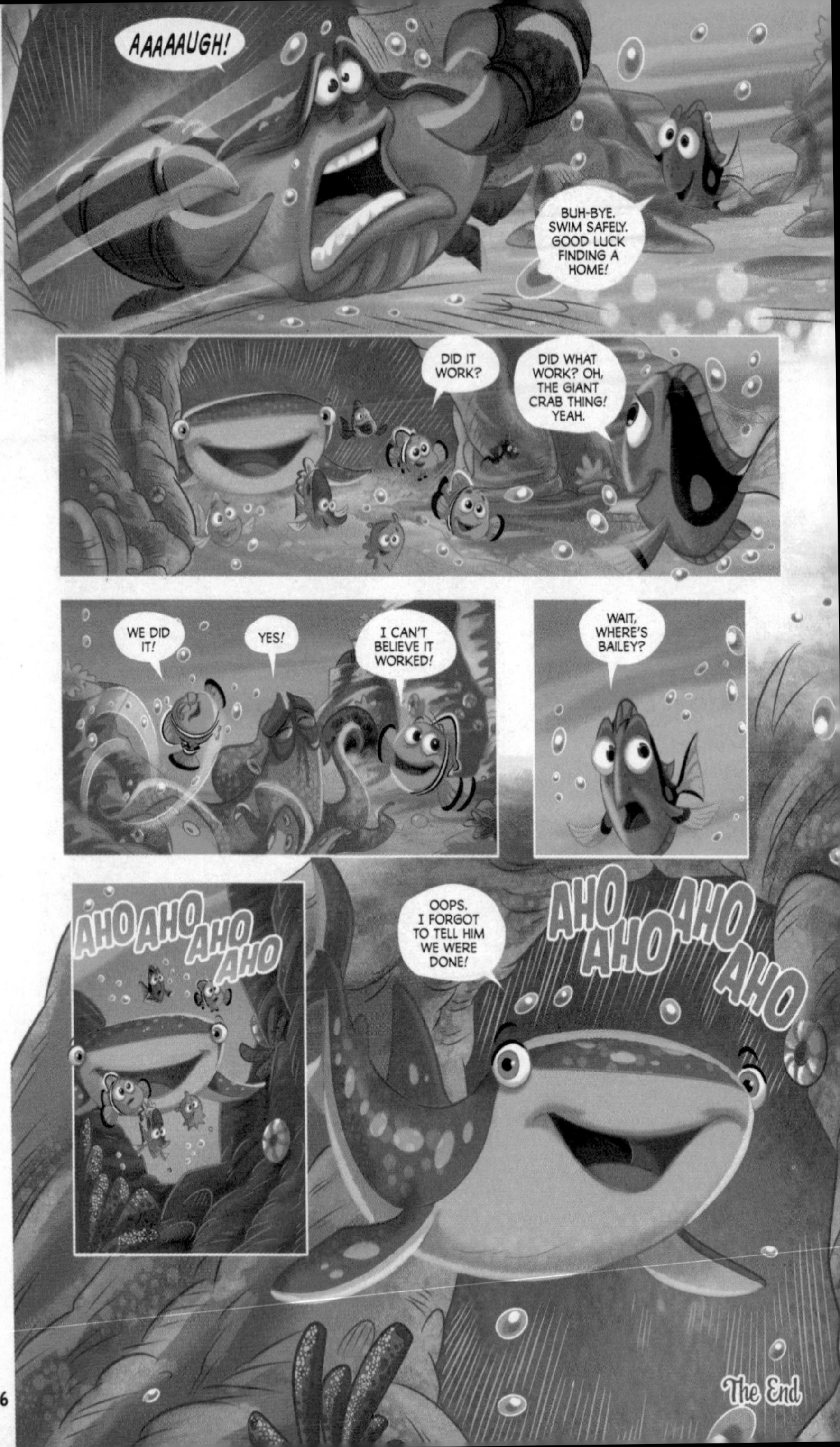
AAAAAUGH!
BUH-BYE. SWIM SAFELY. GOOD LUCK FINDING A HOME!
DID IT WORK?
DID WHAT WORK? OH, THE GIANT CRAB THING! YEAH.
WE DID IT!
YES!
I CAN'T BELIEVE IT WORKED!
WAIT, WHERE'S BAILEY?
AHO AHO AHO AHO
OOPS. I FORGOT TO TELL HIM WE WERE DONE!
AHO AHO AHO AHO
The End

Making Memories

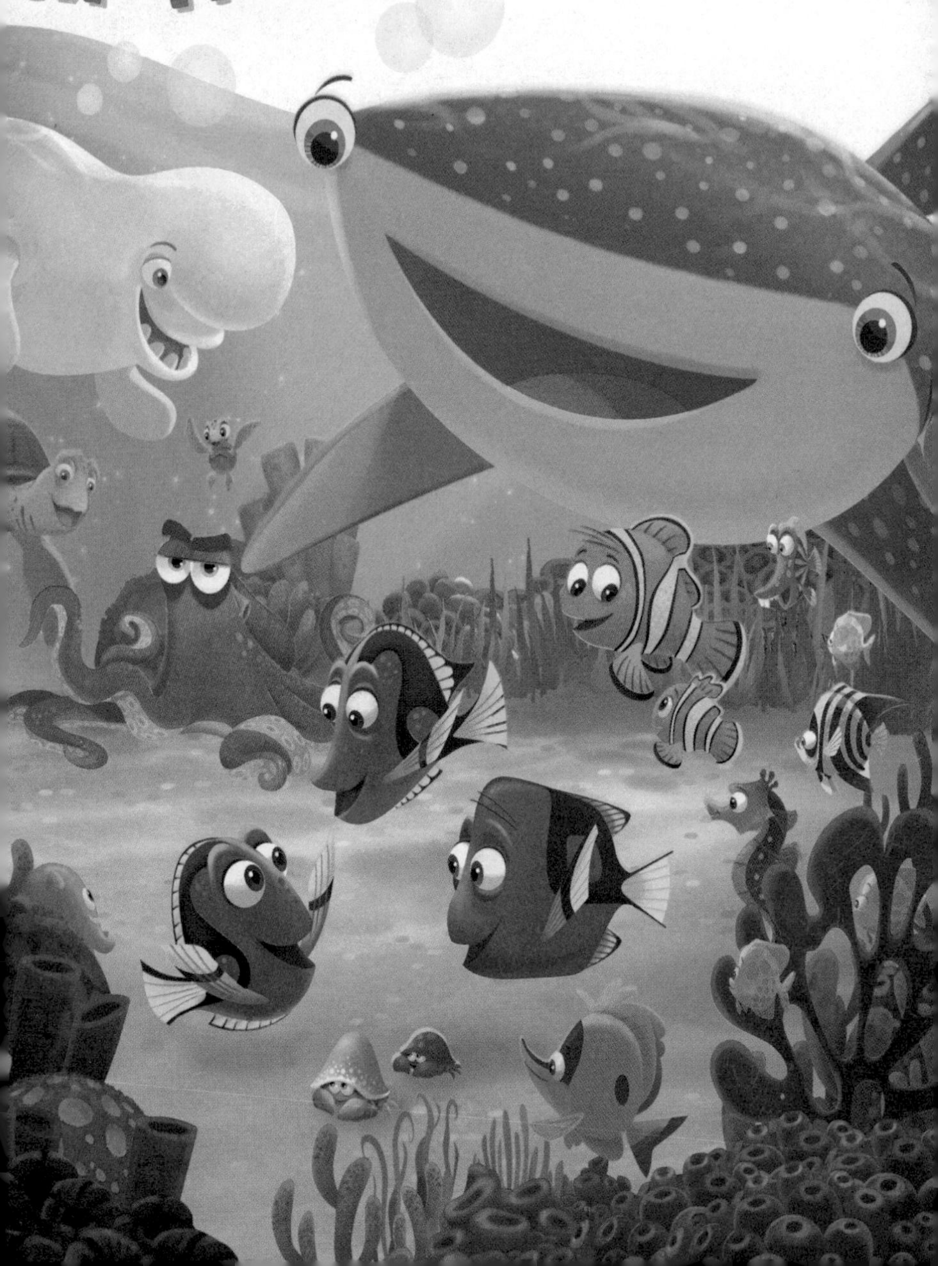

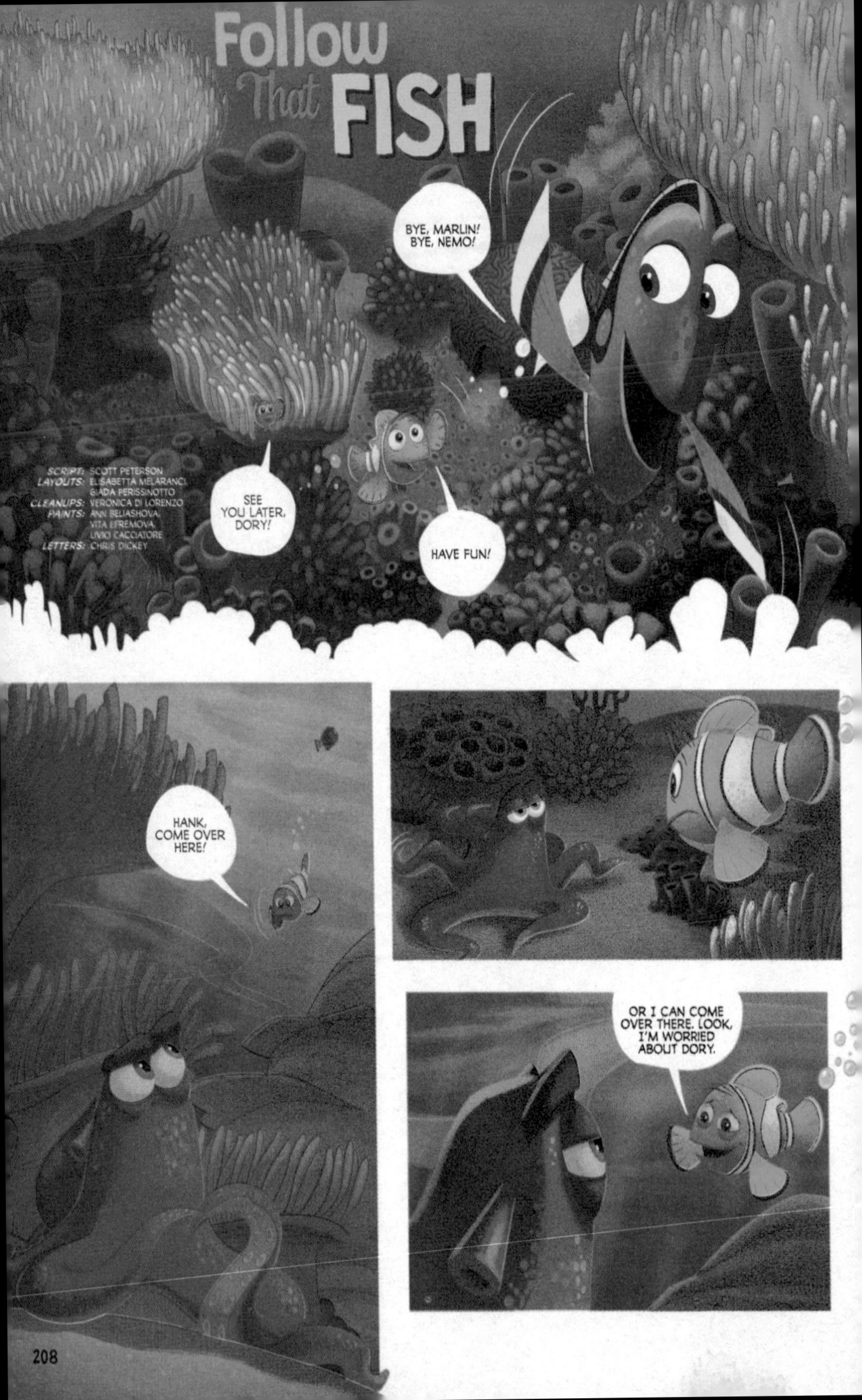
Follow That FISH
BYE, MARLIN! BYE, NEMO!
SEE YOU LATER, DORY!
HAVE FUN!
SCRIPT: SCOTT PETERSON
LAYOUTS: ELISABETTA MELARANCI, GIADA PERISSINOTTO
CLEANUPS: VERONICA DI LORENZO
PAINTS: ANNI BELIASHOVA, VITA EFREMOVA, LIVIO CACCIATORE
LETTERS: CHRIS DICKEY
HANK, COME OVER HERE!
OR I CAN COME OVER THERE. LOOK, I'M WORRIED ABOUT DORY.

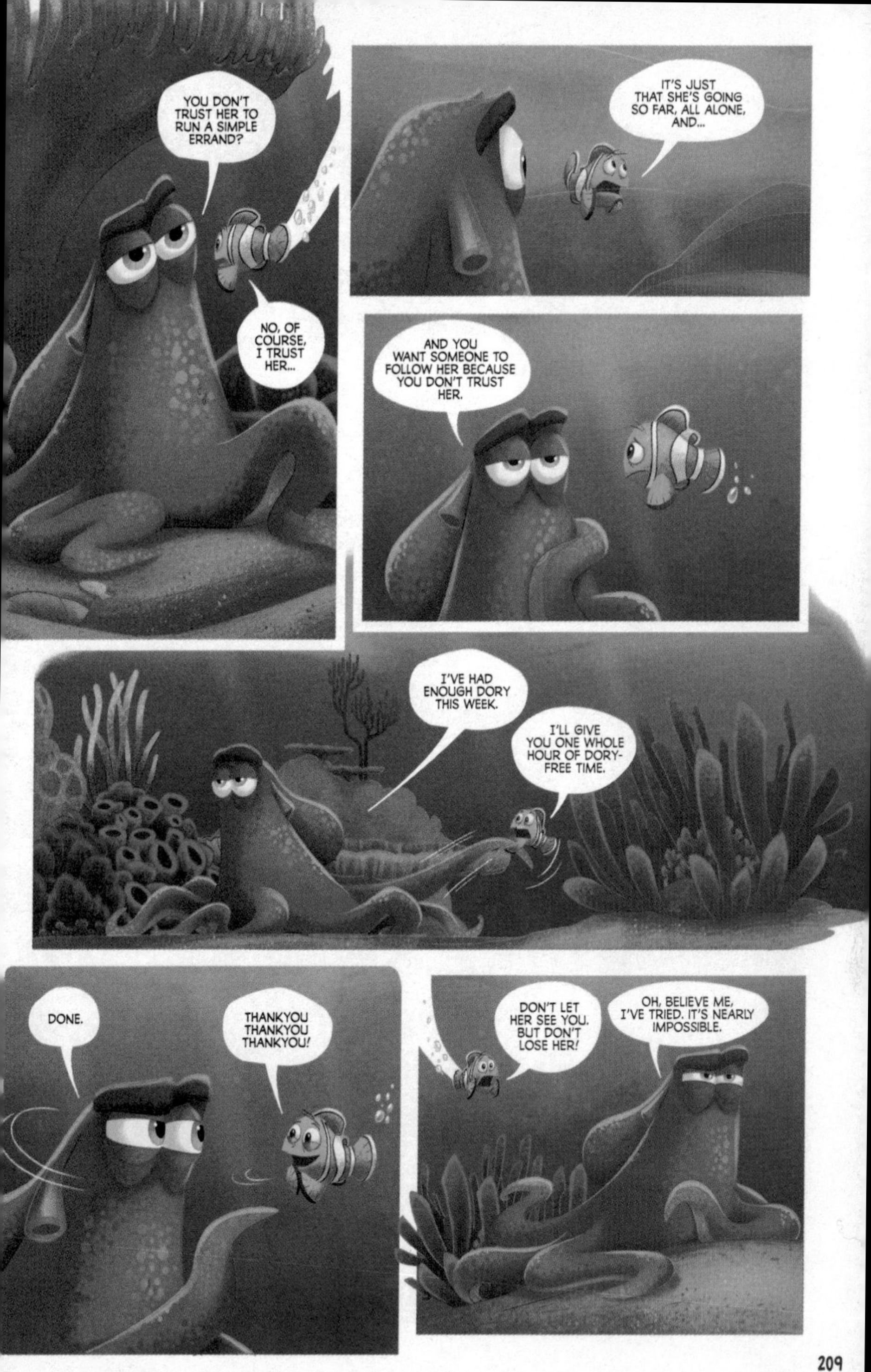
YOU DON'T TRUST HER TO RUN A SIMPLE ERRAND?
NO, OF COURSE, I TRUST HER...
IT'S JUST THAT SHE'S GOING SO FAR, ALL ALONE, AND...
AND YOU WANT SOMEONE TO FOLLOW HER BECAUSE YOU DON'T TRUST HER.
I'VE HAD ENOUGH DORY THIS WEEK.
I'LL GIVE YOU ONE WHOLE HOUR OF DORY-FREE TIME.
DONE.
THANKYOU THANKYOU THANKYOU!
DON'T LET HER SEE YOU. BUT DON'T LOSE HER!
OH, BELIEVE ME, I'VE TRIED. IT'S NEARLY IMPOSSIBLE.

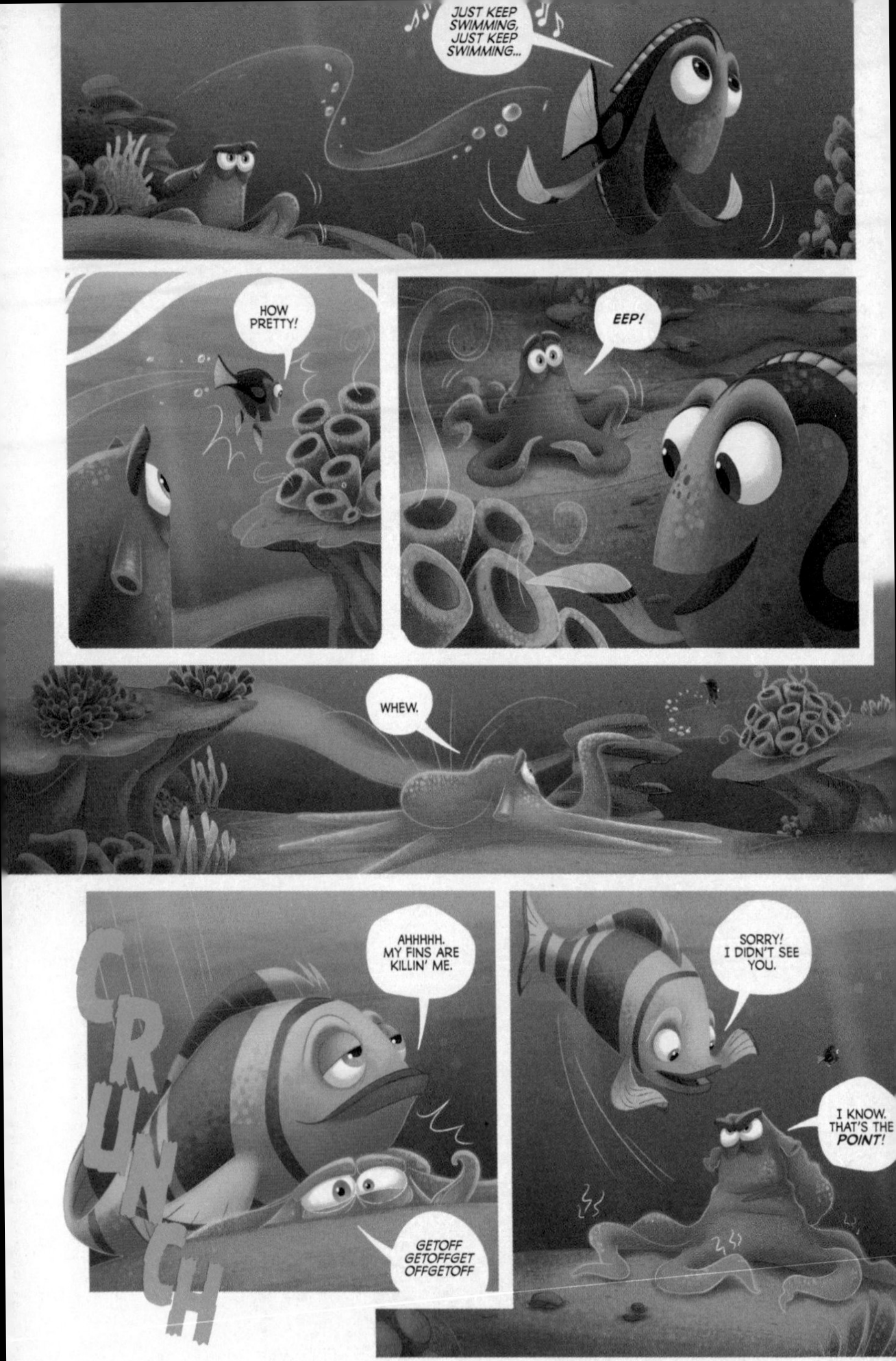
JUST KEEP SWIMMING, JUST KEEP SWIMMING...
HOW PRETTY!
EEP!
WHEW.
AHHHHH. MY FINS ARE KILLIN' ME.
CRUNCH
GETOFF GETOFFGET OFFGETOFF
SORRY! I DIDN'T SEE YOU.
I KNOW. THAT'S THE POINT!

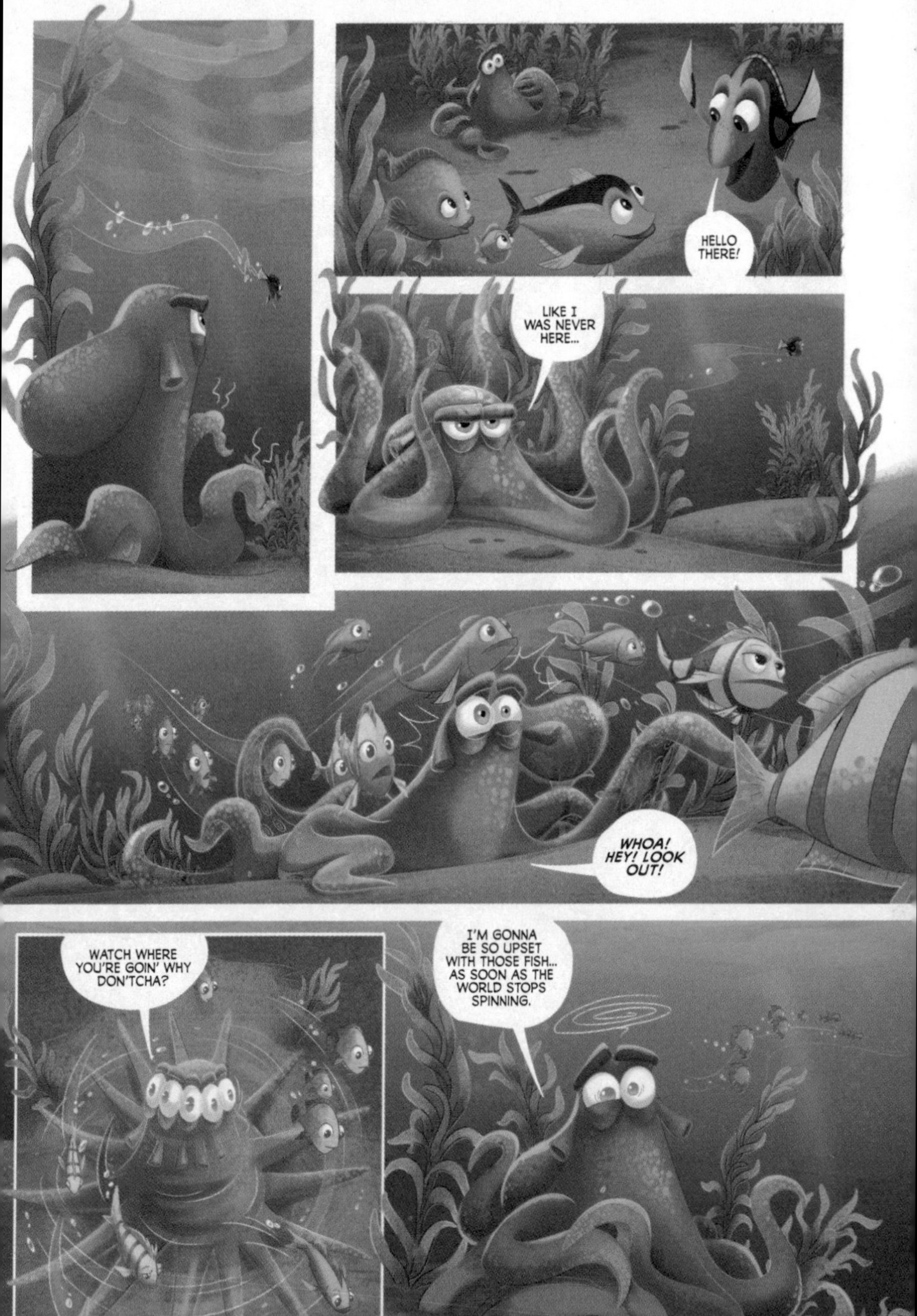
HELLO THERE!
LIKE I WAS NEVER HERE...
WHOA! HEY! LOOK OUT!
WATCH WHERE YOU'RE GOIN' WHY DON'TCHA?
I'M GONNA BE SO UPSET WITH THOSE FISH... AS SOON AS THE WORLD STOPS SPINNING.

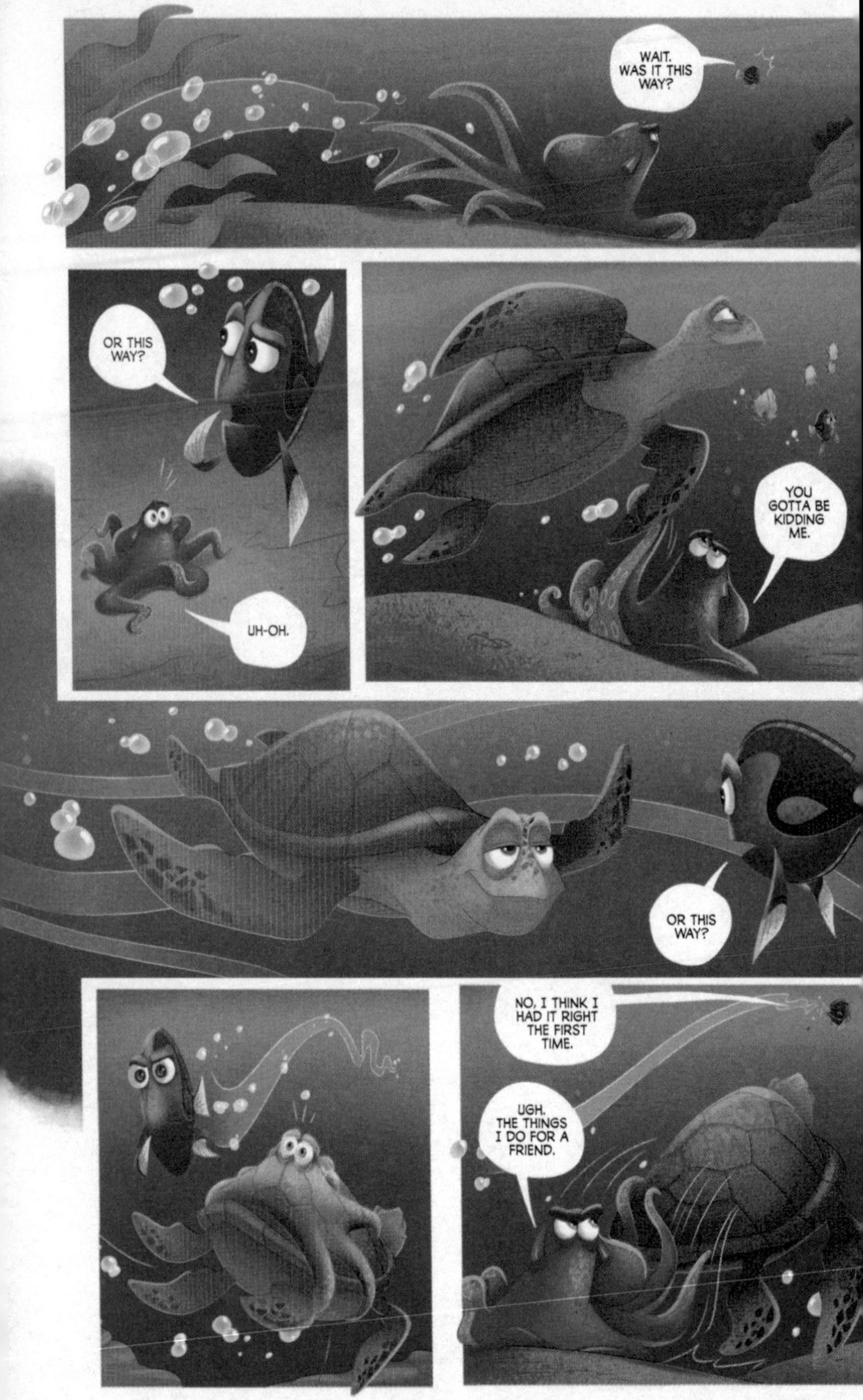
WAIT.
WAS IT THIS
WAY?
OR THIS
WAY?
UH-OH.
YOU
GOTTA BE
KIDDING
ME.
OR THIS
WAY?
NO, I THINK I
HAD IT RIGHT
THE FIRST
TIME.
UGH.
THE THINGS
I DO FOR A
FRIEND.

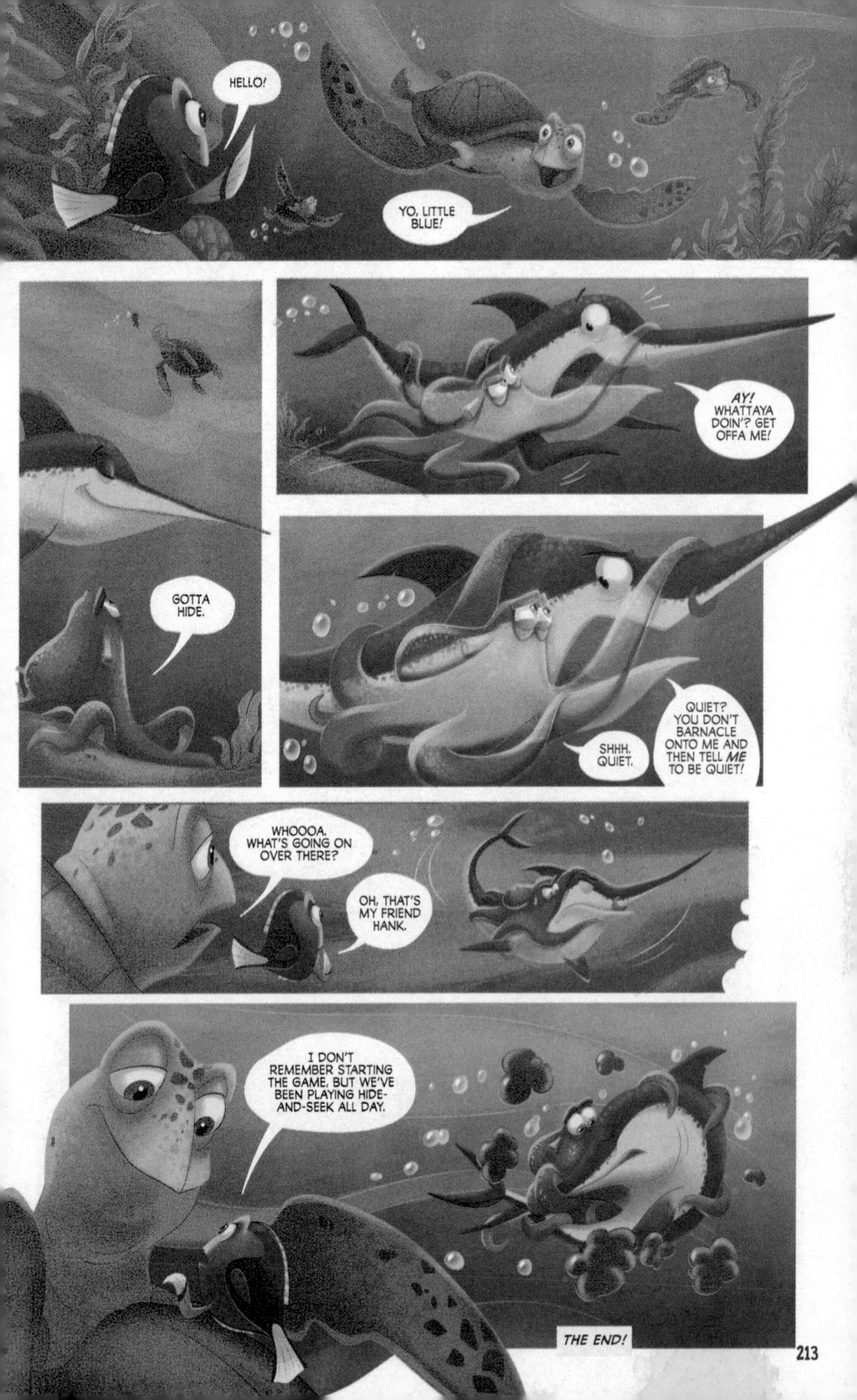
HELLO!
YO, LITTLE BLUE!
GOTTA HIDE.
AY! WHATTAYA DOIN'? GET OFFA ME!
SHHH. QUIET.
QUIET? YOU DON'T BARNACLE ONTO ME AND THEN TELL *ME* TO BE QUIET!
WHOOOA. WHAT'S GOING ON OVER THERE?
OH, THAT'S MY FRIEND HANK.
I DON'T REMEMBER STARTING THE GAME, BUT WE'VE BEEN PLAYING HIDE-AND-SEEK ALL DAY.
THE END!

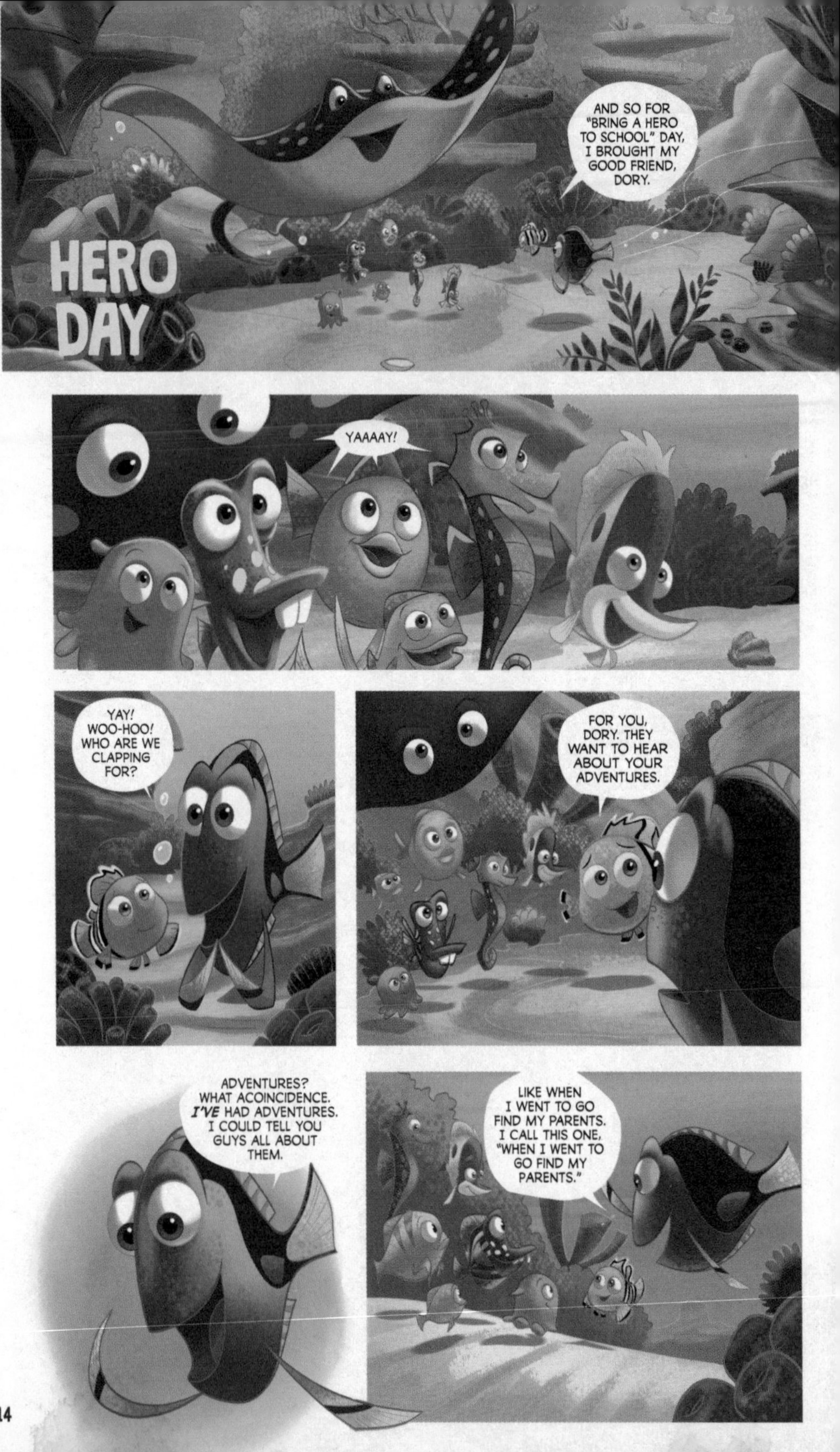
HERO DAY
AND SO FOR "BRING A HERO TO SCHOOL" DAY, I BROUGHT MY GOOD FRIEND, DORY.
YAAAAY!
YAY! WOO-HOO! WHO ARE WE CLAPPING FOR?
FOR YOU, DORY. THEY WANT TO HEAR ABOUT YOUR ADVENTURES.
ADVENTURES? WHAT ACOINCIDENCE. *I'VE* HAD ADVENTURES. I COULD TELL YOU GUYS ALL ABOUT THEM.
LIKE WHEN I WENT TO GO FIND MY PARENTS. I CALL THIS ONE, "WHEN I WENT TO GO FIND MY PARENTS."

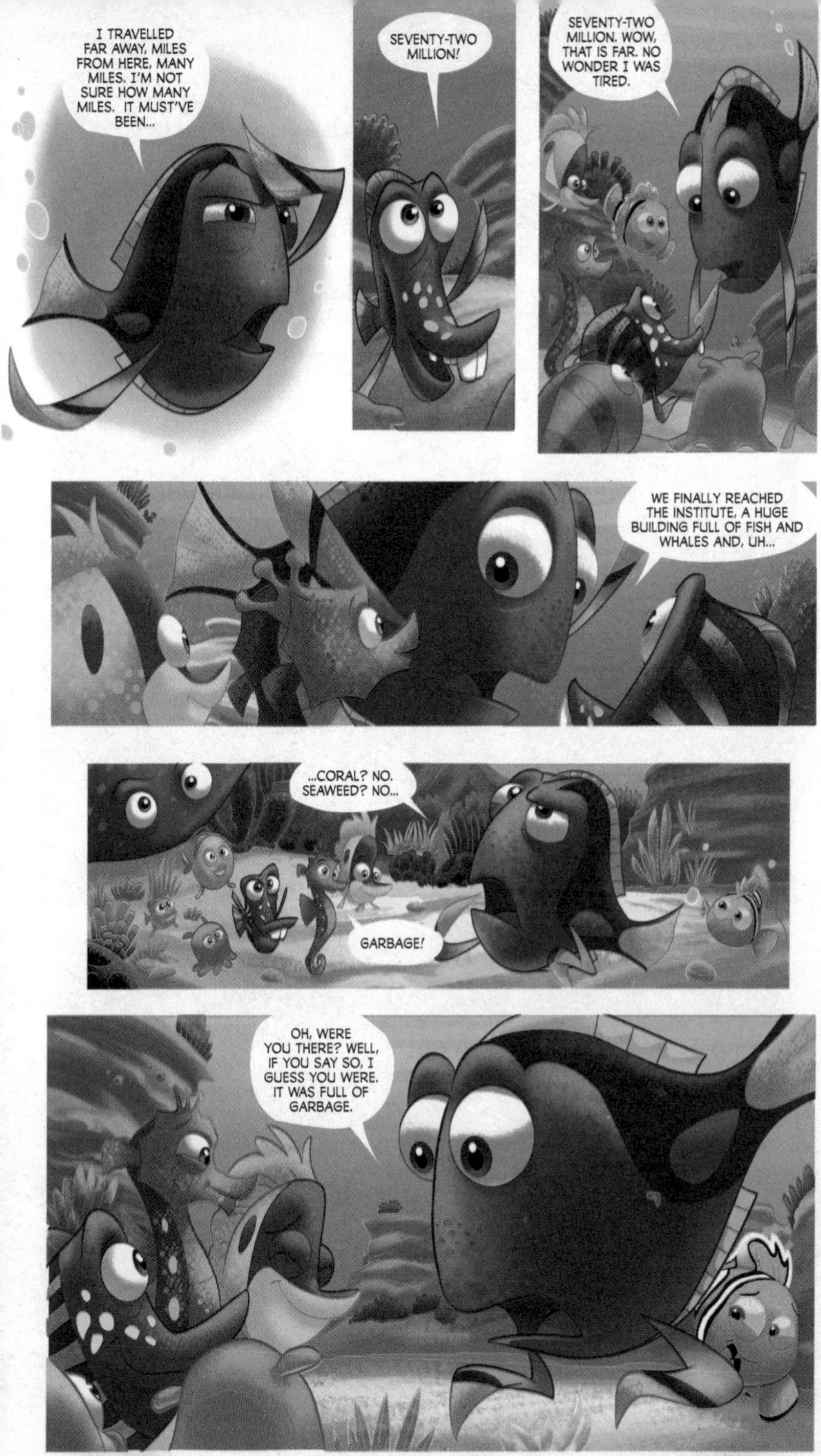
I TRAVELLED FAR AWAY, MILES FROM HERE, MANY MILES. I'M NOT SURE HOW MANY MILES. IT MUST'VE BEEN...
SEVENTY-TWO MILLION!
SEVENTY-TWO MILLION. WOW, THAT IS FAR. NO WONDER I WAS TIRED.
WE FINALLY REACHED THE INSTITUTE, A HUGE BUILDING FULL OF FISH AND WHALES AND, UH...
...CORAL? NO. SEAWEED? NO...
GARBAGE!
OH, WERE YOU THERE? WELL, IF YOU SAY SO, I GUESS YOU WERE. IT WAS FULL OF GARBAGE.

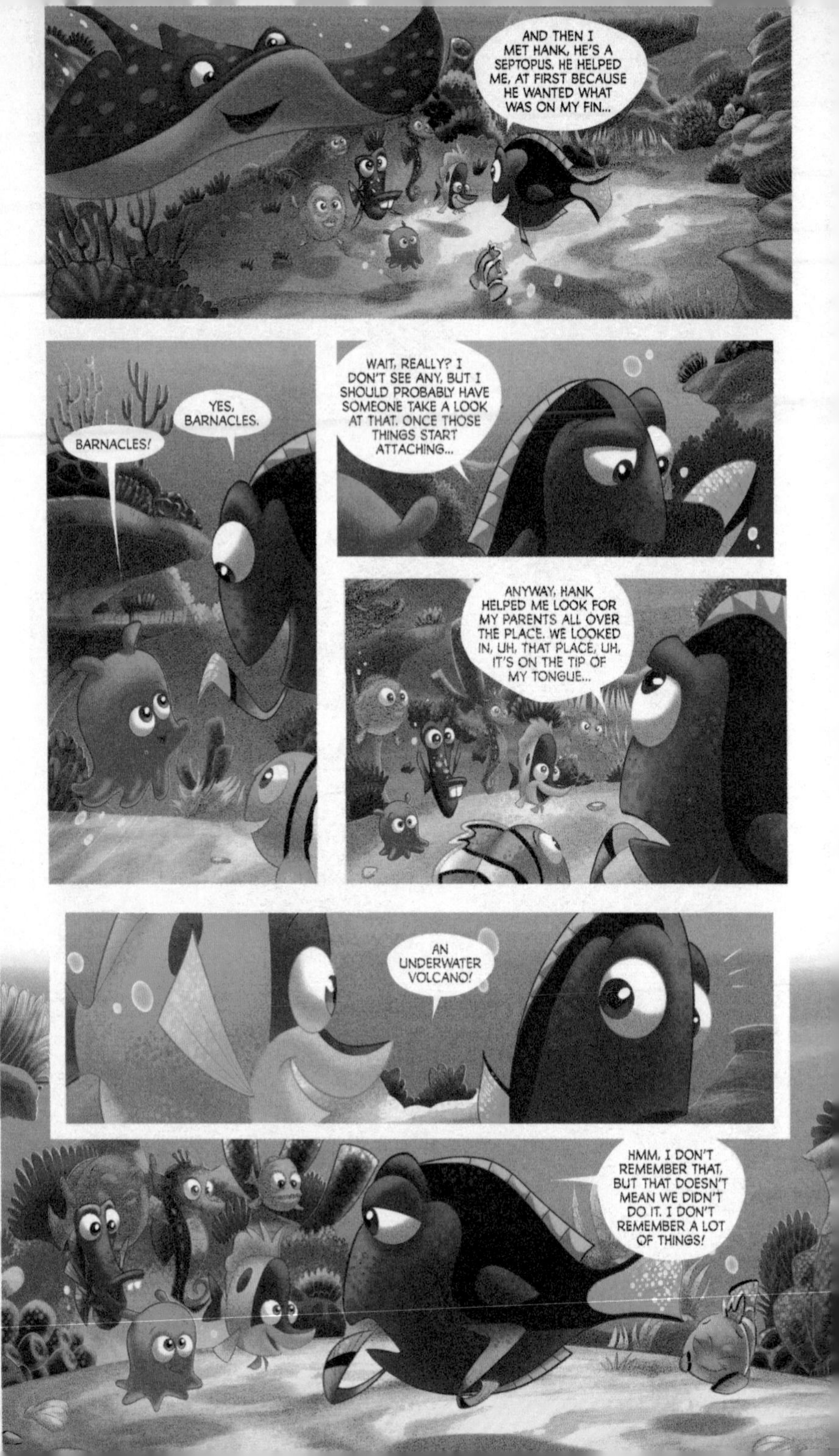
AND THEN I MET HANK. HE'S A SEPTOPUS. HE HELPED ME, AT FIRST BECAUSE HE WANTED WHAT WAS ON MY FIN...
BARNACLES!
YES, BARNACLES.
WAIT, REALLY? I DON'T SEE ANY, BUT I SHOULD PROBABLY HAVE SOMEONE TAKE A LOOK AT THAT. ONCE THOSE THINGS START ATTACHING...
ANYWAY, HANK HELPED ME LOOK FOR MY PARENTS ALL OVER THE PLACE. WE LOOKED IN, UH, THAT PLACE, UH, IT'S ON THE TIP OF MY TONGUE...
AN UNDERWATER VOLCANO!
HMM, I DON'T REMEMBER THAT, BUT THAT DOESN'T MEAN WE DIDN'T DO IT. I DON'T REMEMBER A LOT OF THINGS!

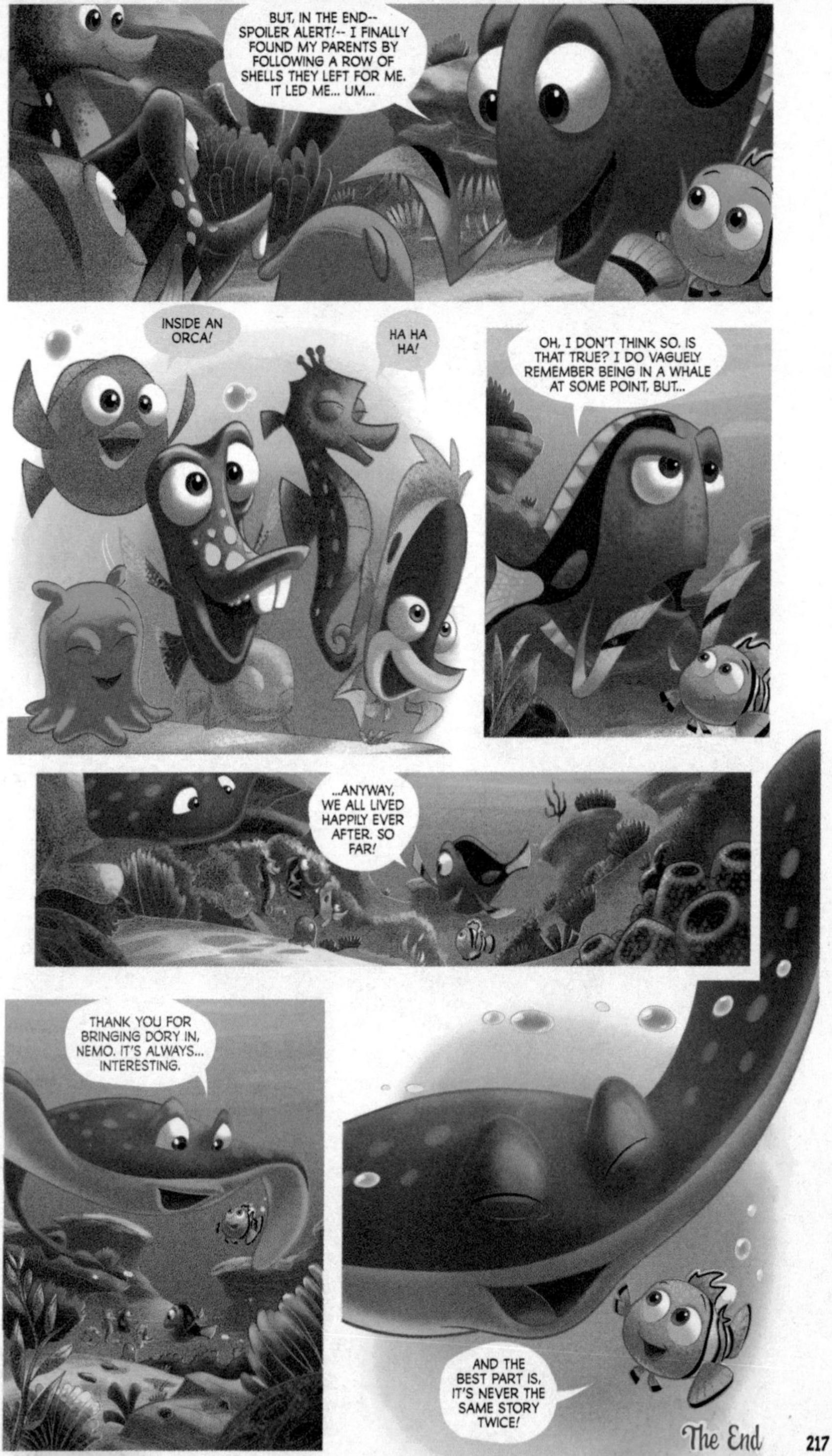
BUT, IN THE END-- SPOILER ALERT!-- I FINALLY FOUND MY PARENTS BY FOLLOWING A ROW OF SHELLS THEY LEFT FOR ME. IT LED ME... UM...
INSIDE AN ORCA!
HA HA HA!
OH, I DON'T THINK SO. IS THAT TRUE? I DO VAGUELY REMEMBER BEING IN A WHALE AT SOME POINT, BUT...
...ANYWAY, WE ALL LIVED HAPPILY EVER AFTER. SO FAR!
THANK YOU FOR BRINGING DORY IN, NEMO. IT'S ALWAYS... INTERESTING.
AND THE BEST PART IS, IT'S NEVER THE SAME STORY TWICE!
The End

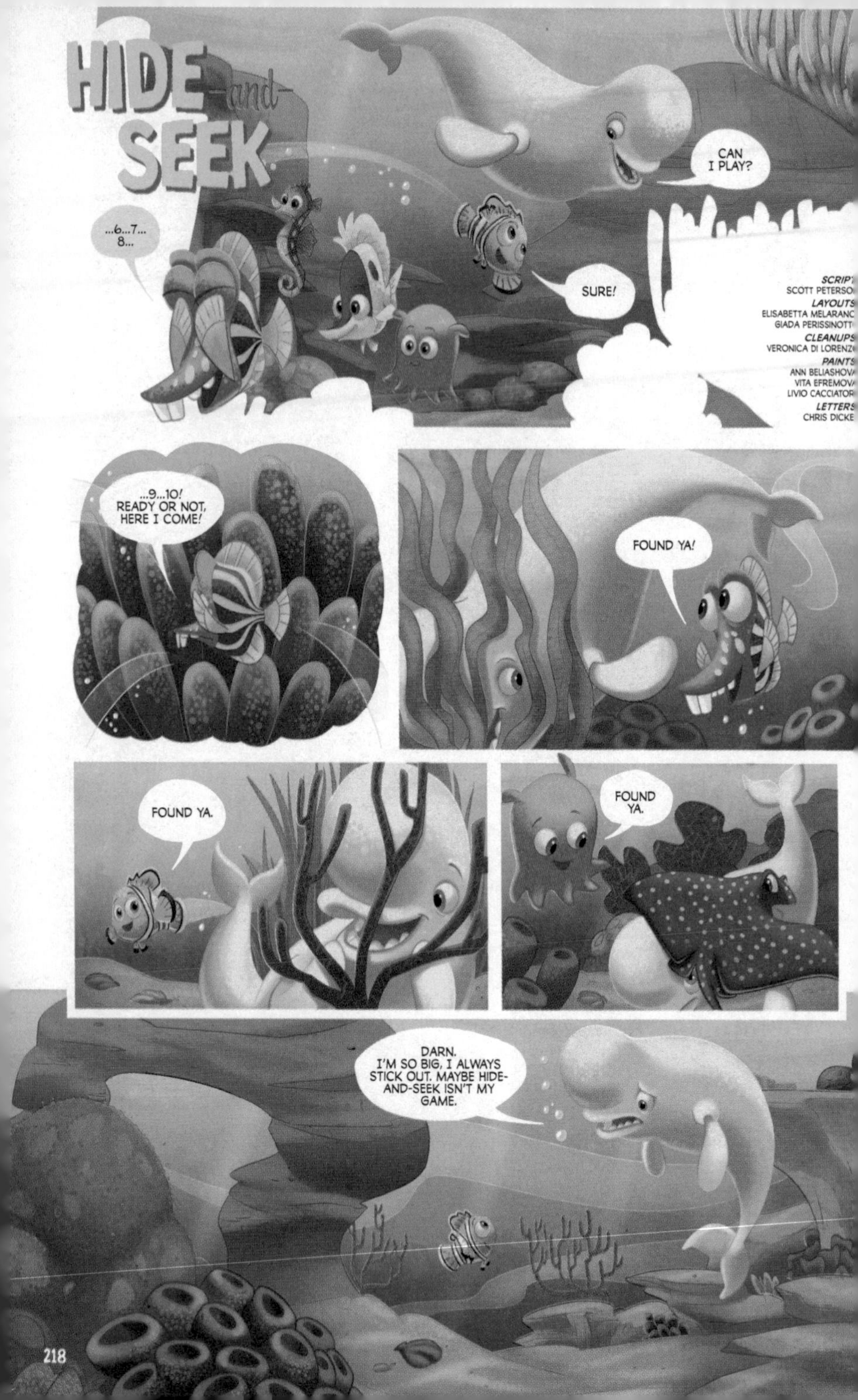
HIDE and SEEK
CAN I PLAY?
...6...7... 8...
SURE!
SCRIP
SCOTT PETERSO
LAYOUTS
ELISABETTA MELARANC
GIADA PERISSINOTT
CLEANUPS
VERONICA DI LORENZ
PAINTS
ANN BELIASHOVA
VITA EFREMOVA
LIVIO CACCIATOR
LETTERS
CHRIS DICKE
...9...10! READY OR NOT, HERE I COME!
FOUND YA!
FOUND YA.
FOUND YA.
DARN. I'M SO BIG, I ALWAYS STICK OUT. MAYBE HIDE-AND-SEEK ISN'T MY GAME.

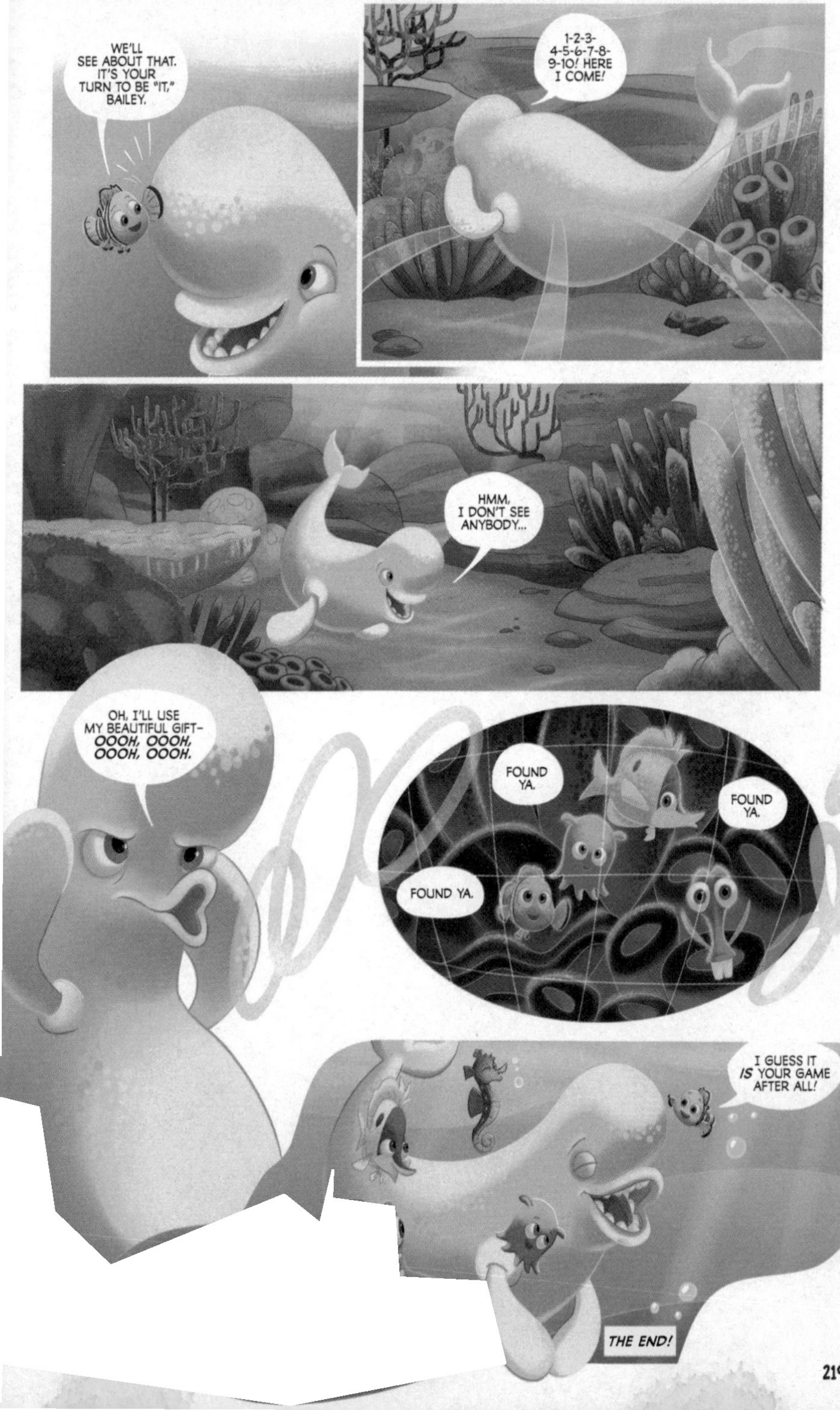
WE'LL SEE ABOUT THAT. IT'S YOUR TURN TO BE "IT," BAILEY.
1-2-3-4-5-6-7-8-9-10! HERE I COME!
HMM, I DON'T SEE ANYBODY...
OH, I'LL USE MY BEAUTIFUL GIFT- OOOH, OOOH, OOOH, OOOH.
FOUND YA.
FOUND YA.
FOUND YA.
I GUESS IT IS YOUR GAME AFTER ALL!
THE END!

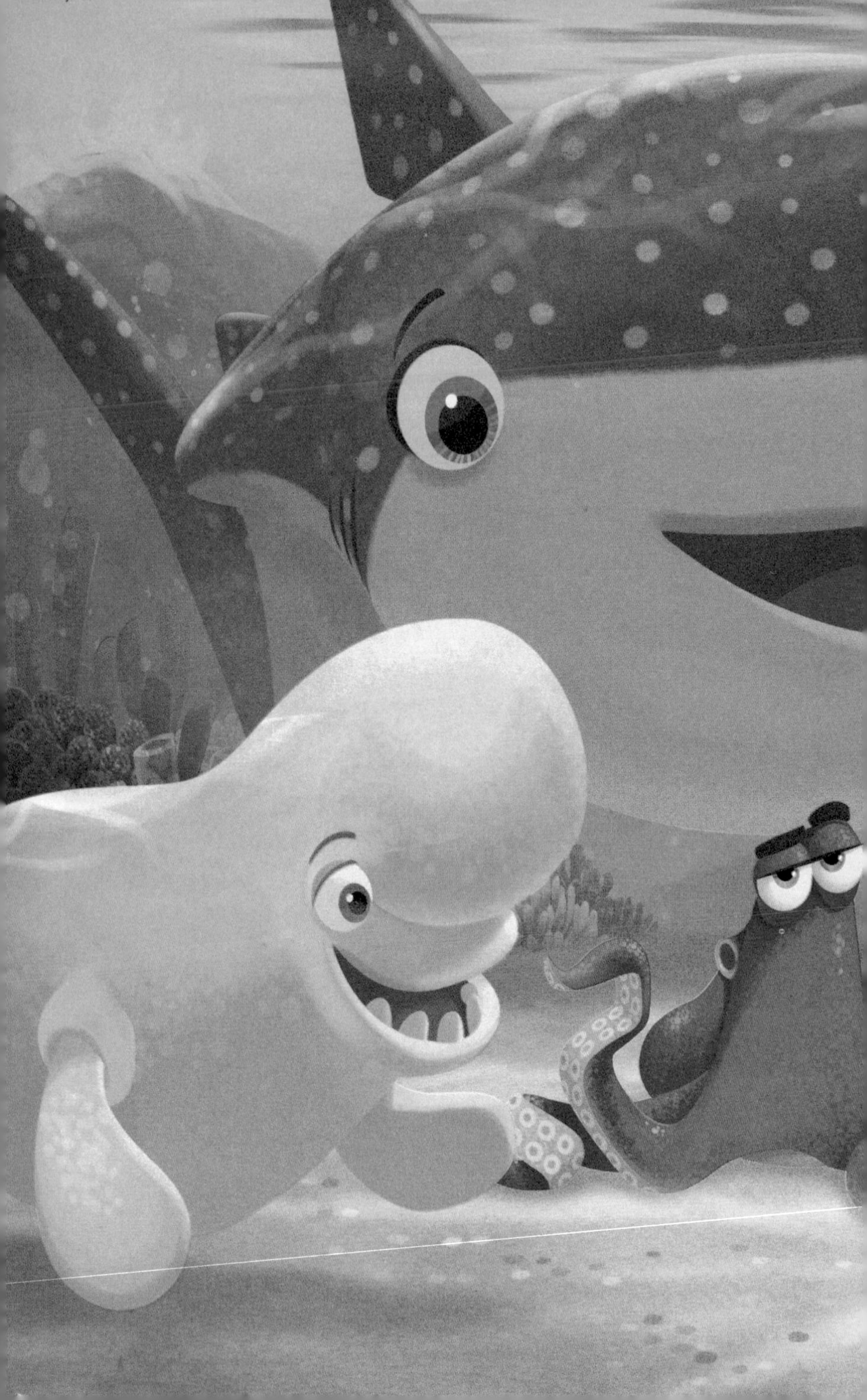

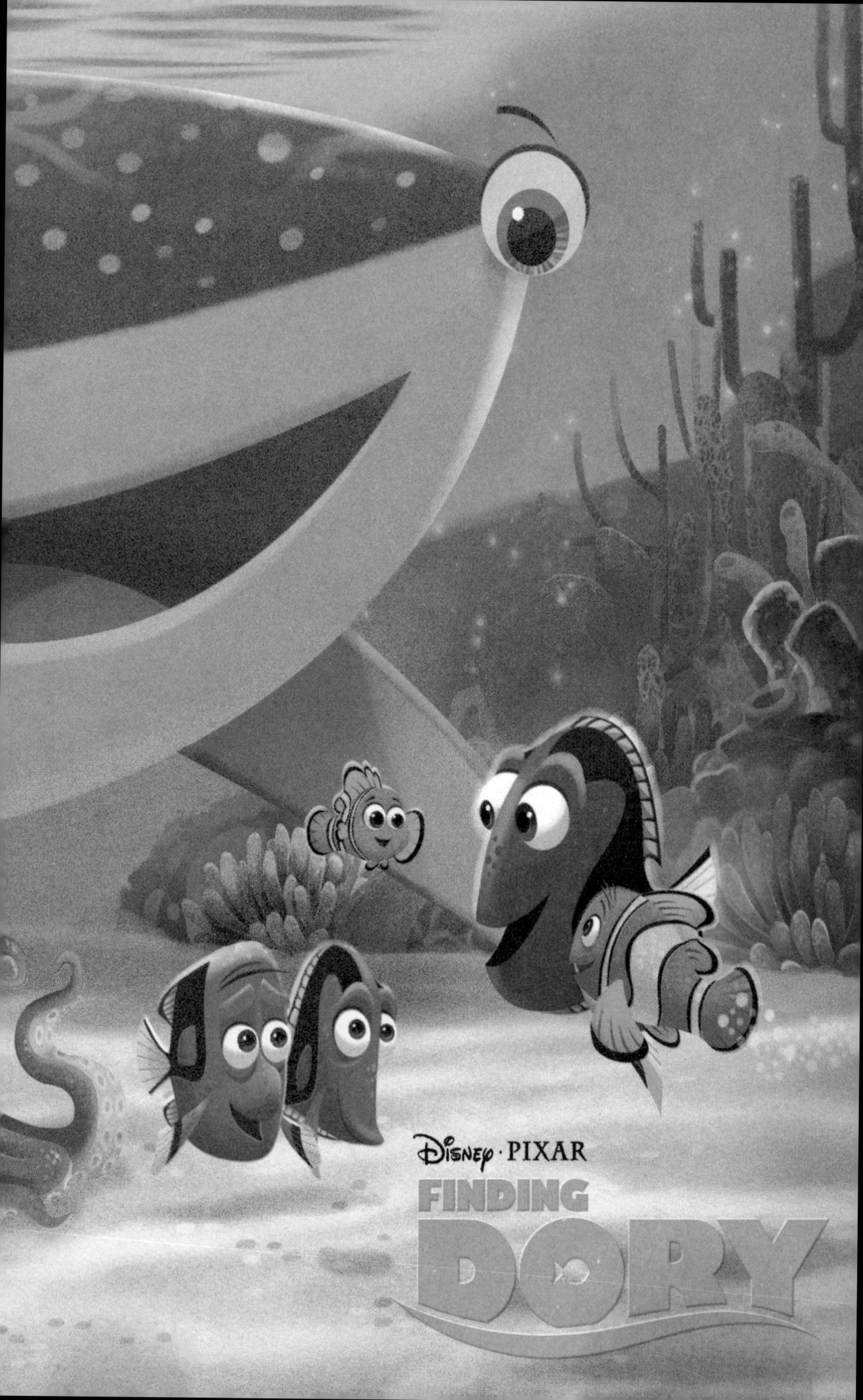

DISNEY · PIXAR
FINDING
DORY

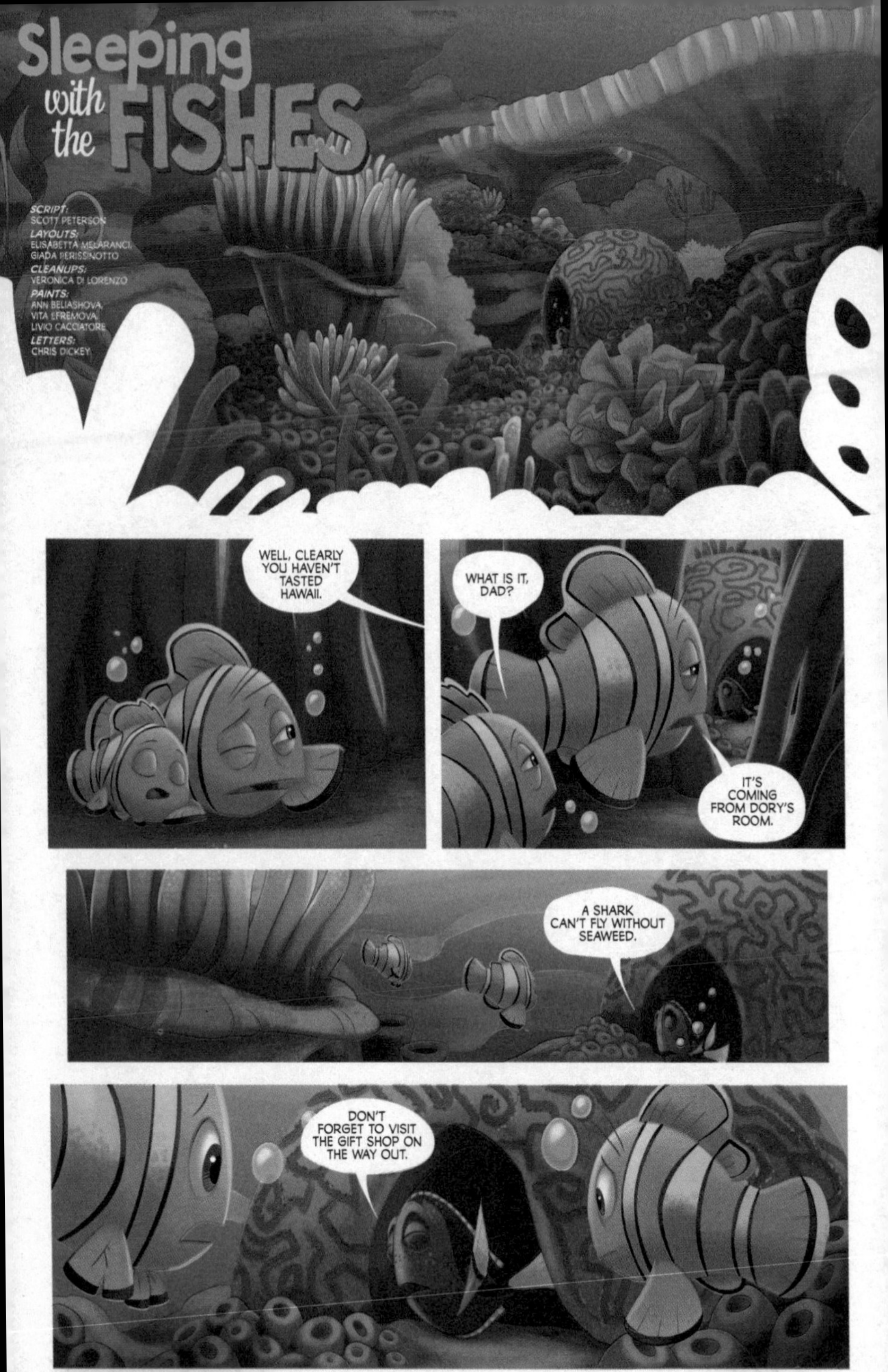
Sleeping with the FISHES
SCRIPT: SCOTT PETERSON
LAYOUTS: ELISABETTA MELARANCI, GIADA PERISSINOTTO
CLEANUPS: VERONICA DI LORENZO
PAINTS: ANN BELIASHOVA, VITA EFREMOVA, LIVIO CACCIATORE
LETTERS: CHRIS DICKEY
WELL, CLEARLY YOU HAVEN'T TASTED HAWAII.
WHAT IS IT, DAD?
IT'S COMING FROM DORY'S ROOM.
A SHARK CAN'T FLY WITHOUT SEAWEED.
DON'T FORGET TO VISIT THE GIFT SHOP ON THE WAY OUT.

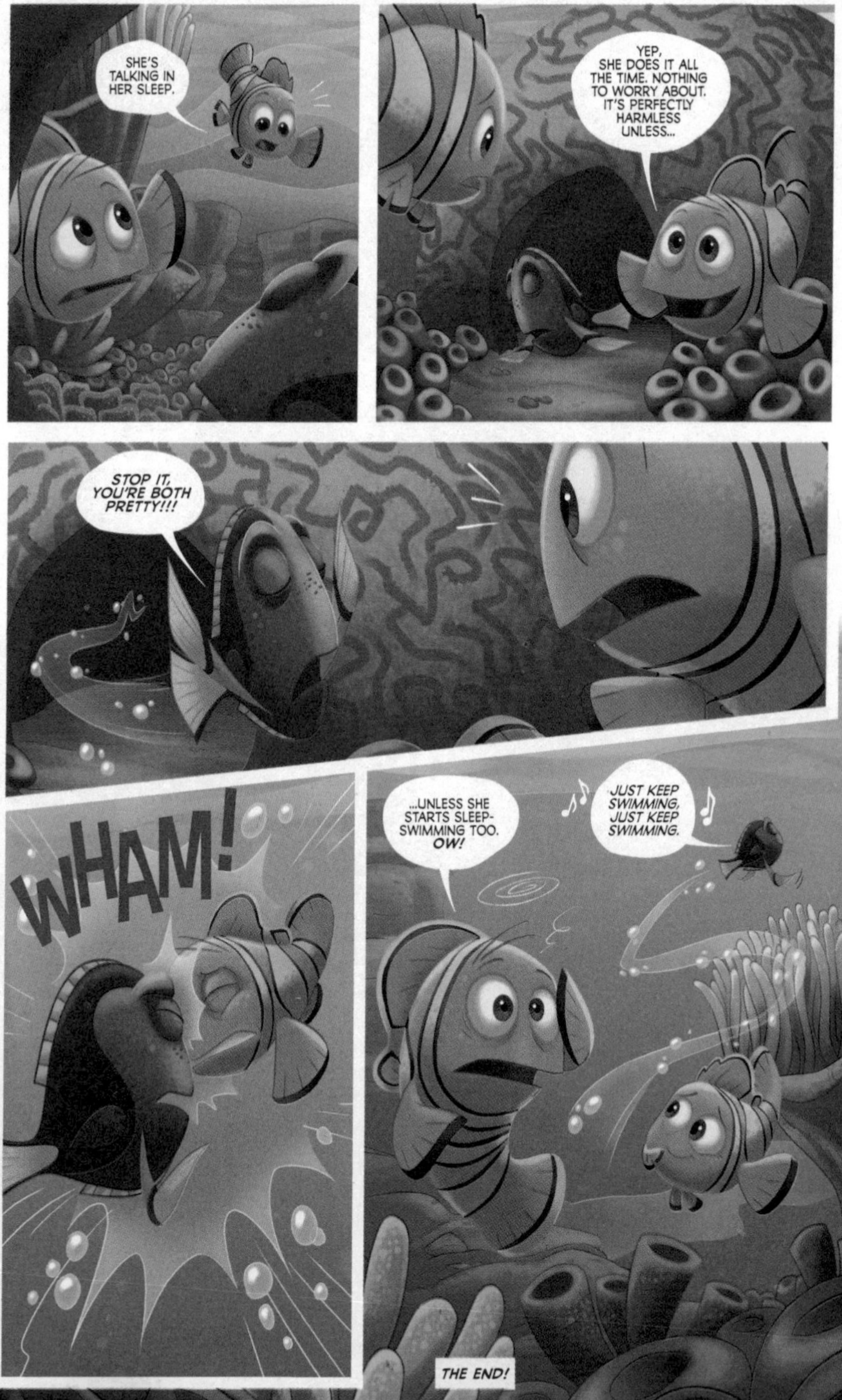
SHE'S TALKING IN HER SLEEP.
YEP, SHE DOES IT ALL THE TIME. NOTHING TO WORRY ABOUT. IT'S PERFECTLY HARMLESS UNLESS...
STOP IT, YOU'RE BOTH PRETTY!!!
WHAM!
...UNLESS SHE STARTS SLEEP-SWIMMING TOO. OW!
JUST KEEP SWIMMING, JUST KEEP SWIMMING.
THE END!

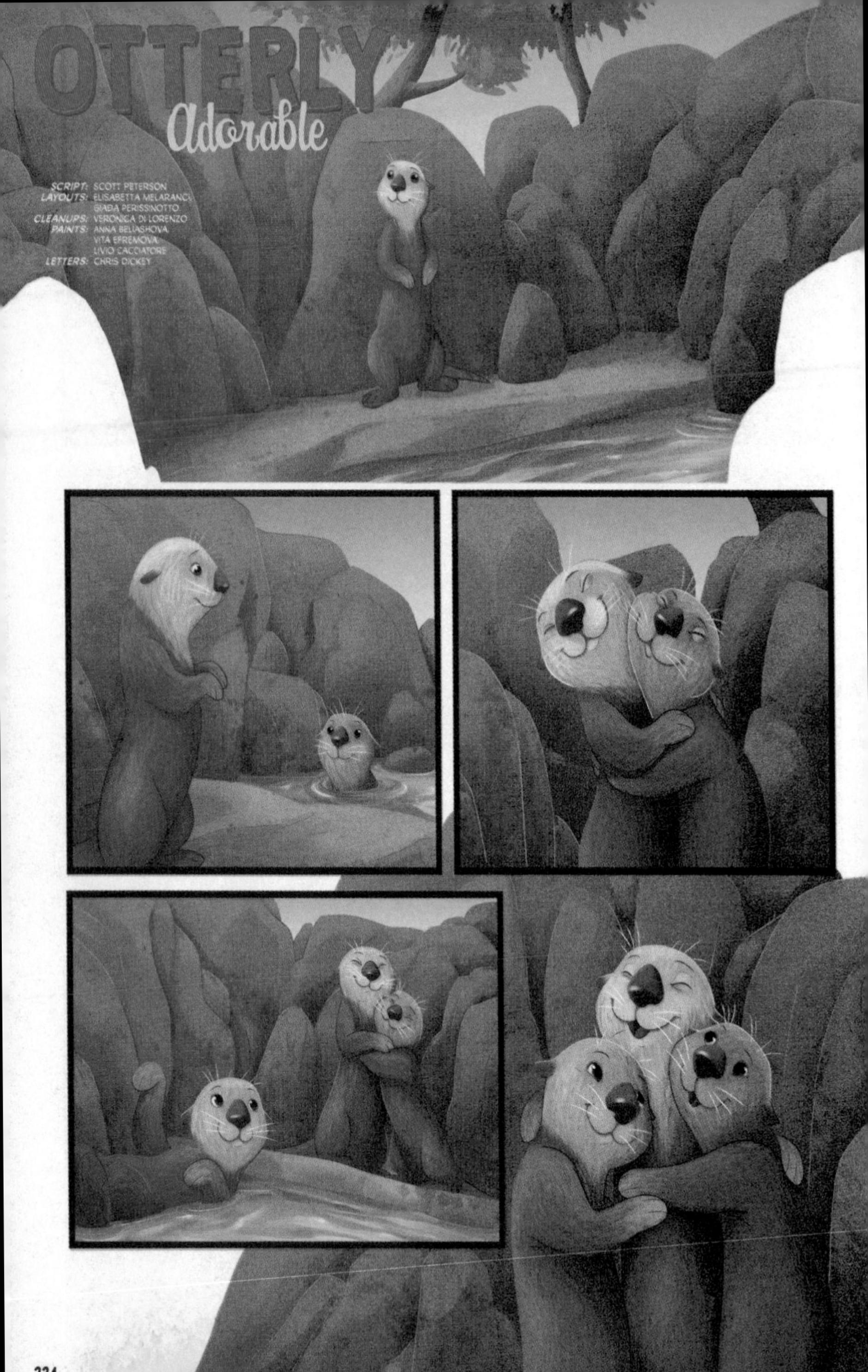
OTTERLY
Adorable
SCRIPT: SCOTT PETERSON
LAYOUTS: ELISABETTA MELARANCI, GIADA PERISSINOTTO
CLEANUPS: VERONICA DI LORENZO
PAINTS: ANNA BELIASHOVA, VITA EFREMOVA, LIVIO CACCIATORE
LETTERS: CHRIS DICKEY

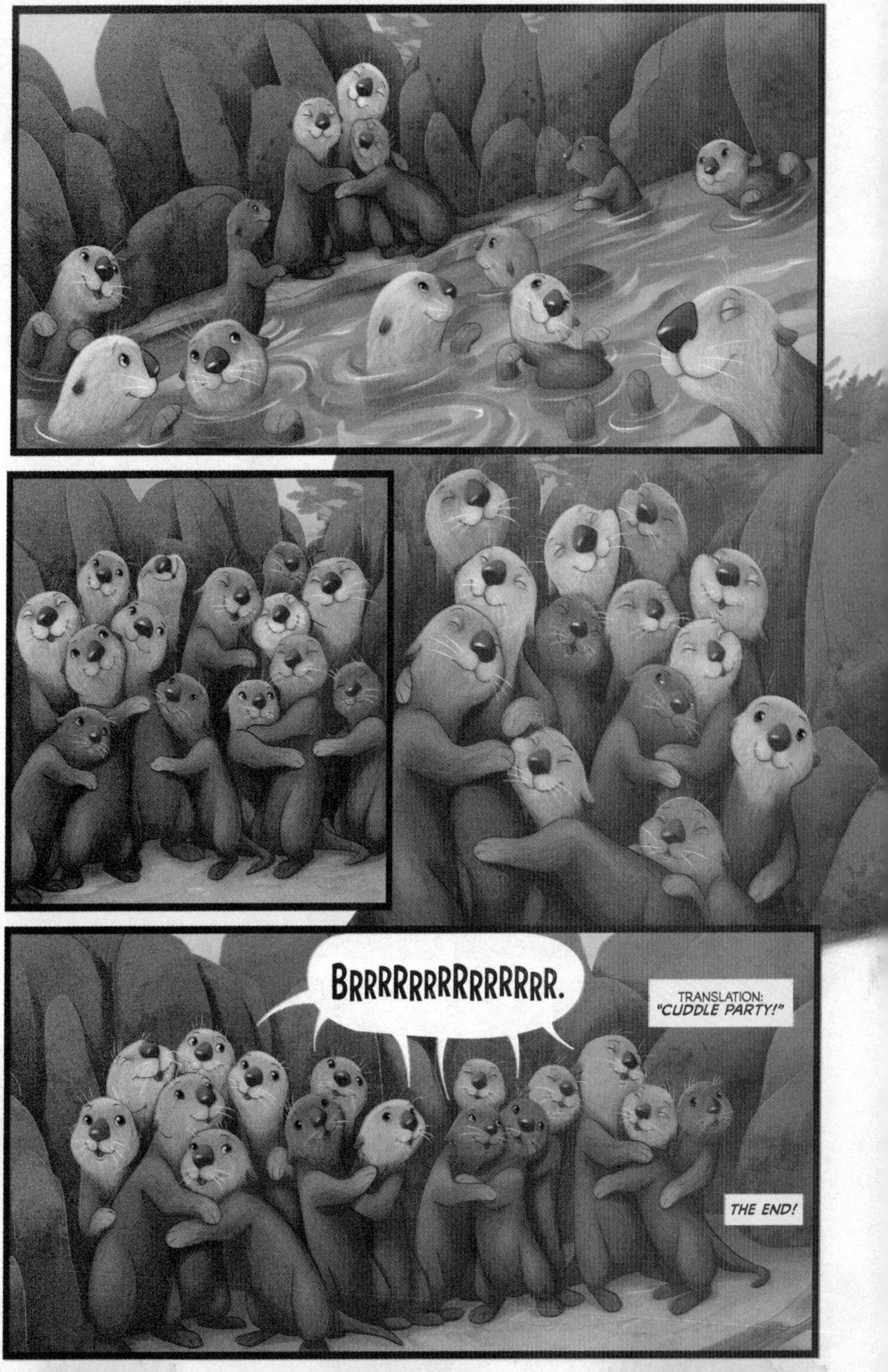
BRRRRRRRRRRRRRR.
TRANSLATION: "CUDDLE PARTY!"
THE END!

In Plain SIGHT

SCRIPT: SCOTT PETERSON
LAYOUTS: ELISABETTA MELARANCI, GIADA PERISSINOTTO
CLEANUPS: VERONICA DI LORENZO
PAINTS: ANNA BELIASHOVA, VITA EFREMOVA, LIVIO CACCIATORE
LETTERS: CHRIS DICKEY

THE OCTOPUS GOT OUT AGAIN.

AND SHE ACTED LIKE EVERYTHING WAS NORMAL...

WELL, CLEARLY THINGS ARE *NOT* NORMAL IF SHE HAS TO ACT LIKE THEY'RE NORMAL, RIGHT?

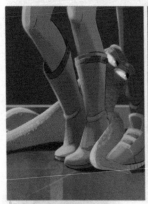

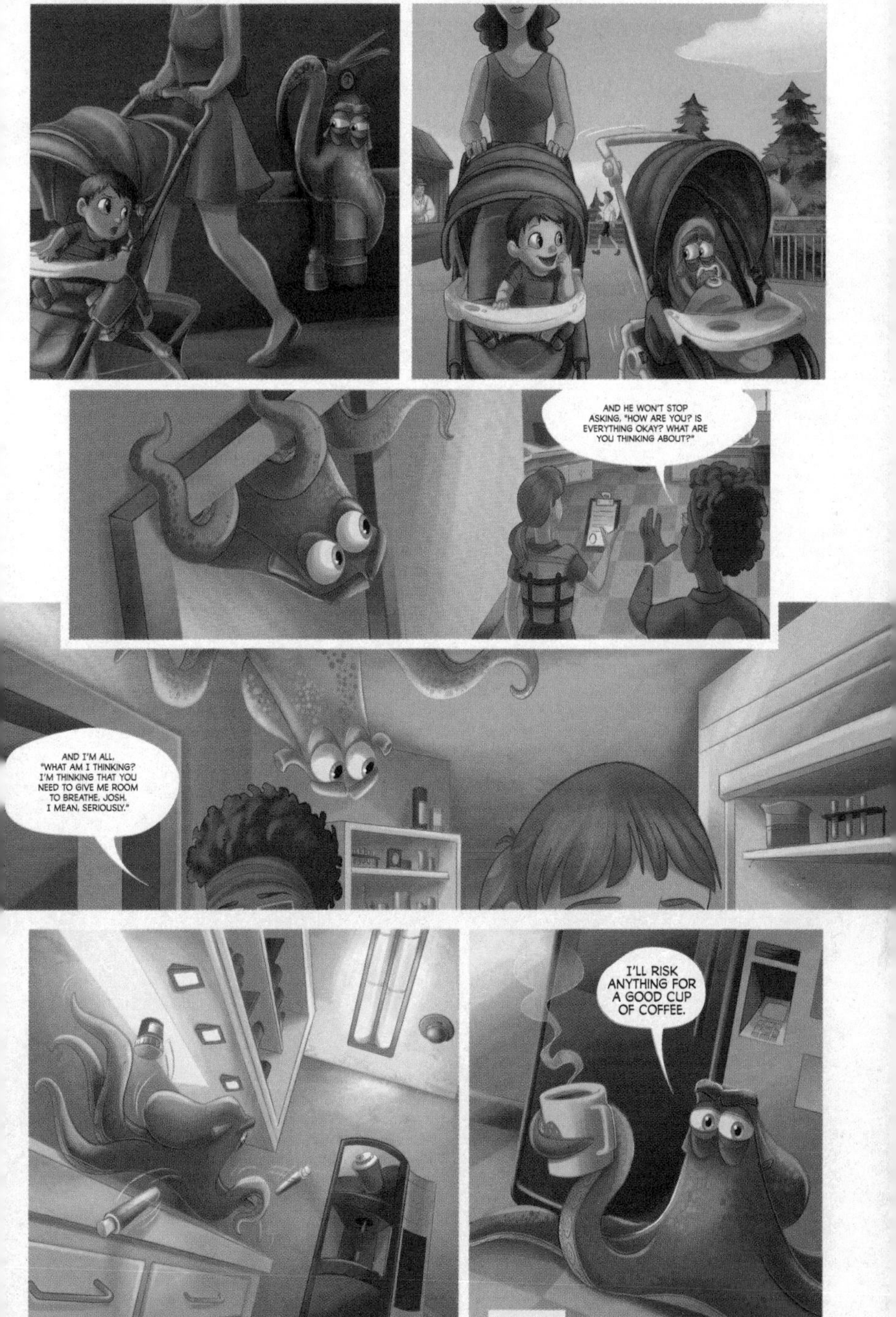
AND HE WON'T STOP ASKING, "HOW ARE YOU? IS EVERYTHING OKAY? WHAT ARE YOU THINKING ABOUT?"
AND I'M ALL, "WHAT AM I THINKING? I'M THINKING THAT YOU NEED TO GIVE ME ROOM TO BREATHE, JOSH. I MEAN, SERIOUSLY."
I'LL RISK ANYTHING FOR A GOOD CUP OF COFFEE.
THE END!

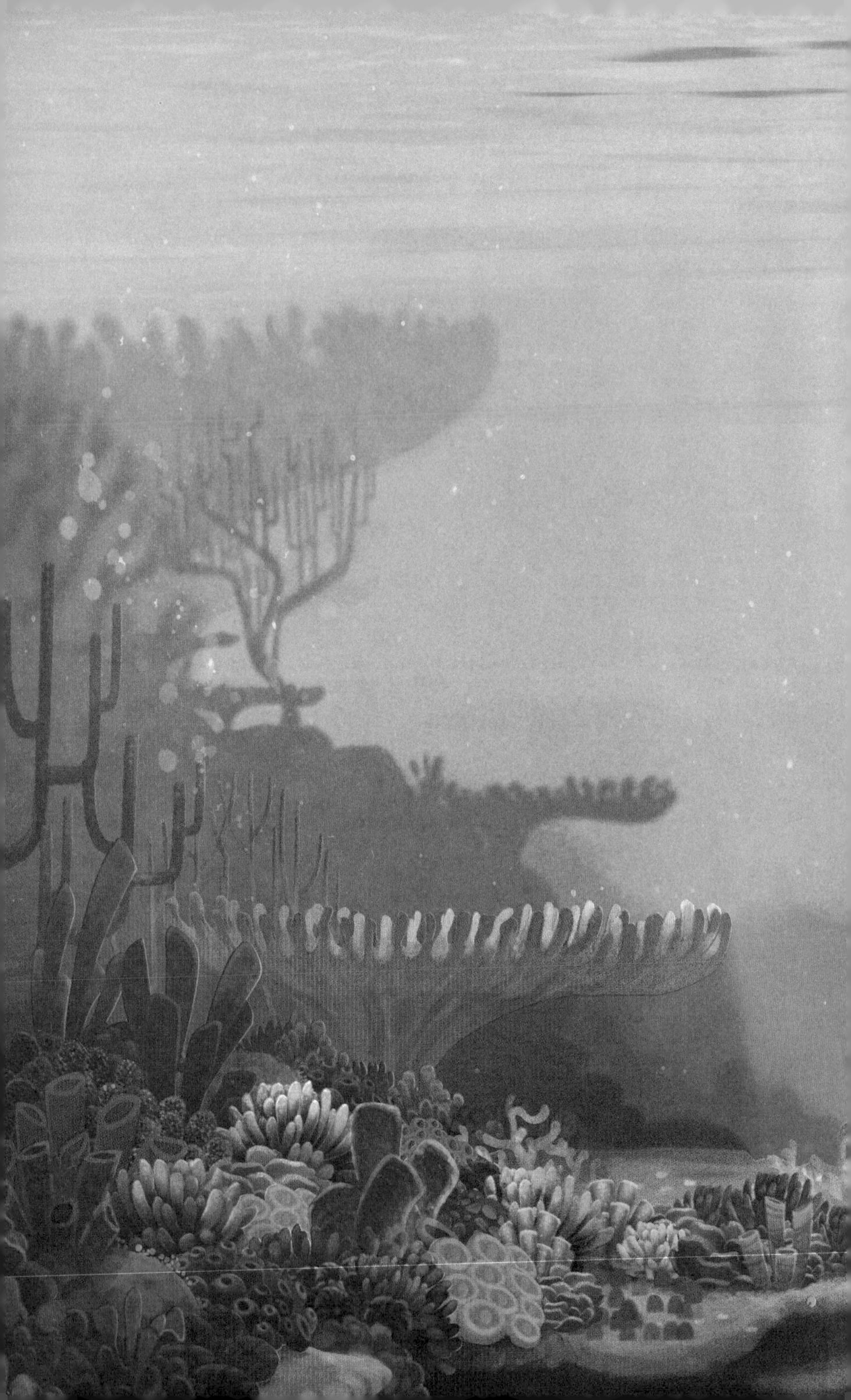

Credits

Disney • Pixar Finding Dory:
The Story of the Movie in Comics
Manuscript Adaptation: Alessandro Ferrari
Layout: Nicola Sammarco • Pencil: Andrea Greppi
Paint: Dario Calabria, Mara Damiani • Graphic Design & Editorial:
co-d S.r.l. – Milano, Chris Dickey (Lettering)
Pre-Press: co-d S.r.l. – Milano, LitoMilano S.r.l.
Special thanks to Laura Uyeda, Scott Tilley

For Joe Books
CEO: Jay Firestone • COO: Jody Colero
President: Steve Osgoode • Publisher: Adam Fortier
Associate Publisher: Deanna McFadden • Executive Editor: Amy Weingartner
Production & Editorial Assistant: Steffie Davis
Sales & Marketing Assistant: Ahlia Moussa

"Neighborhood Watch"
STORY: Scott Peterson • LAYOUTS: Davide Baldoni, Federica Salfo
CLEANUPS: Veronica Di Lorenzo, Livio Cacciatore • COLORS: Vita Efremova, Kat Maximenko
LETTERS: AW's Zakk Saam

"Lunchtime"
STORY: Scott Peterson • LAYOUTS: Davide Baldoni
CLEANUPS: Davide Baldoni • COLORS: Patrizia Zangrilli • LETTERS: AW's Zakk Saam

"Speaking Her Language"
STORY: Scott Peterson • LAYOUTS: Davide Baldoni, Federica Salfo
CLEANUPS: Davide Baldoni • COLORS: Sara Spano • LETTERS: AW's Zakk Saam

"Crab's Coral"
STORY: Scott Peterson • LAYOUTS: Federica Salfo
CLEANUPS: Davide Baldoni • COLORS: Yana Chintsova, Anastasiia Belousova • LETTERS: AW's Zakk Saam

"In the Dark"
STORY: Scott Peterson • LAYOUTS: Federica Salfo
CLEANUPS: Federica Salfo • COLORS: PATRIZIA ZANGRILLI • LETTERS: AW's Zakk Saam

"Little Lost F
STORY: S
CLEA

"Clam Chat"
STORY: Scott Peterson • LAYOUTS: Federica Salfo
CLEANUPS: Rosa La Barbera • COLORS: Ekaterina Myshalova • LETTERS: AW's Zakk Saam

"Intruder"
STORY: Scott Peterson • LAYOUTS: Massimo Asaro
CLEANUPS: Paco Desiato, Rosa La Barbera • COLORS: Sara Spano, Manuela Nerolini,
Jackie Lee, Lucio De Giuseppe, Luca Merli • LETTERS: AW's Zakk Saam

"The Show Must Go On"
STORY: Scott Peterson • LAYOUTS: Davide Baldoni
CLEANUPS: Rosa La Barbera • COLORS: Luca Merli • LETTERS: AW's Zakk Saam

"Home Sting Home"
STORY: Scott Peterson • LAYOUTS: Davide Baldoni
CLEANUPS: Letizia Algeri • COLORS: Jackie Lee • LETTERS: AW's Zakk Saam

"A Stand-Up Dad"
STORY: Scott Peterson • LAYOUTS: Elisabetta Melaranci
CLEANUPS: Rosa La Barbera • COLORS: Manuela Nerolini • LETTERS: AW's Zakk Saam

"Piranhacuda"
STORY: Scott Peterson • LAYOUTS: Elisabetta Melaranci
CLEANUPS: Paco Desiato • COLORS: Ann Beliashova, Kat Maximenko,
Vita Efremova, Anastasiia Belousova, Yana Chintsova • LETTERS: AW's Zakk Saam

Artwork on pages, 89, 149, 163 by Elisabetta Melaranci and Ann Beliashova

Disney Publishing Worldwide • Global Magazines, Comics and Partworks
Publisher: Gianfranco Cordara
Executive Editor: Carlotta Quattrocolo
Editorial Team: Bianca Coletti (Director, Magazines),
Guido Frazzini (Director, Comics), Stefano Ambrosio (Executive
Editor, New IP), Camilla Vedove (Senior Manager, Editorial Development),
Behnoosh Khalili (Senior Editor - Project Lead),
Julie Dorris (Senior Editor), Megan Adams (Associate Editor)
Design: Enrico Soave (Senior Design)
Art and Design: Manny Mederos (Comics & Magazines Creative Manager)